The
Earth Woman
Tree Woman
Quartet

by

Connie Pwll Walck Tyler

Illustrated by Katie Stewart

Berkeley, CA

THE EARTH WOMAN TREE WOMAN QUARTET
Connie Pwll Walck Tyler

The Earth Woman Tree Woman
is dedicated to my ancestors,
the tall, wise oak trees
who spoke to me when I was a child,
and to the wolf who lived back
of a gas station in Alaska,
who dances in my dreams.

———————

Acknowledgements

My thanks go to Kenneth and Bridget Tyler, Lissa Dirrum, Holly Coats-Bash, Dan Ross, Allysson MacDonald, Carina Ho, Carla DeSola and Paul Dinas, Book Editor, for their willingness to read and suggest changes to the manuscript;

to Tony Zaatari of Media Masters for all the help with the recording and mixing of the music; to Katie Winton-Henry for singing The Butterfly Song for me and encouraging me; to Matthew Curtis of Choral Tracks LLC for singing all four parts on some of the songs;

to Goodlifeguide.com for help with formatting and willingness to answer many, many questions; to Katie W. Stewart for her patience and willingness in creating the cover art;

to InterPlay founders, Cynthia Winton-Henry and Phil Porter, for giving me a place to dance and sing my new ideas and dreams; and all the InterPlayers who have given me support through the years (www.interplay.org).

In memoriam, thanks go to Dr. Scott Coulter whose help with the music when I first started this musical novel changed my life forever;

and to my father, Henry Z. Walck, who read and tried to promote the first permutation many, many years ago, and my mother, Florence Powell Walck, who gave me the gift of poetry by reading the poems of William Blake, Robert Lewis Stevenson and Bobbie Burns to me when I was very young.

SONGS

Many of the poems in this book have been set to music.
To hear the songs, go to **www.earthwomantreewoman.com**

CONTENTS

JOURNEY TO NINAS TWEI

Connie Pwll Walck Tyler

JOURNEY TO NINAS TWEI

Invocation

The Tree and the Woman are One

Seas crashing
like thunder rolling,
like drums beating,
a call to the brethren,
a cry to the wary,
the time has come!

Earth woman,
tree woman,
sea woman,
stands revealed.
Windblown, proud she faces the sun!

Wind howling,
grass bending,
pines whipping,
bringing the night,
singing the night,
the Tree and the woman are one!

Prologue:
The Hunters and the Cat

Dark of Hunter's Moon

It was midnight when the hunters tramped out of the forest and down the driveway to the Bidewell house, sitting shadowed and silent in the lee of the hill. "Hey, Amundsen," one of the men called out. "How old's your granddaughter?"

Amundsen kept walking, silent and stony-faced, his old 30-30 swinging at his side.

The deputy answered for him. "Nine. And the missing boy's the same age."

"Old enough for the little *beaner* to get into some mischief," the man muttered.

Some of the men beside him nodded. At least one frowned, but didn't say anything.

The young man walking at the front of the group stopped abruptly, causing a startled halt in the line. "What's that?" he yelled pointing at something standing out near the edge of the cliff.

The group spread out around him peering at the tall dark thing – something tree-like, and yet not a tree – inky black against the moonless midnight sky. The deputy frowned. "Weird."

Shaking his head, he turned, leading them across the meadow toward the strange tree thing.

A small gray cat slipped out from back of the dark house and followed them across the trampled grasses to where the object stood facing west over the ocean, watching as the men circled the tall wooden thing.

"What is it?" they muttered. "A sculpture of something." "A tree…" "Or a woman? I think it's a woman!"

Amundsen's eyes narrowed as he glared at the tree woman.

> *(Seas crashing,* the earth breathed in his ear,
> *like thunder rolling,*
> *like drums beating,*
> *a call to the brethren,*
> *a cry to the wary,*
> *the time has come!)*

"Evil. It's evil," he muttered, pulling his gun up in front of his chest.

The men heard him, exchanging uneasy glances.

> *(Earth woman,* the wind whispered to him,
> *tree woman,*
> *sea woman…)*

Dickerson noticed the little cat who sat, tail curled around his toes, head cocked to one side looking at them. "Hey, look at the way that cat's looking at us!"

> *Ba-a-room!*

A gun went off with a huge explosive noise and all the men jumped.

The cat leapt in the air as a bullet hit the ground next to it. It tore across the yard to the house as two more shots followed, managing to duck under the porch without being hit.

Amundsen lowered his gun.

"Jees," muttered one of the hunters.

The deputy took a deep breath – "Amundsen…" – he shook his head. "Amundsen, I don't think you needed to do that. It was just a cat."

> *(Yes,* murmured the surf on the beach below,
> *Earth woman,*
> *tree woman,*
> *sea woman,*
> *stands revealed.*
> *The Tree and the woman are One.)*

1

Full Ripe Corn Moon

*(T*hree moons earlier in the city of Bayomar on the west coast of the country called Uhs...)*

Thump!

Startled, Giselle looked up from gathering the things on the seat beside her to see a small blue-gray cat peering at her from the hood of the car.

"Where did you…" She leaned over, pushing her hair back from her face as she tried to peer through the windshield at the cat.

The cat sat down facing her through the window, intense green eyes staring at her.

Giselle's eyes were green, too. She'd gotten her black hair from her Chinese great-grandmother, but her skin, her eyes and her upbringing were all a kind of generic "white".

The kitty wasn't very old – not a baby, but not full grown either – and he had the same kind of impertinent stare as some of the teenagers she'd volunteered with a few years ago when she was in college.

He leaned down and licked a shoulder.

No collar. Was he abandoned? He was too in your face to be feral.

She gathered her things and opened the door quietly, trying not to startle the cat as she scrunched her legs out of the car seat, her arms full, her skirt twisting under her making it hard to stand.

One of her sandals fell off.

She rolled her eyes as she poked her bare toes back into the sandal (while trying to avoid stepping in an oil streak), stood up, and shook out her skirt. Her nose wrinkled as she took in the reek of accumulated exhaust fumes.

The cat was unfazed, moving to the edge of the hood and giving a demanding, "Meow!"

Turning in a circle she searched the dark, dank garage.

Her sister, Monica, wasn't home yet, but Monica's husband's car was here so he'd already be up in their apartment. They owned the old building and lived on the top floor. The bottom floor was divided into two small one-bedroom apartments. Giselle rented one of them.

The cat jumped down next to her and flicked his tail. She headed towards the garage entrance, and the cat stepped along beside her. She laughed, shrugged her shoulders and kept on walking.

Once outside she took a deep breath of the cleaner air. Southwest winds. No fumes from the refineries today. The cat flicked his tail, and raised his eyes seeming to search for something.

An older man was leaning against the telephone pole on the other side of the garage entrance. The cat walked over to him, rubbing against his legs.

The man crouched down and caressed the cat.

"Is this your cat?" Giselle asked.

"No," he smiled, his brown eyes glinting in his craggy black face. "I think he's yours," and straightening up, he walked away past the big tree on the corner before Giselle could comment.

A moment later Giselle and the cat were distracted by a shrill, "Kee-ee-ar," as a large bird launched itself from the tree and spiraled up and up above them.

"Kee-ee-ar. Kee-ee-ar," it cried before it gave one last circle and headed north.

The cat gave a satisfied meow, and turned back to Giselle.

"Was that a hawk – a Red-tailed hawk?" Giselle was incredulous. A hawk in the city?

She shrugged her shoulders and headed back down the sidewalk to the front entrance of her building.

As they passed the garbage bin, the cat stopped to sniff the belongings of the old woman who lived in the little cave created between the bin and the garage. "If you stick around, you'll meet her," she told the cat. "That's her home now. She was evicted from the public housing apartment she'd lived in for thirty years when the building was privatized," she added sadly. The woman had worked all her life but now she was living on the street – like so many others.

The cat looked up and gave a small "mew."

Giselle nodded, and continued up the steps to the front door, the cat marching at her side.

A newspaper lay on the top step waiting to be picked up by the other downstairs tenant.

The cat stopped and looked at it, then up at her. "Ten Story Garment Factory in Kanidu Collapses Killing Hundreds," screamed the headline.

Giselle sighed. Last week the explosion of the refinery in Port Blas had destroyed everything for blocks around it. A list of other major industrial "accidents" passed through her thoughts, and she shook her head.

The cat flicked his tail.

It almost seemed as if the cat…

Giselle laughed at herself. *Of course not.* She opened the door.

Head and tail high, the cat stepped past her into the tiny lobby – the Visiting Dignitary. Giselle rolled her eyes, laughing. The dogs whimpered on the other side of her door anticipating her arrival home. "I don't know what the dogs are going to think of you – or you of the dogs!"

He just marched up to her door and sat while she fumbled with her keys.

What would the dogs do? Maybe she should pick him up. She put her things down on the floor and reached for him.

He side-stepped away and meowed loudly. The dogs abruptly stopped their whimpering, listening.

She opened the door a crack.

The cat stuck its nose in and pushed it wider, strolling in past the two sitting, tail thumping dogs, and the potted ferns that lined the entranceway.

Giselle shook her head grinning, "Weird." She picked up her things and followed the cat in.

The dogs trailed the cat as he surveyed the apartment, sticking his nose into the ferns, batting the strands of spider plant that swept downward from hanging pots in the windows, peeking into the bedroom and tiny kitchen, and finally settling in for a wash on the old trunk Giselle used as a coffee table.

Giselle dumped her things on the old oak table in the dining alcove, greeted the dogs, kicked off her sandals, and settled too, sitting on the couch with her feet up on the trunk, next to the cat.

It wasn't long before Monica knocked twice, and then used her key to walk into Giselle's apartment. She was a trim, carefully dressed woman in her late twenties with the same straight dark hair as Giselle, but cut short in a no-nonsense style. A briefcase swung on a strap over her shoulder.

When she saw the cat sitting on the trunk giving himself a bath, she freaked. "Where did that cat come from?"

"He was in the garage. Jumped on my car and followed me in." Giselle grinned, scratching the head of a dog. "I think he's decided he lives here."

"You can't keep that cat, Giselle." Monica leaned forward and her briefcase slipped off her shoulder. Giving an annoyed huff, she pushed it back. "You don't have to give a free ride to every stray animal that comes along."

She paused waiting for a response from Giselle who just shrugged. "You can't keep it," she repeated. "Take it to the pound. I'm your landlord. I forbid it."

Giselle didn't answer. It always seemed easier just to let her sister rave than to try to argue. The words, *'You're not the boss of me,'* popped into her head, just as they had when as children, after their mother died, Monica really was the boss. She smiled, thinking the childish phrase again. *You're not. You're not the boss of me.*

"What are you laughing at?" Monica's voice hit a higher pitch. "It's not a laughing matter. You act like you're living on a farm instead of an apartment in a city! You can hardly walk in here with all these stupid plants."

Giselle rolled her eyes. Then she remembered the newspaper. "Monica." She sat up and looked at her sister, the smile gone. "Did you see another garment factory collapsed in Kanidu?"

"Oh, for heaven's sake, Giselle. You get too emotionally involved in these things. It's a million miles away from here and there's nothing you can do about it." She pointed at the cat. "That cat is here. You need to do something about the cat instead of worrying about people on the other side of the world."

Giselle glared. She could feel the anger simmering in her chest. *Deep breaths,* she thought. *Deep breaths.* "Well, maybe you need to think about whose clothes they're making at slave wages and obviously really dangerous conditions."

Monica had the grace to look a little ashamed. "I try to buy fair trade clothes. It's just hard to find them." She looked away and muttered. "I don't like shopping at GoodButUsed."

Giselle smoothed down her GoodButUsed skirt and took another deep breath. "Monica, I have to finish my summer school report cards. Rod's home. I saw his car. Don't you have report cards to finish, too?"

Monica threw her arms up in the air, yelling, "Get rid of that cat," as she left, slamming the door and heading upstairs to her lawyer husband.

Giselle leaned back on the couch again and looked at the little gray cat perched on the trunk in front of her. He flicked his tail, then curved it gently around a small wooden statue that sat in the place of honor on the trunk – a little Chinese carving of a woman who seemed to be emerging from a tree, with one foot stepping out into the world. It was one of the few possessions Giselle's great-grandmother had brought with her from China when she came to this country as a very young GI bride. Giselle didn't know anything about her, but she loved the little wooden woman.

Monica hated it.

Why? thought Giselle, for the hundredth time. *Why does she hate it?*

She took the statue in her hands. The wood was so warm and smooth, her face so serene and calming, and there was something so promising about the foot stepping out. She'd like to know more about her.

She smiled at the cat whose tail flicked slowly back and forth, back and forth...

The plants became a smoky green aura pushing everything else into the background and she closed her eyes listening sleepily to the swish and thump of the dog tails. That deep dark thinking space inside her head seemed to open out. It felt like something was there... touching her. Something beyond…

A fragment of a melody slipped through her thoughts and then a deep voice whispered in her head…

(Breath).

Breath? It was a voice, not a thought. A voice!

(Whispering breath.)

Her eyes popped open. "Where did that come from?" The cat licked a paw and then turned his head to look at her. She closed her eyes again. This time the voice was singing to the same fragment of melody.

(Breath, murmuring in the wind-whipped grasses.)

She peered at the cat. "Is that coming from me or from you?" He just flicked his tail, back and forth, back and forth…

(Flowing in the waves of the sea…)

She smiled. The song was familiar, but…

(Breath, singing through the voice of the wind.)

Then, spoken, not sung and with more urgency…

(Time. The time is now. Leave.)

Time for what? she thought.

(Time to leave.)

She sat up straight and stared at the cat, who suddenly showed great interest in a paper clip, batting it with a paw.

Giselle sat back again. *Leave?* she thought. *Leave and go where?*

(North,) whispered the voice.

"North," Giselle exclaimed out loud. She laughed and shook her head. "This is idiocy."

She hopped up. "I have to finish my report cards."

Two more days and summer school would be over, then a month off before jumping back into the frenetic activity of the school year. She looked at the cat.

Leave? Go North? "Like that would be possible," she muttered as she turned toward the dining room table and the summer school grades.

But she did have a month off. Maybe she should take a vacation – by herself. Yes. A vacation without big sister hanging over her all the time! And she could go north, too. She could head north along the coast…

It was a ridiculous idea. She pulled her papers out of the basket and set to work.

That Friday evening, after the last day of summer school, the seventeen teachers at Rockland School and their spouses had a gathering at a seafood restaurant across the city next to the bay. The district summer classes had been consolidated at Rockland, the inner city school where Giselle taught – the first time Giselle and Monica had taught at the same site.

The dining room was a cozy dark place with a fire in a large fireplace on one side of the room to fight off the chill of the summer fog, a strange comfortable contrast to the serious talk of the destruction of public education and the use of rote learning to pass multiple choice tests.

Giselle sat and listened. They all seemed to agree about the problem of corporate owned schools and the teaching of rote answers to the tests, but when one teacher expressed distress at the disappearance of art and music in the schools, Giselle was amazed that some of the others disparaged their importance. One even suggested that artists and musicians were purveyors of drugs. From there the group moved into a strident discussion about the War on Drugs.

She sat forward in her seat. "But…," she said several times trying to get a word in edgewise. Each time someone spoke right over top of her voice as if she didn't exist.

Annoyed, she raised her voice. "The War on Drugs isn't really about drugs. It's about racism – a counter to the Civil Rights movement. It's really all about throwing people in jail – people of color. It brings in big money by privatizing the prisons. Actually, lots more money than the corporate schools. One Earth Together says…"

But before she could finish, Monica interrupted, "Don't be silly, Giselle. Everyone knows One Earth Together is full of conspiracy theories."

They all turned away from her, and the conversation went on without her.

Her principal, Samuel, an older African American who was sitting next to her, patted her hand, but said nothing.

When she finished eating, Giselle left the table and moved over to a footstool next to the fire. One Earth Together was a good organization pulling together the concerns of many different organizations interested in social change. Their e-newsletter was one of the best sources of accurate information around and Monica knew it.

Monica often said things like that when they were in public – things that made her feel like a little kid, and then everyone else acted like she was a child. Monica'd done it all her life, or at least ever since their mother died. She couldn't remember what Monica had been like before that.

She felt a familiar lump in her chest. It seemed funny that it never got easier. *And then dad made it worse, saying over and over again that Monica had to take care of me, that I was like our mother – 'imaginative', 'flighty', 'unable to cope with life'. It's not true, she thought. It wasn't true about Mom, either. Imaginative, yes. But there's nothing wrong with being imaginative... Mom was powerful. And I... am I powerful? Am I?*

She felt herself sinking into a dark red tunnel inside herself. The people around her – even her fellow teachers and her sister – seemed like robots, all movement on the outside and no thought on the inside, like she was the only one alive...

(*Listen,* the words sang through the red fog. *Listen,
Breath, warmed by the life-giving sun,
Burn, burn within...*)

Under the logs of the fire she watched a forest alive with dark crevices, bright grottoes, and wiggling creatures made of newspaper ash. A forest, inviting her to... she didn't know what. *I'll just get up and walk out the door, and leave them all behind. Maybe I'll go 'north'.*

She grinned, shaking her head at her childish drama.

Suddenly Monica was leaning over her hissing, "What are you doing over here humming to yourself? We've been calling you."

"I didn't hear you."

"That's because you were being weird again. Get up. We're leaving."

Giselle rolled her eyes, but dutifully got up.

By the time she'd gathered her things and made her way out the door, most of the others were half way down the block to their cars. Samuel and his wife stood a little way down the sidewalk waiting for her.

As she turned to follow them a haunting voice – a beautiful, rich chanting voice – came from somewhere behind her. She turned around, searching the dark, nearly deserted sidewalk for the singer.

In a pool of light on the next corner she saw a shadowy figure.

She moved closer, listening, mesmerized by the minor soaring tones. Not English. Maybe not even words.

A tall black woman dressed in swirling colorful skirts and shawls stood looking out toward the sea, her arms reaching to the sky, her head thrown back as she sang.

As Giselle moved quietly toward the corner, the woman turned and looked directly at her. She was beautiful, with flowing dreadlocks and eyes almost too large for her mahogany face.

> *You will become*, she sang, her voice rich and deep.
> *Like the moon and the stars and the sun,*
> *You will become.*
> *You will emerge,*
> *Step out into the world.*
> *You will go.*
> *You will learn.*
> *You will return.*

She slowly nodded her head at Giselle.

> *You will return.*

Then, lifting her face to the stars, spun away and returned to her chant.

Monica grabbed Giselle's arm. "What's wrong with you, Giselle? Come on." Giselle shook Monica's hand away and reluctantly followed Monica's fast clip, clipping down the street.

Samuel and his wife stepped in beside her and Samuel asked, "What did she say to you?"

Giselle just shook her head. "I don't know. Her voice was so beautiful." They nodded and hugged goodbye before crossing the street to their car. Giselle moved a little faster toward Monica's car, smiling a quick "good evening" to a homeless man sitting on the curb as she passed him. Monica, waiting impatiently, rolled her eyes.

Giselle spent Saturday trying to bring order to the chaos in her apartment after the daily rush of summer school. At the top of her closet she saw the little bit of camping equipment she had bought for a trip with Rod and Monica the summer before – a sleeping bag, a small, one person tent, a little solar stove. Maybe she could go camping.

The cat sat on up on her bed and looked at her.

"Monica thinks I'm weird," she told the cat. "You know what I don't understand? I don't understand why Monica and the others weren't entranced by that woman's singing."

She stood still for a moment thinking of the haunting, wild notes of the woman's song. "And what did she mean, I would 'become,' I would 'emerge…' I would 'go,' but I would 'return?' What did she mean?"

She looked back at the cat, who blinked at her. "You know, if anyone around here is weird, it's you." She pulled the camping equipment down and stacked it on the bed. "No chip, no collar. Where did you come from? What do you want?"

In her head she heard, not the woman's chant, but that earlier little haunting melody.

(Breath, flowing in the waves of the sea…)

Saturday night folk dancing at the little local park had always felt like a kind of ritual to Giselle – a communion – although she'd certainly never said anything about that to Monica, who couldn't understand why Giselle would want to folk dance at all. Monica's big fear was that Giselle would hook up with one of those strange folk-dancing men.

This Saturday night the dancing seemed more than just that feeling of fullness and connection. It was more intense, as if she was entering into some new ritual. The people who lived in the park sat at the edges of the grassy circle watching, their grocery carts filled with their belongings behind them, clapping to the music and sometimes joining the dancers.

The setting sun spread silky pastels over their heads and the small band playing folk instruments began the haunting music of one of her favorite dances.

The dance was a slow, rhythmic circling, each dancer moving with the same steps, but not touching, separate from each other, followed by a unison clapping. Tonight every one clapped together. No one missed a beat. They joined hands briefly, thrusting their hands up and stepping together into the center.

Something electric ran around the circle.

Letting go, they lifted their arms again in a burst to the sky that threw them back to the beginning.

There was a high pitched cry above them and Giselle looked up. A Red-tailed hawk *(like the one I saw before,* Giselle thought) circled overhead as if he were a part of the dance, spiraling downward as the dancers circled again, moving as one, but not touching until the unison clap like a drum beat that called them together, joining them as they reached upwards to the fiery sky and the hawk.

The dance music retreated and the strange familiar song whispered to her again:

(Breath, singing through the voice of the wind,
Dance with me. Dance with me...)

The dance moved on, leaving Giselle rooted in the middle, her eyes on the hawk gliding above her. He swooped down close enough for her to see his eyes peering into her own.

(Go north,) she heard, and the whisper was like thunder in her heart.

Light headed, she crouched, touching the earth. Her fingers tingled and she felt something flowing, filling her. Her own voice drummed thunder in her head: *(Go north,* it shouted. *Go north.)*

"I will," she cried, leaping back into the dance.

When she got home she loaded the camping equipment into the trunk of the car, along with all the dog and cat food in the apartment, a cardboard box full of food, and a duffle bag full of clothes and toiletries.

She wrote a note to put in Monica's mailbox just before she left:

Monica,
I'm going camping. I've got the dogs and the cat, and I haven't left any perishables in the refrigerator. I gave the plants a good watering so they should be fine for a week or so, so you don't have to worry about anything. I have my cell phone. If there are any emergencies just leave me a message.

Love,
Giselle

Sleep didn't come easily. She was both excited and terrified about going off somewhere on her own. Monica would be really angry. But I don't care, she thought. *Time to grow up!*

In the morning she slipped out of the apartment building into that quiet that always marked an early Sunday morning in the city. As she walked past the garbage bin, she saw the old woman tucked into the little space between the bin and the wall of the garage, fast asleep. She smiled and slipped ten dollars under the edge of the quilt Monica had given the old lady in December. Monica wasn't all bad. She let the woman stay, and she gave her money and food. No, Monica wasn't bad – just too controlling.

She laughed. Monica was a helicopter sister!

Heading north on the freeway, past the columns of gray smoke hovering over the bleak neighborhoods surrounding the oil refineries and the stark square buildings of the maximum security prison surrounded by fencing topped with spirals of razor wire, she finally reached the exit for the coastal highway. She breathed a sigh of relief at leaving the freeway and began to relax.

The coast road was beautiful, but dangerous if taken at too high a speed. Giselle loved slowing down, then accelerating slightly into the curves, feeling the tires grip the road. It felt like she was an extension of the car, like she could feel the road through the steering wheel, through "the seat of her pants" like a very slow race car driver.

The cat rode behind Giselle's neck between the top of the seat and the headrest, purring, the vibrations massaging her shoulders. She felt she was breathing in the coastal cliffs, the beaches, the occasional small towns with tiny harbors full of fishing boats, and breathing out all the distresses of the school year, of her life, of her problems with Monica. *And maybe of the world,* she thought. *This frightening world we're living in.*

She shook her head. Hard to escape the world.

Monica did call her cell as soon as she found the note, but Giselle didn't answer. *Let her leave messages. I'll call her back later. After all, I'm not supposed to talk on the phone while driving,* she grinned.

She stopped often, exploring the beaches and hiking trails along the way, and loving every moment, except when occasionally she saw a sign:

No entrance.
Beach eroded.

Once someone had added, "Rising seas – climate change!" in red spray paint.

The first two times she stopped, she saw a hawk circling above her – a Red-tailed hawk like the one she'd seen while folk dancing. When she saw a hawk the third time she stopped, she wondered if it could possibly be the same one.

Once, as the hawk flew down closer, she looked at the little cat and saw he was watching it, too, and then the melody came whispering into her head:

(Breath, flowing in the waves of the sea,
Dance with me…)

She smiled. *Yes, let's dance!*

In the early evening she pulled into a state beachside park, setting up her little tent in one of the numbered campsites. She called Monica back, but was vague about where she was and got off the phone quickly, after reassuring Monica that she was just fine, and yes, she was alone, not with some strange man. *But if I was with some man Monica didn't know, it would be my own business,* she thought as she tucked the phone away.

A strident "Kee-eeeee-arr" pierced the air. Again, a Red-tailed hawk soared above her head, circled and flew away – north.

The next two days followed the same pattern. The mornings were chill and a good time to explore the park trails with the dogs – some winding between tall coastal redwoods, others crossing open grassy meadows – before setting off again up the coast. The cat always ran alongside the dogs for a bit before demanding to be carried balanced precariously on Giselle's shoulder. They were on the road again by ten or eleven in the morning.

Once they were caught in stop-and-go traffic passing an ugly logging camp – a muddy mess of wide redwood stumps and huge logging trucks pulling out into the road. She felt an ache in her chest – a deep vibration wailing through her body.

"The trees crying," she whispered to the animals.

But most of the trip was lovely. She did note how low the water was in the rivers they crossed, deep cracked mud showing between the high-water line and the slow muddy flow. The meadow grasses were usually yellow in the summer, but now they looked almost white and dried up. *I haven't been out in the country to see how bad the drought is,* she thought.

They stopped and explored several times each day. Each time they stopped, a hawk circled and called above them, and the elusive melody whispered in her head.

Last Quarter, Ripe Corn Moon

On the third day the road moved inland a little, meandering through a forested area and past some small steep hills separating the road from the ocean. About noon she came around the curve of a hill to see a meadow that swept down toward the sea. She pulled over to a wide spot on the verge on the left side of the road, and sat with her window open gazing at the water while she ate crackers and cheese. She smiled as she noticed a hawk circling over the meadow. She turned to the dogs, "There's our hawk."

Suddenly the cat hopped from where he had been lying behind her neck to the edge of the window and then out into the meadow. Giselle dropped her crackers and jumped out of the car to rush after him. The dogs leapt out the open door after her and they pushed through the tough yellow grasses afraid they'd never find him again as he led them on a stumbling run down toward the sea. He swerved to the left around the ocean side of the wooded hill they'd just driven past and straight to a little gray weathered house, hidden from the road by the hill. Jumping up on the porch, he turned and sat looking at her, giving his fur a little lick.

Giselle stopped and leaned over, hands on knees, panting while the dogs danced around the house in delight. The cat scrubbed a paw. Walking slowly up to the house, she scooped him up and nervously backed away afraid someone might come out the door and demand to know what she was doing there.

She turned.

Directly in front of her next to a driveway that swerved north through the meadow and then curved toward the road, was a sign on a wooden post:

For Sale or Rent

She turned back to look at the little house. It was sturdy and pretty with a porch running around at least two sides so that it sheltered the front door and the side of the house facing the ocean. Climbing up on the porch, she peeked in the windows at the neat little front room.

On the ocean side a bank of windows looked in on a long bright kitchen with a stove and refrigerator, lots of counters and cupboards. The porch continued around to the back where a door, with a small swinging flap for pets at its base, led out of the kitchen and down some steps.

Spinning in a circle looking at the land and sea around her, she breathed deeply.

The air smelled so clean!

The meadow continued on the other side of the driveway down to a cliff overhanging a small beach. To the south, it narrowed as the hill moved out toward the sea. Here, just a little south and west of the house, was a huge coastal live oak tree spreading its gnarled branches wide and tall over the grasses.

(Waves of things of forms I am,) it murmured.

Her eyes widened. Turning quickly away from the tree, she walked to the edge of the meadow to look down at the little beach and the sea.

The tree's presence behind her felt like something warm on her back. Not a bad feeling. Just scary, like when you meet someone you know is going to be important to you. She looked back at it.

(Waves of things of forms I am,
Exist in dreams within me...)

She looked down at the cat. He wiggled out of her arms, jumping to the ground, and then turned to wind between her legs.

Shaking her head she turned back to the house, keeping the tree a shadow in her peripheral vision.

(Waves of things...,) it whispered.

The dogs ran delighted circles around them, darting at intervals out into the meadow.

(Of forms I am...)

She shook her head again as if to shake the song out of her thoughts and took a deep breath. The cat stood a moment on his hind feet leaning his front paws against her leg and she reached down to pet him.

"Could I rent this house? Could I stay here?" *Monica'd be upset if I moved away from her, but it'd be a good thing for both of us.*

The thought wasn't a new one. "I do love Monica," she whispered. "I do, but..."

She'd have to have a job. She had some money she could use for a deposit, but she'd have to have a job.

She moved slowly back toward the house, thinking. The smaller print on the For Rent sign read:

Country Acres Real Estate
1322 Main Street, Arundel

She scooped up the cat, called the dogs and walked up the driveway to the road and then turned toward the car. "Jee-sus," she muttered, "I left the car door open, the keys in the car."

Putting the car in drive, she drove silently just a little farther north.

The road turned inland and crossed a river before heading into the small coastal farming community of Arundel. The highway took her through the middle of town past a row of stores, the real estate office, an older gas station, and a little farther along, a small elementary school.

She turned around and headed back to the school, pulling into a parking place under some trees shadowing the parking lot. There was one other car in the lot.

She wasn't exactly dressed in job interview clothes, but she was clean.

This will be the test. If there's a job, then I'll move.

Rolling the windows down so they could get out if they wanted, she told the animals to stay near the car.

The school was built along the same model as so many rural schools – two long buildings of back to back classrooms with doors to each room coming directly off the sidewalk, joined by a slightly taller building Giselle assumed was the "multipurpose room" – the cafeteria, gym, assembly room all in one. At the end of the first building was a door marked "Office". The door was unlocked.

No one was sitting at the two desks behind the long high counter, but a door behind them was open. A friendly middle-aged white woman with short gray hair, dressed in jeans and a t-shirt, came through the door introducing herself as Nicki Nichols, the principal, and asking Giselle if she could be of help.

Giselle smiled and explained her situation, including having two dogs and a cat out by her car.

"I do have an opening," she exclaimed. "One of my fourth-grade teachers quit just yesterday. Let's talk outside at the picnic tables. You'll have to tell me how you came to be job searching with dogs and a cat – a cat? – in your car."

She held the door for Giselle and pointed out the tables near the cafeteria. Giselle got the animals and joined her.

Nicki petted the wiggling dogs and the gray cat.

"A cat?" she repeated, laughing.

"The cat just came… I mean, he stays pretty close." Giselle stumbled a little over her words. "This is a sudden decision. I mean applying for this job, but I think it's a good one."

She looked hopefully at Ms. Nichols. "I was traveling up the coast camping. I saw this house for rent just outside of town and it… I just thought…"

20

She took a deep breath. "I love teaching. I don't want to stop. I just want to be here."

Giselle listed her educational background and gave her Samuel's name and phone number.

Ms. Nichols told her about the community. "The school serves Arundel and the outlying farms with two classrooms at each grade level. The older children travel to Robertsville for middle school and high school. Arundel's a nice little town with a few stores and in Robertsville there's a shopping mall with all the modern conveniences."

She leaned back and smiled. "Are you interested?"

Giselle nodded. She wouldn't have to stay here forever if it didn't work out. Besides it just felt like…

The cat jumped into her lap and looked up at her.

"See," laughed Ms. Nichols, "the cat wants you to take the job!"

More than you know, thought Giselle, looking intently at the cat. *Otherwise I'd still hear "Go north!"*

She nodded. "Yes, I want to apply."

They returned to the office and Giselle filled out the forms and made arrangements for transcripts and her credential to be sent. Ms. Nichols would call Samuel for a recommendation.

The principal walked her to the office door. "We should know the answer in a day or two, since I've already interviewed you."

She gave Giselle a searching look. "It's very odd you showing up like this just when we need you… but good," she smiled. "It's good."

Giselle laughed and shrugged.

As she headed back into town she shook her head. "It was like the job was just waiting," she told the dogs. "So strange…"

She just shook her head again.

The real estate office was in a little white house next to the row of stores. The owner, Mr. Humphries, was a jovial older man. "I'd be delighted to show you the Bidewell house," he exclaimed when she told him what she wanted.

As they drove out to the house in her car (because of the animals) he told her more about it. "It's a wonderful little house, lovely views. Comes with a little land – a little meadow and beach. Very nice."

Before they went inside he handed her a sheet of paper with a picture of the house, a description of its physical qualifications, and the very reasonable rent and sale price.

"The rent seems pretty low," Giselle pointed out. "Is there something wrong with the house?"

"Oh, no, nothing wrong," he reassured her. "It's just been on the market a long time. It's a little isolated for most folks. The old folks kept it up very nicely. The wife – the husband passed – the wife pays someone to come in every so often to clean and check things out.

"And you don't have to worry about the rising seas," he added. "The cliff is high and the house is set pretty far back from the edge if the cliff does erode."

Giselle hadn't thought about rising seas. A little shiver went down her spine and she sighed.

"If we were a little farther south," Mr. Humphries went on. "You know, closer to the city – it would have sold in a snap."

"What about local people?"

"Oh, well, they mostly have their own places, and...," he hesitated.

"What?" asked Giselle. "And what?"

He laughed. "Well, local people don't want to live there because of the rumors about some of the hilltops over there." He pointed toward the hill back of the house. "People have a funny thing about the hills – the forest and the hills. Ghosts or something. They never define it, just hint at it. Things whispering in the redwood trees, or something. It's ridiculous of course. No one has ever said anything about the house, though. No ghosts in the house."

Singing, maybe? thought Giselle. *Are they hearing songs, too?*

The house was delightful. Everything seemed well and lovingly cared for. It was small – just the living room and kitchen downstairs, a bath and two bedrooms upstairs.

The view from the oceanside bedroom windows was a spectacular panorama from the meadow to the north to the hillside reaching for the cliff to the south where she could see, through the wide branches of the oak tree, a spit of rocks pushing out into the ocean.

And when she focused on the tree…

(Waves of things,) it whispered. *(Waves of things, of dreams...)*

Ghosts, she murmured to herself.

She'd have to wait to hear about the job, but she really wanted to live here.

Humphries smiled with delight. "I'll be glad to rent this house and maybe you'll want to buy it later. Mrs. Bidewell needs the money. I think you'll get that job. We have a hard time coming up with enough teachers."

As they drove back to town Humphries told her more about the community.

Yes, they had a nice little library – thank heavens it hadn't been closed down like some – and most folks really liked Ms. Nichols, the principal. "Some of the people in the community have lived here forever and tend to be a little provincial."

Humphries shifted a little uncomfortably in his seat. "But there are some folks who've moved in from other places – or been out in the world and come back – like Ms. Nichols – whose attitudes are a little more modern, if you know what I mean."

Giselle didn't really 'know what he meant', but thought about the rumors of ghosts in the woods. Maybe he was talking about that kind of thinking. "I really liked her. Does she live here in town?" asked Giselle.

"No. She lives in Robertsville. A little more privacy I think."

"Privacy? For her family, you mean? I mean… Is she married?"

"Well…" He hesitated. "No, she's not married. Ah… she just lives with a…" He paused. "Well, she has a housemate. Robertsville's just a little farther from the families of her students, and a larger community. That's all."

Housemate, thought Giselle. *Partner, perhaps? Maybe that's how the community is 'provincial'.*

"Did you grow up here?" she asked.

"Oh, no," he exclaimed. "My wife did, though. That's why we moved up here. I took over her father's real estate agency. Don't make a lot of money, but I have a small pension from my old job and it doesn't take a lot to live up here."

He paused looking thoughtful. "Hopefully I'll still have a pension from my old job. The way things are going today…"

She let him off at the door of the agency with promises to call him as soon as she heard about the job and drove off to find the nearest campground – a small county park on a river.

Oh, my god, she thought, what am I doing? This feels right, but scary. She wished she had someone to talk to, but she wasn't going to tell Monica until it was a done deal.

"Oh!" she exclaimed out loud. Ms. Nichols was going to call Samuel.

She pulled to the side of the road and found his number on her phone. He answered on the second ring.

"Hi, Giselle. I hear you're leaving us."

"Wow. She called you already?"

"Ms. Nichols called an hour or so ago. Does your sister know?"

"Not yet. I'm not going to tell her until I know I have the job."

Samuel laughed. "A wise decision."

He paused. "Actually, Giselle, I think this is a good move – moving away from Monica. You're an excellent teacher and I'll have a hard time filling your shoes, although not as hard as Ms. Nichols has. At least we have plenty of applicants. But I do think it's a good thing for you."

Giselle sighed. "I haven't gotten the job yet."

"But you will get it. Trust me."

After the phone call Giselle continued on to the campground by the river. It was a lovely little green brushy spot, with a small sandy beach where the river made a wide curve under overhanging cottonwood trees and you could swim at your own risk. The river was low – to be expected after three years of drought, but there was still enough water to swim. It wasn't very far from the house.

My house, she thought.

She set up her camp quickly, and they all headed for the little beach where the dogs paddled in the shallows while the cat patted curiously at the water with one paw.

Swimming out to the middle of the river, Giselle floated in the dappled light where the sun filtered down through the trees and willfully pushed the future out of her head. *Just floating,* she thought. *Just floating.*

She spent the night in the campground, and much of the next day swimming and exploring. Ms. Nichols called her in the afternoon to tell her the teaching job was hers, contingent on the receipt of her transcripts and credential.

As soon as she was off the phone Giselle rushed to the real estate office to rent the house. She signed the lease and Mr. Humphries informed her she could move in as soon as she wanted.

When she returned to the city, Monica was loud and disbelieving, but Giselle gathered her things, rented a truck for her few possessions, and moved. There would have to be a reconciliation with Monica at some point, she knew, but for now she just needed to leave with as little talk as possible.

Leave, and go to my house, she thought. *My house on the ocean.*

2

Moon of Ripening Fruit

Tata Sundancer circled high in the sunlit sky, gliding over the sea below and then beating his way back up the air currents to the top of the cliffs. He swooped low over the golden meadow, tipping his wings to the ancient oak tree, and then climbed the air currents up the hillside behind, turning higher and higher in the sky until he could see the wiry young man in jeans and well-worn t-shirt seated beside the sacred spring.

Circling above him, he called, "She's come, Yameno Wolfwind," and then took off back into the sky, heading again for the meadow.

Yameno bowed to the little waterfall, renewing his vow to protect the spring as his people had protected it for centuries. He stood, pushing his long black hair away from his face. Singing a low song, he transformed into his Tla Twei – a huge gray wolf – and trotted across the top of the hillside to a place where he, too, could watch the meadow, his silvery fur a shadow under the trees.

Stillness crept over the hillside, muffling the background hum of insects and birds, sung to the deep faint beat of the sea pulsing beyond the meadow.

The Wolfwind, sitting on his haunches between two pines, nodded to the Sundancer flying high above him, and then lay down, feeling the spongy needles under his pads. He nosed a weed away from his face, and peered at the meadow below, watching the figures at the edge of the cliff, his ears perked forward, intent.

The woman, and the small gray cat standing beside her, turned and watched the hawk rise out of sight. The sea wind swirled her cotton skirt

26

around her legs. The wolf's body was tight, unmoving, as he sat watching and waiting.

The beating of the surf on the rocks, the wind swishing through the meadow grass echoed a thrumming in Giselle's chest as she watched the circling hawk. She would do yoga here at the edge of the cliff every day. *Surya Namaskara*, the sun salutation. *What a perfect place to do it – at sunset, watching the sun go down over the sea!* She stretched her arms wide and threw her head back, feeling the pull on her spine reach down the backs of her legs and lift her heels from the ground. *My house, my meadow, my beach, my place! This is my place!*

> *(Breath, sang the earth, the wind,*
> *Listen,*
> *Whispering breath,*
> *Anima of the earth,*
> *Murmuring in the wind-whipped grasses,*
> *Lift my feet and keep me dancing.)*
> *And my song! I hear it! I hear it!*

With a quick release of her breath, she straightened, reaching for the sky, and then contracted in, touching the ground, curling into herself in a deep bow to the earth and the sea and the sky.

> *Breath,*
> *Flowing in the waves of the sea,*
> *Creep into my soul and conquer me.*

The two dogs, who had been racing across the field, came back and ran in wide circles around Giselle and the cat. Caught up in their joy, she ran after them and soon led them around and around, beating a path in the meadow grasses. She tossed her head and laughed and the dogs wiggled and leapt and added small yaps to the whistling wind. Faster and faster they circled, until her breath gave out and she fell smiling on the ground.

> *Breath,*
> *Singing through the voice of the wind,*
> *Dance with me, sing with me,*
> *Take my hand,*
> *Enter me as a lover,*
> *Make me one with you.*

A small breeze caressed her as she lay still, gazing at the sky. The dogs pounced on her, full of licks and rubs, shoving their cold noses into her neck. She held them both close and warm, one under each arm. The cat climbed up on her chest between the dogs and rubbed his head under her neck. "Do you hear the music, animals?" she whispered. "Do you hear it?"

> *Breath,*
> *Warmed by the life-giving sun,*
> *Burn, burn within me, until I am consumed.*

The sun reached the edge of the sea and the jagged rocks pointed from their foam washed bases to the fire-lit sky. The wolf's gaze was drawn from the woman to where the hawk winged a swooping dance across the sinking sun.

Even the dogs were quiet as the pink and orange light consumed the day. The cat rubbed against the woman and she sat up, pulling him into her arms, hugging him tightly, and running her fingers through his fur.

Then the light was gone and the sea turned dark.

The Wolfwind watched the woman return to the house set against the hillside. He lay there for a while after she disappeared under the cover of the porch, and then slipped away, a silver shadow in the dark forest.

Loping tirelessly through the woods to the edge of town where the forest met the cat woman's backyard, he crouched behind a tree and made a small yapping noise. The door opened noiselessly and Luhanada, walked swiftly to the edge of the woods. She smiled and pushed a strand of red hair shot with gray back behind her ear, as she watched the Wolfwind take human form.

"She came," Yameno said, joyfully hugging the woman.

"Yes, Tata told me," she replied.

"Did he tell you of the song that came from the earth? Could he hear it from the sky?"

"Yes, and I could hear it here."

Yameno nodded thoughtfully. "Ninas Twei sent for her. Ninas Twei is calling her – calling us all," he added.

The cat woman nodded. "You'll be able to create the totem?" she asked, anxiously.

"Yes, soon. I'm beginning to understand it," he nodded. "Beginning," he added, smiling. They hugged again before he took wolf form, melting back into the trees.

A large yellow cat came and twined himself around her ankles, rubbing back and forth. She leaned down and picked him up before walking silently back to the house and settling herself in a chair, the cat in her lap, the other cats sleeping or bathing on the sofa and in other cozy spots around her.

The music had started. *Twei* – both music and dance in the language of Yameno's people, the Tuwillians. "Well, cat," she whispered. "Now we gather. First this young woman, then the children. It begins again."

She gave a deep sigh and closed her eyes. Now that the young woman was here she kept flashing on the last time and Mary – dear Mary – falling and falling out of the vortex.

It had been a beautiful autumn day, the sky endlessly, cloudlessly blue, and the air crisp and clean. The woods, as they walked through it to the meeting place, had seemed to bow in anticipation. She had noticed that Gunther seemed to hang back and that Mary had to coax him on, but...

"We never thought he would…" she whispered.

The new woman was a wild card just as Gunther Amundsen had been last time – wild, unpredictable, and afraid – but it was different this time. The woman heard the music. "Please," she whispered. "No accidents this time."

Giselle lit a fire in the small stone fireplace. Tonight was a new beginning. Not just a move to a new town and a new job and her wonderful new house. *There's something else,* she thought. She looked into the fire. *Today, in the meadow by the cliff, a hawk circled and the earth sang. I heard it.*

She looked at the little cat. *Didn't I?*

Waxing Crescent

The morning sun fell across the old oak bed awakening Giselle and the two dogs lying curled one on each side of her. As she rolled over to look at the time, a small gray head popped out from under the covers. The cat climbed precariously up her side to her shoulder and then leaned his head down and rubbed it under her chin. She hugged his whole soft body close to her and let his strong tail run through her hands as he arched and walked away across the bed.

Yameno Wolfwind, welcoming the morning scent of pine surrounding him, lay under the same tree as the day before watching the little house. Tata glided in the swift air currents above the cliff. Both watched as Giselle opened the door and the cat walked out, turned toward the hill and stretched, pulling all his rippling body back and back, fixing his eyes on that particular spot in the pines where the Wolfwind sat. Yameno grinned back, his red tongue hanging from the side of his muzzle. The hawk called and the cat padded down the porch steps and sat looking up at the swooping bird.

Giselle, still in her pajamas, followed the cat and looked up at the hawk, watching until he disappeared around the wooded hillside.

She laughed and shook her head. It was less than two weeks since she first saw this house and here she was living in it! "I'm here," she whispered, moving in a circle, her arms outstretched, stopping as she faced the oak tree's ancient, commanding presence out in the middle of the wild grasses. Now it was... not her tree. You couldn't own a tree. It felt more like it owned her.

Looking out to sea, she felt the warmth of the sunshine sliding down her back. The world seemed friendly, welcoming, as if the air, the atmosphere was caressing her. Even the soil in the garden was just sitting there waiting for her to dig her fingers in, wiggling in anticipation!

She laughed and ran back into the house eager to buy garden tools and other housekeeping supplies. A little later she appeared on the porch fully dressed, leaping down the three steps to the ground. Soon her car was leaving a cloud of dust as she climbed the dirt road to the highway.

As soon as she left, Yameno trotted down the hill to the house, waiting a moment at the edge of the woods to make sure the car was out of sight. The dogs ran out the doggy door, barking, and then crouched to greet him as he took human form. They sniffed him and then rubbed closer, wagging their tails and murmuring little whines. He scratched their ears and allowed them to escort him to the house.

The gray cat sat at the top of the porch stairs and he sat on the steps a moment and scratched his ears. "You've done well, little friend." The cat purred and rubbed against him.

He stood up and went to the window on the left of the door and looked in at the living room. Boxes of books were stacked against one wall, waiting to be shelved on boards and bricks. Across from them, an old trunk sat in front of a comfortable, but shabby looking sofa. There were plants in every window.

The dogs and cat followed him, rubbing and begging for pats and cuddles, as he walked around the porch to the kitchen windows, shading his eyes as he peered in past the plants at the oak table and wooden chairs. He laughed at them, gave them all a little hug, then slipped off the porch and strode up the hill.

When Giselle returned from town a little later, he was sitting with his back against a boulder at the top of the hill reading a book. He glanced down as her car pulled in, shifting his position so that he could see the house without moving his head too much from the book, and returned to his reading.

Giselle went happily to work in her garden. The work was hard, but the chill breeze from the sea made the warm sun on her back welcome. She was able to pull most of the large brush out by hand loosening the soil, and then sort through the dirt with her hands for the offending weeds and grasses.

"I know why the sand box is always the most popular part of the play yard," she informed the dogs. "It feels like the dirt wants your hands in it. Sensual dirt, flowing through your fingers, rubbing against you, loving every minute of your digging in it."

Once she turned up a fat wiggling earthworm. She jumped, letting him fall back to the earth and laughed. "I'm sorry. I do like you, worm. Eat and enjoy! And I hope you have a large family." The worm wiggled off into the dirt.

Giselle stood up and stretched taking a deep breath. The mingled odors of fresh-turned soil, the thick unkempt greenery in back of the house, and the salty sea air seemed as heady as ether. She stretched, taking in the wide circle of her world.

The oak tree in the meadow stopped her.

(Waves of things of forms I am…)

She took a deep breath and walked over to it.

It feels so important, this tree. I want to touch it. I want to climb inside and be this tree. She reached out to its warm trunk. The ridges made a rough bark, and yet each one was individually smooth. She sat between its roots and leaned her head back against the trunk, turning her cheek to feel the rough-smoothness.

Everything seemed so silent – waiting. She heard the sea gulls out by the cliff and the smaller woods birds in the forest on the hill behind her.

The man on the hill saw her smile. He watched the cat walk over and sit quietly by her side. The afternoon seemed to take a deep still breath...

Sinking into the soil and twining into the twisted oak, no longer existing apart, no longer separate from the rest of the universe, she was the soil, the air, the tree...

Waves of things of forms I am,
exist in dreams within me.
Flow through the sap of trees to come
and leaves to come.
Falling, decaying, the soil I am,
a nutrient for things living.
Eating the earth,
the water and sun,
fruit I become,
feeding the unrooted beings
ever I'm giving.

And then I am free!
I stretch my wings
and fling myself into the air.
I sing!
I call!
My joy is beyond any earthly care.
The snap of the jaws of the four-legged one
is only a moment of pain,
for I am living again
with a different name.

And when this life's done
the worms I become,
and pass to the earth
to gain my rebirth.

The sun shifted just enough to fall across her face, pushing away the shade of the oak.

She turned her head to look up at the twisting branches of the old tree and the two songs, the tree's song and the earth's song, seemed to weave together...

Waves of things of forms I am...
Breath,
Live in the wind-whipped grasses...
Earth and tree,
Sun and sea.

The song faded out to a whisper, like the sea breeze in the leaves above her:

(Earth and sea,
Sun and tree,
All one. All one. All one.)

She reached a hand out and rubbed her fingers along a ridge of bark and dug them into a crevice feeling the smooth roundness of years of growing. A warmth tingled from the tree through her fingers and she felt a reluctance to sever the contact. Even after she pulled herself away she felt a strength emanating from it, reaching out like an electrical current from the tips of its branches to the tips of her fingers.

She picked up the cat, pulling him tight to her chest. "I think this is what I'm looking for, but I could get lost. I felt lost, like I was gone and the tree – don't let me get lost, kitty."

Giving the tree a last caress, she ran across the field and returned to her garden. She dug in the dirt, feeling a little shaky. "I like the tree," she whispered. She looked down at the dirt, grinning, "and I like you, earth."

The Wolfwind ran south through the forest and then west to the beach. He grinned at brother sea breeze as it ruffled his fur, his nostrils dilated to draw in the thick sea smell. He loped swiftly along the hard packed sand until he came to a driftwood log, wide at one end with a long, thick fork at the other. Becoming two-legged, he went down on one knee beside it and ran his fingers along its water-smoothed surface.

Tata flew down the beach, landed first on the log, and then flew off onto the beach becoming an older black man, tall and craggy in jeans and black t-shirt.

Yameno nodded at him and pulled a small knife from his jeans pocket to carve at the hard wood. Tata watched silently as Yameno, the wind whipping his hair into his eyes, sliced a hard piece off and examined it.

Yameno sat back and looked at him. "She's the tree."

Tata crouched down beside him, his brown hands caressing the driftwood. "Yes, and the earth. The earth sang to her."

"Earth and tree. I can feel it in the wood." Yameno leaned over and rubbed his hand along the water-smoothed log. "And I am wolf and wind and water."

Tata smiled and touched his shoulder. He turned his black eyes on the sea and gazed out to the horizon and beyond. Standing up, he brushed the sand off his legs and turned back to Yameno. "I feel… it feels like there's some urgency to this. They called her."

Yameno nodded.

First Quarter

A week after Giselle moved in, the dogs barked loudly as the local deputy sheriff drove his car down her driveway and knocked on the door. She had been surprised and a little alarmed to see the officer, a slim fiftyish man with short sandy-brown hair, standing very straight in his khaki uniform and looking a little disapprovingly at her.

"I heard you were living out here all by yourself. Just dropped by to let you know a few things about the county and law enforcement."

"Why, thank you. I'm not quite alone. I have two dogs and a cat," exclaimed Giselle.

He rested one hand on his belt holster, stuck the thumb of the other into his belt, and turned toward the hill behind her house. "I know you just rented this house, but you might reconsider living way out here on your own."

Giselle's brows narrowed. "It's really not very far from town."

"Arundel isn't incorporated. There're no police in town. The county sheriffs take care of it all and there's only one deputy at a time covering this north territory. That's two hundred square miles, I'm talking about."

He waved his arm around indicating the size of the territory. "You have some kind of trouble and call it in, I might be on the other side of the county. If you're in trouble and can't call it in, we'd never know. Not unless we get one of them surveillance drones."

Giselle's eyes widened and she shuttered. *Surveillance drone?* "Do you think I'll have any trouble? Do people usually have trouble out here?"

"No – no." He turned again toward the hill. "No, not much trouble over here, but I never had a young woman living alone out the country to worry about before."

"Have you had young men living alone"

"Of course, but…"

"Well," Giselle interrupted, "I don't think there's anything to worry about. I have dogs to warn me if anyone's around, and frankly I haven't seen anyone out in this area at all. You're the first person who's come down my driveway since I moved in here."

The deputy shrugged his shoulders, muttered something about just letting her know the situation and walked off toward his car. Giselle called out a thank you to him and closed her door.

Full Moon

She felt very safe at her house. Her only human contact was when she went to town. She did keep up with friends, and the sometimes heart wrenching state of the world via email and the internet, following especially the news from One Earth Together knowing that OET consolidated news from many other concerned non-profits. But at home, except for the animals, she was alone.

She'd driven up and down the streets of Arundel looking at the mostly older houses, well-kept with pretty gardens. She'd seen all the stores and a couple of churches, one very traditional looking little white church that contrasted sharply with another very bleak looking church down the street made of gray concrete blocks with a big banner that read, "REPENT AND BE SAVED." There was one small coffee shop in town and she'd been there for lunch once, and out on the highway there was a restaurant with a bar that didn't look like a place where she'd be too comfortable.

As far as people were concerned, she'd already become friendly with Hazel Fraya who was the librarian in the one room library – a delightful woman with a mass of red hair beginning to gray pulled back in an unruly braid, who "kept house", as she secretly confided, for seven plump cats.

She was only on a "Hello, how are you?" basis with the older black man who could be found gardening in one or another of the yards she passed walking from her parking space to the little library or the local stores. He was the only person of color she'd seen in town so far, which seemed a little odd. His eyes, smiling, but intent, always seemed to catch in hers. He looked familiar, but she couldn't think of where she might have met him.

The storekeepers had been friendly enough. There was a hardware store, a variety store, a combination drug and grocery store, and some smaller businesses. In the weeks before school started Giselle visited all of them. She knew once school started she'd meet some local teachers, but meanwhile, rushing to get the things she needed to settle in before school opened gave her an opportunity to meet some of the local people.

Back at home hiking through the woods or down the beach Giselle felt totally alone and free to do as she pleased. Free from anyone human at least! Ghosts? Well... she thought of the song that came to her out on the cliff and her experience with the tree. More like spirits.

Last Quarter

One day, however, she returned from a trip down the beach to discover a small bouquet of wildflowers, their stems wrapped in wet paper to keep them fresh, sitting on her porch in front of the door. There was no note.

She turned full circle looking up at the hills, down the drive and out at the meadow and the tree. No one. Her stomach gave a little twist, but, she thought, anyone could have left the flowers as a welcome, even a child. The deputy had just made her apprehensive.

Every evening she went out to the meadow by the edge of the cliff to do her yoga exercises and watch the sun set. She felt like the sun, and the sea and the earth and the air, too, were holding her, cradling her in their arms. As she repeated her ritual bows twelve times to the fiery sky, it felt like her body melted into the earth and the air, floating in the pink of the ragged clouds, clinging to the sinking sun, rolling in the curves of the waves as they beat their constant rhythm on the beach, riding them like a roller coaster.

The gray kitten sat silently at the edge of the cliff, watching the gulls slide down the air currents whipped over the open sea.

Yameno Wolfwind watched her from his hillside lookout. He studied the contours of her figure, her waist above the small curve of her stomach, the muscular sturdiness of her legs. He came often to watch her bow down to the sun, to capture the feel of her arms outstretched to the sky to translate to the driftwood, to see the swirl of her skirt, and the straightness of her whips of hair in the sea wind. Tata had helped drag the log up the hill to Yameno's home, smiling as he watched Yameno caress the wood, and helping as he turned it this way and that to see the natural curves and crevices. The woman's totem was begun.

"And the children?" Tata had asked. Yameno grinned, pointing to a carving of a squirrel sitting between the ears of a coyote.

That evening Tata also talked to Luhanada about the children, taking a hot gulp of the tea she'd just poured for him. "We need the children to complete the circle."

"They'll come soon," she'd replied pouring her own tea, carefully stirring half a teaspoon of honey into its dark amber depths. "The teacher will help bring them."

3

Moon When Acorns Fall

On the first day of school the sun rose bright and warm and the streets of Arundel sparkled with its dancing light and the boisterous laughs of nervous children. Giselle's students filed into the room, looking around at the bulletin boards and posters before choosing desks and settling down.

In the middle of attendance, the door opened tentatively, just wide enough for a small girl to edge her way around it and stand bewildered next to the wall, staring at Giselle. The child's eyes were an intense, dark blue – the color of the ocean on a clear bright day. Giselle'd known an old man once who'd sometimes look at a child and say, "That child's a very old soul." At the time Giselle had been vaguely amused, but this little girl did seem to her to be 'a very old soul.' She pointed out an empty desk and the girl slid quietly into the chair.

"What's your name?" she asked smiling.

The child whispered something in such a small voice Giselle couldn't hear it. "I'm sorry, I couldn't hear you." Giselle moved closer to the girl.

"My name is Enid Amundsen." She was barely audible. There were smirks and smothered giggles from some of the children. Giselle looked quickly in their direction and they were quiet. She smiled reassuringly and continued with attendance.

One child was still missing. She was passing out paper, pencils, and crayons when the door was thrown wide and a tall boy with a full head of dark curls pushed his way in, making all of them jump as he let the door slam behind him.

She looked over at him and smiled. "You must be Jesús McCrae."

He shoved his hands into his back pockets and shrugged, staring past Giselle at the wall behind her. She pointed to the empty seat next to

Enid. "We're writing a paragraph and drawing pictures of what we like best about school."

He gave her a quick, incredulous look, and turned his eyes back to the wall behind her as he pushed his way to his desk.

Nothing, she thought. *There's nothing he likes about school.*

While they were writing and drawing she called students up to a corner table to check reading and math skills. Between groups she walked around the classroom. Coming up behind Enid and Jesús she bent over to get a closer look at Jesús' picture.

It was the school – not any school, but an accurate picture of Arundel Elementary with a crack down the center exploding with fire. Desks were plunging through the air, and dark smoke mixed with flames reached out long tongues toward a woman flying topsy-turvy through the smoke. The woman had such individuated features – older with short permed hair, a grim look on her face – Giselle felt sure she was a particular person.

She picked up the drawing and held it up to see it in a better light. "This is quite a drawing, Jesús. Who's the woman?"

Jesús stiffened, but didn't look at her, or answer. She stood there for a moment looking at him. Finally she said, "We'll talk about this later. Meanwhile, write your paragraph."

Before lunch she collected papers from each desk group. Jesús hadn't written his paragraph, but there were several drawings on his desk. One was a caricature of her and at the top it was titled, "Bitch." *Well, I guess he can write one-word descriptions,* she thought.

The next drawing was of the sea. He had sketched it in pencil, shading it like a charcoal drawing. The water was tossing and angry. "Can I hang this picture on the wall?" she asked him. "You draw very well."

He shrugged.

Then she held the "Bitch" picture in front of his face. He turned his head away from the picture and Giselle. "But this one's mine," she continued. "Too bad you labeled it. I'd have hung it, too. It's good."

No response.

This time it was Giselle who shrugged. She wasn't sure what she was going to do with the disturbing picture of the school.

The bell rang for the noon recess and the children filed out, their lunch bags or money in their hands.

Giselle waited until the room was empty and then looked again at Jesús' drawings. There was a power in his pictures, as if he had somehow caught the edge of something alive and throbbing. She could almost see the waves rolling, could almost hear the drumming of the surf in the picture of the sea. When she looked closer she saw there were faces in the sea – very subtle, but definitely there. How could a child do that? It was hard for her to pull her eyes away from the picture and she was late for her first day in the teacher's lunchroom.

She felt nervous and awkward as she entered the room – unattached to her brain as if there was cotton in her head. The room was small, just big enough to hold a large table. Around it sat most of the members of the faculty. She had been introduced to them at the short faculty meeting the day before, but none of them had come up to her and introduced themselves as she prepared her classroom – and there was the woman from the picture of the school exploding!

The conversation stopped. She felt their eyes examining her until she was fully inspected. Ms. Nichols, sitting at the end of the long table, rose to meet her, and drawing her forward, named the other teachers, including Rowena Dickerson, the woman in Jesús' picture. Giselle slid into an empty chair and promptly forgot most of the rest of their names.

"Hey, I thought I saw Jesús McCrae come in late and go into your room, Giselle," said one younger male teacher waving a sandwich in her direction. He turned to Nicki. "Did you put Jesús McCrae in her class?"

"Yes, Harding," answered the principal, "that I did."

"Do you think that was a very nice thing to do to a new teacher?" Harding persisted.

"Giselle can handle him," replied the principal.

Giselle nodded in agreement. "Jesús and I will do just fine."

"Oh, you don't know," exclaimed Rowena. "I had him last year. He had to be suspended from school four times!"

"Maybe that's why he misbehaves. So he won't have to come to school," suggested Giselle with a grin as she pulled the lid off her yogurt. There was a brief silence. Giselle noted a few raised eyebrows. Rowena Dickerson was glaring at her. *Oh, oh,* she thought, *I didn't quite mean it to come out like that....*

"Oh, he's terrible," Rowena spit out vehemently. "He ought to be sent to Juvenile Hall, or something. He sits there with his arms crossed and doesn't answer you." She shook her head over the neat, half of a

40

chicken sandwich on white bread she held clasped in both hands halfway to her mouth.

"And his parents aren't any better. His father's part of that McCrae clan of dirt-farming trouble makers that goes way back around here. Quit school and joined the army, and when he came back, he'd married a Mexican. Brought her back here – here to Arundel! She's the only one of her kind here." She looked up at Giselle. "There are plenty of them in Robertsville, but thank God not here." Giselle eyes got wide for a moment, shocked at the overt bigotry. No wonder Nicki lived in Robertsville.

Another teacher added, "Billy McCrae's one of those motorcycle types – has a beard and long hair and everything."

Giselle reached in her bag for some crackers. "Well, it's obvious Jesús' quite a handful, but he's certainly an incredible artist."

"Huh?" Rowena replied.

"Jesús," said Giselle. "He does beautiful art work, doesn't he?"

"I didn't know he did any work," replied the teacher.

"He may not do much," replied Giselle. "He wouldn't write a paragraph for me this morning, but he did several really excellent pictures."

"Well, I certainly wouldn't let him draw when he hadn't done his school work." The older teacher folded her sandwich bag carefully, keeping her eyes on her hands and avoided looking at Giselle again.

Harding grinned at Giselle. "I'll bet he really gave you a rough time this morning."

"Oh, nothing I couldn't handle!" laughed Giselle.

Ms. Nichols grinned. "This isn't Giselle's first year of teaching. She's been teaching inner city kids."

Harding shrugged and concentrated on his sandwich.

"You should've seen my class!" exclaimed another teacher drawing the attention away, much to Giselle's relief.

When Giselle returned to her classroom after lunch she found three boys struggling outside the door. One was Jesús McCrae. Catching Jesús' arm, she said, "Boys, stop this and get in the classroom."

Jesús pulled away from her defiantly.

"Jesús, go in." He shrugged his shoulders and went into the room, followed by the other boys and Giselle, who closed the door behind her. "Sit down."

The other boys sat, but Jesús stood in the middle of the room, glaring at the wall. Giselle ignored him. "Am I right in guessing it was you two against Jesús?"

One boy was quick to take the lead saying he'd come to Joey's rescue because Jesús hit him. Joey blushed and looked at the floor. Jesús stared at the wall.

She spent some time trying to get Jesús to tell his side with no response, but after some futzing around Joey finally admitted he'd called Jesús a "dirty spic."

Giselle took a deep breath. "Do you know what that means?"

"It's a nasty word for someone who's Mexican." The boy tucked his chin into his chest staring at the floor.

She gave them a lecture on ethnic slurs as a form of poison, and sent Joey and his friend out of the room, then turned to Jesús. "It feels really bad when someone calls you a name like that."

He turned his head as far away from her as he could.

She picked up his caricature of her off the desk. "It hurts me when you call me names, too." Jesús' eyes flicked wide for a moment before shuttering down again. "But it's not an excuse for hitting someone. I don't hit you when you call me names and you may not hit any of the other students, for any reason."

She took another deep breath. "I hear last year you were suspended from school four times. What did you do while you were suspended?"

"Went fishing," he muttered. He was still staring at the wall, but his lips lifted in a tiny smirk.

"Did you have fun?" she smiled.

Jesús gave her a startled glance before turning away again. "I caught a lot of fish."

"Well, Jesús, I just want to tell you that I don't care how much trouble you get into, you're not going to get suspended from school this year. You can spend every afternoon in detention if you choose, and that will be less time for fishing. You can save your fishing for after school and weekends."

His eyes met hers for a moment and then looked quickly away.

42

The bell rang and the rest of the children came babbling, pushing, and shoving into the classroom. Last was Enid who crept along the wall to her desk. Jesús walked over to his desk and as he passed her he suddenly pounded his fist down on her desk right in front of her face. Enid jumped and looked at him in terror. Her eyes began to fill with tears.

"Oh, shit," he muttered. He glanced up at Giselle and their eyes met for a moment.

"Detention. Today."

He lowered his head and sat down. *Oh, shit, indeed,* thought Giselle, moving over behind Enid to rest a hand reassuringly on her shoulder.

The rest of the afternoon was uneventful. Jesús accomplished nothing, but he didn't cause any disturbances, seemingly off in a world of his own. He went to detention without a word.

After school there was a long, tedious faculty meeting and Giselle found herself staring out the open window at the aspens that rustled gently in the wind, a whispered song. When the meeting ended she was anxious to leave, but she did take time to ask Nicki if she knew anything about Enid Amundsen.

"Yes, I do." Nicki propped herself on a table top and crossed her arms in front of her chest. "Her mother, Emma, was very young and unmarried when Enid was born. She killed herself when Enid was two. Enid lives with her grandfather, Gunther Amundsen. He's very… difficult. He tried to keep Enid from coming to school, but of course he didn't get away with that."

She grimaced. "I hear he hardly ever comes into town anymore," she continued, "although he used to be quite friendly. But when his wife died – that was a couple of years before Emma got pregnant with Enid – he withdrew. I understand Enid does all right in her school work as long as her shyness doesn't interfere, but she won't read out loud in a group or give reports. She reads and writes quite well."

Nicki stood, thrusting her hands in the pockets of her gray slacks and giving Giselle a brief smile, then strode off toward the office.

Giselle walked slowly to the parking lot pushing unlock on the remote as she walked. The car door was burning hot to the touch from the warm late summer sun.

Later, when Giselle went down to the river at the county park to swim she was alarmed to see a new sign at the entrance:

Due to budget cuts,
THIS PARK WILL CLOSE
November 1

It went on to list the names of county supervisors to contact to protest the closure.

"Oh, no, not this park, too," she whispered. She'd read on One Earth Together about park closures all over the country. Often the land was being sold to private corporations. She took a deep breath and continued down the drive to the river. "I'm not going to think about that right now. I'm not."

The river, edged by the tall slender cottonwoods, wound slowly around the nearly empty beach. It was even lower in its banks than the last time she'd come, but still deep enough to swim. She swam laps back and forth in front of the beach with bursts of joy, feeling her energy, dissipated after her first day of class, return as if it were flowing from the river into her muscles. Floating on her back with her hands clasped behind her head, she felt herself a part of the river itself and she dove underneath the water with an inexplicable yearning to stay under forever.

A willow tree extended from the top of the steep bank on the far side and hung over her, filled with the songs of little birds high in its branches. A scrub jay sat on a limb hanging so low she could almost reach out her hand and slip her fingers down his feathery back.

Something blue fluttered above her on the steep bank next to the willow and the jay flew away.

A man sat cross-legged, leaning against the tree, an open book in his hands. His long black hair was shoved back from his dark eyes. His jeans were patched and faded and his old blue shirt hung open to the breeze, but he didn't have that brittle thin look of the malnourished or drug consumed poor that often made her want to pull them into her arms like a small child. She felt a warmth in her cheeks as she realized she did want to touch the brown hardness of his chest. He looked up from the book and for one short second she thought perhaps he was looking back at her, but then he stood and walked away from the edge of the bank, swinging the book in one hand, and disappeared into the forest, leaving her with a strange empty feeling.

She swam a couple more laps, glancing every once in a while up at the bank. For a moment or two a huge shaggy gray dog sat where the man had been, (*I am the wild, the wild,* whispered a song) but then he, too, slipped off into the underbrush. With a sigh, Giselle swam for the beach and home.

First Quarter

After almost a week of school Giselle decided to talk to Enid's grandfather about her shyness. Since his land was just a little north of her place she thought she would stop by on her way home. She turned off the highway and up the long drive to the small house.

The place was shabby. Peelings of old white paint crawled down the walls and the windows were so encased by dirt that it was hard to believe that anyone could see in or out of them. Behind the house, and in sharp contrast, was a sturdy, well-kept barn. As she climbed out of the car, a tall, grim man stepped out of the barn and stood staring at her, hands fisted at his waist. A dog ran over to Giselle, wagging its tail, and she petted it as she stepped forward. "Hello, Mr. Amundsen," she said, extending her hand. "I'm Enid's teacher, Giselle Raphael. I live close by. I thought maybe we could talk."

"I'm busy," he said, ignoring her hand and turning back to the barn.

Following him and talking at his back, she said, "Perhaps I could return this evening. I just live down the road on the other side of the bridge. It would be no trouble."

He turned and faced her, his hands again braced at his waist. "What do you want?"

"Could we sit down somewhere?"

The man just stared at her.

She began again. "Enid seems to have some problems with shyness. She won't read aloud or participate in most of the class activities. It's very difficult for her and she's missing a great deal. I thought perhaps we could work together…"

The man leaned forward. "Listen, teacher. The law says Enid has to go to school, but that's it. Now leave."

"Mr. Amundsen, Enid's growing up. She'll have to face a world full of real people and be able to survive in it. She hardly survives in a world of children right now."

Giselle's eyes met the washed out blue of the man's eyes. He leaned forward and his right hand, rolled into a fist, beat the air in front of her. She stepped back, alarmed.

"Enid won't need to go out into any world," he roared at her. "She won't need to face any people. She's my punishment and she'll stay with me. She's my reminder. She's a child of sin." He pulled himself up straight mumbling, "I've got work to do," and turned toward the barn.

Giselle was so astounded by his outbreak that it took her a moment to recover. Moving quickly, she stepped in front of him and looked straight into his icy eyes. "Enid needs help, and if you think she's a punishment for you…"

She backed up a step, managing to stop herself before the words "you need help, too" slipped out.

The man didn't answer. His muscles tensed and he leaned toward her.

She stumbled backwards again. *My God! He's going to hit me!*

Suddenly he spun away from her, slamming his fist into the barn door, sending it flying back against the wall. Then he stomped away into the dark recesses of the barn.

Giselle's stomach gave a lurch and she walked weakly back to her car.

When she pulled into her own driveway she felt exhausted. With dragging feet she walked out to the cliff to do some yoga.

Yameno, watching from his vantage point on the hillside noticed the droop of her shoulders and leaned forward when she finally gave up her exercises and sat down with a plop at the edge of the cliff. She sank her head into her arms folded across her knees, and cried until, tears finally gone, she pulled herself up and walked slowly back to her house. He sat for a while looking out to sea, then lifted his head and howled a small song before turning towards home.

Giselle heard the song and wondered – was that a dog up on the hillside? It sounded like the howling wolf video she'd seen online, but there wouldn't be any wolves around here. She looked at her own dogs. They seemed interested, but not afraid. She shrugged her shoulders and went into the kitchen to fix some dinner.

Gunther Amundsen dug the shiny points of the hay hooks into the bale of alfalfa, and bending his knees, heaved the bale into the back of his old green pickup truck.

"Interfering teacher," he muttered, raising his arms on either side and driving the hay hooks into another bale with a *thock*.

46

"So she's shy." Up flew the bale *thunking* on the floor of the truck. "Good. She'll stay with me." Again the *thock* of the hay hooks in the hay and the *thunk* of the bale on the truck floor. "Safe from..." *Thock.* The points slid between the stems of the alfalfa to find purchase. *Thunk*, and then sudden silence.

She lives down the road, he thought. *On the other side of the bridge? Near the forest.* Had the dog barked? *No.*

One of them. She's one of them.

(And the wind whispered, *Breath, breath, all One. All One...*)

Giselle found out more about Enid Thursday afternoon when she visited the little library to return some books. As she was about to leave, it occurred to her that an avid reader like Enid might come to the little library. Maybe the cat loving librarian could give her some information.

"By the way," she said, as she waited for Hazel to process her books. "One of my students loves to read and I was wondering if she ever comes to the library? I can't believe she has enough books at home to keep her occupied."

"Who's that?" The woman leaned back in her chair, eyes alert, pushing wisps of curly red hair back into her braid.

"Her name is Enid Amundsen. A shy little girl..."

"Enid." Hazel leaned forward nodding. "Yes. I know Enid very well. She's my grandniece. My sister Mary was her grandmother." A sad, faraway look came over the older woman's face. "Things have been hard. Life… well… life would have been a lot different for Enid, and Enid's mother, too, if my sister hadn't died."

Giselle pulled a chair close to the desk. "Are you willing to talk about it? Enid is such a special child, and she needs help."

The librarian looked keenly at Giselle and nodded her head. "Yes, she is indeed a special child."

Giselle took a deep breath, "I went out to Enid's house..."

"Oh, my!" exclaimed the librarian.

"And managed to talk to her grandfather," Giselle continued, "but it wasn't very successful."

"I can imagine," Hazel said dryly. She straightened some books on her desk. "Enid comes in here once every couple of weeks. When she first reached school age, he didn't send her to school. I told the authorities and the only reason he sends her to school now is because otherwise they'd take her away from him. There were social workers involved and they insisted she be allowed to see me, but I'm only allowed to see her here at the library."

"You'd think they'd want her to spend some time with you, since you're her great-aunt and she has no other female influence in her life."

Hazel looked away. "Well, there was some controversy as to whether or not I was a suitable influence."

"What? That seems surprising!"

The librarian stared out the window at the back of the library. "One of the local ministers is somewhat opposed to me."

"But you're a librarian!" Giselle sat back in her chair and stared at the woman. "You're an intelligent, educated woman – although in today's misogynist climate that might not be so helpful."

Hazel gave a rueful laugh. "Well, yes."

She rolled a pencil back and forth on the desktop. "There were other factors. Not fair ones," she said looking directly at Giselle, "but nevertheless the minister was able to influence the court."

Giselle waited for Hazel to tell her more about the 'other factors', but instead, she smiled at Giselle and asked what happened on her visit to Enid's grandfather.

Giselle sat forward leaning her elbows on the desk. "He said Enid was his punishment and she'd stay with him forever. Sounds like he plans to lock her up as soon as she's old enough to run away."

"His punishment." Hazel looked away sadly. "Only he has the wrong idea of what he did wrong."

Giselle raised her eyebrows, but the woman only smiled sadly and shook her head.

"When did your sister die?"

"My sister died several years before Enid was born. My brother-in-law never really coped with her death." Hazel sighed. "There were unusual... Enid's mother, Emma, really needed him during that time and he wasn't capable of giving her the affection she needed. He wouldn't let me near her. He... distrusted me."

Hazel looked down at her desk and straightened some books, remembering. *He kept Emma from the forest.*

She turned back to Giselle, "Emma turned to the boys at school for affection and the result was Enid. That, on top of my sister's death, was too much for Gunther, and his fury was more than Emma could bear. She killed herself."

No one knew who Enid's father was, and Jarvis – the Reverend Tarrant – had kept Hazel from getting the child away from Gunther. Nothing had ever been as hard as standing by helpless, watching the children – her niece and now her grandniece – suffer.

"You know, Giselle, what people wrapped up in their own emotional needs – and fears – can inflict on others, and on themselves, is a very frightening thing."

As she was talking, the door opened. The older black man Giselle sometimes saw gardening came in and the librarian's worried face relaxed as she watched him walk over to the desk. He spoke pleasantly with her and said, "Hello, how are you?" to Giselle as he placed a pile of books in the book return basket.

"Have you met Dan Burroughs?" Hazel asked.

"Not really," Giselle smiled up at him.

"This is Ms. Raphael," Hazel added.

"Giselle – Giselle Raphael," Giselle said quickly, and they both smiled at her.

"Good to meet you. You're the new school teacher, I believe."

"We were discussing Enid," Hazel explained. "She's in Giselle's class." She leaned down and patted a blue canvas bag on the floor by her feet. "Your interlibrary loans came."

Dan nodded. "I won't interrupt your conversation," he added and walked over to the history section of the library.

"He's an anthropologist. He's working on ancient Mayan societies right now," the librarian smiled at Giselle shuffling some papers.

"Ms. Raphael – Giselle – I do what I can to let Enid know she has a caring relative when she's in here, but beyond that I can't go... yet... but the time will come when we'll both be able to help her, I hope. Please keep me informed on everything you can about her. I... I..." She looked up at Giselle. "I've felt quite helpless about her in the past, but now maybe some things will change."

Boy, thought Giselle, *I hope she's not expecting me to make those changes. I sure didn't make any progress with Mr. Amundsen.*

The librarian leaned over and patted her arm. "Don't worry, dear. Things are happening."

Dan Burroughs looked over at Hazel from the stacks. Their eyes met. Hazel smiled and looked back at Giselle giving her arm another pat. Giselle watched them puzzled. What did that mean – "Things are happening"?

They seemed almost conspiratorial, but she liked them.

"Well, I'd better get going," she murmured, and saying some awkward goodbyes, she left the library.

Hazel watched as Giselle put her books in her car and crossed the street to the little variety store.

"She seems caring and concerned, and she seems to trust you," Dan said, taking the books she pulled out of the blue bag and handed him.

The librarian nodded. "Yes."

Giselle had found the things she needed at the variety store and was standing by the cash register, when she saw Dan Burroughs leave the library and walk slowly down the library steps. The middle-aged woman who ran the store looked disapprovingly across the street and shook her head. "That man spends entirely too much time in that library. Uppity."

Giselle looked up at her startled. She'd read books using that word, but she'd never heard someone actually say it!

"One of these days someone's going to show him his proper place."

"Oh," said Giselle allowing an edge of disapproval to enter her voice, "and where's that?"

"Not in the library, and that's for sure."

"Well," responded Giselle. "He's an anthropologist. Seems like the library might be where he belongs, with the books he needs for his research."

"Oh, yes, books. He's fond of books. They say he's even written some, but I've never seen any." She shrugged her shoulders dismissively and then leaned forward. "But books aren't the only thing in the library he's fond of," she nodded her head knowingly. "Shameful."

"What's shameful?"

The woman looked outraged. "That he's black and she's white. That's what. It's not right."

Oh, my god, thought Giselle, stepping back from the counter. *I can't believe this. That's the reason why the authorities won't let Hazel see Enid except at the library. Racism. I can't believe she just said that!*

She stood for a moment looking at the woman, her mouth a grim line. "Well, it seems to me Mr. Burroughs' friendships are not my business, or anyone else's."

She picked up her things and left.

When she reached home that evening she was still mulling over the incident at the variety store. It left an unpleasant taste in her mouth. She'd been reading about the rise of overt racism on the OET website – politicians making clearly racist statements, police shooting unarmed black men, people being physically attacked, vandalism, but... *All the ugliness isn't in the city,* she thought, as she reached out to put her key in the front door.

She jerked her hand back. Something was on the door knob. A painting on a piece of bark hung from the knob on a braided vine. When she took it to the edge of the porch to look at it in better light, she saw it was her oak tree. Very simple, very beautiful, definitely her tree and not some random other tree.

She looked out at the hills and the meadow, but of course, there was no one around.

When she set the painting down on the old trunk in front of the sofa, the little gray cat jumped up, tipping his head to one side as if evaluating the painting. Giselle laughed and leaned forward almost nose to nose with the cat. "What do you know about this?"

The cat just stared unblinking back at her. *More than he's telling, I'll bet!* she thought, grinning and shaking her head.

That night Luhanada and Tata crouched in the dark around the fire pit at Yameno's den and listened to the owls hooting in the night. They contemplated the trip to the library. "The linking's begun," said Luhanada.

"Yes," said Tata, "but the boy will be harder."

"He comes to the forest," said Yameno. "We'll find a way."

"And how's the tree coming?"

"It's growing." Yameno gestured to where the driftwood log stood at the edge of the clearing, carved lines beginning to show shape. "Soon."

Waxing Gibbous

Not long past sunrise on Saturday morning Enid slipped out of bed, dressed silently, grabbed an apple and some cheese, and crept out of the house like a little mouse always watching behind her for the cat. In one hand she clutched a book. Stumbling down a path through the forest, she headed for the river.

Her nervousness was more a matter of habit than need. She often slipped off into the woods by herself to play, and her grandfather never gave chase – a dichotomy he couldn't explain to himself. He had forbidden Enid's mother from going into the woods and she died. Emma and Enid were damned if they went into the forest, and because they were Mary's children, damned if they didn't.

Enid was headed for a favorite spot, a hidden crevice behind a rock next to the river where she could sit comfortably and read her book. She spent the morning cuddled there, intermittently reading and napping, and munching on her apple and cheese.

The sun was high in the sky when she heard someone coming toward the river through the brush. Pulling herself closer into her crevice, she peeked around the corner of the rock and saw Jesús McCrae settle himself down with his fishing pole on a rock almost directly in front of her.

Awkwardly bent forward and afraid to move, she watched him for several minutes. When her tightened muscles couldn't hold out any longer she moved one foot just a tiny bit to get into a more comfortable position. The foot touched a small round stone which, like a wheel, pulled her foot and leg further out of its hiding place, and then clattered on down the side of the rock.

Jesús whirled at the sound and Enid tightened herself against the back of her hiding place. "Shit," he mumbled. He leaned in toward her, glaring. "How long have you been there?"

She scrambled to her feet, glaring back.

He moved back a little, holding his hands up in front of himself. "It's okay. It's okay." He looked at the book in her hand. "What are you reading?"

She held the book out – the story of a wild cougar.

He grinned as he lifted his arms and pawed the air in front of her like a menacing cat. "I'm a wild cougar and I'm going to eat you up. Grrr..."

She jumped away from the boy, slipping and tripping over branches and stones until she lost balance and started sliding down the bank. He grabbed her arm just before she slipped out of his reach into the cold river and hauled her back up the bank.

"I wasn't going to hurt you." He shook his head, annoyed. "Go ahead and read."

Enid kept her eyes on him as he moved toward his fishing pole. She was angry. This was her special place. The boy ignored her, leaning back against a rock.

She kept staring. "Stop looking at me," he spat at her. "Read."

She sat down and opened her book. Some minutes passed before the exhaustion of holding her muscles tense became too much and she began to relax, moving ever so slightly into a more comfortable position. It was a lot longer, though, before she really began to read.

Except for the running of his reel and the *plink* as the fly hit the water, they were silent. Enid could hear the low burbling of the river, the chirping of the birds, and finally, a low rustling in the bushes behind her.

She looked back toward the sound.

Two small ground squirrels, particular friends of hers, were rooting round the trunks of the bushes. She kept chicken feed in her pockets and on some quiet afternoons one of the little rodents had even eaten the feed out of her hand. They looked at her expectantly, creeping to the edge of the bushes to peer out at her and then running back to touch noses under the brush.

She glanced at Jesús. He was preoccupied with his fishing. Slipping her hand into her pocket, she crawled over to deposit a small heap of feed next to the bushes, sitting back on her heels near the pile to wait for her little friends.

From the corner of his eye Jesús saw the quiet movement and turned his head to watch. Chirping quietly to each other and their friend, the little squirrels moved to the food and with quick jerky movements began to stuff their cheeks. Jesús watched without moving until the squirrels had gathered the entire pile and moved off with happy little scurries toward their home.

Enid turned back, her eyes widening when she saw him watching.

He smiled. "Do you come here a lot? I've never been to this place before. Is this your special place?"

She looked away from him.

"Do you always bring food for them? That's so cool that they come so close to you. Did you bring me some food, too?" he teased.

She turned and glared at him.

"Did you bring yourself some lunch?" Jesús put his fishing pole down on the rock beside him and looked around. There was no evidence of a lunch. "Were you supposed to go home for lunch?"

She shook her head looking away. "If I went home he might not let me go out again." He voice was so low he could hardly hear her.

"Who wouldn't? Your father?"

"I haven't got a father," she mumbled.

Bit by bit Jesús got her story out of her. Yes, she was allowed to sneak out to the woods every Saturday and she had eaten an apple and cheese, but she couldn't make a lunch. He might wake up and stop her. He wouldn't hit her, but his eyes got cold and his body rigid when she did something he didn't like. She always returned in time to help fix dinner – a very silent dinner – and he never said anything. "He knows I come here, but he doesn't like it."

Jesús looked away across the river. His parents never hit him, but he'd heard about kids getting hit. He knew when his parents were disappointed with him, even when they didn't say anything. He'd feel bad, but he wasn't afraid of them. They were disappointed at him a lot when it came to school…

He looked back at her. "Are you hungry now?"

Enid shrugged her shoulders.

"I have a sandwich. Want half of my sandwich?" Jesús pulled himself up to a crouching position to reach for his jacket and pulled a sandwich out of the pocket.

She looked away and shook her head.

He held a half sandwich out in front of her. "Eat half of the sandwich and I'll eat half."

Enid looked longingly at the sandwich, but muttered, "There are other things I can eat."

"What other things?"

"Plants." She pointed to some scraggly greens growing by the edge of the river a little ways from them. "Over there's some miner's lettuce."

Jesús looked doubtfully at the greens. "How do you know they aren't poisonous?"

Enid picked up a pebble, rolling it with her palms. "I read about them in a book."

He leaned forward. "A book about plants you can eat – plants you could find just growing here in the woods? Do you know of any others around here?" He moved around trying to look right into her face. She inched away.

"There's manzanita berries up on the hillside over there," she pointed toward the coast.

"Manzanita, huh," Jesús looked thoughtfully up at the hillside. "Could you bring the book here tomorrow?"

She shook her head. "We pray on Sundays."

"All day Sunday?" Jesús couldn't believe it. "We go to church, but then I can do whatever I want."

Enid's voice dropped. "He says this forest is evil. We live in an evil forest and we need to pray against the evil."

"A lot of people think the forest is evil, but I like it. It doesn't feel evil to me."

"Me, either." She looked down and began rolling the pebble again. "It's hard to pray against the forest. The forest feels like a friend."

"Did you know some people want to cut down the forest for logs?"

Enid's eyes flew wide. "Cut down the forest?"

Jesús nodded.

She looked out at the trees growing down the hillsides toward the river. Her eyes got wet with tears. Jesús looked at her, blinking his own eyes, and then leaned down to pick up a larger rock, tossing it up and catching it. "Do you just pray on Sundays? Don't you do anything else?"

"Sometimes we sing hymns, and eat, of course." Her face brightened. "I like to sing. My grandfather does, too."

She looked across the river. "But he reads the Bible for a long time."

Jesús thought for a moment. "Could you bring that book about the plants here next Saturday? With a book like that we could live out here forever, and you'd never have to go home to your grandfather and I'd never have to go to school."

He tossed the rock higher and higher until, finally, he missed it again and it bounced onto the edge of the bank, and then rolled down into the river. "Well, anyway," he shrugged his shoulders. "We could have something to eat on Saturdays. You could pick plants for a salad or something, and I could catch some fish and we could cook them."

He began to talk excitedly about what they would do the next Saturday. He shoved the sandwich at Enid. "Eat that half-sandwich. Now," he said firmly. Enid was happy to follow his orders. Jesús wasn't so hungry he missed it, and didn't seem hungry enough to really want to catch a fish, because it wasn't long before he had put his fishing gear away and suggested they go for a walk.

Enid shoved her book in the big pocket of her jacket and followed him down the river. He led her through thickets and over rocks pulling her roughly up over the ones too big for her to climb by herself. He pointed out particularly good fishing holes and talked about the fish he'd caught in them. She was very sorry when the sun slipped below the trees and she knew she'd have to go home.

The boy let her go with a shrug and pulled her back only to remind her to get the book and meet him at the same spot about ten o'clock the next Saturday morning.

When Monday came Enid waited for the boy to give some recognition of their Saturday meeting, but he acted as if it had never happened.

Giselle had had only occasional phone conversations with Monica, since moving up the coast. She kept up on world news online, weeping when she heard of the murder of two indigenous environmentalists in South America, and screaming with anger as she saw new statistics on the deaths of children in the wars in the middle east, the famines of Africa, and the devastating floods in India, Nepal, and Bangladesh. "We could stop this," she screamed. "We could stop this."

But now that the first week of school was past, the house in good shape, and her fall garden planted and ready to grow, it was time to soothe the strained relationship with her sister and maybe catch up on news about her friends and family. Sunday night she called Monica and Rod and invited them to visit the next weekend.

It was hard to sleep that night – her mind was obsessed with both planning the visit and worrying about it. When Monday morning came, she was glad to get involved in her school work and push the weekend into the background.

She set up contracts with each of the children finishing certain sections of the required texts and workbooks (complete with multiple choice tests as practice for the state tests). But Jesús, who would never, she was sure, do any work in any workbook, especially a math workbook, was to design and draw the blueprints for a house and then make a scale model of it. He would have to keep a journal of everything he did and why. She would trick him into becoming interested in math and writing while enjoying himself with his art.

She was delighted to see him set to work immediately, reading the children's books on architecture she'd gotten for him from the library. He clearly didn't have any problem reading the books. "My house is going to be some place in the redwoods," he told her, "and it's going to be so much like the forest you can't even see it."

"That's the way houses should be," agreed Giselle.

"It's going to be totally energy efficient. My dad says this earth is going to die if we don't do something about energy. That's what I'm going to do when I grow up. I'm going to stop global warming."

Giselle smiled at him. That was the most he'd ever said to her at one time. "But you know, Jesús, you can't do that without a good education."

He looked away from her and shrugged.

Knowing Enid would finish her work way ahead of time, Giselle gave her a journal and suggested she write a book on whatever she wanted to write about.

Enid ran a finger over the little unicorn on the front of the journal, and looked up at her and smiled. Giselle smiled back. There was something different about Enid this morning – her head a little higher, her back a little straighter – and a smile.

Full Moon

Late Friday afternoon, in search of wild flowers to decorate her house for her guests the next day, Giselle ventured into the wilderness behind her home. The sea wind, pushing through the trees, whispered gentle songs to the birds whose quiet twitterings made the silence seem even deeper. Something hidden in the deep crevices at the bottom of her spirit expand like helium in a balloon pushing upward until it gained the upper hand.

Oh, joy, she thought. *Oh, jubilation.*

>*(Ecstasy and joy, echoed the trees.*
>*An ether – a flow of life-joy. Ecstasy!)*

"Exhilaration," she returned. "Oh! Life elation."

> *(Rejoice! they whispered. Rejoice!)*
> *Come wind, set limbs to dancing,*
> *Wind song, on our soul harps prancing.*
> *Tree dance, spirit romancing,*
> *Come feet, set life a dancing.*
> *Come voice, let your song go chanting.*
>
> *Come earth, set your heart beat thrumming.*
> *Come sea, set your surf to drumming.*
> *Oh, sing heart. Sing to earth's warm silence.*
> *Dance heart, to this sun heat, to this wind dance.*
> *Oh, earth joy!*
> *Dance heart,* the trees whispered. *Dance heart.)*

Giselle ran. Her wild flowers gripped in her hand sent their seeds flying to the wind as she ran down the hillside out into the meadow, out to the edge of the sea. Yameno, crouching behind the trees she had just run through, laughed and sang a low note to the wind, and the wind ran caressing fingers through his thick ruff in return.

Giselle stopped her downward rush for a moment to listen. It was the wind, she thought. Just the wind singing a peculiar note in the redwoods.

That evening, as she bent low in homage to the sea and sun, she thought of her sister and Rod coming the next day. Would they feel it – this joy?

Enid hardly slept Friday night thinking about meeting Jesús the next day. At last a faint light began to grow in the east and she quietly pulled on her clothes, tucked the book on edible plants and a reading book in one pocket of her jacket, slipped into the barn to fill the other pocket with chicken feed, and ran off into the woods. It was past sunrise when she reached the little niche in the rocks by the river and settled herself in her cubbyhole. The warmth of the sun and her lack of sleep relaxed her, and she fell asleep.

When Jesús arrived at the river, his rod thrust over his shoulder and his creel hanging by his side, he looked down at the little girl curled up in a ball, fast asleep. The books were clutched in her arms and wisps of hair slid down her cheek. He stood for a minute and watched her. Part of him wanted to wake her up by frightening her and part wanted to be soft – perhaps let her sleep a while longer or wake her up gently. Finally he leaned down close to her, saying in a deep gruff voice, "Gotcha!"

Enid jumped and flattened herself against the rock in back of her. He looked away, ashamed, and shrugged. "Sorry."

She rubbed the sleep from her eyes, and handed him the book on edible plants. He took it, sitting down on a rock to look through it.

Enid knew where there was some manzanita on the nearby hillside, so they took the carefully washed out juice can Jesús had brought to cook with to hold the berries and headed up the hill.

They found the patch of manzanita, but it was late in the year and the berries were few and far between. "This is taking too long," complained Jesús. Enid just kept looking for the little berries and tossing them in the can. He handed her the can. "I think I should go back and start fishing. You stay here and when the can's full, bring it back." He ran in leaps and hops down the hillside.

Soon the hill was silent except for the shushing of the wind. Enid moved quietly between the bushes. As she moved around one bush she found two quail noisily pecking at the ground. Crouching, she slipped her hand into the pocket where she kept her chicken feed and spread feed like a fan on the ground in front of her. One of the quail clucked and backed away, but the other stood its ground, turning its head to stare at Enid with a little beady eye. It popped one of the little seeds in its mouth. The other watched carefully for a moment and then joined the feast.

There was a sound in back of Enid so small she felt rather than heard it. She turned her head toward it. Standing behind another bush was a man with long black hair. She jumped up, sending the quail in a half walking, half flying scurry into the bushes.

"I'm sorry," said the man. "I didn't mean to frighten you. It's very rare for quail to be so willing to stay close to a human being. They're timid. You have a special gift, Chachuli." He smiled and moved out from behind the bush. "Why are you picking the manzanita berries?"

She didn't answer.

"I've come to pick some, too, but I see there're not too many left. Pretty soon they'll all be gone and we'll have to rely on something else for the winter." He began to pick berries and drop them into a basket he held on his arm.

As soon as he turned away from her, Enid grabbed the can and ran down the hillside, her hand covering the top to keep the berries from bouncing out. She arrived at the river out of breath and wild-eyed.

Jesús looked at her in astonishment. "What's wrong?"

She sat down on a rock. "A man is picking berries, too," she gasped.

"Did he hurt you?" Jesús stepped toward her.

"No." She pushed the hair out of her eyes. "I was feeding some quail and he watched and called me a name – Chachuli, I think. What's that mean?"

"I don't know. It sounds weird – Indian or something.

"Hey! I know who it was!" Jesús exclaimed. "There's an Indian that lives in the hills someplace – alone – and people don't like him. Haven't you heard about him?"

She shook her head.

"Well, that doesn't mean anything. You're a hermit, too, like him. Why did you run away from him? He lives off the land. He'd know all the plants we've been looking for. He'd know what's good in fall and everything."

Enid glared at him.

"Never mind. We'll probably see him another time when I'm with you and you won't have to be afraid." He pulled a line from the stream. "See my fish."

"Oh, poor thing. Do we have to eat him?"

"My dad says he'd rather eat a fish that's had a good life living free, than some piece of steak from a cow that lived in a feed lot. Have you ever seen one of those feed lots?" He wrinkled his face in disgust. "Hundreds of cows standing there with their feet in a bunch of mucky mud and cow poop. At least a fish gets to live in a clean stream until we eat it."

Enid looked at the fish where Jesús had fastened it so that it hung just barely submerged and still alive in the river. She put her hand down against the fish and it stopped splashing as if calmed.

Yameno had followed the girl down the hill. He crouched behind a tree and watched the children and nodded. The girl's shy, but so much like her grandmother, he grinned, carrying chicken feed in her pockets. He slipped away, loping off toward the bridge and his perch above Giselle's house.

Jesús put his rod down. "Come on. Let's get some wood and build a fire. We can make it in that scooped out place in the rock. It looks like a giant thumb print."

Enid crouched over the place where the fish hung in the water, preoccupied, not listening to the boy. "Jesús," she whispered. "We should... we should thank the fish and the manzanita for providing food for us."

He crouched beside her looking at the fish. "Yeah," he said slowly. "And the forest."

She nodded her head. "We could make it sacred. The fire, the manzanita, and other things too."

"And water," exclaimed Jesús. "The fish came from water. And all these rocks. They feel, you know, holy or something." They glanced at each other and away again.

"Well, let's get the stuff." Jesús got up and began to gather twigs, dried leaves, and dead wood for their fire. Enid ran back up the hillside and broke off a branch of the manzanita bush, its bark still deeply red, with green leaves clustered thickly on it. They laid the manzanita branch along the east side of the fire. Jesús found a flat slab of rock perfect to cook the fish on. He placed it to the north of the fire. Enid took the can with manzanita berries in it and filled it with water, placing it opposite the branch. Taking the fish from the water she placed it on the flat rock. Jesús knelt beside her as she placed her hands on the fish. "Thank you, fish," she whispered. "Thank you, trees, and plants, and water, and fire, and earth."

> *(I am the writer of poetry,* whispered the earth.
> *Voice of the universe,*
> *Fluid as the world of dream.)*

Jesús lit a match and the fire caught quickly in the dry leaves. He put the tin can half full of berries, and half full of water, in the middle next to the biggest log, with the fire burning all around it and, taking out his knife, split and boned the fish, placing it on the rock in the midst of the fire. Enid placed some of the berries on top of the split fish. It took a long time for the water to boil and the fish to cook on their little fire, and the children had to take turns running back into the woods to find more dead wood. By the time their meal was ready, it was late and getting chilly.

They crouched around the fire eating their food with their fingers, yelping as the hot fish burned their tongues. The berries proved a fine addition to the fish, giving them flavor like a sweet sauce. Soon the sun was slipping behind the hills and Enid knew she'd have to leave.

"Let's put the manzanita branch on the fire," Jesús suggested.

"It won't burn," replied Enid. "That red in the bark is some kind of chemical that protects it from burning. But we should put it in."

"Put some more dry leaves in so the fire is burning all around it."

They piled dry leaves on the fire until it blazed up and then placed the green and deep red branch in the middle of the flames. The fire singed the edges of the leaves giving off a sweet smoke, like incense, but the branch didn't burn. "Wow," they whispered, as they pulled the still red branch from the fire.

(I am the echo of creation, murmured the fire.
I see the earth in her splendor.
My hands draw the dreams of the universe...)

"Let's float it down the river to the ocean," said Enid, walking over to the stream and holding the branch close to her face so she could inhale the sweet odor from the burned leaves. She broke off two of the leaves, and giving one to Jesús, thrust the other in her jeans pocket. "Thank you," she whispered, and tossed the branch out into the water. The gentle current caught it and pulled it slowly toward the ocean. They stood in silence long after it had turned the curve in the river and disappeared.

"Do you ever go down to the beach?" asked Jesús.

Enid nodded her head.

"I bet there're things down there we could eat for dinner. We could go clamming! Let's meet here and walk to the beach next Saturday, okay? And bring that book."

Enid smiled and ran off through the increasing shadows of the forest toward home.

Jesús carefully hid the flat rock under some bushes, poured water on the fire with the juice can until he was sure every spark was out, and then packed up his things and strode off through the woods.

Giselle woke up early that same Saturday morning. She had decided to make bread for Sunday morning breakfast with Monica and Rod, and a picnic Sunday noon. When the dough was ready for kneading, she turned it out onto the floured bin table and began to work it in rhythm with the low rumble of the sea she could hear through the open windows.

She pushed into it, and pulled it back toward her, folding the sides into the whole. *Like life,* she thought, *pulls out into individuality and then folds back into the whole, all in rhythm like the rhythm of the sea. Making bread, gardening, even correcting papers, you fall into that rhythm.* She looked out the window, watching birds, hardly more than dots in the sky, dipping down into the ocean. *If Monica was here we'd be talking,* she thought. *We'd miss the rhythm.*

When the bread had finished baking and she'd put it up on a shelf to cool, she decided to take her book down to the beach. The noontime sun was shining brightly and the white breakers crashing against the rocks at either end of the little beach were subdued. She spread her blanket and stretched out with her book. The warmth of the sun massaged her back, the tension went out of her legs and arms, and the raucous calls of the gulls, the incessant rushing of the waves became a lullaby.

Yameno Wolfwind, who had been watching from his usual place on the hillside, loped through the meadow to the edge of the cliff. Making a tunnel in the tall grasses, he laid his head on his front paws, his eyes thin slits in the bright sunlight as he peered down at her, his breath whispering out over the beach…

Sun-warm sand cradles her, the sound of the sea rocking her. The wind slips cool caresses across face, body, touch as gentle as silk. Her body seems fluid, flexible, bent so far back her hands hold her feet, and they dreamdance in the air.

> *Rolling on the air currents, through the wind, her gentle lover,*
> *In her and all around her,*
> *enclosing her,*
> *holding her.*
> *The rhythm,*
> *the drumming of the waves,*
> *pushing insistently into her,*
> *filling her with a shattering light*
> *in the dark cavern of her dream.*

Holding her bound tight, close on a single deep note, and then slipping ever so gently, caressingly away, leaving her in the warm cradle of the sand.

She lay without moving, feeling the warmth of the sun. Sometimes when I lie like this, so still and empty, I could stay forever. It'd be nice to be a rock.

The dogs, bored with sleeping in the sun, began to play on the beach, kicking up sand. The growling yaps roused Giselle. She lay there protecting her head from the flying sand. It was three o'clock, but she felt so peaceful and relaxed, happy with the sea and the sand, the birds and the dogs... and the gentle wind.

She didn't want to return to the house. She wished she had never invited Monica and Rod to visit. Monica was always so full of "shoulds" and "should nots". Sighing, she picked up her blanket and book, and calling to the dogs, climbed the rugged path to the meadow and her home.

Yameno slipped away, bounding up the hillside under the trees toward his own home. Just as she reached her house, Giselle heard a short exultant howl from the top of the hill. She stopped and scanned the hillside. The dog again, she thought, if it's a dog.

At four o'clock Monica's shiny new car pulled into the dirt drive and descended cautiously to the house. Rod and Monica greeted her, commenting about the scenery and the charm of the little house, stepping back awkwardly from the jumping, wiggling dogs. She settled them in folding chairs on the porch to watch the sea and drink cold drinks while she prepared dinner.

"Giselle, did you ever find out why this house was empty for so long?" asked Monica. "It's a nice enough house with a great view."

"Ghosts," she laughed. "Not in the house, but in the forest around here. And not really ghosts – just some mysterious feeling. I've meant to ask some other people about it now that school's started, but I haven't gotten around to it. The real estate agent didn't take it very seriously."

"That's ridiculous," said Rod. "But maybe there's something real behind the rumors. Maybe some shenanigans going on people want to keep hidden. When I was working for the D.A. we often heard about pot growers in the mountains keeping people from nosing about on their property by spreading rumors. Have you ever seen anything strange in the forest?"

"Nothing unpleasant," answered Giselle. But, she thought, I think I've felt a presence. You couldn't ask for nicer ghosts.

Rod's eyes narrowed. "Nothing unpleasant?" he asked.

Giselle averted her eyes and said nothing.

"Ugh!" Monica shivered. "I don't want to talk about this anymore. I don't know how you can live here all alone, Giselle."

Giselle rolled her eyes.

After dinner they made their way down the winding path to the beach carrying blankets, wine and marshmallows. The sun lit its fire across the sky and the breaking waves were crested with red and orange instead of their usual white. They sat in awe on their blankets, silent and serious long after the sun had gone down, finally rousing themselves to search the beach for driftwood to start a small fire.

When they were all comfortably settled around the fire with wine in hand, they began to talk about the sunset. "It's funny," said Monica, "how a sunset can isolate you from everyone else. I'm not sure it's a good thing the way it makes you draw away from other people."

"Maybe we're not drawing away, but pulling into something else, a greater whole," answered Giselle. She drew slow spirals in the sand with her index finger. "Usually at sunset I perform a kind of ritual to the sun. I feel like I'm an extension of the earth instead of just standing on it. It's a kind of expansion…" She struggled with the words. "A becoming the whole… the whole… well, everything."

"A ritual to the sun?" Monica raised her eyebrows.

"I go up to a flat place at the edge of the meadow and do my Yoga exercises, ending with Surya Namaskara, the salutation to the sun. It gives me a feeling of being a part of the sunset, like I'm giving something back to that beauty."

"Oh, the yoga thing, again." exclaimed Monica. "Exercise is one thing, but this…" She shrugged her shoulders.

"Yes," interrupted Rod, nodding his head at Monica, "the thing that bothers me – you moved to this place, and you're more involved in the sun and these animals of yours than in people. You're just hiding from people – avoiding people."

She shook her head slowly. "No, Rod, I think I'm bringing people back again." She paused, peering out at the dark ocean. "I don't know why I said that. I haven't really thought that before, but it seems to me humans have isolated themselves from the – whatever it is – the life-force? From other living things? It's the separation – the false separation that has caused so much destruction, our inability to see how we're destroying the earth with our excessive consumption, our greed. Somehow I'm turning back. Something is turning me."

"But Giselle," Rod interrupted. "I understand your concern about the earth, but how can you change humanity way up here?"

"I don't know, but I have to do it. When I do the Surya Namaskara, the bow to the sun, it's a kind of worship, or…"

"Now it's sun worship," Monica muttered under her breath.

"Or maybe more of a lovemaking," Giselle continued in a low voice still staring at the sea. "It's like a love dance – an immersion in the sun and the sea. In fact," she went on turning to her sister, "my whole life is full of rituals. They give me strength and energy, and joy. Sometimes I'm so full of joy I can't…" She looked at their bewildered faces. "Oh, I don't know."

Rod shook his head. "I think this isolation's getting to you. You're beginning to personify everything, that's all."

"No," Giselle leaned forward urgently. "No, it's there. The life is there, and it's alive and pulsating and thinking. I know it's there."

(Earth and Sea,
Sun and tree,
All one. All one. All one.)

Ghosts, she thought. Ghosts – spirits – something – in everything.

Monica and Rod exchanged looks and Giselle stared at the sand she was sifting through her hands. "I feel like I've found something and I have to keep contact. I don't know what it is, but I know it's there, and it's important."

Monica just rolled her eyes, but Rod looked concerned. "You're so far away from everything, Giselle."

"Well," Giselle spoke quietly. "It all depends on what you consider everything." She thought about the afternoon on the beach. When you've made love to the wind…

The chilly air began to creep up their backs and the dying fire refused to fight it. They drowned the fire in sand and sea water, gathered their blankets and wine, and climbed back to the house.

Sunday morning, Giselle got up early and went for a walk along the cliff before fixing breakfast. Her guests came yawning down the stairs at ten o'clock, exclaiming at the pungent smells of pine and salt air. After breakfast they gathered a picnic lunch, and led by the ecstatic pups, headed south along the cliff to the next little cove. The sun sparkled on sea-washed offshore rocks making them black and shiny as jet. The surf was subdued and the ocean a deep lapis edged with white.

Giselle took a path down to an enclosed beach curving between two points of rock where they spent a couple of lazy hours running, climbing, and talking about non-threatening subjects while they ate. Monica and

Rod had a long drive back to the city ahead of them, so after lunch they gathered up the picnic things and headed back to the house taking the beach route, climbing the protruding rock guardians north of the cove, their rubber-soled shoes wet with spray and slippery, the dogs hopping sure-footedly back and forth between them. They halted for a moment on the rocky point, looking up and down the empty beaches before and behind them, and then pushed on to the beach that stretched past Giselle's house.

As they walked along the water's edge, Rod stopped abruptly.

"Hey, who's that?" he asked, pointing to a slender dark-haired man standing at the top of the cliff where Giselle usually did her Yoga. The man ducked back away from the cliff.

"Who was that man, Giselle?" Monica asked.

"I don't know. He looked like someone I saw at the river once." Her breath caught as she remembered how drawn she was to that man. "But that's a ways from here, over on the other side of the hill. I've never seen anyone around here." But someone's leaving gifts on my porch, she thought, uneasily. I'm not telling you about that.

"Anyway," she continued, "I'm sure I'll see more people around here as time goes on. After all, this is a nice beach and the hills make a great place to climb. I'm not worried about it."

She started walking again and the others followed. By the time they'd climbed the winding path the man was nowhere to be seen, although Rod pointed out a big dog sitting up on the hillside. "Maybe that's his dog," he suggested.

"That dog looks ferocious," exclaimed Monica.

"Looks like a wolf," added Rod.

Giselle laughed. "Come on. It's been a long time since there were any wolves around here."

"Well, maybe it's a coyote," he suggested. "I've heard the coyotes are multiplying."

"It's too big and too fluffy to be a coyote." Giselle peered up at the dog. So that's the dog I've heard howling sometimes. It really does look like a wolf. It looks like that dog I saw at the river – the day I saw that man.

"I don't know." Rod moved the conversation back to the man. "There was something odd about the way he was watching us. Maybe he has something to do with your ghosts."

Giselle just smiled. "You'd better get going or you're going to be driving all night," she urged them. As they gathered their things Rod mumbled about how much better he'd feel leaving her if he knew who that man was, but finally, full of gracious, but distant, "Thank yous," they climbed into their car and drove away.

When Giselle returned to the house she made a cup of tea and sat down on the front porch steps.

Something was tied on the underside of the railing. Her heart beat fast as she unwound a necklace of seashells and acorns, strung on a braided vine, and wrapped around a rolled piece of paper. Unrolling the paper she found a quote in dark green calligraphy framed in vines with little birds peeking between the leaves:

> *As you simplify your life,*
> *the laws of the universe will be simpler;*
> *solitude will not be solitude,*
> *poverty will not be poverty,*
> *nor weakness weakness.*

Henry David Thoreau, from Walden.

"Wow!" she exclaimed. "Just what I needed to tell Monica." *Who left this?* Was it that man she saw at the river? Had he stood on the cliff and watched her on the beach before?

She went down the steps, clutching the rolled paper and necklace in one hand, and looked far around her up the hill. Turning she looked north through the fields and south along the cliff, but there was no sign of anyone. She felt awkward, rubbing her fingers down the outer seams of her jeans sensing every thread and the texture of the weave. She dug her bare toes into the dirt and turned her head this way and that trying to find the hidden eyes. She'd been so glad when Monica and Rod left, but...

Crouched behind a tree high up on the hill, Yameno watched Giselle's nervous search. He saw the necklace clutched to her chest in her left hand. When she finally turned and went inside, he loped off through the trees to the cat lady's house.

She looked at his exultant face, questioning. "Yes, Wolfwind?" He laughed and shook his head, pulling out a chair at the kitchen table. "And?" she asked again.

"She had visitors from the city. They saw me."

"If they frighten her we could lose her. What about the tree?"

"It's finished and waiting."

68

Luhanada sighed, looking out the window over her sink. "Let's hope we can go soon." The wait for the Tree Woman had been very long. It was hard to wait any longer – it felt so urgent.

She turned to the stove and put the kettle on the burner. "Do you want some tea?"

"Yes, please." He propped his elbows on the table and leaned his head into his cupped hands. "I've been leaving her gifts. A picture of her tree. A necklace."

Luhanada raised her eyebrows. "Well, as long as she accepts them..." she hesitated, twisting her fingers in the curly ends of her braid.

"And doesn't get frightened," he added. "Perhaps I shouldn't have, but..."

"You're falling in love with her." The cat woman sighed again. It had to work this time. It felt like she'd been waiting all her life. She pulled a chair up to the table to wait for the kettle.

"And the good news," Yameno smiled. "The children were in the forest yesterday."

"Together?"

"Yes. Enid reminded me of her grandmother. She carries chicken feed in her pockets and feeds the quail."

Luhanada nodded. When they were growing up, Enid's grandmother, Mary, had dozens of strange looking birdhouses all around the yard and at the edge of the woods. Mary'd read carefully to find what to feed each different kind of bird. The birds never came right up to her to eat, but sat on perches close by and sang to her. Luhanada had to keep a good eye on her cats to make them understand they were not to mess with Mary's birds.

The kettle whistled and she hopped up to get their tea. "The children together! That's a good sign."

Giselle went into her house and for the first time locked the door behind her. She tried to think of school, but her mind kept slipping back to the man. How often had he been watching her? Could someone who made such exquisite art work really be dangerous? Someone who wanted to scare her away, like a pot grower, wouldn't give her a quote from Thoreau. When she'd seen him at the river, she'd wanted to know him. Was it such a bad thing if he felt the same way?

But he could be someone with a real emotional problem and still be enamored of Thoreau. She needed to find out who he was.

She didn't sleep very well that night. Hot and uncomfortable, jumping at every sound, she twisted and turned, shoving at the dogs lying tight and close on either side of her.

At midnight she heard the howling again, and it was longer and more beautiful, but still eerie. She shivered and squeezed the little gray cat, but the cat just reached a paw up and patted her reassuringly on the nose. *None of the animals are frightened,* she noted. *Strange the dogs didn't bark and the cat didn't bristle when the big dog howled.*

The next morning she was groggy and foggy headed. As soon as school was out she made a list of things she could buy in the little hardware store with the talkative owner and headed for town.

Waiting until the one other customer was gone, she asked the owner to help her find the items on her list. As they walked past the shelves she said, "By the way, someone was out by my beach yesterday – not that I object to people coming on my property – but no one's ever come out there before. I just wondered who he was."

"Oh? What'd he look like?" Mr. Coffman stopped, frowning.

"He was lean, with long dark hair – wore blue jeans and a blue shirt. I couldn't see him very well from that distance."

"Must be that darned Indian kid." Mr. Coffman looked angry. He pulled a box of nails off a shelf. "These twelve penny nails should be the right size."

"This guy wasn't a kid. He was a grown man."

"That Yameno Wellkeeper's a grown man. I just still think of him as the kid we did so much for who turned around and threw it all away. Do you want one of these foam paint brushes, or one with bristles?"

She picked up a thick bristled brush. "This one looks about right."

The man glanced at her list. "Wellkeeper lives somewhere up in those hills behind your place, although why anyone'd want to live there, I don't know." He plunked the nails down on the counter hard and went around it to the cash register, carrying the rest of her items.

"Why wouldn't someone want to be in those hills?"

He looked down and fumbled around with the nails. "It's just strange up there, that's all."

"Why?" Giselle placed her hands on the counter and leaned forward. "What happens up there?"

"I don't know. Just things." He rang up the nails and the brush. "That Wellkeeper probably likes it. He probably makes it worse. Encourages it."

"Encourages what?"

"The things that happen up there. That's what," he said in an exasperated voice, punching the tax and the total. "Anyway, we've tried and tried to get someone to spook him out of there. He hasn't got any right to live up there like that, not owning the land and not paying any rent. He probably don't even live in a house. If he's living on your land you can get him kicked off. The state troopers would do something about it, if the owner of the property he's living on would complain."

"You mean he's living like a hermit up there all by himself?" asked Giselle.

"Yeah. That's it. He's a hermit, and we should've known before we gave a five thousand dollar scholarship to an Indian that he'd waste it." He grabbed the cloth bag she handed him and stuffed her things in it.

"Oh, who gave him a scholarship? And where to? College?" asked Giselle.

Mr. Coffman leaned on the counter. "He grew up here in town. Went to our schools, and the teachers thought he was pretty smart and should go to college, but his family – well, you know these Indians – they didn't have money for college – even a state college. So the townspeople got together and put in five thousand dollars for him to go to college, and I think he worked, too, while he was there."

Well, yeah! thought Giselle, *and huge college loans, probably.*

"He finished college and we all felt pretty darned proud we'd put him through, because he was in some special honor society and got awards and things."

Mr. Coffman glared. "He was going to go on and get more schooling and become a scientist. By the time he got to graduate school they were giving money to Indians to go to school, just because they were Indians, and anyway, he done so well in school lots of people were offering him money to go. Then in the middle of a school year his great-aunt died and for no darn reason at all, he quit school and picked up his things and walked off into the forest up there, and he hasn't been out since except sometimes he goes over to Robertsville and gets odd jobs and earns a little money, then disappears into the forest again."

Mr. Coffman turned back to the cash register and ripped the receipt off. "We paid good money to send him to school and he could'a been a famous scientist."

"It was good of you to put him in a position where he had the freedom to choose the way of life that was best for him," said Giselle.

Mr. Coffman looked at her with exasperation. "He's mighty strange. And, young lady, if I didn't know you was a respectable school teacher, I'd think you were mighty strange too, living out there all alone the way you do, and as old as you are and not married."

Old, thought Giselle. *Twenty-four is old?*

He stuffed the receipt into her bag. "You better watch out for that Yameno Wellkeeper. You can't tell what a weirdo like that might do to a young woman living out there all alone like you do – and right by those woods, too. Here." He thrust the bag at her. "I've got work to do, and I don't need to stand around talking all day."

Suddenly he turned toward the back of the store. "Tom, you better be working," he yelled at a dark haired, dark eyed teenaged boy standing just inside the doorway to the storage room.

The boy was listening, thought Giselle.

Coffman turned back toward her. "My grandson, Tom," he muttered. Giselle paid her bill, and he stamped off toward the storage room.

As Giselle walked to her car she thought, *Sometimes I feel like I haven't just moved two hundred miles from the city, but hundreds of years backwards in time as well. And then this man, Yameno... living in the hills all alone like a hermit. Mr. Coffman didn't indicate anything like drugs and if he could've, he would've! So much for Rod's pot farm idea.*

Now what? She sat in the car for a moment before driving off, thinking about the situation. *Should I look for him? For his home?* She shivered. *Maybe he doesn't want to be found. But, damn it, if he's watching me and leaving little gifts, I have a right to look for him. And I will. Tomorrow right after school!*

Tata found Yameno on the hillside back of Giselle's house. They moved back into the trees before changing into human form.

Tata crouched down and picked up a stick to doodle with in the pine needles. "Luha told me you thought Giselle saw you the other day. She did." He tossed the stick away and reached for a bigger one. "I was gardening next to the Dickerson's today, and Coffman came to tell him Giselle was in the hardware store asking about a stranger she saw out by her house."

Yameno grimaced and crouched down beside him. "Coffman and Dickerson. I'm never really happy when they're reminded I'm up here."

"Coffman told her about you and was telling Dickerson maybe they could convince her to file a complaint against you, although he did say she was 'weird', so she might have seemed sympathetic to you."

Yameno laughed and reached for a stick to do his own doodling. "'Weird', huh? I guess we're all 'weird'."

He stood up, dropping his stick. "The tree's finished. If she finds it now, it'll be all right." He leaned over and gave Tata a quick embrace.

Tata nodded, and changing, flew off toward town.

Finding Yameno Wellkeeper's home proved difficult. Giselle and the dogs searched the hill back of her house the next day after school, finding a blackberry thicket, but nothing that could be the man's home.

The dogs had run up the hillside behind the thicket barking and then wagging their tails with happy little yips. She'd frowned, wondering what could be up there they would consider a friend, but they quickly skidded back down, jumping and running around her as she picked some blackberries, popping them into the little bag she'd carried a few crackers in for a snack.

The second day of searching was just as disappointing until just as the sun was dipping behind the hill, she ran out of water in the bottle she carried for herself and the dogs. "Water," she exclaimed to the dogs. "He has to have water. He'll be next to a stream or the river!" She laughed as she ran down to the highway, crossing it to a trail to the river where they hiked downstream and then followed a small branching creek until it disappeared into a marshy nothing.

Returning to the river, she sank, hot and exhausted, on the bank. The woods were quiet and beginning to darken around her. The water looked cool and tempting. Taking one last look around, she scrambled out of her clothes, and stepped into the cool water. She was surprised when the dogs didn't join her, instead scrambling up the hillside their tails wagging behind them just as they had the day before at the berry patch, but she was too tired to care.

The river caressed her as she swam leisurely up and down the shallow pool formed by the curve in the river. When she swam into one of the few spots where the sun still shone on the water, she lingered feeling the fondling currents lap at her breasts and slip their tingling fingers round her waist and down her hips. She did back bends in the clear water dipping under until she felt the sand brush her breasts and then circled back to the surface.

As the last of the light slipped away, she dressed and walked wetly back down the river until she reached the highway bridge. Everything was so beautiful and peaceful here. This morning she'd gotten an email from a non-profit trying to get food to starving children in the middle east where a wealthy country was pounding a small country on its borders with bombs provided by Uhs. Here she was enjoying a beautiful park while her country used her tax money to bomb children. She sighed. Guilt, compassion, helplessness all mixed up together.

Calling the dogs close to her, she went back down the road to her house. She was tired and chilled. After making herself a cup of miso soup and taking a long hot bath, she fell exhausted into bed.

Yameno watched her return from his usual spot on the hillside before heading home.

Waning Gibbous

The next day after school Giselle was too tired to hike and settled down under the oak tree with some papers to correct. The blue-gray cat curled up in her lap and batted at her papers while the dogs went on adventures across the meadow and came back to lie panting in the shade of the tree. Birds twittered and insects buzzed, and the sun shone in flickers through the evergreen leaves.

> *(Energy,*
> *universal wanderer,*
> *grabbed,*
> *wrapped in a ball,*
> *bound,*
> *flaming, fiery,*
> *hot, too hot,*
> *escape!*
> *Fly,*
> *speed,*
> *faster than earth, faster than night,*
> *run with the speed of light.*
> *Invade,*
> *bombard,*
> *hit the earth, pierce the earth,*
> *tear through the air,*

embrace,
embrace..)

Giselle smiled. *Ghosts.* Lying flat on the ground, her eyes met the bright eye of a tiny yellow wild flower.

She reached out and touched the five-petaled blossom, gently turning its head toward her. "Five-petaled," she whispered. "Pythagoras's pentagram. Can you tell me where I can find the man, Wellkeeper?"

The flower dropped a petal onto her finger – a petal the shape of an eye without a pupil, silky, almost metallic in its yellowness, a piece of the sun. The breeze caught it and it fluttered away leaving the flower imperfect, whispering:

I am without words,
I cry from my beauty,
a gift from the sun,
the ocean and earth.
I cry of my life joy,
I sing to the butterflies,

And know of my death
from the moment of birth.

Cry I! Cry I!
I shout with no words
from the earth and the sky!
Carry my pledge before I die.

A pentagram,
a sign of perfection,
a sacrifice of one fifth
is to lose the whole.
Not a gift, but a message,
a promise.
Earth honor the pledge of my soul!

Cry I! Cry I!
I shout with no words
from the earth and the sky!
Carry my pledge before I die.

The wandering breeze caught the little flower ripping three more petals from the central hub, but the last remained.

Seek for the answer
at the edge of the sea.
Follow the waters

and climb to the sky.
Find there the man,
the wolf, and the tree.
Carry my pledge
as I fly free.

The last petal was suddenly torn away and carried upward with the breeze. Giselle sat up watching it go. She repeated the last words of the song, "Seek for the answer at the edge of the sea. Follow the waters and climb to the sky."

She called the dogs, and they ran south along the ocean cliffs, passing the little beach where she and her friends had eaten their picnic lunch, and continuing down the edge of the cliffs another half mile. Here the meadow widened and the hill retreated. On the other side of the meadow, some low trees and bushes grew in a line down to the coast. The cliff seemed to dip there as if a stream had cut through its rocky shoulders.

"Follow the waters," she whispered to herself, and she began to run toward the dip. A stream in a steeply cut ravine flowed almost directly east and west as far as she could see back into the underbrush. She turned east and walked along the edge of the ravine.

Soon the ravine got shallower and a ledge led down to the stream where it was easier to walk along the drought dry edges of the bed. The plant smell was thick and heady, and the stream flowed in a pleasant bubbly half-roar over the rocks. It was not very deep – perhaps a foot at the deepest points – but in the winter rainy season – if the rains came this year – it would thicken into a rushing mini-river.

She stopped suddenly as she nearly stepped into a second stream creeping out of the underbrush on the left into the main stream. This stream, though not as wide as the first, was deeper under its covering of brush. The main stream was much smaller beyond this point. Ahead the land lay flat, but to the north were hills. "Climb to the sky," she whispered, and searched for a way through the thick brambles all around the fork in the two streams. Pulling off her shoes and rolling up her pants, she ducked under the brush where the stream poured through, and waded into the green tunnel.

The banks of this stream were high, the plants thick and overhanging. She enjoyed the cool wade under the trees as it wound its way around the east side of the hill. When the brush moved back from the bank forming a little clearing, Giselle climbed up and sat on the edge in a shaft of late sunlight. The water glinted with reflected energy, sparking from the ripples where the water bugs wet their toes, flashing the familiar rhythm:

Sacred waters
from deep in the earth,
flowing with sweetness
to bring the rebirth.
Follow the water.
Climb to the sky.
Carry my pledge before I die.

Pushed by the insistent song, Giselle continued up the stream. The underbrush still grew thickly on each side as the stream bed slowly climbed, the water rushing at her down small rock faces. She stayed close to the edge, holding onto the bank and the bushes, followed by the sure-footed dogs. Turning a corner, she saw the hills close in above her and become one hill. The stream seemed to disappear. Climbing quickly, she found the source of the stream.

Tumbling out of a tiny crevice in the rock face of the hillside, it formed a four-foot waterfall pouring into a little round pool, before it flowed down the streambed. She cupped her hands under the waterfall and took a drink.

The water was clean and cool. Closing her eyes, she breathed in the sweetness of the air stirring about the little waterfall. *Sacred,* she thought, and placed her hands together giving a little self-conscious bow.

A path led around a curve up the hillside to the right of the small cataract.

Pulling on her shoes she plunged up the path trying to grab the dogs as they leapt out of the brush-walled path into an elliptical clearing, but it was too late. They ran laughing and yipping around the clearing and then suddenly disappeared into a little dark building that was so much the color of the ground around it Giselle had not seen it.

His house, she thought. *The dogs went into his house!*

They popped back out, running over to her, their tails wagging wildly. She waited, but the man didn't appear.

All sorts of strange painted and carved creatures peered back at her from where they hung from the trees and stood as if planted in the ground. There were pieces of bark stretched between small tree branches, containing paintings in deep browns and purples of wild-eyed creatures – not grotesque, but beautiful and natural in their wildness. From the ground emerged hand carved totems, modern renditions of the traditional echoing the wild beauty of the painted bark. Interspersed between the paintings and the totems were wind chimes, made from smooth small pieces of driftwood and shells, and delicate mobiles hung with acorns and other strange seedpods hung on braided vines, just like her necklace.

A tall totem grabbed Giselle's attention. She thought it was a tree, but then she saw the wood had been subtly shaped into a woman, her arms and fingers branched and stretched upward, as if pulled by a magnet. The toes of one foot diverged into spidery roots downward into the base. The other reached out, as if about to step down to the ground. "Like my Chinese statue," she whispered, "but different. Mine steps out of the tree. This one is the tree."

It was carved out of one piece of driftwood, gray with age and worn. The artist had followed the shape of the wood; the skirt and hair were exaggerations of the worn lines already drawn in the wood by time and the action of the sea. The face, somehow familiar, was lined with strength. The arms, thrust at the sky, and the head thrown back, gave the figure a sureness and determination that made Giselle shiver.

She walked over and touched the wooden folds of the statue, surprised at how warm and smooth they felt...

Deep in the heart of the wooden woman vibration surged through her fingertips, into her own body. The periphery of her vision closed in, a tunnel, the world around her slowly slipping away. At the edge, soft whisperings and the low whooshing accompaniment of the wind.

> *Warm, warm is the earth,*
> *nurturing life,*
> *giving its fullness*
> *to reach for the sun.*
> *My roots mingling in her*
> *bring me my life blood*
> *and when I die*
> *it's earth they become.*
>
> *But my heart-wood goes sailing*
> *in wintry seas,*
> *tossed by the harsh waves*
> *and rocked by the tides,*
> *rubbed on the warm sands*
> *until I am smooth,*
> *warmed by the sun*
> *until I am dried.*
>
> *Then comes the man*
> *who takes of my shape,*

carving me gently
gives me new form.
Made of his soul-sight,
the earth, sun, and water,
the wind is my brother,
my sister, the dawn.

Suddenly the song became more insistent:

I am the fullness,
I am the secret.
You are the answer,
the bearer of life.
I am the singer,
I am the weeper.
You are the leader,
the edge of the knife.

Giselle jumped back from the totem and shook herself into awareness.

"Me?" she whispered. "Is it speaking to me?"

She forced her eyes away from the beautiful, frightening woman. Trembling, she turned her back and walked over to the little brown dwelling at the edge of the clearing.

It looked like a tent built of wood. The peak of the roof was about four feet above the ground extending in a point at each end of the roof. A ditch on either side of the roof carried rainwater away. The west end was open, and steps descended down to a hard packed dirt floor dug out under the roof. She climbed down and stood at the bottom of the steps looking in. The cozy little room was filled with the paraphernalia of living carefully arranged so that everything seemed to have its place. The roof sloped to the ground on either side of its peak about two feet outside the edge of the excavation, creating a shelf of hard packed dirt under the slope of the roof. She noticed some jars of colored powders and some books sandwiched between the clay figures of a quail and a burrowing owl. Other small figures peeked out from between cooking utensils and folded clothes.

The far end of the room also had a dirt shelf backed by a wide board, painted with wild flowers in faded colors, leaning against the sides of the roof, leaving an open triangular window between it and the peak. A fire pit lined with rocks was in the left hand corner where the smoke could go out the open end of the house. A Navaho rug lined the floor, and in one corner there was a stack of old, but clean, quilts. Hanging from the sloping roof was a fishing rod. In the shadows of the roof she could just barely make out dried, smoked fish hanging like laundry from a string stretched the length of the pole. She wanted to look at everything, to touch the clay figures, but she climbed out quickly, afraid to be caught inside.

Across the clearing from the path to the spring another path headed north, and she took it hoping it would lead to a path home. It curved northwest and climbed a small hill above the waterfall where a meadow washed by the late afternoon sun was partially cleared into a small garden full of vegetables and herbs. Some corn stood tall and ripe in one corner, and acorn squash and pumpkins ripened on their sinuous vines inching out into the uncleared grasses.

The path meandered through the meadow and turned toward the sea, branching. The west path led down to the meadow south of her house; the north headed up the hill behind her house. She took the westerly path and cut across the meadow, arriving home as the sun sank into the sea. Too tired for yoga, she went straight to the kitchen.

It wasn't until she returned to the porch, plate in hand, to eat sitting on the top step, that she saw another bark painting leaning against the post by the steps. This one was of a blackberry thicket, set on a hillside in a sunset lit forest. Hanging over the top of the painting was a sprig of blackberry cane with two or three blackberries on it.

Her hands shook as she gingerly lifted the sprig, watching for thorns, and felt the soft juicy berries in her hand. He must have seen her at the blackberry thicket. She remembered the dogs running up the hillside wagging their tails. *If it was him, they think of him as a friend.* "So, do you trust the judgment of the dogs?" she whispered. "Are they really able to tell if someone has evil intentions?" Had he stuck around and watched her from some hiding place while she picked the berries? What about yesterday at the river?

Her face grew warm. She looked down at the painting. Cutting across the lower corner, almost invisible under the brambles, was a silvery river, glinting with the sunset colors flickering through the trees.

The little gray kitty was sitting on the step beside her and his tail flicked ever so slightly, his head turned just a little bit to one side. "You're laughing at me," she exclaimed, poking a finger at his nose. "You think it's funny."

She peered up at the hillside. "I don't know what to think."

Finishing her dinner quickly, she grabbed a book and went to bed, forcing herself to keep involved in the plot so her mind wouldn't wander. Soon her exhausted body took over and sent her to sleep.

Yameno stood on the path next to his garden looking up at the bright stars hanging close above his head and out at the sea glittering in the moonlight beyond Giselle's meadow. He clasped his arms around his shoulders, a little chilled in the cool night. She'd been frightened of the totem, the tree woman. Would she accept it? *She created it,* he thought. *She danced the earth's song and dreamed the oak tree's dream. It seems so right. But she's afraid. Gunther was afraid, and Mary died.*

He shivered, turned, and descended to his home. He built a small fire in the fire pit, and curled up in his quilts, watching until the last piece of wood turned black and flickered out.

The next morning Giselle awoke with the image of the tree woman in her mind. Seeking an escape among people, she arrived at school early and thrust herself into conversations in the coffee room about which she knew nothing. Finally, feeling hot and silly, she rushed to her room and fussed at papers and bulletin boards until class started.

After school she wandered through the variety store, but couldn't bear the suspicion in the eyes of the unfriendly clerk, who, ever since she had defended Dan Burroughs, had followed her up and down the aisles every time she came in. She bought some barrettes she didn't want and walked down the street staring in the windows of stores. Turning up a side street, she saw Dan Burroughs in one of the yards raking fall leaves. Walking causally in that direction she called out a "Hello."

"Hello," he replied, turning toward her and leaning on his rake. "How are you today?"

"Fine, and how are you?" *His eyes are so intense.*

"I'm just fine." He paused and cocked his head a little to one side. "I hear you're living in the Bidewell house? How do you like it up there? Some people say interesting things about those woods up behind that house." There was just a hint of laughter in his eyes.

"What do they say? People keep hinting around at things, but I've yet to hear anything definite about the forest."

"Oh, they feel strange in the forest." He smiled. It was a reassuring smile, comfortable and inclusive. "I don't think there's anything definite to say. How about you? Have you felt anything strange?" He looked closely at her.

"Not anything I don't like," she replied. *Could she ask him about Yameno? Would he know him?* That didn't feel comfortable.

He smiled at her. "You don't feel anything you don't like, huh? Me, either," he chuckled. "I fish there all the time. The best fishing in town 'cause no one else goes there much." He nodded his head thoughtfully, and then turned his piercing eyes back on hers. "Don't let people scare you with their stories of 'ghosts' in the woods."

He remembered what had been frightening when he'd first come to Arundel many years ago. Mr. Fraya, Hazel's father and the expert in local mythology he'd written to about a college project, didn't know he was black. He'd felt compelled to write him for an interview, but he hadn't understood why, and when he stepped off the bus in Robertsville he'd been terrified Mr. Fraya would tell him to get right back on the bus. He certainly hadn't had any thoughts about ghosts – spirits, really. *And once I did understand? It was scary, but the people in town were – are! – a lot scarier.*

He smiled again and turned back to his raking. "Nice talking to you."

Giselle nodded as she continued down the street mulling over the conversation. *I think he knows something about… well, whatever that is, but how do you ask about something like that? What do you say? 'Do trees talk to you?'*

She was so caught up in her thoughts she didn't see Rowena Dickerson, Jesús' third grade teacher, kneeling in a flower bed in her own yard.

"Giselle, Giselle," she called out, standing up and waving her hand.

Giselle looked up. "Oh, hello, Rowena. How are you this afternoon?" She walked over next to the older woman.

"Glad to be out of that stuffy classroom and working in the yard. Say, dear," she looked down at her gloved hands as she smacked them together trying to remove the dirt. "I saw you talking to Dan Burroughs down the street there."

"Yes," replied Giselle, warily. "He seems a very interesting man."

The woman gave her a strange look. "Well, dear, around here you'd do better if you didn't get too friendly with his kind. It's a mistake around here." She frowned, nodding her head knowingly.

Giselle's eyes narrowed and she frowned back. *No need to be surprised about that coming from Rowena.* "I need to get home," she said coldly, turning her back and walking down the street and around the block to her car.

Instead of going home, she drove to the little park by the river and spent some time swimming, blushing a little at the memory of her swim a couple of days before. The water refreshed and relaxed her. She stared up at the trees and wondered how much longer she would be able to continue her swimming before it got too cold and dark at the river.

Then she remembered. *In November they'll close the park for good. What will become of it then? Will they sell the land for fracking or something?*

As she drove down the long dirt driveway to her house, she saw something on the horizon that hadn't been there before. Something tall and tree-like was silhouetted black against the sunset, right at the edge of the meadow by the cliff where she did her Yoga exercises. She stopped the car, and hardly acknowledging the dogs and cat dashing out the doggy door to greet her, ran across the meadow.

The wooden woman she'd seen at Yameno's clearing stood planted firmly in the dirt, facing out toward the ocean and the setting sun.

Giselle's heart pounded against her lungs and she sank to the ground in front of the prepossessing totem. The sea crashed its eternal rhythm and the wind blew strong across the meadow, rattling the dry grass to the beat of the surf. Sea gulls swooped in the wind, calling the sinking sun in a high pitched minor key. She felt fluid...

Formless, liquid, part of the soil and the air, moving toward the woman, flowing in, taking the form of the woman, her arms stretched and strong to the sky. Filled with joy, strangely alive, trembling. Shadows floating, The spirit of the grass, the lord of the sea, the lithe and dancing wind, singing together in wild and glorious chorus:

> *Seas crashing, like thunder rolling,*
> *like drums beating,*
> *a call to the brethren, a cry to the wary,*
> *the time has come!*
> *Earth woman,*
> *tree woman,*
> *sea woman,*
> *stands revealed.*
> *Wind-whipped, proud she faces the sun.*
> *Wind howling, grass bending, pines whipping*

bringing the night,
singing the night.
The tree and the woman are One.

Giselle sat there, unmoving, drugged with the wonder of it, until the night fell so deeply she could no longer see more than a dark outline of the woman. Slowly she retreated back to herself and walked back to the house. *What's happening to me? Is this something wrong? It feels inevitable, unavoidable… right.* She sighed and pulled her arms tight around her chest turning to stare one last time at the Earth Woman. She was beautiful standing there, a dark silhouette against the starry sky.

As she reached to open the door, she heard the dog howling up on the hillside. It didn't sound lonely or melancholy – more triumphant. The dogs stood looking expectantly toward the hillside wagging their tails. If it had really been a wolf certainly the dogs would be scared – not excited – wouldn't they?

Yameno slipped off through the woods. Luhanada was sitting in her car at the side of the road and he sat wagging his tail for a moment before he changed and walked over to her, smiling as he leaned in the window.

The woman sighed and patted his hand. "Always running through the forest in your gray fur, and everyone just thinks you're a big gray dog."

Yameno squeezed her hand. "Your time will come soon, Luha. Giselle has accepted the totem. She became the woman."

"I heard the music. And the children?"

He smiled. "Tomorrow."

Last Quarter

But the children didn't fall into place so easily.

Saturday was a hot fall day, and the flies and mosquitoes buzzed at Enid as she sat waiting alone at the little place by the river. Noon came and went. She read her book and jumped at every sound. As the sun sank behind the trees, the tears she'd tried so hard to hold back finally came bursting out, and she lay on the ground and sobbed. Jesús wasn't coming.

Yameno, who'd hidden in the underbrush watching her earlier in the day, came back to check on her, creeping under the low branches of buckthorn and laying his head on his paws. She was crying so hard she didn't hear his quiet sympathetic whimpers. He wiggled backwards out of his hiding place and bounded quickly toward town.

Luha was playing with her cats in the wild garden in back of her house. She waved a leaf at a kitten with her right hand, while her left scratched the head of a venerable old fat cat with only one eye, who sat regally on her lap. Suddenly Yameno stood in front of her. She started, but only smiled when she saw the young man.

Yameno returned her smile as he crouched beside her, rolling the kitten on its back and tickling its tummy. "You're needed, Moonmother. Chachuli is crying. Jesús didn't come today. I searched, but he's not in the forest."

The woman stood up. "Where is she?"

"In the place by the river where they meet. I don't think she'll stay there long. It's getting late."

"I'll go right now."

When the tears had subsided, Enid went and washed her face in the river. The sun had been down a long time and it was nearly dark. She ran toward home. As she came down the path toward her house she heard a peculiar noise and froze where she stood. A huge cat moved out on the path in front of her, and sat twitching its long tail. "A cougar," whispered Enid. "It's really a cougar."

The cat's eyes glowed in the dusk as she began to purr – a deep rumbling noise, warm and soft, like velvet and to Enid it seemed the night wrapped its arms around the two of them. The cougar lay down across the path and Enid's fear slipped away. Slipping down to the ground, she put her arms around the large animal and sobbed. The cougar carefully licked all the tears from her face with a rough tongue and the child stopped crying, lying quietly snuggled against her warm body. The cat gave her one last lick and with a queenly "Merrowl," stood up and walked off into the woods. *Linked,* thought Luha. *We're linked now.* She felt a tremendous surge of love and possessiveness… and fear.

Enid picked herself up, and slipped as quietly as she could up the path, into the house, and up the stairs to her room, her head held high. Inside she felt warm and strong. She lay awake for a long time, smiling.

Gunther had been watching for Enid's return. When the sun had set and the twilight gone from the sky, he checked the house to make sure he hadn't missed her, and then, suddenly apprehensive, rushed down the path she usually took to the forest. About fifty feet down the path he ducked out of the way of a branch and around a curve, and stopped short. Down the hill and up on the other side, in a place where the faint starlight lit the path, a cougar and the child lay sprawled, darker figures in the dark woods.

Gunther stiffened and his body trembled. "The she-devil," he whispered. While he watched, the cougar stood and walked away, and the child, too, stood and continued skipping along the path.

He turned before Enid could see him and ran awkwardly back across the yard to the barn, bouncing off the open door as he plunged into its dark recesses. He grabbed an old rifle from the tack room and ran back into the woods, the rifle clutched across his chest, the knuckles of his right hand white where he gripped the stock. "You killed my Mary," he sobbed, but it was dark and the cougar was gone. "You think I did it, but it was you. Not me. Not me."

He stood frozen, remembering. He'd thought it was a game Mary and Hazel's parents played with them as children – a game learned from the Tuwillians. They each had an animal – an animal deity from the Tuwillian stories. Mary was the tree swallow. Hazel was a cougar. They'd told him he was a badger. But then before his eyes Mary became the swallow flying up in the air with wings of iridescent blue and black. She was beautiful. *I was frightened,* he thought. *It was wrong.* "It was wrong," he yelled out loud, as the memory flashed before his eyes – his shaking fingers grabbing at the swallow's wing. The fluttering – the uneven swishing of the one wing fluttering, pulling against him, and then the bird falling, falling, becoming Mary just as she landed, her head striking the rock with a crack that seemed to vibrate on and on. The feathers everywhere.

The cougar's paw prints had been all around Mary's body. The townspeople believed the cat had killed her and they'd scoured the woods looking for it. Gunther never said a word about the game which wasn't a game. *The cougar did kill her,* he thought. "Not me," he whispered. "Not me. It was the evil they were doing. It was Hazel."

After Mary's death he'd taken all her bird feeders and burned them, and Emma – his beautiful daughter Emma – had screamed and screamed. Now she was dead, too. But it wasn't his fault. It was Hazel's. She was a devil in cougar form. She was coming for Enid and he had to stop her. They'd searched for the cougar before. If they searched again, maybe they'd find it this time.

Walking as fast as he could in the dark, he headed back to his barn. Sliding his rifle back of the seat of his pickup, he headed for Al's Cafe – Al's and its telephone. He would call the deputy sheriff and the men in the bar would overhear. The word that the cougar was back would spread quickly.

The sun was low in the sky when Giselle awoke from a long afternoon nap under the oak tree. She had dithered all day about whether or not she should try to find Yameno and ask him about the statue… and maybe the music. She looked up into the leaves of the oak, flashing light and dark in the fading light. "Now or never," she whispered. Grabbing a jacket to guard against the chilly September evening, she called the dogs, and started off across the meadow to Yameno's home.

She climbed the hill, laughing and playing with the yapping dogs, anxious to give the man plenty of warning she was coming, but like before, his clearing was deserted. She checked down by the stream, stopping for a moment to dip her cupped hands under the waterfall and sip some of the sweet, cool water. The splash and gurgle of the water was calming and she felt the tension leave her shoulders and neck, almost as if the very air around the waterfall was massaging her, calming her. She bowed to the god of that place before slipping back up the path to the clearing.

A life-sized sculpture of a Red-tailed hawk riding a cougar sat next to the path. Instinctively she caressed the hawk and the cougar feeling the warmth of the wood beneath her hand. "A hawk," she murmured. "I knew he was part of this. It's strange, a hawk riding a cougar." Walking back to the center of the clearing, she sat down to wait, her back against the tree opposite Yameno's little house. The dogs rushed off, playing and chasing among the bushes for a while, and then returned panting, to lie by her side in the deepening twilight.

Giselle looked at the magical mobiles hanging from the trees, the wind chimes clinking musically in her ears. The wind brushed through the trees with a soft whishing. In the distance she could hear an owl. Across from her, hanging beside the little house, was a painting of a wolf, his dark, shaggy fur forming a cloud around his head. A huge wolf pack filled the background, receding infinitely into the distance.

The painted wolf's gentle eyes met hers. Deep, deep in the back of her mind she heard the sound of howling, like that of the lone wolf seeking his pack – announcing his presence…

> *I am the wild, the guardian, earth traveler,*
> *My soul singing touches the moon and the sun.*
> *I am the herald, the seeker, the messenger.*
> *I bear the song for those seeking the One.*
> *I am the hunter, the knower, the lover.*

My voice like a spear pierces deep in the night.
I am the lone, the many, the mirror.
My call is like lightning, jagged and bright.

And then the pack answered:

We are the pack, the tribe, earth travelers,
touching the moon and the sun.
We are the commune, the lovers and sharers,
joining to serve the One.

I am the wild, the guardian, earth traveler, the lone wolf answered.
I bear the song for those seeking the One.

We are the seekers, they replied.
Voices like arrows pierce through the night.
We are the singers, the callers, the wild ones,
Calling the lightning, jagged and bright.

I am the hunter, the knower, the lover, sang the wolf.
My call is the lightning, jagged and bright.

The howling song stopped, leaving a deep haunting silence. The dogs crept closer and the young one whined. Giselle sat still, wrapped in the night and the song. It was impossible to keep her eyes open.

When she awoke a little later, she groped for her dream. Slowly, a picture of running wolves, brown and gray as the earth and the sky, slipped into her mind. She felt herself in the middle of them riding them like the wind to the soul of the earth where something called to her with the voice of the sun.

She shivered as the night air enfolded her and looked around the clearing, but there was no sign of Yameno. Calling quietly to the dogs, she worked her way down the hillside to her home and endless papers that needed correcting.

The cougar ran through the forest and out into the moonlight shining on the meadow by Giselle's house. There she bowed regally to the Earth Woman Tree Woman, and then sat on the edge of the cliff, singing a piercing song.

Giselle sitting alone on her sofa, her feet propped on the old trunk, heard the song. She slipped out into the night to watch silently as the great cat sang to the sea and the skies.

I am I,
I am now,

I am the protector!
I am the law!

Nameless One called for light!
I am the light of understanding.
Nameless One called for light!
I am the light of justice.
Nameless One called for light!
I am the light of wisdom.
I am the light of Love!

I am I,
I am now.
I am the protector.
I am the law!

Slashing down the skies, the Red-tailed hawk dove at the cat, swooping upward at the last moment, just narrowly missing the cougar's head. The cat batted playfully at the bird and he led the cat in a merry teasing dance around the meadow, swinging low over her head and then high, high again out of the reach of her soft paws. Finally the cat lay down next to the Tree Woman and rolled over on her side. The bird landed beside her. They sat very still looking at each other and it seemed to Giselle they were laughing.

They both turned to look at her as she walked slowly toward them, stopping only a few feet from them. The hawk flew up into the sky, circling higher and higher over the meadow. She watched as he banked his wings and swooped back again for another ride on the wind. He circled, and then circled again, each circle bringing him closer to Giselle. The rush of his wings above her became louder than the roar of the sea, and he descended to perch on the head of the statue. Silhouetted against the moonlit sky, he commanded her attention. Suddenly his scream pierced the night!

Look at me!
I am the wild wings of the earth
and the violent sea.
High flyer!
Look at me!
I am the eyes of the sun, piercing,
I am the key.
Wind rider!
Look at me!
I am the claws of the skies,
bearing the welcome!
Sky diver!

Look at me!
I am the voice of life,
the song of the One.
High Crier!

With a last wordless screech, he launched himself on the rising wind and circled far over the sea. The cougar sprang up, and the hawk dove down from the sky, landing on the big cat's shoulder as she walked off into the night.

Giselle stayed out in the moonlight until the sound of a siren somewhere north on the road aroused her and she went inside. It was late and she was just pulling her big t-shirt on over pajama bottoms in preparation for bed, when a car pulled into her driveway. She pulled her bathrobe around her and went to the door where the deputy sheriff stood knocking, a rifle hanging loosely in his right hand.

"Is something wrong, deputy?" she asked.

"Don't mean to alarm you ma'am, but Mr. Amundsen up the road…" He gestured north with his rifle. "Amundsen saw a cougar near his house tonight and we've been trying to track it down. You wouldn't have seen it by any chance?"

Boy, did I, thought Giselle, *but I don't think I want you and your gun after this cougar.*

She studied the man. He seemed very uneasy tonight. It didn't make sense. Why would a deputy sheriff be chasing a cougar? "Isn't this cougar territory?"

He shifted his feet, ignoring her question. "I didn't think you'd have seen it, but I wanted to warn you. Keep your pets in. We'll probably chase this one down in a couple of days. Then you won't have to worry."

"I'm not worried." Giselle leaned against the door. "I don't understand why you want to chase it down. Has it done any damage?"

"Not yet." He scratched behind his neck with his left hand.

"In Bayomar we have cougars in the hills behind the city and they're protected," Giselle pointed out.

"You haven't been around here long enough to know about… We don't want any cougars here. This place," he gestured to the hills, "This place is wild enough as it is."

Giselle stepped outside, catching hold of one of the porch posts. She looked up at the hills. There was something funny about the way he

90

talked about it – funny and uncomfortable. "But where else should a cougar be other than a wild area? It doesn't seem right to hunt it in its own habitat. Why this area rather than some other area?"

The man shuffled his feet impatiently, shaking his head. "Oh, lady, if you see the cougar, or its tracks, just call us, please."

He moved quickly to his car and drove away.

I don't like it, thought Giselle. *There's nothing evil about that cougar – or the hawk, but there's something very wrong about that deputy chasing it. And Mr. Amundsen was the one who got him started.* She shook her head and went upstairs.

Giselle spent most of the next day sleeping, first lingering in bed, then shifting her position to her favorite place under the old oak tree, and finally in deep meditation in lotus position facing the sea, her back against the Earth Woman Tree Woman. A small yellow butterfly flitted around her head and landed a long moment on her hand.

> *Butterfly winging,*
> *'lights on my hand as I sit,*
> *still as a flower.*

She hardly breathed, feeling the bright feathery touch on her hand, then felt something behind her – a hint of movement which disturbed neither the butterfly, or her mind.

The butterfly flew gently upward and over her left shoulder. She followed with her eyes until it landed on the hand of the man leaning lightly on the shoulder of the Tree Woman. In his left hand he held a wolf formed of clay.

"I am Yameno Wellkeeper, the Wolfwind," he said, as he handed the wolf down to her. As she reached to hold it, the circle was complete – the man to the tree, the tree to the woman, the woman to the wolf, and the wolf to the man…

Sinking into the Earth Woman Tree Woman, becoming the woman, becoming alive, herself and the woman, made of the earth and the tree, the sun and the ocean, supple as the willow and strong as the oak. Man and wolf blurred, floating together, one and wild and freeborn.

Wolfwind reaches, caressing breezes tangling her branches, stroking her body, singing through the leaves of her hair, earth and tree feeding the wolf, bending to the wind. Joining, becoming all things. Wolf and tree, earth and air and water.

Wolf howls, sings to the sea, and she – woman, earth and tree – leaps to his back, her roots circling his ribs, her branches his ruff, as they run, racing the wind along the cliffs. Within her a wild confusion – herself and another, many and All...

> *I am the earth, the growing, the first born,*
> *anchored no longer.*
> *I am the highest form, called the lowest,*
> *synthesizer,*
> *anchored no longer.*
> *I trap the sun spirit.*
> *I am the transformer,*
> *I am the earth, source of all life,*
> *anchored no longer.*

Hair flying, tail flying, they climbed the forested hills and called to the day-moon. They cantered through the high meadows, flying down on the wind to the sea to gallop along the wet beach as the sun sank into the foam, taking the light, leaving the night, the moon shining on wet sand, glinting on the wave swept rocks.

Cold, white light when the earth becomes still, and slowly a tree is a tree, and a wolf is a wolf, and the circle is broken...

He left the clay wolf in her hand, turned and walked back toward the hills.

Giselle looked at the moon. She could see the *Hare in the Moon*, that incarnation of Buddha she'd read about in a children's book, who had deliberately thrown himself in the fire to keep another from breaking a law. The fire burned cold like the moon and did not consume him.

She moved back into lotus position, her back against the Earth Woman Tree Woman and sat unmoving for a long time, frightened, elated, unable to think and not to think. She caressed the warm clay of the wolf and leaned back into the smooth wood of the Earth Woman. Finally the cold drove her indoors.

When Jesús arrived in class Monday morning, he refused to look at Enid, who never took her eyes off him. Finally he whispered, "Stop staring at me. What's your problem?"

She looked at him with big serious eyes. "Why didn't you come Saturday?"

He looked away from her. "It was too hot. I went to Robertsville."

She turned her head away and went back to her work.

He returned to his plans for the house, fiddling around for a while looking through the architecture magazines Giselle had gotten for him, and then asking to be excused to go to the bathroom. He didn't come back.

Giselle was thoroughly annoyed. It was the first time he had ditched school this year. She called Ms. Nichols on her cell phone and Nicki went to his home immediately, finding his mother working in the field behind the house.

Dorotea McCrae pushed her hat back wiping the sweat from her forehead, before leading Nicki back to the house. He wasn't there. His fishing pole was gone and the kitchen showed evidence he'd made a sandwich.

She shook her head. "*Mi hijo*, he is too much like his father. *La escuela…* school goes so much better this year. He likes this teacher, but now… We will talk to him," she assured Nicki.

Back at school the teacher's lunchroom was full of talk of the cougar. Giselle was disgusted at the amount of hatred and fear she saw aimed at the animal.

"It was out near your place, wasn't it Giselle?" Nicki asked, as she unwrapped her sandwich.

"I guess it wasn't too far away. It was Mr. Amundsen, Enid's grandfather, who saw it," she replied.

Instantly all the eyes in the room turned toward her. "Mr. Amundsen!" murmured several voices.

Mr. Harding lifted his eyebrows. "Where do you live?"

Giselle carefully unwrapped her carrots before she answered. "You know the Bidewell house next to the cliffs south of the Amundsen's, and on the other side of the river?"

"You live there?" he exclaimed. "Didn't anyone tell you about that place?"

She dipped her carrot into a little bowl of peanut butter. "Well, no one's been able to tell me anything about that place that makes me not want to live there. I like it."

"Well, let me tell you a few things about that place!" He leaned forward, waving his soda in the air, stopping himself as some soda spurted out the top of the can. "Especially the forest behind that house and the next hill south – nobody here will go into that part of the forest except, you know, the strange ones."

"Harding, don't be ridiculous," interrupted Ms. Nichols, halting her sandwich in midair. "Giselle, every small town has its local tales, and that wood happens to be the local scare tale for this area. Nothing's ever happened there. People have been saying there's a strange feeling in the woods for so long that anyone who goes in there knows before he goes in he's going to feel a strange feeling, so naturally he does. Just a bunch of nonsense."

"I don't think so, Nicki," countered Harding.

"Me, either," interjected another teacher. "How about Mr. Amundsen's wife? She died in those woods, and there was a cougar here then, too."

"Oh, for heaven's sakes." Nicki scowled and threw the crust of her sandwich down on her plate.

"Well," Mr. Harding added, "I don't think there's anything supernatural going on, but I think the rumor has been fostered for a purpose, and the cougar might be there for a purpose, too. Maybe to scare people off from a pot farm. You know that Indian, Wellkeeper, lives up there somewhere, and I'm sure he's up to no good."

"Yameno Wellkeeper!" exclaimed Ms. Nichols, glaring at him. "Harding, you're too young to remember Yameno when he was a child going to school here, but I had him in class. I have a great deal of faith in him. Everyone did then, and I still do. I would never, ever suspect him of any kind of wrong doing."

"Then what's he doing up there?" argued Harding.

"I haven't the slightest idea, but he isn't hurting anybody, so I wish people would just leave him alone." Nicki pushed her chair back and glared at Harding.

"But someone mentioned the cougar and Mrs. Amundsen's death," interjected Giselle. "What's that all about?"

"Oh, that," Nicki answered, gathering her lunch leavings into a paper sack. "Mrs. Amundsen apparently fell in the forest. She hit her head. There was a cougar seen wandering in the forest at that time, too, but there was no indication that the cougar had anything to do with her fall."

"There were tracks near her body!" Rowena protested.

"But nothing to indicate that the cougar had anything to do with her death! Maybe she saw the cougar, was surprised, and fell, but she wasn't attacked by the cougar. There were no marks on her body that would indicate that. You all know that's true." Ms. Nichols threw the sack into the garbage with a resounding clunk.

"But listen, Nicki," Mr. Harding leaned forward in his chair. "I know they said there were no marks, but how did a cougar ever get in the forest? And now there's another one. I just think something funny's going on."

"The population of cougars is growing all over the state," Nicki responded indignantly. "They were endangered and now they're not. We should be happy to see them coming back." She shook her head and stomped out the door, throwing, "I've got to go check the playground," back over her shoulder.

"Yeah, right," muttered Harding. "The weirdos stick together. Believe me, if this job wasn't so convenient, I wouldn't stay working here."

"Well," added Rowena, "If they sell the park for logging, like they're talking about, that would take care of the forest."

"Logging!" exclaimed Giselle.

Rowena just shrugged her shoulders and smiled, and no one else seemed to know anything about it.

Giselle was glad to get back to class and away from all the crazy talk. The talk of logging really alarmed her. Still, she did know the cougar wasn't just an ordinary cougar.

When Jesús reached his fishing spot, he didn't see Yameno Wellkeeper sitting quietly beside a rock until he'd settled into his fishing. He nearly fell in the river when Yameno spoke to him. "Well, here you are today when you should be in school, and on Saturday, when you should've been here, you weren't."

When Jesús' heart stopped racing, he asked, "You're that Indian, Yameno, aren't you?" Yameno just nodded. "How did you know I was supposed to be here Saturday?"

"I saw a little girl crying."

Jesús rolled his eyes and turned elaborately back to his fishing. "She would be dumb enough to cry about the whole thing."

"Did you think she wouldn't?"

Jesús shrugged his shoulders and looked away, dragging his fishing line slowly through the water, pretending to be intent on the fish. Finally he turned to Yameno, who sat waiting patiently. "We've been trying to live off the land, like you do."

"I know," Yameno nodded.

"How do you know? Hey," the boy looked at him suspiciously. "Have you been watching us, or something?"

"Or something," agreed Yameno, but said no more.

"People in town think you're strange. Maybe they're right."

Yameno smiled. "They don't say very nice things about you either. Are they right?"

Jesús looked at him, as if weighing the statement in his mind, then shrugged.

Yameno stood up.

Jesús reeled in his fishing line. "Where are you going?"

"To my home."

"Do you really live in the woods? Can I go with you? Can I see your home?"

Yameno nodded his head, and turned off up the river toward a place where he could ford it. "Come along."

Jesús rushed to put his fishing gear away, and followed him up the river.

When they reached Yameno's clearing, Jesús stood at the edge, awed. As he walked slowly around the clearing, peering at the bark paintings and touching the wood and clay sculptures, he found a carving of a sitting coyote with a small squirrel crouched between his ears. He caressed it. "You sure put strange creatures together. I'd think a coyote'd eat a squirrel."

"They're Kumni and Chachuli," replied Yameno. "They belong together. Coyote, like humans, is creative and inventive, but if he's cut off from the voice of the lifeforce, his creativity is destructive. In my nation's mythology – and also in Norse mythology – the squirrel runs up and down the tree of life carrying messages from the gods to humanity."

"Chachuli? Is that the name you called Enid? She said you called her something like that."

"Perhaps," Yameno walked over to the cougar and the hawk. "When you see Enid, tell her about this cougar."

"Oh, yeah, she was reading a book about a cougar." Jesús reached down and caressed the little squirrel. "I've never done any wood carving."

Yameno smiled. "I have some small pieces of driftwood. Would you like to learn how to carve them?" Jesús nodded eagerly and they spent the afternoon together each working on a carving.

As the sun began to reach toward the horizon, Yameno got up. "You should leave now, so you get home before dark. I'll walk with you to the road."

"Can I come again tomorrow?" Jesús asked, as he gathered his tools and scraps.

"Yes." Yameno nodded his head slowly, "but after school. You have a good teacher. There's no reason to ditch." He picked up Jesús' carving, stroking it a little before he placed it on a shelf inside his hut.

"I know." Jesús followed behind him. "I only did it because Enid looked so... I don't know." He hung his head.

"You felt guilty." He raised his eyebrows. "Right?" Not waiting for an answer, he turned and started down the path.

Not long after Yameno had left him at the road, a large Red-tailed hawk came swooping past Jesús and landed on a fence post. It sat there a moment, preening its feathers. As Jesús stood on the road, astonished that the big bird should come so close, it fluttered its feathers and turned its unblinking eyes on him. Finally, it shrieked, spreading its huge wings. Lifting into the air with a mighty thrust, it flew in a circle over Jesús' head, then headed out over the ocean to ride the wild air currents. Jesús continued home not knowing what to think of the strange encounter.

The next day in school, during morning free time, Giselle was startled out of her reveries when she saw Jesús and Enid, heads together, whispering eagerly in the corner where the children hung their coats and kept their belongings. Jesús had just returned from the office where he'd been lectured and given detention for ditching, but Giselle saw no trace of either contrition or anger.

"And one of the sculptures he'd made was a cougar with a hawk on its back. He told me to tell you about that one," Jesús told Enid.

"A cougar? He told you to tell me about a cougar?" exclaimed Enid. Her mouth dropped open in astonishment. "Jesús, on Saturday... Didn't you hear about the cougar?" She dropped her eyes. The experience with the cougar had been so important she wasn't sure she wanted to tell anyone – even Jesús.

"Yeah, I heard about the cougar. Did you see it? I thought your grandfather saw it."

She shrugged and started to walk away. "What?" Jesús grabbed her and turned her toward him. "Why won't you tell me what happened?"

Giselle, seeing the discussion had become physical, was about to interfere when Enid put a hand on top of Jesús' hand where he held her arm and pulled his hand away. Still holding his hand she began to whisper earnestly. "On Saturday when I went home after you didn't come... it was nearly dark, and I was feeling very sad..."

"You were crying. The Indian told me."

"Well, I wasn't crying then. I was just going home and there was this large noise, an animal noise, and this huge cat was standing in the path. A cougar!"

"What did you do?"

"It started purring and lay down across the path. It was... it was meant for me, and... and..." The rest was so personal, so private, she didn't want to tell.

Jesús shook her hand. "And what?"

"I lay down next to it and it... it licked my face."

His eyes narrowed. "Are you sure it wasn't a big dog?"

"It was a cougar!" Enid roared her answer, and tears spurted into her eyes. She let go of his hand and turned to stomp away.

He grabbed her shoulder. "Wait. I'm sorry. I believe you."

"I knew I shouldn't tell you. I knew it." Enid started toward the reading corner, but turned just in time to see a wide eyed Giselle looking at her. She ducked her head, grabbed a book, and scrunched herself way back in the corner where a bunch of pillows lay haphazardly on the small rug.

Giselle shook her head trying to decide whether to interfere or not. She decided to leave them alone now, but keep an eye on them, hoping some day she had the good fortune to find out what it was all about.

By the time lunch recess came around, Enid had calmed down and was willing to talk to Jesús again. Slipping away to a hiding place inside a large, brightly painted, concrete pipe at the far end of the yard, they sat facing each other with their feet stretched up the curved walls. "I think Yameno – the Indian – must've had something to do with your cougar," Jesús suggested. "Otherwise, why'd he tell me to tell you about the cougar sculpture?"

Enid nodded thoughtfully. "I want to go there with you. I want to see that sculpture and talk to that man."

Jesús flipped a twig in the air. "You had a chance to talk to him before, but you didn't."

"Well, this time I will." Her head was high and determined, and there was no sign of the timidity he was used to.

"Boy, you've changed!" he exclaimed.

She looked at him, her face straight and solemn. "It's the cougar," she said. "The cougar was for me." The bell rang and the children walked silently toward the classroom. Without even thinking Jesús held the little girl's hand. When they returned to the room, Giselle didn't notice their newly obvious friendship. She was too distracted with thoughts of the lunchroom conversation.

"The Reverend Tarrant's holding a town meeting tonight on the whole subject," Rowena Dickerson was saying as Giselle walked into the lunchroom. "He says the cougar is evil. He says we need to kill the cougar."

"What a bunch of nonsense!" Nicki shook her head. "He'll get a mob of people up there with guns, and someone'll get killed."

"Well, maybe, Nicki," intervened Harding, "but on the other hand, it might flush out whatever's going on up there."

"With a mob of idiots that think a cougar is a reincarnation of the devil? I doubt it." She packed up her lunch and left.

Harding waited until the door was closed and leaned forward conspiratorially, rolling his eyes. "Well, none of us are surprised by her reaction, are we?"

Giselle sat down and opened her lunch. "Where's this meeting going to be held?"

"You should go and find out about it," Rowena urged. "Your house is right out there near where they saw the cougar."

"Well, I might go to the meeting, but..."

Rowena interrupted Giselle. "I know you don't believe in any of this, but if you went to the meeting and found out about what's gone on before. If you knew about poor Mary Amundsen, you'd think twice about having a house up in those woods."

"My house isn't in the woods. It's by the beach."

"Well, all the same. It's near the forest. You said you go walking in those woods. And besides, you're kind of different yourself. I saw you talking to Dan Burroughs." Rowena nodded her head firmly at Giselle.

"What has Dan Burroughs got to do with this?" Giselle said incredulously.

"Plenty. He talks to that Hazel Fraya all the time in the library. They're friends," said Harding.

"Well, I know she's Mrs. Amundsen's sister, but that doesn't mean she had something to do with the cougar," exclaimed Giselle. *But… she* thought. *But maybe… maybe Hazel and Dan did have something to do with the weird stuff – the songs, the cougar and the hawk playing together. There was something about the way they acted… But, not something bad. I don't think it's bad, and I don't think she caused her sister's death!*

"Gunther thought Hazel had something to do with it," Rowena stated firmly. "And the Reverend Tarrant has always thought she was right in the middle of it – whatever it is – and he grew up with her."

Giselle shook her head. "Well, where is this meeting going to be held? I'd better go find out what it's all about."

"At the *Church of Those Born Again in Jesus* at seven-thirty tonight."

Oh, yeah, she thought, *I remember that church. 'Repent and Be Saved.'* "All right, I'll be there." She ate her lunch in silence, while the conversation milled about her. Nothing more was said about the cougar or the "ghosts". She thought of Nicki's exasperation. *Only she thinks the cougar is just an ordinary cougar.*

Giselle pulled up across the street from the church a little early that evening and watched as people got out of their cars speaking to each other as they headed in the door. Although she recognized some of them, the only person she knew was Mr. Coffman. She'd thought Rowena Dickerson would be here, but it was mostly men. She considered going home, but took a deep breath and walked quietly into the church.

It was impeccably clean, but except for a few very severe looking banners – "Except ye repent ye all shall perish, Luke 13:3"; "The Penalty of Sin is Eternal Torment" (no Bible reference she noticed); and one that made Giselle shiver: "Therefore as the church is subject unto Christ, so let the wives be to their own husbands in every thing, Eph.5:24," – the church seemed bare. The altar, a table with an altar cloth across it and a brass cross in the center, sat at the front of the chancel with a pulpit to the right and a smaller lectionary to the left. A step ran the length of the chancel. On the far right was a small upright piano.

She hesitated at the back a minute or two before choosing a seat halfway down a row of folding chairs against the side wall. From her seat she could see not just the front of the church, but the audience as well. She noted a young man wearing a Yarmulke and a woman wearing a clerical collar sitting together in the fourth row.

A middle aged gray-haired man, neatly dressed in slacks and a dress shirt, came down the center aisle and stood on the first step of the chancel facing the people. He raised his right hand to get the audience's attention.

"Folks! Let's settle and get down to business."

Waiting a moment, smiling nervously with his mouth, but not his eyes while there was a last minute settling into seats, he leaned forward onto the tips of his toes and back to his heels, before continuing. "For those of you who don't know me, I'm Reverend Jarvis Tarrant. We're having this town meeting here tonight to discuss a very serious matter."

He paced along the step toward the right side of the church, away from Giselle, and then quickly turned back to face his audience. "A cougar has been sighted."

He paused, leaning forward. "Yes, a cougar." Another pause and then, moving his eyes across his audience, "Not just an ordinary cougar. A manifestation of evil."

Stepping forward off the step and up the center aisle, he added, "This is not the first time this cougar has come to Arundel."

He looked over his audience, nodding at the two in the fourth row, pausing again when he saw Giselle – Giselle wondered if it was because he didn't know who she was, or because he did – and then turned back to the front. "This is not the first time it's come to that place – those woods." He waved an arm in the direction of the western hills. He smiled. "Hopefully some day in the future the forest will be logged and the wood put to good use…," (Giselle shuddered) "but that's a ways off. Right now we have a problem – a problem that has to be taken care of now, not in the future."

He mounted the steps again. Facing his audience, he spit out the words. "The cougar is here again. It's here and it's time to get rid of it before we have another tragedy like the one that befell Mary Amundsen."

The lady sitting next to Giselle leaned over to her husband and whispered, "Some tragedy. She brought it on herself, if you ask me, messing around in those woods."

"It's time," continued the preacher, "to organize a posse and kill that cougar."

A group of young men in the back cheered.

In the fourth row, the young man with the yarmulke stood up. He held up his hands for silence. Leaning both hands on the chair in front of him, he said, "Reverend Tarrant, if I may interrupt for a moment."

"Certainly, Rabbi Levinson." Reverend Tarrant stood on the step facing the Rabbi with his hands grasped behind his back.

"Reverend Yates and I are here from the Robertsville Interfaith Council. Many of us on the council have congregants from Arundel. We're both fairly new to the area and we don't know any of the background about this cougar, or why people think it's a manifestation of evil. Could you tell us more about this Mary Amundsen?"

"Yes," Reverend Tarrant nodded. "We'll start with Mary Amundsen, and then go back over the other sightings of the cougar."

He rocked on his feet for a moment. "Twelve years ago Mary Amundsen was apparently walking out in the woods back of her house – and let me interject here," he said, looking directly at Rabbi Levinson, "that lots of people have had uncomfortable feelings in that woods."

He continued, "Her husband, Gunther, went out looking for her and found her dead. She'd fallen and hit her head on a rock. A cougar had been seen nearby and the police found cougar paw prints near her body."

"But, Reverend Tarrant," interrupted Reverend Yates, jumping to her feet. "A cougar could have killed her without being a manifestation of evil. Also she could have just seen the cougar, been startled and fallen. Cougars don't often attack adult human beings."

"Well, yes," responded Reverend Tarrant. "They have attacked humans, but not often. That's true."

"And it can't be the same cougar," Reverend Yates added. "Cougars don't live that long."

"Ah, yes, but this isn't a normal cougar. Around here we have a history of unnatural cougar trouble that goes right back to the Indians." He gestured toward a gray-haired lady. "I've asked Muriel Chase, Dr. Chase's wife and our unofficial town historian, to talk to us about that very thing. She's going to give us a rundown of all the cougar sightings that've been recorded over the years."

As she stood he pointed to the right. "Bring your notes up to the lectionary, Mrs. Chase."

Muriel Chase, a slight, twinkly little woman with long gray hair twisted haphazardly on top of her head and a sweet smile, moved up to the podium.

"Let's see," she said, adjusting her glasses on her nose. "We'll begin with the local Native Uhseans, the Tuwillian people. The information comes from a fascinating book about their mythology, written by a woman who actually spent time a hundred years ago interviewing and talking with a lot of natives who lived right here."

"Mrs. Chase," the Reverend interrupted. "I'd like to add here…" He hesitated. "We have to be careful when reading material about the Indians. Some people seem to idolize them, but they were heathens – godless. We need to read between the lines."

"Oh." Mrs. Chase's eyes opened wide at Tarrant. She cleared her throat and opened her notebook, licking her forefinger as she peered down through her glasses and turned the pages. She found the correct page and smiled at the audience again. "Here it is: 'The cougar was a vastly important part of the local pantheon.'"

The Reverend moved up the step and touched Mrs. Chase's elbow. "May I interrupt again, Mrs. Chase?"

"Yes… yes, sure…" She blinked her eyes and backed away.

The Reverend turned and frowned at the audience. "A pantheon is a group of gods believed in by heathens – false gods, of course." He turned back to the little woman. "Please go on."

Giselle noticed Mrs. Chase's eyes narrowing as she looked at Reverend Tarrant. "Thank you." She nodded her head several times and returned to her reading. "'Luhanada was considered to be the judge and the lawgiver.' The cougar, that is. Luhanada is the Tuwillian name for cougar."

Again the Reverend interrupted, holding up a hand in the traditional stop position and shaking his head apologetically. "I must add there is, of course, only one law giver and judge, and He certainly is not a cougar."

She frowned at him, then shrugged her shoulders. "This is mythology, Reverend."

Giselle almost laughed. This woman probably was not one of his parishioners.

"Ah," he interjected with a raised finger and a smile on his shaking head, "but the Indians believed it to be true. It was a false god."

Mrs. Chase stood looking at him blinking her eyes for a moment. "Or a metaphor."

She looked back at her notes. "But, here comes the part of local significance." She turned back to the audience and smiled sweetly again, lifting the book:

> To the Indians of the Tuwillia River there was an even greater importance, since a cougar had frequently been sighted by the young men and women of the village when they made their dreamfast at the age of fifteen. This cougar had seemed to them to be almost human. In fact, it is clear that the ceremonies of the secret society of the village almost certainly involved this cougar in some way. But when I questioned Chief Yanada about this, who, as I have already said, was a very important member of the secret society, he would only smile in that charming way of his...'"

"You can see as well as I can," Reverend Tarrant interrupted, "the author of this book – a woman," he smiled, and shook his head knowingly, "was being, as she put it herself, 'charmed' by this heathen."

Mrs. Chase raised her eyebrows and looked at the Reverend. She carefully closed her book. "So," she turned toward her audience, "A cougar has been sighted several times under strange circumstances, way back before the Europeans came to this community."

"And of course," added the Reverend, "I think all of you know where the Indians lived. They lived right next to the river where it flows through the forest, the very part of the forest we're talking about!"

Rabbi Levinson stood up. "Mrs. Chase, this is very interesting. Thank you for sharing this information, but can you tell me – at that time weren't cougars a natural part of the environment around here? They were part of the original habitat, were they not?"

"Oh," she responded, "I suppose they were, but you understand, this cougar was supposed to act differently – human."

"Yes, I understand that," he said, as he sat down.

"Now," Mrs. Chase smiled, and then looked hesitantly at Reverend Tarrant in case he wished to interrupt again, "that takes care of the earliest written records about cougars in our area. Let's see," she peered through the bottom halves of her bifocals at the notebook as she flipped through the pages, again pausing every so often to lick her index finger. "Here it is. Let's see. About forty years ago... Let's see, yes. Well, actually thirty-nine years ago there was a cougar sighting by one Albert Swenson. He was out hunting in the forest and this is what he told the newspaper reporter."

Mrs. Chase's voice changed as she read the article and Giselle smiled at how well the little woman was able to assume the character of the hunter:

> I saw this big red-tail hawk sitting up on the limb of a tree, and I was going to take a shot at it, and I had my gun up and was just about to pull the trigger when this huge cat comes leaping out at me and knocks the gun out of my hand, and then turns around and knocks me right over. The hawk flew up in the air, then came over our heads and flew off back of me, and the cougar took off in the same direction. Well, I thought I'd bag me a cougar, and I grabbed my gun and ran after it, but instead of the cougar, the next thing I saw was Hazel Fraya sitting on a log. And you know what she said? She said she never saw the cougar.

"Yes! Yes!" The Reverend banged his fist down on the podium for emphasis, startling poor Mrs. Chase. "She said she never saw the cougar, but of course, none of us believe that. Nobody did then either, because I remember the incident."

His eyes almost flamed!

"We were both in high school at the time, and that Dan Burroughs had just come to town and was working with her father, and Hazel was spending a lot of time sitting out on the steps talking to him."

He cast his eyes from one end of the audience to the other. "And you know what else? Her parents didn't say one word to her. They didn't seem to think there was anything wrong with her being so friendly with him. I believe they not only did not disapprove of her friendship with Dan Burroughs, but were a part of this whole thing. Way back then," he thumped his fist again. "I think that whole family was involved in this."

There was an angry murmur of sound in the audience. Giselle noted the reactions of Mrs. Chase, who was looking at the Reverend with a bewildered expression, and the rabbi and minister from Robertsville, who were frowning. *Mrs. Chase doesn't quite buy this stuff,* thought Giselle. *And oh,* thought Giselle, *the minister who kept Enid from visiting Hazel! I'll bet this Tarrant's the one. He has some kind of serious problem with Hazel. Is it about racism? Does racism really explain all of this?*

"No," continued the Reverend, "we certainly didn't believe her, but we didn't realize then just exactly what was involved. We just thought she was in the forest up to no good with that Dan Burroughs." He shook his right index finger wildly. "As far as the cougar was concerned, everyone thought it was just a dangerous animal that needed to be eliminated. The men all went hunting it, but they couldn't find it."

He began to pace back and forth on the step. "It wasn't until later that we began to really understand what was going on here. That was when Mary Amundsen was killed."

He turned to where the rabbi and minister sat in the audience, "Yes, Rabbi Levinson and…" he hesitated, his voice almost a sneer, "Reverend Yates, this you will find very interesting. Please, Mrs. Chase, tell us what Gunther Amundsen said to the police officer when he reported his wife's death."

"All right." She turned toward the rabbi and minister. "Gunther was apparently quite excited and frightened when he talked to the police officers about his wife's death. He kept repeating – and I quote from the officers' written report – 'I thought it was evil, but they were all involved in it.' But when the police asked him later, he wouldn't talk about it."

"And that," added the Reverend, "is when he withdrew – stopped going to church, stopped talking to anyone. He knows something, but he's too afraid to talk."

He looked directly at Reverend Yates. "I think they were involved in devil worship."

Reverend Yates who'd looked questioning, if not skeptical, before this, was now slowly nodding her head. "I see you nodding your head," said Reverend Tarrant. "Now you're beginning to believe."

"Well," replied Reverend Yates, sitting forward in her seat. "I would want to look farther into the matter, but, yes, I do begin to be more suspicious when someone mentions more than one person involved, and being afraid. But not of a cougar. I don't believe a cougar…"

Rabbi Levinson stood up. "Yes, not a cougar. Reverend Tarrant, before you go off cougar hunting, I really think it would be a good idea to call in some experts. In our Robertsville Interfaith Council we actually have a Catholic priest, Father Keegan Gilchrist, who has done some studies on Satanism and similar cults. He wanted to come to this meeting, but had to go out of town."

"No," yelled someone in the back. "Let's kill the damn thing. We don't need no help from no Catholics."

"Or Jews either," yelled someone else. "Yeah, yeah," echoed a lot of voices.

Giselle shuddered. *Oh, my god. Jews and Catholics. If there were any Muslims here they'd probably lynch them.*

Reverend Tarrant smiled uncomfortably. "Ah, Rabbi Levinson, suppose you go ahead and contact your expert. We'll go ahead and kill that cougar, if we can, but those woods will still be evil. And when your expert gets here, why, he can exorcise the woods. How's that?"

"Not okay, really," responded the rabbi, sitting back down and crossing his arms. "Taking a mob of people out into the forest armed with rifles is asking for trouble. People will be killing each other instead of the cougar."

"Yes," agreed Reverend Yates, "And if it is a manifestation of evil, you won't be able to kill it with a rifle."

"Oh, well, neither of you have been around here very long," Reverend Tarrant responded in a voice that began to sound impatient. "We're perfectly capable of handling a hunt safely."

"Yeah," roared the young men at the back of the room.

Reverend Tarrant smiled again. "You just call your exorcist or whatever he is out here. I think that would be just fine, and he can exorcise Hazel Fraya, and that Dan Burroughs and the like, but we'll take care of the cougar."

The two religious leaders shook their heads. "We're not talking about exorcism – he's not an exorcist. He studies Satanism and other cults. But I will call, Keegan… Father Gilchrist," Rabbi Levinson added.

Suddenly, Mr. Coffman from the hardware store stood up. "I vote we get planning this hunt. We should do it Saturday." He turned around in a circle looking at all the members of the audience. "Are we all agreed, men?" There was a cacophony of foot stamping and applause. Giselle noticed the startled look on Mrs. Chase' face.

"Then Saturday it is," Tarrant shouted out over the din. "Coffman, why don't you organize the details? Where to meet and so forth."

Coffman nodded his head in agreement and walked to the front of the church.

This is crazy, thought Giselle. *I can't stand listening to this anymore.* Trying to be as unobtrusive as possible, she stood up and made her way quietly toward the door. She noticed the two religious leaders from Robertsville and Mrs. Chase doing the same. One group of people turned their heads toward her as she passed. A middle-aged man leaned over to another man sitting in front of him and she heard him whisper, "Look, there's that teacher who bought that old Bidewell house out there by the beach in front of the forest. I wonder why she's leaving now. You'd think she'd want to stay and find out what's going on."

She grimaced and rushed out the door.

Outside Mrs. Chase, the rabbi, and the minister were talking. "I'm glad you told us about this meeting, Muriel," Reverend Yates was saying. "This is alarming."

The rabbi turned to the minister, "But surely you don't believe there are Satanists involved in this, Clare?"

The minister shrugged. "I don't know, Micah. A few years back there were rumors of horrible things happening. Not here, but..."

Mrs. Chase reached out to Giselle. "I think you're the new teacher. I'm Muriel Chase, and this is Reverend Clare Yates." She gestured toward the woman and then the man, "and Rabbi Micah Levinson. I attend Clare's church, Robertsville Methodist."

Micah Levinson smiled at her. "What do you think of all this?"

Giselle shook her head. "I don't think it has anything to do with evil." She turned to look at Clare. "Or Satanists either. Have you ever met Hazel Fraya and Dan Burroughs?"

Muriel nodded and smiled. "Yes, they're very nice people. I don't for one minute think they're Satanists."

"Well, probably not," Clare conceded. "I just think Father Gilchrist should check it all out. That's all."

Giselle excused herself and headed for her car.

Waning Crescent

The next day at lunch the room was a-buzz with discussion of the meeting. Rowena Dickerson's husband had gone and was excitedly making plans to join the hunt on Saturday. Giselle couldn't stand it and left. On the way to the office to check her box for messages, she ran into Ms. Nichols. "Nicki," she asked. "I wanted to ask you — well, I guess I'm concerned. I went to that meeting last night about the cougar, and the Reverend Tarrant..."

"Oh, that Jarvis Tarrant," Nicki shook her head in disgust. "The thing that's so maddening about him is he should be an intelligent man! You know, Giselle, I don't think he's all bad. He and I are about the same age. I grew up in Robertsville, so I didn't know him as a child, but when I first started teaching here I was only about twenty-two years old. He had just gotten back from some Bible college in the east and was ready to start this little church he runs. He was an idealist of sorts, really. At least, he was enthusiastic about his church."

"When did he change?"

"Well, twelve or thirteen years ago, when Mary Amundsen died, he got real excited and was talking about the devil. Actually though, he's always been a little crazy where Hazel Fraya is concerned."

"And she's so nice," exclaimed Giselle. "She's been so helpful to me in the library. She seems like an intelligent and genuinely good person."

"To me, too," Nicki nodded her head. "But Jarvis has always been upset about her and especially about her friendship with Dan Burroughs. And…" Nicki lifted her index finger and shook it significantly, "Jarvis has never gotten married. I kind of think he had a thing for her once, and Dan Burroughs came along..."

"But she never married Dan?" Giselle interrupted.

"No, I've never understood that – or maybe I do. They'd have to leave and go to a city or something if they got married, because people here would make life intolerable for them. Well, they do anyway. But why haven't they left? Why does Dan Burroughs stick around a place where people are so crude and nasty to him? He's an intelligent, educated man. He's had three books published. Why is he working in Arundel as a gardener, when he could be working in a city some place at almost any job he chose?" Nicki shrugged her shoulders.

"Tarrant said he came here to work for Hazel's father."

"That's right. He came here when he was about twenty for his summer vacations. He was going to college down in Greenville. Hazel was just finishing high school. He came and worked with Hazel's father, who had a small farm. Jarvis said he didn't think her dad really needed help."

"Well, maybe her dad was just helping Dan out."

"I don't know. It seems to me I remember something about him doing research, too. He has a doctorate, but he came back every summer when he was getting it, and then when he was finished, settled here." Nicki shoved one hand in the pocket of her gray slacks, and ran the fingers of her other hand through her hair.

"You know, Giselle, the only thing I do really know about this whole thing, is that if they felt they could organize a hunt for Hazel and Dan, they would. They're afraid of this cougar, but they're really afraid of Hazel and Dan… and Yameno Wellkeeper, too."

"They're different. People are afraid of people who are different."

"That's right."

"Scary."

"Yes," Nicki nodded. "Yes. Very scary." She looked out the window.

Scary for her, too, if she's lesbian, thought Giselle.

She felt agitated and upset all afternoon. *What can I do? Maybe go to the library and talk to Hazel Fraya – warn her about the hunt, if she doesn't already know.* She looked out over the heads of her students who were deep in silent reading. Maybe the librarian would tell her what it was all about. Maybe. But why would the woman trust her?

When she walked into the library that afternoon, she found Dan Burroughs there sitting in a chair beside Hazel's desk. Both looked up at her warily as she came in the door, and Dan stood.

"Hi," said Giselle awkwardly.

"Can I help you, dear," said the librarian.

"No, I mean… Well, I just came here because…"

She pushed her hair away from her face and walked over to the desk. "This is probably none of my business," she started again, "but people are worked up about a cougar and – this sounds so strange…"

Hazel interrupted. "It is strange. We understand."

"I just wanted to warn you."

"To warn us?"

"Yes, they – they're going to hunt for the cougar on Saturday."

Hazel and Dan shot an alarmed look at each other.

"You didn't know?" continued Giselle. "They're forming a posse to hunt for this poor cougar, and somehow they connect it with you."

Dan sank back in the chair. "We knew Amundsen saw the cougar, but we didn't know about the hunt."

Hazel gestured at the other chair for Giselle. "Tell us, dear."

Giselle told them everything and they listened intently. She paused after telling them the stories of the newspaper clipping and of Mary

Amundsen's death, but they didn't comment. After she finished, Hazel leaned over and put her hand on Giselle's arm. "Thank you, Giselle. Thank you."

Giselle waited a moment. She wanted to talk about the cougar and the hawk, about her experiences with the Earth Woman Tree Woman, but Hazel and Dan didn't say anything, and she didn't either. Instead she went home and sat for a long time leaning against the wooden woman.

That night Luha and Tata, climbed the path to Yameno's.

Holding hands and leaning into each other, they sat quietly next to the little waterfall while Yameno sang:

> *Water of life,*
> *Purify me.*
> *Water of the soul of earth,*
> *wash me in your love.*

Dipping their hands into the pool they drank of the sacred waters feeling the spirit of the earth pour over them, the silence of the night thrumming like a drumbeat, a heartbeat.

> *Come, come, whispered the night.*
> *Hammer your feet*
> *to the beat of the drum.*

"Did you hear?" whispered the cat woman.

> *Come, come, answer the call*
> *of the earth and the sun.*

"Ninas Twei is calling us," Yameno added.

Tata nodded. "Hunt or no hunt, we have to go as soon as we can all gather"

"Saturday," added Luha.

4

Dark Hunter's Moon

Jesús continued to visit Yameno after school while the town planned the cougar hunt. By the end of the week he had fashioned his own rough version of a squirrel. On Saturday he carried it with him to his meeting with Enid at their spot by the river.

"Look." He shoved the squirrel eagerly at the little girl. "This is the squirrel I carved with Yameno. Do you like it? Do you think it looks like a squirrel?"

Enid rubbed her hands down the ridges of the rough carved wood and smiled. "It's really nice. It looks like my little squirrels under the bush."

"Take it. I mean..." Jesús shrugged his shoulders and looked off to one side. "If you'd like it, you could have it. It's not that great or anything."

"Oh, yes," she smiled broadly. "I really like it." She brushed the wooden fur with her hand. "Can we go there?"

Jesús nodded and they ran off through the forest toward Yameno's clearing.

All that Saturday morning Giselle felt restless as she tried to settle down to her school work, her eyes constantly drawn to the Earth Woman Tree Woman. Later this afternoon the forest would be full of hunters, tramping around with their guns, hoping to find the cougar at dusk when it might be hunting for food.

She thought the cat wouldn't be found. She'd heard it sing and knew it was something more than a real cougar, but still, no good could come out of all those men out there with guns.

She went to sit by the wooden woman, the dogs and the cat beside her. Suddenly she felt overwhelmed by some urgency, some need.

The cat patted her arm and she looked down at him.

Go. Go now, whispered the voice in her head. *Go!*

Giselle took off at a run, the dogs flying at her heels. She slowed, panting, as she climbed up the hill behind her house and walked down the ridge to the little meadow and Yameno's garden. As she came down the path to the clearing, she heard low voices and a child's laugh. She almost turned back, but the dogs ran on into the clearing and she followed, stopping short in surprise when she saw Jesús and Enid sitting cross-legged on the ground beside Yameno as he poured tea into small carved cups in front of them.

The children jumped up startled, "Ms. Raphael!"

Yameno paused for a moment smiling up at her, and a warm shy joy spread through her. His eyes filled with sweet laughter as he stood and bowed slightly, holding out his hand in welcome. "Please join us, Ms. Raphael."

Giselle walked over and sat with them in the circle around the teapot, the dogs lying quietly behind her. Yameno slipped into his little house and returned with another carved cup. As he handed it to Giselle, she saw that it was an oak tree, earth-rooted at its base, twining around the cup, and up the handle.

"Look," Enid said, thrusting her cup at Giselle. "Mine's a tree squirrel and Jesús's is a coyote."

Giselle admired the cups, adding, "But what are you children doing here?"

The once shy child began chattering like the squirrel on her cup. The story of meeting Jesús in the forest and the friendship they had formed with each other, and with Yameno, just spilled out of her.

Jesús, too, loosened under the influence of the smiling adults and urged Enid to show Giselle the ground squirrel he had carved. Giselle took the carving in her hands and looked carefully at the workmanship. "Very nice, Jesús."

Enid's eyes opened wide and she turned to Yameno. "I forgot about the cougar. You told Jesús to tell me about the cougar."

She stood up, looking around until she saw the carved figure emerging from the woods at the other side of the clearing.

Yameno looked at her, his face as serious as hers, but with a small smile lingering on the edges. "Her name is Luhanada."

"It was real, wasn't it?" Enid walked over to the sculpture, running her fingers over the cougar's head. "There really was a cougar, wasn't there, and she was for me, wasn't she?"

"Yes. She was for you."

"Did you know there's a hunting party looking for that cougar?" interjected Giselle.

"Yes," Yameno nodded.

Giselle leaned forward. "Perhaps we shouldn't be here at all. Perhaps you shouldn't be here." She wanted to say, they might hunt you instead of the cougar.

He shrugged his shoulders. "But we have to be here."

We have to be here? She looked at him, but didn't ask the question.

Enid returned. "Why do you call me Chachuli? What does it mean?"

"It's the Tuwillian name for squirrel, or tree runner."

"Like the squirrel on my cup."

Yameno nodded. "Now, my name, Yameno, is also a Tuwillian name." He raised his cup to her. "I'm the Wolfwind."

Giselle reached out her hand to look closer at the wolf cup. Her eyes met Yameno's. She looked away, feeling her face warm as she released the cup and Yameno placed it carefully in front of him.

Jesús picked up his cup. "You told me coyote was like humans, creative and inventive."

"Yes – although sometimes he gets man in a lot of trouble!" replied Yameno. "Kumni is his Tuwillian name."

"And the Earth Woman Tree Woman?" Giselle asked.

"You created her, although there's plenty of mythological precedence for tree women – and for earth goddesses, too. But not in Tuwillian mythology."

Giselle became very still. *I created her?*

She felt a power like thunder surging through her. *What am I?*

Yameno laughed – a quiet, joyful, expectant laugh.

One of the dogs sat up with a sharp bark. "Someone's coming," exclaimed Enid, jumping up, and the others hurried to their feet.

"It's all right. They're expected." Yameno moved to greet Hazel Fraya and Dan Burroughs as they stepped into the clearing. Giselle looked intently at their faces. *The cougar and the hawk,* she thought. *Of course.*

Hazel flashed a smile at the children, and then walked over to Giselle, taking her hand.

"Come and sit," offered Yameno, gesturing toward the circle where he and Giselle and the children had just been sitting, but Enid backed away, moving instinctively to the carving of the cougar for protection.

Hazel smiled. "Do you look to the cougar – to Luhanada for protection?" Enid tipped her head to the side and looked at her aunt.

Yameno interrupted. "Come back to the circle, Chachuli." She nodded and returned to the circle, sitting between her aunt and Jesús. Yameno went into his hut and returned with two more carved cups and a carved pitcher. He handed Enid a cup. "Chachuli, will you give this to your aunt."

It was a cougar, its tail curved to form the handle. Enid looked from the cup to her aunt. Luha smiled and nodded as she took the cup from the child's hands.

Yameno handed a cup carved like a hawk in flight, with its head thrust up in a silent shriek, to Dan. "Do you children know Dan, Tata?"

Jesús looked at Dan. "The hawk."

Tata smiled, his eyes bright and piercing.

"I don't understand," whispered Giselle.

Dan nodded, reaching out to touch her hand. "We don't any of us really understand, but we've done this many times before and it's good – it's right."

"The shape changing?" Giselle asked.

"Yes. We become our Tla Twei, our 'one dance/song' in Tuwillian."

"And the Tla Twein travel to Ninas Twei, the place where all life dances," added Hazel.

But I still don't..., thought Giselle.

Yameno took Enid's cup, pouring the tea on the ground and washing it out with water from the pitcher. He did the same with Jesús' cup and then put both cups back in front of them, turning to Giselle. "I promise you this has to do with good, not evil; life, not death."

He held the carved pitcher high over his head, and Giselle felt exultant as she saw it was a carving of the Earth Woman, Tree Woman riding the back of the wolf. Yameno leaned down to pour the liquid from it into their cups.

"Water from the sacred spring," he intoned. "Water is the most magical thing on earth. My people have been the protectors of this spring for hundreds of years. Now I am the last Tuwillian here in Arundel."

"The last Tuwillian!" exclaimed Giselle. "Coffman said your great-aunt died. That's why you quit school and came back."

He nodded. "She was the last of our people here. Someone had to come back and protect the spring." He sat back and took his cup in both hands, the head of the wolf rising above his fingers, its mouth open as if to sing. Each of them followed suit, holding their cups before them.

> *Water of life, he sang, Purify me…*

and they all repeated:

> *Water of life,*
> *Purify me.*
> *Water of the soul of earth,*
> *wash me in your love.*

Hazel raised her cup, "To the journey."

Dan responded, "To Ninas Twei."

As Giselle drank from the cup, she heard the wolves singing, encircling, coming close, and closer. As they sang, a pale blue mist wove its way around the circle in undulating waves, winding about them, catching each of them in its wispy caress. She felt Yameno's hand on hers, pulling her to him. As she moved, she became the Earth Woman Tree Woman, and he, the Wolfwind.

"The journey," she whispered, and as she jumped onto the back of the waiting wolf, she felt a pull like a cord drawing her gently, insistently, linking her to the life force, an umbilical to the mother. They raced away through the mists, the cougar ahead of them, the hawk clinging to her back, her mouth open in a haunting caterwaul, pierced by the hawk's harsh cry. Behind them ran the coyote, the little squirrel riding between his ears.

The Journey to Ninas Twei

As they raced through a thickness darker than night, warmer than light, the air vibrated like a taut bow string, singing of many feet thundering, drawn to the One, to the source. On either side of her came the music of the wolves, the cougar, the hawk, singing their songs:

I am the wild, guardian earth traveler, sang the wolf, followed by the cougar's high pitched chant:

I am I!

High flyer! skirled the hawk.

We are the lone, the many, the mirror, came the howling chorus of the pack.
We bear the songs for those seeking the Dance!

Suddenly the song surged within her, and her voice sang out into the whirling mists, mingling with theirs.

I am the fullness. I am the secret, she called.
My soul singing touches the moon and the sun, joined the wolf.
I am justice. I am wisdom, sang the cougar.
For I am the wild wings of the earth, cried the hawk.
I am the answer, she whispered. The bearer of life.
We bear the songs for those seeking the One.

Their voices reached a peak of intensity, shattering the mists, throwing points of glittering light against the whirling blue walls around them, and then there was silence like an explosion.

Quietly, slipping into the silence like a rabbit into a forbidden garden, the children joined the song:

I am the writer of poetry, sang the little squirrel.
Voice of the universe,
Fluid as the world of dream.
I see the whole in every part,
I see the things that aren't seen.

And then the coyote's brassier voice:

I am the echo of creation.
I see the earth in her splendor.
My hands draw the dreams of the universe,
The human heart at its core,
So the joy of humanity can soar.
So the joy of humanity can soar.

Then all around them hundreds of voices joined together as one:

Seas crashing, like thunder rolling, like drums beating,
a call to the brethren, a cry to the wary,
The time has come!
Come! Come! Hammer your feet to the beat of the drum.
Come! Come! Lift up your voices to answer the One.
Come! Come! Answer the call of the earth and the sun!

They were swept onto the rim of a swirling vortex and they slid, round and down, pulled ever toward the center, chanting with rolling thundering drums:

Come! Come! Come!

They fell into the heart and the heat, and were the heart and the heat and all things, and the Earth Woman Tree Woman, who was all things and one thing, felt an elation, an ecstasy...

The drum stopped and there was a sudden sharp pain. Unbearable pain. She cried out, "What is it? What is the pain?"

"Danger," cried the others. "Danger."

The pain came again, and it was cold like a knife of ice piercing the heart.

The voices cried out again, "Danger. Danger."

Out of the darkness a voice called in anguish, "The pain!"

Then the drums began to beat again, a weak fearful beat.

Life, they whispered. *Life, life. Live, live. Come, come...*

The drums strengthened. The mists whirled them around and around and down and down into the center and the song began again:

Come, come! Hammer your feet to the beat of the drum.
Come, come! Lift up your voice to answer the One.
Come, come! Answer the call of the earth and the sun!

The voices waxed stronger, the mists began to lighten, and as the world around them stopped spinning, they could see towering walls of rock, and far above them, stars, clear and bright almost as the moon.

They were standing in a vast bowl, a valley of stone surrounded by jagged mountain peaks. Carved in the rock cliffs were steps, circling higher and higher on the mountainside, twisting in and among each other in impossible spirals. As they watched, the steps filled, as if from nowhere, with a multitude of color and movement, leaving some profoundly empty places here and there. The music slowed and slowed.

"Where are we?" whispered Earth Woman Tree Woman, feeling her roots cling to the rock beneath her feet.

Yameno answered, "We're at Ninas Twei and this is Din Tsin Twei, the place of the dance of life."

The little coyote leaned against Earth Woman Tree Woman's trunk, and she felt Chachuli's little squirrel paws climb onto a low hanging branch.

Tsin Twei

The music stopped.

All movement stopped.

The huge amphitheater dropped suddenly into silence – deep, hypnotic silence.

The stars pulsed with a rhythmic brightness that was almost sound, like a deep, deep drum beat, and the Tree Woman felt far within her something welling, something rising to the surface. It crept upward into her consciousness and as it flowed to the surface. All of the spirals drew breath as if they were one creature and chanted:

> *We are the One and the many.*
> *We are the life force,*
> *We are the center,*
> *We are the all,*
> *The nameless and the named.*
> *We are the whole, greater than the parts.*

Then the chanting divided, and the spirals began to move. Enid jumped higher into the Tree Woman's branches, climbing to get a good view.

One spiral, full of quivering greens like light on silk, spotted with reds and blues and yellows, glimmering with purples and pinks, sang:

> *We are the kingdom Plantae.*

A second spiral, the brown of velvet flickering in candlelight, shot through with the blues and reds of feathers, the shimmering of silvery scales, and the grays and whites of fur, with large polished areas of lacquered black, returned:

> *We are the kingdom Animalia.*

The spirals danced, parading their beauty in front, above, and around the Tla Twein.

Monera, sang one, *Fungi,* sang another, and the one flickered with unrecognizable light and dark, while the other's browns and greens and yellows began to take shape and divide. *Myxomycophyta,* called the green, silken flowing of the slime molds. *Eumycophyta,* answered the others and began to divide again. *Chytridionmycetes, Oomycetes, Zygomycetes, Ascomycete, Basidiomycetes.*

"Look, mushrooms," whispered Kumni, jumping up against the Tree Woman to nose Chachuli's fore leg.

Suddenly a different spiral started to flicker and wind its way in front of them. *Protista,* they chanted and then they divided and called their names to each other.

Chrysophyta,
Pyrrophyta,
Euglenophyta,
Flagellata,
Ciliata,
Sarcodina,
Sporozoa.

They began a graceful dreamy dance, some moving with the swooshing motions of their flagella, and others flowing their shapes out and in and around, in a constant rhythmic pulse. Then the flickering green of the *Plantae* swirled forward again, and the *Tracheophyta* twined themselves like vines through the pebbled greens and browns and reds of the *Chlorophyta,* the *Phaeophyta,* the *Rhodophyta,* and the *Bryophyta,* singing sweetly of the beauty of their colors and scents, and their love of the sun, and the earth, and the waters that feed them.

"Look," whispered Chachuli, "Flowers – so many flowers – and so many colors. Like paint dripped on oil and swirled and whirled together."

The flowers whispered back, *Angiospermae.*

"I'm overwhelmed," the Tree Woman murmured. "I'm speechless."

Luhanada twitched her ears forward and nodded her head. "This isn't the first time for me, but its beauty and wonder has never lessened." She shivered, remembering the last time, when they had not made it as far as Ninas Twei. "We're here," she whispered to herself, blocking Gunther's hysterical screams about evil and the devil from her memory. "This time we made it. We're here."

"Look," cried Kumni. "Look at the animals!" and they watched the swirl of *Animalia* in all its awesome variety.

Parazoa, cried a small group, fantastically shaped.

"Can they be animals?" asked Chachuli.

"They're the sponges," answered Yameno. "The line between animals and plants is sometimes smudged."

Metazoa, cried the rest.

Cnidaria, came a treble song of sea anemones, corals, and jelly fish in bright pastels.

Next came twining worms, like ribbons and hair, long and short, round and flat, dancing in undulating waves of luminescent beauty, and their chant was like the whispering of wind through the grass.

Platyhelminthes,
Orthonectida,
Nemertea,
Acanthocephala,
Rotifera,
Gastrotricha,
Kinoryncha,
Nematoda,
Nematomorpha,
Priapulida.

Their song slipped off into the edges of the spiral as the sudden trumpeting of the mollusks sang out.

Amphineura, boomed the chitons in a deep bass and the others responded in harmonic quaverings. *Monoplacophora, Gastropoda, Scaphopoda, Bivalvia, Cephalopoda.*

They, too, faded into the distance as a high-pitched whining flew in, circling above their heads as it reached its ear piercing crescendo.

Anthropoda, they buzzed.

Above their heads they saw a cloud of bright colors, and lacquered blacks and browns: The *Chelicerata,* with their spiders and scorpions, and the deep voiced, ancient horse shoe crab, and the *Mandibulata,* with its *Crustacea,* and centipedes and millipedes, and the thousands and thousands of insects.

"Oh!" whispered Chachuli. "Oh! Oh!" Her little squirrel eyes were round and bright as she stared open mouthed at the multitudinous cloud.

Again the spirals swirled, and out came the *Echinodermata.*

"Are these the plants again?" asked Kumni.

"No," murmured Tata. "They're animals, just like us – we're still seeing the *Metazoa*." He stood with his taloned feet curled around the top of a stone wall behind the other Tla Twein. *If only we could have gotten Gunther this far*, he thought. *He couldn't have thought this was evil.*

"Oh, a starfish!" cried out Chachuli. Tata spread his red tail and the chanting continued:

> *Hemichorcata,*
> *Chordata.*

"That's us," Tata explained and the swirling creatures divided again.

> *Urochordata, called one group.*
> *Cephalochordata,* called another, and then, *Vertebrata.*

"That's us, too," Kumni called out. "We have back bones. We're vertebrates." Tree Woman smiled and dropped her branched hand on his furry coyote shoulder.

> *Agnatha,* called some fish.
> *Chondrichthyes,* answered the sharks.
> *Amphibia,* rumbled the salamanders, toads and frogs.
> *Reptilia,* hissed the snakes and the lizards, and,
> *Aves, aves, aves,* whistled and twittered the multicolored birds of
> the air.

Last of all came the parade of the larger animals.

> *Mammalia,* they cried in unison.
> *Monotremata,* intoned the three egg bearing species, as they
> moved ponderously up the spiral.

"A duck-billed platypus! I've always wanted to see one," exclaimed the Tree Woman.

A kangaroo hopped by singing,

> *Marsupialia,*
> *Macropodidae,*
> *Megaleia rufa,*

followed by the shrill songs of many other furry creatures singing,

> *Marsupialia,*
> *Tarsipes spenserae, and*
> *Marsupialia,*
> *Phascolarctos cinereus.*

And they came and came – the *Insectivora*, the *Chiroptera*, the *Edentata*, the *Rodentia*, the *Lagomorpha*, and the giant whales and playful dolphins of the *Cetaceans*. The *Proboscidea* lumbered by, singing their names in their trumpeting voices, followed by the gentle sea cows and manatees of the *Sirenian* order. The horse of the *Perissodactyl* galloped and shook his mane at the children while the *Artiodactyls* calmly chewed their cuds.

"Oh, my," exclaimed Enid, as the large *Felidae* of the *Carnivore* order proclaimed their names.

> *I am Felis yagouaroudi...*
> *And I am Felis rufa, they called.*
>
> *And I*, roared the largest of all, *I am Leo leo,* its voice booming through the universe.

The spiral wound on, and as the next order came on the heels of the roaring lion, Giselle noticed that one of the vacant spots was here.

Primates, sang out the lemurs and monkeys and apes, but their voices were thin as if some essential harmony were missing.

We're the ones, thought Giselle. We're missing. Among all this vast multitude of living things, this endless listing of names, this communing of the life force, there is no representative of Homo sapiens.

The Hunt: Missing Children

At seven o'clock that night, Coffman's grandson, Tom, went looking in the forest for his granddad and the rest of the hunters to tell them the little Amundsen girl was missing. The deputy sheriff was gathering people to look for her, afraid she'd been attacked by the cougar. "Mom's calling everyone. The deputy says we should all meet back by the road where you parked your pickups."

The hunters headed back to their trucks as more cars and trucks rumbled down the highway, filling the cleared space at the edge of the road. Men climbed out, their rifles in hand, ready to search for the child, the cougar, and anything else strange to be found in the forest. The deputy's black and white pulled in with them, and they all gathered around.

"Amundsen says she goes out in the woods to play every Saturday, but she's always back by dark," said the deputy.

"What's a little girl like that doing playing in these woods, that's what I'd like to know?" one man asked, shifting his rifle back and forth between his hands. "Didn't his daughter die out in the forest?"

"No," said the deputy, "that was his wife. His daughter killed herself."

"Anyway," Coffman added, "he shouldn't of let the girl go out there every Saturday. He's crazy."

The deputy thought so, too. He remembered when Amundsen'd found his wife dead in the forest. He'd thought the man was insane. At first Gunther had yelled all this stuff about the devil and evil and the cougar – mostly he'd yelled about the cougar – and there'd been cougar prints on the ground all around the woman, but the body hadn't been touched. There were no bite marks or bruises, except where her head hit the rock, and a bruise on her arm. The other strange thing had been the way Gunther had reacted to the feathers. There'd been feathers on the ground near her – just ordinary feathers – and Gunther had mumbled about pulling the feathers out of her wings. But the cougar prints were there, and the whole thing'd been odd.

He surveyed the crowd. "Looks like almost all the town's here, but where's Dan Burroughs? I stopped by his house on the way here. I thought he'd be a help, since he knows the forest so well. His car was there, but he wasn't."

Harding frowned. "He comes into the forest often enough to fish – he says." He turned to Tom. "Your mom might not have called him."

Coffman interrupted. "There's no way she'd know *his* number." He spit on the ground.

"Maybe he's with Hazel Fraya," smirked Dickerson. Some of the men laughed and some frowned.

"Maybe they're already in the forest," muttered Coffman.

"Maybe they're looking for the child," suggested Dr. Chase, the historian's husband.

"Hah!" exclaimed Dickerson. "You must not of been at the meeting last Monday night, or you'd know those two have something to do with the bad stuff happening here. They're devil worshipers!"

Dr. Chase frowned at him. Muriel had told him about the meeting and they'd both agreed the devil worship thing was crazy. When Tom's mother called this evening to tell them about the missing child, he'd headed for the search and Muriel'd called Reverend Clare asking Clare and some of the others from the Robertsville Interfaith Council to join them on the hunt to help defuse any trouble.

Dickerson waved his old rifle over his head. "But we'll fix 'em. You know what I got? I got a 400 grain mold for this rifle and I cast up some silver bullets last night. I got 'em right here. Melted down some of my wife's silverware she got from her grandmother. That devil's not going to get away from me."

"Well, good, Dickerson," Reverend Tarrant slapped him on the back. "We don't know just what it'll take, but sometimes these old folk tales have some truth to them."

Dr. Chase frowned. "Hazel Fraya's the little girl's aunt. She probably *is* looking for her."

Reverend Tarrant shook his head, as he pulled his rifle up close to his chest. "Who would have told them? Not Amundsen. There's no love lost between them."

"And my daughter wouldn't dare call her, not if she knows what's good for her," muttered Coffman.

Tom looked at the ground and pushed some leaves around with his foot.

"Well," the deputy cleared his throat. "Let's figure out where to begin."

While he was pulling out a map and spreading it across the hood of his car, Gunther Amundsen walked out of the forest, his old 30/30 in his hand, and stood silently, not meeting anyone's eyes.

It was Harding who finally spoke. "Don't worry, Amundsen," he said. "We'll find your grandkid."

Amundsen scowled. *If it's not too late. If Hazel and Dan hadn't already taken her to that place with the fog and the drumming, losing her body to some animal.*

The deputy nodded at him. "You have any idea where in the forest she hung out?" he asked, pointing to the map with his flashlight. The man shook his head.

Just then an old pickup drove up and a bearded man jumped out, his eyes scanning the crowd warily until he found the deputy.

Harding's eyes narrowed.

The man walked quickly to the deputy.

"What, McCrae?" the deputy asked curtly.

"I just heard the girl's missing. My son's missing, too. He went fishing in the woods and hasn't come home."

"Is that unusual?" The deputy glared at McCrae.

McCrae bristled. "He's usually home by dark."

The deputy sighed and turned to the crowd. "So we're looking for two children." He raised his voice. "Listen up, everyone. The McCrae kid is missing, too."

Harding stepped over next to them, pointedly ignoring Billy McCrae. "They know each other," he told the deputy. "They're both in the same class with that new teacher, Giselle Raphael."

The deputy nodded his head. "I've met her. She lives through the forest over on the coast."

"Hey, Amundsen," Harding called out. "Listen to this."

Gunther Amundsen walked over, his face locked in its stony frown.

"Do you know Jesús McCrae?" Harding asked. "He's in Enid's class and he's no good."

"Hey," yelled McCrae, but Harding ignored him.

"One day I saw them together out on the playground, and they were sneaking around inside the cement pipe out there, and when they came out they were holding hands. I'd have done something about it, but that teacher of theirs, Ms. Raphael, protects that Jesús, and Ms. Nichols…" He drew out the "Ms." and sneered. "Ms. Nichols backs her up, so I didn't say anything. But it struck me at the time he had your girl under some kind of control. He's a mean one, that Jesús, and your girl is scared as a rabbit of anyone. I'll bet they've been meeting in these woods. I'll bet he makes her meet him, and he's done something to her now. That's what I bet."

McCrae pushed his long brown hair away from his forehead. "I know my kid's had trouble at school, but he's not like that. He wouldn't hurt the girl. Underneath he's a good kid. A thinking kid – more than a lot of the others, but he just don't fit in school."

"Oh, shut up, McCrae. We know what kind you are." Coffman pushed between McCrae and Harding. "There's something going on here all right. Both these kids are in that Ms. Raphael's class. She came into the store one day asking questions about that Indian, Wellkeeper. He was messing around her property. And Harding here says she protects that Jesús. I'll bet she knows more about this than she's telling."

"The Indian?" interjected McCrae. "He's a nice man. He's been giving my son art lessons." Coffman, Harding, and the deputy turned and stared at McCrae.

"Your son has been messing around with Wellkeeper?" laughed Harding. "Well, well!"

"My wife saw that teacher talking to Dan Burroughs," added Dickerson.

"Well, folks," Reverend Tarrant stepped in, his lips smiling, but his eyes and his body were tense. "I've heard about this Ms. Raphael. Now, I think she's like the little girl, an innocent being pulled into the whole deal."

"Yeah," mused Harding. "I tried to warn her, but she just couldn't believe this stuff. I think you're right." He stared out into the woods. "Anyway, we're beginning to figure out who's involved in this. Wellkeeper, of course. We've always known he was up to something up here, and Dan Burroughs…"

"…with his goddamn eyes that look straight at you, instead of down where they belong," interjected Coffman.

"…and if Burroughs is involved, ten to one Hazel Fraya is, too."

"Someone should go check Hazel's house, see if she's home. You go, Tom," said Coffman waving his grandson toward his pickup.

"And that Jesús. My wife had him in school last year and said he wasn't human. I'm not surprised he's in it," added Dickerson.

"That poor little girl. What do you think they're doing to her?" murmured one of the other hunters.

"Well, my theory," answered Harding, "is it's some kind of Satanism cult. God only knows what they're doing to that child."

Satanism, thought the deputy. *Well maybe that would explain it.* He'd thought maybe drugs before, but there wasn't any evidence anywhere. "That Ms. Raphael lives just through the forest here, over on the coast not too far from your place, Amundsen." He nodded at the older man, who just glared back.

Turning back to the map, he traced a route with his finger. "We should follow the river through the forest, and then check in with her and see if she knows anything."

"Dickerson, you wait here for Tom," snapped Coffman, "and then drive around and meet us." Nodding at the deputy he headed for the forest.

Ninas Twei: Singing Swan

The Earth Woman Tree Woman watched as the spirals of the Tsin Twei settled onto the stone steps of the mountainside until the only movement was a slight shimmering across the surface of the crowd.

Finally the life forms seemed to fade away, leaving a mist, and then, empty tiers – a vast empty bowl.

Behind them a white swan stepped out from where he stood at the side of the rocky valley, his diamond shaped black beak and black webbed feet setting off the pure white of his feathers. "Welcome back," he said, with a slow bow of his head to Luhanada, Tata, and Yameno, his shiny eyes glittering in the upper point of his beak. "At last, after many years, you've returned. I've feared for your well-being. Yameno, you were just a child the last time I saw you and now you're a grown man."

Yameno nodded and Luha added, "And Tata and I were teenagers."

"Your sister's not here or your parents – or your grandfather, Yameno. Well, perhaps there'll be time to hear why it's been so long."

He nodded at the Earth Woman Tree Woman and the two children. "I see you've brought others with you."

Luha sat on her haunches, curling her tail around her front paws. "Our new companions are the Earth Woman Tree Woman, Kumni, and my grandniece, Chachuli," she said, nodding at each of them. "This is our good friend, Singing Swan."

Singing Swan bowed. "Earth Woman Tree Woman. This Tla Twei does not come from the stories of our people. It's very interesting."

He turned to the children. "Ah, Chachuli the squirrel, messenger to the gods." His eyes twinkled. "And Coyote who represents both what is good and unique about *Homo sapiens,* and the source of all our troubles! These two are well linked."

Luha laughed. "We're glad to be here, but sad to lose those who traveled with us before, and to find ourselves still excluded from the Dance – the Tsin Twei."

"Yes," exclaimed Giselle, her leaves rustling as she moved. "Why aren't *Homo sapiens* a part of this Tsin Twei?"

"Come to my home and we will discuss this and other things," said Singing Swan, turning and walking down a winding path that led behind one of the rocky hills that walled Din Tsin Twei. They followed him down the steep path and before long the stone gave way to dirt, the hills fell away, and they found themselves at the edge of a grassy marsh. In the distance they could see the silver shimmer of a river.

Singing Swan led them down a narrow pathway, between the high grasses and tulles etched in silhouette against the starry night. The tulles got higher and higher, twining together above their heads to form a high arched tunnel that smelled sweet, like fresh mown hay. The tunnel widened into a large oval room, the grasses woven and braided together to form a vaulted ceiling. The floor was carpeted with rushes, and at one end of the room were some soft cushiony mounds made of straw and feathers. In between the soft mounds was a fallen tree that had been split in half, perhaps by lightning. The split side faced upward, like a table.

"Please, have a seat," Singing Swan indicated the mounded hay.

The Tree Woman grinned as Yameno, Kumni, and Chachuli each jumped on one, and circled twice, making a little nest before settling in. Luha reclined on hers wrapping her tail in front of her, while Tata perched on the edge of his. She sat down, wiggling to shape it to fit.

Singing Swan carefully set out pottery bowls and a basket full of nuts, lifting them in his beak. His mouth closed over the handle of a pitcher, carefully pouring juice in each bowl. Then he climbed into his own nest and looked at the Tree Woman. "You asked why *Homo sapiens* is not a part of the Tsin Twei."

She nodded.

"There was a time when *Homo sapiens* was a part of this dance, when every living species was a part of the Tsin Twei."

"What happened?" Kumni asked.

"Man hasn't always been as different from other animals as he is now. When he first evolved into *Homo habilis* from *Australopithecus*, he was still very much a part of Tsin Twei, the dance of the species you just watched. He had become a hunter as well as a seed gatherer, but many species are hunters of flesh, and we all depend on each other for food. Tsin Twei helps us to understand and accept that."

"Please," Chachuli said in a low apologetic voice. "I don't – I mean the dance was beautiful, and I kind of understand, but I don't really know what the dance – this Tsin Twei… what it is?"

"Ah," smiled Singing Swan. "That's a good question little Chachuli." He rubbed his beak musingly under his wing. "First you need to know who the dancers are. Each one is the grandsoul of a particular species – which should be all the souls of the members of that species living today joined together into one grandsoul – and they usually are. Some species do have individual members who don't remember how to become a part of the grandsoul, but there're still enough members of the species to have a grandsoul. Tsin Twei is where all the grandsouls of all the species join together in one dance for the continuance of life – the dance of life. In the Tsin Twei they become aware of each other, and of each other's needs. It's this awareness of each other that makes life work."

Kumni sat up on his nest and curled his tail tightly around his feet. "But the humans have forgotten how to become a grandsoul?"

"Well... yes," answered Singing Swan. "As *Homo habilis* developed tools and became more able to alter their environment, and *Homo erectus* built huts, clothed themselves in skins, and built fires, and were able to conquer problems – like how to live with the changes in weather through the ice ages – more and more individuals dropped away from the grandsoul. Finally – not until three or four thousand years ago – too many individuals dropped out, and suddenly there were not enough who remembered how to become a grandsoul. It's not a coincidence this is about the time some people began to exploit the labor of others. If you're going to enslave someone it's not convenient to be able to understand their needs, their pain, as we would if we were joined in a grandsoul. Greed overcame compassion."

He shook his head. "It was the first time since the evolution of *Homo sapiens* there was a hole in Tsin Twei."

"But there were other holes in the dance," exclaimed Giselle. "I saw them."

"Are they when animals go extinct?" asked Chachuli.

"Oh, no – well, yes, but not in just the ordinary way. Many species have become extinct. Why *Homo habilis* and *Homo erectus* are both extinct and they were once a part of Tsin Twei, but their place was gradually taken by *Homo sapiens* as they evolved, and that's happened to many species. The spaces are where that hasn't taken place. Species like the passenger pigeon who became extinct abruptly because of *Homo sapiens*."

"Oh, yeah, I remember them," Kumni nodded. "They were the ones that people hunted to sell for meat, and the hunters killed all of them."

"Yes, and many millions of years ago there were spaces when many of the dinosaurs disappeared, but those spaces have been filled in."

"Why did they die off so suddenly?" asked Chachuli.

Singing Swan ruffled his feathers. "My species wasn't here then. I don't know."

"Are you the grandsoul of a species?" asked the Tree Woman, tucking her woody legs up under her chin and folding her arm branches around her knees.

Singing Swan looked at her. "I'm a human being... like you," he replied.

"You're a human being!" exclaimed Kumni. "But you look like a swan!"

"And you look like a coyote."

Yameno laughed. "Singing Swan came here in the same way the rest of us did, only a long time ago."

"And you stayed here forever?" Chachuli stood up, alarmed. "Are we going to stay here forever, too?"

"No, no." Luha curled her tail around little squirrel, who sat down again, uneasily. "We'll return. Singing Swan died on earth and came here."

"How did you die?" asked Kumni.

Singing Swan preened his wing feathers for a moment before speaking. "It was when the white men discovered gold in our country. Other white men had come before and enslaved us, and brought terrible diseases, and my people were already greatly diminished. We wanted only to keep living in our village next to the sacred river and near the sacred spring as we always had, but they wanted the land we lived on. They spread rumors about us. They said we were attacking them, even though we weren't."

He sighed. "One night they came very late with torches and guns. I ran to the dance ground in the middle of our village and danced to Mother Turtle." He looked at the others. "We were powerless. I didn't know what else to do." The feathers on his back stood up as he opened his wings and danced a little on the floor in front of them singing:

> *This is our place, our earth,*
> *our sacred waters.*
> *This is our place,*
> *Given to us by you, Great Mother Turtle.*
> *Help us.*

"And then words came to me. Words for my people." He began to dance more fiercely.

> *This is our place, our earth.*
> *Go from it.*
> *This is our place, our earth,*
> *Our sacred waters.*
> *Hide from those who would steal it.*
> *Hide from those who would steal our place, our earth,*
> *Who would destroy our sacred waters.*
> *Hide from those who would steal our lives*

Given to us by Great Mother Turtle, who lives in the river.
Hide now.
Hide now.
This is our place, our earth,
Our sacred waters.
Great Mother will come again.
We will live again in this place, our earth,
This is our place.
Hide now.
Hide now.

"As I danced, I transformed into the trumpeter swan, the Tla Twei I had always used when we visited Ninas Twei. The white men saw and were frightened. I sang, and I flew up in the air on my mighty wings. They shot me."

He sat down again, lowering his head and closing his eyes.

Finally he looked up. "They burned our village to the ground, but all of my people managed to escape into the forest while the white men were watching me. I was the only one who died. I died as a swan, so I came here."

They were all silent, thinking of the little village. "You were very brave," whispered Chachuli.

Singing Swan shook his head. "I couldn't think of anything else to do."

The Tree Woman nodded her head slowly, her branches whispering a chant for the little village as they rubbed together. "You had come before you died – to Ninas Twei, I mean. How do living people get here? How did we get here?"

"Well…" Singing Swan wiggled himself into a more comfortable position on his mound of grasses. "For my people, it first started about 300 years ago in our small village near the Tuwillian River."

"Oh, Yameno's people who used to live where we live!" Chachuli exclaimed, her tail bouncing with interest.

"Yes," nodded Singing Swan. "At that time we thought there was something about those particular woods and the sacred spring that enabled people to visit Ninas Twei, even though *Homo sapiens* as a species can't form a grandsoul. Many people of my village visited as their Tla Twei."

"And when they died did they all come here?" asked Giselle.

"No, only a few of us have come here – those of us who died as our Tla Twei." He looked around at all of them. "Those of us who come here, dead or alive, do have a purpose. We come to help find some way for *Homo sapiens* to rejoin Tsin Twei."

"Our Tla Twei – as a coyote, but why a coyote? What is Tla Twei?" asked Kumni.

"The shapes we all wear except for the Earth Woman Tree Woman come from the stories of my nation. Over the years other people have worn your forms, but I have always worn mine."

"At the meeting at the church," Giselle asked, "they talked about a cougar being seen many years ago by the people of your village. But Hazel couldn't be..."

Luha's whiskers twitched. "No, I took this form after my grandmother died and left me her totem – a small wooden cougar. It was used by a Tuwillian woman and given to my grandmother when the woman died."

"So Reverend Tarrant was right when he said he thought your family had all been involved in this."

"Yes, Jarvis guessed that correctly." She looked down at her paws and her voice dropped to a whisper. "Poor Jarvis. When we were children we were friends."

Tata added, "Luha's family – Hazel's family – learned about the woods and Ninas Twei from the Tuwillians, so it was natural for them to take on the forms of the Tuwillian pantheon, just as the Tuwillians had. And for me, too."

"Yes," said Singing Swan. "But there are others here from other places in the world who come in the Tla Twein of their own mythology..."

A deep thunderous rumble interrupted him and all their heads popped up, listening.

The earth began to shake, moving faster and faster until the woven tules waved frantically above their heads.

"It hurts!" Chachuli cried out.

The Tree Woman was tossed off the edge of her cushion to the floor. Tata flew up in the air while the others clung to their nests with their claws. The pottery pitcher bounced on the split log and fell to the ground with a crash.

Chachuli ran to her aunt's side and burrowed under her fur. "It hurts," she moaned. "It hurts."

Just as suddenly as it had started, it stopped.

"What is it?" whispered Giselle. "What is it?"

The Hunt: The Forest Good or Evil?

As soon as Reverend Clare got off the phone with Muriel Chase, who was asking her to bring members of the Interfaith group to join the search for the little girl, she called Father Keegan and Rabbi Micah. Now she was waiting for them to pick her up so they could join the search together.

She shook her head, trying to understand. Muriel had been sure that Hazel Fraya and Dan Burroughs would never hurt the child, so what was going on? After the meeting at the church in Arundel she and Micah had met with Keegan Gilchrist, the Catholic priest who had studied Satanism, to tell him about the meeting.

"The demographics are wrong," he'd said. "I've never heard of a Satanist group that crosses cultures – a white woman, a black man, and a Native Uhsean? Not too likely. Mostly people who call themselves Satanists are white men rebelling against the church they were brought up in, and they aren't really doing evil. The ones who do atrocities are usually teenaged boys. And a cougar as a devil? Probably just a cougar."

He'd smiled. "You know real evil is caused by our own personal 'demons' – the things in our childhood, in our culture that cause us to pull in so we can't see the needs and hurts of others."

Later that same day Clare had found time in her busy schedule to ride up to the part of the forest Reverend Tarrant had said was evil. She'd gotten out of her car and walked around a little bit, and then gone down by the river. The woods had felt cool and pleasant and she'd felt tuned in to the vast silences of the forest as if in the presence of Spirit.

Tarrant had mentioned this forest might be logged. She thought about the logging sites she'd seen, muddy with caterpillar tracks running through where the trees had been. Ugly.

That would be true evil. Could this whole thing be a ruse to get the woods for logging? But now a child's missing, she thought.

A car horn beeped. She pulled on her jacket and locked the door behind her as she headed for the car and the hunt for the child.

The three religious leaders discussed the missing child, and the idea that the forest might be evil, in the car on the way to the hunt. Clare pointed out she'd felt close to Spirit in the forest and thought it would be very wrong to allow logging there. The others agreed. Keegan added, "There have been places where I've felt some kind of palpable evil. Sometimes in some of our most revered…" He paused. "Money, greed. Jesus spoke of it. It seems to be destroying…"

"Well, the logging certainly would be greed," added Micah, "but until we find both children, we really can't make any decisions about what's going on."

The deputy sheriff and the hunters tramped through the forest toward Giselle's place, stopping halfway when they discovered Jesús and Enid's meeting place by the river.

"Look, someone's had a fire here," said Reverend Tarrant, panning his flashlight over the depression in the rocks.

The men spread out around the area looking for clues. Harding poked back into the little crevice where Enid had waited for Jesús. "Hey, I found a pencil here. I think it has a name on it." He focused his flashlight on the top of the pencil, awkwardly balancing his gun and the pencil in one hand, and the flashlight in the other. "Enid Amundsen. This is the girl's pencil!"

Amundsen stalked over to Harding and took the pencil out of his hand. "One of the pencils Hazel gave her." His eyes smoldered as he stared at it. Suddenly he whirled around and threw it forcefully into the river.

"Well," said Harding, looking warily at Amundsen and taking a step backward. "At least we know she was here."

"Here's a fish hook, too," added Coffman, stooping with difficulty to pick it up. "Hey, Amundsen, would your girl be fishing?"

Amundsen shook his head.

"So that adds Jesús into it," said Harding. "It looks like they were both here, and they had a fire too."

"But not today," said the deputy. "This fire was from a week or so ago at least. And the pencil's clearly Enid's, but the fishhook could be anyone's. Besides they could have dropped those things at separate times."

"But I'll bet they didn't," muttered Harding.

Ninas Twei: Pain!

"What was that pain?" cried the Tree Woman, pulling herself to her feet from where she lay on Singing Swan's floor.

Singing Swan leaned down to pick up the pieces of the pitcher with his beak. "I don't know, but Ninas Twei is in danger! This happened earlier – maybe just as you were coming – but not as bad as this!"

"Yes, we felt it in the vortex. Has it happened before?" Tata asked.

"No, but there have been times when I've felt… something."

"Something?" Luha prodded.

"Yes." He poked at his nest with his beak and finally fluttered back up onto it. "I don't know how to explain it – a vague uneasiness that was on the edge of pain. But this was like an earthquake and there was pain, too."

Luha's tail flicked back and forth, back and forth. "If this place is destroyed, what will happen to the world?"

"I don't know," he shook his head.

Tata stretched out his wings, the light flickering over his feathers. "I think we're the ones who need to find out what's happening."

Luha nodded, adding, "Maybe that's why we felt compelled – drawn to come here now, today."

"But where is it coming from? Is it someplace we can go?" Kumni asked.

Chachuli scampered off her nest and emphatically pointed her nose back toward the entrance to the room. "It was back that way. I felt it. It was in that direction."

Luha stood and faced the entrance, her tail lashing back and forth. "How do you know, Chachuli?"

"I just know." Her little eyes flashed.

Luha nodded. "Our messenger." She turned toward the rest of them. "That's back toward Din Tsin Twei. Let's go and investigate at least."

"Wait," Kumni demanded. "I want to go, but how long have we been here? What about Chachuli's grandfather?"

"My grandfather will be upset, but it doesn't matter." Chachuli stood up on her hind legs, her nose lifted quivering in the air. "This is more important. I feel… I feel… I can't explain, but we have to follow the pain."

136

Luha flicked her tail. "Chachuli's grandfather knows where she is. He's very frightened, but he knows."

"It's too bad we can't go back keeping others from knowing we've gone," Tata added, ruffling his feathers. "Especially with that cougar hunt going on, but we need to pursue this pain. We're the only ones who can."

"Please, let's go now!" pressed the little squirrel, running back and forth between her aunt and the entrance.

Singing Swan led the way up the steep path from the marsh back to the mountain bowl with Chachuli close on his heels. At Din Tsin Twei, she took over the lead, crossing the middle of the vast empty space. She was headed for a large crack in the rock, wide at the bottom and narrowing, as it led up the rock, to a thin line.

"This wasn't here before," exclaimed Singing Swan as he looked into the deep crevice. "I can see a lighter spot like an opening at the end. I've never been able to get to the other side of the amphitheater. When I try to fly over, it just gets higher."

The little squirrel started to go through the tunnel created by the open crevice.

"Wait, Chachuli, wait." Giselle, grabbed the squirrel.

"Can we all fit through there?" Yameno crouched before the opening, his ears laid back on his head.

"We can try," Luha replied.

"But I need to stay here," Singing Swan said regretfully, "to protect Din Tsin Twei."

The Tree Woman let go of Chachuli who darted into the crevice, her fluffy tail straight behind her. The base was wide, but the roof was low. Kumni was able to follow her with only a little uncomfortable crouching through places where the ceiling dipped lower. Luha crawled through after him with Tata gripping her neck, wings outspread and curved down over her back, head tucked low behind hers. Giselle found her form was flexible; like a human she could crawl, and her branches, seeking the light, stretched ahead of her down the tunnel. Yameno followed, creeping on his stomach.

The squirrel stood silhouetted in the opening at the other end then scampered back to the others to offer encouragement. "On the other side there's a forest – like our forest. It's beautiful."

As they clambered, not without a little squeezing and grunting, out of the tunnel, they found themselves in a small clearing between a dark, rustling forest, and the steep stone cliffs that rose on this side of Din Tsin Twei. Above their heads the stars twinkled large and clear.

Yameno lowered his nose and sniffed along the edge of the forest. "There are several old paths here," he said, raising his head to look into the dark under the trees, his tail wagging encouragement.

"Which one do you think we should follow?" asked Tata. "Chachuli, do you still feel the direction of the pain?"

"Yes." She scurried directly to the faint beginning of one of the paths, and stopped to sit back on her haunches and sniff the air. "It's down here."

The path was old and overgrown, the night dark under the trees where the starlight made only tentative inroads into the shadows, but before long they came to a wide, deep meadow. "What a beautiful place," whispered Chachuli.

Giselle looked around her at the meadow, enclosed by yellow-leafed aspens, looking as if hung with drops of silver in the starlight. She heard a gentle susurrus as the light breeze played the leaves like a wind chime, and then continued on to rustle the meadow grasses, sprinkled with the night-closed blossoms of autumn wild flowers.

A large upended oak tree sat at the far side of the meadow, its roots a darkness protruding into the night, and its lightning scarred trunk extending up and away from the travelers, resting in the branches of another tree at the far edge of the meadow. At the upper end of the tree, where some of the limbs dragged the ground, and some reached as high toward the star filled sky as many of the surrounding upright trees, the light seemed to gleam off something that stretched between the branches.

"Look." The coyote pointed his nose at a faint separation of the grasses. "The path goes on here out into the meadow."

"Toward that tree," added Tata.

"It must have been huge when it stood," Yameno pointed out. "That's not a fresh fall. The wild flowers are growing around the roots as if it's been that way many, many years."

Luha sat and moved her tail slowly through the grasses, sending off a faint, sweet perfume as it gently knocked the closed blossoms of the wild gentians. "Something at the other end is... something different."

"It looks like a huge spider web," Kumni added.

"Yes." Yameno's tail drooped behind him. "But the shape, somehow..."

"I'll check it out." Tata leaped forward, moving his wings in large undulations as he pushed himself into the air over the meadow. He circled high over the tree, and then lower and lower, finally landing in front of the unknown webbing. He walked back and forth, turning his head from one side to another. The rest watched anxiously at the top of the meadow until with slow powerful wing beats, he flew back to them.

"What is it?" Chachuli asked eagerly.

"A loom."

"A loom?" Giselle peered at the tree.

"Yes, but..." He stopped and shrugged, his shoulders lifting his wings up and back down again. "You need to come see it," and he turned and flapped off toward the tree again.

The cougar loped down the path after him, followed by the coyote, the squirrel hanging onto his ruff. The wolf and the Tree Woman came more slowly after, Giselle walking instead of riding, and stepping carefully to avoid crushing the fragile grasses. As they approached the upended roots, they could see the others standing at the other end of the tree looking bemused. "The tree isn't dead," Yameno pointed out. "It's fall, so the leaves on it are dying, but some are still green."

"Yes, and a lot of the roots are still firmly in the ground," Giselle added. "Come on. Let's go see the loom," and she half-ran to where the others stood, with the wolf loping beside her.

It was indeed a loom made of the many huge limbs reaching fifty feet into the air above them. Stretching between the thick limbs, the meadow grasses grew and reached, weaving themselves, and the wild flowers that grew in their midst, in and out, in and out, between the still growing branches of the tree and each other. There was no shuttle, no hand working the loom, and yet the grasses twined and braided themselves through the woof and the warp of each other. The flowers, their colors twinkling in the bright starlight, studded the weaving like jewels.

"It's... It's...," whispered Chachuli.

"Beautiful and strange and wonderful," Luha whispered back.

The Tla Twein stood looking at the be-woven oak tree in awed silence. The weaving stretched on different planes from one limb to another and the starlight flickered over it, bringing out a pattern here, a shape there. *A face,* thought Tree Woman. *I saw a face.* It glimmered high on one side. She moved in closer. Many faces! A child… She saw:

> Small girl swinging on a wood and rope swing hung from the high branches of a towering old willow tree, singing wordlessly in a high clear baby voice, long straight blonde hair flying behind her. A happy song. A smiling happy child...

> Older now, arguing with perturbed, amused parents, who allow some and forbid some, a teenaged girl with short straight hair that flops on her neck as she nods her head to make her point...

> College – some ecstatic joys, some heartfelt tears. Working, marrying, having children, and grandchildren. Growing old. Dying.

Tears slid down the Tree Woman's cheeks. "What's wrong?" Luha caught the Tree Woman's hand in her mouth.

Giselle started, turning to look down at Luha. "There was a woman – a child and then a woman. Her whole life is there."

The others gathered around her and peered into the weaving. "I can't see anything," said Yameno, "except how beautiful the flowers and grasses are all woven together."

"And patterns – I can see patterns," Kumni interrupted.

"Yes," added Giselle excitedly, "and people's lives add into the patterns. See!" she pointed. "My woman's life's here where the pattern's light and simple. I wonder..."

She walked over to where the pattern was difficult and uneasy. "Oh, no!" she cried out, as she watched a tiny girl go flying across the floor after the man backhanded her. The child huddled whimpering in the corner, but didn't cry.

> And she didn't cry at thirteen when her stepfather hurled her out of the house and told her never to come back. Or when, on the filthy streets of a large, impersonal city, she took her first dope with her first john.

> The tears came later when the young community organizer said, "Yes, you can sleep here. Yes, there is food here. Yes, we can find you a job." And much later again, as the girl, now a woman, a social worker helping abused children, held a small, beaten boy in her arms, and whispered, "It's all right now. You're safe now. We won't ever let it happen again."

140

"A more complex pattern," whispered the Tree Woman, "but still a good part of the whole thing." She turned to look at her companions. "People's whole lives are in this tapestry. There are so many faces, I think there must be billions of lives."

Chachuli examined the tapestry. "Do you think everyone's lives are in it? Are our lives in it?" Giselle's eyes widened and she turned back to the woven tree. It was huge. How would you find yourself in such a giant weaving?

"Yes," came a rumbling voice, "of course your lives are in the tapestry. All lives – even the torn ones – are in the tapestry."

Everyone turned, startled, to face the owner of the strange voice. A turtle large enough for a small child to ride on, the markings on its shell dark lines in the starlight, made its ponderous way around the end of the Weaving Tree toward the travelers.

"Who are you?" exclaimed Kumni.

"I'd ask you the same thing," responded the turtle, "if I didn't already know." She stopped in front of them, allowed her shell to rest on the ground, and stared at them.

Chachuli giggled.

The turtle stretched her neck toward her. "Well, my little Chachuli, do you find me amusing?"

"Well…" The little squirrel sat up on her haunches. "You're looking at us, and we're looking at you. We'd introduce ourselves, but you said you already know who we are, but we don't know who you are, so you should tell us."

"So," the turtle lifted her head up into the air. "Chachuli, the youngest of us, dares to speak of manners to the oldest one of all."

"Or Ratatosk." Luha gave a small laugh.

"Yes, perhaps it should be the Norse Ratatosk. But then, perhaps you are not Luhanada. Are you either Bygul or Trjegul, Freyja's blue cats?"

Luha laughed. "I'm not blue."

The turtle nodded her head on her long neck. "Now we have this Earth Woman Tree Woman who isn't Tuwillian. We need to think beyond our nation to include the whole world. Yes, Chachuli can also be Ratatosk, messenger God of the Norse people."

Luha flicked her tail. "Are you Tuwillia, the turtle?"

The old turtle nodded.

"Are you one of the Tla Twein of the Tuwillians?" asked Kumni.

"I took the Tla Twei of Tuwillia the Turtle, the ruler of water, the form chosen by the Nameless One when she created the earth and the sacred spring. But I came here many years ago, before even Singing Swan."

"Singing Swan doesn't know you're here," added Tata. "How do you know about him? He said he couldn't get to the other side of the mountains. Can you go there?"

"I knew when he came. I watch the people of my nation in the tapestry," rumbled the old turtle. "But I don't try to find them. It's too hard to walk that far. I guard the tree and protect the tapestry."

Giselle stepped forward anxiously. "What is the tapestry?"

"Perhaps you can guess, Madame Earth Woman Tree Woman," Tuwillia nodded her head knowingly. "It's the tree of human life. In its branches is the weaving of the lives of all humans together that should make a grandsoul. It is this weaving into a grandsoul that allows a species to join the dance, the Tsin Twei. But you can see, the tree of *Homo sapiens* has fallen. At the edges of the weaving are rents that spread."

The travelers looked at the edges, and saw the torn places. Giselle looked closely:

> A small black child, wearing only a loin cloth, running happily down a path in a garden is suddenly kicked aside by a large white man, who then pulls him up by the hair and drags him out of the garden.

> "You don't belong in here. Get out."

> The boy is shoved out into the dry yellow dirt.

> The child grows. The land his ancestors lived on sustainably for centuries has been devastated. The trees have been cut, the water polluted. His baby sister is stillborn. His younger brother, stomach extended with malnutrition, lies still on the cot, large eyes pleading for food. His mother fades away to nothing with a cancer brought about by the polluted water. He has barely enough to eat, and watches hungrily as the white children play in their large gardens, get in and out of their large cars. He carries their heavy suitcases with bent head and shuttered eyes that burn beneath their lids with coals of hate, as the white children leave to attend their foreign schools, and there is no school for him.

And when the revolution comes he swings a large machete.

"Oh," cried Giselle. "Poor child – poor children."

"The torn children," muttered Tuwillia. "Their lives are torn asunder, and they turn and tear the lives of others."

"All of their lives were torn – not just the black child," whispered the Tree Woman.

"Yes. Racism, oppression, and hatred tear the lives of all who touch it. On the weaving we can trace the rips back and back.

"But compassion and love can mend the tears. Look here." She followed a thread from the boy down to his granddaughter as she joins a group of African women planting native trees where they had been destroyed by the oppressors. The leader of the group tells how the fig tree, revered by their people, provides not only fruit, but water, because its roots dig deep into the rock providing a path for the water to come to the surface. She urges the women to listen to the wisdom of their ancestors.

"I remember reading about this leader on OET – the One Earth Together site," Giselle smiled. She saw that the threads woven by the women were weaving themselves back into the past, pulling the torn sides together, creating colorful new patterns as they repaired the rips.

"I saw one whose life should have been destroyed, but she repaired her own life by becoming a counselor for children like herself."

"Ah, where one of the community organizers works." Tuwillia nodded her head knowingly on her long neck. "The torn lives need help or they tear away at the rest of the fabric. Where many of the community organizers work the lives are badly torn, but often they do mend them. That's why the pattern is so complex."

"Look at the rents here," exclaimed Giselle, pointing to a particularly blighted part of the weaving that grew larger and larger as she looked at it.

"War," muttered Tuwillia. "War ravages thousands of lives. It destroys the lives of people who live where the war is fought – innocent men, women and children, not to speak of the land, and the animals and plants that live on the land."

"'Collateral damage'," muttered Tata.

"It destroys the lives of the soldiers who fight it. It destroys the lives of the people in the far off lands who are sending the soldiers to fight the wars, even though often they don't see the lines of connection. But see, here, on the weaving how the rips travel long distances and cause more rents over here where the weaving looks strong?"

Giselle peered at the weaving. "It's undermined with rips and destruction. It will fall apart! How can we stop that?"

Her eyes traveled over the weaving. "And look at this! This is the source of the rips that lead to the war. Greed, and the oppression that comes from greed. Can you see that? Large corporations making money selling weapons, or worming their way into the armed forces as providers of services, and siphoning off huge amounts of money." She pointed to a particularly large, almost colorless, pattern that was surrounded by rips. *How is it held in place?* she wondered. *It seems suspended, unconnected.*

She moved in to look closer. Suddenly, she could see clear ropey strands that extended from it out to other almost invisible colorless patches all over the weaving. "What's this strange pattern?" she murmured, but she couldn't penetrate past the pattern, as if some screen wavered in front of it blocking her view. She felt a deep chill. Something here was very wrong.

Yameno peered at the pattern. "How come Giselle can see these lives – these people – and we can't?"

"Because she's the tree," rumbled Tuwillia. "She's the earth and the tree. She can see the lives of people. She can mend the torn ones, and you, too, will have to learn to mend the torn ones, if we're ever going to rejoin the Tsin Twei.

"The fabric rips more every day all over the world." She moved ponderously over to another side of the weaving. "See how the weaving doesn't connect from place to place where it has been rent almost from one end to the other?"

Giselle looked closely. There were the colorless ropes again, not connecting, but separating, strangling the others.

"Not only is it destroying the fabric of *Homo sapiens*," added the turtle, "but it's destroying the Tsin Twei and the earth. I felt Ninas Twei shake with pain tonight and the center of the pain was here."

"We felt it, too," exclaimed Chachuli. "It opened the tunnel in the mountains that rim Din Tsin Twei. That's how we got here."

"Singing Swan hasn't been able to find a way over to this side of the cliffs before this," added Luha.

Tuwillia nodded. "The trees are protected from discovery."

"The trees… There's more than one tree like this one?" Yameno lifted his muzzle as he looked around at the other trees.

"Each species has a tree with roots deep in the soil of Ninas Twei," she said solemnly, pointing her head toward the earth beneath their feet. "But not right here. They have their own special places."

Tata looked at the dry roots of the tree. "When did our tree fall over?"

"The tree fell when *Homo sapiens* left Tsin Twei, when some people began destroying each other's lives on such a huge scale that we could no longer form a grandsoul. It perpetuates itself. The destroyed becomes a destroyer. The child who is hurt lashes out at other children, at his own children."

"Compassion," whispered Giselle. "They lost the ability to be compassionate."

"But lots of people do understand other people's pain," Yameno insisted his tail sweeping back and forth. "Not everybody is – well – unconnected."

"That's true," answered Tuwillia. "Just look at the weaving. You can see lots of connections. Look at this one."

The Tree Woman focused where Tuwillia pointed. The fabric was beautiful here – a myriad of interconnected spirals of wildflowers reaching out to touch upon other spirals and then into the center to gather strength.

The center of one was a service group in a small town where the people helped feed members of their community in need.

"And here." Tuwillia pointed to another spiral – a group in a large city that came together to dance, sing, and tell their stories. Paths from this spiral radiated out all over the weaving to other cities and small towns, even other countries, where there were groups doing the same thing.

"Oh!" exclaimed Giselle. "These folks use the Internet to stay connected with other people all over the world!"

The spirals from both the service group and the dancing community connected to other spirals in their own communities where there were schools, religious congregations, hospitals, community centers, and jazz clubs. One had an interfaith group of teenagers painting the walls in an apartment in a tenement building a bright clean color to brighten the lives of the refugee family that lived there. In return the refugee family – part of another spiral that had its center at a temple far away – showed the young workers the precious few things they'd brought from their homeland: a shrine portraying their own much revered ancestors, a fancy comb that had been a grandmother's.

That same youth group touched other spirals, which were their churches, synagogues, temples, and mosques, and all of them connected to a food bank, which connected to a mental health advocacy committee, a homeless shelter, and a political protest group. Woven between and in and out of these various spirals, were smaller spirals of folk dancers and soccer players, quilters, and neighbors drinking coffee together.

Giselle smiled. "Just people," she said, "doing their thing! And look here! Here's a radio station creating community by spreading important information. See the spirals moving outward, some going around the world through the Internet. Here's another one spreading hate. See how the rips move out from it."

She looked closer. One of those clear strands connected here and the pattern was losing its color. She tried to follow the clear strand and found a place where the strand was blocked by a very complex – maybe even chaotic – pattern of color. Here a bank had tried to foreclose on a house belonging to an elderly woman. A mass of people from many different groups – churches, synagogues, mosques and temples; schools; labor unions; political action groups – had come together to stop it. Some had signed a petition on the Internet, others were lawyers and activists making phone calls, but overlaying it all were the people who marched in front of the house, camped out in the front yard, and stood up to the police who came to enforce the eviction. Some were tear-gassed, some were clubbed and dragged away, and still they stood strong. "And they won," she whispered. "The woman didn't lose her home!"

"Here's one of my favorites." Tuwillia pointed with her head.

Giselle laughed. "Making connections beyond humanity!"

"What is it?" asked Chachuli.

"A group of people on a small boat interfering with an artic oil expedition – one of those groups out to save the oceans."

"Yes," said Tuwillia, "saving the whales and other endangered species is just as important as saving people." She moved over to another place on the weaving. "Look here. The spiral this group connects to is huge, and getting larger all the time, reaching out to people and animals all over the world."

Giselle followed the pattern as it wove itself in and out of spirals all over the fabric. "It's OET – One Earth Together. They bring all kinds of groups together." She looked up at Tuwillia. "They're all so different, and yet there's the same kind of joy and earnestness in all of them."

"You will find that joy anywhere people are reaching out to each other, and the rest of the world," Tuwillia agreed. "Of course, sometimes people are reaching toward each other, but hate the rest of the world." She pointed to a place where the weaving stood all by itself and was not connected to the rest at all. It was a church group not too different from the others she had seen, but the faces were cold and stern.

"And here," pointed Tuwillia. "And here."

Tree Woman saw a white supremacist group in Uhs, a Christian fundamentalist group, a fundamentalist Muslim group in Pakistan, a group of Israeli settlers on the West Bank, a Hindu fundamentalist group in India. Even though their clothes, and their skin and hair coloring, were very different, the expressions on their faces were the same. Fearful. Angry.

She looked closer. In each case there was a colorless strand worming its way through it.

"And the joy isn't there either," added Tuwillia. "It can't exist with hate."

The bright light of the stars dimmed for a moment fading the weaving to black and white. Giselle blinked and looked around her, but the light was back, and the colors.

"What about the pain we felt?" asked Yameno. "Is that part of the weaving?"

Tuwillia patted the ground with her right front foot. "I felt it in the earth below the tree – in the roots of the tree."

Tata looked toward the upended roots of the tree. "Perhaps when the tree fell over, the roots were damaged."

"But if the tree has fallen over and the roots are damaged – we couldn't put it back," cried Chachuli. "Will we ever be able to rejoin Tsin Twei?"

The Hunters and the Cat, Reprise

Clare, Micah, and Keegan drove up to the clearing at the side of the road where the hunters had gathered earlier just as Tom arrived from checking on Hazel Fraya.

"Well, was she home?" Dickerson yelled at Tom.

"No, I checked up at Amundsen's, too, and the people waiting there for Enid said she hadn't shown up yet, and Hazel hadn't been there at all."

"So that cinches it," exclaimed Dickerson. "Hazel's involved in this whole thing. How could she do it to her own niece?"

"Do what?" Keegan interrupted.

"Well," sputtered Dickerson, "whatever she's doing to her. Who are you, anyway?"

Micah stepped forward. "This is Father Gilchrist. He's an authority on Satanism."

"Oh, all right!" said Dickerson. "Well, you're just the man we need, 'cause for sure, there's some kind of Satanism going on here."

"And what makes you think so?" asked the priest.

"Where's my Grandfather?" interrupted Tom.

"Oh, yeah, we need to go join the others up at that teacher's house. You come too, Father. Then you can talk with Reverend Tarrant. He knows all about it. Come on Tom."

Tom left his truck parked with the others and jumped into Dickerson's car. Clare, Micah, and Keegan got back in their car and followed them up the road to Giselle's. When they arrived the hunters had just reached Giselle's place and discovered she wasn't there.

"Was Hazel at her house?" demanded Coffman, before Tom had a chance to get out of the car.

"No one's at Hazel's and her car's still there," Tom answered.

"The teacher's not here either," added the deputy, "and there's her car." He pointed to where it stood in the driveway. "Just a cat," he said, swinging his flashlight to pick up the gray kitty sitting on the porch.

"Where's that Wellkeeper live?" asked Harding. "I'll bet if we could find it, we'd find them."

"Good idea, Harding." Reverend Tarrant patted Harding's shoulder and walked toward Clare, Keegan, and Micah. "So, Rabbi Levinson, you've come to join us... and Reverend Yates," he added. "Reverend Yates, I hope you aren't intending to come with us. This is no place for a woman."

Clare raised her eyebrows. "Well, I'm sure you think the pulpit is no place for a woman either, but I'm there."

Micah laughed, interrupting before the discussion went any farther. "Reverend Tarrant, I'd like to introduce you to Father Keegan Gilchrist. He's an authority on Satanism."

Reverend Tarrant nodded and shook Keegan's hand. "So I understand you haven't found the child yet. Have you seen the cougar?" Keegan asked.

"No, we haven't found anything very helpful, but there are some people we haven't found that's been helpful. The children's teacher lives in this house, and as the Deputy here was just pointing out, her car is here – so where is she this time of night? We haven't found Hazel Fraya or Dan Burroughs, and both their cars are at their houses, so where are they? Interesting, isn't it?"

"Perhaps." Keegan tucked his hands behind his back and rocked on his heels, looking around him.

"Hey, what's that?" yelled another man, pointing toward the tall dark shadow of the Earth Woman Tree Woman – tree-like, and yet clearly not a tree – standing black against the starry sky, near the edge of the cliff.

The men turned to stare. "We should check it out," muttered the deputy, and they all followed him across the meadow. The small cat padded across the trampled grasses behind them. The men circled to the front of the woman where it faced out over the ocean, muttering, "What is it?" "A carving of a tree…" "Or a woman."

"Looks like both," added the deputy.

Amundsen's eyes narrowed as he glared at the tree woman. "The devil," he whispered. "The devil is here."

> *(Seas crashing, the earth breathed in his ear,*
> *like thunder rolling,*
> *like drums beating,*
> *a call to the brethren,*
> *a cry to the wary,*
> *the time has come!)*

"Evil. It's evil," he muttered, pulling his gun up in front of his chest.

The men watched him, exchanging uneasy glances.

> *(Earth woman, the wind whispered to him,*
> *tree woman,*
> *sea woman…)*

Keegan frowned as he looked at the man.

"That Giselle's a lot weirder than I thought she was," Harding added.

The little gray kitty sat watching them, his head cocked to one side. "Look at that cat!" exclaimed Dickerson.

"Oh, Dickerson, you're getting a little spooked. It's just a cat."

"No, it's not. Look at the way it's looking at us."

Ba-a-room! A gun went off with a huge explosive noise and all the men jumped.

The cat leapt in the air as a bullet hit the ground next to it. It tore across the yard to the house as two more shots followed, managing to duck under the porch without being hit.

The group froze, wide-eyed. Amundsen lowered his gun.

"Jees," muttered one of the hunters.

The deputy took a deep breath – "Amundsen…" – he shook his head. "Amundsen, I don't think you needed to do that. It was just a cat," but Amundsen didn't seem to hear.

Father Gilchrist thrusting one hand behind him, and stroking his chin with the other, looked closely at him, frowning.

> *(Yes,* murmured the surf on the beach below,
> *Earth woman,*
> *tree woman,*
> *sea woman,*
> *stands revealed.*
> *The Tree and the woman are One.)*

Ninas Twei: The Fall!

Tree Woman looked back to where the roots of the fallen tree thrust themselves out of the earth that encrusted the trunk. "Are they permanently damaged?" she asked, looking at Tata.

He flew back to the bottom of the tree, scratching in the soil with his talons. The others followed.

"It looks like it's still growing, but I wonder if there're enough roots left in the soil to sustain it. Even if we were able to right the tree, Chachuli," he said, turning and smiling at the little squirrel, "the old roots have dried out. Once they're dried out they can't be brought to life again. But new roots can grow."

"Can a tree survive with most of its roots out of the ground?" Giselle asked.

"For a while, but unless the remaining roots are strong and well connected to the earth, it will eventually die."

He turned to Tuwillia. "Has the tree been growing? Have the branches been sprouting?"

"Yes. Every spring the branches grow higher and there's more weaving." The turtle paused and stretched her neck toward the other end of the tree. "But as the years go on it seems more and more disconnected."

Tata nodded. "The root system is not sufficient."

"What are we going to do?" Chachuli cried out.

Tata looked thoughtful. "Well, maybe there needs to be more weaving to support it as it grows so big."

"Not more weaving, but more connected weaving," added Luha.

"But it goes both ways," added Tata. "The weaving helps the roots, but the roots also need to be strong to support the weaving."

Giselle crouched down by the roots and stuck a branched hand into the hole Tata had made with his talon. She felt a thick, moist root, and encircled it, extending down, down. She seemed to flow in and out of the roots, the myriad thin root hairs caressing her, drawing nutrients, minerals, and water from her.

The earth, she thought, *I am the earth. Dirt and rock. The roots of the tree drill into me letting the water flow through for the tree and all the others, plants and animals, who need it.*

Then she became the root, strong and firm, but dry —almost brittle. Why were the roots so dry?

I am the tree, she thought, *and I am dying.* But even as she thought of death, she could feel herself flowing and dividing, and dividing again, and drawing the moisture and the minerals from the soil – from herself and from the trees of the other species! She was reaching and growing toward the others whose roots were firmly dug into this soil, this earth.

I can become the tree. Joy welled up, like the water in the roots of the tree. *I can be the tree! And I can be the earth that feeds it.* She flowed and divided and felt the myriad tiny hairs sucking and sucking at the soil, touching the apes, the hawks, the songbirds. Mingling, becoming the squirrels, tiny mice, a sea otter. A jellyfish. Such an alien feeling. A worm.

Growing rooted. Rooted in the earth and in the life of the earth. Losing, losing the self into the soil, the air…

Then… touching something else – something hard, impenetrable. Alien.

Suddenly there was pain and a ripping sensation. Her roots were torn from the soil with a terrible wrenching. Chachuli cried out and Kumni wrapped his front paws around her, pulling her close to his chest. Tata and Luha grasped at each other, and the Tree Woman wrapped her limbs around the Wolfwind's neck. Tuwillia withdrew within her shell.

The ground shook and heaved, bouncing them around, against each other and away again as they screamed with fear. The children clung to each other, and tried to cling to a rock across from the tree as the ground tried to shake them free of it.

The pain subsided and they all lay panting on the ground. The children leaned back against the rock. Tuwillia stuck her head tentatively out of her shell.

Suddenly the shaking came again, greater than before. They cried and grabbed at each other as a crevice opened at the base of the rock.

With frightened shrieks, the children fell into the abyss.

Tla Twein Forever

After finding the sculpture at the edge of the cliff, the hunters continued their search for the children and the missing adults. The men, and Clare Yates, poured up the hillside back of Giselle's house, and just as the morning light was beginning to creep into the sky, they found the path Yameno always took from his hiding place on the hill behind Giselle's house to his home.

"Now I think we're getting somewhere," mumbled Harding. "You know, I really think Giselle is an innocent victim – hypnotized or something."

"Maybe so," countered Reverend Tarrant. "A young woman living out here alone could easily get caught up in something."

"What do you think, Father Gilchrist?" asked Harding. "Don't you think she could have been hypnotized?"

"Perhaps – if there is indeed something evil going on," he replied, picking up a large branch to use as a walking stick.

"Now Hazel's another matter," added Coffman. "She's always been strange. Look at all those cats she has."

"Yes," agreed Tarrant bitterly. "Hazel has always been strange, even when we were children."

Dickerson called out to Amundsen who was walking grimly ahead of the others, who were giving him a wide berth. "What do you think Amundsen? She's your sister-in-law."

Amundsen looked out into the dawn. "She's evil." The words seemed to spit from his mouth, and everyone took another step away from him.

(I am I, whispered the earth.
I am now,
I am the law.)

"Don't talk to him, Dickerson," whispered Coffman. "He might do something crazy."

"Yes, indeed, he might," muttered Micah to Keegan, whose only response was a slow nod of his head.

They came upon Wellkeeper's vegetable garden first.

Amundsen stopped abruptly and stared at the garden. The others flowed around him.

"So this is how he managed to live up here," muttered Coffman.

Tarrant found the path down to his hut and the others followed as he lead the way down, half turning and holding up one hand, his other hand gesturing for silence as he reached the edge of the clearing.

The dogs jumped up, growling, from where they lay back of Giselle, who with the three other missing adults was sitting in the circle just as she had before the journey. The adults were holding hands, but Hazel and Dan each had an empty hand extended as if holding the invisible hands of two missing people. Six cups sat on the ground, one in front of each of them and two where the missing people would be.

Tom pulled out his cell phone.

"Wow, look at all that strange stuff hanging around on the trees and things," said Dickerson, in a stage whisper.

Yameno's head came up and the travelers all dropped hands looking disorientedly toward the hunters, and then around the clearing.

"The children," whispered Hazel, her fearful eyes meeting Dan's.

Yameno stood up, taking a step toward the hunters. Coffman raised his gun. "Just hold it where you are."

"Hey, what's that they're drinking?" exclaimed Harding. "Some kind of drug?"

Giselle stood up. "What's going on?"

"That's what we want to hear from you, young lady," replied the deputy. "Where are the children? What have you done with Enid, and that kid, Jesús?"

Oh, my god, the children, thought Giselle. *Where are the children? They fell and they didn't return with us! And these people. How can we go back for the children with them here?* Her thoughts raced. *Look at all those guns. They won't believe us if we try to tell about Ninas Twei or the Tree.*

"No. It's important. You've got to let us continue. We need to help the children."

"So, you did have something to do with the children," exclaimed Harding. "What've you done with them?"

"My son," cried McCrae, pushing his way into the clearing. "Where's my son?"

What can we say? Giselle thought. *I don't know what to say. Oh, no! There's Enid's grandfather, and he looks – something – he's going to...*

Amundsen had been standing at the edge of the clearing staring at Hazel and Dan. He raised his gun. "It's her," he muttered. "She's evil and I'm going to kill her."

"Wait, Amundsen," cried the deputy, grabbing his arm.

Hazel and Dan jumped up. *Oh, god,* thought Giselle. *He'll kill them.*

Suddenly Hazel and Dan were not there. Instead, a cougar was rushing down the path out of the clearing, a hawk, wings stroking cumbrously, above her head. Amundsen shoved the deputy out of the way, knocking him to the ground, and raised his gun. Two shots rang out in rapid succession and two screams rent the air.

"No," cried Giselle, "No!"

"What happened?" whispered Harding.

"It was the cougar," said Coffman. "He killed the cougar and a hawk."

Jarvis Tarrant froze. *Hazel was dead. The bodies were a cougar and a hawk, but it was Hazel – Hazel and Dan.* Numbness crept through him – his fingers, his toes. Cold, then a sick churning in his stomach.

Amundsen had pulled the trigger, but he, Jarvis, had killed Hazel because he'd brought these people here.

When we were children she was beautiful, and wild, and different from all the rest of them even then, and I loved her. I loved her. Tears filled his eyes. "I didn't know," he whispered, shaking his head, still staring at the dead cougar. "I didn't know I loved her."

She wore pants rolled to her knees – my mother hated that! Girls weren't supposed to wear pants. And those thick braids of hers! They danced when she ran. He smiled thinking about the curls that would slip out around her face and ears.

And she loved cats even then. They were constantly on her shoulders, or in her pockets. She was wild – a tomboy – but she was the gentlest person I've ever known.

I remember one day on the beach… One grain of sand. She held one grain of sand between her fingers, holding it up to the sun, squinting and peering at it when it was so small, she couldn't have seen it. She chanted that poem over and over so much I can still remember it. "To see a world in a grain of sand, and heaven in a wild flower, hold infinity in the palm of your hand and eternity in an hour."

William Blake. I read it in high school years later. But by then I hated her – and the poem.

"Why?" he murmured to himself. "Why?"

His parents had always distrusted her family. When they drove past her house his mother always had something to say. "Those Fraya's ruin the town. The forest is growing right into their yard and they do nothing to stop it! And they spend all their time and their money, too, on books, and not on the right book, either." She'd tremble all over with anger and smooth her skirt down over her knees over and over again. "Jarvis," she would shake a finger at him. "Jarvis, you just stay away from that wild girl of theirs. You stay away from her."

She knew! She knew and I didn't know it myself. Did she feed the hate? Love turns to hate easily, he thought. He'd been confused. He wanted to agree with his mother, but he liked Hazel. He'd liked Hazel until… until Dan Burroughs came to town.

Hazel stopped doing things with the rest of the gang – no, that wasn't true. We stopped doing things with her because she always brought Dan with her. It was one thing letting weird Hazel trail along, but no one was going to have a nigger hanging around with them. Hazel had a choice – and she chose Dan.

I felt so ugly and strange inside, and I hated her. I hated her, thought Jarvis. He looked over at the bodies of the cougar and the hawk. And now they're dead – transformed in some unknown way to a cougar and a hawk. He saw it happen. They were dead.

The deputy stepped over to Amundsen, taking the gun from his hands. Amundsen let go willingly, turned, and walked off down the mountainside. No one went after him.

Giselle ran to the cougar and the hawk, sobbing as she crouched and stroked the dead animals. Yameno joined her, trying to find some sign of life in the bird and the cat, with no success. "He killed them," whispered Giselle. "He killed them.'

Yameno stood up and looked after Gunther. "He should be stopped."

"Shut up." muttered the deputy without much conviction, as he pushed in next to the cougar, placing his hand on the still warm body. Clare moved instinctively to put her arm around Giselle while Coffman, Dickerson, and the other townspeople stood bemused, focused on the dead animals.

The deputy stood up slowly. "Well," he said, "It looks like you got what you came for. You got the cougar."

No one spoke as he moved away from the animals, but there was a visible relaxing of bodies in the crowd – just a cougar and a hawk.

"About the hawk, though," he continued. "It's illegal to kill hawks, so Amundsen's going to have to deal with the Fish and Game on that one."

Yameno turned and looked steadily at the deputy. "Is that what you believe? That he killed a cougar and a hawk?"

"Shut up!" the deputy glared at Wellkeeper. "Just shut up!"

"No!" Giselle grabbed the deputy's arm. "They weren't a cougar and a hawk. He killed Hazel and Dan! You saw it. You know! He killed Hazel and Dan."

Clare gently pulled Giselle back from the deputy, who, turning a rigid back on her, carefully surveyed the crowd.

(Tom moved behind the other hunters, hiding his cell phone.)

The deputy looked quickly away from Father Gilchrist's piercing gaze, noted the anguished look on Reverend Tarrant's face as he continued to stare at the cougar, and the relief on the faces of the rest of the crowd. He dropped his eyes.

"He killed a cougar and a hawk. That's what you came for, now let's go."

"Hey, wait a minute." Tom slipped his phone into his back pocket as he strode forward from where he'd stood toward the back of the crowd. "What about the girl? Where's the girl?"

"And my son," added McCrae, reaching out to grab the deputy's arm. The deputy pushed his hand away, glaring at him.

"Yeah," added Coffman. "What were these people doing here? Was it Satanism? Aren't we going to arrest them?"

"Yeah," echoed Dickerson. "Are those drugs in those cups? Aren't you going to investigate?"

Yameno leaned across the bodies of the cougar and the hawk and touched Giselle on the arm. "They died as a cougar and a hawk," he whispered. "That means they're there with Singing Swan and Tuwillia."

"Yes," whispered Giselle. "They'll look for the children." *But still they're dead. He killed them.*

Clare's eyes narrowed as she listened. The children? The hawk and the cougar were dead, but somehow Wellkeeper and Giselle thought they were alive somewhere looking for the children? Where were the children?

They were interrupted by the deputy, who took Wellkeeper by the arm and pulled him away from Giselle. "All right, you two are under arrest. Just get away from each other and no more talking. Reverend Yates, you take the woman, please, and Reverend Tarrant, you take Wellkeeper."

"No one has to take us," said Yameno quietly. "We'll go with you."

"All right, but you just stand over there by Reverend Tarrant while I get this all straightened out."

Dickerson started to wander over by the place in the clearing where the travelers had sat drinking their spring water.

"Hey, Dickerson," yelled the deputy. "Stay away from that stuff. That's evidence."

Giselle looked at Yameno. "Should we tell the truth?" she said in a low voice.

Yameno shrugged his shoulders. "I don't know what else we can do."

"Who would believe us?" answered Giselle. "But yes. What else can we do, but tell the truth."

The sun rose unseen on the eastern side of the hills as the strange procession wound its way down the mountainside to Giselle's house. The deputy led the way, followed by Jarvis Tarrant and Wellkeeper, side by side wherever the path would allow. After them came Giselle and the dogs, followed by Clare. The hunters, except for Tom who stayed to guard the clearing, came behind carrying the bodies of the cougar and the hawk hanging from a long tree branch across the shoulders of two of the men. Keegan and Micah came last. The deputy would take the prisoners into the county jail in Robertsville, and then return with the proper equipment to gather the "evidence".

Giselle looked out toward the Earth Woman Tree Woman, standing at the edge of the cliff, and tried to remember the magic, but could feel nothing but a cold fear at the pit of her stomach. What happened to the children? What was her sister going to say? What would people say when they heard the truth? Would anyone believe it? For sure she'd lose her job. Ninas Twei and the Weaving Tree floated farther and farther away in her mind, like a good book she had once read. All she could feel was the cold frightening reality of now.

Micah looked over at Keegan, but the older man seemed deep in thought. *What did we see? Was it the Almighty, or something evil? All these people are pretending they didn't see it – but I know I did. And Keegan saw it, too,* he thought. *The teacher spoke to Wellkeeper about telling the truth and said no one would believe them. Dear Hashem, help me know what to do? I feel certain I'll believe them.*

Jarvis Tarrant moved up next to Yameno again after a narrow place in the path. *Why?* he thought. *Why do I feel this need to be close to this man? He seems so calm. He doesn't feel "evil".* He felt the weight of his gun pulling down on his right arm. *What if I had shot the cougar? What if I had shot Hazel?*

That damn Amundsen, thought the deputy. *If he hadn't shot them this craziness wouldn't have happened. I wonder how many of those men saw it? No one besides the kidnappers said anything. If nobody else says anything we'll be all right. We'll just pretend Hazel and Dan never were a part of this thing.*

Dickerson, walking toward the end of the line, broke the silence. "Well, what do you think of that, Coffman? Amundsen killed a devil and he didn't even need my silver bullet. It was Hazel, you know. Did you see it? She was a devil all these years, and we didn't even know it. Remember when we were kids and she used to play with us? She was probably a devil even then. I'll bet being devils runs in her family. Wait 'til my wife hears about all this."

Well, that will take care of it, thought the deputy. *Those who saw it will think that Hazel and Dan were devils. That won't be taken seriously in court. So, the only bodies are of a cougar and a hawk, and that's that. We need to find the children, but a search of the woods should do that.*

Luhanada

Waves of pain filled the vortex as Luha tumbled through it. Gray – whirling swirls of dark and dirty gray, and so much pain.

No sound.

Time – stretched.

She floated, aware, unaware, feeling, unfeeling, floating.

Is this forever? Did I fail? And Dan – Tata? She tried to look, but all she saw was the swirling dark gray.

Alone. No arms, no legs, no paws – nothing. Nothing but gray.

She remembered everything: Gunther lifting the gun. Changing. Running. Tata flying down the path ahead of her. Tata screeching and falling. Her cougar voice screaming. And then darkness. Where was he? Where was she? Shouldn't they be like Singing Swan and Tuwillia? Shouldn't they be at Ninas Twei if they died as their Tla Twei?

Did Ninas Twei die, too? All that pain. All that pain at the dance.

She sank into despair, and time stretched some more.

Tata

"Tata, Tata."

He could hear her calling, but it was so far away, and her voice seemed to be fading farther and farther from him as he tumbled through the darkness and the pain of the vortex.

"Tata."

He stretched his wings, finding balance.

The pain seemed to slip away, and the darkness grew lighter.

"Tata."

Perhaps she lived. Maybe that was why her voice was so distant. Maybe she was alive! He stretched his wings, gliding in ever widening circles. The vortex pulled him. Energy popped around him like fireworks and matter swirled in beautiful spirals of pale color. He thought he heard one last "Tata," – a whisper, maybe only a thought, and her voice disappeared.

THE
LOST CHILDREN
OF
BAYOMAR

Connie Pwll Walck Tyler

THE LOST CHILDREN OF BAYOMAR

Invocation:

Breath

Listen,
Whispering breath,
Anima of the earth,
Murmuring in the wind-whipped grasses,
Lift my feet and keep me dancing.

Breath,
Flowing in the waves of the sea,
Creep into my soul and conquer me.

Breath,
Singing through the voice of the wind,
Dance with me, sing with me,
Take my hand,
Enter me as a lover,
Make me one with you.

Breath,
Warmed by the life-giving sun,
Burn, burn within me, until I am consumed.

1

Hunter's Moon, Still Dark

As the sun came over the eastern hills flicking reds and golds over the meadow and the ocean beyond, the little gray cat sat on the front porch of Giselle's house watching the procession of the deputy and the hunters flanking Yameno and Giselle moving slowly down the hill.

With a querulous "meow" the cat slinked down the steps to peer through the tall grass beside the driveway watching the hunters mill about for a moment. He hissed and snarled as he watched the deputy sheriff push Giselle and a handcuffed Yameno into the back seat of Dickerson's car to ferry them to where the patrol car was parked at the clearing near the river.

The two dogs were pushed roughly out of the way as they tried to follow Giselle into the car. They retreated, whimpering, to the porch.

The cat's green eyes narrowed, tail flicking as he watched Tarrant climb into the car with Rabbi Micah, Father Keegan, and Reverend Clare, listening as Keegan and Clare explained that they had to rush to their Sunday morning church services, but would drop Micah and Reverend Tarrant off at Tarrant's car on the way. Micah and Tarrant would follow the deputy to the jail to see what they could do to help Giselle and Yameno.

Asked about his own church service Tarrant just shook his head.

As the two cars left the driveway for the highway the cat stood and paced silently back to the porch where he rubbed up against each dog in turn, then stretched out between them to watch the rest of the hunters head off through the woods to their cars and their homes.

At St. Francis Catholic Church in Robertsville Father Keegan went through the routine of the mass in a daze. When it was over he had no idea what he'd said for a homily. The news of the morning's events was already moving through the gossip mills, and after the service, when he stood by the door shaking hands with his parishioners, many of them started to ask him about the hunt and the arrests. He put them off, shaking his head and asking them to pray for the children, suggesting they join the search.

Jesús' mother was also there, and waited hidden in the shadows of the narthex until everyone else had left, before approaching him.

"Dorotea." Father Gilchrist took her hand in his. "I know you must be very worried."

"Yes." She wrung her hands together, willing herself not to cry. "I don't know what to think. Often, Jesús has gone to the woods to fish. But just last week he met Yameno Wellkeeper – the Indian. Jesús said Mr. Wellkeeper was teaching him how to carve animals. He liked Mr. Wellkeeper. I can't believe…"

She shrugged, her face twisted with anguish. "They are looking for him and the girl. Billy – my husband is with them. And…"

She looked at Keegan, fear and uncertainty flashing across her face. "Father, Billy told me you were there. You saw…"

Her eyes flicked away and she hesitated before speaking again. "You saw when they captured the teacher and the Indian."

"Yes."

Her eyes slid down to the floor. "He said… He said…" She looked up at him and he nodded. "He said something very strange. Something I cannot believe."

Keegan sighed. "Yes. I saw it, too, Dorotea. I don't know what to believe myself."

She looked up at him with fearful eyes. "Is it the devil, Father? They say it is the devil."

Keegan turned to look out the door, over the roofs of the houses, toward the treetops covering the hills between Robertsville and Arundel. He sighed again and looked back at Dorotea. "No. I don't think so."

"Billy didn't think so either. He said… He said there was something… something…"

"I know." He shook his head. "I can't explain it, but, yes. There was something very…" He hesitated. "Something important happened."

164

He took her hand. "Waiting is hard, but it's the only thing we can do now. Wait and hope they find the children. And pray."

"And the little girl?" she whispered. "Sometimes Jesús got in trouble, but he never was mean to anyone who wasn't mean to him first. I can't believe he'd hurt the little girl."

He reached up and touched her shoulder. "I can't believe it either, Dorotea."

"Thank you, Father."

She turned and started down the steps, turning halfway down to look back at him. "Perhaps Billy will want to talk to you."

"That would be good. Yes. I'd like to talk to him, too."

She nodded and continued on down the steps to her car.

On Monday morning, the religious leaders all attended the arraignment at the courthouse in Robertsville. Dorotea and Billy McCrea, and Muriel and Mark Chase sat with them. Giselle's sister, Monica, was across the aisle. She and Rod, who was acting as Giselle's lawyer, had rushed up the freeway to Arundel Sunday afternoon.

The judge made sure that Giselle Raphael and Yameno Wellkeeper were not in each other's presence when they told their stories. There was no real discrepancy in what they had to say, but the prosecutor presented Giselle and the children as innocents duped by Wellkeeper, Hazel Fraya, and Dan Burroughs, and Wellkeeper as an evil perpetrator of a strange cult. "Why," he asked, "if this was a voluntary 'trip'…" He paused and smiled at the word 'trip'. "Why would the children be included in this?"

Yameno responded it had always been done this way. "When I first went I was only five years old. I was full of wonder and delight. The Tsin Twei – the dance of all the species is beautiful."

The prosecutor turned away from him raising his eyebrows at the audience. Some laughed, but the religious leaders just stared back at him.

Reverend Clare turned to look out a window. Inside she felt a kind of longing – something deep, and still.

After the hearing, Micah suggested a walk in the woods behind Giselle's house before returning to Robertsville. Jarvis Tarrant asked to join them. They stopped to look at the Earth Woman Tree Woman before climbing through the woods back up to Wellkeeper's clearing.

They spent some time in silence looking at each hanging painting and wooden sculpture.

That night, after dinner, they all met at Father Keegan's rectory, making themselves comfortable on the sofas and arm chairs of the living room.

Keegan mused, looking out the window at the tree-lined street. "I have no trouble believing that a man who lived 2000 years ago was really the son of God, but to believe that some people today've seen something miraculous – that I have trouble with. It makes me wonder about myself."

Clare spoke hesitantly. "After the arraignment I was speaking to Muriel Chase and her husband, Mark – you remember, she went to that meeting as the 'unofficial town historian'."

Keegan nodded. "He's the retired doctor. He was with us on the hunt and I've met them at Interfaith Council meetings."

"They suggested it could be a mass vision. The tree and this dance – this Tsin Twei could be a symbol or metaphor, and a hundred other symbols or metaphors could give the same message. Muriel said the metaphors didn't matter – it was the message that counted."

Micah shook his head. "But I believe it's more than a vision. I saw them transform, and so did you."

Clare nodded. "No, I don't think it was a vision either, and the children are missing. That isn't a vision. But still the thing that keeps coming to my mind is what Muriel Chase said. 'It's the message that counts.' It isn't an evil message."

"Yes, yes… but," Keegan grabbed the top of his head in frustration, digging his fingers into his thick curls. He leaned forward, looking intensely at Clare and Micah. "I saw a man and a woman turn into a cougar and a hawk, and I have no doubt about it, but what of this dance – this Tsin Twei? We didn't see the dance."

"No, we didn't see it, but I believed it," Clare added. "There's nothing in their story that doesn't agree with the message of that man, 2000 years ago. 'Love thy neighbor as thyself,' for instance."

"Which he learned from our traditions," interjected Micah.

"Yes, love and compassion are the important message from this dance, and from Jesus, and the Jewish tradition – most religions," Keegan agreed.

"But, like God, the devil works in mysterious ways. I remember once watching some ladies teach some children how to protect themselves from strangers who wanted to harm them. They said, 'Trust your funny feelings. I thought at the time, that's how I decide if someone is not trustworthy. None of these people – these travelers to this place of the dance – give me funny feelings."

He stretched his legs out and folded his hands together in his lap. "That's all I can say. None of these people give me funny feelings."

He shook his head and shrugged. "But is there room in the church's story for this dance – for this woven tree?"

Micah laughed. "Well, we Jews have lots of stories this might fit with. The Tree of Life, in a little different form, is the central symbol of Kabbalah. I don't think I have to worry about that, but I am worried about these people who think it's evil, and most of all I'm worried about the missing children."

"Yes," agreed Keegan. "The missing children. We need to think about how to find the missing children."

He looked down at his hands, his fingers woven together. "The closest thing to evil I can find is Amundsen. But even Amundsen – I can't believe he's evil, only afraid, and cut off from people. And I don't think – I hope he hasn't anything to do with the missing children."

Jarvis Tarrant had been so silent they'd almost forgotten he was there. Suddenly he spoke. "Amundsen doesn't have anything to do with the missing children. I'm sure it's exactly as Yameno and the teacher told it. I believe them. I saw Hazel…"

His voice broke and tears slipped down his cheeks. "I saw her change. I saw her become…," his voice dropped to a whisper. "I saw her become the cougar."

He shook his head, his voice catching. "Hazel was good, not evil. I've always known that really, even though I worked hard to deny it… to deny it to myself."

He looked up at them. "I loved … and then I hated. I hated her and now she's dead."

Keegan sat forward in his chair, nodding. "But Jarvis, you did have 'funny feelings' about her before. And those other people – Coffman, Dickerson, and that Harding – they all did too."

Micah stood up, shaking his head, "No, but…" He walked around to the back of his chair. "This is something I know about."

Gripping the chair back so tightly his knuckles turned white, he leaned across it. "All of them are racist. They're ready to hate those who're different from themselves. Their feelings are tainted by the racism."

He straightened and shook his head again. "Something like racism… It corrupts those 'funny feelings'."

Jarvis nodded his head. "Yes," he whispered. "We were racist… and I was jealous. I was jealous of Dan Burroughs."

Giselle looked out her living room window at the wooded hills behind her house where so much had happened just two days before. She felt bewildered and bereft as she tried to block the strident tones of her sister's voice out of her head.

It was Tuesday afternoon. Monica and Rod had bailed her out after the Monday morning arraignment, but Yameno was still confined at the county jail in lieu of bail.

"Well," exclaimed an indignant Monica. "I can't believe you've done this to me. This ridiculous story has been all over the papers and television, too."

She paced Giselle's living room in angry spurts. "Giselle, you've gone nuts! I knew you shouldn't move up here. You were… strange before you left and now you're just – you're just plain crazy!"

No one had believed Giselle and Yameno's story, of course, least of all her principal, Nicki. She'd been pretty upset with Giselle when she'd talked to her Monday, after the arraignment.

"Giselle, you're an excellent teacher," she'd exclaimed, "but I can't keep you teaching after something like this. I can't believe you were doing anything to hurt the children, and I don't believe Yameno would hurt anyone either, but this cock and bull story about turning into animals and traveling to some other world – I can't buy it! I mean all this wonderful stuff about returning to some dance with all the species, and loving the torn people and all that – it's great, but it's a fantasy Giselle!"

"It's not, Nicki," she had replied in a quiet sad voice. "It's real, but I don't blame you for not believing it."

She had looked across the courtroom to the door where two guards had taken a shackled Yameno, and then turned back. "You know, Nicki," she pleaded, "We both told the same story, and we weren't together. We didn't hear each other's stories."

"Well, that would hold water," Nicki'd replied, "if there was an ounce of possibility in it, but there isn't."

Giselle had seen the religious leaders – Rabbi Levinson, Reverend Yates, and the priest – sitting with Reverend Tarrant at the arraignment. She'd felt that in some way they were sympathetic – even Tarrant – but none of them had said a thing.

The television reporters had gotten hold of Dickerson and Coffman, so the devil story was running rampant across the country. Rod hadn't allowed Giselle to tell the reporters anything, and Yameno hadn't been given the chance to talk to them, either.

The worse thing was the deputy's bright idea that Hazel and Dan were still up in the woods somewhere – that they hadn't turned into animals, but had slipped away just as Amundsen killed the cougar. Since he hadn't found any evidence of drugs or any wrongdoing in the clearing, he suggested that Hazel and Dan had come back and removed the evidence.

Coffman's grandson Tom, who'd been left to guard the clearing, had been adamant that no one could've gotten past him to mess with the stuff there. He had explored around the clearing some, looking at the paintings and sculptures, fascinated, but the cups and stuff had never been out of his sight.

He'd peered down the path to the spring, too, and seen the stream, but he hadn't gone down there until after the deputy got back. Then he'd gone down the path and looked at the beautiful little waterfall and drunk some of the water, wondering if there'd been a time when all water tasted that good. He thought he'd go back there sometime when no one else was around.

"But Tom's young," the deputy had insisted despite Tom's denial. "I shouldn't of left a young kid there guarding the evidence. And there's no sign of the children anywhere, and that teacher whispered something to the Indian about Hazel and Dan looking for the children."

Of course the deputy didn't buy that stuff about Ninas Twei, and the children falling down a crevice. "Those two are still around, and they have the children somewhere. Hazel's the girl's great aunt and she's tried to get her away from Amundsen before."

Giselle couldn't tell if the deputy had invented the alternate story to hide what he had seen, or if he was genuinely deceiving himself.

The woods had been full of searchers, and the air full of helicopters. The highways had blinked Kidnapping Alert signs, but no one had found anything. The deputy finally concluded that Hazel and Dan had left the area, taking the children with them, even though their cars were still at their homes, there were no reports of stolen cars, and no one at the bus station in Robertsville had seen them.

"You're just lucky to have a good lawyer like Rod to represent you, although I can't imagine what he can do to save you," continued Monica. "How in the world could you get mixed up in such an awful thing? Kidnapping! I don't believe it! I don't believe it!"

"Well, don't believe it," answered Giselle, exasperated. "It's not true. We didn't kidnap Enid – or Jesús. They came of their own free will."

"All right. Suppose I believe that," answered Monica. "Then why are these two characters – this Hazel and Dan – why are they hiding out instead of coming forward? Why did they run away?"

"They didn't run away!" screamed Giselle. "They're dead. Amundsen shot them right there in front of everybody. They all know it. The deputy knows it, but he doesn't want to admit it. He doesn't want to deal with it."

"That's ridiculous. You're crazy," Monica yelled back.

"Yes, yes," said Rod, coming out of the kitchen where he had spread out his law books on the big table, "and that's what we're going to plead. Innocence on the basis of insanity."

Monica had been uncomfortable with the idea, but Rod pointed out they could have Giselle committed to a private institution in Bayomar, away from the bad influences here in Arundel, and get her some counseling.

Giselle had protested, but it all happened so fast she hadn't a chance to figure out what was going on. The district attorney, eager to have one less trial to deal with, had agreed to drop the charges against her if she were committed. If she'd been willing to change her story and "admit" that the transformation into animals and the trip to Ninas Twei was a lie, they wouldn't have had grounds to commit her, but she couldn't do that – she couldn't betray the rest of the travelers. She signed the necessary papers.

Tom waited two days before using a pseudonym to upload the video he'd taken with his cell phone to VidYou. It showed the whole thing. Amundsen shooting at Dan and Hazel, the transformation of Hazel and Dan to cougar and hawk, and their dead bodies. It was shaky, and blurred, but still, it went viral.

2

Waxing Crescent in Bayomar

Giselle found life at Kavanaugh House, an institution for the mentally ill, strangely calm and peaceful. The first couple of days she felt empty – silent, wordless – as she was shuffled, first to the Admissions Counselor, then to group therapy, art therapy, meals, and finally bed in a small private room.

When she allowed herself to think of the journey to Ninas Twei, and her companions, she became restless and agitated wondering what had happened to Dan and Hazel, fearing for Yameno and the children. But when she asked for information, for access to a computer or a phone, they politely refused and suggested a tranquillizer.

What a schizophrenic society we live in, Giselle thought. *If we think someone doesn't fit the norm we hand out drugs like candy, and yet we throw hundreds of thousands of people in jail with huge sentences in our 'War on Drugs.'*

The building where the institution was housed was old and not kept up as well as it could be, but there was an attempt at making the rooms friendly and warm. Despite the programmed "therapy", she had plenty of free time to wander, finding a rather pitiful library and a lovely little garden with a fountain.

She finally found her tears when she saw the life-sized stone statue of an Asian woman riding a dragon next to the fountain. The woman looked like the little Chinese figurine of a woman stepping out of a tree trunk that had come from China almost a century ago with her war bride great-grandmother. She yearned for the little wooden statue that probably still sat on her old trunk in her living room in Arundel. How could she have forgotten to bring it?

But I didn't remember anything, she thought. *Monica packed my things.* Monica would never have packed the little wooden woman.

Monica came to visit her in the institution every evening, clearly frightened and worried, her fears associated with what their father always called "being imaginative" and somehow rooted in their mother's death.

Giselle had been quite young when their mother died, but not so young she couldn't remember her. Every day after Monica left for school, she and her mother had danced in the living room or taken hikes in the park. Sometimes they created collages and mobiles from the leaves and seedpods they found. Giselle had loved prancing around singing made up songs and she remembered her mother following her, writing down the words of her songs in a notebook. What had happened to that notebook?

The little Chinese figurine had been very important to her mother. It stood on a table in the living room. Giselle had loved to hold it, running her fingers up and down the silky polished wood. Sometimes her mother lit a candle next to it while Giselle took her nap, her head in her mother's lap. Her mother would sit very still watching the candle.

The day her mother left for the weekend retreat, she kissed Giselle and told her to take care of the little wooden woman while she was gone and Giselle had dutifully picked it up each morning, giving it a little hug.

She remembered acutely the moment she was told her mother had died in an automobile accident on the way home. She had pulled away from her father and run to the living room to the table where the statue sat.

Her father had tried to take the statue away, but her mother had told her to take care of it. She screamed and screamed, and finally he had given up. She wrapped it in her arms and carried it close to her heart for months… or years. She couldn't remember when she had finally put it on her bedside table, touching it every night before she slept.

What kind of retreat was it? No one ever told her anything about the retreat. Why did Monica have so much fear connected with what she called "being imaginative" around that accident? Was there was something hidden, something secret about their mother's death?

Nicki had taken Giselle's dogs, and unbelievably, Reverend Tarrant had taken the little gray cat. Nicki had reassured her that the cat would be safe with him. "He's had a change of heart," she said, "and he and Muriel Chase are taking care of Hazel's cats, too."

But what happened to her other things? Where was the little wooden statue? The next visit from Monica she asked about all of her possessions.

"They're still at your house. I thought I would pay someone to pack up the small things and put them in a storage unit," she answered. "You have such a lot of clutter, I don't want to deal with it, and we can't just leave it there in the house. They might want to rent it to someone else. Nicki took all your plants to her house."

"They mustn't rent the house. I want to buy it. Mrs. Bidewell knows that."

"Well, Mrs. Bidewell told the realtor she wants to hold it for you, but you aren't going back there."

Giselle glared at her sister. "I am – and right now I want the little wooden woman that was great-grandmother's."

"That stupid little Chinese thing?" Monica began to rant. "Why do you want that thing? You're just like Mama. Daddy would be so upset to hear you asking for that – thing. He should have thrown it away, instead of letting you take it and carry it around like a baby when mama died."

Giselle tensed. "Mama asked me to take care of it while she was gone. It was our great-grandmother's," she repeated.

"It was why Mama went to that retreat." Monica was nearly shouting. "It was a retreat about that Chinese stuff. It was because she wanted to know more about it that she went. She never would have wanted to go and find out about all that religious stuff, if it hadn't been for the wooden woman. She wouldn't have left us. And she wouldn't have died."

Giselle looked at her sister, her eyes wide with astonishment. "She died in an automobile accident."

"Yes, but she was coming home from that retreat. That wooden woman made her go."

Giselle took a deep breath. "The woman made her go? How could a statue make her go?"

Monica jumped up and went to the window, her back and neck rigid with emotion. *Anger or fear,* thought Giselle, *or both?*

"Monica," she said. "Monica, tell me about it. Please."

"I don't know if I should." Monica paced the little room, wringing her hands together.

"I was so young, Monica. I don't remember all these things. Maybe I never knew them. You were older. Please tell me."

Monica turned to Giselle and shouted, "Daddy didn't want her to go."

She sat down in a chair, staring at her hands clutched in her lap. Her voice dropped and she wiped away the tears flowing down her face. "He didn't want her to go. He said she was letting her imaginative side take over, reading all that stuff about Buddhism. But Mother said she needed to understand her roots. She said the things she read 'spoke to her,' and that the woman 'spoke to her'. Those were the words she used – 'spoke to her.'"

Monica looked up at Giselle. "I know what that means. I know she didn't mean it literally. But sometimes I'm not sure. It always bothered me, Giselle." Her voice caught. "I might have been older than you, but I was still just a little girl. And there were these things 'speaking' to her, 'calling' her, and they called her away from us."

She looked down at her hands. "And now you're talking about being called by some kind of dance in some imaginary place. You're crazy just like her."

Monica stood up and walked to the window. "Mama said she wasn't going away forever – just a weekend – but it wasn't true."

"But Monica, you just said she was on her way home when the accident happened. She didn't run away from us. She was coming home."

"But she didn't get home. She died." Monica screamed. "I know she didn't do it deliberately, but she said she wasn't going away forever, and then she did." A deep wrenching sob escaped and she collapsed on to a sofa in a storm of tears.

Giselle went to her and held her in her arms. Something deep inside her released – a tightness she hadn't known was there. She had always seen Monica as the strong one. She'd thought she'd been the one hurt by her mother's death, not Monica. Monica was daddy's child, daddy's right hand. But Monica was a child, too. And mama was also her mother. This was why Monica so mistrusted their Chinese heritage, why Monica was so afraid of what she called Giselle's "imaginative" side. She associated their mother's death with "imagination", with seeking.

"I don't know why Daddy let you have that statue. He should've thrown it away."

"But Monica," Giselle pushed Monica's hair away from her face. "It was the only thing our great-grandmother brought with her from China. It would have been terrible to throw it away." *And the wooden woman is one of the most important things I remember about our mother. But Monica was at school. She didn't have that special time with mama and the statue.*

Monica pulled away. "I know," she whispered. "I know."

Giselle had a flash of the weaving tree at Ninas Twei. *Torn people. We're torn people, Monica and I. We've never recovered from the rip in our lives caused by our mother's death. And then later, daddy...*

She smiled with a sudden insight. *This is the beginning of our recovery. We're weaving a new pattern of how to be with each other, and we'll repair the rip. We'll be stronger than ever.*

She pulled Monica into her arms again. "We're going to be all right, Monica." She felt Monica tentatively hug her back. *Now I'm the strong one,* she thought. *She took care of me the best she could all those years of our growing up and now I can return that. I can give her strength.*

That evening at dinner she noticed the other people confined in the institution.

Torn people. She was confined in an institution full of torn people.

Is this where I'm to start? It wasn't easy to think about mending torn people, when it felt like you were one yourself. Giselle began that night with small smiles, and direct eye contact, but found it incredibly difficult. There were a few tentative smiles in return, but most ignored her.

She took a deep breath. *One step at a time,* she thought.

First Quarter in Bayomar

The next day Giselle spent the whole afternoon in the little garden with the life-sized statue of the Chinese woman standing on the back of a dragon. The statue was placed in a corner, with a wide circle of pavement in front of it. Alternating between walking the paths, and sitting on a stone bench placed opposite the woman so that the sitter could gaze on the stone statue and the fountain next to it, she barely noticed an older Asian man pulling weeds and planting new plants near the fountain.

She was thinking of returning to her room to prepare for dinner when she looked up to see him leaning on a rake looking at her. She smiled at him and he smiled back.

"May I sit with you a moment?" he asked.

She moved to the side of the bench to make room.

"My name is Shen Ch'i. I'm a volunteer member of the staff here." He pointed to the badge hanging around his neck. "And yours?"

"I'm Giselle." She turned away. *It's funny,* she thought, *how even saying my name feels strange.*

"I can see you like my little Kuan Yin corner."

Giselle turned to look at him. "Your what?" she asked.

"Kuan Yin. That's her name."

"Her name. Kuan Yin," she smiled up at the statue. "Her name is Kuan Yin." She brushed away tears. She'd always wanted to know who she was.

Looking back at him she asked, "She's yours?"

"Yes. Well, no. The sculpture, the fountain, and the plantings in this corner are a gift to Kavanaugh House from me, so it's not mine."

"It's beautiful."

"I put this corner together for my daughter who was a patient here."

Giselle cocked her head as if to ask a question, but wasn't sure it was all right to ask.

Shen Ch'i smiled. "There was a gang shooting. My wife and my fifteen-year-old daughter were caught in the crossfire. An Lien, my daughter, was injured, and my wife was killed because she threw herself in front of my daughter to try to save her. While my wife was dying, my daughter was lying beneath her, and was helpless to save her."

He shook his head pausing for a moment. "We were both very...," he looked down at the ground. "I wasn't able to be there for her because I felt guilty, too."

He looked up at Giselle. "Survivors guilt they call it. Her legs are paralyzed and she uses a wheelchair. I found myself hiding from her, unwilling to look at her. I buried myself in my work, and she turned to drugs."

He sighed, looking up at the smiling stone woman.

"Finally, we both got help and she came here to rehabilitate. She missed her mother very much. I thought perhaps Kuan Yin could be a mother to her. I wanted her to know that Kuan Yin was here, hearing her cries."

"Hearing her cries?" asked Giselle.

He gave a slight nod of his head and Giselle noticed how very warm and sweet his smile was. "Do you know about Kuan Yin, about how she hears the cries of the world?"

176

"No." Giselle leaned forward. "But I want to learn about her. My mother had a little wooden statue my great-grandmother brought with her when she came from China and I cherish it, but I didn't know her name. I don't know anything about her. My wooden woman is stepping out of a tree, not riding a dragon, but I'm sure she's the same woman."

He nodded. "There're many myths about Kuan Yin. One is that a sculptor found her hiding in the trunk of a willow tree he was carving. Another," he gestured at the tall sculpture in front of them, "is that a fisherman, fighting a storm, saw her riding the back of a dragon swimming through the ocean."

"But who is she?" Giselle asked.

"Ah." Shen Ch'i sat back, crossing an ankle over his knee. "Kuan Yin is the bodhisattva of compassion. She hears the cries of the world. She heard my daughter's cries and led her back to me. She healed her – and me."

"Bodhisattva?" asked Giselle.

"A Bodhisattva is an enlightened one, who refuses Nirvana until all of earth's beings have achieved it. Kuan Yin stays in this realm helping others achieve enlightenment instead of entering Nirvana, even though she has earned it."

"What is Nirvana? Is it heaven?"

"No, it isn't heaven." Shen Ch'i laughed. "There are many debates about just what Nirvana is. But all agree it is to be without cravings and suffering."

"So Kuan Yin could be without cravings and suffering, but she chooses to still suffer?"

"I think, myself, that she has achieved a place where she has no cravings for herself, and thus no suffering, but chooses to have compassion or 'karuna'."

"Karuna?"

Shen Ch'i smiled. "It's hard to explain, but it's more than compassion; it's empathy; it's the deep sorrow and understanding that comes from feeling at one with someone else."

Shen Ch'i smiled and shook his head a little. "Seems so impossible to think that there would ever be a time when everyone would be healed. Yet, Kuan Yin vows to keep on being present to the suffering of others until that time comes."

"I don't know how she could do that." Giselle's voice dropped to a whisper. She looked away so the man wouldn't see the tears in her eyes.

"I don't either, but I think there must be something about having achieved a state of detachment that puts her in two places at once, or two minds at once."

He uncrossed his legs and leaned forward, looking at the path. "I think she must be able to feel both the joy of the universe, the joy of detachment from this life, and the pain of the sufferers at the same time. I think feeling the joy makes it possible to bear the suffering. My daughter told me she learned something very important from Kuan Yin while she was here. She learned that if she danced while she cried, she could tap into a kind of joy that made it possible to live with the tears."

He paused looking searchingly at Giselle. "Does that make any sense?"

Giselle nodded her head. *It did. Somehow it did. She remembered dancing and singing with her mother in the living room, and the Kuan Yin was there. How happy her mother had seemed then!*

"Where… how did your daughter dance?"

"Right here, in front of Kuan Yin, in her wheelchair." He pointed to the circle of cement. "She would dance and cry, and sometimes she would sing and cry."

"And did she get better?"

"Yes, she did." He smiled. "Now she teaches others to dance and sing, and be healed! She also has a day job as an internet researcher and website designer."

"Oh, that's wonderful! I was a teacher. I loved teaching."

"Me, too. I teach physics at Bayomar U."

He looked at his watch. "I have to go, but if you would like to learn more about Kuan Yin, I can get you some books. Would you like that?"

Giselle nodded her head. "Yes, very much."

The next day Shen Ch'i brought her a book about Kuan Yin. She moved from the stone bench to sit with her back to the trunk of an old pine tree and read. It didn't feel like her oak tree, but it was living, and underneath it there was the soft spongy soil of decaying pine needles. When she sat there she could feel a faint tingling, the suggestion of a song. She dug her fingers into the soil and could hear the branches of the pine tree whispering:

> *Breath,*
> *Live in the rich brown soil,*
> *Merge with my hands and start me singing.*
>
> *Blowing through the limbs of the tree,*
> *Creep into my soul and 'waken me.*
> *It's still there,* she thought.

One of the branches of the tree stretched across the path and hung over a young black woman, who clutched the iron bars of the fence separating the little garden from an alley. She was pulling herself against it and thrusting herself away from it in a monotonous rhythm, chanting angry-sounding nonsense syllables.

Giselle watched as an attendant walked past the woman as if she were a part of the fence. She dug her fingers back into the earth. *She's a torn person. I should help her. I should see her, when no one else does.*

"No," she whispered. "She'll be angry. She'll yell at me. She won't want to be touched." And she pushed herself back in – back to the farthest corner of her mind. The breeze shushed in the branches above her, and a small bird sang. The sun felt warm on her lap.

> *Breath,*
> *Warmed by the life-giving sun,*
> *Slip into my mind and strengthen me.*

Giselle stood up, took a deep breath, and walked over to lean against the fence next to the woman. "Hi," she murmured.

The woman didn't appear to hear her.

Giselle cleared her throat. "Hi," she said again, a little louder.

The woman froze for less than a second before continuing her endless banging and chanting.

Giselle reached over and lightly touched the woman's arm. "Hi."

She jumped back as the woman leaned right into her face. "Grarr," she yelled with a deep almost animal sound.

Their eyes made contact.

Giselle was shaking and her heart beat fast. The woman went back to banging on the fence, but this time she sneaked peeks at Giselle out of the corner of her eyes as she banged.

Giselle smiled.

The woman kept banging, but Giselle noticed just a twitch of a smile at the corner of her lips. Giselle started to laugh and the woman's smile got bigger. Soon they were both laughing. The woman didn't stop her rhythmic banging, but she was laughing.

Giselle looked around her, a big grin spreading across her face. *This place is full of torn people I can help mend. And when I get out...* She laughed again because she knew – she was sure she would get out of this place, and soon. *Even,* she thought, *if I have to break out. When I get out, the world's full of torn people to mend!*

Her heart leapt with joy at the thought. *I'm not scared. I'll go where they are and I'm not scared any more.*

She looked up at the branch, and for the first time, noticed the small green nodules at the ends of little twigs. She crouched, thrusting her fingers into the soil. She felt the flowing and the stretching, the seeking and dividing as she reached deep into the soil, down into the richness of the earth. "This is me," she whispered. "This is me."

Tuesday evening, Monica and Rod took Giselle out to dinner at a restaurant with an art gallery in an adjoining room. While Rod and Monica were still mulling over their orders, Giselle looked around. She could see a large painting through the doorway between the restaurant and the art gallery. There was something familiar...

Her breath caught, eyes widened. She glanced back at Rod and Monica, but they hadn't noticed.

The painting was the one of the wolf from Yameno's clearing – the one with the generations of wolves flowing into the distance back of him – the one that sang to her! How could it be here? She excused herself to go to the Ladies room and slipped between the tables to the art gallery.

I am the wild, the freeborn, earth traveler, whispered the painting.

"Yameno," she sighed, blinking her eyes.

A man approached her. "We just got that in. It's painted on bark using paints made from plants. The artist's just been discovered, but he has a large body of work – not just paintings, but sculptures out of wood and clay. I got a carload of them on Monday and I haven't put them all out yet. Look at this clay quail. Amazing, isn't it?"

Giselle looked at the clay bird. It was Yameno's, too. She had seen it in his hut. How could his art be here?

"What's the artist's name?" she asked.

"Yameno Wellkeeper. He's a member of the First People. Lives up the coast."

"Yameno," she whispered. He was free? What had happened? She'd asked Monica about him, but hadn't gotten an answer. She'd assumed he was still in jail.

She looked up at the man. "What do you know of him?"

"A priest brought his work to me yesterday. He brought it down from where he's living up the coast. Father Keegan Gilchrist. We're old friends."

"From Arundel," interrupted Giselle.

"Wellkeeper is from Arundel." He smiled at Giselle. "Do you know anything about him?"

Giselle nodded glancing back at the dining room. She leaned toward the man almost whispering. "Do you have a telephone number for Father Gilchrist, or an email address?"

The man cocked his head and looked at her for a moment, but didn't ask her any more about Yameno. "For Father Gilchrist, yes, but not for Wellkeeper. The Father said he was handling all of this for Wellkeeper. Gilchrist's a good man. I trust he's got the man's best interests in mind."

He walked over to his desk and moved his fingers over his computer keyboard pulling up his address book. "Here's an email address and phone number. I don't think he'd mind if I gave it to you."

He wrote the email address and phone number down on the back of his card and handed it to her. Giselle slipped it into her pocket.

"Thank you. I can't buy anything now, but maybe I'll be back."

"That would be nice," he smiled. "I'm glad you like his work."

"Oh, I do, I do!" she exclaimed.

Monica appeared in the doorway. "Giselle, what are you doing in here? Come on."

She glanced around at the paintings and frowned. "Your salad is here."

Giselle obediently followed her sister back to the table. She spread her napkin in her lap and picked up her fork. "Rod?"

"Yes," he answered, taking a bite of his salad.

"What happened to Yameno? Is he still in jail?"

Monica and Rod exchanged glances.

"You'd better eat your salad before…" said Monica.

"Before what? It gets cold?" Giselle laughed. "No, Monica. You need to tell me now. What happened?"

She glared at Rod. "Rod? Tell me."

Rod sighed and put down his fork. "The charges were dismissed. Insufficient evidence."

"So Yameno's not in jail."

"No."

"And if I'd gone to court, the charges would've been dismissed against me, as well."

"Probably." He shrugged his shoulders. "It's hard to know. It's always different for each person."

Giselle leaned over the table. Her voice was low, but angry. "So why am I still in prison?"

Monica interrupted. "You're not in prison, Giselle. You're in the hospital. You're sick. You need help."

"I don't think so," said Giselle angrily. "I'm not sick and I never was."

"You signed the commitment papers, Giselle." Rod opened his hands as if to say that she was the one who had done it, not him.

Giselle sat back in her seat, crossing her arms in front of her. "You got me into this, Rod, and you're going to get me out."

Rod glanced at Monica and didn't answer. They both returned to their salads and not another word was spoken.

Waxing Crescent in Arundel

But Yameno had not been released right away – not until the Thursday after the Monday arraignment.

The day after the arraignment, while Giselle was still in Arundel listening to her sister rant, Billy and Dorotea McCrae had gone to morning Mass. After Mass they'd asked Father Gilchrist if they could meet with him and he led them to his small office moving behind his old wooden desk.

Billy started talking before they could sit down. "After the arraignment we decided," Billy began.

Dorotea interrupted, moving up to the edge of the desk. "We must find a way to go to this Ninas Twei, Father. That's the only way we will find our Jesús. This Yameno and the teacher – what they say is truth, I am sure. We must go to Ninas Twei."

Billy glared at Keegan, challenging him to disagree. "We believe them. We want to talk to that Yameno Wellkeeper and see if we can go find the children. We want you to help us get to talk to him in the jail. He's the one who'll help us find Jesús. Not that deputy."

"We called the teacher last night," added Dorotea, "but her sister wouldn't let her talk to us and I think they are taking her away someplace."

"Besides," Billy interrupted, "that Yameno's the one who knows how to do it, more than the teacher. He's the one who can help us. And," he added, placing his hands on the desk and leaning towards Keegan, "I don't care if you don't believe it or think it's something of the Devil. We need to go and find Jesús, and little Enid, too."

Keegan nodded. "I'm with you, Billy." He pulled out his chair. "Let's sit down and figure this out."

Billy pulled two straight chairs closer to the desk, visibly relieved, and he and Dorotea sat down.

Keegan leaned forward across his desk. "Last night the other ministers – and the Rabbi – you saw them at the arraignment…"

Billy and Dorotea nodded.

"We met to talk about it. I think we all agreed – even Jarvis Tarrant – that we think the story is true. We all want to do something to bring the children back, but we don't know what." He picked up a pencil and tapped it on the desk. "But this idea of talking to Yameno. That's a good idea. I'll see what I can do."

The phone shrilled and they all jumped. Keegan hesitated and then picked it up.

It was Nicki, who was also a member of Father Gilchrist's parish. She had overheard some of the children at school talking about their parents' plans to go up in the hills to Yameno's place and destroy all the 'devil's work'.

"I think Giselle and Yameno are deluded," she added, "but I can't believe they're evil. Yameno's artwork needs to be kept safe no matter what really happened. The artwork isn't evil."

"Hold on a second, Nicki."

Keegan turned to Billy. "People are talking about smashing up Yameno's artwork. This is Ms. Nichols, at the school. The children are talking about it."

"Billy told me of how beautiful it is. We must not let them hurt it!" exclaimed Dorotea.

"I can take the little tractor up there. We can haul it all down here," added Billy.

"And we can store these things in our barn," added Dorotea.

Keegan turned back to the phone. "We'll take care of it, Nicki. Thanks for letting us know."

He put down the phone and looked for a moment at the McCraes. "The tractor, yes, but I'm not sure your barn's a safe place." He punched Jarvis Tarrant's number into the phone.

"These people who want to destroy the art are my parishioners." Jarvis moaned. "This is all my fault."

"No," Keegan soothed him. "No. It's time for healing now, not blaming."

He looked at Billy and Dorotea for a moment. "Jarvis, Billy McCrae has offered to bring the artwork to his barn, but I'm not sure it's safe there." He looked at Billy. "Do you understand why, Billy? Because people are…"

Billy interrupted. "Racist and they don't like us. I get it."

"I have a big garage," Jarvis interjected. "Let's put it there for now."

Keegan got on the phone again, first with Micah and Clare to ask them to join them rescuing the art, and then with the prosecuting attorney, who argued and then finally agreed that the McCraes could talk to Yameno as long as Keegan was present, but not until Wednesday morning.

Dorotea's eyes flashed. "He's not a parent or he would not make us wait."

Keegan nodded. "I know this is hard, Dorotea."

Billy stood up. "But we can rescue the art work right now. Let's do it," and before noon Billy and Dorotea, with their mini-tractor and trailer, and the four religious leaders had gathered at Yameno's clearing.

Dorotea was astounded. "*Asombroso.* This is… this is… *Es muy… Es* beautiful." She turned in circles in the middle of the clearing. "Jesús was here. I know that he loved this. It must be kept safe."

The others nodded in agreement, wandering from painting to painting, sculpture to sculpture.

"It's too bad it couldn't be displayed right here," Clare added. "It belongs right here."

Keegan shook his head. "It's not safe."

"I know. I just wish…"

"Look, down here," Billy called out and they all followed him down to the little waterfall.

"A spring," exclaimed Micah, as he crouched down and cupped his hands under the water. "We didn't see this Sunday!" He sipped the water and turned, smiling towards the others. "It's so sweet."

One by one they followed suit, cupping the cool water in their hands and drinking…

The forest stilled, a deep breath. The branches and bushes rustled and whispered.

> *Water of life,*
> *Purify me.*
> *Water of the soul of earth,*
> *wash me in your love.*

Micah looked around him, "Did you hear…"

"Maybe…" Keegan muttered, looking up at the trees, listening to the wind in the branches. "Maybe."

"*Es sagrado,*" whispered Dorotea.

"Yes," added Clare. "A sacred spot. If we were Shinto we would bow down to the God of this place." She folded her hands together and bowed her head over them.

Billy took Dorotea's hand and they all stood silent for a moment.

Finally, with a sigh, they returned to the clearing and their work.

Micah came last and looked back at the spring from the top of the path. "This must be a very deep spring for the water to be so cool and clean. Very deep."

"*Es Sagrado,*" Dorotea repeated. "*Sagrado.*"

Back in the clearing they began the work of lifting down paintings from the tree branches and layering them with newspaper for protection.

They wrapped the smaller sculptures and placed them next to the stack of paintings.

Billy examined each of the larger sculptures, trying to decide which should go in the trailer first. When he came to a life-sized black bear he called Dorotea over. "Look," he pointed to the bear's shoulder.

She moved over beside him, smiling as she saw the little killdeer perched on the shoulder, one wing dragging down the bear's arm as if it were broken. "The little bird who pretends to be hurt, to lure those who'd eat her children away from her nest. They look so real, yet so impossible."

Billy reached out to touch the bear and Dorotea caressed the little bird.

Keegan smiled as he watched them. Looking around, he saw Micah was fascinated by a painting of a gray fox, Jarvis was running his fingers over the ridges on a small carving of a horned lizard, and Clare held a life-sized mourning dove carved out of gray driftwood cupped in her hands. *It's all so wonderful,* he thought, *but we've got to keep working or we won't be able to get it all out of here in time.*

He went over to the little house that crouched like a mushroom on the ground at the edge of the clearing, climbed down inside, and stood waiting for his eyes to adjust to the dim light. The deputy sheriff had obviously gone through Wellkeeper's things. The string of dried fish lay on the floor as well as most of the other foodstuffs, tools, and books. He picked up the small clay figure of the burrowing owl that lay on top of a pile of clothes. It felt warm, almost alive in his hands. The large round eyes seemed to look right at him, demanding. *Wisdom,* it seemed to whisper:

> *Wisdom comes,*
> *not from judgment,*
> *not from fear.*
> *Wisdom is seeing in the dark.*
> *Wisdom is listening, not talk.*
> *Wisdom is flying close to the ground.*
> *Wisdom is seeing all,*
> *seeing all,*
> *all around.*

Keegan shook his head as if to shake the words out of his brain. Moving out of the little house holding the owl, he called out to the others. "There are more things in here. We need to clean everything out of this building."

With the aid of the tractor, they were able to bring all of the art and Yameno's belongings down before the sun set Tuesday evening. Just before their last trip down the hillside, they stood in the clearing, now empty except for the little house. "The house is quite wonderful," said Micah. "Too bad we can't save it."

Keegan looked at him and smiled. "You know if Yameno's released he won't be able to return here. He won't be safe."

Clare sighed. "Where will he go?"

"He'll come live with me." Jarvis sighed and touched a tree where a willow tree painting had hung not too long before. "His artwork is safe with me, and he will be, too."

He looked around the clearing again. "And he'll teach me. He'll be my teacher."

Keegan rocked back on his heels and smiled.

Wednesday morning, Keegan and the McCraes met in front of the county jail in Robertsville. After being searched and put through a lot of hullabaloo, they were admitted to a small room with a table and four chairs. Soon after, Yameno was brought in, his hands handcuffed in front of him, a chain reaching down to his cuffed ankles. Keegan introduced himself, Billy, and Dorotea.

"You're Jesús' parents." Yameno looked anguished, shaking his head. "I'm so sorry. I don't know what happened. I don't understand it."

He walked to the window looking out. "I need to get out of here. I need to go back." He turned back to them. "I need to find the children."

"That's why we're here," Billy exclaimed. "We want to know how to go there – to this Ninas Twei – so we can go and find Jesús and the little girl."

"Let's sit down," urged Keegan, gesturing to Dorotea and Billy.

Yameno moved to the table and Keegan helped him to sit.

"I don't know if you can go without me and without being called," Yameno answered. "We always had six before and they all'd been called by their Tla Twei. It was the way we did it even when I was a small child – the tradition of my people. And we always drink from the spring before we go."

"We did," exclaimed Dorotea. "We drank from the spring and it was so sweet." Her voice dropped. "It sang to us," she whispered.

Yameno leaned toward her. "It's the sacred spring of our people. It sang to you?"

"*Si*," Dorotea nodded. "*Es sagrado.*"

"It sang?" He looked around at all of them as each nodded.

Sitting silently looking at his hands cuffed on the table in front of him, he took several deep breaths. "I've been worrying about who will guard it now. There's no one left to guard it."

Keegan moved forward in his chair. "Yameno, while you think about this let me tell you – we went up to your clearing and brought all your things – all the paintings and sculptures – down and stored them in Jarvis Tarrant's garage."

Yameno's eyes grew wide. "Jarvis Tarrant?"

Keegan nodded. "Yes, Jarvis Tarrant. He had an epiphany, Yameno – an awakening, I think you'd say, when he saw Hazel transform and die. He was in love with Hazel."

Yameno looked thoughtful. "I think Hazel knew that."

He lifted his handcuffed hands up so that his elbows could rest on the table and leaned forward. "When we walked down the hill he stayed beside me, but it didn't feel as though he was guarding me. It felt... I don't know." He shrugged his shoulders. "And he was there when they brought me to the jail, too."

Billy nodded. "I can tell you, Yameno, he's different. He always looked at me – if he even looked at me – like I was dirt. Now it's as if he sees me, really sees me."

"And he smiled when he helped me wrap your sculptures," added Dorotea.

Keegan agreed. "Yes, I believe the change is real. He says he wants you to be his teacher, Yameno, and he offered his garage for your artwork because he felt it would be safe there."

Yameno pushed his hands together as much as the handcuffs would allow, touching his forehead with his fingertips. "I have to trust. Just trust."

The cuffs rattled on the table as he brought his hands down. "What about Giselle? Is she in jail? What did they do with her?"

"She was released to her sister." Keegan patted his hand reassuringly. "They've taken her back to Bayomar."

"I'm glad she's not in jail, but I hope she's…" He looked back at the window. "I have to get out of here."

Sighing he turned back toward Keegan. "At the arraignment they said they were holding me while they did further testing on the cups. But there were no drugs in those cups. Just water. There's no evidence of any of the things they've charged me with. Don't they have to let me go?"

Keegan nodded. "Yes. I think so."

Billy slapped the table with his hand. "But it won't happen unless someone puts pressure on them. I know! I've been there."

"Yes, I think you're right, Billy," Keegan agreed, "and this is a good job for religious leaders. I think it's time three ministers and a rabbi paid a visit to the District Attorney."

Dorotea wrung her hands. "It will take too long. We need to go now. What if the children are hurt?"

Yameno reached over the table, his handcuffs scraping the wood, and took her hands. "Hazel and Dan are there. I'm sure they're there and they're looking for the children. They may've already found them. If the children are hurt they'll take care of them."

Dorotea peered at him, hoping he was right. Finally she nodded. "And you will get out, and we will find a way to go there and get them and bring them back. You will get out and help us. You will."

That afternoon Jarvis Tarrant went to the jail to visit Yameno, making arrangements for Yameno to live with him, at least for a while.

"Why are you doing this?" Yameno asked.

Jarvis looked out the little window, and then back at Yameno. "I was confused. I was in love with Hazel, but I got it all mixed up. I thought I hated her. When I saw her change to the cougar – saw her die – I knew the truth."

Yameno reached over and touched his hand. "Reverend Tarrant, I think Hazel knew you loved her."

There was a long silence before Jarvis continued. "I'm glad she knew." His voice dropped to a whisper. "Perhaps she understood, just a little, why…"

Yameno just nodded and patted Jarvis' hand.

"And now I want to know more about this. It's like this… this dance of all the species – it feels like I've been looking for this all my life. I got blinded by hate. But Yameno," he leaned forward, "I'm not blind anymore, and I need your help. I need to know more."

Yameno looked at his own hands for a moment, then back at Jarvis. "I'm happy to help you, but I have to find the children and I have to protect the spring. Those things must come first." *And Giselle,* he thought. *I have to find Giselle.*

Yameno was reluctantly released on Thursday morning after all four religious leaders, Dr. Chase, and his wife had called and talked to the prosecuting attorney.

Jarvis picked him up at the jail. "I think you'll be safe at my house, but you need to know my parishioners don't understand yet, and some of them think I've turned to the devil. Perhaps Sunday I'll be able to turn some of them, but..." he paused, "you could also go live with Micah – Rabbi Levinson. He lives in Robertsville and you might be safer."

"No." Yameno shook his head. "No, I need to be here. I need to be able to get to the spring."

Jarvis nodded. "Micah went up there yesterday to see if everything was okay. Nothing had been touched. You're not thinking of moving back up to your hut, are you?" Jarvis glanced at him anxiously. "That wouldn't be safe right now."

"I know..." Yameno sighed. "My focus has to be on the children and the spring – and Ninas Twei. Something bad was happening at Ninas Twei and we might be the only ones who can help."

But I have to find others to go with me to find the children, he thought. *They need to be called. And Giselle...* There was a deep ache in his chest. *Hazel and Dan... and Giselle.*

When they reached Jarvis' house, they went into the garage to see Yameno's artwork. Yameno smiled at Jarvis. "Thank you for saving my things."

Almost immediately Keegan, Clare, and Micah drove up in a car, followed by Billy and Dorotea in a pickup truck. "We brought lunch," explained Clare, holding up some takeout bags. "We thought we needed to talk as soon as possible about the children."

Dorotea touched Yameno on the arm. "We must go to this Ninas Twei soon."

They gathered for lunch at a round oak table in the big kitchen of the former farm house. The little gray cat stalked around them and then wove himself in and out of their legs.

Yameno reached down to touch the cat. "You've taken in the cat – the one who lived with Giselle."

Tarrant nodded. "He's… I don't know," he shrugged.

Yameno laughed. "Yes, he is!"

The cat seated himself under the table, back and head upright, tail wrapped around his feet, sitting resolutely at the exact center of the circle.

Over lunch Yameno explained about the journeys to Ninas Twei. "Always before we've had people who were called to their Tla Twei. We sat together in the clearing by the waterfall and sipped the spring water. Sometimes we've said, 'To the journey,' before we drink, but we didn't do that when I was a child – maybe that was added by Hazel's parents – a European type toast." He looked around at the others. "Then it just happens."

"But how are people called?" asked Micah.

Yameno shrugged his shoulders. "I was so little when I first went as Yameno, the Wolfwind, I felt I was always the Wolfwind. Hazel and Mary gave Gunther and Emma their Tla Twein. Back then all of our Tla Twein were animals native to this area and sacred to my people – some might call them gods – but when Giselle came…" He paused.

"What about the past, Yameno?" Clare interjected. "What is the history of this… this being called?"

"The first I knew of the journey was when I was quite young. My grandfather was part of a group that went to Ninas Twei often and when I was born he dedicated me to the Wolfwind. I grew up knowing about it. Members of our nation had been going to Ninas Twei as our Tla Twein for centuries, but by the time I was born those who went with my grandfather were not all members of our nation. Many of our people were leaving the area. The elders were dying." He stopped talking and watched the flickering leaves of a live oak beyond the kitchen window. "Now I'm the only one left."

He continued. "Hazel's grandmother, Greta, was nursing an elder who was very sick. The elder's Tla Twei was the cougar – the wise one – and when she died in Greta's arms the shaman saw the cougar like a shadow around Greta. So the shaman invited her to travel to Ninas Twei – and later Hazel and Mary's parents. They went with the elders of the nation. The two Fraya children, Hazel and Mary, started going when they were five and seven years old, I think, when their grandmother died. Hazel took her grandmother's cougar Tla Twei. The year I was born, Grandfather, the Fraya's – Hazel's parents and the two girls, Hazel and Mary, who were teenagers by then – and Dan, who had come to live with the Fraya's – went together. Then Mrs. Fraya – Hazel and Mary's mother – died suddenly."

He looked out the window. "I remember how sad my grandfather was. They were all very good friends. I was five years old and I became the sixth person."

He looked around at all of them, smiling. "It was incredible. We went several times that year, but then my grandfather died and we were without a sixth again."

He shook his head. "I don't know why we needed six, but that had been the tradition for hundreds of years. We never tried to go with less.

"It was a long time before we tried to go again. Mary married Gunther Amundson, and they had Emma. We thought Gunther would make the sixth and began telling him just a little about Ninas Twei, but then Mr. Fraya died. We thought we had to wait until Emma was a little older – well, Gunther was reluctant, unsure. He was a little older than Hazel and Mary. We thought when he saw the Tsin Twei, he would be okay, but he never gave it a chance."

Keegan leaned forward. "What happened to Gunther's wife – to Mary?"

Yameno sighed. "The mists and the singing had started…"

He looked up. "When we go there're always swirling mists and singing. We sing our own songs, and then there're other songs that join us."

"Songs," murmured Keegan, nodding his head.

"We heard that song when we drank the water at the spring," added Micah.

Yameno nodded at him thoughtfully, and then continued.

"We'd just begun to transform – and somehow Gunther didn't. He grabbed Mary's wing just as she started to fly. She was a beautiful tree swallow – they were also water protectors. She fell and transformed back at the same time, and her head hit a rock. She died instantly. Emma never transformed. She watched her mother die. She was ten."

He shook his head. "And then Gunther wouldn't let her see us or even go into the forest. He said the forest was evil. She got pregnant when she was fourteen. She'd never tell who the father was, but we think it was one of several boys in high school with her in Robertsville. She may not have even known which one. Enid was born and then Emma killed herself."

Yameno leaned back in his chair, shaking his head. "He wouldn't let us near Enid either, but Hazel went to court for visitation rights."

He looked out the window for a moment. "For some reason Gunther let Enid play in the forest even though he'd kept Emma away. Strange, but good."

The listeners sat, heads down, or looking out the window, processing what they'd heard.

Keegan leaned forward. "I believe Gunther needs to be healed. We need to find a way for him to understand what happened and let go of the need to blame you – and himself."

Yameno looked doubtful. "Maybe."

Keegan nodded his head. "Yes. He needs to heal. He'll be my project."

Clare nodded agreement. "What animal was he to be?"

"A badger. We thought the badger would be our protector…"

"And did you try again before this last time?" Micah leaned forward.

"No. That left just Hazel, Dan, and myself. We waited and waited. This last year we began to realize that Enid and Jesús were a part of it, because they came so often to the woods."

"How did the teacher become involved?" Billy asked. "She's new to Arundel. All the rest of you – well not Dan, I guess…"

Yameno grinned, shaking his head. "You'll have a hard time believing it."

"It's all pretty strange!" Clare exclaimed.

He shrugged. "I guess. Yes, to others it's strange. I grew up with it."

"Please," pleaded Dorotea. "Tell us about the teacher. And then we must figure out how we can go."

"Hazel had a dream. She's always had a lot of cats. There was a young blue-gray cat who just showed up at her door."

He grinned and pointed down under the table.

Clare leaned down and looked at the cat who stared unblinkingly back at her. She sat up, and grinned at the others shrugging her shoulders.

Yameno laughed and continued. "When she woke up from the dream the cat was sitting on the bed right in front of her face looking at her.

"She said it was a little disconcerting!

"Anyway, the dream was that she should take this cat to Bayomar and he would find the sixth person. She was very insistent that it was a real dream – that we should do it. So we did. We took the cat down to the city, and as we stopped at a stop light, he suddenly leapt out the open window and ran down the cross street.

"We pulled over, not certain what to do. Dan transformed to Tata Sundancer – the hawk – and flew down the street, following the cat who went into an apartment garage.

"Then a few minutes later the cat came out of the garage with a young woman and went in the front door of the apartment building.

"Dan flew back and told us. Hazel and I returned to Arundel, while Dan stayed behind to watch."

Yameno sat back smiling. "Less than a week later Dan followed as the cat came back bringing Giselle."

Keegan shook his head, laughing, too. "The cat. I heard about the cat! You know, Nicki – Mrs. Nichols, the school principal. She told me about that cat one day after church. The homily had dealt some with animals – some apparent miracles having to do with pets. Nicki told me the day she hired Ms. Raphael the cat was with her – and two dogs. She said the cat seemed to be listening to the interview and urging her to take the job. She was joking, but…"

Dorotea jumped into the conversation. "Is that how we are called? An animal calls us? We cannot go unless an animal calls us?"

"No, I don't think so," Yameno reassured her. "It doesn't have to be a living animal – and Giselle's Tla Twei isn't the cat. I saw her dance on the cliff and there was a song."

"Music," Micah nodded. "If there's a dance, there must be music…"

"I could see the Earth Woman Tree Woman like a shadow around her," Yameno continued. "So I made the totem."

"A song," whispered Keegan, looking at his hands folded in front of him on the table. He looked up. "When we were bringing your art down from your clearing…"

He paused. *Such a private thing to say out loud.*

Finally he spoke. "When I picked up the Burrowing Owl I heard…"

"Did you hear a song?" Clare interrupted. "I heard a song. The mourning dove…"

Micah was nodding his head. "For me it was the gray fox."

Jarvis stood up and reached for the carving of the horned lizard sitting on the counter behind him. He held it up and then put it on the table in front of him as he sat down again.

"And the bear and the killdeer for us," exclaimed Dorotea, jumping up from her chair. "Yameno, I am sure we're called. We're called and we can go look for the children now."

She placed her hands on the table and leaned over, looking at each of them in turn. "We must go now."

"There are seven of us, not six," Clare pointed out.

"Yameno, Dorotea, and Billy should definitely go," added Micah.

Jarvis shook his head. "I don't deserve to go."

Keegan spoke up. "Actually, I think you should go. I think the seventh person will be needed to guard the rest. What if Coffman and some of his crew go up there? We really don't know what they're up to. I should stay behind and guard."

Yameno looked at Jarvis who was caressing the horned lizard. He nodded his head. "Yes, Jarvis, I think you should go. I think… Hazel talked about you as a child – how different you were then. She said you were friends. I think you're meant to go."

They agreed to meet at five at Giselle's house. Before leaving Jarvis' house, at Yameno's urging, they each took the totems that had spoken to them. It took four of them to load the bear and killdeer into the McCraes' truck. "It will be *maravilloso* in our back garden," exclaimed Dorotea. "When Jesús comes home he will love it."

Micah, Clare, and Keegan followed them home to help place it in the garden.

Later that afternoon, Harding finished correcting papers in his classroom and drove down the coast road. He found himself behind Jarvis Tarrant's car and watched it turn into Giselle's driveway.

"Was that the Indian with him? Why'd they be going there?" he muttered. "Giselle's down in Bayomar."

He pulled over to the verge and got out, peering over the meadow grasses towards the sea. "Uh, oh," he muttered, jumping back in his car.

Driving around a curve where he couldn't be seen from Giselle's driveway, he parked again and pulled out his cell phone to call Coffman. "There were a bunch of cars down there. I saw Tarrant, and the Indian was with him, and the McCraes' truck was there. Those ministers from Robertsville and the rabbi were standing there, too."

Coffman, still at the hardware store, thumped a fist down on the counter, startling a customer. Moving to the back room he lowered his voice. "What are they up to? One of them might go out to her house to check on something for her, but all of them?"

"It's the easiest way to get up to Yameno's shack," Harding replied.

"Yeah. Find a way to watch them. I'll be there as soon as I can."

He pushed the "off" and then punched in a number. "Tom, get downstairs here and cover the store," he commanded, disconnecting before Tom could reply, and punching in another number. "Dickerson, meet me out on the coast road by the old Bidewell place. I'll be there waiting," again disconnecting before there could be a response.

Harding left his car parked on the verge behind the hill and hiked back toward Giselle's driveway just in time to see the group set off hiking up the path that led to Yameno's clearing. He called Coffman, who was already in his car headed out of town.

"Follow them," commanded Coffman. "We won't be far behind you."

Harding took off across the meadow toward the path. He could hear them chattering ahead of him so it was easy to stay far enough behind to keep out of sight. When he reached Yameno's vegetable patch, he slipped into the trees away from the path and worked his way down toward the clearing, so he could see them through the brush. He crouched down to watch.

Yameno pulled a backpack off his shoulders, and knelt down to pull out six simple wooden cups and a pottery pitcher. *That looks like the kind of paraphernalia they had the last time,* thought Harding. *Not the same stuff, though, 'cause I know the deputy still has that. Said he wasn't going to give it back. It's evidence.*

He watched a while longer, and then slipped back down the hillside to phone Coffman. "They're setting up to do the ritual thing again," he whispered into the phone. "They've got cups, and Yameno went down to that waterfall to get water in a pitcher."

"Get back there. Stop it if you have, too. We're coming," Coffman yelled at his cell phone.

When Harding got back, six of them were sitting in a circle and Keegan stood with his back to the path to the garden. He watched as Yameno poured water into each cup, as they lifted their cups and Yameno said, "To the journey," and the others repeated, "To the journey."

A mist seemed to gather around them… *What the fuck is that?* he thought, grabbing the tree beside him to keep from falling over. He tried to shout, "Stop. Stop that," but it came out as a whisper. like when you were asleep having a nightmare and trying to yell and your voice wouldn't work.

Suddenly it became a scream, and he managed to make his muscles move, pushing his way out of the brush into the clearing.

"Stop that," he yelled again. Coffman and Dickerson came running down the path from the garden, their guns swinging in their hands. Coffman was yelling, "Stop! Stop!" and Dickerson added, "You better watch out. I've got my silver bullets."

They came to an abrupt stop practically nose to nose with Father Gilchrist, who stood with his arms crossed over his chest, blocking the path.

"Move out of the way, you," screamed Coffman, trying to push the priest to the side.

Father Gilchrist proved surprisingly strong and unmovable. "Calm down," he demanded. "Stop this yelling and put those guns down before someone gets hurt."

Coffman straightened his shoulders and thrust out his chest. He didn't put his gun down, but he didn't try to get past Gilchrist.

Harding was more successful, running right into the middle of the circle of travelers.

The mist dissipated quickly, as if blown away by a stiff breeze, and the six travelers blinked their eyes looking up at him.

Dorotea was the first to react, springing up and launching herself at him, pummeling him with her fists. "*Pendejo, idiot!* You have kept us from finding the children. *Dónde es mi Jesús?* How will I find *mi Jesús?*"

Billy grabbed her, pulling her gently away from Harding. She turned into his arms, sobbing. "*Mi Jesús. Mi Jesús.*"

As the others stood up, Harding backed quickly out of the circle before they could surround him.

Jarvis walked across the clearing to stand beside Keegan. "This isn't your business, Coffman. You need to leave."

Coffman crossed his arms, and his gun, across his chest. "I'm not going anywhere until you go." Leaning forward into Jarvis' face, he spit out his words. "I don't know what happened to you, Jarvis, but you're double crossing us. You leave here, and don't try this devil stuff anymore."

"We can't go to Ninas Twei this way," Yameno said in a low voice to the others around him. "We need to leave and try again later." Dorotea drew a sobbing breath, and Billy pulled her closer. Yameno reached over and put a hand on her shoulder. "I'm so sorry."

Keegan looked around. "I think it's time for all of us to leave. All of us," he reiterated looking back at Coffman. With little more said, both groups went slowly down the hillside.

When Coffman's group got back to the hardware store, Harding told what he had seen. "I think there's something about that water," he added. "The water from the waterfall on the other side of Wellkeeper's clearing."

Tom, listening from the storage room, froze in place. "The spring," he whispered. "That beautiful sweet spring."

That night after Jarvis had gone to bed, when the house and the town lay in darkness, Yameno slipped out of the house and into his wolf form. Running swiftly on back streets to the woods, he loped through the forest and up the hill. He stopped for a moment to look at the emptiness of the clearing, and at his little house, which had been broken up by vandals, and then turned urgently down the path to the spring.

It looked untouched. He leaned over and lapped some water. It was still clear and pure. The vandals hadn't been here.

He sighed with relief and changed to his human form. Stripping himself of his clothes, he stepped into the pool and sat cross-legged under the waterfall clearing his mind of all thoughts, letting the water pour down his head, over his shoulders, cleansing himself of the jail, the despair, and of the fear.

> *Water of life,* he sang.
> *Purify me.*
> *Water of the soul of earth,*
> *wash me in your love.*

In the silence he heard a voice deep, deep in his head. His grandfather's voice…

> *The ancestors gather.*
> *The forces of justice are coming, running.*
> *The forces of justice are drumming and coming.*
> *Gather your people and join.*
> *Come, come to Ninas Twei.*

Friday morning was the monthly meeting of the Robertsville Interfaith Council. Micah, Clare, and Keegan were regulars of the group comprised of Christians, Jews, Muslims, Hindus, Sikhs, atheists, and Buddhists. Most of the religious leaders in Robertsville attended, and many of their congregants, including Muriel and Mark Chase, Nicki Nichols, and her partner, Penny Waite. Jarvis had never been a member in the past, but at Micah's urging, decided to go.

They told the Interfaith Council about the missing children and Ninas Twei hoping the council would be a support for them even if they didn't quite accept it as truth – and some of them didn't, of course.

Nicki was astounded. "It's like you really believe all this stuff about another world, about this dance of all the species."

Keegan responded, "I was there, Nicki. I saw Hazel and Dan turn into a cougar and a hawk. I saw them shot. I touched their bodies. I believe."

Mark added, "I've been a doctor for many, many years, and I've seen some very strange and wonderful things – spontaneous healing, for instance. Things I didn't want to believe. I'm not so quick to pooh-pooh things anymore. The universe contains more than we understand."

The Sikh Gyani, Giaan Singh, suggested that people could just 'suspend their disbelief' and wait and see what happens, and Penny Waite, Nicki's partner, agreed.

"New adventures, Nicki," she exclaimed.

After the meeting the four ministers met with Yameno and the McCraes at Clare's home. Mark and Muriel Chase joined them.

Keegan talked to Yameno about his art. "I have a friend in Bayomar who runs an art gallery connected with a restaurant. I've already talked to him about taking some of your art to sell in Bayomar and he's interested. What do you think? I need to go to Bayomar on Monday and I could take some of them."

Yameno looked down at his hands. "I did sell my art right after I left collage in a few galleries in small towns along the coast in order to pay off my collage loans. But now I think of it as a gift to the earth. I like to give it away."

Keegan smiled at him. "But if it's kept in a garage how can it have an effect on others? It needs to be seen and people need to have it in their hands. Perhaps it will call to other people just as it has called us. And you can keep the prices low, but as Jesus says, *'the laborer is worthy of his hire'* – the artist is worthy of his pay."

"We're afraid it's not safe in Arundel, Yameno," Micah added. "With all this craziness about the devil what if someone decided to break into Jarvis' garage to destroy it?"

Yameno nodded, "Giselle's somewhere in Bayomar. Perhaps the art being there, too…"

"Yes," Keegan agreed. "Perhaps the art work will find its way to her somehow. She'll recognize it as yours, I'm sure."

"But the problem of violence in Arundel is much bigger than just the artwork," Jarvis added. "I started this business about the devil. I don't know if I can stop it."

"Perhaps if you preach about it?" Muriel suggested.

"Last Sunday I didn't show up for the service. I wanted to be with Yameno at the jail. The men who were there with us on the hunt all knew I was at the jail, but they didn't know I had changed my…"

He hesitated. "But they all know by now. They know I brought Yameno home from jail, and helped rescue his art work. And last night, Coffman…"

Clare smiled at him. "I think they'll be there this Sunday to find out why."

"Yes," agreed Keegan. "And some will be ready to listen to you. Many were taken aback by Amundsen's violence."

Dorotea had been fidgeting impatiently in her chair. "Yes," she said, jumping up, "but when will we try again to go to Ninas Twei? Shall we go now? Or tonight? We must rescue my Jesús and the girl."

Clare shuffled her feet nervously. "They'll be watching for us. They know we're trying to go to Ninas Twei."

"But we must go soon," argued Dorotea. "Tonight!"

Keegan shook his head. "They'll be watching all weekend. We need to go when they're doing something else – like working. Monday morning might work."

Yameno nodded his head. "Yes. They'll be at work, and if there's anyone reporting back to them maybe they'll know Keegan's headed to Bayomar on Monday. They might think we wouldn't try to go without Keegan guarding us."

"But we need someone to guard us," exclaimed Clare.

"Mark," Micah added, turning toward the doctor. "Mark can guard us."

"Yes, certainly. I'd like to," Mark agreed.

Billy turned to Dorotea holding her hand. "It's hard to wait, but if we're going to get there, we have to wait – just three more days."

Tears slipped down Dorotea's cheeks, but she managed to nod as she wiped her face with the back of a hand.

Something else of importance had happened at the Interfaith meeting that morning.

Micah turned to Yameno to tell him. "The county park – I think actually your clearing and the spring are a part of it. The county is thinking of selling it for logging."

"Logging?" asked Yameno, alarmed.

Micah continued. "The county is being pressured by the Greenlog Corporation to sell the park for logging. That would take in all the land from the campground to the ocean just south of the old Bidewell place."

"South of Giselle's house!" exclaimed Yameno. "The spring!"

Dorotea's eyes met Yameno's, and she cried out, *"No el manantial sagrado!"*

"The spring?" asked Muriel.

"Yes," answered Clare. "Yameno is charged with protecting a sacred spring at the top of the hill just south of the Bidewell place. Next to his clearing."

She turned to Mark. "Did you see it? It's very beautiful, a very holy place."

"Sacred to the Tuwillian people?" Muriel interrupted.

Yameno nodded.

"Perhaps we can fight the logging by proving this is a holy place to the local natives," she suggested.

"Or," Micah added, "When they find out about it they'll want to put a water bottling factory there and sell the water."

Eyes rolled and heads shook.

"They're also talking about fracking!" added Muriel, explaining that the Baptist minister had reported that one of his parishioners – a county employee – had told him. "He can't reveal the man's name, but an oil company has approached the county about using fracking to extract the oil in the shale in the coastal hills. They're working together with the logging company. Some of the county supervisors have been wined and dined."

"But," Mark hastened to add, "the Buddhist nun, Nanda, agreed to chair a committee to fight it. They'll talk to officials, get articles in the paper, and go to council meetings."

They'd also planned a demonstration coordinating with the One Earth Together worldwide demonstration at the end of the month. Nanda, he explained, had been excited about the totems that helped people become their Tla Twei that Clare'd told them about when talking about Ninas Twei and the children.

"This could be a way to show all the animals affected by the logging," she'd suggested. "We could carry pictures or sculptures of the many, many animals that make their homes in the forest. We could tell their stories."

"Pictures of animals and humans, too," Muriel had added. "Humans will be affected – children who swim at the river, fishermen. The river will be polluted by the logging. Our water supply will be contaminated. Especially if there's fracking."

"In our hills!" another woman had exclaimed. "No, we can't allow this. And we can't allow this spring to be destroyed. We must stop it!"

First Quarter in Arundel

It was after midnight that night when Yameno was finally able to get away from Jarvis' house to go check the clearing and the spring. His anxiety about the spring had grown from moment to moment.

The quarter moon made a path through the forest for the silver wolf, as he climbed the hill to his clearing, loped across, glancing at his broken house as he went by, and started down the path to the stream, stopping short when he heard muffled sounds.

Crawling down through the underbrush, he peered out at the waterfall. There was very little water in the pool and someone was standing in front of the crevice where the water usually poured out, pulling on something and sobbing. "No. You can't do this. You can't destroy it. I won't let you."

The person banged a hand against the side of the rock face by the hole. "Please, let me pull you out of there. Please!" He fell against the rock face, his arm under his head, weeping.

Who is this? thought Yameno. *What happened here?* He took human form and stepped out on to the bank. "Stop. What are you doing?"

Tom jumped away from the rock face, and Yameno could see that something had been jammed into the hole, damming the water so that only a trickle ran down the side of the rock. "They tried to destroy it," sobbed Tom. "My grandfather and the others tried to destroy it. I've pulled out a lot of the smaller stuff, but this one…" He turned and tried again to pull out a huge rock that had been jammed into the hole.

"Here." Yameno stepped into the pool beside Tom. "Let me help." He looked at the rock, and then hammered with his hand on one side so that it moved a little to the left where the top of the hole was just a little bit higher.

"I think they used a hammer to push it in," muttered Tom.

Yameno nodded. "Yes, but we'll get it out."

He turned to Tom. "I'm glad you care about the water, Tom." He looked carefully at Tom, noting his black hair, cut very short, and his dark eyes, his skin a much darker tone than that of his blonde grandfather.

"Tom, you live with your grandfather and your mother, right?" Tom nodded. "Who's your father?"

Tom shrugged. "I don't know. They won't tell me, and when I ask, my grandfather gets mad at my mother. Sometimes he hits her, so I don't ask anymore. She was married. She did tell me that."

Yameno nodded and turned back to loosening the rock. He remembered a story he had heard when he returned home for vacation his first year in college. A Tuwillian man, Yono – a little older than he was – had married a girl from town in secret. The man had left town suddenly. He'd never heard who the girl was. He'd thought she'd gone with him, but… The next time he came home for vacation there were only three Tuwillians – all elders – still in Arundel. Everyone else had left looking for work elsewhere. No one had said anything more about Yono and the girl. A few years later, his great aunt, the last of the elders, died and he'd returned to protect the spring.

The rock came loose and Tom helped him lift it back down into the stream bed. They watched as the pool began to fill again.

Tom wiped his eyes. Somehow he just couldn't stop crying. "How could they do it? How could they ruin this beautiful…" he sobbed. "The water is so sweet. They must never have tasted the water. They couldn't…" He turned his head away trying to stop the sobs.

Yameno smiled. "The water is running again. Come, let's offer a song to the water. I'll teach you." He sat down beside the pool, patting the ground beside him.

Tom wiped his eyes and sat. Yameno sang:

> *Water of life.*
> *Purify me.*
> *Water of the soul of earth,*
> *wash me in your love.*

"Wash me in your love," whispered Tom, reaching into the waterfall and splashing the water over his head.

It was a crisp, clear autumn Sunday morning when Muriel and Mark pulled up to Jarvis's little church.

They slid into a back pew. Mark noticed many of the men who'd been a part of the cougar hunt, including Coffman, were scattered with their families around the church, but most interesting was the underlying whispering and pointing at two banners, handwritten on rolls of shelf paper, that lined each side of the church.

"God is Love," they proclaimed in huge letters. The banners hadn't been there when Muriel had come just a week and a half before to the meeting about the cougar hunt.

The pianist played an introduction to the opening hymn, and the congregation stood for the processional of two people: first, a man Mark had seen at the hunt who was holding a Bible, and then Reverend Tarrant.

Jarvis turned just before the step and faced the congregation. "Oh, Lord, be with us as we explore your mysterious ways. Help us let go of old ideas and embrace new ones, as you present them to us. Amen." He turned and moved to a chair next to the pulpit.

The congregation sat, and the man who had processed with the Bible stood up and placed his Bible open on the lectionary. "A reading from Isaiah 29, verses 13 through 24:

> *These people draw near me with their mouth,*
> *and with their lips do honor me,*
> *but have removed their heart far from me,…*
> *Therefore, behold,*
> *I will proceed to do a marvelous work and a wonder, …*
> *And in that day shall the deaf hear…*
> *and the eyes of the blind shall see …*
> *the meek also shall increase their joy in the Lord,*
> *and the poor among men shall rejoice …*
> *For the … scorner is consumed*
> *and all that watch for iniquity are cut off…*
> *They also that erred in spirit shall come to understanding ….*

He closed the book and looked up at the congregation. "All rise and sing hymn number 370, *This is a Day of New Beginnings.*" The pianist played the introduction and the congregation stood and sang.

As the congregation sat after the hymn, Jarvis moved to the podium. "Let us pray: Isaiah says, 'They that erred in spirit shall come to understanding.' Lord, I have allowed my own fears to rule my life and this church. I have turned my love into hate, and have preached that hate when I should have preached love. My eyes and my ears have been closed to you, and you have been 'like a book sealed from me'. Hear my confession. Amen."

He raised his head and looked at one of the banners. "God is Love," he whispered, and turned to face the congregation leaning with both hands on the podium.

"Once when I was a child, I knew and loved another child. She was my friend and a delight to my heart."

He looked out at his parishioners. "Many of you also knew that child, and have known her as an adult as well. That child was Hazel Fraya."

The congregation stirred and muttered. Mark noticed particularly the way Coffman sat up and hunched forward, anger written on his shoulders and rigidly held head.

"Most of you know the story," Jarvis continued, "of how a young man came to town – a dark skinned man who went to live with Hazel Fraya's family. Many of you were among my friends who refused to allow that young man to participate in our teenage activities. Many of you, and I foremost among us, gossiped and railed against the friendship that developed between that young man and Hazel."

He sighed, looking down at his hands and then back out at the people. "Oh, Lord, I confess today my recognition that my behavior toward Dan Burroughs and Hazel Fraya was sinful – a degradation of two of your people, your creations. Lord, and my congregation, I ask your forgiveness."

The congregation seemed frozen, wide-eyed, as they stared at Jarvis, most leaning forward in their seats.

Coffman broke the silence, standing suddenly and shaking a fist toward Jarvis. "What are you doing? They're sinners. They're the devil. You know it."

Jarvis raised his hand to silence Coffman. "Wait, Coffman. Wait and listen. When I'm finished you can speak your thoughts."

Coffman looked around at the people in the congregation, and reluctantly sat down.

"Last Saturday," Jarvis continued, "many of you were with me when we went cougar hunting, but surely also hunting for Hazel and Dan, and Yameno Wellkeeper."

He paused and looked out at Coffman. "Many of you witnessed the miracle I witnessed."

"Miracle?" yelled Coffman skeptically.

Jarvis held up his hand again. "Yes, miracle, and most of you, I know, have heard the story told by the school teacher and Yameno – a story of hope, of community, and surely of God."

He leaned farther into the podium looking at each of his congregation in turn, and took a deep breath. "I had an epiphany that morning, a revelation. At the moment of Hazel's death – that moment when, just after she manifested as a cougar, the bullet struck her, and she screamed and died – I was stunned, struck by my sins."

He took a deep breath and turned away for a moment, running a hand across his eyes.

Turning back, he continued: "Memories of our childhood flowed through my mind – of the way she cared for her little sister, of the kittens in her pockets and on her shoulders. Many of you remember that happy child."

He paused, and Muriel looked around the congregation. Some were nodding their heads.

"I loved her, and yet I turned away from love and learned to hate her, and then I promoted that idea of hate to all of you. Hazel and her family understood about God's acceptance of all peoples, no matter what the color of their skin. It was her family that loved and accepted Dan Burroughs and Yameno, as equals, as God's creatures. The rest of us, in turning toward bigotry, turned away from God."

"No," yelled Coffman, standing and stomping his feet, quickly joined by some of the other men. "No! They're the children of Ham. They're consorting with the devil. They're evil. You lusted after Hazel and she's used that to turn you to the devil."

Jarvis's eyes were wide. He held his hands up trying to calm Coffman.

A woman pulled on her husband's arm, whispering to him, trying to get him to sit down. "Silence, woman," the man yelled, raising his hand in a threatening manner. "A woman's to be silent in church, and obey her husband."

Muriel gasped. Mark started to stand, reaching toward the man.

Jarvis stepped out from behind the podium. "Enough. Sit down, all of you." His voice was quiet and yet carried throughout the little church. One by one the men sat down.

When Coffman was the only one still standing, Jarvis looked at him and waited. Finally, he sat.

Jarvis continued, his eyes boring into Coffman, his voice rich and full. "The story they told was about God's creations. It was about community, and love, and caring for the earth. Psalm 24 says, 'The earth is the Lord's and the fullness thereof; the world, and they that dwell therein… Who shall ascend into the hill of the Lord? Or who shall stand in his holy place? He that has a pure heart.'"

He stepped forward and surveyed the people. "Not – as Isaiah pointed out in the reading this morning – not 'the scorner,' or those that 'watch for iniquity' – that is, those who point out the sins of others – but," he paused, his eyes searching through the congregation, "but 'he that has a pure heart.'"

He looked down at the floor for a moment, an audible breath catching in his throat. "You'll all have to make up your own minds. You can listen to me, and Ms. Raphael, and Yameno Wellkeeper. You can listen to your friends," he nodded toward Coffman, "who were also there, but it's a time for opening your eyes and your ears – and most of all your hearts – listening and making your own decisions. Not a time for blind following."

He turned toward the pianist. "Let's sing the closing hymn, number 203, *Amazing Grace.*"

Mark smiled. *A good song,* he thought, *written by the captain of a slave ship, who came to understand his own evil – slavery, greed, the overwhelming desire for money, and the things it can buy, that blinds us to love.*

The pianist began the introduction to the song. The congregation rose to sing, but as they began, Coffman pushed his way out of the row and down the aisle toward the door, pushing his daughter and Tom in front of him. He was yelling, "Sinners. You're all sinners."

A few of the men followed, dragging their wives after them, but the rest raised their voices, first tentatively, and then with more strength:

> *Amazing grace! How sweet the sound,*
> *That saved a wretch like me!*
> *I once was lost, but now am found,*
> *Was blind, but now I see. (John Newton)*

Dorotea in Ninas Twei

Dorotea thought Monday took a long time coming. She had gardened and fidgeted all Sunday afternoon and hardly slept at all Sunday night.

There were no cars on the coast road at all when they turned off at Giselle's place at 9:00 that morning. Mark had picked up Billy, Dorotea, Jarvis, and Yameno hoping his car would not be recognized. Micah came in Clare's car and both drivers managed to pull their cars up beside the house so they were hidden from the road.

They climbed as silently as possible up the trail to the clearing, settling in a circle as before. Dorotea held tight to Billy's hand as they drank the water, and watched the mist form around them.

It was an incredible experience, full of spiraling mists and joyous music – wonderful to be a killdeer and to see Billy as a big hairy bear! The mourning dove, and horned lizard were also delighted with their new personas. The fox pranced.

Then there was the glorious dance of all the species – the Tsin Twei. She would never forget it – never in her whole life. But still one part of her mind focused on Jesús.

After the Tsin Twei they met Singing Swan, who was overcome with joy to see Yameno. "You returned to the world on your own," he exclaimed. "I was so worried when the ground shook so hard and you didn't come back."

But he knew nothing about the children, had not seen Luhanada Moonmother or Tata Sundancer. He pointed at the place in the Din Tsin Twei where Chachuli had led the others through the crack in the cliffs to the other side, looking for the source of the pain.

"Later that day," he said, "there was more pain, and the earth shook again. There was a rock fall inside the tunnel blocking it."

He shook his feathered head at Yameno. "You never came back."

"It must have been the same earthquake we felt – the one that opened the crevice the children fell down."

"Yes," nodded the old swan. "But now you're here. That's a good sign. Perhaps we'll find another way to the other side of the cliffs."

"And maybe Luha and Tata are there trying to find the children," added Yameno.

Dorotea, the killdeer, peered into the blocked tunnel, and then looked up at the towering cliffs. "Maybe the mourning dove and I could fly over?"

She looked up, and up. The cliffs seemed to reach the sky.

Singing Swan shook his head. "I've tried. The higher I fly, the higher they get."

But she needed to try, so the little killdeer and the larger mourning dove, launched themselves in the air and circled Din Tsin Twei going up, and up, and up. It seemed they would never reach the top.

Suddenly, they felt a sharp jolt of pain, the earth shook below them and rocks rolled down the cliff sides. They flew as fast as they could down to the others, who had been thrown to the ground, and the killdeer dug her claws into the bear's thick fur.

The world whirled around them, gray spiraling mists seeming to clutch at them as they tumbled and fell back to the clearing, sitting in the circle, the empty water cups sitting on the ground in front of them.

Singing Swan, who had fluttered into the air when the earth shook, flew anxiously back and forth in the amphitheater trumpeting his distress. Finally the shaking stopped and he landed back on the amphitheater floor.

The travelers had all disappeared. *Back to the world,* he hoped, shaking his head sorrowfully.

"What's happening to Ninas Twei?" he whispered, looking around at the cliffs soaring above him, the wonderful craggy rocks that so often held the dancers, the grandsouls of all the species except his own.

What will happen to the earth, he thought, *if something happens to Ninas Twei?*

He swung his head back and forth checking the spiraling rows of the amphitheater looking for damage. High on the cliffs in a line above the blocked tunnel, blue sky shining through a crack caught his eye — a new, narrow crack very high in the cliffs, but right above the blocked tunnel!

He launched himself into the air, and pushed with his powerful wings — up and up until he could fly past it. *Another very small tunnel to the other side,* he thought. *Too small for me, but a killdeer could fit through it — a killdeer, and maybe the dove, too.* As he glided back down to the ground, he hoped they would come again soon, before this crack was swallowed up by the earthquakes.

Micah called Keegan's cell as soon as they returned from Ninas Twei.

"We went and it was beautiful!" he exclaimed. "I've never seen anything like it, but the end was a disaster."

He told of the closed tunnel, of Dorotea and Clare's attempt to fly over the cliffs and the sudden earthquake that sent them back to Yameno's clearing. "We tried to return to Ninas Twei right away," he added, "but nothing happened. We couldn't go back."

It was the next night that Giselle went to dinner with Monica and Rod at the restaurant in Bayomar and discovered Yameno's paintings.

210

3

Hunter's Moon, Waxing Gibbous

A stony silence prevailed over the rest of Giselle's dinner with Monica and Rod. When they turned her over to the night shift nurse at Kavanaugh House, Giselle broke the silence only to glare at Rod and repeat, "You got me into this, Rod, and you're going to get me out."

Rod exchanged looks with Monica and neither one of them said a word as they left.

Giselle turned to the nurse. "I'd like to use the phone."

"I'm sorry, dear, but you're only allowed to call your sister," the nurse returned, taking Giselle's arm to propel her toward her room. Giselle shook her off and walked rapidly down the corridor staying ahead of the nurse who followed and whispered something to the aide who sat guard in the hallway.

Giselle slammed her door. There was no lock.

The next day she waited anxiously for Shen Ch'i. When he arrived she told him everything.

He listened gravely, nodding his head. When she came to the part about Ninas Twei, he looked directly at her for a moment. "I saw something about this on the internet. "I'm not sure…" His voice faded away.

She continued, asking him if he wouldn't at least contact Father Gilchrist for her and find out what was happening to Yameno.

"Yes," he said, "I'll be glad to contact this Father Gilchrist. I'll also go and look at these paintings and sculptures at the gallery."

He paused, thinking. "And yes, I don't believe you belong in here, although this story of journeying to this other place – another dimension, perhaps – is very… well, shall we say, out of the ordinary?"

He smiled. "But we can take one step at a time. I was planning to ask if you'd like to go tonight to the InterPlay class my daughter teaches at Shanti Place. It's a shelter for homeless teenagers."

"Will they let me go with you?"

"Yes. I can get permission to take you. Actually, I was thinking, since you're a teacher, and they badly need people to teach the young people who come to them for help, you might be willing to volunteer there. Patients who are nonviolent are often allowed to work or volunteer on the outside.

"Also…" he smiled, "I looked at your case papers. It may seem as if your sister is in control of your life, but she isn't your legal guardian. You actually signed papers yourself to come here. Some staff have a tendency to act as if the relatives of patients are 'the boss', but it's not legally true when patients come voluntarily. You can leave whenever you want to. I think you should make sure leaving doesn't put you at risk of jail before making a decision to go, but you can go with me to Shanti Place tonight and volunteer there without your sister's permission."

Giselle was elated and apprehensive at the same time. She paced the paths of the garden all afternoon, waiting for dinner, and for Shen Ch'i to pick her up afterwards.

Shen Ch'i made arrangements for Giselle to go to the class with him and then went to the art gallery to see Yameno's paintings and sculptures. A vivid painting in beautiful greens and browns of a vine wrapping itself around a giant oak tree with roots that spun around a miniature earth caught his eye almost immediately. It was set in a universe of whorls of deep blue inlaid with spirals of yellow.

As he looked closer, he realized it wasn't just a vine wrapped around an oak, but hidden in the vine and the tree was a dragon. The scales and the wings of the dragon were formed of leaves. The feet were five-lobed oak leaves with tree roots for claws. The earth was the dragon's crystal ball, painted in luminous greens and blues, and the deep red and orange trumpet flowers flaming joyously out toward the universe came from the dragon's mouth.

Golden eyes pierced with black peered at him. He shivered. A whispering sound, a song…

212

Rooted in the soil
My flames fire the skies
Union of heaven and earth.

Shen Ch'i looked around. No one was there.

He turned back to the dragon, seeing something deep in the golden eyes, some small flash of light in the middle of the black, black pupils. *Are you singing?* he thought. *Are you singing to me?*

Earth crystal my home
Universe my joy
My deep hymn to creation.

And then louder, fiercer…

Rooted in the soil
My flames fire the skies
I am the union of heaven and earth.

He shook his head and smiled at the proprietor as he pulled out his wallet. "It's Ti-Tien-Lung, the dragon of heaven and earth. I have to have this."

The man nodded. "It seems to be that way. Either people don't notice this man's work at all, or they get caught up in one piece, and then pull out their wallets! I have one myself that I just couldn't put on display. I knew when I saw it, it was mine."

He laughed and shrugged his shoulders. "Hard to explain, exactly."

Shen Ch'i nodded, smiling.

He took his painting home and placed it on a table leaning against the wall, so that he could look at it while he telephoned Father Gilchrist. He explained his connection to Giselle and that she'd told him about the journey to Ninas Twei.

"What's your feeling about all this?" he asked.

"Ah," Keegan replied, pausing. "Either several of us have been having a mass hallucination or it's all true. I'm not sure how a physicist would explain it, but…"

He told Shen Ch'i everything he'd seen and heard, and about the latest trip to Ninas Twei and the failed search for the children. "So you see, I'm not alone in believing Giselle and Yameno's story, and some of the others have actually experienced Ninas Twei and the Tsin Twei – the dance of life – as well."

His voice dropped almost to a whisper. "And I hope I get to go there, too."

"Yes, I see," Shen Ch'i responded. He told about finding the Ti-Tien-Lung.

"Maybe the Ti-Tien-Lung's your Tla Twei," Keegan suggested. "Maybe you're a future visitor to Ninas Twei."

"That, I think," responded Shen Ch'i, "would be a great privilege."

"Yes," Keegan agreed. "A privilege."

For a moment both men were deep in thought, then Keegan spoke. "Please report what's happening here to Giselle, and you and I must meet, maybe on my next trip down to Bayomar."

In the car driving over to the class at the homeless shelter, Shen Ch'i told Giselle about his trip to the gallery, and his conversation with Gilchrist.

Giselle was delighted with the story of the dragon, but anxious when she heard about the failed search. "I want to be there."

"Maybe you're meant to be here."

"But the children…"

"Yes, they're worried, too. They think – they hope the cougar and the hawk are there with the children. Right now it seems we have to wait. This class tonight will help with that, I think."

Giselle sighed, and then asked him to tell her more about the class.

"The kids move, dance, sing, and tell stories to one another. They can express themselves freely in words, and non-verbally, with their bodies and their wordless voices." He smiled at her. "Sometimes we can't use words to tell our stories. Sometimes we don't even know our own stories in words, but our bodies, when we let them just move, find a way to help us see our stories and give us answers, too."

He was silent for a bit. "You'll see. You'll find your answers, too."

The shelter was mostly one really big room in the basement of a church. There were folding tables which were put away at night so the youngsters could curl up to sleep in blankets and sleeping bags laid out on foam pads. There was a kitchen to one side where the meals were

214

prepared, with the help of the youngsters who took turns cooking, serving, and cleaning up. One corner held a couple of old sofas.

A shelter counselor sat at a desk by the front door.

When Shen Ch'i and Giselle arrived, the tables had already been put away in anticipation of An Lien's class. Shen Ch'i introduced Giselle to the woman at the desk and they walked into the room.

The youngsters ranged in age from twelve to seventeen. They were a mix of ethnicities, and some of them, Giselle noticed, had dogs.

Shen Ch'i explained. "The dogs are very important. They're their family. As long as the dogs are well behaved they're welcome, but the staff's very strict about doggy behavior! Some dogs and owners have been sent to the animal shelter for obedience training."

Some of the young people hung back against the edges of the room, arms folded defensively in front of their chests, but many came eagerly up to Shen Ch'i, giving little bows with their hands pressed together in front of them.

Shen Ch'i returned their bows.

One younger black girl bowed and then quickly hugged him. He returned the hug, smiling sweetly. "Good evening, Miesha. How has your week been?"

Before she could answer, an older black boy, who hung back on the edges of the group, interrupted.

"Hey, Shen, who's the babe?" He nodded at Giselle.

Shen Ch'i motioned toward the young man. "Giselle, this is Sidney. Sidney, this young *woman*, is a teacher. Her name is Giselle Raphael."

"Hey," Sidney nodded at her, and with a small apologetic grin added, "Sorry for the babe comment. I forgot that's not okay, but I'm learning."

Giselle gave a nod and a smile, "Glad to meet you, Sidney."

Just then a slender young woman in a wheelchair came in the door behind them. Miesha ran over to her and got a really big hug.

"An Lien, An Lien, guess what I've been doing?" She didn't wait for an answer. "I've been singing on the street! Just walking down the street singing!"

An Lien laughed, nodding and clapping her hands, her short black hair flying around her face.

Sidney rolled his eyes. "She did. We all hung way back so's no one'd think she was with us."

The girl punched him in the arm. "You did not. You told me to sing. You dared me and I did it."

He grinned down at her, rubbing his arm.

She turned back to An Lien. "And you know what? In that OET demonstration, we're all going to sing and dance right down the middle of the street."

An Lien grinned. "Good. We'll all be there! We'll dance and sing together!"

"They're participating in the demonstration?" Giselle asked Shen Ch'i, quietly.

One Earth Together, she thought. *She hadn't been online to find out what was going on with the demonstration and the world since she was arrested.* She remembered how important OET had been as a connector of people on the Weaving Tree.

"Yes," he smiled. "It's just a couple of weeks away – a big demonstration here and all over the world. People marching for peace and justice, for sustainable living, for dealing with global warming – all of it!"

He gestured toward An Lien, "This is my beautiful daughter."

Giselle felt an immediate bond with An Lien. *Safe,* she thought. *I feel safe with her and with Shen Ch'i.* She felt her body sigh with relief.

An Lien's class was amazing. Not all the young people participated, but Giselle noticed that the ones rolled in their sleeping bags against the walls were quiet – were listening.

First they did some exercises, stretching their hands upward – "running their fingers through the milky way," as An Lien described it – reaching toward the floor, swinging their arms around themselves and more. Giselle joined in, but also watched with delight the grace and beauty of An Lien's movements, the way the chair became one with her as she moved it back and forth, and spun it around.

After that they did what An Lien called a "walk, stop, run"; moving around the room forwards and backwards; laughing and saying, "Thank you," when they bumped into each other; following each other's antics; taking off suddenly pushing An Lien's chair in a careful "run", and giggling. Lots of giggling.

But the part Giselle loved the most came after when they gathered in a circle, humming together and then breaking out into incredible wordless harmony. An Lien led them in a spiraling path around the room, first into the center and then back out again, the harmonies soaring and dipping, the children adding rhythms, clapping their hands and drumming on their bodies.

And the room disappeared, filling with a swirling mist, the dancing bodies swirling into the center, the harmonies a background accompaniment as Giselle heard again the song of Tsin Twei, the dance of life.

(We are the One and the many.
We are the life force,
We are the center,
We are the all,
The nameless and the named.
We are the whole, greater than the parts.)

She sang a whispered counterpoint:

Come, come! Hammer your feet to the beat of the drum.
Come, come! Lift up your voice to answer the One.
Come, come! Answer the call of the earth and the sun!

And was that the Wolfwind by her side…? A shadowy… something?

It was a wonderful evening. Giselle hated returning to her empty room at Kavanaugh House.

The next day Shen Ch'i made arrangements for Giselle to start work at Shanti Place. She was to remain at Kavanaugh House for the moment and go to Shanti Place by subway for part of the day to tutor the children, who were not allowed in the Bayomar School District because they didn't have a home address in the city.

She was offered a small salary. Not much, but it would probably cover the cost of renting a room when Giselle could move out of Kavanaugh House – something Shen Ch'i was also working on. *It can't happen quickly enough,* thought Giselle.

She started teaching Friday morning.

Shanti Place offered some counseling, some food, and a place to sleep, but had no resources or authority to force the children to come to class.

Giselle noticed that the teens split themselves into several different groups. Miesha and Sidney were in the most open and friendly of the groups, mixed in ethnicity, gender, and sexual orientation, including a transgendered girl, Maria. She had met a lot of the members of this group in An Lien's class.

Sidney seemed to be their leader, and when she arrived, at Sidney's urging, the kids in his group quickly gathered at the tables shoved together in the middle of the room. The other kids sat on the floor up against the walls in small closed circles communicating only with each other; some were rolled up in sleeping bags, apparently still asleep.

Deborah, one of the counselors, took her to each group, introduced her, and tried to get the young people to come to Giselle's class.

Most of them barely acknowledged the introduction.

Giselle was struck by their homogeneity. One group of seven was all black, mostly boys, and another smaller group, all Latinos. A third group contained only three Asian boys, and a fourth larger group was all white.

Giselle spent the morning finding out how many of the students at her tables had been in school before and for how long. One of the youngsters said he was just dumb – he would never be able to learn anything.

"No," Giselle, responded with a smile. "Everyone can learn, but we all have different ways of learning, and a different speed. No one's dumb."

"We all different, huh." agreed Miesha. "We just different. Don't mean we aren't okay."

"Yeah," agreed Giselle. "Exactly. We're all a little different from each other. Some learn better with their eyes, and others with their ears, for instance. Some learn better dancing."

"Dancing!" exclaimed one boy. "How can we learn while we're dancing?"

"It's true, it's true." Miesha did a little dance move with her hands. "I learn all kinds of things when I'm dancing with An Lien."

"Oh, shut up, Miesha," yelled someone from one of the outer groups.

Miesha glared at him, but Giselle took note. The folks in the little closed groups, even if they pretended not to participate, were listening.

After that first teaching session, Miesha, Sidney, and Maria showed Giselle around the neighborhood. Giselle noticed that Maria stayed close either to her, or to Sidney. *She doesn't feel safe,* she thought. *She's right. Even here in Bayomar she's not safe.*

First they proudly toured their urban farm, located in a vacant lot across from Shanti Place. "We get a lot of our food from our garden. We're planting winter stuff now, like squash." Sidney wrinkled his nose and laughed. "I'm learning to eat all kinds of weird stuff."

Some of the young people who had been in class with her that morning were working in the garden under the supervision of Reverend Meg, the minister of the church, and Yasar, a sweet Palestinian man who volunteered.

"He volunteered to help us learn how to garden," explained Sidney later, "but he listens – really listens to us. Sometimes Rev-Meg refers to him as the 'listening post.'"

The children explained that they planned to take some of their vegetables to display as they marched in the OET demonstration. "We'll show them even city homeless kids can grow their own food," one girl told her earnestly.

"Yeah," said another, "in an urban garden."

As they moved on down the street, the students introduced Giselle to several friendly homeless adults.

Most responded to her, "How are you?" with, "I'm blessed."

It always seemed incredible, this response, "I'm blessed." *They have to scramble for a bed in one of the shelters at night, and are kicked out during the day. They have very little food, no money, no way to get a job, and yet they say, "I'm blessed." It's an affirmation,* she thought – *a way of affirming to themselves that no matter what, they are human, they are real, they are okay.*

As they came around a corner Giselle could hear someone chanting. She looked up to see a tall black woman with beautiful big brown eyes, her dreadlocked hair gathered in a scarf at her back. She was dressed in long ragged skirts over skirts, like petticoats, with a full sleeved top under a long tunic, all covered by a long, faded cape.

The chanting woman, she thought. *This is the woman I saw last summer outside the restaurant! The woman who sang to me.*

As before, the woman was chanting in some unknown language, her hands raised to the sky. People walking on the streets glanced at her and then away, avoiding getting too close and yet clearly fascinated by the beauty of the song.

Miesha walked over to her, trying to catch her eye. Gradually the woman became aware of her, and brought her chant to an end, lowering her arms and turning to smile at the girl.

"Ayoabia Asukiye, this is our new friend – our new teacher, Giselle." Miesha pulled Giselle close.

Ayo looked for a long moment at Giselle and then nodded. "You have returned."

She started singing:

> *You have become.*
> *You have emerged.*
> *You have returned.*
> *You have returned!*

Giselle felt a wild thrill vibrating through her, a desire to answer the chant with one of her own.

"I have returned," she whispered, and then a little louder. "I have returned!"

She's right, she thought. *I have. I have returned. I am the Earth Woman Tree Woman and I have returned!* And she thrust her own arms wide singing:

> *I am the fullness,*
> *I am the secret.*
> *I am the answer,*
> *the bearer of life.*
> *I am the singer,*
> *I am the weeper.*
> *I am the leader,*
> *the edge of the knife.*

And the woman joined her in a duet winding her words through Giselle's:

> *I am the fullness, the secret,*
> *You are the singer, the weeper,*

I am the secret, bearer of life,
The answer, the edge of the knife!

Mists wound around them, spiraling in and out between them, dancing in muted colors and Giselle thought she heard the faint howls of a wolf pack:

I am the singer, the weeper,
You are the fullness, the secret,
I am the answer, the leader,
The bearer of life,
The secret, the edge of the knife!

Ayoabia smiled. "You are," she whispered. "You are."

A small movement brought Giselle's awareness to Miesha who was looking at her intently. The girl turned toward Ayoabia and their eyes met.

Ayo smiled and nodded.

Miesha smiled back her eyes twinkling with suppressed excitement.

Then Ayoabia turned back toward the street and raising her arms again continued chanting.

Miesha grabbed Giselle's hand and pulled her away. "You sang, too! You sang like Ayoabia." She clapped her hands and danced around, grinning. "I'm gonna sing on the streets, too. I am!" She leaned in and whispered. "We gonna do it together!"

Then as they continued on down the street, she added in a low voice, "Some people think she really crazy. Do you?"

Giselle looked at Miesha. "I'm not sure what it means to be crazy, but no, Miesha, I don't think she's crazy."

When they arrived back at Shanti Place, Deborah was waiting for Giselle. "I want to talk to you before you return to Kavanaugh House."

They sat down in Deborah's tiny office – clearly once a closet. "Do you have any questions?" Deborah asked.

"Yes, actually. I didn't think to ask Shen Ch'i about the origins of Shanti Place. I thought it might be Buddhist, because of its name, but it's located in a protestant church."

"It's not Buddhist. It's not any one religion. The name comes from both Hindu and Buddhist traditions and means 'peace'.

"Shanti Place was formed by a group of women – Christian pastors and priests, nuns, Jewish rabbis, and Buddhist priests. We started getting together to work on the sexism we were experiencing in our various congregations, but then found we had a lot of other, more positive common ground between our religions – like the imperative to serve the poor. We decided we wanted to do a project together. The project was Shanti Place."

She shifted in her seat and leaned closer. "But I want to talk to you about some of the groups at Shanti Place so you'll understand – well I don't understand." She smiled and shrugged her shoulders. "But at least you'll know about some of the problems."

She took a deep breath before continuing.

"They really come from every ethnic group. Of course, the poorest groups contribute the most kids – although until recently we had few Latinos. But that's changing. Now we're seeing kids who were born here whose parents have been deported, or taken to detention centers."

She looked up at Giselle. "Detention centers owned by private corporations who are making a mint off the 'immigration problem.'"

Giselle nodded. "Yes, I know about the private detention centers and prisons."

Deborah sighed. "As for the rest, most have been kicked out or have run away from abusive situations. Some of them are gay or lesbian and have been rejected by their families. They're all forgotten by the world."

Another head shake. "They should all be working together to make the world better for themselves, and each other, but instead they gather in these little groups – you saw them this morning. A group of white kids here and another group of black kids over there. They spend a lot of time dissing each other. I try hard to keep it from happening here, but out on the streets there're stronger influences."

"I noticed that they seem to hang together by their ethnicity – except for the group that's working with me – Sidney's group."

"Yes, Sidney's group. He's wonderful. He really sees everyone as being okay, rather than getting entrenched in this 'my group is better than your group stuff.' His group is the only one really open to the gays and lesbians, too – although sometimes the gays and lesbians form their own little groups, too."

Giselle interrupted. "But racism's everywhere in our world. It's hard for them to escape it. They grow up hearing stereotypes, and ugly lies about the groups they aren't a part of."

"Yes," Deborah nodded, and then went on to explain the different groups. "Dirk is the leader of the current group of white boys. They call themselves The Avengers." She laughed. "I don't know what they're 'avenging' but they really believe white people are better than everyone else and the bad things that have happened to them can be blamed on black people and immigrants – mostly Latinos – but they don't like the Asians either."

She grimaced. "Like almost everyone else here, the families are very poor, mostly they come from homes where their parents were very young when they married – if they married – and the fathers deserted the mothers. A lot of them have never known their fathers."

"Are they all boys?" asked Giselle.

"No, but the girls that hang with them are very subservient. They get treated really badly, but they come out of the same kinds of homes. They've seen their moms treated badly, so they think that's the way it has to be. This is true for the girls in all the groups other than Sidney's group. He won't allow it."

She leaned forward. "But we do have more success with the girls than the boys in all the groups. The girls – oh, and the gay boys, too – are more open to the possibility of personal change. Just accepting for themselves the idea that they're gay means they don't have to follow the stereotype of the 'real man'. They're not caught up in that macho thing – the need to be tough.

"The straight boys have a harder road because of the roles that society imposes on them and they don't want to blame the situation they find themselves in on the people they think of as heroes – role models. So the boys in the Avengers blame it on the blacks and Latinos. We try hard to change that model."

She sat back. "Of course, we have had groups that were all girls, too. Very anti-men. We lost a group like that not too long ago."

"You lost them?"

"Yes. They disappear. They just don't come back and we don't know where they go."

"Is it just a turn over? They travel on or something?"

"Maybe. There're outside influences and I haven't been able to figure out who they are, but the kids leave as a group. They're just gone – down the road to some other town, I guess. We have no way of knowing. And," she shook her head, "this is the weird thing. They leave their dogs behind. The dogs return here, and someone else adopts them."

"That's very strange."

Deborah shrugged. "We can't figure it out. It's all… well, odd."

When Giselle got back to Kavanaugh House that afternoon, she found that Shen Ch'i had talked to Rod, and to the prosecutor in Arundel. Both had reluctantly agreed that there was no legal way they could keep Giselle at Kavanaugh House, if she didn't want to stay.

"Where can I go?" Giselle asked him. "Should I return to Arundel? I don't have a job there now, but I love it and…" *Yameno,* she thought. *I want to be with Yameno.*

Shen Ch'i looked at her thoughtfully. "I don't know, but I think you're meant to stay here – to work at Shanti Place, for a while at least."

A smile flashed over Giselle's face as she remembered the encounter with Ayoabia. *Yes,* she thought, *I've returned. Ayoabia predicted it and it happened.*

She nodded her head. "Yes. It feels right to be at Shanti Place, but… I want to see Yameno. And my dogs and my cat…" It felt like she was torn in two.

"Well," he smiled at her. "I had this thought. We can find a place for you to live near Shanti Place this weekend. Then next weekend, we can go together to Arundel. I'd like to meet Yameno and Father Gilchrist. An Lien could come, too. You could bring back some of your things, maybe the animals, too. The van is big even with An Lien's chair in it."

Giselle nodded. "I can't tell you how much I appreciate your help. I don't know what I would have done." Her eyes filled with tears.

Shen Ch'i patted her shoulder. "But you've also brought me something precious – a new purpose to my life."

Giselle spent the rest of the afternoon packing the few things she had at Kavanaugh House.

In the evening, Monica came to visit. Giselle stiffened her back prepared for a fight, but her sister didn't seem to have any fight left. She handed over Giselle's cell phone and her keys.

"But you're staying in Bayomar, right?" she added. "You're not going back up there?"

Giselle explained she would be looking for a room near Shanti Place.

"That's a dangerous area where that Shanti Place is. I don't like the idea of you working there, much less living there. We've rented your apartment, so you can't come back with us, but there are places nearby. We could find you a place nearby."

Giselle just shook her head.

"It would be expensive," Monica continued, "and you aren't getting paid much to work in this Shanti place. But if you weren't paying rent on the place in Arundel…"

"No." Giselle took a deep breath and smiled gently at Monica. "I'll be fine. I'm doing what I need to do. And Monica," she took her sister's hand, "you did a good job raising me, but now you need to let go. I'm not your responsibility any more. Let go. It will be better for you, and for me."

A few tears rolled down Monica's cheeks. Giselle stood up and pulled Monica up into her arms. They stood together, hugging and rocking, until Monica's tears stopped.

When Monica pulled away, she looked at Giselle and nodded her head. "Okay. Okay, I'll try. I'll try to let go."

She looked away for a moment, and then back at Giselle adding fiercely, "But you better not get hurt. You better not do anything stupid and get hurt."

Giselle started to laugh. "Oh, Monica," she exclaimed. "I can't promise that, and you can't promise me you won't get hurt driving down the street. Let's just love each other now and not worry anymore."

Monica nodded her head, and finally, smiled.

After Monica left, Giselle called Father Gilchrist asking how she could contact Yameno. He gave her Jarvis' phone number.

Yameno was overjoyed to hear from her. "Giselle, I was so afraid…"

He told her about the new group and the trip to Ninas Twei on Monday. "We've tried three times to go since then, but we've failed every time. Absolutely nothing has happened. No mist. No music. I'm frightened for the children and for the Tsin Twei."

Giselle shivered. "I hope Hazel and Dan…"

"Yes, me too…" His voice trailed off.

"Oh," he added, "I didn't tell you about the spring and Tom."

"Tom?"

"Yes, Coffman's grandson. I think he's half Tuwillian. His father might be…" and he went on to tell Giselle about the attempted sabotage of the spring and meeting Tom.

"Another guardian?"

"Yes. I don't feel so alone trying to protect… and the members of the InterFaith Council, too. They'll help protect the spring."

Giselle told him of Shanti Place, of Shen Ch'i thinking she was needed in Bayomar, and of singing with Ayoabia. "It was like when we sang going to the Tsin Twei. When our voices mixed it was… it was… I don't know how to describe it – and Yameno, when An Lien led the InterPlay class singing and dancing, I heard the music of the Tsin Twei – and there was mist, and I thought you… at least the wolf pack…."

"But you didn't go to Ninas Twei?"

"No, but I heard the music as if there was a connection… And it felt as if you… Well, like you were there with me."

"We're linked, you know," he whispered. "Earth and tree, wolf and wind and water. Linked."

"Wolf and wind, earth and tree, and water," she repeated. "Yes."

And it was if she could feel the wolf sitting right next to her, leaning into her…

She pushed the phone closer to her ear, listening to his breath.

Yameno broke the silence. "I wonder who Ayoabia is? Singing Swan said there're others who come to Ninas Twei from other places. Is she one of them? Or something else?"

"I don't know. She's just… different. She's – I don't know what to say, but she feels right. She feels important."

"Yes," Yameno agreed. "Yes."

He was silent, thinking. "We were able to go to Ninas Twei once without you. I don't think the problem for us is here, but at Ninas Twei. The earthquake…"

Giselle shuddered remembering the pain the last time.

Yameno's voice dropped. "But I miss you."

"Me, too." Her eyes filled and she rubbed the tears away.

Not long after breakfast on Saturday morning, Shen Ch'i and An Lien came to take Giselle room hunting. "There's a building across the street from my apartment that has rooms to rent," exclaimed An Lien. "It's just a few blocks from Shanti Place. It's not fancy, but it's clean and the landlady is nice."

She looked back and forth between her dad and Giselle. "Should we try there first?"

Giselle nodded and Shen Ch'i smiled at his daughter. "Excellent. Things are falling in place. A good sign."

The building was old and shabby, but the room was full of light, with tall ceilings and big windows. It had its own small bathroom, obviously added in recent years, but no cooking facilities.

"If you want, you can eat breakfast and dinner at Shanti Place with the kids. The kids are on their own for lunch," added An Lien. "The kids and the staff would like that. Then you wouldn't have to worry about where to eat."

Giselle nodded her head. The room felt comfortable – right – and An Lien was just across the street. She could see the entrance to An Lien's new six story building from her window. It would be fun to eat with the kids. She'd get to know them better and maybe they'd trust her more.

At An Lien's suggestion, Shen Ch'i gave Giselle a small futon he had stored in his attic which, for now, would be her only furniture. He would bring it the next day when she made the move from Kavanaugh House.

"Now let's go celebrate over lunch," he suggested.

"Oh, yes," agreed An Lien. "Let's go to the restaurant with Yameno's art. I want to see the paintings."

In the end, it wasn't the paintings that drew An Lien, but a life size carving of a laughing dove. The wood was smooth and silky under her fingers.

"They come from Southern Asia," Shen Ch'i explained. "They're sweet birds who seem to chuckle."

An Lien grinned. "A sweet, gentle, chuckling bird. I love the way it feels in my hands."

"A peaceful dove," added Giselle, "with a sense of humor! A lovely Tla Twei, I think."

An Lien looked up at her father. "Maybe as a dove I'll learn to fly."

Sadness passed over Shen Ch'i's face, quickly replaced by a smile and a nod. Then he laughed. "Dragons can fly, too! Maybe we'll fly together!"

4

Full Hunter's Moon

It didn't take long Sunday afternoon to settle Giselle's few belongings into her new living space. Shen Ch'i had added some sheets, a blanket and a pillow to the loan of the futon, which doubled as a sofa.

It was close to three o'clock when Shen Ch'i and An Lien left, leaving Giselle alone in her new home. She stood at the big double windows at the front of the room and watched people down on the street for a few minutes before deciding to go exploring. Wandering in the direction of Shanti Place, she saw Sidney sitting at a table outside a little coffee shop. He was alone and seemed to be deep in thought.

"Hi, Sidney," she smiled at him. "A penny for your thoughts."

He laughed. "Probably not worth a penny. What're you doing down here?"

"I just moved to a room near here." Giselle pointed back up the street. "I guess you're going to see a lot of me."

"I can live with that," Sidney grinned, and gestured toward one of the other chairs at the table.

"Thanks," Giselle smiled back as she pulled out the chair and sat. But Sidney's smile disappeared as he focused in on a group of kids walking down the opposite side of the street. The Avengers.

"That's Dirk's group."

"Yeah." Sidney hesitated, looked up at Giselle, and then down at the table. "I'm just wondering when they gonna disappear."

Giselle nodded at him. "Deborah was telling me about that. What do you think's going on, Sidney? I mean, I know they're really racist, so maybe you want them to disappear, but…"

"No, no," Sidney shook his head. "It's not just the white kids. It's all the groups – the kids in them are all alike, you know what I mean?"

"Homogeneous," added Giselle. "A group of people who are all alike."

Sidney laughed, "Yeah, whatever! Anyway, I don't want them to disappear. There be something bad about it. I can't figure it out, but it be something bad."

They both watched the group until they reached the corner, and turned down the next street. "So they form groups – all white, or all black, or all Latino, Asian, gays?"

Sidney nodded his head. "It's like gangs, but different. They're not the regular gangs that've been around all along."

He stood, flipped his chair around, and sat on it backwards, crossing his arms across the back. "They got recruiters. One tried to recruit me a while back – a black guy. Kept talking to me about how bad blacks are treated, and how it was all the fault of white guys, which might be sort of true, you know?" He looked at her for confirmation.

She nodded her head.

"Yeah, but I didn't trust this guy. It's like the drug dealers who try to hook the pretty boys and the young girls, so they can turn them into hookers. I haven't seen no drugs, but it feels the same somehow. I just didn't want to get involved in that."

He leaned back, straightening his arms out in front of him, still holding the back of the chair, and then leaned in again. "It's all this hate. I be better off loving people than hating them, I think."

Giselle grinned. "Yup, me too."

"Also, Ayo – she talk to me, tell me not to get involved in the hate."

"Ah," nodded Giselle. "Does Ayoabia know more about all this?"

Sidney shrugged. "Maybe."

"I should go talk to her."

Sidney laughed. "Sometimes that be hard. Sometimes she talk a sentence or two, and sometimes she just sing. Sometimes she just sit and stare."

"What about drugs, and cigarettes, and alcohol, Sidney? Do the kids at Shanti Place use drugs?"

"Not much. It's not allowed, but that wouldn't keep it from happening outside. It's too expensive. Nobody got any money. Kids hooked on that stuff still be out on the street – selling their bodies. Sometimes they come by for a day or two."

"Well, who was this guy who tried to recruit you… and are there others?"

"Yeah, there are. White guys for the whites, Latinos, more than one kind of Asian – they break up into groups by where they come from… They change, but I know who some of them be."

"Can you show them to me?"

Sidney looked at her for a moment. "Yeah, but you be careful. This maybe's not a place for a white woman."

Then he turned his head to the side and looked at her. "Maybe you not all white?"

Giselle laughed. "White and one eighth Chinese. Maybe the Chinese one will try to recruit me. Maybe then I could find out more about them."

Sidney shook his head. "They call you a mongrel. But even if they do accept you," he looked directly at her, "remember, they all disappear. Don't you disappear."

She shook her head. "No, I don't intend to disappear."

They sat companionably in silence for a while. Then Sidney started to speak in a small voice, looking down at the ground. "Um," he said.

"Yes?" asked Giselle.

"Ah… when you and Ayoabia sang…"

"Mmmm," Giselle nodded her head.

"I saw something."

"What?" Giselle looked confused. "What did you see?"

He looked directly at her. "I saw a shadow around you looked like a tree."

Giselle's eyes got wide. "A tree?"

"Yup, a tree."

I don't want to explain this, thought Giselle. "Weird," she muttered.

"Sometimes when Miesha sing I see…" He shook his head and got up quickly. "I gotta go."

"Wait, what do you see?"

He just shook his head. "I don't know. Just something. I gotta go," and he strode off down the street.

Giselle watched until he went around the corner and then slowly got up to continue exploring the neighborhood.

The buildings were old, and some of them were empty, boarded up stores, with graffiti all over the boards. Giselle stopped to examine the graffiti. Some were quite wonderful; others seemed to be messages – some written in Spanish, others with various different forms of calligraphy that might have been different Asian languages, and one that looked like Arabic.

She found one from the Avengers.

"Avengers Avenge!" it proclaimed. "Tuesday midnight under the bridge. All others stay away, or else!" This was followed by a gory picture of a skull with blood running out of its eyes. She rolled her eyes. How sixth grade!

But Tuesday under a bridge… I wonder where the bridge is? Would it be possible to spy on them?

That night Giselle went to Shanti Place for dinner. The tables were set up in three long rows down the room and the meal was served cafeteria style from a table near the kitchen door. The "crew" lists where the kids signed up for different jobs were hung on the wall. Some of the kids were setting up to serve and some were in the kitchen cooking. Dirk and his group, who had signed up for clean-up, were leaning up against the wall waiting.

She added her name to the clean-up list just as one of the cooks clanged a spoon against a metal pot and everyone lined up to go through the food line.

Giselle got on line right behind Dirk's group.

The food was simple vegetarian fare – beans and rice, tortillas, and a salad. She followed the group to a table toward the back of the room.

Choosing a seat across and one person down from Dirk, she pulled out the chair. "Mind if I sit with you?" she asked as she sat down.

Everyone looked at Dirk, who gave her a quick hostile look, shrugged and turned back to his food.

She turned to the young woman next to her. "I'm Giselle. Did I meet you Friday? I can't keep up with everyone's names."

The girl looked at Dirk, who wouldn't look back at her.

She muttered, "I'm Kim – Kimberly."

"Glad to meet you, Kim."

She took a bite of the beans. "And you're Dirk, right?" Giselle looked at him, waiting for a reply.

He raised his eyes and stared at her.

"I remember meeting you."

No response.

"I hope you'll come to my classes."

He shrugged.

She turned back to Kim, smiling warmly. "How about you, Kim?"

Kim looked at Dirk, back at Giselle, and then down at her plate. "Maybe."

The boy opposite her had a dog sitting quietly at his side.

She smiled at him. "I don't remember your name either."

"Charlie. I'm Charlie."

"Glad to meet you, Charlie. I like your dog!"

Charlie grinned. "His name is Bandit."

"I have two dogs and a cat, but they're not with me right now." She paused. "I really miss them. Maybe they can come live with me soon."

Kim looked at her. "You look sad."

Giselle nodded. "I am sad about the animals."

As the room filled up, the chairs next to Giselle and Charlie were left empty, leaving a little boundary between Dirk's gang and the rest.

Giselle picked up her fork again. "I've just moved into a room a couple of blocks away. I'm hoping some of you'll show me around the neighborhood. I need to know where to wash my clothes, and stuff like that."

"There's a laundromat over on Tenth Street," Kim volunteered.

"Great! Could you show me where it is?"

Kim snuck a look at Dirk, who still wouldn't look at her. "I guess I could."

"Thanks!"

The conversation stayed light and awkward, but by the time they were all in the kitchen washing dishes, or out in the main room wiping down the tables, at least Kim and Charlie were more relaxed with her. Both seemed to be vying to tell her about the neighborhood, different stores, and the closest park.

Dirk seemed to be staying close by, listening, even though he wasn't willing to get involved in conversation. A couple of times, Giselle was able to catch his eye and smile, but he just turned away.

After dinner, the kids brought out cards and board games from a cupboard, and settled down for a comfortable evening playing games and chatting. One end of the room was left empty, and before very long some of the girls were dancing to CDs on an old boom box.

Some of the young people, including Dirk's gang, went out to the streets again, even though they were discouraged from going out at night. Deborah told Giselle the doors were locked at eleven o'clock. If they didn't get back in time, they had to stay out all night.

"But," she confessed, "we often sneak them back in when they come back late. We really don't want them out on the street at night at all."

"Where are you going?" Giselle had asked Kim.

She'd shrugged, and just said, "Out."

Finally, Giselle decided it was time she got home, and amid lots of good byes and hugs from Miesha and some of the other girls – and some teasing from some of the boys, who said they wouldn't mind hugging her, but didn't actually step up to get a hug – she headed for her room.

Giselle's cell phone rang just as she unlocked the door to her room.

"Remember we talked about One Earth Together?" An Lien asked. "They're having a meeting tomorrow night to work on the demonstration. Would you like to go with me?"

Giselle was delighted and they agreed to meet outside An Lien's building at seven.

She felt unaccountably happy. It'd been a great day, a great evening. She felt at home with the children, and appreciated. She liked them.

They liked her. She was going to be friends with An Lien and she was going to get involved with OET. What could be better?

Yameno, a little voice whispered in her head.

"But that can't be helped," she said aloud

She did wonder where Dirk's gang was, and if they'd get back by eleven. *I hope they don't disappear. I feel certain,* she thought, *whatever's happening to the kids who disappear isn't good.*

The next day Giselle returned to Shanti Place for breakfast. She'd spent a cozy night in her room with a good book, but really missed her dogs and the little gray cat.

Dirk and his gang had come back before the curfew the night before. She checked the job lists and found they had signed up for set-up. She added her name to the list and started helping set up the tables, gently urging still sleeping youngsters toward the edges of the room.

She smiled at Kim, but Kim looked away and then went to a different place in the room to work.

Dirk glared at her and went over to check the job list. He walked up to her, standing so close she couldn't keep unfolding the legs of the table she was setting up. "Are you following us around?"

"Following you?" asked Giselle.

"Yeah. You signed up for the same jobs as us, you sat with us last night, and you're asking lots of questions. Why?"

Giselle shrugged her shoulders and smiled. "Why not?"

"Because you're not like us. Your real friends are those mongrels," he spit out the words. "Blacks and mongrels like Sidney and Miesha."

"Whoa." Giselle raised her eyebrows at him. "I intend to be friends with all of you, but I'm not going to tolerate racism, Dirk."

"They're the racists," interrupted Dirk.

"How's that?" Giselle looked over at Sidney's group, who were preparing to serve the food. "Looks to me like they accept everyone regardless of race."

"Yeah, mongrels. They hate whites – pure whites like me. They're out to kill us all off."

Giselle's eyes got wide. *Pure whites?* she thought.

"Dirk, there's no such thing as 'pure whites'. Who's telling you things like that? It's…"

She stopped, noticing his balled fists and glaring eyes. "I don't agree with you, but I'd still like to be friends."

She put a hand tentatively on his arm. He turned his back, jerking his arm away, and walked off.

Giselle sighed, and turned back to setting up tables. What had happened? Last night she felt like Dirk was coming around, and Kim and Charlie, too, but now this morning…

Where did they go last night? she wondered. *Did they meet with the 'recruiter'?*

When it came time to eat, she found an open seat next to the Latino group. This group proved to be more receptive, asking her questions about how she had ended up at Shanti Place, and telling her some of their stories.

Their leader was a tall handsome boy named Angelino who openly flirted with her, while keeping an arm possessively around the pretty girl on his left, but she found herself more interested in Dario, a quiet young man who seemed to be Angelino's second in command.

"My parents were deported to Mexico," he responded in answer to her question about how he ended up on the streets. "I was born here. I'm an Uhsian. When they picked up my parents, I was fourteen. The young kids went to live with *los padrinos* – do you call them God-parents? – and I did, too, but the house was so crowded." He looked bleak. "I thought it would be better if left – if I tried to find a job."

His voice dropped lower. "It's hard." He looked down at his food. "I hung out on the corners where people look for workers, and sometimes there was a job, but then the police started making us move on. I don't know how to find jobs now. When people find out I'm only fifteen, and on my own, they want to call social services."

"Come to my classes, Dario," she urged him. "I'll help you get your GED."

Dario glanced at Angelino, and then down at the table. "We have other plans," he muttered.

"What are they?" asked Giselle, but he just shrugged and wouldn't answer. She looked at the others, but they all avoided looking at her.

Angelino picked up his tray and headed for the kitchen. The rest quickly followed suit, leaving her alone to finish her breakfast.

236

When everyone had finished eating, they cleaned off the tables, and pushed some of them into a square for her class. Sidney's group all eagerly found seats, but Dirk's group and Angelino's headed out the door. She noticed Dario looking somewhat wistfully toward the class, before the door shut behind him.

After class Giselle went home, picking up a takeout of curried noodles on the way at a small Thai restaurant. She spent the next couple of hours reading and napping, and feeling a little lonely, but then decided to go out and see what the kids did when they weren't at Shanti Place.

She found a lot of them panhandling near the subway station, a few blocks away. The white kids had the places closest to the station. Some of the black kids were dancing to a boom box with a cap out in front for donations.

She stopped to watch for a while, dropping some coins in the cap. They were really good. She wondered if some of them rapped. *Poetry from the oral tradition,* she thought. *Maybe I can get them to the classes by getting them to rap, and to talk about it.*

As she wandered a little farther away, she heard a sweet voice singing and followed it.

Miesha was standing in front of a small group, including Sidney and Maria, who were sitting on a retaining wall drumming on plastic buckets and bottles. Her voice soared in pure flutey high notes and sometimes Maria added a deep rich harmony. They also had a cap out for donations.

Giselle stood and listened, applauding loudly when she was finished. "This is a great way to pull in a little money! It's a real gift to the people walking by."

She looked around at all of them. "The drumming's great, too! The rest of you could add your voices, as well. The other day when you were toning in An Lien's class it was beautiful. You could do a whole improvisation performance!"

"Yeah," grinned Sidney. "We be working up to it. We had to get Miesha and Maria going first."

Miesha stuck her tongue out at him.

Giselle laughed, "They're very good."

"And we made us some money, too," added Miesha pointing to the cap.

"Yes, and I'll add to it." Giselle dropped some coins in.

"Hey," exclaimed one of the kids. "Looks like another train came in."

He pointed toward the subway station, where a crowd of folks were ascending the stairs to the street. "Sing some more, Miesha."

Miesha took a deep breath and started to sing. Maria wove a deep counterpoint under Miesha's voice. *They're really good,* thought Giselle, *as she watched the commuters lift their heads and smile, some of them dropping coins in the cap.*

She perched on a fire hydrant and allowed herself to sink into the music – into the mists that seemed to float in and out around the singers forming something shadowy – something surrounding Miesha. It was shaped like a woman, but where her legs should be the shadow curved up behind her.

She glanced at Sidney, who was also watching Miesha. He turned his head and met her eyes for a moment, and then shrugged as he returned his attention to his drumming.

It's here, too, she whispered. *The Tsin Twei, the dance.*

After a while she moved off to look for the rest of the kids, but never found the Latinos or any Asians. That night while setting up for dinner she asked Sidney about them.

"They don't never panhandle that I can see. I don't know where they get money. But there never be that many of them. They people take care of them, mostly."

"What about your people, Sidney? Where are your people?"

Sidney sighed. "My mom, she died giving birth to my brother. He died, too. My gramma raised me, but then she died – pneumonia – so I don't got a family now, except these kids here. They my family," and he looked up and smiled, "and they be a good family, too!"

"Yes, I think they are, Sidney."

"What about you, Giselle? You got a family?"

Giselle laughed. "Just a little family. I have a sister, and she's married, so I have both of them – her husband, too. My parents are both dead. My mom died when I was five."

"Yeah, me, too," Sidney nodded. "And I never knew who my dad was. I don't think gramma knew either."

"Well, I guess I was lucky." Giselle smiled at Sidney. "I had my dad until I was almost through college, and I still have my older sister."

The sauce pot clanged for dinner, and she and Sidney moved to get in line. She found a seat next to the three Japanese boys, but had absolutely no luck in getting them to talk. They totally ignored all her opening questions as if she wasn't there at all!

Finally, she laughed out loud, shook her head, and applied herself to eating her dinner. She needed to hurry so she could meet An Lien.

Full Moon Waning

On the subway ride to the meeting, An Lien talked about the One Earth Together group. "They're all good people involved in their own causes. The problem is they argue about which cause is the most important – which one the march should focus on."

"I thought OET was about all the different issues – about how they're related. I thought they brought together lots of different groups."

"Yes, you're right, and the marches all over the world will be focused on many different issues, but each place tends to focus on the ones related to their area. Maybe the problem is that we're many different groups brought together. We're just having a hard time coming to a decision about what issue ours will focus on – and the march is just a week away!"

Giselle nodded. "What are the issues they're vying about?"

"There're four basic ones. Poverty: the lack of jobs, the attacks on poverty programs like food stamps, social security, Medicare. The attacks on unions. That's one. And then there's the militarization of Uhs, of the police forces, the rise in police killings of innocent civilians, excessive incarceration, and the racism associated with all of that. The third is the environment – climate change, deregulation of corporations so more toxic materials are in the environment, destruction of the rainforests, watersheds, and so much more, and then there's a large contingent of women who want to focus on women's health issues. Personally, I think the issue of violence against women is very important."

Giselle nodded and An Lien continued. "I've been doing some research tracing the source of the problem for some of these issues. Almost all seem to be connected with corporations. Sometimes there're subcontractors of subcontractors involved, sometimes there're subsidiaries of other corporations, and if you trace them to the top of the pyramid of corporations you often find that it's the same mega-corporation that's destroying the rainforest, that's polluting in Bayomar, funding legislation to defund food stamps, and they also own the private prisons and detention centers that are making so much money on the incarceration of black and brown people. Actually," she added, "I should say corporations, because it's more than one.

"And it's weird what they're funding. One big corporate CEO who's involved in a lot of this funded a campaign in a small town to re-segregate the schools. I mean, I expect them to be funding lobbies to get legislatures to deregulate industry, but the racist stuff – and for one small town – was kind of a surprise."

"I think a lot of the stuff that's going on is subtly racist," Giselle noted. "I've read stuff about the prisons – about the 'War on Drugs' – that suggests that the whole thing is about circumventing the Civil Rights Movement. If you can't keep blacks out of your schools and restaurants, you just send lots of them to jail."

An Lien nodded. "And it's a profit-making deal. You build private prisons, charge the states and feds lots of money to run them, and then have the prisoners make things for very little pay and rake in the profits – a new kind of slavery. And here's a really weird one. The state gets charged for a certain number of beds in these 'for profit' prisons regardless of how many prisoners are actually there. So the state has an incentive to fill those beds. And the stupid thing is, it costs more to put someone in prison for a year than it does to send someone to a private university for a year!

"Here's where we get off," she added, rolling toward the subway door. Giselle moved behind her to help her through the door.

The meeting was held in the parish hall of a local church. A stage with a wheelchair ramp was at one end of the large packed room. Giselle found an aisle seat and An Lien maneuvered her chair next to her in the aisle.

Before the meeting started the facilitator asked everyone to turn off their phones and reminded people no filming or recording of the meeting was allowed. "People need to feel safe to say whatever's on their mind," she added, "without finding themselves posted all over the internet. And, as always, we need to make sure all who want to be heard are heard."

She outlined the facts of the situation – that the march would happen the next Tuesday, that although they'd informed the city of the march, it would be a march without permits. "We're taking back the commons," she added.

"We're still trying to decide the focus of our protest," she pointed out, and from there the meeting moved into a restatement from various different speakers of the reasons why one or another of the four issues should be the focus.

The argument remained polite but testy for a while and then got contentious, with members of one group standing and yelling at members of another.

Giselle and An Lien raised their eyebrows at each other. *Why do we have to choose?* thought Giselle. *These issues all have the same source.* She wanted to stand up and speak, but she was a newcomer. Anyway, who could yell over this pandemonium?

One man, wearing a baseball cap with the word "POW!" on it, seemed especially disruptive, yelling first, "We want jobs. No one cares about any of you other people's stuff. Jobs," and then, a little later, "We need to take out the cops!"

When the people near tried to calm him down he got worse and started pushing them.

Giselle and An Lien sat wide-eyed watching.

A faint sound floated into the room from the street slipping under the sounds of screaming voices. *Music. It's...*

You have become, the words whispered.

Giselle strained to hear it.

You have emerged.

Ayoabia, she thought. It's Ayoabia!

You have become.
You have emerged.
You have returned,

and then louder.

You have returned!

Yes, I have, Giselle thought.

You are the singer, the leader!

Ayoabia's voice grew stronger and pierced the tumult, like a lightning bolt aimed at Giselle.

Giselle leaped up, trying to speak over the yelling voices. "All these problems have the same source," she called out, but nobody heard her.

An Lien shrugged her shoulders at her, and she tried again. "All these problems are important..."

Her voice faded away in the tumult. One group was threatening to leave, noisily getting out of their chairs, pushing through the others.

Ayoabia sang again, higher.

> *You are the answer,*
> *the edge of the knife!*
> *You! You are the answer!*

She wants me to speak, but they won't listen.

She pulled her shoulders back, lifted her head, and repeated Ayoabia's words, "The edge of the knife, I am the answer. I am the Earth and the Tree, the Earth and the Tree."

Her voice strengthened, her back straightened, and she remembered her first wild ride across the hills as the Earth Woman Tree Woman gripping the back of the wolf.

How strong she had felt! I could do anything joined with the Wolfwind. Community makes us strong, she thought. We saw it in the weaving and we must make it happen here.

She jumped as something moist and cool pushed into her hand where it hung loose at her side. Startled, she looked down.

A shadow stood beside her – large and dark, transparent, but clearly there.

"I am the wolf, the wind and the water," the shadow whispered.

An Lien gave a small surprised, "Oh!" and pushed herself backwards leaving more room for the tenebrous wolf who stood there with a laughing face and a gently wagging tail.

Giselle grinned. Energy surged through her. She lifted her head and resting her hand on the back of the shadowy wolf she moved out of the row and strode down the aisle to the stage.

"Yes," she whispered. "Yes!"

Someone called out, "Look, look," and then, "A tree and a wolf. A really big wolf!"

The tumult stopped as if someone had flipped a switch – sudden silence except for the swish and squeak of chairs as everyone turned to look.

"Can you see it?" someone whispered starting a spate of murmurs.

"Is it a shadow?" "There's a tree in back of her." "No, she's the tree, and do you see the wolf?"

242

Giselle's arms reached up, disappearing into the shadowy tree. Startled, she looked back at An Lien, who gave a surprised laugh and nodded her head.

Tree Woman and Wolfwind walked up the ramp to the platform growing as they went, her limbs shadow, but wide and leafy, reaching up and out to fill the upper reaches of the room, snaking down the corners, making the room a dusky forest.

She raised a leafy hand and the whispers stilled.

"Sit," she called out, and everyone sat down without a word – even the man with the POW! cap.

She began to sing.

> *Breath,*
> *Singing through the voice of the wind,*
> *Dance with me, sing with me,*
> *Make me one with you.*

She paused, and in the silence you could hear the wind rustling through the branches overhanging the room.

Then her voice rang out.

"We're here for the earth, for all. We need to make ourselves one with the spirit of our earth and with each other. We must have unity in our diversity. You've divided yourselves into different groups vying with each other for prominence, but all of these problems are important, all need to be set forth, and… and you're forgetting something important."

She smiled down at An Lien and then turned back to the group.

"You're forgetting that the source, the root of all these problems is the same. It's the source of the problems that must be our focus. Like the roots of a tree, the source is buried deep, not, like a tree, in good clean earth, but in confusion and obfuscation – confusion created by a kind of sleight of hand on the part of the ones at the source."

She paused looking around the room. Some seemed stunned, but others were nodding their heads. *They all know this,* she thought, *but it's hard to grasp.*

"The source of it all is greed – greed for money and for power, and a kind of game, a contest to be the wealthiest, the most powerful."

She lowered her eyes a moment, thinking.

When she raised them again she was shaking her head and overhead the leaves rustled as if in the wind before a storm.

"Who are these people who feed on greed? Someday we will need to figure out why they're able to commit such horrendous crimes against the earth and the creatures who live on it; why it is that they have no compassion, no empathy for those they run rampant over; what is it about our society that allows this to happen? A big job for the future."

She sighed.

There was an anxious stir in the audience and she held up her hand again.

"Yes, greed is the source, but it's the people who feed on greed that we need to find and focus our march on. We must stop them before they destroy us and our earth."

The room erupted in applause and cheers.

Tree Woman raised her branches for quiet, and as the group settled, several yelled out questions: "How do we find them?" and, "Who are they?" and, then, "Who are you? How…"

Tree Woman answered, gesturing to the wolf and her tree self. "We are the Earth Woman Tree Woman and the Wolfwind. The 'how' I don't understand myself."

"I saw that video…" called out one man, and, "I read in the newspaper…," added a woman.

Tree Woman shook her head, and the room quieted.

She beckoned to An Lien with a branched hand. "An Lien, we need to know about your research."

An Lien started up the ramp, and someone in the front row jumped up to help push her up the ramp to the microphone, lowering it to her height.

An Lien began. "Our culture of suspicion towards those who are different makes it easy for the greedy to succeed – and they're everywhere – but right now a small group of elite corporations are responsible for most of our problems."

Tree Woman and the shadowy wolf stood to the side of the platform while An Lien outlined what she had found, tracing a path through the tangled pyramids of power.

"Do you see the man sitting on the aisle with a cap on?" the wolf muttered.

She looked at the frowning man in the fourth row holding his head at a strange angle. "He was a big trouble maker."

The wolf nodded. "Look at his cap." The 'POW!' was written in black letters across the front of the cap. The center of the "O" seemed to reflect the light.

"A camera!"

The wolf's tail swished in agreement.

The man was holding his head so the hidden camera would focus on An Lien who was listing the connections between small corporations who turned out to be subsidiaries of the same larger corporations – sometimes subsidiaries of subsidiaries of subsidiaries.

"Mega-corporations," she added, "who are also the largest donors to non-profit organizations influencing legislation, and think tanks providing inaccurate information to the media. You'll recognize some of the names, but some are kept quite private. Wiebe Armaments, Worldwide Media and Communications, Goldstream Oil, Tutiso Security, The Chaford Corporation, and Audamar Corporation – did you know they're the largest bank in the world? And another one is the Lugas Group, although they don't seem as connected to the same stuff as the others. And there are others, not as powerful, but still up to no good. Many of their assets and their connections are hidden in off-shore banks and corporations with phony names."

An Lien turned toward Tree Woman, not sure whether or not to go on.

The POW! man turned his head toward her as well, and noticed that the tree and the wolf were watching him. He jumped up, heading quickly up the aisle toward the doors.

"He has a camera," Giselle exclaimed, and the man began to run.

The room erupted in noise and some people started up the aisle after him, but he was out the door and down the street before anyone could catch him.

The few who followed returned moments later. "There was a car waiting for him," they explained, out of breath. "He jumped in it and they were gone."

"He was an outside agitator, I'll bet," someone shouted from the back.

The facilitator looked over at Giselle. The shadowy wolf and tree were gone leaving the unknown young woman who had been the tree standing at the edge of the stage.

Giselle looked down at the empty place where Yameno had stood, then silently moved down the ramp and back to her seat. The facilitator watched her go and seemed about to say something, but Giselle looked up and shook her head.

The woman turned to the crowd and held up her hand for silence. "Never mind the camera," she said. "We can't do anything about him. And," she hesitated for a moment looking again at Giselle, "never mind what we just saw."

There was a murmuring in the audience, but most looked back at the facilitator who turned toward An Lien, "An Lien has given us important information and we still have decisions to make."

The audience settled, most nodding their heads, still a little bewildered looking, but ready to move on. A dark-haired woman waved her hand wildly, not waiting to be recognized before she exclaimed, "We can make signs holding those corporations accountable. We can get all this information out to the people. Signs with sound bites telling the stuff An Lien just told us."

The facilitator nodded and held up her hand again. She turned to An Lien. "An Lien, have you anything to add?"

"Yes," she replied, moving back to the mike again. "There are a lot of people involved with these corporations with lots of influence – not just CEO's and presidents of corporations, but legislators, judges, and more – but there's one man who seems to have more power than any other. He's the owner of Goldstream Oil, Kasimir Goddard. He has shares in all the other corporations, except the Lugas Group, and gives a ton of money to LCU – you know, Legislative Committee for Uhs – and the Birthright Foundation. He's a powerful man.

"One of the things he did was fund an election attempt to re-segregate the schools in a southern town. I think that was part of a calculated attempt to use our culture of racism to divide us against each other instead of against the huge power of the corporations and banks. Our signs need to make that clear – make it clear that we stand together regardless of our race, our many different gender types, our religious affiliations, our abilities and disabilities. And beyond this march, we must work hard at helping others understand racism and privilege and how it undermines us all."

The room erupted with applause. The facilitator laughed as she tried to call them to attention. Finally, they broke into groups and got to work planning the march.

Giselle and An Lien talked quietly while helping to make posters. "We don't know what that man's going to do with the video," Giselle pointed out, "but I do think it's weird a car was waiting for him. He did leave before you mentioned Kasimir Goddard, which is probably good."

An Lien shrugged. "Maybe, but I think he's a spy from the police, or the NIO."

"Just be on the alert, An Lien. These people are dangerous."

The next afternoon Kasimir Goddard sat behind a big mahogany desk in his office in the central tower of the Seaview Business Park – owned by one of his subsidiaries. This wasn't his public office, but one he maintained quietly in Bayomar where he could meet with people out of the limelight. He'd been contacted that morning by Peters – his liaison with TigerSNake Limited (TSNL) – a little known company that provided information as needed to many different large corporations, including Goldstream Oil. They also provided contract workers for the UhsSA – the Uhsian Security Administration. They had information to sell on many fronts.

One of their jobs for Goldstream was infiltrating OET groups all over the world – not only collecting information, but fomenting disruption as well. Howie, the man in the POW! cap who was filming the meeting in Bayomar was one of their operatives. The night before they'd downloaded the file from the camera in Howie's cap and searched for a list of key words. An Lien's presentation had contained almost all the English words on the list.

"Bring the video to me. I want to see it," Goddard had demanded, "and bring the operative who filmed it. I want to question him."

Now Goddard was staring at a laptop. Howie and Peters stood on either side of him watching both the screen and Goddard. On the screen An Lien was explaining the connections between the various corporations and subsidiaries. Finally, the camera followed An Lien's glance toward Giselle and Yameno.

Howie shook his head. "It didn't photograph them, but they were there – a tree and a wolf. Like shadows. You could see through them, but they were there. You heard the people exclaiming about them. You heard them!"

"Yes," agreed Goddard. "I heard them, but I don't see them. And that's not really what I care about right now."

"Remember that video that went viral about some people who changed into a cougar and a hawk? This same woman was in that video. I read about them, and they talked about some place where…"

"Yes, yes," Goddard interrupted impatiently. "My concern is this An Lien. What's her last name?"

"I don't know," Howie squirmed.

Goddard turned to Peters. "Find out. Find out anything you can about her."

He turned away from the computer, waving his hands dismissively at the men. "Go. Go."

"But Mr. Goddard," Howie interjected. "The other woman – the one who was a tree and who had the wolf beside her…"

Goddard raised his voice. "I'm not concerned with fairytales. Find me the woman in the wheelchair. Go!" Peters grabbed Howie's arm and steered him out of the room.

Goddard stared out the window at the dark sky. Suddenly he turned and slammed his fist down on the desk. "She knows too much, damn it! I think she knows."

Arundel

Yameno sat by the side of the waterfall thinking about the link he'd had with Giselle in Bayomar. "It's something different," he whispered, "and something strong."

He sipped the water and sang, dancing at the edge of the pool. He was no longer there with her, but he could feel her. *Connected,* he thought. *We're like the Tsin Twei – like her speech at the meeting. We're ourselves and we're One. Unity and diversity.*

The need to bring *Homo sapiens* back to the Tsin Twei had always felt like a world-wide – maybe even universe-wide – problem, and yet for him it had been contained in this one little place, at this one little spring. Now, suddenly, as he thought of the OET meeting, it was global.

Distressing things had been happening here with the threat of logging and fracking, and the county talking about fencing the park area in. It would make it more difficult for him to get to the spring, though not impossible, but it would be impossible for the wildlife of the park.

The Interfaith Council would be meeting in the morning and talking about their own OET demonstration. He had been invited to join. "After all," Muriel had pointed out. "This tradition of traveling to

Ninas Twei certainly is a faith journey. You belong with us." The question would be, just like the questions in Bayomar, should their focus be on these local problems or on the bigger national problems?

But it's all related, he thought. *If we trace the logging company and the gas company back to their origins, we might find the same corporations An Lien was talking about.*

He looked down at the bubbling water. *My job is to protect the spring. Is that only a local concern? Without water there'll be no life for anyone, anywhere. Water is a global concern and our little spring is a part of that. And what about Enid and Jesús. Just two children. The world's full of suffering children. But these two are ours.*

Dorotea had sunk into a deep depression after the last failed attempt to visit Ninas Twei. Keegan had been visiting her every day with little success. *Will we ever be able to go back?* Yameno wondered. He leaned down and scooped a handful of water from under the little waterfall and slowly sipped.

> *Water of life.*
> *purify me.*
> *Water of the soul of earth,*
> *wash me in your love.*

Keegan had also been visiting Gunther Amundsen since the Tuesday morning after his hurried trip to Bayomar – after the others had made another failed attempt to visit Ninas Twei. He found Gunther wherever he was working on his little farm, and settled himself nearby, making occasional comments about the weather, about whatever Gunther was doing.

For the first couple of visits the man only grunted in response, but Keegan counted it a success that Amundsen didn't yell at him and chase him away. Gunther dug into the dirt, or swung an ax, as if angry at the ground or the wood, but the anger wasn't aimed at Keegan.

Local gossip noted Gunther had never asked the deputy sheriff, or anyone else, about the search for Enid and Jesús – he hadn't come into town the entire week after Enid disappeared. Some had even speculated he was responsible for the children's disappearance since he didn't seem concerned, but Keegan was pretty sure Gunther's lack of interest in the search was because he believed Yameno and Giselle's story. He knew the sheriffs weren't going to find the children. *Maybe,* he thought, as he watched Gunther working at a furious pace as if driven by demons, *he's in a fierce argument with himself. Is he angry at Yameno, or is he angry at himself?*

After two days of sitting nearby making one-sided small talk while Gunther worked, Keegan decided to push a little farther.

"Gunther," he said. "I've heard Yameno's story of what happened when Mary died. I'd like to hear your version."

Gunther's shoulders stiffened and he paused for just a moment, but then turned back to digging his spade deep in the dirt of his vegetable garden plot, and turning the remaining debris from his string beans into the soil.

Keegan waited.

When Gunther spoke, his voice was so low Keegan could hardly hear it over the *thunking* of the spade. "He told you I killed her."

"No." Gilchrist shook his head. "No, he said it was an accident. That you were afraid."

Gunther kept digging. "I tried to save her."

He turned some of the dirt, chopping the vines with the spade before covering them with more soil. "I tried to save her, but I killed her."

"No," Keegan repeated. "No. It was an accident. You were afraid for her."

Gunther tried to keep digging, but it was as if the spade was stuck in the soil and he didn't have the energy to pull it out. Tears slid down his face. "I killed her. I wanted to save her, but I killed her. And then I drove Emma to kill herself."

He brushed his sleeve across his eyes. Taking a deep breath and pulling his shoulders back, he tried to control his tears. "It was my fault."

Keegan said, very quietly, "You were afraid," and Gunther let go of his breath in a big sob. He pulled his arms across his chest and leaned over, his shoulders heaving as he tried to hold in the tears. When he collapsed to the ground, the sobs turned into a wailing as he beat at the earth with his hands and his feet.

Keegan moved over next to him. "Tears are cleansing, Gunther," he murmured. "Tears are a gift from God."

Gunther sat up and turned toward Keegan. "Now I have killed Hazel, too. I killed her!" he yelled. "I shot her, and that Dan, too."

His voice dropped to a whisper. "And maybe I've killed Enid."

He looked anxiously at Gilchrist, and the words that had been locked up inside him poured out. "Maybe I've caused Enid to die, or worse, because she's there in that other place, and I can't get there. No one can get there, because I killed Hazel and Dan. And I know… I know Yameno can't go there alone. He needs six. That was the way it was. The teacher left, and the children aren't here. It's just Yameno, and he can't go alone."

Keegan touched his shoulder. "Listen, Gunther. Listen."

He sat down next to him. "One of the things they found out this time is that people who've been there – travelers from here who go there who die as their Tla Twei – like Hazel and Dan – those people go to that place and live there as their Tla Twei."

Gunther looked at him, bewildered.

"They go there as cougar and hawk, Gunther, and they can find Enid and Jesús."

He leaned forward placing his hands on the ground between them. "A new group went to Ninas Twei on Monday. There's some kind of problem at Ninas Twei – you know from what Yameno said at the hearing that there're problems. They couldn't get to the place where the children fell, but they'll keep trying."

Gunther looked at him, pleading. "Who went?"

"Yameno and the boy's parents – Billy and Dorotea McCrae – and Rabbi Levinson and the Reverends Yates and Tarrant."

Gunther's eyes opened wide. "Jarvis? Jarvis Tarrant? Jarvis was so angry at Hazel."

Keegan smiled, nodding his head. "Yes, but he's had an… awakening, I guess you'd call it. He loved Hazel, but jealousy turned that love to hate."

Gunther looked down. "I loved Mary. I loved her."

"Yes," answered Gilchrist, "but perhaps you didn't trust her."

"No," whispered Gunther, "I didn't trust any of them."

Keegan smiled and patted his shoulder. "It will be all right. There will be healing, Gunther."

Gunther stared at the ground a long time, and finally he looked up at Keegan. "I want to go," he pleaded. "This time I won't be afraid."

Keegan took a deep breath and sighed. "Yes, I want to go as well, Gunther, and I hope both of us get the chance."

5

Waning Gibbous in Bayomar

Tuesday afternoon Giselle looked for the bridge where the Avengers were to meet at midnight. The only bridge nearby was an interstate fly over. The area under it was overgrown with weeds and trash, but she found a thin path leading to a circular clearing where the weeds had been trampled down. To the right, the ground rose in a bank where pillars held the bridge up over the street. Heading back up the path, she followed the street to the underpass, working her way around the pillars until she found a place where she could crouch and peer through the weeds down at the clearing.

She returned to her room for a nap in preparation for a late night.

That evening, as she left her building to head back to Shanti Place for dinner, she noticed a man standing in a doorway next to An Lien's apartment building. Something about him looked familiar.

Looking in the other direction she saw a black car with tinted windows idling on the corner.

As An Lien came around the corner on her way home from work, the man pulled back into the doorway letting her roll past, then started after her.

Giselle dashed across the street, yelling, "An Lien, behind you!"

The man glanced at Giselle, but kept moving toward An Lien, who had spun her wheelchair around to meet him. Another man jumped out of the waiting car running to grab An Lien's chair from the back.

A deep surge of sound erupted in Giselle's chest as she yelled, "Stop! Stop!" and grabbed the arm of the wheelchair trying to hold it against the two men, one pushing and the other pulling it toward the car.

The man who had been in the doorway looked at her, startled. "You're that tree woman," he sputtered.

It was the man with the camera!

"Yes, I am," she replied, and suddenly her voice soared over the city noise:

> *Breath, flowing through the depths of the earth,*
> *Grow in me,*
> *give me strength,*
> *I AM ONE WITH YOU!*

Her roots dug deep into the concrete, holding fast in the earth below. Some of her branches flew high in the air, but those that had been her arms twined themselves around the arm of the wheelchair and out to weave a protective barrier around An Lien, holding her safely in the chair.

The men froze, wide eyed, and when they felt the hot breath of the shadowy wolf snapping at their heels, they took off running toward the car.

The car wheels screeched as they spun out and flew down the street. Giselle's branches and roots slowly withdrew and she was herself again.

Yameno was gone.

An Lien was staring at her, eyes and mouth wide open. She shut her mouth with a snap. "Well," she exclaimed, "you're getting better and better at that!"

Giselle gave a shaky little laugh. "She just takes over!"

"No kidding!" An Lien grinned and shook her head. "That certainly set my adrenaline flowing!"

She looked around her. "The wolf is gone."

"But he's with me," Giselle almost whispered. "He's always with me now. We need to call the police, but no mention of the tree, or the wolf, please!"

An Lien already had her phone out, pushing her emergency number. "Of course not."

It wasn't long before the police car pulled up. The officer who responded seemed sympathetic until they mentioned the OET meeting — that the man with the camera was one of the kidnappers.

"You get involved with something like OET, you get what you ask for," he muttered.

Giselle stepped forward. "Do you have a family, Officer?"

He looked at her suspiciously, but nodded.

"Are your children in the public schools?"

His eyes narrowed. "What business is that of yours?"

Giselle smiled. "How big are their classes? Too big? How's their health? Any of them have asthma from the pollution? And how about your pension? Didn't it get cut? Oh, and I think you haven't had a raise in a while. Not enough tax money available. Of course, the CEO's of the big corporations have had huge raises – large enough to pay salaries for thousands of workers if they would – but those corporations and their CEOs hide their income in overseas banks and don't pay their fair share of taxes."

He glared at her.

"Aren't you concerned about these issues?" she continued. "Maybe you should join the march."

He snapped his notebook closed and tucked it in his pocket as he turned toward his car. "You didn't get the license number. Not much we can do."

He dropped his keys twice as he tried to get the door open, but finally scrambled into the driver's seat and roared off swerving to keep from hitting a car coming down the street from the opposite direction.

An Lien rolled her eyes, then turned toward her apartment door. "Come up with me."

An Lien's apartment was on the second floor. Giselle looked around as they went through the wide doorway. The large room held exercise equipment, and something that looked something like a hospital table in one corner that An Lien explained would tip her upright so that her body had the benefit of standing vertically. There were lots of bookshelves full of computer books, novels, and Buddhist tracts, and a desk with a laptop computer and a large screen.

Giselle found herself drawn to a beautiful painting on the wall over the desk. Half the painting was a beautiful dark wooded area and the other a majestic city with tall shadowy buildings. A sunlit path led between them narrowing into a mountainous misty future.

"My mother painted that," An Lien explained.

"I love paintings that draw my eye like that – that make me want to just look and look into them. Like meditating." She smiled at An Lien. "Your mother was an artist?"

An Lien nodded. "Yes. She was very good."

She pointed to several other paintings and Giselle looked at each of them. "Yes, she was. I'd like to see more of her work."

"But," she turned to An Lien. "We need to talk … Whoever's behind the filming of the OET meeting's figured out who you are and where you live. You should go stay with your dad for a while."

An Lien rolled over to the window and looked out. "If they know where I live they probably know where my dad lives. They probably know where I work."

She turned back again. "Maybe you scared them off."

"We can't count on that, An Lien."

"Yeah. You're right. Okay, I'll call my dad."

She pulled out her phone. "Were you headed to Shanti Place for dinner? Maybe you should go so you won't be too late."

"I guess, but are you all right?"

"Yeah, I'm fine here. They can't get in here."

Giselle hesitated, taking a deep breath before heading for the door.

At the door she turned back. "I'm going to hide at the bridge where the Avengers are meeting tonight and watch what happens."

An Lien looked at her for a moment. "I was going to suggest you not go alone, but I guess we just found out you can protect yourself!"

Giselle laughed. "I guess so… and I'm not alone. Yameno…"

She shook her head. "But you – An Lien, do you promise you're going to call your dad?

"Yes, I promise. I'm not dumb."

Giselle left and An Lien pushed her father's number on her phone.

Kasimir Goddard's tower office had windows on three sides looking out at the city and the ocean. The two men who attacked An Lien, and Peters, who'd been driving the car, stood near the door to the outer office, and two more men – one older heavyset man with gray hair, the other younger, both chic in silk suits and expensive Italian leather shoes –

sat in comfortable arm chairs beside the desk watching Goddard pace back and forth across the whole expanse of the office.

"I don't give a damn if all of you saw it," Goddard glared at the standing men. "It's not possible. You're deluded."

He went to the window looking out over the city, trying to see the street where An Lien had not been captured.

He turned back shrugging his shoulders. "Oh, hell, the damage is done." He sat back down in his chair behind the desk.

The younger seated man added, "It could be worse. There are no names mentioned on that video – I mean besides company names – and they don't know about the…" He stopped abruptly, looking at the men by the door.

Goddard glared at him and the gray haired man rolled his eyes.

The young man ducked his head down and remained silent.

After dinner the Avengers all left Shanti Place in a group.

Shen Ch'i called Giselle on her cell phone and they discussed the attack.

"It must be related to one of the corporations she mentioned while the guy was filming," Giselle explained. "I think they're afraid she found something in her searches that they don't want found."

Shen Ch'i agreed and said An Lien would stay with him for the next few days, at least until after they all returned from the trip to Arundel planned for the weekend. She could continue her searches and email the OET members her findings. He would make sure she was never left alone.

For the rest of the evening Giselle played cards with Miesha and even took a turn at dancing. She didn't leave for her hiding place under the bridge until eleven o'clock. The Avengers hadn't returned when she left.

The ambient light of the city made it easy for her to find her way back to the bridge, but as she crept through the weeds to the little alcove tucked in under the pillars, it suddenly seemed very dark and isolated, even though she could hear the muffled sounds of the cars rushing by overhead. Looking down, she saw that the street lights pushed the bridge shadows back, making it easy to see the clearing.

No one was there.

It was nearly midnight before the first people arrived, walking quietly up the path through the weeds to the clearing. One was a hefty blonde man, and the other a thinner brown haired man. The blond was carrying a tote bag.

Sidney's 'recruiters', she thought.

He set the tote down and began taking plastic glasses and a bottle of some amber liquid out of it. He looked up when they heard the sounds of teenagers chatting and horsing around.

The kids came up the street and turned down the path.

The blond stood up and welcomed the group as they entered the clearing. Giselle saw Dirk, Kim, Charlie and Bandit, and a couple of others she'd seen at Shanti Place, but some of them weren't familiar looking, so it wasn't just kids at Shanti Place pulled into this.

"Make a circle," the blonde man urged. "It's almost midnight."

They circled up and Bandit, the dog, settled at Charlie's feet. The men passed around plastic cups, and then poured a little of whatever was in the bottle in each one.

"I don't drink," one girl protested.

"Oh, this is just a little whiskey — not enough to hurt. You need it for the ceremony."

The girl looked at Dirk, who nodded at her. She shrugged and let him pour.

"Don't drink yet," added the blonde. "We have to say the pledge together." As he spoke they picked up the extra glasses and the bottle, stuffing them into the tote as they moved to the outside of the circle.

They placed the tote by the path, and then began walking in opposite directions, touching each of the youngsters on the back as they passed them. When they met, they passed each other and kept going until they were opposite each other.

"Repeat after me," proclaimed the blonde in a large voice. "We are the Avengers."

The group responded.

"We are the pure. We are the white, the bright, and the right. God keep us pure."

He raised his glass into the air. "Now, again, louder and all together and when you're finished, drink."

The youngsters raised their glasses into the air, their voices ringing out in the night:

We are the Avengers.
We are the pure.
We are the white, the bright, and the right.
God keep us pure.

They drank, and suddenly – except for the two men who were outside of the circle and did not chant, and did not drink – and Bandit, who stood up whining and looking wildly around him – they all disappeared. They just weren't there.

Giselle gasped. *My god,* she thought. *My god! What happened here?*

She looked down at the two men.

The blond tossed his glass into the weeds, and swiped his hands together as if to wipe off some dirt.

He laughed. "Done."

They grinned, picked up the tote, and headed up the path to the street. Bandit ran after them, but the smaller man turned around and kicked him back into the clearing.

The dog yelped, and crawled over to the place on the circle where Charlie had been.

Giselle waited in the shadow of the bridge until she heard car doors slam and a car drive off. *Poor dog,* she thought, as she made her way down into the clearing. Bandit crawled over to her, and she carefully felt along his ribs until he stood up and shook himself. He stuck close to Giselle as she circled the clearing looking for some clue.

Nothing remained except the plastic glass tossed in the weeds.

"What should we do?" Giselle addressed the dog. "How can we tell anyone? If I call the police they'll never believe me. They'll send me back to Kavanaugh House!"

She shook her head as she climbed back to the street, tears slipping down her cheeks, walking slowly back toward her apartment. Bandit stuck close beside her looking anxiously up at her face.

As she rounded one corner, she became aware of some faint music.

Singing, she thought, stopping to listen.

Ayo! It's Ayo singing. She started running, following the sound to a small grassy park. In the middle, she could see swirling colors, and as she came closer she realized Ayo was dancing and singing on a circle of blacktop in the middle of the park.

"Ayo," she whispered, as she ran up the path.

Ayoabia paused for a moment and looked at her. She was weeping, tears streaming from her large black eyes as she threw her hands up in the air and began a wailing chant, circling slowly. Gradually the chant grew louder and faster, and she turned faster and faster, until she was spinning, her skirts circling wide around her, her shawl held in one hand and flying even farther out, like a single wing undulating around and around.

Giselle found her own voice rising in the same wordless, wailing chant, while tears ran down her face. She moved out onto the blacktop and she, too, began to circle in place, faster and faster into a whirling wild spin.

Her eyes were open. She could see Ayo and the city spinning around her, and then something else. Something dark, confined, as if she were inside some small dark round room. Something was screaming at her. Still spinning she covered her ears with her hands. Then the vision was gone.

Ayo's chant went higher and higher, their two voices split apart in a strange harmony, weaving in and out of each other, and then, slowly receded, flowing downward in pitch and volume. The dance followed, slowing and slowing, until both women were standing swaying across from each other, humming a low minor hum, gradually fading until there was nothing.

Ayo opened her arms. "Come, girl," she whispered, and Giselle moved into her arms, feeling like a child in the tall woman's embrace. They stayed there hugging and crying together for a long time, before Ayo gently pushed Giselle away. "I can't bring them back," she whispered. "I've tried, but I can't bring them back."

"Where did they go?" asked Giselle. "I saw… I saw something dark, something like a prison."

Ayo shook her head. "A bad place. I don't know where."

"What can we do?"

Ayo just shook her head again. Finally, she gathered her shawl around her. "Go home now. Go home," and she turned her back on Giselle and walked away.

Giselle looked down at the dog, who was laying down, his head on his paws, at the edge of the blacktop. "Let's go, Bandit. We need to call Shen Ch'i."

She took a deep sobbing breath. *More children gone.* "Please let Hazel and Dan find Enid and Jesús, or let Yameno get to Ninas Twei and find them," she whispered. "I think I have to find these."

When she got back to her apartment, she fell down on the futon and into a deep sleep. The dog stood next to the futon and watched her for a long while before he too, curled up on the floor to sleep.

When Giselle awoke Wednesday morning, she thought everything she'd seen the night before was a dream. Then she heard a whimper and turned over on the futon finding herself nose to nose with Bandit, sitting up with his head resting on the edge of the mattress.

Oh, god, it's true, she thought. *I have to call Shen Ch'i. S*

he sat up and looked down at her wrinkled clothes. "Wash my face first," she muttered.

When Shen Ch'i heard her story, he told her to meet him as soon as possible at Shanti Place. "I'll bring An Lien. Bring the dog. First we'll make sure the Avengers haven't returned."

The Avengers had indeed disappeared. They weren't at Shanti Place for breakfast, and when Sidney and his group spread out and searched the streets, they couldn't be found.

Giselle checked the boarded up store where she'd seen the graffiti telling the Avengers to meet under the bridge. It'd been painted over.

Before dinner Giselle, Shen Ch'i, and An Lien met with Sidney's group, Deborah, and Reverend Meg in the corner of the room with the old sofas.

"Dad and I tried to find Ayo," An Lien said, rolling her chair up across from them.

"I found her." Miesha perched on an arm of the sofa. "She asleep in a cardboard box in that alley off Eleventh Street. I tried to wake her up, but she ignoring me."

Sidney shook his head. "She don't talk unless she wants to."

"I think she saw it, too – the dark room – but I don't think she knows any more than what we saw last night," Giselle mused.

Shen Ch'i nodded, "I think she does her best. When she can tell us something she will."

Giselle continued. "And the graffiti on the store front that told about the Avengers meeting – it's gone. It's been painted over."

"But now there's one in Spanish on Tenth Street," Maria added anxiously. "Says the same thing – almost the same. It's *Los Gallos* this time. It says for *Los Gallos* to meet under the bridge tomorrow night."

"Is that Angelino's gang?" exclaimed Giselle, looking around the room. They weren't back from the streets yet.

Maria nodded.

Shen Ch'i stood up and started pacing. "We need to talk to them."

Deborah shook her head. "But they won't listen. We've tried to talk to them before."

"Yeah," Sidney added, "but we got more information now. We can tell them more about the bad stuff."

Giselle looked thoughtful. "I wonder what they do know? Dario said they had a plan."

Sidney nodded in agreement. "Usually when we talk to them they just laugh – like they know something we don't know. The recruiters tell them something that makes them want to go with them."

Los Gallos had signed up to do cleanup, and they didn't come in until just before dinner was served. When they sat down to eat, Giselle, Shen Ch'i, An Lien, Deborah, and Sidney all sat at the same table, surrounding them.

"Angelino, we need to talk to you," Shen Ch'i said.

Angelino shrugged his shoulders and rolled his eyes, but didn't say anything. Dario looked troubled.

Shen Ch'i sighed, and went on. "Angelino, do you notice none of the Avengers are here?"

"Thought we weren't supposed to use gang names," muttered Angelino.

"Shall I name them all?" Shen Ch'i paused. "Look around the room. You know who's missing."

"So, that's nothing new." Angelino looked at Sidney. "You told us before that groups disappear."

"Yeah, I did." Sidney leaned forward, "But I didn't tell you where they go, did I?"

Angelino got a smirk on his face. "That's because you don't know where they go."

"And you do?" interjected Deborah.

Angelino just grinned.

"I don't think so," added Giselle. "I think you think you know, but you don't really know."

Angelino gave a little laugh and took a bite. "And you do?"

Shen Ch'i sat back. "Tell him what happened last night, Giselle."

Giselle put down her fork and told the story of watching the children disappear, of the two men laughing and smacking their hands together, of the dog kicked and left behind, pointing at the dog who sat against the wall.

"Charlie's dog," muttered Dario.

Giselle nodded. "Yes, and where is Charlie? I think I saw where they are," she continued. "I had a…" she paused, a little embarrassed. "It was like a vision. I saw a place. It was dark and small, like a prison, and I was…"

She stopped. Suddenly she knew. "It wasn't me. It was like I was Charlie, Bandit's owner. I was alone in this small dark place, and there was a voice screaming at me." She felt a tightness in her chest, difficulty breathing. "It was frightening."

She looked around at each of them. "I couldn't help him."

Sidney leaned forward. "Somebody told you something that isn't true. You think you going somewhere good, but you not."

Maria interrupted. "I saw the sign. I saw you're supposed to meet tomorrow at midnight. Don't go. Don't do it."

Angelino put his fork down on his plate with a loud clank. "*Mierda*, you…"

He paused, looking quickly at Dario, and then at Shen Ch'i, who said, "Careful, Angelino."

Angelino looked back at Maria. "You stay away from me, Manolo Ma-ri-a…" He stretched out the syllables of her name, then turned back to Sidney. "*Todo eso es mierda.* Those white trash do go to a bad place, but not us."

He looked around at his followers. "Time to clean up. Leave these people."

Giselle noticed there was a little hesitant pause before they all pushed back their chairs and headed to the kitchen. Dario, especially, seemed reluctant, looking first at Maria with a small apologetic smile, and then turning toward Giselle, meeting her eyes for a minute, looking away as he followed the rest.

Giselle gathered her dishes. She walked into the kitchen and stood beside Dario who was rinsing dishes, preparing them for the dishwasher.

"Dario," she said. "It was like a prison. Dark… and small, and very frightening."

He didn't respond.

"What did they tell you? Where did they say you would go?"

He kept his eyes on the plates, rinsing and stacking them for the next person.

"Did they tell you about the ritual? About the chant? They probably have a special chant, designed just for you, about the purity of being Latino."

Dario's eyes flashed in her direction for just a moment.

"Did they tell you that you would just disappear from here, or something else?"

He threw down his dishrag, and left the kitchen. Giselle followed him as he headed out the street door, glancing over at Shen Ch'i as she went.

Angelino came to the kitchen door just as they left, frowning. He started toward the street door, but Shen Ch'i stopped him. "I want a word with you, Angelino."

Angelino tried to push past him, but Shen Ch'i moved to block him. "No, we need to talk. You're leading your people into disaster."

"*Mierda.* We're going to a better place than this."

"How do you know? Who told you this?"

"Someone who cares about Latinos, who knows we're better than all of you, even you chinks."

"What does he say? And how do you explain that the same thing happens to people of other ethnicities – like the Avengers?"

"They are bad. Bad things happen to people who are bad. Leave me alone," Angelino pushed Shen Ch'i out of the way and headed out the door, but by the time he hit the street, Dario and Giselle were nowhere to be seen.

Giselle had to run to catch up with Dario. "Dario, please. You know I care. I don't want to see you hurt."

He walked on with his head down, but slowed his pace so Giselle could keep up with him.

"Tell me what they told you," Giselle urged him.

"There are two Latino men. They are very – I don't know – they seem to care about us, but sometimes I have a bad feeling about them."

They came to a little park. Dario stopped and looked around.

"Shall we sit down?" asked Giselle.

Dario shook his head and started walking again. "They're wealthy and educated. They wear suits. They say the reason we are treated badly here is that people are jealous of us, because we're really better than everyone else."

"Do you agree?"

"I don't know. Sometimes I think…" He sighed, and stopped for a moment.

"And what do they say about the other ethnic groups disappearing?"

"They say they are being tricked. They are being taken away to make the world better for us."

"So someone is saying the same thing to them these guys are saying to you, but in their case, it's a trick."

Dario was silent for a moment. "I don't know. Sometimes I think they're playing a game with us – leading us on like a bull with a nose ring. But Angelino is my cousin. We need to stick together."

"I think you're right about the bull with the ring through his nose. I think that's exactly what's happening."

Dario looked at her for a moment, and then looked away. "But why?"

"I don't know." Giselle shook her head. "This whole thing is too strange. All I know is what I saw last night – all at once – poof! Just as they finished the words, they were gone. And then later, I saw Charlie… No, it was as if I was Charlie. I was inside some small dark prison, with a loud yelling voice."

264

"What did the voice yell?"

Giselle thought for a moment. "It was instructions. 'Find the' – something – 'plug into…' I couldn't understand it all. 'Tighten knob'… It was loud and it was mechanical." She shook her head. "None of it makes any sense."

She looked at Dario. "What did they tell you will happen Thursday night?"

"They're going to take us out of here to someplace where we will be taken care of. There will be plenty of food. We will be part of an army of Latinos who will conquer the world."

Giselle shook her head. "Don't do it, Dario. Don't do it."

Just then Angelino came around the corner. He stopped for a moment when he saw Dario, and then ran toward them. "What are you doing?" he yelled. "What did you tell her?" He grabbed Dario by the arm, and pulled him away from her down the street.

"Stop it!" Giselle ran after them. "Let him go!"

Dario put a hand out to stop her. "No. It's all right. Leave it. It's all right," and walked off down the street with Angelino.

When Giselle got back to the shelter, Shen Ch'i and An Lien had managed to talk two of *Los Gallos* into staying behind. Sidney's group took charge of them, making them feel welcome, and one of them decided to adopt Bandit.

"I think," added Shen Ch'i, "this is our best strategy. We have to approach them one by one and try to change their minds. It's too hard for them to speak up against Angelino and the whole group."

"Dario senses something's wrong," added Giselle. "Perhaps he'll be able to talk Angelino out of it."

"We only have tonight and tomorrow," An Lien sighed. She spun her chair around so that she could see all of the young people in the room. "We need to tell all of them about this. They all should be warned."

Giselle nodded, and Deborah called a meeting of everyone in the room.

Giselle told her story. Some of the young people looked at each other and smirked, but others nodded their heads. One young African American girl from The Commandos said, "Ayo, she told me. She told me that man gonna do bad stuff to us."

Rashaun, the leader of the Commandos grabbed her arm, trying to silence her, but Sidney moved between them, adding, "Ayo know more than she tell. You listen to her."

Again, some of the others smirked, but many nodded.

When eleven o'clock came, neither Angelino nor Dario had come back. Several other members of *Los Gallos* were also missing. After talking to the night counselors, making sure that anyone who came back late would be let in, Giselle and the others had no choice but to go on home.

An Lien Searches the Web

An Lien often had trouble sleeping at night, and tonight, back home with her dad, she was wide awake thinking about the disappearance of the Avengers. She pulled herself out of bed and into her chair, moving over to the table she used as a desk and opening her laptop.

Is this the only place this is happening? How can I find out? What can I search on?

She typed "recent disappearances" into the search engine. "Two million results!" she exclaimed out loud.

Refining her search to eliminate the disappearance of individuals, and of bees and other animals, she found several news items about recent disappearances of groups of people. All of them were closed secretive groups, and none of them seemed to cause a big stir. *People without connections. No one who cares enough about them to make a big stink. Just like our kids.*

She opened a new file and carefully documented each disappeared group she found as she scrolled down the list.

She had rolled on past one headline, "Crowd sees shot woman turn into Ibex as she dies," when she realized what she had seen and scrolled back up. It was about a demonstration in a small country, where the people were demanding that their dictator step down and allow a democratically elected government.

The army had been called out and had fired on the demonstrators, killing several people and one Nubian Ibex – a kind of wild goat that didn't even live near the city where the demonstration took place. Many of the demonstrators swore that it was not really a goat, but a woman – a pregnant woman from the dry hills of the countryside who had been part of the demonstration. This woman couldn't be found anywhere.

Like Hazel and Dan! An Lien thought.

The woman, whose name was Djeserit, had been known as a holy woman, a healer.

She started to call out to her dad, stopping herself as she realized how late it was.

It can wait until morning. It can wait. She turned her chair back toward her bed, and then paused. *But I can't wait! I want to know more.*

Turning back to the computer she began a new search – "People become animals" – finding nothing useful – mostly articles about people behaving badly. *I wonder if they find an animal behaving horribly to its fellow animals, they say they're animals acting like humans.*

She sighed. *Probably have to have the name of the specific animal,* she thought. *But maybe I can put a question out on the internet somehow.* It'd only been a couple of weeks since Giselle and Yameno's story had flashed across the web complete with a video someone had taken with a cell phone.

"Just saw a story about a demonstration in Yerainia where a woman seemed to change to an Ibex when she died."

She pasted in the URL and continued. "Has anyone else heard any stories like this? Please share."

She closed down the computer and went back to bed.

When she awoke the next morning, she opened her bedroom door and called out to her dad, returning to load her computer while she waited for him.

"One group was a cult in Canada," she explained after telling him about the search. "A religious group that was very private and closed. There was only one relative, and she couldn't get anyone to pursue their disappearance. The authorities just seemed to think they had gone together somewhere in the wilderness to start a commune. The one thing the neighbors knew was there'd been a strange man seen with them for a couple of months before they disappeared – someone new to their group.

"Another was a whole extended family in East Asia somewhere whose neighbors got alarmed when the house seemed empty for several weeks. The father was very authoritarian, and the mother, her sisters, and the children were seldom seen out of the house. The authorities just dismissed it, saying they probably moved, and again, the neighbors had seen a man – very well dressed – who was a stranger to them, going in and out of their house for a few weeks before they disappeared."

She paused for a moment. "There were others like these from all over the world, and there was always an unknown man, sometimes two men."

"Strange, very strange," muttered Shen Ch'i.

"But dad, the strangest one is about something else. I've found another person who turned into an animal when she died."

She told him about the Ibex. "I tried to search for more, but really didn't know what to search on. I posted this one on LifeFriends, asking people to tell me if they had heard any other stories like this."

"Did you get any response?" he asked.

"Just a minute," she muttered, clicking on LifeFriends.

"Yes, there's a response!

> When I was working on ecological issues with the indigenous people of the Amazon last year, I heard a story about a tribal protest against a lumber company, where the lumber company guards shot and killed a number of people, and among the bodies they found three giant otters. The tribal people said they were humans who turned into otters. I never could substantiate the story, though.

That's it."

"Very interesting," mulled Shen Ch'i. "I wonder how many people are at Ninas Twei living in their Tla Twein? Are there any more responses?"

"Not yet. But I posted it very late last night."

"Well, keep an eye on it and talk to Giselle at breakfast this morning. We'd better get down there and see if we can save any more of *Los Gallos*."

Much to their relief, when they got to Shanti Place they found that Dario, Angelino, and the other *Los Gallos* members who had been missing the night before, had come back to get some breakfast. An Lien, Giselle, and Shen Ch'i decided to talk again with all the residents and see if they could get some of the children who were in the gangs to talk about their own experiences.

As soon as An Lien started talking about the disappearing groups she'd found out about on the internet, Angelino jumped up and ordered his gang to leave. "We'll get something to eat somewhere else."

Dario, and some of the others, hung back. "Wait, Angelino. Let's just hear what she has to say."

"*Vámanos! Apúrate!*" Angelino grabbed Dario's arm and pulled on it.

Dario pulled back. "No. I'm staying and listening. If you insist on going tonight, I'll go with you, but only to help rescue you when we get wherever they're taking us."

He pried Angelino's fingers off of his arm, and pushed him away.

Angelino stomped out of the room. Two of his gang members followed him, but the others remained behind.

An Lien continued telling about the missing groups.

When she'd finished, Shen Ch'i added, "These groups all have something in common. They've isolated themselves from other people. They have few friends to worry about where they are. They all think they're better than other people and…" He stopped and looked first at Dario, and then at the other gangs in the room. "And, each time, there was a strange man, or men, seen meeting with them before they disappeared. Men who appeared to be just like the people in the group, but more prosperous."

Dario turned to the other Gallos. "It's just like us. They aren't all Latinos, joining together to save the world for Latinos, like he tells us. They're all different kinds of people probably being told the same thing we are – that they are better than everyone else. *Es una mentira! Es un truco!* It's a trick. We are being led like a bull with a ring through his nose!"

Rashaun laughed. "You all being fooled! Demont, he tell us the truth. We gonna rule the world."

Sidney stood up. "Rashaun, listen to yourself. This guy telling you the same thing these other guys telling Dario. They both con-men. They both leading you around by the nose."

He turned and looked around at the other young people. "How about you Jingang Ninjas? Someone telling you the same thing?"

The three boys glanced at each other. Finally one said, "Maybe."

"You think it's true? You the best? You gonna be saved?"

The boy shrugged. Another one spoke up, "We're the smartest."

"Not smart enough to get classes and finish high school when you got the chance," laughed Sidney, nodding toward Giselle. The boy blinked and sat back in his chair, looking a little startled.

Dario stood up. "What is important is Alberto and Luis are going to take Angelino, Pedro, and Roberto tonight. We must find a way to stop them, or I'll have to go with them. Angelino is my cousin. I can't let him go alone."

Giselle nodded. "We could just go there and interrupt the ceremony. That would at least stop them tonight."

Dario stood up. "Yes, you do that. I'll find Angelino. I won't tell what's going to happen, but I'll stay with him."

Before she headed to work An Lien talked to Giselle about the stories of the woman who turned into an Ibex and the Brazilians who turned into otters. Sidney, who was standing nearby turned and looked directly at Giselle. "This related to that tree shadow thing?"

Giselle looked at An Lien raising her eyebrows.

An Lien grinned and shrugged.

Giselle turned back to Sidney. "I think I need to tell you about this." They headed for one of the sofas in the corner while Shen Ch'i took An Lien to work. Later Giselle and Shen Ch'i decided Sidney should go with them the next day when they headed to Arundel.

The night was very dark by eleven o'clock when Giselle, Shen Ch'i, and Sidney sequestered themselves under the freeway bridge.

Giselle and Shen Ch'i had come together, but Sidney had sneaked in from the other direction. They had decided not to hide where Giselle had hidden before, in case Angelino told the men about her and they checked to see if she was there. Instead, they hid on the other side of the clearing from the entrance. They spread out, ducking behind higher clumps of weeds close to the circle, so that they could easily interrupt the ritual.

They waited.

Giselle looked at her watch. *Eleven-fifty. They should be coming very soon. The men were already here by this time on Tuesday.*

They sat motionless and still no one came. Finally, Giselle looked at her watch again. *Twelve-thirty!* She heard a slight rustling and found Shen Ch'i next to her, talking in her ear. "I think they got wind of us. I don't think they're coming."

They both stood up and Sidney joined them. "What if they come late?" Sidney asked. "Maybe they're watching and waiting for us to leave."

"We should check back at Shanti Place and see if they came in. Maybe Dario talked them out of it," whispered Giselle.

"You two go." Sidney motioned toward the path. "They most likely watched you and didn't see me. I'll wait here. You check Shanti Place and come back. If they come and start the ceremony, I'll interrupt it."

"Be careful," warned Giselle. "Don't go into the circle."

"No, I'll stay outside. I'll run around the circle, knocking the drinks out of their hands. Just hurry back."

Shen Ch'i nodded. "Come, Giselle. We'll both walk out together, and go down the street and around the corner, then you run to the shelter and see if they're there and I'll sneak back to hide with Sidney."

Giselle ran as fast as she could to Shanti Place, only to hear that none of the missing *Los Gallos* had returned. She returned to the bridge, being careful once she got close to stay in the shadows, and slipped down through the undergrowth to where Sidney and Shen Ch'i were hiding. They looked at her expectantly and she shook her head.

They settled down again to wait.

Around one-thirty they heard something – someone singing.

"It's Ayo," whispered Sidney. "She be singing her sad song."

"Oh, no!" Giselle found tears flowing down her face.

"They gone. She singing because they gone."

Shen Ch'i sighed, shaking his head. As he pushed himself into a standing position, he suddenly seemed old. "Let's find Ayo. Maybe she'll tell us something. If not, we can at least all mourn together."

They pushed their way out of the weeds, down the path, and down the street to the park where Giselle had found Ayo before.

The gibbous moon seemed to shine directly on Ayo as she spun, her arms stretched out, her skirts flying. Her head was thrown back and out of her mouth came a mournful wailing. Tears streamed from her eyes.

They stopped at the edge of the circle and watched.

She abruptly stopped her spinning and singing, standing tall, looking at them. "They steal my power," she muttered. "They steal my power, and they do bad things with it."

Shen Ch'i came up next to her and very gently placed a hand on her shoulder. "Your power, Ayoabia?"

But she just shook her head, and pulling away from him, started to spin again, wailing her weeping song. Giselle began singing and spinning as well. After a moment Sidney joined them.

Shen Ch'i seated himself on the ground in lotus position, his hands resting palms upward on his knees. They stayed that way, singing, spinning, and meditating, until the moon dipped behind the western buildings and Ayo sank to the ground in a heap.

Giselle went to her. "Ayo, come with us. Come to Shanti Place."

Ayo shook her head. "I be all right. Just go away now. I be all right."

Giselle sat next to her and gave her a long hug. The men knelt and embraced both of them.

They headed back to the shelter, leaving Ayo huddled on the blacktop.

The next morning Angelino, Dario, and the others did not return. A search of the neighborhood told them what they already knew. The meeting place had been changed. *Los Gallos* had been taken, and with them Dario.

EARTH WOMAN TREE WOMAN QUARTET
BOOK 3

LUHA
AND THE
GIANTS OF GOD

Connie Pwll Walck Tyler

LUHA AND THE GIANTS OF GOD

Invocation:

Like a Tiger, I am Growing

Like the lotus I am blooming.
Like the lotus I am blooming.

I, daughter of the mountains,
Fierce mother of all,
Sounding the great Om with my conch,
Firm as thunder, am I,
Striking the demons like lightning
With my sword of knowledge.

I, daughter of the mountains,
Fierce mother of all,
Like the lotus I am blooming.

I, daughter of the mountains,
fierce mother of all.
Like the tiger, I am growing.

1

Luhanada Moonmother

Grayness – whirling swirls of dark and dirty gray still surrounded Luhanada, as she slipped back into awareness after a long period of no time, no sound. Shades of gray whirling like the vortex that brought them to Ninas Twei, but no colors, no song.

And pain.

She moaned aloud – a small whisper of a moan, but sound.

Sound! *Can I sing?*

She tried to whisper her song out into the mist:

> *I am I.*
> *I am I.*

Flashes of music.

> *(Come, come.)*
> *I am I, she cried out.*
> *I am I.*

Oh, God I can't do this alone.

Faintly again she heard:

> *(Come!*
> *Come!*
> *Hammer your feet*
> *to the beat of the drum.)*
> *Nameless One called for light, she whispered.*
> *Nameless One called for light, for me, for me.*

Still, she was tossed in the gray whorls of mist, spinning, spinning alone, throbbing with pain. *This is death,* she thought. *With Tata beside me it was life and joy.*

"Tata!" she cried out. "Where are you?"

A whisper.

A whisper a long, long way away:

> *Look at me!*
> *I am the wild wings of the earth*
> *and the violent sea.*
> *High flyer!*

"Tata!" she called again, louder.

> *I am the eyes of the sun,*
> *piercing.*
> *I am the key.*
> *Wind rider!*

But the song was disappearing into the mists.

> *I am the voice of life,*
> *the song of the One.*
> *High Crier!*

…and the last words faded away to nothing.

"Tata," she whispered. *I can't,* she thought, and *s*he felt herself slipping again into deep, gray nothingness…

Time passed.

Deep inside she heard Tata's voice – or was it her own?

You must. You must.

> *Come!*
> *Come! sang the whispers.*
> *Lift up your voice*
> *to answer the One.*
> *Come! Come!*
> *Answer the call*
> *of the earth and the sun!*

I am I, I am now, she sang, her voice just barely sounding in the gray nothingness.

I am the protector, and her voice became stronger.
I am justice.
I am wisdom.
I am Love.
I am Love!

"I'm needed. The children need me. Ninas Twei needs me. Just sing," she whispered to herself. "Sing."

I am justice. I am wisdom.
I am I.
I am I.
I am the protector.
I am the law.

First faintly, and then louder and louder, she heard the answer.

Seas crashing,
like thunder rolling,
like drums beating,
a call to the brethren,
a cry to the wary,
The time has come!

She joined the chorus.

Come! Come!
Hammer your feet
to the beat of the drum.

And the gray began to turn to blue – swirling mists of blue.

Come! Come!
Lift up your voices
to answer the One.
Come! Come!
Answer the call
of the earth and the sun!
We bear the song for those seeking the One.

Suddenly she found herself crouched beside the Weaving Tree, her long tail flicking back and forth. *I'm here,* she thought. *I'm here like Singing Swan and Tuwillia. I'm a cougar and I'm here forever.*

She looked around her, searching the path, the rocks, the tree. "Where is Tata?" she whispered. "I heard his voice, but so far away." Laying down, resting her head on her paws, closing her eyes, and breathing slowly she let the tears pour down her cheeks. *I wonder if real cougar's cry?* she thought and fell into a deep sleep.

Tata Sundancer

Look at me! sang Tata.
I am the wild wings of the earth
and the violent sea.
High flyer!

"Yes, look at you," voices whispered. "Look at you, look at you."

"Who are you?" he asked.

"Who are we?" the voices laughed. "Vibrating strings, vibrating strings of things," they said, joyfully. "Quarks, photons, electrons. Strings."

Voices called out all around him, "Up, Down, Charm, Strange, Bottom, Top. Yes, and Leptons – Muons, Tauons, Neutrinos, Electrons." And a very deep, slow voice, "Neutralinos.... the dark,... heavy ones... floating... between."

"What?" he asked. "I don't understand?"

"Energy," said some, and "Matter," whispered others. "We... are the universe," rumbled the Neutralinos.

"The universe?" he asked.

"We are the whole, and the parts. You, too, are the whole and the parts of the universe. Come dance with us. Follow the light back to the beginning. Come with us."

"But Luhanada and the children; Earth, Ninas Twei... I'm needed at Ninas Twei." He spun in space looking for earth, looking for Ninas Twei.

"No," the deep slow voices of the neutralinos rolled past him. "In time,... in time,... but not now. Now... you are needed... here. The Tsin Twei... needs you... here," and Tata felt himself flowing down paths of light and color, surrounded by the vibrating strings of things, soaring back and back in time until he found himself in a hot, hot squished-in place – a murky chaos, without space or time. He was himself, and he was more than himself. He was All, the totality – pulled in, sucked in, to a tiny lump, rolled into a tightly loving ball of oneness – rolled in with all the quarks, and leptons, and dark neutralinos.

Words sang:

There was neither existence nor non-existence then.
No realm of space or sky.
There was neither death nor immortality then.
No sign of night or day.

Death and life,
Neither death nor life.

The Rig Veda, he thought, the beginning of time.

He was One and All, a singularity, the whole. He felt ecstatic, filled with joy, and he sang his own song, and All sang his song, together.

Look at me! (Look at us, Look at the me/us, the We.)
We are the wild wings of the universe.
High flyer!
We are the eyes of the suns and the stars, piercing – the key.
Wind rider!
We are the voice of life, the song of the One.
High Crier!

"Ten to negative forty-three seconds," whispered the All. "Vibration. Vibration in vacuum. False vacuum. Quantum fluctuation. One thousand billion degrees."

"Thick," whispered one. "Dense," whispered another, with a little wiggle.

Tata felt everything beginning to move, and again the voice sang from the Vedas:

What stirred? Where?
That one breathed, Windless,
By its own impulse.
Darkness, hidden by darkness.
That one arose through the power of heat.

Tata laughed. The All, the We laughed.

Vibrating strings, they sang out.
Vibrating strings of quarks.
Particles, anti-particles, things, not things, popping in and out.

Laughter and delight whispered around him.

Existence, nonexistence.
Things. In and out.
Where? When? Uncertain, unknown.
Popping, colliding particles, in a hot! hot! hot-hot plasma!

And a raucous chorus of:

Energy/pop/particle/pop/energy/pop/particle/pop, pop, pop, pop.

WHOOSH!

Tata felt himself, the whole, the We, expanding, bursting outwards in a leap of rambunctious delight!

Annihilation, the Strings sang.
Radiation, inflation,
creation inflation,
flying outward, every-ward,
faster than light, faster, faster, faster than light.

And then – fluctuations.

There was a cooling and a joining, a becoming, and a separating.

Tata felt confused. There was a yearning for the whole, and a curiosity, a questing in the separateness that was a joining in new ways of the parts that were once the whole. There was a freshness in the cooling, and yet, and yet, still a yearning for the hot dark lump of oneness.

One second, sang the All.
Time is.
Matter binding, twisting, twining.
Becoming.
Becoming.
Three minutes, sang the All.
Nuclei forming,
but still inflation, creation inflation,
flying outward, every-ward, faster than light.

Tata felt this outward flinging of self, wholeness, but at the same time a clumping, pulling into separateness, separate things. Deuterium, helium formed, laughing with delight at their birth. Still Tata felt a confusion of wants and desires. A yearning to return to the hot singularity, and a joy in the creation of newness, of things. *Of me, perhaps,* he thought. *Eventually me.*

The cooling continued, and he felt a slowing as the forming, becoming, grew denser, and yet more separate. There was a floating, a kind of endless, slow growing.

"Not seconds," whispered the One. "Not minutes. Years. Five hundred thousand years. Electrons whirl, nuclei curl, atoms form hydrogen, helium, free-floating in space," and Tata floated, drifted, a kind of slow dance through time, watching as the electrons were pulled into a bond, becoming hydrogen, helium, and lithium atoms, forming clouds, drifting through space. Drifting..., and then a pulling, the first feeling of gravity, a sucking inward again, but not the whole. Separatenesses becoming. Parts that gathered, and collapsed, and ignited.

Sheets of light swirled into clusters and lacy formations, pulling the Separatenesses inward.

"Whee," cried the Quarks, as they slid down filaments of light and lace, forming galaxies in the giant web of the Universe.

"Whoa," cried the Neutralinos, as they begin to cool and condense.

"Not seconds. Not minutes. Not years." shouted the Leptons!

"Eons," muttered the Neutralinos.

"Gravitation pulls hydrogen, helium," the Strings explained. "Hydrogen fuses, stars form, stars shine," and they laughed with glee, "Stars shine!"

Tata looked around him at the coalescing stars, as he became the stars. He was filled with joy and awe. "I can still feel the whole," he murmured, "and yet I am separate, pulled into starness."

"Hydrogen, Helium," the elements introduce themselves. Their laughter is a little lower pitched now, but the giggles of the Strings are still there, echoing in the laugh. Then a tightness, a pulling of that part of him that was the star into tight, tight, hotness, heaviness, until... "Carbon, Oxygen," a still deeper laugh, and then deeper still, "Silicon, Titanium, Manganese," and deepest of all, "Iron," but Tata could hear the Stringy giggles, still there, a descant over the deep harmonies of the heavier elements. "Gravity pulls, and pulls," the Quarks explained. "It crushes, cooks, changing hydrogen and helium, smashing hydrogen and helium, gathering into heavier and heavier forms until they form iron. And then..."

"Too tight, too hot," called out the elements, now heavier, deeper. "Push, push back."

Suddenly a huge explosion thrust Tata out, out, scattered, here, there through space. "Supernova! Explosion," giggled the Quarks and Leptons, roared the heavier elements, "flinging nuclear matter into space."

Tata felt himself flung outward, and then pulled inward, in an endless creation and destruction of stars, and galaxies, and new elements. Created and destroyed a million times, first part of one thing; then part of another, flowing, bursting, decaying, ever becoming.

Earth, and his life on it, receded into the background. What difference did it make what happened on earth faced with the glorious continuity of the universe? Here he just was. No words. No plans. No thoughts. Just being – endless being – swooping through the universe, like riding the thermals at the edge of a cliff. Sliding through the various irregular shapes of smaller galaxies, and spinning in and out of the larger spiral galaxies. Some older ones were like hills he flew up and slid down, and the oldest were elliptical, sending him round and round, until he flew off to find another.

As he explored, he saw millions of stars with billions of planets in each galaxy. Billions of planets!

Then something felt … he was spinning though a spiral that felt familiar, like home. Home.

"It is home," explained the Quarks and Leptons. "The Milky Way. This is where you lived when you were Dan."

Tata spun around, looking for Earth. There were so many stars that could be Sun, many with planets.

"Billions of stars," laughed the Quarks. "Billions of planets," added the Leptons.

"But my world has life on it," said Tata. "Won't that help me find it?"

The Quarks and Leptons collapsed in gales of laughter. The Neutralinos whispered in their deep, deep dark voices. "There are millions of planets with life on them. Millions."

"Millions?" exclaimed Tata. "How could there be so many planets with life on them?"

"Us," called out Nitrogen, Phosphorus, and Sulfur. "We're all over the place."

"Me, too," interrupted Silicon and Carbon in unison. "Sometimes me. Sometimes you!" They pointed at each other, and their laughter ricocheted off the nearby stars.

"They need us," – suddenly Tata felt a wetness as Hydrogen and Oxygen sprayed him with water – "but we're abundant!"

"What color is your world?" asked the Strings.

"Blue and green," Tata answered. "Beautiful blue and green with swirling white clouds. But wouldn't all planets with life be blue and green?"

"Oh, no," answered the strings. "Look here," they pointed to a planet that was mostly red and orange. "Lovely life down there."

"Red?" exclaimed Tata. "Red life?"

"And yellow, too," said the Strings. "And all of it, us. We are them and they are us." They chanted and danced joyfully. "We are them and they are us. We are them and they are us. We are all..."

"But... not... everywhere," muttered the Neutralinos. "Some... are gone. Yours..., too..., will be gone... soon."

"What?" exclaimed Tata. "What do you mean?"

Soft as a whisper the deep voice replied. "Gone."

A smell wafted past him. An odor of burning plastic.

"Follow it," whispered the Neutralinos, and Tata followed the stink back to the ugly lump of a planet that still smoldered with the poisons that had killed it.

"Life... was here," they rumbled. "Magnificent complex life. Thinkers. Doers. Users." As they got closer Tata could see crumbling buildings, different from those of Earth, but not unrecognizable as buildings.

"What happened?" he asked.

"Greed," rumbled the Neutralinos.

"Stupidity," trilled the strings. "So smart, and yet so ignorant."

"Indifference," whispered the Oxygen and Hydrogen. "They destroyed us."

"They... knew... better," boomed the Neutralinos, "but they couldn't let go. They wanted more... and more... and more."

"More," murmured the strings, no longer laughing. "And they hurt each other, destroyed each other."

"It happened here," said the Neutralinos, sweeping him off to another distant solar system, "and... here," and another, "also here, and soon, Earth."

Tata felt a deep longing. "What can I do? Can I stop it? Can we stop it?"

Luha Down the Crevice

Luha awoke in the dark to a wild shaking, the ground rolling and undulating under her. Pain shot through her. She dug her claws into the ground and screamed a high pitched cougar scream. The ground stopped shaking as abruptly as it had begun and she closed her eyes.

Tuwillia cleared her throat. Luha's eyes popped open. "I see you have finally joined me, Luhanada," grumbled the old turtle.

Luha stretched her back legs out behind her, looking around at the shadowy tree and the bright stars overhead. *Ninas Twei,* she thought, and remembered.

"Gunther shot us." She looked around. "But where is Dan? I thought... I felt... I mean..." She paused, shaking her head helplessly.

"The hawk, Tata?" questioned Tuwillia.

Luha nodded, "I know he died with me. Do you think he's with Singing Swan?" She jumped up. "I should go look for him."

"No, he's not with Singing Swan. He's not at Ninas Twei."

Luha felt tears flow down her face again. "Is he alive? Could he have lived?"

Tuwillia slowly shook her head. "I don't know. He's not here, but you are, and you have something important to do." She paused. "Did you forget about the children? Did you forget about the Tsin Twei and the pain?"

Luha sat back down, her tail flicking in back of her. "No. Yes, for a moment, but no, I didn't forget about the children – or the pain, the danger to the Tsin Twei."

Tuwillia's voice lowered. "And my pond. The water in my pond is sinking. My pond is drying up." She pointed her head in the direction of the weaving, and the crown of the tree. Beyond the tree Luha could just see a silver glint of water where the meadow sloped downwards.

"Your pond?" asked Luha, her voice rising. "Ninas Twei should be safe. How can the water at Ninas Twei..." *So many things going wrong,* she thought. *How can I...?*

Tuwillia just shook her head and walked slowly over to the edge of the crevice the children had fallen down, yawning just a few feet away. "I've watched this crevice for many days, but there's been no sign of the children, and there's been much pain and shaking."

"Many days?" questioned Luha.

Tuwillia nodded her head. "The sun has risen and set many, many times and the children..." She looked back at Luhanada. "I can't get down there."

Luha rose to her feet, moving cautiously to the edge, peering down. It was steep and deep, and the bottom seemed to curve away under a ledge. But the walls were not sheer. There were ledges all the way down. There was no way a turtle could go down it, but...

Luha's human self saw the leaps from ledge to ledge down the crevice that had swallowed the children as frightening – maybe impossible – but the cougar in her laughed.

"Piece of cake," she whispered, launching herself down to the closest ledge.

There was a kind of exhilaration in the thrusts out across space and Luha found herself moving from ledge to ledge faster and faster, as she became more and more comfortable with her cougar self. When she reached the bottom of the crevice she saw that the floor extended under the last ledge making a small cave. Light shone dimly through an opening on the far side of the cave.

She crept to the opening and saw a wide flat plateau ahead of her that seemed to end at another drop off. Crawling out and looking up, she saw that the outer wall swooped upward to form a high wide dirt dome reaching out over the plateau, and whatever lay beyond the drop off. Directly opposite the plateau on the other side of the dome, steep cliffs worked downward to another cave – but very large and dark, filled with shadowed geometrical shapes.

A huge cavern, she thought peering into the heights of the dome. *It looks unnatural, like a quarry, like the dirt has been removed leaving these rough orange cliffs.*

There was light here, but she couldn't tell where it came from. There was no sky, only the orange and gray dirt ceiling of the cavern, which seemed to be covered with something tangled and snaky hanging down from it.

"Roots!" she exclaimed out loud. "The tree. The roots of the tree hanging out where they can't be nourished by the earth." There were so many of them and they looked so dry, so lifeless.

But where were the children? If they had fallen and died their bodies would have been at the bottom of the crevice. She peered out at the edges of the plateau hunting anxiously for any sign of life.

On either side of the opening she had come through, piles of rubble from small avalanches ran like rivulets out onto the ground. Had they tried to climb up the dome? It was very steep, and even her cougar self wouldn't be able to climb where it began to swoop inward to form the ceiling. It would make more sense to climb back up the crevice, and they hadn't done that.

She lowered her head to the ground and sniffed. How strange. No scents of wild life

Chachuli! A very faint scent. *But she's Enid, not Chachuli!* Whatever happened, the children – at least Enid – had changed back to human form. *But I didn't change. I'm dead.*

She followed the faint scent cautiously across the plateau, looking back once, making sure she could find the small opening to the crevice. Creeping toward the edge, she swung her head back and forth, sniffing and watching for danger. She saw no one, nothing except the muddy sides of the dome, the hanging tendrils of the tree roots high above her. There were no plants, no greenery anywhere on the plateau or the sides of the cavern. Even the faintly lingering scent seemed remote, as if only the smallest wisps of odor remained after a cleansing.

As she got closer to the edge, she realized the geometric shapes in the dark cave on the other side of the canyon were buildings – luxurious, modern buildings with expanses of steel and glass built into a wide, deep dark cave carved into the far wall of the larger cavern, its floor just a little lower than the plateau.

The buildings, starting with one story in the outer circle, stepped upward in four concentric circles until they reached a tall octagonal building with a tower in the middle – a building tiered like a concrete, glass, and steel wedding cake, each level a little smaller in circumference than the one below, flowing up to the tower.

The outer circle of the little city was incomplete, partially cut off by the canyon so that the buildings actually backing on the canyon were the two story buildings in the second circle. On either side of the outer circle, the cave floor, filled with what appeared to be bushes, sloped gently upward. A tall chain-linked fence walled these sloping brushy areas and the buildings off from the canyon.

A small city, she thought. *This doesn't fit with the concept the Tsin Twei. It's too… manufactured.*

There were no lights on in the buildings. It was so dark in the smaller cave she wondered if anyone was even there.

Pressing herself closer to the ground, she followed the elusive scent, creeping closer to the edge of the plateau where the Enid scent faded into nothing.

Peering over the edge she saw a dry lifeless canyon, with sides that went straight down, as if cut by a machine. Halfway down, there was a heavy metal net stretching across the entire canyon. Wafting up from below was the smell of sweat – human sweat, and fear.

Under the net, the canyon floor was almost completely filled with some kind of large gray, egg-shaped bubbles set on their sides in even tightly packed rows, the pointed ends all facing to the right and touching the broad end of the next egg. It was hard to tell how big they were, but she thought they might each be the size of a garden shed.

Lines of heavy cable came out of dark square holes in the cliff under the little city and crossed the canyon under the net, but above each row of eggs. Above the net was another set of square dark holes.

To her right, the canyon ended in another straight wall. Above the plateau it curved upward enclosing the cavern. The end of the canyon on the left was much closer, and again, dropped straight from the plateau to the canyon floor with no ledges to provide a way down. Unless there was an opening in the cave wall behind the city, Luha could see no exit from the cavern except the crevice she had come down – the crevice that had not been there before the earth shook and the children fell.

But at this end of the canyon something did stretch across the cliff from the plateau toward the buildings on the far side – a thick protrusion, with thinner lines of gray stretching at angles above and below it. Something metal.

A bridge? But if the children went that way, wouldn't she catch their scent?

She looked back down the plateau to the right. Maybe there were other caves like the one at the bottom of the crevice she had come down. She moved quickly towards the farther end of the canyon, keeping close to the wall looking for openings, and constantly moving her head to catch any smells. The wall angled closer and closer to the edge of the canyon until she found herself on a small ledge looking down again at the canyon floor.

At this end of the canyon there was a space under the net without any eggs. What looked like large metal pipes stretched across the floor in rows, and the cables stretched above them. *A place for more eggs?* she wondered.

She peered across the canyon at the dark square holes in the wall, but could see nothing. "And no children," she whispered.

She heaved a sigh and ran swiftly back toward the other end of the canyon and the place opposite the crevice where she had caught Enid's scent. Crouching down to peer over the edge, she examined the canyon again.

They must have fallen. But the net. If they fell off the cliff they would land in that net and then where would they go? Could they have crawled over to those openings under the city? Were they in that city, or below that city wherever those openings led to?

She looked again at the strange metal thing at the near end of the canyon. Staring up at the roots, hanging dry above this possible bridge, she saw something else. Something gray like the bridge below it attached to the sides of the dome. She loped quickly toward the bridge.

Scaffolding, holding the metal bridge to the side of the cliff, stretched across the wall just above the edge of the plateau. A slopping path carved into the edge of the plateau, led the few feet down to the walkway, which hugged the side of the cliff as it crossed the cavern to the dark cave with the buildings.

High above the bridge, hidden behind the roots, was a wide pipe coming down from the cavern ceiling and stretching across to the city where it disappeared again into the wall of the city cave.

Is it coming from or going to Ninas Twei? she thought. *What was in the pipe?* It just didn't fit. Ninas Twei didn't have pipes and metal bridges.

Her cougar self was suspicious of the bridge.

She smelled it and could find no trace of the children. If they had been here, their scent had been completely scrubbed away.

They fell, she thought. *I'm sure they fell and went in one of those openings under the city.* She would have to go over the bridge and find a way down into those openings.

"Oh, Tata," she whispered. "I wish you were here doing this with me."

She put one tentative paw on the metal pathway, and pushed. Solid. Slowly she crept out on the bridge, following as it hugged the edge of the cavern, gaining more confidence as she moved along. Occasionally she glanced down, but saw nothing but the earth-raw edges of the canyon and the gray of the egg-shaped bubbles under the net.

As she came closer to the city in its dark cave, it seemed even more artificial. The buildings had a strange regularity to them, and the shiny gray of the steel beams seemed a very unnatural contrast to the muddy orange-brown of the cavern walls.

At the end of the bridge, near the top of the slope filled with bushes on this side of the city, there was a gate that connected to the chain-linked fence that edged the canyon. It was padlocked, but it stopped four or five feet short of the top of the bridge's scaffolding. She scrambled up and over, leaping onto the path that ran between the fence and the green bushes.

Green, yes, she thought as she looked around her. *But plastic!* The mass of plastic bushes covered the slope down to the edge of the city and the leaves of the bushes were dusty as if the area wasn't used.

If Tata was here he could look for the children from the air.

But... but... She sniffed the air, the ground again. *No birds! No mice! No other small creatures. Plastic plants, no animals.*

"This can't be part of Ninas Twei," she whispered. "Where am I? Where is Tata?"

She gave a big sigh and turned to survey the city.

There were no paths through the bushes. The one she stood on ran down between the chain-link fence and the plastic bushes, and then past the houses edging the canyon.

Four one story buildings lined the bottom edge of the park – rather elegant residences made of concrete and steel, with big plate glass windows that faced out on the bushy slope. Their front doors opened out on the outer circular path which continued to the right, until it merged at the bottom of the slope into the path she stood on – the one that edged the canyon. From here she could see that straight paths cut across the circles, moving between the buildings in radial lines toward the center. More plastic greenery hugged the walls of the buildings, making a border along the edge of both the circular and the radial pathways – a green trim against the concrete, steel, and glass of the buildings.

She tested the air and the ground for scents. A few people had used this path recently, but not the children.

Creeping down past the plastic bushes to the edge of the little park, she crouched, surveying the dark, quiet one-story houses to her left, and the taller ones in the second, two-storied circle of buildings in front of her. The two story buildings looked like duplexes.

The light in the cavern remained uniformly bright, but the darkness in the city cave began to change, the cave ceiling gradually brightening as if simulating daylight. Lights began to appear in some of the buildings, and she could see the shadows of people moving behind the curtained windows of the duplexes.

People, she thought, *in human shape, not in their Tla Twei form. This can't be part of Ninas Twei.*

Slipping behind the nearest house in the outer circle, she tried to see inside, but the curtains hid the occupants.

A radial path ran to the right of the house. The greenery lining it was a perfect hidden tunnel toward the center of the city. As she crept through it she flared her nose, constantly seeking the children.

She had made it to the first circular path, separating the large houses of the outer circle and the duplexes in the next circle, when a carillon rang out, startling her. She pulled herself tight against the ground listening to a familiar triumphant marching melody. *A hymn, or something from an opera?* She couldn't remember.

A door opened somewhere and she froze. A man came out of one of the houses farther around the curve and headed up the nearest path toward the center of the city.

As soon as he was out of sight she scanned right and left, then dashed across the circular path, tunneling through the bushes past the duplexes, and up to the next corner. Men were coming out of each of the circular paths ahead of her, and heading up this path toward the center of the city.

Crouching beneath the plastic greens, she waited.

At the third circle she had a longer wait as more men came out of the three-story buildings.

Apartments, she thought, looking up at the balconies on the second and third floors. She waited until all had reached the next corner before dashing across.

The path ended at the innermost circular path. Across the path was the obtuse angle of one corner of the octagonal central building. An artificial tree whose branches reached up past several tiers of the building was "planted" at the corner.

The men were turning right and climbing some steps to a wide, cement apron, like a stage, which centered on another corner of the central building, this one facing the radial path ending at the canyon. Tall doors cutting into this corner stood open and they were greeting each other and men coming from the opposite side of the building jovially as they moved purposely through the doors. Most of them were white, but a few were brown skinned, and some looked Asian. Many were clothed in casual, but expensive, western attire, but those coming out of the doors of the buildings backing on this inner circle wore camouflage, like a uniform.

She slipped under the green tunnel next to the building to her right, coming almost immediately to an opening in front of this building's entrance. From there she had a good view of the apron and the central building's tall steel doors etched with circles within circles.

Directly across from her on the lowest tier of the building was a *bas relief* of a naked muscled giant, with books and scrolls cradled in his right arm, raising another book in his left hand so that it reached over the doors. The naked figure towered over the heads of etched crowds of much smaller, clothed people – men, women and children – who, by their clothing, represented many different cultures. Across the bottom was an ocean with large waves rolling over the little people who were raising their arms in anguished pleading toward the giant towering above them.

Her ears flattened against her head and a shiver slipped down the fur on her back.

The men poured into the building, the doors closed behind them, and the song ended leaving a clanging last chord echoing behind it.

The paths were empty again. She waited, ears perked, listening.

When she was sure no one else was coming, she crept carefully onto the path and looked up at the *bas relief*. The words THE CHRONICLES OF THE GIANTS OF GOD were carved on the book held up over the door. The books in the naked giant's right arm had titles of scriptures from all the major religions.

Her tail flicked and she turned to circle around the back of the tall, tiered building, sniffing for the children. There was an artificial tree at each of the eight corners, and across from each of them, radial paths back to the outer circle. Two smaller windowless steel doors were set in the middle of sides three and six, and when she looked down the radial on the very back corner she saw, rather than dead ending at the edge of the park, it led to the double doors of a utilitarian looking one story building on the outer circle.

All eight sides of the building held a *bas relief,* each with a naked muscular giant with the little pleading people overrun with waves below. To the left of the book-holding giant, the huge naked figure was juggling newspapers and magazines, computers and televisions, his eyes turned upward toward the circling objects, a wide grin on his face.

Around the next corner was a giant with a war plane in one hand, and a missile in the other.

The fourth naked giant wore a helmet and combat boots, an automatic rifle at ready rest in his hands.

The first giant who actually looked down at the little people was on the other side of the back corner. He had a bag in one hand and was scattering toys, electronic equipment, and appliances down on the little people, who were grabbing the objects, fighting over them even as the waves reached up to drown them. This giant had a strange satisfied smirk on his face.

Luha's nostrils flared and her mouth curved up showing her eye teeth.

The next giant stood sideways in front of a table piled with what looked like coins. His eyes were on the table, but one hand reached down toward the little people.

At first she thought he was pouring streams of money down at them, but when she looked closer she realized the money was flying upward from the people to his hand and another stream was flowing from him into the cupped left hand of the seventh giant, who stood with his right hand held high in the air, fingers spread in a vee. At his feet were a group of buildings that looked like state and country capitals, court houses, and municipal buildings.

The last wall, on the other side of the tall main doors, held a two-headed giant with oil well derricks balanced on three of his four hands. Luha's eyes grew wide as she realized the fourth hand was gathering coins flowing from the government buildings in the last panel.

Who would ever create sculptures like these? she wondered, shaking her head, as she padded quietly toward the open space in front of the cement apron and the tall main doors facing the canyon.

She froze, overwhelmed by the scent of fear. Her teeth bared in a snarl she moved her head back and forth, nostrils flared.

A frightened crowd had been here and their scent over-laid the ground like a multitude of ghosts! Who were they? Not the men who'd gone in the building. Others.

Where were Enid and Jesús? *Are they hiding someplace below this city, or do these people have them? Please,* she thought, her tail snapping back and forth, *please don't let them be found by these people.*

She needed to get down below the city where those dark openings were. Was the way down inside this central building? The doors were the only way in. Even if she could open them with her paws they might lead right into the midst of the men.

She swung her head back and forth, back and forth. Where should she go?

Control, she whispered to herself. *Keep control.* She would have to hide and watch, bide her time. Perhaps when the men...

Wow, no women, she thought, startled. There were no women in the group headed in the doors, and there were no women among the giants in the *bas reliefs* although there were many in the small people below them. *And in the scent of fear... many.*

She shuddered and crawled under the greenery. Pushing herself back against the wall of the triangular building across from the giant with the books, she curled into a tight ball, tucking her nose under a paw.

The carillon rang again, this time ringing the melody of a grandfather clock sounding the hour, and tolling nine times. No one left the central building and when the last bell faded, the city sank into silence again.

She laid her ears back and a low snarl rumbled in her throat. She would have to search the city. Pushing her nose slowly out under the greenery, she sniffed and listened and looked, finally crawling back out on the path.

The building she was next to was triangular except for a flattened area at the point facing the central building. Double doors decorated with hammered copper sculptures of men lifting heavy loads, and soldiers with guns filled the flattened point. Above the hammered copper was a small window.

She pushed herself up on her hind feet, leaning her forepaws against the door, so she could peer in the window at the small hallway with an elevator across from the door. She could just read the floor numbers above the elevator – 1, 2, 3, 4. No basement.

She turned and trotted down the path that went from the temple doors to the canyon, her head moving constantly back and forth, testing the air, ears alert to any sound.

Peering down the next circular pathway, she noted that the wide backs of the four-story buildings had something that looked like stores opening at street level. On the upper floors, balconies suggested apartments.

Afraid she might be seen through the plate glass windows of the stores, she continued down the path past the next circle – the three-storied apartments. They had entrances on both sides of the buildings decorated with circles of a light gray metal, stamped with abstract designs that seemed to be related to the concentric circles on the temple doors. She didn't dare look in the windows in these doors. One side faced the stores and the other the duplexes.

When she turned to look back toward the temple she noticed a sign on the building on her right, on the corner closest to the central building – NICKEL ONE, written in steel letters a little above the eye level of a human. The building across the path also had a NICKEL ONE sign. Looking back at the buildings on the inner circle, she could see that there was a word on the corner of those buildings as well. She ran back to look.

COPPER ONE – and again the same word on both buildings.

Turning back towards the canyon, she trotted to the circle of duplexes, sniffing the crisscross of human scents, many edged with fear. The words SILVER ONE were on the inner corner of these buildings and there were signs of life in the ground floor windows of the duplex on the right – lights on, curtains open, and some shadows moving in the background.

She loped on down the path to the edge of the canyon.

Slinking down past the greenery on the circular path back of the duplexes to the next radial path, she found herself back where she'd first entered the city. There were no words on the elegant one-story houses, but when she turned to look at the duplexes, she saw the sign SILVER TWO. *The second radial path,* she thought. *Numbers for the radials; words for the circles. 'One' goes from the central building to the canyon.*

She sat, reaching around to smooth her fur with her tongue, trying to decide where to go next. A small sound alerted her, and she pushed herself under the greenery just as the back door of one of the duplexes opened a crack, and then a little farther. A head peeked out, and looked up and down the outer path. The woman slipped furtively out and quickly into the back door on the other side of the duplex.

Frightened, thought Luha.

She stayed where she was, hoping the woman would come out again. Could she ask her about the children? Would she be frightened of her cougar form? She flicked her tail nervously. She had to find the children. She laid her head down on her paws and waited.

Her ears perked. Footsteps and low voices coming around the circle from radial One. She pulled herself in, crouched, hidden, waiting as two men in camouflage, with pistols at their hips, came strolling toward her, chatting.

She held her breath as they passed, not relaxing until they moved out of sight around the circle.

As soon as they were gone, the woman slipped back out of the neighboring door, her eyes on the path where the men had been, and into her own door so fast Luha didn't have a chance to speak to her. A moment later the carillon started chiming again, this time ending with twelve gongs.

Luha started back down radial Two towards the central building – maybe the men would all leave and she'd be able to get in – but as she got to the Silver circle, several young boys in maroon pants and white shirts came around the path toward her. *A school uniform*, she thought. At the corner they split up each going into a different duplex. She snugged herself behind the greenery. If the boys came out again, she would follow them. *Perhaps the children...*

She was dozing when the carillon rang again, this time chiming the three quarter hour. The boys came out of the duplexes and headed back clockwise around the circle.

She followed.

She was about to dash across the next radial when she heard a murmur of voices and footsteps from the Nickel circle. She pulled back into her tunnel and watched as men came around the corner of the Nickel path and headed toward the temple.

The carillon rang again, signaling one o'clock. The paths emptied. Leaping across radial Four, she dashed for the corner of radial Five. The boys were gone.

Left to right, left to right, nostrils flared, she listened.

Hurried footsteps to her left – a child running on the outer circle. She reached the circle just in time to see him dash through the double doors of the one-story building she had seen from the back corner of the central building.

This building was flanked by two paved play yards. The plastic park extended behind the play yards on each side, but the building itself was backed by the wall of the cavern. *If there's a way out of here through the cave wall, she thought, it's behind this building – this school.*

Crouched and wary, she moved back and forth on the paths from the school testing the air and ground for scent of Enid and Jesús.

Nothing.

Crawling into a green tunnel hiding place, she waited.

The silence was broken again by footsteps and chatter, this time from deeper in the city. Peering up the radial she saw the two men in camouflage pass on the Copper circle. Their footsteps faded quickly.

A buzzer sounded. The doors opened and boys came walking silently, in single straight lines, from each door – ten to fifteen boys in each line. The ones coming from the door on the left were younger, the ones on the right older, but all wore the maroon slacks and white shirt.

She searched the younger group carefully as they waited, silently watching a man who had followed them out the door. The man clapped his hands and they broke out into noisy play. There were a few boys of color, but no one even resembled Jesús.

She focused on the older boys. Still no Jesús.

The buzzer rang again. They lined up and marched back into the building.

Her ears perked. Footsteps again – a little closer, but still on an inner circle. She watched the two men pass over the radial at the Nickel circle, and a while later, at the Silver circle. *This circle will be next.*

She waited.

The carillon rang three o'clock. The front door opened, and the boys filed out, separating into smaller groups headed in different directions. There were no girls, and no Jesús.

Luha sighed and put her head down on her paws. Even if Tata was here, he couldn't fly around looking for the children. He'd be seen. Ears alert for the patrol, she followed the outer path to the other side of the city passing over three of the radial paths and coming back to radial One.

Like the other side, there were four large single residences.

Eight residences and eight sides to the central building, she thought. *Eight giants in the 'bas reliefs'.* One duplex in each of the eight segments of the circle. Sixteen homes in the duplexes and who knows how many apartments in the two other circles. Why weren't there more people wandering around? She couldn't see any activity in the three-story or four-story buildings, but she knew there were people – women and the boys, at least – in the duplexes.

Voices, footsteps again. She crouched to watch the two men pass, this time on the outer circle.

Well, she thought, as she crept back counter-clockwise around the Silver circle testing for scent at the intersections, *this stupid plastic greenery has certainly served me well. I'll bet that wasn't the intention!*

She had just crossed radial Eight when the carillon sounded again, this time signaling five o'clock. Three men came down the radial from the central building. She crouched lower, her side rubbing against the wall of a duplex, the step to the front door a few feet in front of her nose. She tucked her tail closely around her body. *No twitching, please,* she thought, holding tight to her tail muscles.

Two men turned right, and headed away from her, but the third turned up the short path to the duplex door. Her cougar self, Luha, knew about stillness, about not looking directly at the man. Her Hazel self held her breath.

He didn't look in her direction and the door slammed behind him.

She waited.

Nothing.

She let her breath out in a quiet sigh and dashed past the door, continuing on around the circle, but the noise level was increasing. At the next radial she watched several groups of men strolling around the Nickel circle, stopping to talk to one another. She heard laughter and occasional good-natured shouting.

Damn, damn, she thought. She'd have to wait until the city went totally dark again to explore that circle and try to get into the central building.

Her head moved back and forth, tasting the air. The slope of the park on this side of the city caught her eye. A safe place with a view.

The outer canyon remained light but the domed ceiling of the city cave began to get dark an hour or so after Luha settled under some bushes on the brushy slope looking down into the city. There were lights over the entrances of each building, and the store fronts on the Nickel circle were still brightly lit.

The outer cavern, too, remained lit. The men wandered talking and laughing up and down the streets and she catnapped until the carillon rang again, this time chiming midnight.

As the reverberations of the carillon floated away she heard a deep whooshing sound, like a strong wind, from the other side of the canyon. She felt a mild, almost imperceptible, shaking of the ground.

Some kind of machine? she wondered, peering across the canyon, but she could see nothing. When she looked back at the city, the storefronts were dark and the lights over the doors were off. The only light was the little that leaked in from the larger cavern. The city had fallen silent.

She padded quietly down the radial toward the central building.

When she got to the Nickel Seven sign, she heard footsteps. She hid as the patrol passed on the Copper circle, waiting for silence, before moving to the right on the Nickel path, checking for scent.

The storefronts were restaurants, a grocery store, and game arcades.

She was almost to radial One when she heard the footsteps again, this time coming toward her. She pushed quickly under the bushes just as they came in sight.

"Did you see something move up there?" muttered one man.

"No. Where?"

"By the arcade."

Luha pulled her muscles tense ready to launch herself at the men if they saw her.

They moved around in the path looking right and left, but not low, not under the bushes. "There's nothing here," the second man said. "Come on." They continued to radial One and turned down toward the Silver circle.

She breathed.

The last storefront in the Nickel circle had heavy wire netting stretched in front of the windows. Beyond that she could see only empty space. Was it some kind of prison?

She sniffed under the crack of the door. Sweat. Male sweat.

A muffled "Oh!" sounded behind her, and she whirled around, crouching, to face a young, dark-skinned girl who stood on the corner not ten feet away staring at her.

They peered at each other for a heartbeat, the girl's eyes wide, mouth still circled in the "Oh!" before the girl turned, and dashed back down the radial toward the temple, the thin skirt of her dress – really more of a tunic than a dress – flying around her knees.

Luha leaped after her, noting that the girl's bare feet made hardly a sound on the paved pathway. *I could catch her,* she thought. *She might know...*

But she would scream. Luha slowed to a trot and followed.

When the girl got to the inner circle, she swerved to the right around the back of the central building, and then right again down radial Four to the outer circle. Luha reached the outer circle just in time to see her slip silently into the nearest back door of the duplex between radial Four and Five, across the street from the school.

Footsteps! She flattened herself behind a bush as the patrol passed on the Silver Circle.

Close, thought Luha. *Close for both of us.*

Would the girl tell? *She was sneaking around too,* she thought. *Could she have told me something about the children? But the patrol...*

She waited and listened. Nothing. The duplex remained dark and the girl didn't come back out.

The patrol was on Silver. She dashed to the school yard to explore behind the school building before they got to the outer circle, but the cave wall behind the school was just as smooth as the rest – no exit – and no scent of the children.

Returning to the storefront where she'd been interrupted by the girl, she sniffed the door again and pressed an ear to doors and windows. She couldn't hear anything.

The door handle was a lever. She pushed it expecting it to be locked, but it clicked and the door swung inward. Pushing in with her shoulder, she stood peering into the shadows.

Her shoulders relaxed. *A handball court. The mesh over the windows was to protect them. Plenty of man scent, but no Enid, no Jesús.* She backed out to the pathway, carefully letting the door close without a sound.

That left the central building.

Listening, she heard the patrol on the outer circle. She headed to the door under the *bas relief* of the man showering toys and appliances on the people below.

This door also had a lever. *Lucky me,* thought Luha, as she pushed at it with a paw. Locked.

She trotted around to the door on the other side, but it, too, was locked.

Slinking up the steps to the front doors, she hooked a paw in the round steel hoop handles and pulled. *Locked, of course.*

She heaved a sigh, and laid down in front of the doors.

She felt groggy and confused. What was going on here? What did it have to do with the children, or with Ninas Twei? Should she return to Tuwillia and see if she had some answers? *No, she thought, Tuwillia was just as bewildered by the crevice as I was, and Singing Swan didn't seem to know why the pain was happening. No, I think both the source of the pain and the children are here, and I have to find it... alone.*

She roused herself, and slipped down the steps to her place under the greenery on the corner of radial One, almost opposite the big front doors. She would watch for a chance to get into the building during the day. There was no other way.

The Judgment

She shook herself awake when she heard the carillon playing the same familiar song and watched the men coming from the different paths around to the front of the central building. The first to arrive, two men in army camouflage, opened the doors. She crouched, poised to slip in the door after all the men were in, but just as she tensed her muscles to leap up the steps, the two who had opened the doors pulled the doors closed behind them.

Growling low in her throat, she trotted around the building pawing the levers on each of the side doors, but they were still locked. She sighed and returned to her hiding place. She didn't bother to rouse herself when the carillon struck nine o'clock. The boys would be headed to school.

Sometime later she was startled awake by a loud dissonant clanging from the tower. When the bells stopped, she heard running feet and saw women, some dragging small children behind them, running towards the temple. Soon the courtyard was filled with women, girls, and small children in a great diversity of ethnicities and clothing styles. The only sound was the whisper of shuffling feet. Even the smallest children were silent. They exuded that overwhelming odor of fear.

Slowly, the big steel doors opened and the men – wearing white and silver robes! – filed out and stood in ranks at the back of the stage followed by four of the men dressed in camouflage who moved – two to the left and two to the right – down the steps at the sides of the stage. Then a man with a shaved head, wearing a gold robe, walked through the doors, followed by two more men in camouflage, one carrying a whip and the other an automatic rifle.

Whoa! Luha sat up behind the bushes. *What's going on here?*

The men in camouflage stopped at either side of the door, while the man in gold stepped to the front of the stage. His voice rang out. "It is," he said, speaking slowly, and turning his head so that his eyes wandered

300

over the entire crowd before him, "the hour of judgment. Accusers step forward."

A short middle aged man, in a white robe, stepped forward. "Deirdre," he called out.

The crowd moved away from a young white woman, leaving her exposed with a path to the steps in front of her. The woman looked wildly around her, as if for some help, but no one would even look at her.

"Deirdre," the man called again, in a more demanding voice.

Reluctantly, the young woman walked toward the stairs. As she paused before the steps, the guards each grabbed her by an arm, dragged her up to the stage, and threw her at the feet of her accuser.

"You are accused of laziness, of keeping a less than perfect house, of shirking your duties."

She rose up on her knees, saying, "But I was sick."

He slapped her down with the back of his hand, and she fell to the ground.

The bald man announced, "Extra lashes for speaking back, for trying to avoid acceptance of your just punishment." He turned away from her, and she lay where she fell, her body stiff, tight with fear.

Luha looked at the faces of the men ranked behind the woman. Many of them were grinning. *My god,* she thought. *My god, what is this?*

"Next accuser." The words rang out almost louder than bearable.

A tall, large-boned, blond man, in a silver robe, stepped forward, crossing his arms across his chest, and glared out at the women. "Kujakali."

Again, the crowd parted, revealing a small dark girl, with long straight black hair that swung down to her hips.

That's the girl I saw last night. Luha moved quietly so she could see more clearly.

The girl could not have been more than fourteen years old. She raised her head defiantly, and walked to the steps and up onto the stage, crossing her arms just as the man had crossed his, and stared at him. He lowered his eyes, then looked quickly at the other men.

"On your knees," he yelled, grabbing her and throwing her down on the hard cement of the stage. She lay still where he had thrown her. "You are accused of resisting your connubial duties."

The girl turned her head and glared at him.

Again, he looked away, this time staring out in space.

Connubial duties? A bolt of anger shuddered through her body, and deep, deep down inside her she felt Luhanada Moonmother rising. Luhanada, the judge, was rising, like burning bile in her throat.

The bald man stepped forward again. "Women, remember this is the first commandment of the Chronicles of the Giants of God." Another man handed him a book. He opened it, and began to read:

> As woman was created as a gift to man, it is clear that women are to be subservient to their husbands, fathers, brothers, and sons; and are indeed, as was known for so many years in the past, the property of their men. They must obey their men in all things.

He raised his head again, turning so his eyes swept over all of the women in the courtyard in front of him. "These commandments are found in common in all right thinking religions. To refuse sexual favors, and any demands your men make, is the greatest of sins."

He turned back to look where the girl lay on the cement. "Kujakali, too, shall have extra lashes for defiance."

Luha's mouth curved in a snarl, her muscles poised to leap.

Just at that moment a tiny girl, really just a baby, standing with her mother not far from Luha, started to cry. The women and children started, and then froze.

The man in gold looked out at the group. "Bring her forward," he said, his voice deep and ominous.

The woman lifted the crying child, and walked slowly toward the closest steps.

"Faster," he yelled, and she began to run. The two men stepped out to meet her and grabbed her from both sides, pulling her, and the child in her arms, to the top of the stairs, pushing them forward toward the man in gold. She quickly dropped to the ground in front of him, covering the child with her body.

From the back of the stage, the man with the whip came forward. The bald man stepped back, and the man with the whip started to lash the woman and the child.

Luhanada's ferocious scream reverberated off the walls of the buildings as she bound forward through the crowd parting, terrified, before her. She leapt to the stage, knocking over the man with the whip, and stood growling over him.

Chaos erupted among the men, some of them running for the doors, momentarily impeding the man with the rifle, who pushed his way through the robed men until he had a clear path to the cat.

The *rat a tat tat* of the automatic rifle rang out, echoing from the walls of the central building and the buildings surrounding it.

The women in the courtyard dropped to the ground, covering their heads and their children. The man kept firing, until he found himself no more than five feet away from Luhanada, who turned to him, crouched and growling.

The bullets hit her... and disappeared.

There were no holes in her body. No blood.

Suddenly she screeched and leapt at the gunman, knocking him to the ground.

"Retreat," yelled the bald man, and all the remaining men pushed and shoved back into the building, dragging the man with the whip and the gunman with them. The doors closed.

Luha stood panting and looked around her. The little girl was cuddled in her mother's arms, and both were weeping. The teenage girl lifted her head cautiously, staring at the large cougar. The other woman lay very still, but her eyes were wide open, and she, too, stared at Luhanada.

Out in the courtyard, the women and children had begun to pick themselves up.

At first they all stared at the almost empty stage, the closed doors, and the cougar. Then, one woman grabbed her child and ran off down one of the pathways, and soon many of them were following suit, but not all.

Some moved cautiously closer to the stage and Luha, whispering among themselves. "The bullets passed through it. I saw it." "But they disappeared. The bullets didn't go through it. They disappeared." "The gun was right in front of it. He couldn't have missed."

Luha looked at the women on the stage. "Get up. You're safe for now."

The crowd exclaimed and murmured. "It talks. It can talk."

Luha looked at them. "Yes, I talk." *But it isn't safe here*, she thought. *We're too close to the men.*

"Go home now. Be safe. I'll return."

She turned to the women on the stage. "But you're not safe. Come with me. We'll find a place to hide."

The girl, Kujakali, quickly jumped to her side, but the other accused woman, Deirdre, shook her head. "No. There's no safe hiding place. If we run and they find us, they'll torture us, and torture us, and then kill us."

She pushed her hands out toward Luhanada. "Go away. You've just made things worse for us."

Kujakali stood beside Luhanada defiantly. "I'm going with the lion. The lion is sent for us, and I'm going with it." Deirdre just shook her head, and scampered quickly down the stairs and down one of the pathways.

Luha turned to look at the mother, who was now sitting on the cement, the child cradled in her lap, rocking back and forth. "I don't know what to do," she murmured. "I don't know what to do."

Suddenly automatic gunfire exploded from the roof of the first tier of the building. The woman jumped to her feet, holding her child cradled in her arms, threw herself first against the wall of the building, out of sight of the gun, and then edged down the steps. When she was far enough out of reach of the bullets, she ran across the open space to a radial pathway, and with the remaining women from the courtyard, ran for home.

Luha nudged Kujakali with her head. "Run! Stay in front of me, keep me between you and the gun, but run."

Kujakali turned for just a moment to whisper, "Follow me. I know where we can hide," and then she ran, her small legs flying across the courtyard.

Luha leapt after her, the bullets hitting her body and disappearing. *Oh, Tata.* She whispered over and over in her head. *Where are you?*

The girl ran as hard as she could down the path to the outer ring of houses, Luha close behind her. *Where can I hide her?* thought Luha. *She'd be a sitting duck trying to get over the gate to the little bridge and I don't want to lead them to Ninas Twei. We need to hide until night.*

She glanced behind her. No one was following yet.

At the edge of the park the girl dropped to all fours, plunging into the plastic bushes and climbing upward under the greenery. As Luha crouched to follow her, she noticed the tracks the girl's hands and knees made in the dirt and swept her tail back and forth in the dirt behind her, erasing the signs of their passage. The girl reached the cave wall and turned to follow the wall to the right, still crawling under the bushes.

Luha followed her, crouched close to the ground between the wall and the bushes until suddenly, the girl disappeared.

Behind one of the bushes planted next to the wall, was a hole just big enough for the small girl, or a lithe cougar, to crawl into. Luha followed crawling along a short passageway that curved to the right, and within a few more feet curved again to the left. The tunnel continued beyond the curve for another few feet, where it opened into a small, dimly lit cave.

Luha stood and stretched, and then moved over next to the girl. "Does anyone else know about this place?" she whispered.

The girl shook her head and whispered back, leaning in toward her so she could hear. "No, it's mine."

The sound of plastic bushes rustling, and voices calling, came faintly through the tunnel.

Luha turned toward the entrance. "They're looking for us." The girl just nodded and they sat in silence, waiting. Finally, the carillon chimed twelve and the rustling and voices stopped.

Kujakali crept out of the tunnel and peeked over the edges of the bushes. When she came back in, she was smiling. "They've gone to lunch. No one is out there now," she whispered.

They both relaxed, Kujakali sitting cross-legged, leaning against the wall of the cave, and Luha stretching each leg behind her, and then curling up on the floor.

"You say this cave is yours?" she asked.

"Yes. I've been sneaking out food, and supplies – things they won't notice are gone." She gestured to the back wall where some cans and boxes were stacked.

"But how did this cave come to be here?"

"I dug it out myself. I made the tunnel curve so they couldn't see the light." She grinned. "I stole the light from the walls of the City Cave."

Luha looked up, and saw a small, round plastic light set in the ceiling.

"It's wired to the other lights."

Luha looked at her with disbelief. "But how long did it take you?"

"A long time. I started it when I was just ten years old. I've been working on it for four years."

"Four years!" exclaimed Luha.

The girl nodded. "It gave me hope. I thought someday I would just come here and stay. I would never go back."

Luha sat up and looked at her. "But is there a way to escape from here – back to the world?"

"I don't know a way, yet. But I hope someday to find one."

"There's the bridge to the other side of the canyon. Do you know about it? That's how I got here." Luha circled and lay down again, curling her tail around her.

"But you can't go over there," the girl exclaimed out loud, and then quickly dropped her voice again. "The wind comes and pushes you into the net, and you become one of the workers in the eggs. We've all seen it happen."

"The wind?" asked Luha. *Was that what I heard last night – wind?*

"Yes. It knows when someone is there. It comes whenever humans find their way to the large cavern. That's how they get their electricity. The workers pedal something – I don't really understand."

"The eggs?" questioned Luha. "Those gray bubble things I saw at the bottom of the canyon contain workers?"

"Yes, I've seen it. The wind captures them in the net, and they are grabbed by a machine and put in the eggs. They told us that the workers are all alone in the eggs. They work until they die, and there are always more workers to take their place."

She looked puzzled for a moment. "I don't understand where the workers come from. No one from the city would go over there. They just suddenly appear, and then the wind roars up and sweeps them over the side of the cliff."

Maybe that's what happened to Enid and Jesús, thought Luha.

She remembered the moment Enid and Jesús fell down the crack in the earth by the Weaving Tree. The crack had not been there before. One of the tremors had opened it. Did Enid and Jesús get caught up in this wind by accident, or did all the workers come by way of Ninas Twei?

Kujakali looked anxiously at Luha. "Did you come from over there? And there was no wind?"

Luhanada's tail flicked back and forth. "Yes. I came from over there, but there was no wind."

"The wind must not know you're there. You must not trigger the wind. Like the bullets can't hurt you, the wind can't see you."

Luha nodded her head. *It's because I'm dead,* she thought. *No double jeopardy for the dead!*

"Are you a god?"

"A god?" Luha looked startled. "No. I'm not sure what I am, but I'm sure I'm not a god."

Kujakali head bobbled a small yes-no. "Where do you come from?"

Luha looked up. "Above this cavern is another place. A beautiful place called Ninas Twei. Have you heard about it?"

Kujakali shook her head. "No. Is it part of the Giants of God?"

Luha's tail flicked. "Is that what this place is? A place for something called the Giants of God?" *The title of the book in the sculptured giant's hand,* she thought.

"Yes," nodded Kujakali. "This is the retreat center of the Giants of God. It's where they meet in secret to talk about running the world."

"The Giants of God run the world?"

"Yes," nodded the little girl earnestly, "They say they run the world and they are the true children of God – the world was created for them, and everything in it is theirs."

"And they go back and forth, from this place to the real world."

"Yes. It's magic. I was little when they brought me here, but not so little that I didn't see how they did it."

She moved over to her food supply, and got a box of crackers. "Would you like something to eat?"

Luha shook her head and sat up. "But how was it magic?"

"I was about eight years old – maybe. I'm not sure of my real age. My mother died when I was very little and I was living in the streets with lots of other children. There were grownups who helped us if we would give them the money we earned when we begged.

"One day a strange man was with Aadi – the man we gave our money to. He was a tall, blond man. It was Eric – you saw Eric. He owns me. He accused me."

"Yes," Luha nodded her head.

"He looked over all of us children and he called me to him. He crouched down and smiled, but he looked to me like a hyena who wanted to eat me. He asked me if I would like to go with him, but I didn't like him. I said no and tried to run away, but he grabbed me and picked me up in his arms. I was kicking and screaming, and he just laughed. He liked it that I was fighting him.

"He held me harder." Kujakali voice dropped even lower, and she started to shake. "He was pinching my buttocks and touching me..."

She paused and shivered. Luhanada's ears went back, the corners of her mouth moving up in a snarl. "I tried to hit him, but he had my arms pinned. Aadi told me to stop fighting, but I didn't and Eric just laughed."

Kujakali looked down at her hands for a long time. "Now I'm used to these things."

She took a deep breath and continued. "He just tucked me, screeching and kicking, under his arm and walked off with me. I was very small and he was very big." Her eyes were wet with tears.

Luha whispered, "I'm sorry this happened to you, Kujakali. I am so sorry."

Kuji wiped her eyes. "You can call me Kuji," she smiled.

"How did he bring you here?"

"That night we went to this place a long ways away on the other side of the city where there were other men, and other children, too – girls and really little boys. The men made a circle and put us in the middle, and then they drank something and began chanting these words in English, and everything went smoky – an ugly yellow and black – and when the smoke cleared, we were all inside the temple."

"The temple. Is that the central building?"

"Yes, they call it the temple. Then they took us to their homes in the city."

"But I didn't see any older boys in the group in front of the temple this morning, just women, girls like you, and small children."

Kuji looked down. She was silent for a few moments, then she whispered. "The boys they bring in for sex... the boys don't live."

Luha's tail flicked back and forth, back and forth and then stopped. "But I saw boys yesterday, and a school."

"They are their sons. Sons by the captured women, but they are raised as Giants of God."

"But what about the daughters?"

"Daughters are often traded... and sometimes they don't live either."

Luha's ears lay back against her head. Her tail was flicking angrily. A low ominous growl rumbled in her throat. *How could this be? The ritual sounded so much like the ritual that brought them to Ninas Twei. This place was right below Ninas Twei – below the Weaving Tree. The roots of the tree hung in this canyon. Yet certainly this abomination could not be related to Ninas Twei or the Tsin Twei. It had to be some kind of aberration.*

She lay down, taking a deep breath and willing her cougar body to let go of its tension. Finally, she asked, "And you've been here ever since?"

"Yes. For the first couple of years I could do nothing. He had other women to do the housework. He used me only for sex. He let me do many things, as long as I stayed in the house and garden. I could play. I could dance and sing. When I was dancing and singing I felt stronger."

She looked at Luha as if to dare her to doubt her.

"Singing and dancing are sources of power," Luha agreed.

"The men are not always here. They all come and go at different times. Eric has a family in the other world. When he's not here I look at his books, and Sarah – she's one of the grown women. She does his housework now, but she used to... You know."

She glanced at Luha and Luha nodded. "Sarah taught me the alphabet when he wasn't around to know – but I think he does know."

She shifted her position a little. "They sometimes have a meeting to tell us things and they tell us some of the history of the Giants of God, and they read from that book – *The Chronicles of the Giants of God.*"

"That's the one the man in gold read from this morning, about women being the possessions of men?" Luha asked.

"Yes, that's it. It is like the *Bhagavad Gita,* a holy book."

"Very bizarre," Luha shook her head.

"And they told us how they brought in big machines to dig the City Cave out of the Giant Cavern in just the way they brought us in – making a circle and chanting. Many of the women believe they really are Giants of God and all powerful because they can do these things."

"You don't believe it?" Luha's ears perked forward.

"No," grinned Kuji. "Eric has temper tantrums like a little boy sometimes. And once I bit him and he bled. He's human just like me. Anyway," she continued. "When they talked about digging out the cavern, I got an idea. The back garden to Eric's house is across from the school yard, and back of the school yard is the park. When he's gone, no one watches me much and I sneak into the park. I just have to watch for the patrols. I used to crawl under the bushes to the top of the hill, and sit and look down at the city. Sometimes I dug in the dirt. I dug a little tiny cave, and I was playing that some broken twigs from the bushes..." She made a face. "They are not real bushes, you know, just plastic."

She had pretended the twigs were girls who hid in a cave, and then decided to make a cave herself. It took a long time digging the dirt with a big spoon and spreading it under the fake bushes. She pulled one of the lights in the ceiling into her cave, made the entrance tunnel curve so the light could not be seen, and took food and bottles of water in small quantities that wouldn't be noticed to hide in the cave.

"But now you're gone, and they'll notice that," Luha pointed out.

Kuji nodded, "But also, I know that often when a woman tries to run away, they don't pay any attention. Sarah says that's because they know if the woman gets to the other side of the canyon she'll be captured by the wind, and if she stays on this side hidden, she'll die of starvation. They always come back."

She shook her head. "That's why I thought my cave would work. They wouldn't look for me, and when I didn't come back they'd think the wind took me."

She sat for a moment, her elbow balanced on a knee, her head cupped in her hand. "But you're different. I would think they'd try to find you. They're frightened of you."

She laughed, thinking about how the men ran into the temple when the screaming cougar leaped up on the stage.

"Hunh," muttered Luha. "I guess if I were them, and knew that bullets didn't stop me, I might be afraid, too. I'd try to think of another way to stop me. Do they have dogs for tracking?"

"No, there're no animals here at all. When I was little," she said wistfully, "I missed the wild dogs on the streets and the cows who were beggars, too." She looked up, alarmed. "But maybe they could bring some, just like they brought us."

"Then we need to get you out of here as soon as possible – up to Ninas Twei, I think."

The carillon rang twelve forty-five. "Lunch is over. They might start looking for us again although I think they will search the houses now," Kuji pointed out.

"Then we need to stop talking," added Luha. They decided to take turns listening in the tunnel and napping, to be rested for the night.

The afternoon passed slowly. Occasionally they could hear voices calling and bushes rustling, but no one ever came very near the cave. They shook themselves awake when the carillons chimed five o'clock. They hadn't heard any rustling, or any voices, for quite a while. "Perhaps they've given up," Kuji suggested.

Luha nodded. "Perhaps. When it's fully dark, I'll go out and see what's happening. We'll need to wait until it's dark to cross the bridge."

"Cross the bridge?" the girl exclaimed. "It's never dark in the big cavern – and there's the wind. I think it's much worse to be a worker and be put all alone in one of the eggs."

Luha nodded. "When you were brought here, were the men still surrounding you, still chanting, when you arrived?"

"Yes," she nodded.

"And when these people come on the other side of the cavern, are the men around them?"

"No. The men never go over there. I think they're afraid of the wind, too." She grinned. "The people who come are always in a circle. And chanting!"

She looked at Luha. "They're chanting, too, but they aren't Giants of God. Sometimes there're only men, but they're swept away by the wind, too. Sometimes there're only women. Most of the time there're men, women, and children." She shrugged her shoulders. "So I think even the Giants of God would be swept by the wind, if they were there."

Luha nodded her head slowly. *I'll bet this is what happened to Enid and Jesús. Oh, dear Tata! How will I ever rescue them?*

When Kuji's stolen light dimmed, and finally went completely off, Luha crept out of the cave to explore the possibilities of getting Kuji across the bridge to the crevice, and up to Tuwillia. She crept silently under the greenery, hanging close to the back wall of the cavern, until she was halfway to the path by the bridge. Suddenly her cougar self was aware of a scent – human scent. She crouched low letting her senses appraise the situation. *By the bridge. There was a human by the bridge.* She raised her head slowly, so that just her eyes showed above the greenery. Ahead of her, at the entrance to the bridge, stood one of the men in camouflage holding an automatic rifle. He was looking out at the greenery, but not in Luha's direction. She turned her head carefully toward the city and saw several more armed men edging the park, looking upward. She crawled silently back down under the bushes to the cave.

"They've posted guards all around the park," she whispered to Kujakali. "We'll have to wait them out."

"I have waited for years," Kuji smiled. "I can wait more if I have to."

Luha reached out a paw and patted her.

But how long could she wait? How long could the children wait? The bells of the carillon chimed midnight. As the resonance from the last chime dissipated, Luha and Kuji heard the unmistakable sound of the wind sweeping across the plateau. It lasted only a moment, and then was silent again. "I wonder who they captured this time?" whispered Kuji into the darkness of the cave. "If we'd been there, it would have been us."

"Does it always happen at midnight?" Luha asked.

"No." Kuji shook her head, and Luha could hear her hair swish across her back. "No, we've seen it happen during the day. There's no one time that the wind comes."

"Listen!" Luha hissed.

Voices.

"I think they're out on the paths," whispered Kuji. "Not searching the bushes."

Luha waited until the voices were silent, and then slipped out again. The guards were still at the bridge, still surrounding the park with their rifles in their hands. *The voices were a changing of the guard,* she thought.

She sighed, and returned to the cave. Her tail flicked with impatience. "We'll have to wait until tomorrow night," she told Kuji. "We don't dare try to cross the bridge in the daylight." She felt the girl stiffen beside her. "Don't worry," she whispered. "I won't let the wind catch you."

312

They waited. Every once in a while, one of them crept to the entrance and peeked out to see if the guards were still there. When the carillon chimed noon, they heard voices again, which faded away as if they were walking back into the city. The next time they looked, the guards were gone.

"They seem to have given up," Kuji whispered to Luha after the third time of peeking out of the cave.

"Perhaps." Luhanada's ears perked forward. She wondered if Kuji could sit on her back, or would she just fall through, or worse, like the bullets, disappear.

The girl placed her hand on the cougar's back. "It feels solid." She began to stroke her. "Soft and silky."

Luha reached around and gave her a lick with her big tongue. Kuji giggled, then climbed onto her back. She didn't fall through, she didn't disappear, and she wasn't too heavy. Luha knew she could carry her up the crevice to Tuwillia and Ninas Twei.

"Tuwillia?" asked Kujakali.

"Yes. She's a little gruff, but a good woman – or turtle. She once was a woman." Luha laughed. "Like me. I was once a woman, too, Kujakali."

Kujakali just blinked her eyes and nodded. Then she sat down and began to plait her long black hair into five thick braids. These she pulled into a bunch at her back, using one of the braids to tie the others together. She shook her head, proving that the braids were secure. "I'm ready to ride," she declared.

It seemed a long time before the carillon chimed five. Kujakali pulled out a long piece of silk, like a wide long scarf – the sari she had been wearing when Eric kidnapped her. She wrapped it around the cougar's body, crossing it over Luhanada's back, and then tying it in front of her furry chest, so that it wouldn't slip. She tucked a box of crackers into the folds of the scarf. "In case I am hungry," she added.

They waited another impatient time for the lights in the City Cave, and the one in Kujakali little cave, to dim, and go out, before creeping out into the night, moving slow and low, watching for the patrol.

"They just crossed Silver Two," Kuji muttered.

"On my back, quickly," Luha whispered, crouching down to make it easier. Kujakali climbed on, holding on to the silk harness. "Make yourself as small as possible. Lie along my back, but make sure your feet don't touch the ground."

Kujakali leaned way over Luha's neck. "They've passed Silver Three."

"Now," whispered Luha, and ran for the bridge. "Hold tight!" She scrambled over the gate, leaping out on to the bridge, and bounding as fast as she could over the canyon, up the path and over the plateau, not stopping until she had soared to the first ledge inside the crevice.

"Are you all right?" Kuji whispered. "Am I too heavy?"

"No, it feels like you belong there."

Luha looked up at the ledges that climbed the crevice. "We have to go up there. You'll need to hold on very tight and warn me if you're slipping." She vaulted up to the second ledge and from there to the third. As she went she could feel Kujakali gripping her fur with both hands, and yet the scarf felt tight, as if she still had her hands entwined in it. As she landed on the fourth ledge, she heard Kujakali gasp.

"Are you all right?" She twisted her head around to look at her and saw a hand balancing a lotus flower. She bent farther around and saw a hand raised in the air, gripping a thunderbolt thrust toward the skies.

Kujakali moaned, "What's happening to me?" Luha looked to the other side, and saw two more upraised arms holding a sword and a conch shell. "Luha, I have extra arms. I'm becoming something else."

Transforming to her Tla Twei, thought Luha.

"It's all right, Kuji. Hold on." She felt the two hands grip her fur tighter and two more pull themselves tighter into the scarf. She surged upward again, up and up, and as she landed on the ground beside the Weaving Tree she heard the deep trumpeting of the conch shell!

Kujakali, wearing a red silk sari, with her pallu pulled up between her legs to create a split skirt, a golden helmet crowning her head, leapt from Luhanada's back, her eight arms, holding their sacred objects, dancing in the air as she sang:

> *Like the lotus I am blooming.*
> *Like the lotus I am blooming.*
> *I, daughter of the mountains,*
> *Fierce mother of all,*
> *Sounding the great Om with my conch,*
> *Firm as thunder, am I,*
> *Striking the demons like lightning*
> *With my sword of knowledge.*
> *I, daughter of the mountains,*

Fierce mother of all,
Like the lotus I am blooming.

"Well," a dry old voice commented. "So you are."

Luha laughed. "Tuwillia, let me introduce you to Kujakali."

"Yes," nodded Tuwillia, moving her head high on her long neck to look at Kuji through hooded eyes. "Durga," she muttered. "First we have this Earth Woman Tree Woman, and now we have Durga."

"Durga? The mother goddess?" asked Kuji.

Tuwillia nodded at the girl. "Your name tells the story. Kuji – the knowledge of Durga – and Kali – the fierce aspect of Durga, killer of demons."

Kali's eyes grew wide.

Tuwillia looked at Luhanada. "I feared for you. I was afraid the crevice had closed up." She began a slow walk to a sheltered place beneath the Weaving Tree.

Behind her, Kuji relaxed, her arms coming down at her side. The objects that had been in each hand, and the golden helmet, disappeared. She unwound her old sari and the crackers from Luha's back, and they followed Tuwillia. She looked up at the tree, lying on its side, with some of its roots dark protrusions waving in the air against the night sky. The branches, and the colorful weaving stretching through all the long limbs, gleamed in the moonlight. "What is this tree?"

"It's the tree of all human life," Luha replied.

"It feels hurt. Demons beset it," exclaimed Kujakali. "Why has it fallen over?"

"Actually," Luha answered, as she made herself comfortable next to Tuwillia. "I think I've figured it out – some anyway."

"Oh?" Tuwillia's head went up. "What have you found?'

"Down below the tree – down where this crevice leads, is another world – an ugly world where people are enslaved."

"The world of the Giants of God," added Kuji. "Luhanada rescued me from them."

"The roots of the tree hang out dry at the top of a huge cavern," continued Luha. "These Giants of God seem to get to this cavern very much like we come to Ninas Twei – with a ritual, and sharing of drink. But it's an ugly place. There's a city where these men – they're all men – enslave women and children and treat them unspeakably."

A shiver rippled down her fur, as if she were shaking off the ugliness.

"And then there are these huge gray eggs down in a canyon that divides the floor of the cavern. Kuji says they contain other enslaved people – men, women and children – who work there alone until they die. The workers appear on the canyon edges, and a huge wind grabs them and throws them into a net, where they are captured for the eggs. I think the children are there, in the eggs. Enid and Jesús..." She paused.

"Kumni and Chachuli... Our clever coyote and our wise little messenger." whispered Tuwillia.

"I wish she could get a message to me," muttered Luha. "And I wish I knew where Tata is. I need Tata."

She sighed and slowly stood up. "I need to go back down there and find them before it's too late." She turned to Tuwillia. "I brought Kuji to stay with you. She isn't safe down there."

"And you are?" questioned Tuwillia.

"Yes. I'm dead. They shot bullets at me and nothing happened. I didn't even feel them."

"But I want to go back," Kuji exclaimed. "You need me to help find others in the city. I want to help them to escape, too. I want to get Sarah out." She looked at Luhanada with pleading eyes. "You said it felt like I belonged on your back. When I'm on your back the wind can't get me."

"But the bullets can." Luha's tail flicked back and forth. "And what if the wind is triggered by something else? Will you be able to remain on my back? I might be blown over the edge, too. We don't know." She sighed. "There is so much we don't know, yet. Stay here," she urged her. "Let me explore. I'll need you later, I'm sure. But for now, stay here," and she turned and leapt back down the crevice.

Kuji stood and looked down the crevice, watching Luhanada leap from ledge to ledge until she disappeared. Finally, she looked back at the old turtle. "What shall I do while I wait?"

"Sleep. It's late." She pulled her head back into her shell.

The girl stood looking around her. It was dark, but the stars were clear and bright across the sky, the almost quarter moon sinking in the west.

Tuwillia pushed her head back out. "Perhaps in the morning, you, too, can explore. I'm too old." She cackled for a moment. "I was old when I died. That hasn't changed."

She turned and nodded her head towards the exposed roots of the tree, and the path beyond. "The cat and the others came down that path. They crawled through a crack in the mountains that contain the amphitheater where the Tsin Twei takes place. Perhaps you can find your way to Singing Swan and tell him what happened."

"Yes!" Kuji spun in place, her eight arms and her braids flying outward. "I'd love to explore. Perhaps there're other people here, too."

Tuwillia pulled her feet in, and settled her shell on the ground. She started to pull her head into her shell. "Go when it's light. Watch your path. Don't get lost. I'll stay here to watch for Luhanada."

Her eyes had closed almost before her head disappeared into her shell.

Luha Explores the Temple

Luha crouched where the crevice opened on to the plateau and watched the city. It was still dark and she couldn't see any movement. Creeping along the edge of the canyon wall, she headed toward the bridge, camouflaged in the muddy color of the ground and cavern walls. She looked down at the net, and the eggs lying below it, and peered back and forth along the edge of the canyon, hoping again to find some way down without having to go back into the city.

Nothing.

Darting across the bridge and over the gate, she thrust herself under the greenery of the park, and waited. Nothing moved. No lights went on anywhere. She crept slowly to the edge of the park, then trotted silently toward the center of the city, listening at each intersection for the patrol until she determined they were on the outer circle on the other side of the city. Creeping around the inner circle, she looked for some way into the temple she might have missed before.

There were no windows in this bottom tier, but there were the plastic trees at each corner of the building. They had wide trunks and were set out from the wall about a foot. They branched just beneath the top of the first tier and stretched much higher, beyond the edge of the second tier. The first branch was about twelve feet up, running alongside the temple wall. Too high for a human to jump and reach, but not a cougar!

Piece of cake, her cougar self muttered.

She took a deep breath, crouched, and then sprang upward, landing awkwardly across the branch, but quickly righting herself. From there it was an easy leap to the wall that enclosed a cement floored patio circling the second tier of the temple. She jumped down to the patio, and slinking in the shadow of the building, circled the tier, pausing at each of the sliding glass doors – two to each of the octagon's sides – to carefully peer inside. The ambient light from the larger cavern allowed her to see shapes that looked like desks and chairs, but nothing else.

When she had almost completed the circle, she tried opening one of the glass doors, listening first for the footsteps of the patrol, sounding clearly in the silence. They were still on the outer circle, but on the other side of the city. She pushed at the handle with her paw and was surprised when it moved easily enough to open a space in which she could slip a paw, and then her whole body. Leaving it open, she crept into the room.

It was a moderately sized room with three metal desks and chairs, some file cabinets, and a couple of extra chairs. There were computers on the desks. She headed for the closed door and looked at the doorknob, mentally smiling as she remembered her house cats trying to turn the knobs on her doors at home. They never could reach quite high enough, but the motion of their paws made it clear they knew that turning the knob would open the door.

Sitting on her haunches, she put both paws around the knob, extending her claws so that they hooked under the edge. A slow turn and the door popped open with a click. She slipped a claw in the crack, and pulling the door just wide enough to push her head through, peered out into the dimly lit corridor beyond.

The corridor was narrow. A short plastic balustrade with a built-in bench in front of it lined the opposite side, topped by open space. Above that, each of the tiers of the building seemed to reach a little farther into the center until at the very top the tower stretched quite a bit higher than the last tier.

She waited and watched.

Silence. She put her front paws up on the bench and peered over the balustrade down into what appeared to be a chapel. She climbed up, so she could see more.

Rows of padded pews faced a raised triangular alcove tucked into the back corner of the building where dim lights lit an altar. A suspended sculpture hung over the altar, made of four concentric closed circles, each circle a little smaller, and a little higher, than the one below. The topmost circle appeared to be gold, and the one below it, silver. The next circle down was light gray, but not shiny – *nickel*, she thought, *like the circular path* – the last one looked like copper. It must have been suspended from very thin wire, or perhaps clear plastic rods. The effect was of the circles suspended in the air.

In front of the altar there was another larger version of the concentric circles, this time set in mosaics in the floor. As she studied the altar, she realized she was seeing more and more detail — a silver tray holding a large gold pitcher, surrounded by small goblets, appeared out of the shadow on one side, and a book on the other.

It was getting lighter.

The carillon started ringing and she jumped off the bench, peering under it. There were solid braces at intervals of about six feet leaving plenty of room between them for her. She crawled under, pulling in her legs and tail.

Kuji and Peeka

The rising sun warmed Kuji's face and she opened her eyes, remembering where she was when she saw Tuwillia still sleeping in her shell. Looking up, she saw how beautiful the weaving in the tree of human life was in the sunlight — full of bright colors. Still, she could feel that demons beset it.

She was staring at Tuwillia, trying to decide if she should waken the old turtle and tell her she was going to look for Singing Swan, or just go, when Tuwillia stuck her head out of her shell. "Go, go," she said nodding her head in the direction of the path toward the Tsin Twei, and then pulled her head back in and resumed her sleep.

Kuji walked slowly, looking all around. She had never been in a meadow before, had not seen many trees, except in pictures in Eric's books. Sarah had talked about meadows and woods with a great wistfulness. "I miss them more than anything," she had said.

I love this, Kujakali thought. *I love this quiet, this real green.* She touched the leaf of one of the meadow flowers. She gaped at the silvery trunks of the aspens and the yellow flickering leaves. The dirt was brown and crumbly, not orange and packed like the dirt in the City Cave. She remembered a hidden garden in the big city she had come from when she was little. The owners hauled water from the river and grew lovely things to eat, but you didn't dare steal them! The garden had seemed like paradise to her, so still and green. The air even seemed to smell better. The air here smelled wonderful!

Soon she was through the meadow and under the trees. She could hear birds singing and insects buzzing and the light flickered green and orange as the sun shone down through the leaves.

When she looked back she couldn't see the Weaving Tree and became afraid of losing her way. Taking three sticks, one with a fork at one end, she stuck them in the ground in a triangle with the fork up, leaning the straight sticks into the fork like a teepee and delighting at the ease of making this when you had eight hands to hold things. She piled rocks around the bottom, and put some wild flowers where the tops of the sticks came through the fork.

Stopping every time she thought it might be hard to find the path coming back, she made lots of pretty markers with tall sticks, stones, and flowers.

It wasn't long before she came out of the woods to the rocky place in front of the steep cliffs back of Din Tsin Twei, the amphitheater where the dance of life was held.

Looking around, she saw there were other paths into the woods much like the one she had come down. Creating a triangle of sticks and stones with branches that were almost as tall as she was, she marked the path back to Tuwillia, then turned and studied the rocky bottom of the tall cliffs, looking behind the piles of rocks, and clumps of green grasses and weeds for an opening.

She found a small cave big enough to crawl in partially hidden by a scrawny bush, but when she looked in, she saw only darkness, not the light of an opening at the Din Tsin Twei that she expected.

She crawled into the cave on four of her hands and her legs, curling the other four arms across her chest. She hadn't gotten very far into the tunnel before she ran into a pile of rocks and dirt. *A cave in!* She poked at it a little, and more of the rock and dirt came tumbling down, forcing her to scramble backwards as fast as she could to the entrance. She pulled herself out into the light and stood up, brushing the dirt off her clothes and hands.

A small rodent dashed past her, making her jump!

He skidded to a stop shrieking, "It's closed. The earth shook and it opened, and I saw the others go through and I followed them, and they went to the tree, and then the earth shook again, and two of them fell and the others disappeared, and I ran back and ran in the tunnel and the tunnel was closed, and I tried to find a way through and there wasn't one, and the dirt slipped and slid, and..."

He stopped as suddenly as he had begun.

Kujakali stared at him wide eyed. "Who are you?"

"I'm Peeka. I'm a pika." He laughed. "Peeka, the pika. At least that's my name now."

"Are you a human who died?"

"Yes. Yes. But the others I followed, they were alive, but they disappeared. But two fell."

"I think you're talking about my friend Luhanada and her friends! When the earthquake came they ended up back in the other world, where they came from. They were still alive then."

She moved closer to him, fascinated. "Who were you when you were alive?"

Peeka sat back on his haunches. "So long ago." He shook out his fur. "I was Ay-demir, Moonlight. My family wandered the Central Plains of Asia at the edge of the mountains. We lived under the Great Blue Sky, and moved with our reindeer, and horses, and goats from pasture to pasture."

Kuji crouched down so she could look more directly at him. "And your people visited Ninas Twei?"

"Oh, yes," he nodded his little head. "We worshiped the Great Blue Sky and the Earth Mother, and they led us to Ninas Twei. I was studying to be a Shaman. When we came here I took the form of the little pika who lives and loves under the Great Blue Sky, and gathers hay in the summer so he may live through the winter."

Kujakali turned her head to one side. "You were studying to be a Shaman, but you never became one?"

"No. I was only twelve winters. One day when I was playing in my pika form, a hawk swooped down and carried me away. I died in my pika form and came here."

"Oh, dear!" Kuji exclaimed.

"No, it's okay. Everyone must eat, even the hawk. And it's fun to be a pika!" he laughed.

"How long have you been here?"

"A long time. A very, very long time."

He ran back and forth in front of her. "But we must hurry, hurry. We must find the others. We must find a way back to the Din Tsin Twei, to the river, to Singing Swan, and my other friends."

"But how will we do that?"

He sat back on his haunches again. "I don't know. I've tried going along the side of the cliffs in both directions, but there're just more cliffs that bend and close us in."

Kuji sat down on the ground, crossing her legs and resting her head in two of her hands, elbows propped on her knees, her other hands resting on the ground at her sides. "I wonder if Tuwillia knows another way. She told me to go this way because this is the direction Luha and the others came from. She thought the tunnel would still be here."

The little rodent turned his head to one side. "Tuwillia?"

"Tuwillia's a turtle who lives down by the tree of human life. You don't know her?"

"No. No." He started to run back and forth again. "Did I see her? I did see her – with the others. Small like a rock. Well..."

He stopped and looked up at her. "Bigger than me, but smaller than they were. I was a long way away. They moved too fast. I couldn't keep up."

He demonstrated by running past her again. "She was small like a rock, but she was with the others when the earth opened and two fell, and the others disappeared," he continued. "Back to the living, you say?"

"Yes, she was there."

"But she didn't disappear." Again the pika sat back on his haunches. "I should have known. I thought she was a rock. I should have known she was one of us. When they disappeared, I went back. I didn't know she was a turtle."

Suddenly he scampered up into Kujakali lap. "You carry me. We'll go faster. You carry me, and we'll go ask Tuwillia."

Kujakali cradled Peeka in two of her hands and hurried back along the path, following her markers until she reached the meadow and could see the tree. As they approached the tree, Peeka exclaimed, "I saw this tree before. Something's wrong. What happened to this tree?"

"This is the tree of human life," explained Kuji, "and it's fallen over. The roots are hanging out in a cavern below it – drying out. The cavern is an evil place."

"Yes, yes," asserted Peeka. "We must hurry and rescue it. I knew we must hurry. What is this cavern?"

"It's a long story. Look, there's Tuwillia. Let's talk to her first. Then I can tell you more about the cavern."

The old turtle lay as Kuji had left her, sleeping inside her shell next to the crevice. As they approached she poked her head out, opening one eye. "Back so soon?"

"The tunnel was blocked with a rock fall, probably right when this crevice opened up," Kuji explained. "And I found Peeka."

She thrust out the hands holding the little rodent. "He was a nomad in Asia. He was training to be a Shaman, but he died when he was twelve."

She placed Peeka on the ground in front of the turtle. "He followed Luha and the others through the tunnel, and then couldn't get back."

"We need to get back to Din Tsin Twei. We need to find the others. There is danger. I feel it!" Peeka declared.

"Yes," muttered Tuwillia, moving her head around so she could better see the little rodent. "And you know others like us?"

"Oh, yes. I know some. I know Singing Swan. We have a story about a White Goose, but it's not a swan. He's yours."

Tuwillia blinked her eyes. "Yes, I know."

"There are others, and they need to know about this tree."

"And who are the others?" she asked.

"Oh, the Giant Otters from the Amazon, and the Iriomote from Okinawa. And those tough little fish, Mbuna, from Malawi. Lots and lots."

"Fish? Is there a lake or a river?"

Peeka nodded his head. "Yes, yes, both. A lake and a river. The river goes to the lake."

Tuwillia poked her legs out of her shell, and stood up. "Then maybe..." She paused, turning her head toward the crown of the tree where the branches spread out toward more woods. "Maybe I know another way to get back to Din Tsin Twei, and to these other people."

She turned, and moved slowly toward a path into those woods. "I'll show you, but I'll stay here and watch for Luhanada."

"Where are you going?" asked Kuji.

"Home," muttered the old turtle.

Kujakali scooped up the little pika and skipped up ahead of her. "But where is home?" She jumped out of the way as the turtle came up to her. "You move faster than it looks like you're moving!"

"Humph." Tuwillia just kept moving.

"But where is your home? Should we come with you?"

Tuwillia nodded her head, and kept on walking past the top of the fallen tree and down a small hill.

"Oh, a pond," exclaimed Kujakali running ahead of the turtle. "Of course, you live in a pond." She ran back to the turtle. "Where shall we start exploring?"

Peeka scampered down to the ground and ran to the edge of the pond. "What's wrong with this pond?" He turned to look at Tuwillia coming steadily behind him.

"The pond is drying up," she murmured.

"But this is Ninas Twei! How could the water dry up?" exclaimed the little rodent running back up Kuji's sari. Kuji caught him up in two of her hands.

Tuwillia just shook her head and continued her ponderous journey toward the far end of the pond. "There is a creek from the pond. If you follow the creek perhaps it will lead to a river."

"Yes," shouted the little pika. "The river, and the otters will be on the river, and the river will lead to the lake and the marshes where Singing Swan lives. Yes," he wiggled around in Kuji's hands, and ran up an arm to her shoulder. "I can sit here. I can see from here. Let's go."

Kuji laughed, but Tuwillia just nodded her head to the right. "The stream leaves the pond in that direction. "Surely it leads to bigger streams and a river."

Parade of the Gods

They're playing the same song as before, Luha thought, as she listened to the ringing carillons. Perhaps it calls the men here in the morning. Oh! she laughed to herself, shaking her head. It's from one of Oosnof's operas. It's the 'Parade of the Gods.'

Soon she could hear the men talking and joking downstairs, but heard no one coming up to this floor.

The carillon stopped ringing and a recording of an organ playing the same music started up in the chapel below her. Peering carefully in each direction, she crawled out from under the bench and up on it again, crouching behind the balustrade and tucking her ears flat against her head so that she could peer down into the chapel without much of her head visible from below.

The men, wearing their white robes, processed down the center aisle in twos, silently moving into the pews to left and right, leaving the first row empty and empty seats in each of the rest of the rows. They remained standing and she could see a pointed hood hanging down the back of each robe. In the first rows the hoods were trimmed in light gray, but those in the rows back of them had hoods trimmed in a coppery color. Silver or Nickel? Copper? Again like the circular paths. She wondered what they would look like if they pulled the hoods up over their heads – the Ku Klux Klan?

The music soared to a triumphant march, modulating to a higher key, repeating the musical introduction and the men began to sing. The melody was from the opera, but the words were their own:

> *We are the Giants of God.*
> *We inherit the earth.*
> *All the world bows to our glory,*
> *Never knowing our secret story.*
> *We are the men of power and glory.*
> *We are the Giants of God.*

As they sang, another group of men came down the aisle, single file. There were six of these men, each wearing a silver robe. They filed into the front row, leaving ten empty seats, and again remained standing. As the verse ended everyone turned to face the aisle. The tempo slowed, and they all sang:

> *Eight shall lead us.*
> *Eight shall guide our ways.*
> *Eight shall be our victory.*
> *Eight for all our days.*

Four men, wearing gold robes, walked solemnly down the aisle and up the three steps to the dais, sitting two to a side in four of the eight throne-like chairs that faced the pews on either side of the mosaic floor pattern. One of them was the man with the shaved head who had presided at the 'judgment' the day before.

When the hymn finished, Shaved Head stood and nodded his head toward the pews.

All the men sat.

"We have an urgent problem to deal with this morning, so we'll suspend our reports until tomorrow." He looked down at the first row. "Eric?" Eric stood quickly. "Has the girl returned?"

Eric shook his head. "No and I'm sure none of the women of my household have seen her."

"You interrogated them?"

"Yes, of course."

"And this cat thing – has it been seen?"

All the men shook their heads.

One of the other men in gold – older, heavier, with gray hair – stood up. Luhanada pulled her head a little farther down so that only her eyes were above the wall as Gray Hair addressed the group.

"I wasn't here. I didn't see this cougar or whatever, but I do know we haven't been able to bring any living animals or plants here. So, how did this animal – if it is an animal – get here?"

"And invulnerable to our guns," added the first man in gold.

Another of the men in gold came forward. This one had thick black hair.

"Seb, this is a trick," he said, addressing Shaved Head. "The women are behind it somehow. Or maybe just one woman in a costume that acts as a shield against the bullets. Someone who's set herself up as superwoman or something."

Seb shook his head. "I don't think a woman, or any human, could move the way that animal moved. Besides the bullets disappeared."

"Oh, nonsense, Seb," said Black Hair. "You were startled, and it just seemed that way. There can be no other explanation."

Seb's eyes smoldered, but he didn't say anything.

Luha, her eyes barely visible as she peered over the edge of the balustrade, watched as Black Hair turned toward the assembled men, ignoring the still smoldering Seb. "The cougar's one of our women. We need to search all the houses for the costume. Think which of your women might have had access to materials to make it. Whoever it is is still among us and has the girl hidden someplace."

He looked directly at Eric. "And you, Eric, need to question your household more. The fact Kujakali wasn't afraid to escape with the so-called cat indicates she knew something beforehand."

The gray-haired man in gold leaned over to the fourth gold robed man – a tall middle aged man with white hair – and with a concerned look, whispered something. The white haired man looked annoyed, shaking his head. Then White Hair stood up and walked forward. The rest turned to him deferentially.

"Thanks, Todd," he patted Black Hair on the back and turned to the congregants. "This is all very well and good, but a minor problem really. If the women escape they end up in the eggs. This is not a real threat."

He turned toward Seb. "Sebastian, I disagree that reports should be put off until tomorrow. The world is our first concern, not some minor revolt among the women here. Our little 'retreat center' here is fun, but we need to remember our larger goals. You can handle this among yourselves."

The gray haired man stood up moving forward hesitantly. "But Kas, what if this is connected to that woman who turned into a tree?"

Luha's ears perked up. *A woman who turned into a tree? Giselle?*

Kas glared at the man. "I told you, Stuart, that's a fantasy. I think Todd's right. This is one of our women." He looked at the other men in gold. "Who's here the rest of the week?"

"I am, Kas." Todd smiled.

"Good, Todd. After the meeting, you meet with the men who will be here this week," Kas nodded his head out toward the congregants, "and figure this out."

He turned to look out at the rest of the men. "I can't emphasize too much the need to keep our organization secret. We're powerful, but we also have powerful rivals. The Lugas Group and their allies, for instance. We have enemies on two fronts – the protestors and the other large corporations. This OET demonstration is potentially a big problem. This is not just a game. It's a war, and we want to win."

Returning to his seat he added, "Now, please, let's go on with reports."

There was silence for a minute, then Seb turned back toward the congregants. "Who has reports?" Many hands went up. He nodded at a man in silver in the front row. "Kevin."

Luhanada was amazed at the breadth of the issues described in the reports, which seemed to be summaries of activities. They talked about attempts to privatize cities and towns, even states, their success in third world countries and some cities and states in Uhs; about the deregulation of many industries, including the communications industry; breaking labor unions in both the private and public sectors; corporate takeover of public schools, prisons, and detention centers for immigrants, and how disaster economics made this easy; taking control of the International Financial Agency, and the consequent bankruptcy of whole countries; the hordes of information they had access to through the tapping of cell phones and computers by the UhsSA; and the War on Drugs.

She fought to control a deep growl as she realized these people might be connected both to the politicians advocating military intervention in countries where there were large drug cartels, and to the drug cartels themselves! But the men seemed to think it was funny, laughing outright at the chaos they had caused with the drug war.

One man mentioned a new book linking the War on Drugs to racism and opposition to the victories of the Civil Rights Movement.

Todd dismissed it with a wave of his hand. "Who's going to read it? White people want to believe they're better than other people. They'd much rather think blacks deserve to be in prison."

"They do," a voice muttered. The few men of color looked around them suspiciously, but couldn't tell who the speaker was. Todd just smirked.

The report on global warming, talking about how to continue keeping the majority of people ignorant about the reality and extent of the ecological problems occurring, was the most disturbing. "There's a fool born every day," Todd laughed. "We bring in someone with a degree, make him sound like some big expert, and he pooh-poohs global warming." They all laughed.

"Yes," replied Kas. "It won't work forever. But people love to stick their head in the sand and ignore problems – especially when it means giving up things they like having. I think we have a few years left for the oil industry, but we've got to get the major pipelines we need, down through Uhs and Western Asia. The big die-offs are still in third world nations, where no one with any power cares. By the time it starts happening in the first world, it will be too late."

Luha had the distinct and horrifying impression that the purpose behind the global warming policy was not only to keep the governments from regulating big business, but also to allow the effects of global warming to kill off as many people as possible, leaving the spoils for themselves. The men clearly believed it was really happening.

Who are these people? she thought. *Why are they doing this?*

The meeting ended and Seb stepped forward. "Those who are leaving, disrobe." The men on the outer edges of the rows followed Seb up the aisle, away from the altar followed by Kas and the gray haired man in gold.

Todd and the others sat and chatted until Todd hit a gong sitting at the edge of the altar alcove.

Immediately they all stood, and turned toward the aisle to watch the others return and walk silently up to the altar, each taking a goblet and moving to stand on the outermost circle of the mosaic flooring. Seb went to the altar, picked up the golden pitcher, and walking on the inside of the circle, poured a small amount of liquid into each goblet. When he had finished, he poured some into a goblet for himself, returned the pitcher to the tray, and joined the circle.

Then Todd stood and picked up the book that sat at the other end of the altar, turned, and remaining outside of the circle, began to read:

> And it came to pass, when men began to multiply on the face of the earth, and daughters were born unto them, that the sons of God saw the daughters of men that they were fair; and they took them wives of all which they chose. And the LORD said, My spirit shall not always strive with man, for that he also is flesh: yet his days shall be an hundred and twenty years. There were giants in the earth in those days; and also after that, when the sons of God came in unto the daughters of men, and they bore children to them, the same became mighty men which were of old, men of renown.

He finished with, "So saith Genesis 6:1-9 of the Bible of the Judeo-Christian tradition," and all the men responded in unison, "We are the descendants of those Sons of God, we are the Giants. It is we who shall inherit the earth."

The men in the circle lifted their goblets and drank… and disappeared. *Whoa*, thought Luhanada. *Like going to Ninas Twei, but…*

As soon as the ritual was over, Todd went to the edge of the podium and addressed the remaining men. "I think we should deal with this problem of Kuji and the woman who's pretending to be a mountain lion immediately. We'll surprise the women with a search. If you don't find anything, return here in an hour. That will be enough time to waste on this nonsense." The men stood and left the chapel.

Luha slipped into the office behind her, and out onto the patio. She peered over the top of the outer wall, watching the men move down the radials away from the temple. She noticed that Todd went with them — searching his own home, she presumed.

Back in the building she found a stairway and an elevator at the end of the corridor and took the stair down to where it ended in the chapel. She could see another stairway on the opposite side of the chapel, but there were no stairs going further down there or here.

A wide doorway at the top of the center aisle led past a corridor circling outside of the chapel to a large hallway and the tall steel doors out to the courtyard. Open doorways on either side of the hall revealed dressing rooms with hooks hung with robes lining the walls, and a strange contraption like an airport scanner next to each door.

Down the corridor behind the chapel she found a door with long plate glass windows on either side looking into a large office space. She could see one of the smaller outside doors across from the window.

Further down the corridor was the terminus for the elevator, and then a dead end. She turned and crept past the chapel doors down the corridor in the other direction finding another windowed office space, and another elevator terminus. The floor indicator over the elevator read, "C1, C2, C3, 1, 2, 3, 4, 5." Number one was lit.

This is floor one, she thought. *The C numbers must be lower floors.* She started to reach a paw up to hit the down button... *But if there's someone down there, they'll hear the elevator. Much riskier than stairs... but the stairs don't go down.*

She paced for a moment in front of the door. *I'm already dead. I don't think they can hurt me. But can they capture me? Kuji can sit on my back. I am, in some way, solid.*

She sighed. The children.

She sat up on her haunches, but just as she started to push the down button, the outer temple doors opened and she heard men's voices in the front hall. She batted at the up button. The doors opened and she leapt into the cab pawing at the button for the second floor until it lit up. The doors closed slowly behind her and the elevator moved up. She looked at the buttons arrayed on the inner wall beside the door. One, two, three, four, five, and below them three buttons labeled Cellar 1, Cellar 2, Cellar 3. *Cellars. Yes.* Should she change her mind and go down?

Muffled voices came up the shaft. "Look, someone's in the elevator." "But I thought we were the first back in the building."

The first floor button lit up just as the doors opened onto the second floor corridor. She leapt out, sprinting down the hall to the open door of the office where she had entered the building. She could hear the elevator doors close behind her, the cab descending to the first floor to pick up whoever had pushed the call button. She wavered for a moment, her head turning back and forth, to the door, to the bench, back to the door.

Taking a deep breath, she ducked under the bench again, making sure all her paws and her tail, were well hidden.

Almost immediately, the elevator doors opened. Footsteps came rapidly down the corridor and stopped outside the open door – two pairs of feet, one clad in black and green sports shoes, the other in expensive brown leather loafers.

"Look at the patio door." The voice was deep and gravelly.

The other spoke with authority, "Check it out, but carefully," and they moved slowly through the room to the patio.

Then she heard a voice in the chapel below her. "Take her up front."

They had one of the women! Her tail started to switch angrily and she held it tight to the ground.

The men returned from the patio.

"Whoever it is might still be inside," gravelly voice suggested.

"Or long gone," muttered loafers. "That Kujakali a slick little brat. I wouldn't be surprised to find her running all over the place. We better report downstairs."

Luha waited until the elevator doors closed, before slipping out from under the bench and climbing up to peer down into the chapel. This time the men entered without singing or processing, and without their robes. Two men were holding a slight, brown-haired white woman tightly by her upper arms.

A moment or two later, two more men, one wearing the black and green sports shoes, and the other the brown loafers, entered with Todd.

"Order," Todd called out as he climbed the steps. "We've had an intruder. Came in through the patio door in your office, Fenmore."

He glared at a man sitting in the fourth row, and then back at the whole group. "He – or probably she – may still be in the building. We need to do a search. Silver and Nickel, head for your own offices. Search your own floor thoroughly – your offices, and the offices of those who aren't here. Copper spread out through the whole building."

One of the men holding the woman said, "What shall we do with Sarah?"

Kuji's friend. Luha's tail started flicking.

Todd turned to them. "You stay here with her."

Some of the men headed for the stairs, and others down the center aisle – *Going to the elevators*, she thought – *all moving fast.*

Todd followed them.

She held herself tightly in check until the two men holding Sarah were the only ones left in the chapel, and then, leaping up on to the top of the balustrade, screamed loudly and soared down into the center aisle. The two men yelled and let go of Sarah, turning to run toward the outer aisles, calling that the cat was back as they went.

"To me, Sarah," Luha commanded, and Sarah ran up the aisle toward her.

The men who had been holding her started running back. There was loud confusion on the stairs as some of the men turned to run back toward the chapel.

Luha crouched. "On my back. Hold tight." Sarah straddled her, wrapping her fingers deep into her fur, and Luhanada took off up the aisle.

"Keep low," she urged.

Sarah wrapped her legs around the cat's body, and her arms around her neck, pressing her cheek into the back of Luha's head. Luhanada bounded through the hallway, past the corridors where the men waiting at the elevators were now running back toward the chapel doorway. The big front doors were wide open and she flew out the doors, leaping down off the concrete apron, and up the pathway toward the park, heading for the bridge over the canyon.

"Hold on," she called to Sarah, as she bounded up the path and crouched for the leap over the chain link gate. "Hold on tight, keep your feet up, and you'll be safe."

Sarah tightened her grip as they sprinted across the bridge, and then across the plateau, finally reaching the crevice.

Luha leapt up to the first ledge and stopped for a moment, panting.

Sarah took a sobbing breath.

"It will be all right, Sarah," Luha urged her. "Just hang on. No matter what, just hang on." She took another deep breath, and leapt up to the next ledge, and the next. She felt Sarah begin to change.

"What's happening to me?" whispered Sarah digging her claws into the cougar's back.

"It's all right," Luha soothed, as she reached the top of the crevice. "You can get down now."

Sarah Wood Thrush flew off her back, landing on the ground near the Weaving Tree. "Where are we?" She looked around her. "This is a beautiful place."

"This is Ninas Twei. You're safe here."

The little bird nodded her head. "But... but I'm..." Suddenly she broke into a beautiful fluty song and just as suddenly stopped.

"I'm a bird." She looked at Luhanada. "Am I a bird?"

Luha laughed. "Yes, for now. When humans come here, they come as their Tla Twei – it's hard to explain."

She told her a little about Ninas Twei. "I think you're a Wood Thrush. You're very pretty."

Sarah twisted her head around, and stretched out her wings, looking at her feathers. "When I was a little girl I used to play in a wood full of Wood Thrushes. I loved their songs." She laughed with delight. "And I can sing, too." She broke into her whistling song again.

"You're Kuji's friend, aren't you?"

"Yes." The little bird hopped toward Luha. "Where is she? Is she all right?"

Luha looked around her and then called out, "Kujakali? Tuwillia?"

"Ummm," came a rumbly voice from down the path. Luha and Sarah turned to look as the old turtle made her way toward them. "Tuwillia, this is Kuji's friend, Sarah."

"Lady Thrush," Tuwillia gave a little bow of her head. "I was called by your beautiful song."

Sarah nodded back. "Thank you."

Tuwillia told of Kuji's unsuccessful attempt to get to Singing Swan and her discovery of Peeka. "I sent them down the creek that leaves my pond, to find this river Peeka spoke of – and Singing Swan, and the others."

She settled herself down on her shell pulling in her legs. "What have you found? Did you find the children?"

"No, but I found an elevator that goes to floors below the temple. Those openings in the canyon wall above and below the net must lead into rooms beneath the city. I hope I can get to them using the elevator." She turned to the thrush. "Perhaps you know something about the eggs we don't know."

Sarah cocked her head to one side. "I don't know very much except what I've heard when the men talk. Once I heard them talking about how clever it all is. How the people in the eggs provide the electricity for the city by pedaling – I don't know what, but something like a bike.

They said it was very automatic – hardly any humans involved, except the people pedaling in the eggs."

Tuwillia slowly nodded her head. "You go, Luhanada. Try to find the children. We will work here to gather people to help."

The thrush hopped into the air. "I can fly and find Kuji, and take messages between you." She broke into a joyful song, flew in circles around their heads, and then landed in front of Luha.

"I've been imprisoned for so long, and now, suddenly, I can fly." She shook her head. "It's so hard to believe." Luhanada touched her gently with a paw.

Tuwillia rose slowly to her feet. "Go, Luhanada. Lady Thrush will fly to Kujakali. I'll show her the stream and she can fly down it looking for them. I'll wait here for messages." She turned toward the path to her pond. "Come, Sarah."

Luha turned and leapt back down the crevice. At the bottom, she crawled forward until she could see the whole city. It was crawling with activity, especially in the parks on either side. Men were combing the plastic bushes, and moving in and out of the buildings, searching, she thought, for Sarah, Kujakali, and the mysterious cougar. No one seemed to be looking on this side of the canyon or even on the bridge.

They feel so sure of the danger of the wind they aren't looking for us here. She sighed, and took the time to lick the fur between her front paws, pulling out dirt and pebbles caught between her claws. Keeping a low profile, she reached around and licked her underside, getting the dust off her belly. How long would it be until the lights faded in the city cave? She licked as far as she could down her back, and caught her back paws between her front paws so that she could clean their claws.

It would be late before she could get back into the temple. She crawled back to the crevice, and settled herself down, tucked close to the wall where she could see out, but where it would be hard for others to see her in the shadow.

2

The Piercing Voice

Enid shoved at the translucent gray plastic material that made up the walls, ceiling, and floor of the small egg shaped room. If she pushed the sides, they gave like elastic, but she couldn't break through them. She could make her container rock just a little when she sat on the bench stretched along the left side of the egg from the wide end at the back to the more pointed end in front. It felt like it pushed into something else equally elastic, like she was inside a really thick-skinned egg-shaped balloon, in a cluster of balloons.

She was incredibly tired, but the short sleep periods were the only time she could work at escape. During the work periods, if she slowed down her pedaling, the voice came and yelled at her with a piercing sound so loud it hurt – a terrifying, loud voice. During work periods she worked – and remembered.

She had been terrified when they fell down the crevice. She had managed to cling to Jesús as they bounced off the ledges, even as they changed back to human form, only to be torn away from him by a rush of air, a wind like a tornado, that sent them rolling like tumbleweeds across the plateau at the bottom to fall again down another cliff into a steel mesh net, which rolled them slightly downward across a canyon, until they were caught in the center of the net.

As they crawled over the net, desperately reaching toward each other, Enid was only peripherally aware of the gray bubbly stuff that covered the floor of the canyon. Jesús had almost caught her outstretched hand when a long metal arm, with a pincher on the end like two huge fingers, flew out of a dark square opening in the far side of the canyon, and grabbed him, tearing him away from her.

She had screamed and screamed, as she watched him disappear into the opening. She had not seen Jesús again.

When the arm came back for her she'd tried to scramble away from it up the net, but the net shook, and she fell back to the bottom where the pinchers caught her. The arm pulled her into a dark window in the cliff and dropped her through a hole into the egg which immediately closed above her head. She'd tumbled back and forth, slamming into the pedals and the pipe, finally grabbing on to the plastic bench, as the egg moved – swaying as it went – then was lowered, sliding back and forth until the square metal pipe in the middle of the egg slipped over a metal box that protruded up into the egg.

Then the piercing voice began:

> FIND WIRE AND PLUG HANGING FROM CYLINDER
> UNDER PEDALS;
> PLUG INTO BOX;
> SIT IN LEGLESS PLASTIC CHAIR;
> MOVE CHAIR ON SQUARE BAR
> UNTIL FEET CAN PUSH PEDALS;
> TIGHTEN KNOB HOLDING CHAIR IN PLACE;
> PEDAL.

She pedaled.

The instructions continued, but if she kept peddling at the right speed the voice dropped to a barely audible level. If she slowed down, the voice got louder. She soon learned how to keep the voice soft.

But where was Jesús?

Jesús hated the screeching voice. He'd curled in a ball on the bench, holding his ears, refusing to follow instructions.

After a while a pain had shot through his body – an excruciating pain – and in the end he'd had to give in. He plugged the wire into the box and climbed on the seat and pedaled – he pedaled and fell into a dark despair broken only by the automatic movement of his legs. He'd lost Enid. He'd wanted to protect her, but he'd lost her.

During the rest periods he fell into a deep sleep. He didn't notice when the wall sometimes puffed inward, as if something were pushing it from the outside.

Another sleep period, but Enid wasn't sleeping. She didn't know how long they'd been here. Many, many work periods, but were they days?

She remembered, vaguely, seeing the valley full of gray bubbles, as she and Jesús tumbled down the cliff, and scrambled across the net toward each other. *There must be eggs on either side of me, and in them other workers, isolated and alone, and pushing, too, against the sides of their prisons,* she thought. *Jesús must be in an egg somewhere.*

Her eyes widened. "If the eggs were placed in the valley in order of their capture, Jesús might be right next to me. Oh, I hope he's right next to me," she whispered, and fell asleep.

"AWAKEN. NOURISHMENT," the voice boomed.

She gave a little cry of despair. The sleep period was over.

A metal bucket, suspended on a long pole, pushed down through the ceiling, hanging for a moment beside the bench. She jumped up to grab the bar of food and the plastic bottle of water it contained before it was pulled up again. Not that it really qualified as food. There was no taste to it at all. As for waste, there was a hole at the end of the bench, but if you got off the chair to use it, the voice screamed. You had to hold your waste until the sleep period.

She watched as the skin of the egg's ceiling closed up after the bucket was pulled back through it. It reminded her of the way you can draw your arm out of water, and the water will flow instantly into the place where your arm had been. But when she tried to force an arm through the sides of the egg, the plastic simply poked outward like a balloon, but didn't break. She couldn't reach the top where the bucket came through.

Two work periods later she started singing.

The singing was amazing. She didn't think, *I'm going to sing.* Suddenly she was singing and the more she sang, the more strength poured into her. The harsh voice of the instructor became, instead of an irritant, a background percussion.

Except for the Sunday hymns, her grandfather hadn't had much music in the house. In school a music teacher came to their classroom once a week for six weeks out of each year with an electronic keyboard and paperback songbooks, and Enid, without singing a word out loud, had learned all the songs by heart. By herself in the woods, she had sung those songs with the birds.

Now she sang them to herself.

Down by the station early in the morning, she sang out, as she pedaled thinking of herself pedaling right through and out of the plastic egg. *She'll be Coming Round the Mountain* was Luhanada, not driving six white horses, but galloping toward her in cougar form. When she got tired, *Amazing Grace* gave her endurance. Finally, she thought of the songs she and Jesús sang as they traveled with the Tree Woman and Yameno, Luhanada and Tata to Ninas Twei:

> *I am the writer of poetry,*
> *Fluid as the world of dream.*
> *I see the whole in every part.*
> *I see the things that aren't seen.*

She sang it over and over again. *Maybe if I sing loud enough, Jesús will hear me,* she thought. And she began to sing louder, and to make up songs that incorporated his name:

> *Jesús, Jesús, I'm singing for you.*
> *Hear me singing, hear me singing.*
> *Jesús, Jesús, I'm singing to you.*
> *Are you near,*
> *Can you hear,*
> *Can you hear me singing?*

Jesús was deep in a stupor, pedaling without much awareness of what he was doing, when he first heard someone whispering – someone singing his name. It was a soft, higher pitched voice than that of the machine that gave him orders – a child's voice. Then he caught some of the other words – *poetry and dream.*

That was Enid's song – the song she sang on the journey to Ninas Twei!

It's Enid! he thought.

He yelled out her name, but the voice kept singing as if she hadn't heard him. He pedaled and listened. The words were so faint. How was he hearing her, and yet she couldn't hear him? He kept pedaling, but as he pushed the pedals the rhythm of the pedaling began to feel like a dance, like a song, and the words of his own song began to slip like the rustle of leaves, into his head. He whispered:

> *I am the echo of creation.*
> *I see the earth in her splendor.*

Louder and louder, he sang until he was shouting!

> *I am the echo of creation.*
> *I see the earth in her splendor.*

My hands draw the dreams of the universe,
humanity's heart at its core,
So the heart of humanity can soar.
So the heart of humanity can soar.

As he sang, he felt his back straightening. *I can survive this. And Enid's near. In the silence I can hear her. She's singing, too.*

But maybe that was it. She was singing. Perhaps she couldn't hear because she was singing. He would wait until the pedaling stopped for the rest period and until her voice stopped, and then he would respond as loud as he could.

Enid sang through every work period, alternating the children's songs she had sung in school with her new made up song for Jesús, always ending with the song she sang as they traveled to Ninas Twei, before falling into the deep sleep of the rest period.

At the end of the third work period of singing, as she finished her last notes, she thought she heard a faint echo of her song. In the sudden quiet as the pedals stopped, she heard a deeper voice ever so faintly.

When it stopped, she sang again:

Hear me singing, hear me singing.
Jesús, Jesús, I'm singing to you.
Are you near,
Can you hear,
Can you hear me singing?

She heard a whispery response:

Enid, Enid,
Are you near,
Can you hear,
Can you hear me singing?

"Yes," she cried out in her loudest, shrillest voice. "I'm here. I hear you."

Jumping off the bike she poked as hard as she could at the gray walls in the direction of the voice.

Almost immediately the walls poked back at her!

It's Jesús, she thought as she pushed her arm back into the wall. Then, through the plastic skin of the walls she could just barely feel another hand wrapped around hers. She started to cry.

Her arm got tired and she had to release it, but almost immediately the plastic poked in on her side, and she reached up and caressed the hard bump it made. Then it, too, receded.

She pushed herself up as close to the wall as she could and felt the wall curve around her, as if Jesús was curled up on the other side next to her. Faintly she heard:

> *I am the echo of creation.*
> *I see the earth in her splendor.*
> *My hands draw the dreams of the universe,*
> *humanity's heart at its core,*
> *So the heart of humanity can soar.*
> *So the heart of humanity can soar.*

… until they both fell asleep.

"Nameless One called for Light"

Luha roused herself when the carillon rang five o'clock and watched as the men stopped their search. She saw some enter homes and apartments, while others headed for the restaurants. About an hour later the bells rang again and the men flowed back down the radials toward the temple. The doors, which had been closed at five o'clock, were opened again, and the men went inside closing the doors behind them.

The streets were empty except for the patrol walking now on the outer circle. Waiting until they disappeared back of the temple, she crouched low to the ground and sprinted to the bridge, where she hunkered behind the posts for a minute. The patrol was on the other side of the city as she ran quickly across the bridge, scrambled over the gate, and dashed into the cover of the plastic bushes in the park.

The entrance to the cave didn't look disturbed. The odor of the men was all around it, but not behind the bushes next to the wall where the only scent was of Kuji and herself. She'd wait here until midnight, and then get into the temple and down that elevator.

Much later she heard voices outside of the cave. She crept quietly down the passage until she was right behind the first bend after the short entrance tunnel.

Two men seemed to be searching the undergrowth near the cave. "It can't really be here," said one. "It's been a long time and we haven't seen any movement. Either it has some way to escape, or it's in one of the houses."

Their voices faded as they pushed through the bushes and down the hillside. "Todd said we'd quit at midnight." "I don't know why they couldn't have turned the lights back up for the search."

"Nobody knows how. The mechanism's in the cellars. Nobody goes down there anymore."

A pause. "That's stupid."

"Everything's automatic. Everything works really well."

"Except for strange cats that can't be killed."

The other one gave a laugh. "Right."

Luha gave a sigh of relief as the voices faded away and the carillon rang midnight. She crept to the entrance of the cave, listened for a moment, and then crawled out, standing just tall enough to peek over the tops of the bushes.

No one. She couldn't even hear the footsteps of the patrol.

She slipped down to the edge of the city, and waited before creeping down radial Three toward the temple, listening and looking before crossing each path.

When she reached the Copper circle, the city was totally silent except for a low hum from the canyon. She dashed across to the tree and crouched ready to jump.

A swooshing sound from above startled her and she looked up in time to see a large net falling from the first tier. She screamed and twisted, trying to leap out of the way, but the netting fell on her head and caught under her feet, tripping her.

Men in camouflage rushed out of the doors of the buildings across the pathway and circled around her, standing on the edges of the metal netting. They quickly locked their arms together, walking forward on the netting until they had her tightly closed in. "We've got it! We've got it," they yelled, and more men came from around the corners and squeezing out the side door.

Luha shrieked again and again, clawing at the netting, throwing herself against the men, and trying to grab them with her teeth, but it was a heavy metal mesh. She couldn't bite through it, she couldn't tear it, and the men stood firm shoulder to shoulder. She was caught.

She gave one more ear piercing screech. *Be still,* she thought. *Fighting isn't helping.* Suddenly calm, she sat down on her haunches, tucked her tail around her feet, and looked regally around at her captors.

"Gees," muttered one of the men.

She stretched her cougar mouth in as much of a grin as she could and said, "What now, gentlemen?"

The men stared at her, and she grinned back, occasionally flicking her tail.

Three more men came walking around the building from the front entrance, and inserted themselves into the circle so they could see her.

"Well, well," said Todd.

"Well, well, yourself," she responded.

Todd's eyebrows shot up.

One of the two other men – short, wiry, with brown hair – looked closely at her and said, in a German accent, "Clearly, it talks. And it could not possibly be a woman dressed as a cougar."

Todd ignored him, glaring at the cat. "Who are you?"

"Me?" Luhanada pulled herself up into a standing position, maneuvering against the netting, until she was facing Todd. "I," she said in a menacing voice, "am Luhanada."

"Luhanada," Todd responded laughing. "And just who is that?"

Deep in her chest she felt something welling, breath gathering, pouring upward and emerging in a huge rich, resonant voice:

> *Nameless One called for light!*
> *I am the light!*

Some of the men took an involuntary step back as she leaned into the netting, her voice piercing the night.

"Don't move," yelled Todd.

> *I am I,*
> *I am now,*
> *I am the protector,*
> *I am the right!*
> *I am justice,*
> *I am wisdom,*
> *I am the law!*
> *I am I,*
> *I am I,*
> *I am the light.*

(Suddenly, out of the rainbow mists of stars and galaxies, orange and red, blue and green living planets, and barren dead planets, Tata heard something – something very far away. Even the strings were silent for a moment as the attention of the universe turned toward the faint voice:

> *I am I,*
> *I am now,*
> *I am the protector,*
> *I am the right!*

"Luhanada," he whispered. "Luhanada," and his voice got louder. "Luha, I hear you."

He turned to the Strings. "She needs me. How can I find her? How can I help?"

"Blue-green," they whispered. "Search for the blue-green." Their voices echoed through the galaxy, and all the playful strings of things swirled in circles looking for the blue-green. "Here," cried one. "No, there," cried another. "Look, look..." "Seek, seek...")

Todd's eyes narrowed. Looking around at the others, he said, "You're the devil."

"No," she answered in her huge echoing voice, singing:

> *No!*
> *You are the devil.*
> *I am the judge.*
> *I am the law!*

Todd shivered, but responded, "Yeah, right."

He turned away calling back to one of the men, "You handle it, Don," as he disappeared around the corner.

Luha turned toward Don, mocking Todd. "Handle it, Don. How are you going to handle it, Don?" She flicked her tail.

Don fought the urge to step back and pulled himself up straight. "Warren and Marius, get the rope."

Two men left the circle at a trot and headed across the path to the door of the building across the street.

"Tighten the circle."

The men pushed their feet even farther in on the net. Don stepped out, pulling the men on either side of him together.

"Tighten it more." Luha kept herself standing, pushing outward against the netting as much as she could, but feeling the wire pushing tighter into her skin.

Warren and Marius came back, each carrying half the coils of a long nylon rope. "Circle it," demanded Don, and the two men circled her twice with the rope, pulling it tight against her legs until her feet slipped sideways from under her and she fell over on her side.

As the men began to drag her toward the open door behind her, Luha's eyes met those of the man with the German accent, who was following close by her head looking down at her. *He almost looks concerned,* she thought.

They pulled her through the large open office space she had seen before from the corridor, out the door into the hallway, and into the elevator. When the elevator reached the third floor they pulled her down the hall to an office with a cage with thick woven wire sides in one corner of the room.

Pushing her into the cage, they loosened the rope, and pulled the rope and net out, tumbling her onto the floor of the cage. Don slammed the door and fastened a padlock on it. He looked in at her and grinned. "You asked what I was going to do. Now you know. Done!" He smacked his hands together.

"You can go now," Don waved the men out of the room. "Get some rest."

The man with the accent was the last to leave, walking out the door looking back over his shoulder at her, a quizzical look on his face.

Don spoke to him. "Pretty weird, huh, Ranulf?"

Ranulf just nodded and headed down the hall.

Don looked back at Luhanada where she sat staring at him flicking her tail. Finally, he turned his back on her, grabbing a blanket and pillow sitting on one of the desks. He carefully spread the blanket on the sofa, placing the pillow at one end, then lay down and curled up in the blanket. It was a long time before he went to sleep.

Luha paced quietly around the cage, checking its strength enough to know that she couldn't break out of it easily, if at all. She curled up in a corner.

The artificial daylight of the City Cave filled the room when Don and Luha were awakened by a rapping on the open door.

Warren stood there with a tray. "I brought you some breakfast, Don."

"Oh, thanks, Warren." Don sat up on the couch and stretched, as Warren placed the tray on one of the desks. Luha lay still, her eyes half closed, watching and listening.

"Did it keep you awake all night?"

"Nope. I think it slept, too."

They both turned to look at the cat, who opened her eyes wider, and stared back. "It's spooky," muttered Warren.

Luha sat up and began to wash herself, stopping every other lick to stare at them.

Don watched a moment. "Sure seems like it's a real cougar."

"Yeah, and it felt real when we were bringing it here. But we've never been able to bring real animals in here before. No dogs, no cats, no chickens."

Don laughed. "Of course, real dogs, cats, and chickens can't talk."

"Shows how much you know," she muttered.

"Human languages, anyway," added Don.

"They did teach some chimpanzees sign language." Warren looked anxiously at Don.

Luha gave them a look, and then stretched out a back paw so she could lick between her toes. Finally, she sighed and sat up again. "So, Don, how come you get to be my caretaker?"

Don grinned. "I planned the whole thing. I'm the one responsible for capturing you."

"Very clever."

She leaned around and licked her shoulder, then sat back up. "So, who are the Giants of God? Why don't you tell me about yourselves?" She drew her voice out in a slight sarcastic drawl. "About the Giants of God, rulers of the world," she laughed. "Then maybe I'll tell you about myself."

Don looked at her and slowly nodded. "I'll think about it, but first I think I'll eat my breakfast. Hungry?"

"Nope," she laughed.

"I've got work to do, unless you need me." Warren headed toward the door.

"No, I'm fine here, Warren." Don sat at the desk and began to dig into his food. "So, what do you want to know?"

Luha cocked her head. "Well, for starters you could tell me why you think you rule the world."

Don chewed his toast. "Because we do. The heads of most of the biggest corporations in the world are Giants of God – actually, by definition."

"By definition? How is that?"

"Because we can tell who is selected as a Giant of God by how much power he has. If a person is given power, then God must be behind him."

"Not the devil?"

Don glared at her for a moment. "There's only one power, and that's the power of God. God grants that power to those he favors. Anyone who gains great power or wealth must be a descendant of the Giants – the sons of God who married the daughters of man."

"From Genesis in the Judeo/Christian Bible," added Luha.

"Yes," smiled Don.

"A little perverted," she added.

"No, the words in Genesis are deliberately obscure, but we have the truth."

"Sure," laughed Luhanada. "So that justifies anything you do."

"Yes," Don nodded, "it does. It's clear we're the best and the brightest of God's creatures."

"What if one of these powerful people refuses to work with you?"

Don laughed. "Then they find they've lost their power."

Luha's ears perked as she heard someone moving stealthily out in the corridor, listening, but Don kept talking. *Don doesn't know he's there,* she thought, deliberately lowering her ears. "So you're fundamentalists? You follow all the rules in the Bible?"

Don shook his head. "No way. We aren't like those fundamentalists – even though we pretend we are so we can use them. We believe in Darwin's survival of the fittest."

346

"Darwin didn't coin the term, and it didn't mean to him, the same thing it means to you."

"Whatever." Don dismissed her comment and went on. "We know the weak must die, so the strong can live. We'll never achieve our potential, if we spend our time taking care of the weak."

"How many of you are there?"

He laughed. "Legions."

"This place can't hold 'legions'"

"Oh, most of them don't even know about the City Cave. Only the elite of the elite get to come here, or even know about it. But we have minions working our will all over the world. Only those who seem ready are actually asked to join the Giants."

"And if they refuse to join?"

"Rare, but if they do…" He moved his hand in a slashing movement across his throat.

"And yet your big boss – that Kas fellow – when he was talking in your temple yesterday mentioned other corporate enemies. Sounds like you haven't destroyed them all."

Don shrugged. "Not yet." He moved from the desk to the armchair next to her cage, and whoever was in the corridor moved back a little. "We rule the world, and that means anything we need to do, we do."

"So cheating is okay? On the *bas relief* around this building, it looked like one of your Giants is a banker. Is he responsible for all the foreclosures?"

Don stretched his legs out in front of him grinning. "The mortgage stuff was one of the best of our moves," he chortled. "You put the rules and regulations in really small print, full of obscure industry lingo, and convoluted language. Then you set yourself up as the sympathetic expert who will explain it all. Voila, millions of dupes on the street, and before long either dead or in jail, where they can't breed. And it affected the economy all over the world."

"Can't breed?" she asked.

"Yeah, we're ridding the world of dupes."

"And people of color."

"Well, yeah," he shrugged. "Of course."

Luha flicked her tail back and forth. Why was this man so willing to tell her all this? *He thinks I'm going to die, or be caged here forever. He's not worried about me telling anyone, and he's bragging. Probably doesn't get to tell this story – it's running out of him like effluence from a broken sewer.*

She continued probing asking about climate change, to which he replied, "So what? The earth is overpopulated."

She pointed out that if humans would share and use renewable resources, there would be enough for everyone. "And," she added, "when people's needs are met, they have less children."

"We don't want to share. Why shouldn't we have everything we want?" Don's fist hit the arm of the chair. "Why share with the scum, the mongrels? People who don't have enough sense to get rich."

"Or people who've been badly exploited by people like you, or people who don't see having piles of stuff as the purpose of life."

"No." He leaned forward and spit out the words. "No, people who are genetically dumb and aren't meant by God to survive. People of inferior races. God put them here for us to use, just like the animals."

"Slavery." Luhanada glared at him.

He shrugged. "It shouldn't have been outlawed, but we have ways around it." He laughed. "Like the War on Drugs."

She sat back and nodded. "Incarcerating people of color for doing the same things white people can do with impunity."

He nodded. "Yes, indeed. We're getting it all under our control. Industry, media, politics..."

He leaned back, clasping his hands behind his head. "War is a great one. We get people to kill each other off. Our biggest industries make lots of money on weapons – sold to both sides. We make it so most kids not rich enough to go to college, go into the army – or else they get sent to jail for minor drug offences. We encourage young men in other countries to become terrorists, and then we attack the countries we blame for it, and kill off millions."

"How about the powerful in those countries? Are they Giants of God?"

"Some of them."

"But most of you're really from one country."

He began to push the papers around on his desk again, keeping his eyes away from Luha. "Well, one group of countries. Clearly, the sons of the 'sons of God and the daughters of man' come mostly from the traditionally white countries. We've proved ourselves. We're the smartest, the strongest."

"And this place?"

Don leaned forward, looking at her again. "This place is the proof. God showed us this place." He got up and pulled a book down off the shelf.

Luha sensed a slight movement in the corridor. *I wonder who that is? Is Don going to get in trouble for telling me all this?*

Don sat back down and held up the leather-bound book. "*The Chronicles of the Giants of God.* This book tells it all." He leaned forward shaking the book at her. "There were eight powerful men meeting to read the scriptures, and they were reading the very passage in the Christian Bible that tells about the Giants."

He opened the book and read, "'When the sons of God came in unto the daughters of men, and they bore children to them, the same became mighty men.' *Genesis 6:1-9.*"

He looked up at her, and then back at the book, reading:

And then one of those eight powerful men said, 'We are the descendants of those Sons of God, we are the Giants. It is we who shall inherit the earth.' Then they drank together, and suddenly they were in the cavern of the Giants.

He closed the book.

"Of course, the cavern wasn't like this then. It was just a small cave filled with dry roots hanging down from somewhere – and with no opening. But we figured out how to use it. We carved out the City Cave and created electricity by using the workers in the canyon."

Luha sighed. "And where do the workers come from?"

"We have our ways." Don leaned forward. "But now it's your turn. Who are you?"

"I told you. I'm Luhanada."

"Yeah, right. And who is Luhanada? Do you think you're some kind of god?"

"No. I'm not a god. What I am is not so easily defined."

She began to pace back and forth in the cage. Suddenly she stopped, her head thrown up as she felt the song well up in her again. Her voice rang out, echoing through the temple:

Nameless One called for light.
I am the light of understanding.
Nameless One called for light.
I am the light of justice.
Nameless One called for light.
I am the light of wisdom.
I am I,
I am now.
I am the protector.
I am the law!

She heard the person in the hall stir restlessly, and sent that line out again on a piercing high note.

I am the protector!
I am the law!

She paused for a moment looking at Don, whose eyes were wide, and then sang again on a softer note:

I am wisdom.
I am Love.
Nameless One called for light.
I am the light of wisdom.

There was silence when she finished, and then footsteps running up the stairs at each end of the hall. The listener in the hall moved back down the hall somewhere.

Hiding, she thought.

Don shook his head. "Gees, you've stirred up the militia." His words were flippant, but his hands trembled.

He stood up and went to the doorway just as the first men arrived from the stairs. "No worries," he laughed. "I just made the mistake of asking it to tell me what it was."

There were nervous laughs. "We could hear it all over," exclaimed one man. "It's got..." "'She', I think," someone interrupted. "Yeah, she's got a really big voice." "What does it mean," asked someone else, nervously. "Nameless One. Is that God?"

"All right, everyone." Todd's voice broke over top of the others. "We know that this thing can't be associated with God. If it was, it'd be one of us. And it wouldn't be female."

"Right," echoed another voice.

Todd continued. "It's some kind of trick. We'll figure it out. Now all of you get back to your business."

As the rest headed back to their offices, Todd walked into the room and stared at Luha. "Don, what the fuck is this thing?"

(And the song moved faintly through the universe, just a little bit louder than before:

> *Nameless one called for light.*
> *I am the light of wisdom,*
> *I am the light of love.*

Tata threw back his head and responded:

> *I am the wild wings of the earth*
> *and the violent sea.*
> *High flyer!*
> *I am the eyes of the sun, piercing.*
> *I am the key.*
> *Wind rider!*
> *I am the voice of life,*
> *the song of the One.*
> *High Crier!*

The strings and quarks cried, "Yes, we are. Yes, we are!" as they spun through stars and planets seeking, seeking.

> *The song of the One, the voice of life, sang the neutralinos.*
> *You... are needed. We... are needed.*

Luha... Luha, thought Dan, where are you?)

Todd and Don stood in front of the cage looking at Luha, who was busy washing herself. Todd had an arm folded across his chest, the elbow of his left arm balanced on it, his chin resting on his fist. She heard the listener creep out of his hiding place, and come a little closer to the door. Don's hands were in his pockets, and he rocked a little on his feet. "Physically, it seems like a real cougar."

"Cougars can't talk," muttered Todd.

"It doesn't seem to be hungry either," Don added. "At least it said it wasn't hungry when I asked it this morning."

Luha looked up at them, trying her best to produce a grin.

"Gees," Todd's eyes got wide. "It's baring its teeth."

Luha laughed, and returned to her washing.

"It's laughing! I don't believe in this kind of thing." Todd shook his head. "I don't believe in the supernatural."

Don looked at Todd, "But..." He paused. "But, how about how we get here – to the City? That's pretty weird, too."

Todd threw his hands up in the air, and turned toward the door. Luhanada heard the listener slip back down the hall.

Todd stopped at the door and turned back. "God. That's God." He looked at Luha again. "It's got to be something of the devil. It's got to be."

"We've always said there wasn't really a devil," muttered Don.

"Well, we must have been wrong." Todd whirled around and dashed out the door, heading down the hallway in the opposite direction from the listener.

Don turned away from the cage and sat down on the sofa, leaning over with his head in his hands.

Luha spoke. "It might be..." she paused. "It might be that you're the ones doing the devil's work."

Don's head shot up. "Shut up. Just shut up."

She laughed.

"Are you a woman? Are you a human woman?"

"Do I look human?"

"No, but you sound like a woman."

"And we all know where women fit into your hierarchy."

Don grinned. "God gave us women more than any of the other creatures. Women are our particular servants."

"More like slaves, I think," interrupted Luhanada.

"Yeah, slaves." He sat back on the armchair, putting his hands behind his head. "Men have big appetites. We were created that way by God. Women are here to fulfill them."

"Including little girls."

"Especially little girls." Don grinned. "And little boys, too. It's good training for them."

"I see." Luhanada's tail lashed back and forth. "And just how far are you willing to take your appetites?"

"As far as they go."

He laughed.

"And women, more than any others, are to be subjugated, because they're the source of all evil."

"I thought you didn't believe in evil – or at least in the devil."

Don shrugged and rolled his eyes as the carillon started ringing the operatic march.

"Meeting time," Don announced as he turned to leave the room. "Have a good afternoon!" His laughter could be heard as he loped down the hall toward the stairs.

The bells stopped ringing and she listened carefully, sniffing the air, trying to find the secret listener, but he was no longer there. She could hear voices coming from outside and downstairs, then singing from the chapel. After that, talking, but she couldn't understand the words.

Every once in a while someone came to the doorway and looked at her, but no one came in, no one spoke to her.

Don didn't return until late in the evening. The meeting hadn't gone on that long, so Luha supposed he had been out doing other things. She wondered if he had a woman here, too. When he finally returned, she asked.

He laughed. "Of course. A couple. One's a little girl. Want to hear about it?"

"No, I don't."

"Can't do anything about it from in there, can you?" He giggled.

A moment later, Warren came and stood in the doorway.

Don turned to him. "Come on in. She can't hurt you from in there." He pointed at the blanket and pillow. "You can sleep there. You don't have to stay awake. She can't get out."

He turned to Luha. "Bye, bye. See you in the morning."

And to Warren, "I'll be back about nine, after the meeting."

Warren just nodded.

After Don left, Warren turned out the light, gathered the blanket around him and curled up on the sofa, his head turned toward Luhanada.

"So, Warren," Luha asked. "Tell me about yourself."

"Shut up," muttered Warren and closed his eyes.

She sighed. *Don't think I'm going to get anywhere with him.* Several times during the night she was aware of the listener in the hall. He seemed to be coming from a lower level, checking on them for a few minutes, and then leaving again.

Kuji Gathers her Band

Kuji and Peeka followed the stream, sometimes having to move a little inland to get around heavy growth, and sometimes scrambling down the bank to walk along a rocky beach. Kuji found blackberries to eat and they drank the fresh, sweet water from the little stream. They walked and chattered, telling each other about their lives, as the sun rose high in the sky and back down again, seeming to get bigger as it approached the horizon.

"Is it going to be dark soon?" Kuji asked anxiously.

"Yes," Peeka nodded. "Maybe we'll stop and sleep."

They were looking for a good place to spend the night, when a small bird came flying down the middle of the stream, chirping loudly, and then calling, "Kuji, Kuji, it's me."

Kuji turned to watch the bird, startled by the loud chirping. The Wood Thrush landed on the branch of a tree next to her, laughing. "It's me – Sarah."

"Sarah," Kujakali exclaimed. "Sarah?"

"Yes. I'm a Wood Thrush here. I can fly! And I can sing!"

She sang a little song.

"You've always been able to sing, as long as Eric wasn't around," laughed Kuji.

Sarah cocked her head and looked at her. "I can see it's you, but you really look different. You've got a lot of arms!"

Kuji lifted one hand to the little bird. "Tuwillia says I came here in the form of the deva Durga. It's quite useful to have eight arms. Did Luha bring you here?"

"Yes, she rescued me."

The little bird hopped on Kuji's hand. She looked over to where Peeka had started running up and down another one of her arms. "Is that Peeka?"

Peeka chattered, "You're Kuji's friend. You're Sarah who helped her when she was a little girl. Kuji told me about you."

Sarah smiled. "Yes, and Tuwillia told us about you. I was afraid I wouldn't find you before dark."

"We're looking for a place to spend the night," Kuji explained, as she started on down the bank with the little pika on one hand and the bird on another, holding them close into her body, so they were next to each other. She used her other arms to balance and push branches out of their path.

The last of twilight seemed to be leaking out of the sky as they rounded a turn in the stream and came upon a little clearing under a tall oak tree where they settled down for the night.

Kuji sat with her back to the wide trunk of the tree and looked up at the night sky full of stars. "I remember stars, but I don't ever remember seeing so many at one time!"

Sarah nodded. "You lived in a city. The lights make it more difficult to see the stars. When I was little I lived in the country and the stars were like this."

Peeka turned his head to one side. "I've never seen a city. Is the place you came from – the place of these Giants of God – a city?"

Sarah laughed. "It's like a pretend city. It's not that big, and there're no stars – not even pretend stars."

Before they slept, Sarah told Kuji of her narrow escape from the temple.

Kuji cupped her close in her hands. "Oh, Sarah, it's my fault. I'm such a trouble maker."

"No, Kuji," chirped Sarah. "It's important to stand up to them, and now maybe we'll have help. Now sleep."

"Yes, we'll sleep," muttered Peeka, his little eyes almost closed. "We're safe here."

The sun woke them early the next morning. "I'm hungry," Kuji exclaimed.

Peeka looked at her with concern. "There's plenty of food for Sarah, but we'll have to find more blackberries for you."

The morning went much like the day before, with occasional blackberries, lots of brush, and some rocky beaches. Sarah had flown ahead and back several times before she reported that the stream flowed into a small river just ahead.

Kuji, Peeka cradled in one of her hands, rushed forward to stand at the point where the two waterways met. "Is this the river?" Kuji asked anxiously, as she held him high so he could see.

"This seems very small. The river is wider. We should head downstream. Maybe it'll get bigger."

They headed off down the bank, Sarah perched on one of Kuji's shoulders and Peeka on the other. The path was a little easier now. The brush didn't grow quite as close to the edge of the river.

"This must be a trail for larger animals," Peeka suggested. "The dirt is packed down and the seeds don't grow. Look," he dug the claws of a back foot into her ear as he leaned forward, pointing at the path. "There are hoof prints like those of reindeer – only they're straighter. Reindeer make a curved print."

"Ouch," muttered Kuji. "Don't pull on my ear!"

"Oh, sorry," Peeka laughed. "But I need to hold on!"

"Not by my ear," she exclaimed. He let go, still laughing, while Sarah fluttered off ahead again to see if the river got wider.

They rounded a bend and found themselves walking beside a grove of tall straight trees, whose branches were much higher than those of the rather sparse undergrowth crowding the edges of the path. "Those trees are very different," exclaimed Kali. "Look how the bark peels off them."

Just then Sarah came flying back. "Come see what I've found!" she exclaimed.

"Yes, but look at these trees." Kuji waved an arm at the tall trees.

"The tall ones are Eucalyptus and those other trees are some kind of pine," answered Sarah, flying in a circle around Kuji's head. "Come on," and she flew off around another bend.

When they turned the bend, they saw Sarah perched on a small branch hanging over the path, conversing with a creature who looked like a giant guinea pig.

"I found another person who came here after death!" Sarah fluttered up and down on the limb. "She's a wombat from Tasmania in Australia."

The creature grunted a little grumpily as Sarah introduced them, adding, "I've told her about the cavern and the Giants of God."

"This story is much like my story," the creature said, scratching at her tiny ear.

"Can you tell us your story?" asked Kuji, plopping herself down on the ground at eye level with the wombat.

The wombat waddled over to the side of the path, giving them a look at the hard furless skin of her nearly tailless rump, and took a bite of some tall grass. "Don't need to eat, but I like to," she muttered while chewing. Finally, she moved back in front of Kuji, standing proudly, her head up.

"My name is Tinaluirga. I was one of Tarenorerer's raiders when I died. She was a great warrior. We lived in the place you call Tasmania."

She paced back and forth in front of them. "When I was young the white men came and took us – just the women and girls. They took us to the islands to kill the seals for them."

She stopped pacing, her body rigid, her eyes turned away from them, her voice low in her throat. "They did... they did unspeakable things to us."

She turned back to look at Kuji and continued. "Some of us escaped the sealers and followed Tarenorerer to fight for our land. She was young and fierce. The other raiders called me wombat because I was quiet and small, but when I was attacked I was... surprisingly dangerous."

She lifted a paw and flexed her long claws, and then sat and scratched her ear again. "The men the bird told me about – these Giants of God – sound a lot like the sealers. They did horrible things to us. The white people did horrible things to our people all over our land. They killed us all off – men, women and small children. Tortured us. Tied us to trees and used us for target practice. Thought it was funny. The only ones who survived were the children of woman who were raped by white men.

"We had lived on Tasmania by ourselves for more than 9,000 years. We were wiped out in less than a hundred." She heaved a sigh.

"Tarenorerer led us in raids against the whites. I was killed in a raid. I took on my wombat spirit form just before I died and came here."

"I'm so sorry," whispered Sarah.

"But did you know about Ninas Twei before you died?" Kuji asked.

"Oh, yes. My people visited Ninas Twei in our ceremonies for most of the many thousands of years we lived on Tasmania before the white man came. When the white people first came we finally understood why we were not allowed to be a part of the Tsin Twei."

"Well," said Peeka, running down one of Kuji's arms. "If we are to stop more horrors from happening, we must find the others who are here, and gather them to help us."

He sat up on Kuji's hand. "Even if we don't think about the need to rescue the women, and the two children who fell down the crevice, we must consider that the crevice opens a way for the Giants to come here, once they discover it. We must protect Ninas Twei, and especially the Tsin Twei or... or..."

Kujakali seemed to grow upward from where she was sitting, until she was standing tall and imperious. Her arms, with all their symbols grasped in their hands, formed a circle. Peeka scurried down to her shoulder, to hide in her hair, as she danced:

> *I, daughter of the mountains,*
> *fierce mother of all,*
> *sounding the great Om with my conch.*
> *Firm as thunder, am I,*
> *striking the demons like lightning*
> *with my sword of knowledge.*

As she sang and danced wildly, the others scattered backward from her path.

> *I, daughter of the mountains,*
> *fierce mother of all.*
> *Like the tiger, I am growing.*

She stopped, and shrank back to her Kuji self, seating herself again on the ground.

Peeka slipped out from under her hair, and ran back down one of her arms to her hand. "Are you finished?"

Kujakali smiled down at him. "I think so."

Sarah flew over to her shoulder. "Durga is a fierce goddess, defender against demons."

"Demons, yes," replied Peeka. "These men – these Giants of God seem possessed by demons."

"But we need to keep moving. We need to find Singing Swan," exclaimed Kuji. She turned to the wombat. "Are you coming with us, Tinaluirga?"

Instead of answering, the wombat walked over to a Eucalyptus tree next to the path, and peered high up into its branches. "Barega, come out here."

Kuji, Peeka, and Sarah looked up the tall trunk of the tree, searching for whatever it was Tinaluirga was calling to.

Very slowly, a large black nose poked out from between the leaves, followed by small black eyes, a gray moon face, and finally very large ears.

"Oh, a koala," exclaimed Sarah.

"Barega. Get down here. They're not going to hurt you," demanded Tinaluirga.

The head disappeared, and a round, thick-furred body appeared on the trunk of the tree, climbing slowly down, and then jumping to the ground and running to hide behind the wombat.

"This is Barega. His people come from the Australian mainland."

"Hi," whispered the little koala, peeking out from behind the wombat.

"Did you hear everything?" asked Tinaluirga.

The little koala nodded his head and backed up into the wombat, who gave him a bump back toward the others. "Don't be shy. These people are friends. Tell your story."

Barega fidgeted a little, then spoke in a very small voice. "I only lived nine years. We lived near the Forrest River Mission. Sometimes the white men would come and demand that the women... that the women – you know..." He ducked his head behind the wombat who pushed him out again.

"Finally Lumbia killed one of the white men because the man tried to steal his wife."

He scuffed his feet on the ground a little. "Then all the white men came and shot the people, and me. When the white men shot me, I looked up into the Eucalyptus trees and saw a koala looking out at me. As I died, I became koala..."

He turned to the wombat and whispered in her ear. "Is that enough, Tina?"

The wombat nodded her head. "We should go with them to find the others, and make a plan to save Ninas Twei."

Barega nodded his head again, but crowded quite close to the wombat, looking quite as wide-eyed as his little black eyes would allow.

"Well, let's get on with it," exclaimed Peeka. "Up, Kuji!"

"Up, Kuji?" she complained. "Am I an elephant?"

Peeka just laughed, and Kuji stood up. As they continued down the path, the wombat waddled beside them, but the little koala climbed back up into the Eucalyptus and hopped from tree to tree. After a short ride on Kuji's shoulder, Sarah launched herself into the air. "I'm flying ahead."

"She's impatient with my slow progress," muttered the wombat, "but I can go very fast when I need to! Very fast."

"I'm sure you can," soothed Kuji.

When the sun was halfway down the western sky, Sarah rejoined them, and they stopped for a brief rest. Kuji, Sarah, Peeka, and Tina all drank from the river.

Barega declined. "I get my water from the Eucalyptus."

"I wish I could eat Eucalyptus," muttered Kuji. "I'm hungry."

"I wish I could sleep," muttered Barega.

"He sleeps a lot," added Tina.

Sarah fluttered up to a low hanging branch. "Other rivers and streams join the river on the other side and it gets a little wider as you go down it, but not as wide as you describe it, Peeka. We need to keep moving."

As they walked, the trees began to change to tall pines and cedars overshadowing bushy rhododendron and laurel. Deeper in the woods the leaves and branches were rattling and shaking.

Barega looked up in alarm as a large, dark gray monkey, with a black face surrounded by long silvery hair, came swinging through the trees, landing on a branch next to him. He dropped to the ground and ran to Tina.

"Oh, sorry," exclaimed the langur, in a sweet apologetic voice. "I didn't mean to scare you."

She moved down closer to the group, looking them over. She saw Kujakali and exclaimed, "You aren't dead!"

Kuji smiled and shook her head. "We're here to try to save Ninas Twei."

"I've felt the ground shake and the pain!" exclaimed the langur.

"We might have found the source of the problem," Peeka chittered running up Kuji's hair and perching on her head. "Come with us. We'll tell you what we've found, and you can tell us about yourself, but we must keep moving."

"I'll come gladly. My name is Nima Rinzen. I'm from Tibet."

She jumped down to the path, loping on all fours beside them. "I haven't been here very long."

She gazed off into the trees. "I was a nun – a Buddhist nun in Tibet. The Chinese occupied our country. Last year the nuns of my monastery organized a big peaceful protest, using the Internet. I was arrested by members of the Chinese army who wanted me to tell them all the people who were involved."

She shivered, and the shiver rippled through her skin. "They stripped me and beat me. They used one of our sacred..." she paused. "They used it to inflict sexual wounds on me. Then they tied me naked to a post in the snow and threw pails of water over me that froze on me in the night."

The others looked at her in horror.

"They are inhabited by demons," she said, sighing and shaking her head a little.

"I was sending waves of hate out at my tormentors as I hung there on the post, and then, suddenly..."

Nima took a deep breath, sighing audibly. "Suddenly, I had a vision of one of the beautiful, black faced monkeys I played with as a child. It was standing in a warm green forest, surrounded by light. Then the monkey sang to me. She sang the words of the dharma. About how I must learn to let go of my hate:

> *Nima, Nima,*
> *Hatred is never ended by hatred.*
> *Remember,*
> *fear breeds hate,*
> *hate breeds violence.*
> *Only love,*
> *only love can stop hate.*
> *Violence can be stopped with violence,*
> *but not ended.*

Violence only ends with compassion.
Hatred is never ended by hatred, but by love.
Nima, Nima, remember.

She stopped and looked at the others.

"And I remembered. I remembered the dharma. I remembered that hate only breeds hate – the words of Siddhartha."

Looking out at the river, she continued. "I breathed... I breathed out the hate, and left my body behind. I became the monkey, and then I was here. Here with this beautiful warm air, and green growing things, and the silvery river."

She turned back to them. "I think I am here to help save Ninas Twei and the Tsin Twei."

"It's hard not to hate," muttered Kuji.

"But I don't think we can save the Tsin Twei with hate."

Nima turned her sweet black face up to Kujakali. "Hate invites in the demons. We can have compassion toward these people who do evil things. We are instructed to have compassion for all beings."

"But how do we stop the evil?"

Nima curled her tail gently around Kuji's leg. "Having compassion does not mean allowing evil things to be done. We can find ways to stop them and we must help them change."

Kujakali shook her head. "You haven't met them."

"But I have," answered Nima. "I have met them in Tibet."

Kuji was quiet for a moment.

"Yes," she replied. "I guess you have."

"I think we've all met them," muttered Tinaluirga.

"We need to keep moving," chirped Sarah. "We're almost at the wide river. Up ahead another river joins this one, and it gets very wide."

The monkey let go of Kuji's leg and lopped off down the path, followed by the others. It wasn't long before they came around a curve and saw their river, now rushing between its wide banks, flow into a much larger one.

Peeka climbed up on Kuji's head, and looked, and looked. He seemed bewildered. "Where Singing Swan lives – near where I lived – near the Din Tsin Twei, everything was green and lush." But the land here was dry like a desert.

362

There were hills further down the river, and they looked greener. Peeka thought maybe they were the beginning of the hills that held Din Tsin Twei.

Sarah launched herself again, climbing in circles higher and higher in the air, and wider and wider, so that she was traveling down the river as well. The others followed as she became just a speck in the sky ahead of them.

Finally she headed back, landing on the hand Kuji held out to her. "It becomes greener, and the hills are higher, almost mountains. But it's a long way."

Close to the river, there was a narrow belt of greenery, mostly grasses, which tapered off at the edge of the sandy hills. "Might be delicious if you were a cow... or a wombat," muttered Barega.

He moved out of the way as Tina kicked at him, saying, "You don't need to eat. You're dead."

"And no trees. Not safe," he added, as the little group continued on down the river.

It was still light, but the sun had set when Kuji, and the others, heard a strange sound, almost like a human baby crying for its mother, coming from behind a hill that blocked their view around the next curve of the river.

Sarah headed in the direction of the sound and they all picked up speed, following her around the hill.

"More friends," she called out, landing on Kuji's shoulder. "Meet Djeserit and her baby. They're Ibex. They just arrived here."

The mother Ibex looked warily at them. The baby, still wet with his birth sac, and very wobbly on his legs, tried to get to her teats, but she pushed it away.

"Are you dead or alive?" Kuji asked. "The baby seems hungry."

The Ibex gave herself a shake, and her skin rippled down her back. There was a long silence while she looked at all of them.

"The soldiers shot us. We had gone to the city to protest. We had no weapons. They surrounded us, and shot at us."

She stamped her foreleg and threw her head back. Her voice rose to a wail. "My child!"

Her voice dropped. "My baby was inside me. Without me he would die. I wanted him to live." She gave a fierce, almost painful cry, and then shook her head back and forth, as if to release the pain.

She glared at them, her odd yellow eyes bewildered. "I thought if he did live, perhaps they would let him feed from my friend, the wild Ibex who lives on the hillside by our village. And then... then I was here. I was an Ibex and my baby was coming. Right then. I gave birth to my baby right then and he was a baby goat – an Ibex," she wailed.

Nima moved over next to the sweet baby, petting him gently. The kid looked up at her. "Ma-a-a. Ma-a-a," he cried.

"He's alive – he's a human, Djeserit, but here he's in his Tla Twei. He's in the form of an Ibex, like you, and he's hungry."

She brought him over next to his mother. "Let him try to eat, Djeserit. Please?"

The Ibex stood rigid for a moment, and then sighed, releasing the stiff muscles in her legs. Nima pushed the baby towards Djeserit. The baby grabbed a teat and sucked hungrily. The tension seemed to slip from Djeserit's body, and she turned her head back toward the baby and nosed at him gently, beginning to lick at his wet fur.

When he was finished, Djeserit looked back at the group. "My grandmother told me about a place. Reqsh Alheyah [رقص الحياة].

Dance of life. Is this that place?"

"Yes," Sarah nodded. "Yes, this is Ninas Twei, home of the Tsin Twei which is called the dance of life."

Suddenly the ground began to shake and they all cried out, losing their balance.

Kuji fell to her knees and Sarah flew up into the air. A sharp, intense pain shot through each of them.

Then it was over.

"What was that?" asked Kuji.

"That was the pain we've been feeling," exclaimed Nima.

"And the shaking," grumbled Tina.

"The danger!" added Barega.

"Oh, dear." Sarah landed next to Kuji. "We need to hurry. Ninas Twei is in danger. I hope that didn't close up the crevice down to the Giants of God."

"Luha," Kuji cried out. "Oh, I hope Luha is all right."

She and Sarah stared at each other in horror.

Sarah jumped into the air, "I need to go back and find out about Luhanada."

But it was dark. Night had fallen. She landed back on Kuji's shoulder. "I'm tired," she whispered. "I'm too tired to fly back."

The baby had finished eating and was curled up in the grass, falling asleep almost instantly. Djeserit stood looking around her. "I don't understand. What was the shaking?"

"We'll stop here for the night and we can explain it all to you," Nima pronounced, "and tomorrow we'll walk as long as we have to to find Singing Swan's marsh."

Sarah began pecking around on the ground, finding seeds to eat. Kuji watched her longingly. Her crackers were gone and there had been no blackberries for a long time.

"Kuji," Peeka exclaimed. "You're hungry, too!"

"Kuji is hungry?" asked Djeserit.

"Kuji and I are still alive, like your baby," explained Sarah. "There's plenty for me to eat, but Kuji..."

Djeserit stood quietly looking at Kuji. "She can drink my milk. The baby won't need it all."

"How do I do that?" Kuji's eyes were wide.

Nima laughed. "We used to squirt it in our mouths when we were children."

"Me, too," exclaimed Djeserit. "It's warm and sweet. Try it, Kuji."

In the end, it was Nima who squirted the milk into Kuji's mouth, and it was warm and sweet, and tasted very, very good. Afterwards Kuji curled up next to the baby goat, with two arms wrapped around him. Sarah tucked herself in by Kuji's shoulder, and they all fell sound asleep. The others gathered in a circle nearby and talked long into the night telling Djeserit their stories and listening to hers.

When Kujakali and her friends woke at dawn the next morning, Peeka said, "I think we're closer to Singing Swan than Tuwillia. If we get to the amphitheater, Sarah, you can fly over the top, and then it's just a short distance to Tuwillia's home."

They walked and talked, and as they went, the grass on the hills got greener, and more bushes and trees appeared. The sun was not far up the horizon when the vegetation began to look tropical, with tall trees hung with vines. "Oh, I think we're coming to the place where the Giant Otters live," exclaimed Peeka. "That's just down the hill from the Din Tsin Twei, just before the river flows into the lake by the marshes where Singing Swan lives."

"Let's hurry," exclaimed Kuji, and they walked faster, the baby goat constantly scampering ahead, and then returning to his mother. The river narrowed and rushed more quickly, curving first one way and then the other and they came to a place where the bank had a muddy groove down it.

Peeka scrambled up Kuji's arm. "That's an otter slide."

He sent out several shrill, high-pitched whistles. Kuji fastened a pair of hands over her ears and glared at him.

"That'll bring them. If they were alive they'd probably want to eat me," he giggled. "But we're friends now."

Soon the otters came bounding down a path on the opposite bank. They were big and sleekly black, with backs curved like a crescent moon, ending in a long pointed tail. They emitted a melodic, "Ya-ah, ya-ah, ya-ah," and then a deeper "Br-r-r, br-r-r," and pushing their fore legs back at their sides, their hind legs stretched behind them, slid down a muddy slide on that side of the river landing in the water with a splash. Propelling themselves with their strong tails, they swam swiftly across and pulled themselves up on the bank next to the travelers.

Peeka greeted Aucapomi and his family, and introduced Kuji and the others. "We're headed to find Singing Swan," he added. "Ninas Twei is in danger and we need to gather people to help."

"Yes," said the female, Illari. "We have felt the pain."

The otters joined them and the group moved down the river to a path headed into a marshy area. "Singing Swan lives up here," explained Huayna, Illari and Aucapomi's young son.

The marsh was full of tall tulles, and as the path led them through they noticed the tulles began to bend over their heads, weaving themselves together to form a roof. Peeka gave another shrill whistle and was answered with a low honking sound.

Singing Swan appeared on the path ahead of them, bowing his head with its diamond-shaped black beak. "Welcome."

Peeka scrambled down Kuji's leg and ran up to the swan. "I followed the travelers through the tunnel in the wall of the Din Tsin Twei. When I tried to come home, it had been closed by a tremor."

"Yes, it closed. I worried about the travelers, but one came back just a few days ago with some others. They told a sad story of the ground opening and the children falling."

"We know," Kuji nodded. "The rest found themselves back in the world when the ground shook, and when they got there, two of them were shot."

"Do you know any more?" asked Singing Swan. "Do you know anything about the children, or about Luhanada and Tata?"

"Yes, Luha – Luhanada – transformed and came here – to Tuwillia and the Weaving Tree on the other side of the cliffs. She doesn't know what happened to Tata."

"I see," he said, nodding at Kuji and Sarah, perched on Kuji's shoulder, "you are still alive. Come," he said, turning back the way he had come, "we will have some food and drink while we talk."

He turned back and smiled at Kuji. "Unlike the rest of us, living Tla Twein get hungry." He gestured at the baby goat, who was taking advantage of the moment to grab a little milk from mama.

When they had all settled down in his comfortable home, he produced juice and cakes, while Peeka told what he knew of the story of the Giants of God.

"I didn't know of this tree of human life and Tuwillia until Yameno came back." Singing Swan looked thoughtful. "Tuwillia must be one of my people."

"Yes," agreed Kuji. "But she lived a long, long time before you."

"We need to get back to Tuwillia and make sure Luha is all right," added Sarah. "I can fly over the Din Tsin Twei and take the path to the tree."

Singing Swan shook his head. "I've never been able to fly over the top of the cliffs that rim the Din Tsin Twei, but there was another tremor and it opened a new crack in the cliff right above where the tunnel opened up before. I flew up and could see trees on the other side. It's too small for me to go through."

He turned to Sarah, "but I think you could fly through."

Sarah jumped into the air. "Let's go." Singing Swan nodded, and led them out another grassy tunnel to the Din Tsin Twei. He pointed a wing toward the top of the cliff and they looked up at the opening where they could see a small patch of blue sky.

Sarah leapt into the air and flew in circles higher and higher and then right into the crack, momentarily blocking the patch of blue sky. When they could see the sky again, Kuji yelled, "She's through!"

Kujakali's tall path markers were easy to see, and Sarah flew carefully down the path finding Tuwillia sitting right at the edge of the crevice, looking worriedly down it.

"Tuwillia," she called out, as she landed beside her and peered down the large crack in the ground. "Is the crevice still open?"

Tuwillia looked up. "I think so. But Luhanada hasn't come back, and twice I've heard her sing her song."

She stared back down into the crevice.

"But what does it mean that Luha sang her song?"

"I don't know, but it's been a long time, and she hasn't returned."

Sarah nodded. "We were worried too, but..." She moved toward Tuwillia eagerly. "There're many of us now, Tuwillia. Many to help," and she told Tuwillia about all the people they had gathered.

"They're all dead like you and Luhanada – except the baby Ibex. They'll be able to go down to the cavern and not be killed, just like Luha." She peered down into the crevice, "If they can get down those ledges."

A huge noise, a rumbling sound erupted from the crevice. Sarah flew up in the air, her wings fluttering wildly as the ground began to shake violently.

Tuwillia tried frantically to push herself backwards, but she was too close to the edge. The dirt under her feet slipped and slid toward the crevice, pulling her with it. Sarah grabbed at Tuwillia's shell with her claws and beak, but the turtle was too heavy and slid head first over the edge tumbling to the first ledge where she just barely managed to twist herself so that she landed on her feet.

The shaking stopped.

Sarah flew down to the ledge next to Tuwillia. "Are you all right?" she cried out.

Tuwillia was trembling inside her shell. "Fine. I'm fine," she answered, looking up at the nearly sheer sides of the crevice. "But I can't get up from here, and I don't think you can help me."

The top seemed a long way away.

"I'll go for help." Sarah flew back up to the top calling behind her, "They have to find a way over the top of the cliffs, and come and help you. They have to."

She flew away back down the path as fast as she could toward the Din Tsin Twei.

When she arrived her friends were struggling to crawl over rubble piled at the bottom of a large crack from the top to near the bottom of the cliffs.

"What happened?" she called.

Djeserit, who was standing at the top of the rubble, her baby standing between her front legs ma-a-a-ing gleefully, answered. "The earth shook and the mountain cracked open right where the tunnel was before. We can get over it now."

Peeka and the otters were climbing gingerly down the rubble toward Sarah. "Mountain climbing is not our strongest asset," laughed Aucapomi.

Singing Swan flew over. "Ah, Sarah, good. We were coming to meet you. Kujakali and Nima are helping Tina, and Barega is staying with them."

Soon the rest came scrambling down, Kuji and Nima lifting Tina over the largest boulders, and sometimes giving Barega a little boost as well.

"The tremor shook Tuwillia off the edge of the crevice," exclaimed Sarah. "She's on the first ledge down. She's all right, but I can't help her."

Kuji scooped Peeka up. "Let's go quickly," she cried, and took off down the path followed by the otters who outpaced her with their graceful lope.

She was startled when Tina came running past her, too.

"Wombats can move fast when they need to," the little wombat muttered.

In no time they were all gathered around the crevice, peering down at Tuwillia.

"I can get her!" Nima was already feet first down the crevice as she talked, her silver hair flying around her sweet black face as she disappeared over the edge, and dropped to the ledge. The large tortoise was heavy, but she gently lifted her and tucked her under one arm. Gripping with one hand and her prehensile feet, her tail swinging to keep her balanced, she scrambled back to the top. Tuwillia dug her feet into the fur on Nima's chest as best she could, and Nima could hear her muttering, "Careful, careful."

Kuji reached three arms down and dragged Tuwillia up as soon as Nima had one hand over the top edge, freeing Nima's other hand so she could pull herself up.

Everyone cheered.

Kuji cuddled Tuwillia to her chest for a moment, a few tears dropping on the turtle's head, until Tuwillia snaked her head out, and gave her a little nip. "That's enough, young lady. Put me down."

Kuji set her gently down, rubbing the nipped place with another of her hands. "Ouch," she whispered.

Tuwillia looked around at all of them. "Luhanada hasn't come back and I've heard her song twice. I think she's in trouble. If she was in hiding, she wouldn't sing her song so loudly that the crevice reverberated with it."

Kuji peered down the crevice. "Do you think the crevice closed up where we can't see it?"

"No," Tuwillia shook her head. "The song came from farther away."

Kuji's eyes got wide. "Did they catch her? I have to rescue her."

Sarah grabbed her sari with her beak. "No, Kuji. You can't go. I can't either. We're alive. We'll turn back into women and the wind will catch us if we try to go over the plateau. We'll just make things worse."

"That's right, Kuji," agreed Peeka. "It has to be one of us who's already dead."

"It has to be me," interrupted Nima. "I don't think anyone else can get down the crevice."

"I can," said Djeserit.

"But you need to stay with your baby. If your baby goes down there, he might turn into a human baby."

Djeserit blinked her eyes and looked at her baby. "My baby is human," she whispered.

"So it's me." Nima looked around. "But Kuji and Sarah, we must talk first. You must tell me everything you can about this city before I go."

Tuwillia turned toward the shade of the tree. "We will sit and talk."

Hatched

At the end of the rest period, Jesús watched the food bucket come down through the ceiling of the egg. There wasn't an opening in the ceiling, but when the bucket came down the plastic flowed away from it, closing back around the metal rod the bucket hung on. He knew when the bucket went back up the plastic would push away from it. What made the ceiling open? Was it something on the bucket? He grabbed the bucket, pulled the food bar and water out of it, and then held on to it as it tried to pull back up.

Something on the edges of the bucket was different from the rest of the bucket, not sharp like a knife, but a different texture. He pulled hard and twisted trying to break the bucket off the post which was pulling the bucket back up. Something cracked and he could work the bucket back and forth on the post, but then the bucket jerked out of his hands and headed back to the ceiling. It had trouble breaking though the plastic, but in the end it disappeared, the plastic flowing back to cover the opening.

All during the next work period he waited for some consequence for breaking the bucket, but nothing happened. Everything seemed so mechanized. Was it all done by machines and computers? Perhaps real humans would never notice.

The next rest period, Enid and Jesús curled up again so they could feel each other through the plastic skin of the eggs. Jesús placed his mouth against the plastic, pushing it outward, hoping she could hear him better. He began to sing:

> *Enid, Enid, listen to me.*
> *Do you hear my words?*

Enid could just barely hear the faint singing, and put her ear up to the place where the plastic bulged. Jesús felt the pressure against his mouth and sang again:

> *Enid, can you hear my words?*

Then he felt her move so that her mouth was against the plastic.

> *I hear you,* she sang.

He leaned his whole face into the plastic so that his ear was against her mouth, and his mouth pushed against what he thought must be her ear:

Are you all right? he sang.
I'm all right, she sang back. *And you?*

It was hard to talk, and to listen, and they were so tired. He tried to sing about the food bucket moving through the skin of the egg:

Tried to break it.
Maybe it will cut the egg.

Yes, she answered.
I'll try, too.

"Good." He sighed.

Good. Now sleep, sleep, and she joined with him in the little lullaby,
Sleep, sleep.

He slept fitfully despite his exhaustion. When the voice signaled the end of the rest period, he jumped up quickly, waiting anxiously for the food bucket.

At first it had a hard time getting through the skin. One corner came through and seemed to stick at an angle, but then it broke through and descended. *It wasn't repaired,* he thought, grabbing it and pulling hard, twisting it back and forth, and finally breaking it off the rod.

He turned immediately to Enid's side of the egg and pushed the bottom of the bucket against the skin. It cut through the skin like a knife through butter.

"Enid," he called, putting his mouth up to the bucket, which amplified his voice. "Enid!"

Enid had slept well and at the end of the rest period, when the bucket pushed down through the ceiling, she was ready. She grabbed the food bar and the water bottle, dropping them at her feet so that she could hang on to the bucket with both hands, using all her weight to swing it back and forth, back and forth until she felt something crack. When the rod started to pull the bucket up, she hung on, letting it pull her into the air, swinging her whole body as hard as she could.

She heard Jesús calling her name.

He's much louder! she thought, but she hung on and swung even harder. The bucket had almost reached the ceiling when it came loose in her hands and she fell to the floor, curling in a ball around the bucket.

She lay there stunned for a moment, before she saw Jesús' bucket protruding through the skin of her egg over the bench. There were only a few minutes left until they would need to pedal to keep the voice from getting louder and louder. She scrambled to her feet and shoved her bucket into the wall next to his.

It slipped through easily!

"Hurray!" she called out. "Jesús, Jesús!"

"Push the two buckets apart and see if we can make a hole," he responded, and they both pushed the buckets sideways away from each other. A hole formed, but the plastic started to flow down to fill it. They let the buckets snap back next to each other.

"END OF REST PERIOD," shouted the voice.

"We need to pedal until the next rest period," Enid called through the buckets. "We need to think."

"Yeah," Jesús agreed, "but we're going to do it! We're going to find a way out!"

They both scrambled up into their seats and pedaled, eating, and drinking their water as they pedaled. Before too long Enid started to sing. Faintly she heard a voice join her. *Jesús is singing, too, and because of the buckets, I can hear him!*

As she sang Enid surveyed the inside of the egg. *We need something to push into the egg, something to keep the hole from filling.* But there really wasn't anything. The bench was too big. The pedals weren't a good shape, and they were attached to a wide metal box which went down through the bottom of the egg and would be impossible to move.

She closed her eyes as she pedaled trying to rest and pedal at the same time. The seat felt hard under her buttocks and she wiggled pushing against the back to get more comfortable.

The seat! She sat up trying to keep pedaling and twist so that she could look at the seat. The voice got louder.

She sat back and pedaled. "I don't need to look at it," she whispered to herself. "I know I can move it right off the end of the square bar it's attached to."

She laughed out loud, and sang out to Jesús:

I know the answer. I know the answer.

She could just barely hear his response. "What? What did you find?"

You're sitting on it, she sang out.

She heard him laughing. "Yes," he yelled. "Yes!"

When the work period ended, they both leaned over their seats, reaching for the knobs that tightened the seats to the bar, loosened them, and slid them off.

Enid called through the buckets. "I have mine."

"Me, too," Jesús responded. "Try yours first. I'll hold the buckets apart."

The buckets moved apart and she slid a corner of her seat into the hole, pushing it farther in. It didn't move as easily as the buckets – it couldn't cut – but it did push the plastic apart. Gradually she pushed it upward until the seat was sitting on its side pushing the plastic farther up than the buckets.

"Push it against my bucket," Jesús suggested. "Then I can push and pull too."

With a lot of pushing and pulling they maneuvered the seat so that the bottom was resting against one bucket, while the back pushed across the top of the hole resting an edge against the other bucket. The gray plastic was trying to fill in the hole from the bottom.

"Now mine," Jesús said.

Enid put her hands in the hole, holding the chair seat back on one side and the bucket on the other, while Jesús pushed the other seat in so that the two seats made a square, with a large hole in between. The two children grinned at each other through the hole.

"High five," yelled Jesús, and they smacked their hands together, and then grabbed each other's hand squeezing them together.

Tears rolled down Enid's cheeks as she leaned in trying to be as close as she could to Jesús.

"Don't cry," he whispered, wiping his own eyes with his other hand. "We have too much work to do."

Enid wiped her own eyes, nodding.

Jesús looked up at the ceiling of his egg. "I wonder how much time we have before rest period is over? We won't get any more food, you know. We need to get out now. We need to get into one egg and then use the buckets to go through the skin on the side near the pointed end of the egg," he added. "There must be a space between eggs there."

Enid put her head through the hole and looked down Jesús' egg. The point was in the same direction as her egg. There would have to be a space.

"I'm coming into your egg," she declared and knelt on her bench and pushed herself, arms first into the hole.

"I can fit through, but I wonder if you will?" she said anxiously.

She pushed herself farther in, feeling the plastic give around her, the edges of the seat pushing on her stomach. "The seats are moving."

Jesús grabbed the seats pushing them back as she pushed forward.

"The egg skin pushes away. It'll be harder, but you can do it, too, I'm sure," she panted.

Scrambling so that her feet were on the bench, she pushed, her arms reaching for the floor of Jesús' egg next to the square rod that had held his seat. The plastic bent slowly downward with the weight of her body and she thrust with her feet, curling downward.

She was in such a silly position, she started to giggle, and then to cry again.

"Keep going. Keep going," muttered Jesús, pulling on her shoulders.

She gave a thrust of her feet and pushed herself the rest of the way through, sliding head first down the side of the egg to the floor where she curled in a ball at Jesús' feet, the two of them squished between the pedal mechanism and the wall, panting, crying, laughing, and holding on to each other, rocking each other in the tiny space.

"We have to keep moving," Jesús whispered, and they unscrambled themselves.

Jesús pulled the buckets loose, leaving the chairs holding the hole. "Don't pull them yet. Not until we know we can actually get outside the eggs."

He crouched at the pointed end of the egg, pushing the buckets through the skin where the egg started to slope upwards just before the point. They slipped through much easier than before.

He grinned back at Enid. "It's only one layer of egg skin!"

They pulled the buckets apart and Jesús peeked through. "I can see the point of your egg, and dirt on the ground. Let's do it."

Pushing the seats into this hole was easier, but a little trickier, because they were maneuvering them from only one side.

They'd just got them in place when they heard the voice, "REST PERIOD IS ENDED," and the creaking of whatever it was that brought the food buckets.

"You go first," whispered Enid, "so I can push you if you get stuck. I know I can get through."

"And to check for danger," added Jesús as he pushed his arms, then his head and shoulders, through the opening, twisting and turning himself as he pushed forward.

Enid alternated holding on to the seats and pushing from behind and he slid out, diving head first down the side of the egg, balancing on his hands as he twisted so that his feet rested on the ground between his egg and Enid's. Enid held tight to the seats pushing his feet up so they didn't hook and pull them out of place.

Jesús looked around. Nothing but gray plastic eggs to left and right, forward and back – sides pressing against sides and the pointed end of each touching the wider base of the next. Way above, he could see the net, and below it, steel rails that crossed the canyon over the rows of eggs.

A train of food buckets was traveling down the rails, each one in turn sliding into a small cross bar right over the center of an egg.

He watched the two bucket-less rods slide over the eggs he and Enid had been in. Then the rods telescoped downward, plunging into the eggs. A moment or two later they pulled back up.

By the time he turned back to the egg, Enid was halfway through the opening. He grabbed her under her arms, and pulled her out.

As the two of them slid down to the ground, crouching in the space created by the curved sides of the four eggs around them, Enid whispered, "Hatched!"

Madre de Dios

"Yes!" Jesús laughed. "Hatched." He grinned at Enid for a moment, and then stepped farther into the open space between the four eggs and turned to watch the traveling buckets return to a wall on the far side of the canyon.

"Ugh, we smell." Enid laughed. "And I feel so sticky! I want a bath!"

"Not going to happen. But it does smell a little fresher out here."

Enid nodded. She and Jesús looked thinner, their faces gaunt, but the muscles of her legs and arms felt hard and strong.

"Look," he pointed up at the opposite wall.

Large rectangular openings – one above and one below the net – opened above each row of eggs. Steel rails hung from the top of the lower openings and reached across the canyon.

"The buckets come from that side. We should go the other way." He pointed to the left at the steep wall of the canyon about six eggs away.

"We need to take the buckets and the seats with us," Enid pointed out as she pulled, first the buckets, and then the seats out of the side of the egg. "There got to be people in these other eggs. We need to help them."

Jesús nodded, as a low hum started.

"They're pedaling again," murmured Enid.

"We need to find a way out of here first – before we help the others escape. If there's no way out of here…." He gave Enid a meaningful look and she sighed and nodded back.

"I know," she whispered.

Jesús went first, thrusting a leg over the place where the narrow points met the flatter bottoms of the eggs in the next row. The egg bent slightly beneath him as he slid down the other side. Enid handed him the buckets and seats, and a bit more awkwardly, followed. They were experts at egg climbing by the time they made their way to the side of the canyon, stopping one egg away from the wall.

Vertical metal posts were set in cement against the canyon wall. The horizontal rails looped around the top of the posts.

They turned and looked up at the rectangular openings where the rails disappeared on the other side of the canyon.

"Do you remember?" Enid asked. "The pincher things grabbed us from the net and pulled us into one of those window things."

"Yes." He shivered. "Maybe all the people who run this are on that side of the canyon."

"I hope so," whispered Enid, looking anxiously around her.

"I wonder how long it'll be before they discover we aren't in our eggs." He peered up over the eggs toward the ones they had escaped from. "If no one's ever escaped before, maybe they won't figure it out right away."

"What if people get sick and stop pedaling? What if someone dies? They must have something they do?"

"But then they'll just get louder and louder with the instructions – at least at first, and then, the pain."

He shook himself, as if to shake away the pain and pulled himself up higher, looking carefully around.

"Look," he pointed to the top of the cliff, above the openings. "It looks like there might be buildings up there."

Enid stood up and looked where he was pointing. "There weren't any buildings on that flat place where the wind blew us, the place we landed when the ground opened up. Maybe that flat place is on this side."

She turned to look at the wall behind her. It was impossible to see what was above the wall. "If we could get up there, maybe we could find our way to the place we fell down."

They both looked up at the sheer wall.

There was no way they could climb it. Enid sighed and looked down the canyon to the right and left. If they went to the left, the end of the canyon was closer.

Jesús pointed to the right. "There's something there. Something up above the net that's attached to the end wall. Do you see it?"

Enid squinted, trying to see through the net at that end of the cavern. "But I can't see what, and it's above the net. We'd have to get above the net to get to it."

It seemed best to try the near end first. Staying one egg away from the wall they crawled on their bellies under where the sides of the eggs touched, pushing the plastic seats and buckets in front of them to the next row.

It was a tight squeeze, first over a large square pipe and then an even larger one. Enid noted that the smaller pipe connected to a big square box coming out of the bottom of the egg – probably the one below the pedals in the eggs. The larger pipe was clearly connected to the waste hole in the end of the bench.

Rising to a crawl between the rows, and squirming again under the next row of eggs, they headed toward the end of the canyon.

Jesús had crawled under eight rows, when he realized Enid wasn't keeping up and turned to wait for her. When she came squirming through after him, he whispered, "We need to rest."

Enid collapsed gratefully, lying flat out on the ground, panting. They curled up under the edge of the nearest eggs, and closed their eyes.

After a while Enid yawned and sat up. "Thirsty," she whispered.

"Yes." Jesús roused himself to look down the rows at ground level. "I don't know if we'll be able to find water or food. But we need to keep going."

Enid nodded, and gestured to Jesús to go ahead of her.

Two rows later they heard a sound coming from behind them. Very carefully, Jesús stuck his head up to see over the eggs back of them. A large convex circular object was emerging from one of the dark openings on the far side of the canyon, hanging from beneath the track like the food buckets. It traveled down the track, coming to a stop over an egg. "Maybe that's one of our eggs."

She stood up beside him to look, as the circle dropped down and the egg seemed to rise to meet it. "Like a magnet," muttered Jesús.

They watched as the egg went swinging back to the canyon wall.

Enid looked at him, wide eyed. "Now they'll know we're gone. We need to find a hiding place." They both dropped to their stomachs, and scrambled as fast as they could toward the end of the canyon.

The area between the last row of eggs and the end of the canyon was flat. There were no eggs, but the horizontal pipes were already set in place on the ground making room for ten more rows of eggs.

Jesús crouched on the ground under the slopping point of the egg on the right, and Enid crawled up next to him. They stared out at the open area, peering to the left and right, and up the canyon walls. Enid noted the metal boxes that stuck up from the pipes. "I'll bet the edges are made of that material that cuts through the egg, like the edge of the buckets."

"They're waiting for more eggs," Jesús added. "I don't see anywhere to go, do you?"

The walls were sheer. No crevices, no way to climb them in any direction.

Enid found herself shaking as if she were chilled. Would they never get out of here?

Jesús put an arm around her and pulled her close. "There has to be a way out of here. There has to be…"

A blasting sound thundered above them.

"The wind," exclaimed Jesús, and they scurried back under the sides of the eggs, squishing together, and holding on to each other.

They could hear the wind roaring above them, but it didn't reach into the canyon. The sound went on for a few minutes, and then silence.

They had started to crawl out again when they heard a clicking sound, and then a purring like an electric motor. A long steel bar moved slowly out of the opening in the far cliff, crossing in front of them. The front part of the bar was doubled. When it reached their side of the canyon, the doubled part opened downward, and anchored itself in a metal stump standing upright at the edge of the wall. Soon eggs began to emerge from the opening, hanging from convex disks like the one that had picked up the egg earlier. One would move out and then sit still for a moment or two before another egg would follow it out.

"It's another track," muttered Jesús. "They're placing more eggs down there."

The eggs traveled across in front of them until the first one ran into the vertical bar. The disks holding the eggs were lowered on telescoping bars like the ones that brought the food buckets. The eggs seem drawn to the right spot, as if there were magnets in the metal box and the square pipe pulling them into place. There was a snapping noise as they pushed down.

The children lay on the ground, peering under the pointed end of the egg next to them, while ten eggs fell in place. Not the full width of the canyon. The sound stopped. Enid turned pleading eyes to Jesús. "More captives. We have to get them all out."

"Yes, but we have to have some place to go with them. We need water and food and a place to hide."

"I wonder how safe it is here under the eggs. It can't be too easy to look for us here." Enid looked at Jesús hopefully.

Jesús nodded. "Let's go in toward the middle – away from the canyon walls, and back from this end. If they start looking for us, we'll see them, or hear them. We can move away."

As they scrambled over and under the ends of eggs, pushing their chair seats and buckets in front of them, the background hum stopped. "Rest period. You sleep and I'll keep watch," Jesús whispered.

Enid collapsed, exhausted, and so thirsty, putting the seat and bucket on the ground beside her. "And then I'll keep watch," she muttered as her eyes closed.

When Enid awoke she found Jesús standing and peering around him. She tried to pull some moisture into her dry mouth. Her head felt like it was full of cotton balls.

He crouched down next to her. "I think we have to go to where the tracks go into the openings in the wall over there." He pointed at the wall with the openings. "We know there's food and water there, because that's where it comes from to go to the eggs.

"I don't think there're people there," he continued. "The machines took both our eggs, and both eggs were replaced, but there hasn't been any alarm. No one has even looked out one of those openings. They're wide enough for an egg, so a person could look out easily. I don't think they know we've escaped."

Enid stood up and peered at the openings. "I don't know."

"But we really have no choice," Jesús interrupted. "We need water, and food, too."

She nodded slowly. "But we also need to rescue the people in the eggs."

He nodded. "Yes."

He sat down, drooping. "But I'm tired. I think I'll have to sleep some before we do anything."

"Yes, it's your turn. You sleep. I'll watch."

Enid sat up, resting her back where the end of one egg met the beginning of the next one and looking at the openings in the cliff on the far side of the canyon, where the tracks disappeared.

While she watched, the meal buckets began to flow across the underside of the tracks positioning themselves above each egg, then plunging down into the eggs. *I wish I could see some way to get to those buckets,* she thought, thinking about trying to climb the posts at the end of the rows.

Oh, no! she thought, as she realized they couldn't steal from the buckets. Someone in an egg wouldn't get any food! She sighed and moved to a more comfortable position. Soon the buckets returned to the openings and the humming of the pedals started again.

She looked up through the mesh, past the openings above the net, at the buildings. The angle was too great to see much and she didn't see any humans. *But there're buildings there. There must be people somewhere.* As she watched, it got darker and darker around the buildings until she couldn't see them, except for a few lights in the windows.

The rectangular openings in the wall remained dark, both above and below the net. *If there were people there they would turn on some light,* she thought. *But if we get up there and people come, we won't be able to protect ourselves. We need to release some of the people in the eggs so there're more of us, before we try to get up to those openings.*

She dragged herself upright and picked up the buckets from where they lay on the ground next to the sleeping Jesús. Struggling to place them against the side of the nearest egg she leaned in to them. They slid easily through the plastic skin and she managed to pull them apart enough to slip one hand, and then the other, in between them.

A voice exclaimed, "*Madre de Dios!*"

"Are you in there?" she whispered through the opening, turning her head so that she could see through to the inside of the egg. "Is someone in there?"

Two dark eyes peered back at her. "Who are you? How did you do that? Can you help us?" exclaimed the occupant.

"Yes, yes, we can get you out." Enid tried to push the buckets apart, but it was hard.

The person on the other side stuck his hands through, too, and pushed the buckets wide enough for her to see his face – a young Latino teenager, older than Jesús and herself.

They both jumped as the mechanical voice in the egg got louder and louder and the eyes looked alarmed as he turned his head toward the voice.

"Keep working," Enid called over top of the voice. "We'll get you out soon. I promise."

He pulled his arms out of the opening, and Enid pulled hers back, leaving the buckets stuck in the egg. She turned back to look at Jesús.

He was sitting up watching her. "Let's do it. Let's break him out."

"Right now? But we should wait until the sleep period."

"That's a long time away!" he exclaimed. "Anyway, I don't think it matters. I think the sooner the better, and the more the better."

He hopped up, grabbing the plastic seats. Enid pulled the buckets apart while he thrust the corner of a chair into the hole rocking it back and forth to get it farther in. Pretty soon the young man was back with his own chair, pushing it in from the other side.

"Can you get through?" Enid called in. The young man's hands and forearms pushed through. They grabbed his arms and pulled as they saw his head enter the opening. The seats pushed out and up as they pulled him through, but seemed to stick as the widest part of his shoulders entered the opening.

"Push, push," called Jesús, and they felt an extra shove as the older boy pushed with his feet.

They pulled harder, reaching farther up his arms to grab closer to his shoulders. Suddenly his shoulders popped through, and they both nearly fell over. He came flying out and tumbled to the ground. Enid and Jesús pulled themselves back against the egg on the other side to give him room in the small space.

The teenager pulled himself stiffly to a crouch, and then stood up and looked around. "Where are we?"

"We don't know," answered Jesús, telling him what little they knew.

"I'm Dario," he told them. "My cousin and my friends are here, too. Can we find them? Perhaps, like you, our prisons are next to each other."

He turned to the egg behind him, and they set to work getting the occupant, who turned out to be Angelino, out. The cousins hugged each other for a long time before turning to the job of releasing the other members of *Los Gallos*.

It was not long before Enid, Jesús, Dario, Angelino, Pedro, and Roberto crouched in the spaces between two of the eggs. They had clung to each other for a few minutes when they first came out of the eggs, then spent some time looking around, and being introduced to Jesús and Enid.

"We need to find a way into the openings over there, where the rails come out of the wall," explained Jesús. "We need food and water, and that's where it comes from."

Dario looked at the dark openings. "They're like truck bays in a factory. I think they are big enough for a man to stand up. I wonder if there isn't some way in there to release everyone from the eggs that's easier than using the buckets."

They all turned to look at the wall.

Pedro looked dubious. "What if there're people in there?"

"We've watched a lot and haven't seen anyone," explained Jesús. "Maybe they never look out the openings, but if they're there, you'd think they'd walk past some."

"Also," added Enid. "When it got dark where those buildings are up above, lights went on in the buildings, but no lights came on in the openings." She hesitated a moment. "But if there are people there, there need to be enough of us to resist them."

Dario nodded. "We need to find out more. Perhaps two should explore the wall, and see if we can find a way up, and the rest should continue getting people free."

He looked at Enid and Jesús. "We're bigger than you. It's easier for us to pull people out of the eggs. We should continue with the eggs, working our way toward that wall, and you two should go and see if you can find a way to get up to the openings."

Jesús and Enid looked at each other. Was it wise to trust these boys with the precious buckets and seats?

Dario sensed their distrust. "I know. We don't know each other, but we must have trust. Otherwise we will never get out of here."

Jesús nodded.

Enid looked troubled. What Dario said was logical, but… "Okay," she muttered.

He raised a hand. "But go carefully. If you find a way up, don't go in by yourselves. Wait for us to get there. We'll have a lot of people by the time we make it to the wall."

Jesús and Enid clambered over the ends of the next eggs, and headed for the wall.

Dario turned to Angelino. "I have something I need to say first."

He took a deep breath. "I think we must stop hating other people and work together. I think it was the hate that Alberto and Luis taught us that made us willing to follow them, and it was Alberto and Luis who brought us here."

The other boys nodded.

"It's my guess," Dario continued, "that all the groups who disappeared from Shanti Place are here, brought here by the same kind of hate. If we're to get out of here, we'll have to work together."

Angelino looked down at the ground, nodding his head. "You tried to tell me. I'm ashamed I didn't see this before, but I've thought about it a lot these long days in this prison. I'm sorry to all of you who followed me in this stupidity."

Pedro and Roberto scuffled their feet and nodded their heads. "We didn't have to follow you," added Pedro. "We were stupid, too."

Dario patted Angelino's shoulder. "We have no time for shame, only for changing our ways, and breaking these other people out of the eggs."

The first man they pulled out was an older man with a long beard, whose white cloth hat fell out on the ground as he was pulled out of the egg. He wore a long shirt over white pants and spoke with a deep accent.

"Shukran, shukran. Thank you, thank you," he repeated over and over again, with a bow. "I am Imam Labeeb Aalim. But where are we? Where are my people?"

Dario and Pedro explained what they knew, and suggested that his people might be in the next eggs down the row.

"We must get them out," he exclaimed.

Soon the boys figured out a system where one of them went ahead with Jesús and Enid's buckets as soon as the seats had been pushed into an egg creating an opening. They had each escapee pass out their own chair seats before leaving the egg. There was no way to collect more buckets. They divided into teams – a bucket team, and several seat teams – getting more and more people out of the eggs.

In the next row over from the Imam they helped another older man out of his egg. This man had a long beard too, but on his head was a small black skull cap. He had a hard time standing, and the boys lowered him carefully to the ground.

"My legs are weak from pedaling." For a moment he held his head in his hands.

They crouched down next to the man and introduced themselves.

He looked up at them. "I am Rabbi Abraham Cohen." Then he looked around him. "What is this place?"

"We don't know, but each prisoner is held alone in these eggs."

"And my people? There were people with me when I came. Where are my people?"

Roberto pointed. "Probably in the next eggs. Our eggs were all next to each other. A young boy and girl figured out how to break out, and they got us out of our eggs. Now we are helping others get out."

The old man struggled to his feet with the help of the boys. "We must help the rest of my people to get out of this prison. I'm sure this is a trick of the Muslims."

"I don't think so." Angelino looked at Roberto for help.

"It's hate," added Roberto. "It's hating other people that brought us here."

The man just shook his head and pointed at the next egg. Angelino and Roberto helped him crawl over the ends of the eggs, and he sat again while they got the next man out of the egg who was, indeed, one of his people.

As they pulled people out of the eggs they explained their plans as quickly as they could to each newly released captive. Some were able to jump right in and help, but others seemed to be in shock. Some were overwhelmed with fear. Some refused to come out of the eggs and the boys reluctantly left them behind leaving a seat in the side of the egg in hopes they would change their minds.

They moved as fast as they could, but they wished they had another set of buckets. "But there's no way to get them before the end of the next rest period," Angelino pointed out. Eventually they figured out that with some more muscle they could make an opening with just one bucket and things began to move faster.

The Long Dark Room

When Enid and Jesús reached the last egg before the wall, they stood for a moment looking up at the sheer side of the canyon. Jesús stepped back to look at the openings far above them. "I don't know how we can get up there. Even if you climbed on my shoulders, or if Dario climbed on Pedro's shoulders, we couldn't reach the openings."

Enid nodded, "Maybe there's another way farther down the canyon."

They started the crawling, wiggling scramble under the eggs toward the other end of the canyon. Each time they reached a new row they stood and stared at the wall, and each time they found nothing but blank wall. They crawled on under nine more eggs.

Enid was the first to crawl out from under the tenth egg and stand up.

"Look, Jesús." Enid pointed at the wall, a big grin on her face. A ladder was set into a recess in the wall, making it invisible from an angle. It went straight up the wall ending a little higher than the lower bay, just

386

beneath the net and the upper bay. The wall between the bay and the ladder was cut back, creating a ledge so someone could step easily from the bay to the ladder, or vice versa.

"I'm going to climb up there and just peek in," muttered Jesús, sliding across the point of the egg to get to the ladder.

Enid grabbed his shoulder. "Shouldn't we wait…"

A faint musical sound interrupted her.

She cocked her head to one side. "Listen!"

A clanging like church bells came from far above them. It sounded the same tune as Enid's grandfather's clock and then started chiming the hour.

Enid counted. "It must be twelve o'clock in that city," she whispered. "It's night time because it's dark. Maybe everyone's asleep."

"Then this is the best time to go up the ladder. I won't go in. I'll just look. I'll be very quiet."

Jesús scrambled up the ladder pausing every few rungs to hang on and pant. His legs were strong from pedaling, but he was weak with thirst.

The water's up here, he thought. *I just need to make myself strong enough.*

Finally, he reached the ledge by the bay. The bay was very wide and much taller than he was. The metal track hung from brackets at the top with enough space below it for the eggs to move through.

Metal handles were set in the wall between the ladder and the bay. They would be just above his head, if he were standing even with the ledge. He looked down at Enid for a moment and smiled reassurance, then climbed up so his feet were even with the ledge, grabbed the closest handle and moved his left foot carefully out, keeping himself hidden behind the edge of the opening.

Enid held her breath, her hands gripped tightly together, as he moved onto the ledge and then peeked around the corner of the bay into the room. *Oh, Jesús,* she thought, *please be careful.*

The window opened into a long room with huge square metal pillars set about six feet back from each opening. The tracks the eggs had hung on traveled across the ceiling to a wide opening in the pillars. Toward the back of the room, little lights blinked. *Computers,* he thought, *but still no people anywhere.*

He wanted to climb into the room and look more, but he could almost feel Enid below, her eyes boring into his back.

No, she's right, he thought, *I have to go back and tell them what I've seen, and there need to be more of us up here exploring.*

Slowly he moved back out of the opening, off the ledge, and down the ladder. He was still thirsty. He hadn't seen anything that looked like food and water in there, but it had to be there.

When Angelino and Roberto came to the next to the last egg in one of the rows, the young man they pulled out was Dirk, head of the Avengers.

The three boys stood silently looking at each other for a moment. "Dario," yelled Angelino. "We found Dirk."

Dario came crawling under several rows of eggs to scramble up next to Dirk.

"Dirk," he said. "We're glad to find you."

Dirk's eyes narrowed. "Glad?" he said.

"Yes," nodded Dario. "We, too, were caught up in this trap."

Dirk looked around him at the hundreds of eggs. Some of the people who had been released were visible over the sides of the eggs in both directions. He turned back to Dario, his face impassive.

He's afraid, thought Dario. *Of course. So are we.*

He took a deep breath. "Dirk, it's because of the hate we ended up here. If we hadn't been willing to believe the message of hate from Alberto and Luis – that we were better than everyone else... I know you were given the same message, only it was us you were superior to." He shrugged his shoulders. "We thought ourselves superior to you."

He sighed. "Don't you see? They used that message to capture you, and to capture us."

He looked at Dirk. Dirk seemed to be thinking about it. "We must now work together to escape this place. We must no longer hate each other."

Dirk turned away and stared at the wall. He ran his arm across his eyes.

Tears, thought Dario, *a good sign.*

Dirk turned back. "I know we were betrayed. That I know."

He looked around him. "Where are the rest of the Avengers?"

"You can help release people and find your friends."

They moved to the next egg where they found Kimberly.

Dirk and Kimberly were still clinging to each other when they heard loud voices down the rows to the right and Dario and Angelino scrambled quickly under the eggs in the direction of the voices.

The yelling was coming from the two old men and their followers, screaming at each other over the sides of the eggs, each blaming the other group for their captivity.

"Be quiet," Dario grabbed the Rabbi's shoulder. "They might hear you."

The Rabbi turned to Dario. "It's their fault. They imprisoned us here. They hate us."

"We, too, were imprisoned. It is your people who want to take our lands. You are the ones who imprisoned us," answered the Imam.

"No, no," Dario got between them. "It's someone else who imprisoned all of us. We don't know who, but we do know how they're able to do it. It's hate. There were men who encouraged us, and they led us into this."

The Rabbi and his people looked at each other, and the Imam looked around at his people. The low voices of the others around them releasing prisoners, explaining, and moving on to release the next prisoner was like a low buzz in the otherwise silent canyon.

"It's true," said one of the Rabbi's people. "Amos and Isaac were the ones who led us here. We came here after the ritual with them."

He looked around him. "And where are they? We haven't found them here."

Dario turned toward the Imam's people. "We also had two men who encouraged us to think we were superior to all other people. Then there was a ceremony, and we were here. And you?"

The Imam slowly nodded his head. "Yes. Yes. It was Mohammed and Ali. Ha!" he laughed. "Perhaps their names weren't real. Who knows who they were?"

Dario took a deep breath. "We can't afford to hate each other anymore. If we're going to get out of here, we must work together."

The Rabbi sighed and nodded his head. "I'll need to think about this, but for now, yes, we must work together."

The Imam looked at the Rabbi for a moment, and then shrugged his shoulders. "Yes. We must get out of here. Then we will find out who does this thing. Then we will see."

The noisy shouting had started while Jesús was climbing down the ladder. He leaned out looking down the rows of eggs toward the noise.

Enid looked up at him, alarmed. "What's going on?"

"I don't know. Some of the people who were released seem to be mad at each other. Dario and Angelino are crawling down there now."

He hung there watching while Dario reached the men, quieted them down, and then seemed to solve the problem.

When things were quiet again he leaned out from the ladder, waving at them.

Pedro, who had just released Charlie – Bandit's owner – was the first to see him. "Dario," he called out down the rows of eggs. "Look up."

Dario looked up and laughed. "They found a way in."

Slowly the crowd, crawling under and over the sides and ends of the eggs, moved up to the eggs surrounding Enid and Jesús. Dario pushed his way in, so that he was standing with Enid right below the ladder. When they were all as close as they could get, Jesús climbed a little way up the ladder, leaning out so they all could see him. "The room's very long – the length of this canyon maybe. I didn't see any people. I think we need to have a team that goes up to explore – enough people so if anyone comes we can overcome them."

"It's after midnight in that city," added Enid, scrambling up the ladder next to Jesús. "We heard a chiming clock. Maybe the people are just all asleep right now."

Dario nodded. "Then we need to work fast."

He climbed up the ladder a couple of rungs and looked out at the escapees gathered below. "We must all work together," he called out, clinging to the ladder with one arm and gesturing with the other. "We cannot allow hate, or believing that we are better than others, to keep us from working together."

He looked around at the people. Some were nodding. Some wouldn't meet his eyes.

He took a deep breath and went on. "We need some people to go up and explore for food and water – those who haven't been here long and are still strong. Perhaps we'll find a way to release all the eggs up there, but meanwhile, I think those who don't go up need to keep releasing people."

"I saw some computers," added Jesús. "If anyone is good at computers, they should come."

A young black woman called out. "I'm a techie. I'll go."

Jesús started back up, and Dario moved out of the way so the techie and others could follow.

Enid scrambled up after him. "I'm going with Jesús."

"We're coming." Dirk pushed his way toward the ladder, followed by Kim and Charlie.

"Dario, you and Roberto go," Angelino urged. "Pedro and I will stay here and help release people."

Dario nodded and followed the rest up the ladder.

Jesús climbed to the opening, and then helped each of the others as they came up the ladder. "We need to find food and water and search for a way to release all the prisoners in the eggs," he explained to them as they moved from the ladder into the room. "Enid and I have missed two rest periods – two water bottles."

The woman who said she was a techie introduced herself as Adia. She headed for the bank of computers lining the wall on the side of the room across from the opening. Two others followed her. They looked over the computers and talked together in low whispers.

The others clustered near the opening, looking first one way and then the other. "This is a huge room," exclaimed one man.

Another pointed to the wall to the left of the bay where a picture of a ladder was etched in the concrete. "Maybe there're more ladders. We should look for this picture."

"Look down there." Dirk pointed in the direction of the near end of the canyon. "Looks like more eggs stacked on top of each other."

They all peered in that direction, where the rounded sides of the eggs were just visible in the dim light.

"They're waiting for new prisoners."

Some shuddered, some turned their heads away, and one man whispered, "God help us."

Dario, Enid, Jesús, and Roberto stayed by the ladder across from the computers, where they could keep touch with the people in the canyon and the rest could report back to them. A gray-haired woman who introduced herself as Sister Maureen led a small group down the far side of the room heading away from the stacks of eggs, while a small dark haired man named Fadil led another group in the same direction, but along the window side looking for more ladders. Dirk, Kim, and Charlie headed toward the much closer end of the room with the stack of eggs.

Dario leaned into the opening of the metal column, looking up and down. "This goes down to a floor below us and up to the next floor. There are complicated looking pulleys in it. I think the food comes from above or below."

"Or people come," suggested Enid, "and distribute the food."

Dario pushed up his sleeve to look at a battered watch. "I've timed the breaks. They come every twelve hours at three o'clock for three hours. Back to work at six o'clock. It's now fifty-two minutes to break."

"The food comes at the end of the sleep period," interjected Enid. "That gives us about three hours before someone might come."

Dario looked out the opening. "We have to find the food supply and the buckets, too. We can use more buckets to speed up the release of people."

Dirk, Kim, and Charlie were the first to return from exploring. "We don't think there's anyone in those eggs. It's just like here, except for the eggs. There's a hole right above the one closest to the opening in each row."

He looked up. "Look there's a hole next to this opening, too." They all stared at the square hole in the ceiling that seemed to go up to another dimly lit floor.

"Up there's where that pincher thing pulled us," added Kim. "And then it dropped us into the egg through that hole."

The rest of the searchers returned reporting they had found two elevators and three more ladders down into the canyon. Adia reported that they had found some programs that ran the electric system, but hadn't found anything that opened the eggs.

"We need to guard those elevators," Enid exclaimed, to a chorus of yes's and nods. Adia returned to her computer, but the rest all headed for the elevators.

As they approached the first elevator, something started to hum.

Some froze in place while others ran toward the elevator.

"Someone's coming. Everyone hide," exclaimed Roberto.

Jesús grabbed Enid, and they crouched behind one of the metal columns, where they could watch the elevator door.

Enid's heart pounded with fear. *Oh, no,* she thought. *Oh, no. We can't be caught now. We just can't.* She gripped Jesús' hand tightly and tears ran down her cheeks.

EARTH WOMAN TREE WOMAN QUARTET
BOOK 4
TSIN TWEI
THE DANCE OF LIFE
Connie Pwll Walck Tyler

TSIN TWEI, THE DANCE OF LIFE

Invocation:
The Wolves Song

I am the wild, the freeborn,
earth traveler!
My soul singing touches the moon and the sun.

I am the herald, the seeker,
the messenger.
I bear the song for those seeking the One.

I am the hunter, the knower,
the lover.
My voice like a spear pierces deep in the night.
I am the lone, the many,

the mirror.
My call is like lightning,
jagged and bright!

1

Hunter's Moon, Waning to Last Quarter

On that terrible morning, after Giselle, Shen Ch'i, and Sidney knew they had missed saving *Los Gallos*, An Lien and her dad went home to pack for the trip to Arundel while Giselle taught her class. There was nothing they could do to help *Los Gallos* at the moment, so postponing the trip would serve no purpose. The Commandos and the Ikemen Ninjas, shaken by the events, joined Giselle's class. Deborah and the other counselors planned extra activities for the afternoon to keep them busy.

An Lien had suggested they could make a video to post on VidYou interviewing Giselle, Yameno, and the others involved in the trips to Ninas Twei, but meanwhile, she posted a short version of the story on LifeFriends and referred to the anonymous video that showed the murder of Hazel and Dan. She also mentioned the story about the woman demonstrator who apparently became an Ibex when she died, and the giant otters in Brazil. There was no way of knowing if any of them had ever visited Ninas Twei.

Could people who gave their lives for a cause that helped the Tsin Twei, focus on a totem, transform, and go to Ninas Twei? She posed the question on LifeFriends and watched as a lively discussion grew up around it.

Many people mentioned having totem animals, or favorite saints, or mythical heroes. One person mentioned the OET demonstrations. Perhaps, if people had a totem to focus on, he suggested, they could take on some of the attributes of the totem to help them stand strong against the police. "Those of us who are Native Americans will be having drumming circles and dances, that day, too, in solidarity with OET," added one woman. "We've always had totems."

An Lien's father poked his head in her bedroom door asking her if she was ready to travel.

"I'll pack quickly," An Lien promised, shutting down her laptop.

Shen Ch'i took the inland freeway, rather than the more picturesque, but much longer coastal route Giselle had taken on her summer trip north. Giselle, An Lien, Shen Ch'i, and Sidney had lots to talk about, filling each other in about their pasts, bandying about different ideas on how to keep more homeless youth from being pulled into the influence of the recruiters, and wondering who it was that tried to kidnap An Lien. "At least you should be safe up here," added Sidney.

They planned to stay at Giselle's little house on the coast, but stopped first in town at Jarvis Tarrant's home to meet over a potluck dinner.

Yameno was waiting for them in the shadow of the doorway, moving out to greet them as they pulled up in front of the house. Giselle climbed out of the van and into his arms. He held her and she felt the whisper of the wind in her hair.

Almost all the second group of travelers to Ninas Twei and their supporters were there. The religious leaders Jarvis, Clare, and Keegan (but not Micah who was celebrating the Sabbath); Jesús's parents, Dorotea and Billy McCrea; the doctor and historian couple, Mark and Muriel Chase, and this time the group included Giselle's old principal, Nicki, and her partner, Penny.

Nicki had brought Giselle's dogs.

Giselle cried as she cuddled the dogs' wiggling bodies and let them lick her face. The gray cat, who was living with Yameno and Tarrant, waited patiently for his turn and kindly allowed her to gather him into her arms for a long hug.

She was startled to see Gunther Amundsen hovering in the background as they got their food, and found chairs and floor space in the living room.

She looked at Yameno who smiled encouragingly, and in a low voice said, "It's okay. Keegan has been working with him. He's one of us now."

"But he killed Hazel and Dan!" she whispered back.

He nodded. "Yes, but... he's different now. Keegan would call it an epiphany."

Gunther, seeing her look at him, walked slowly over .

"Ms. Raphael, please..." He hesitated, his voice almost a whisper. "Please... I'm so sorry. I know you only had Enid's best interest at heart."

Giselle looked at the floor, for a moment at a loss of words. "But Hazel and Dan..."

He turned his head away, but not before she had seen his eyes fill with tears. "There is no way I can be forgiven for that," he whispered.

Giselle took a deep breath and turned toward the window, staring out into the dark. Yameno touched her shoulder and she looked up at him. Could he forgive Amundsen for killing his closest friends?

She thought of Kuan Yin reaching out to hear the cries of the world and the Weaving Tree full of rips needing repair.

Breathing deeply she turned to face Amundsen. She reached out a hand. "Yes, Mr. Amundsen, I would rather be friends than enemies."

He took her hand. "I'm Gunther," he added.

"And I'm Giselle."

The cat twined himself in and out of their legs.

When they were all settled Yameno told about their failed attempts to return to Ninas Twei. Giselle told of the disappearance of the Shanti Place young people and An Lien added what she had found on the internet about groups that disappear.

Sidney spoke up. "Do you think they related? I mean the traveling to Ninas Twei, the children falling down that crevice, and the disappearance of our kids and these other groups?"

Clare spoke up. "It seems to me it can't be a coincidence – Giselle coming up here and finding out about Ninas Twei, and then Giselle going down there and finding out about these disappearances."

"And this woman, Ayoabia," added Muriel. "She seems to tie both things together... somehow."

Giselle looked around the room. Everyone was nodding. "They feel very different. Going to Ninas Twei was so beautiful, so ecstatic. The place I went to – where it seemed like I was Bandit's owner – was horrible – and the Avengers and *Los Gallos* disappearing makes my stomach hurt. Ninas Twei felt right. This feels wrong."

She paused for a moment. "But so did our arrest, and...," she paused, "Hazel and Dan..."

"Yes," nodded Keegan. "They seem like opposites, but there's something similar."

"But the travelers to Ninas Twei are concerned for the whole world," Clare exclaimed.

"And the gangs that disappear are... ho-mo-gen-e-ous." Sidney said the word carefully, turning and grinning at Giselle. "And they're haters."

They also talked about the OET meeting – how Yameno was there in shadowy wolf form supporting Giselle in her shadowy tree form.

Giselle told of the man filming An Lien and the later attack on the street, how she became the Earth Woman Tree Woman, and again, Yameno was there. "And the Tree Woman wasn't a shadow either," added An Lien. "She was tall and rooted in the sidewalk. If I hadn't seen it, I wouldn't believe it."

Nicki looked skeptical, but the rest just nodded.

"An Lien has found some other interesting stuff on the internet," Giselle added, telling about the woman who turned into an Ibex, and the Brazilians who became Giant Otters. "She's started a discussion on the internet and related it all to our journey to Ninas Twei."

"People are talking about using totems in the OET demonstrations," added An Lien. "About how they could draw strength from them."

Muriel laughed. "That's great. Our Interfaith Council is doing something very similar for the demonstration." She told about Nanda's idea for choosing local animals and making posters talking about the effect of logging and fracking on the local wildlife.

"How about you, Sidney?" Yameno smiled at the young man. "Have you chosen a totem? I've heard about Shen Ch'i and the dragon, An Lien and the Laughing Dove, but I haven't heard that you've chosen something."

Sidney grinned. "I been thinking 'bout that. I like the African Gray Parrot. Smart and chatty – like to live in a large community and cooperate with others to get food and stuff. 'Observant of other cultures, and capable of mimicking them.' That's what it says online. Also good at camouflage." He laughed.

Shen Ch'i laughed. "That's perfect."

Yameno reached down under his chair and pulled out a wooden image of an African Gray Parrot in flight. Its extended wings reminded

Giselle of the usual depiction of an archangel's wings, its feathers long and separate as they extended outward from the curve of the wing bones. It was carved out of gray driftwood. Red-stain covered the fanning tail and just touched the tips of the wing feathers. He handed it to Sidney.

Sidney took it in his hands and caressed it lovingly. "How did you know?" he whispered. "How did you know?"

"I felt compelled… I felt compelled to carve it." Yameno smiled, shaking his head a little. He'd carved it sitting by the spring – guarding the spring.

"And this one, too." He reached down again and pulled out another carving. This one was of a beautiful young black woman, her head thrown back, her mouth open in song, as she rose up out of ocean waves, holding a crescent moon in her hands. A dolphin tail rose out of the ocean behind her. "Who is this one for?"

"Miesha," exclaimed Sidney. "It's Miesha."

He turned to Giselle. "It's what I see in the shadow around her when she sings. I see her, just like that."

"Yemonja," said Muriel. "It's Yemonja. She's an Orisha from the Yoruban tradition. She's goddess of the oceans, a mother goddess, and a healer of sadness."

Sidney laughed. "She got to grow up a little to take that all on, but that sounds like her. She a healer of sadness right now!"

Shen Ch'i, An Lien, and Giselle all nodded their heads, smiling.

"She's thirteen," Giselle explained. "And I think she has a kind of secret connection with the woman, Ayoabia. They seem sometimes to communicate silently."

Sidney nodded his head. "Yes. She real close to Ayo."

Yameno handed the carving to Sidney. "Will you take this to her?"

Sidney nodded. "Maybe we're headed to Ninas Twei, too."

He looked around at all the smiling nodding faces and turned to Giselle, "And maybe Ayoabia…"

He didn't finish, but Giselle understood. Ayoabia was involved in this somehow.

Shen Ch'i turned to Yameno. "And your group will be trying again, very soon?"

Dorotea, who had been sitting silently throughout the conversation, spoke up. "We have to keep trying. Over and over again until we get there."

She wiped her eyes on her sleeve, and Billy put his arm around her.

Yameno nodded. "Yes. I don't know what else to do."

Before they left to go to Giselle's house for the night Yameno told them to be careful. "People have thrown rocks through the windows of Jarvis's church and spray painted 'Church of the Devil' on the wall. I'm worried they'll find out you're back at your house. Just be careful."

Giselle nodded and after a lot of handshaking and hugging, the Bayomar group gathered back in the big van and headed to the little house by the ocean, accompanied by the two dogs and the gray kitty.

Saturday morning Giselle, followed by the dogs and the cat, slipped out of her little house early and went to sit by the Earth Woman Tree Woman, first sitting facing her, drinking in her treeness, and then leaning back against her looking out at the ocean.

She breathed deeply, and slowly found that her muscles – so tight for so long – were relaxing.

> *Warm, warm is the earth,*
> *nurturing life,*
> *giving its fullness*
> *to reach for the sun.*
> *My roots mingling in her*
> *bring me my life blood,*
> *and when I die,*
> *it is she they become.*

Tears rolled down her cheeks.

It had been so wonderful, that trip to Ninas Twei, and yet so frightening – the pain they had all felt, like Ninas Twei itself was in pain – the children falling, and then finding themselves back at Yameno's clearing surrounded by those men and their guns.

But now there was Bayomar and Ayoabia – and through OET, the rest of the world. *All connected,* she thought. She put her head back against the Earth Woman Tree Woman and closed her eyes again. The cat crawled into her lap.

There was a rustling sound, and she heard someone beside her.

She opened her eyes to see Yameno kneeling next to her. "Have you been there long?" she asked.

"I've been out here all night, guarding."

"Guarding?"

He shrugged. "Just in case. I don't think Coffman and his crew have had time to know you're back, but…" He reached over and wiped the tears off her face.

"I want to stay here," she whispered, "and I want – I need to be there."

He pulled her into his arms, tumbling the cat out on to the ground. "Come with me to the spring," he whispered, becoming wolf. Giselle, slipped easily into her Earth Woman Tree Woman form, riding the Wolfwind as he circled the meadow and dashed up the path, his feet barely touching the ground, slowing only as they approached his clearing.

She cried out as they passed the remains of his little house. "No matter," he howled. "All that matters is the spring," and he slipped quietly down the path to the edge of the little pool.

They took human form and Yameno knelt and reached under the waterfall with cupped hands. Giselle knelt next to him and he brought his hands up in front of her, and she cupped her hands under his and drank. Then she reached her cupped hands into the fall and brought water to him, and he drank.

> *Water of life,* he sang.
> *Purify me.*
> *Water of the soul of earth,*
> *wash me in your love.*

She joined him, and their voices rose together, the rhythm of the falling water singing beneath their song.

> *Breath,*
> *Singing through the voice of the wind,*
> *Dance with me, sing with me,*
> *Take my hand as a lover,*
> *Make me one with you.*

"You're the earth and the tree," he whispered. "I'm the wind and the water. We need each other. No matter how far apart, you can call me and I will come."

"And can you call me, as well?" she asked.

He nodded, smiling, and pulled her into his arms.

When they returned to the house, they found breakfast was waiting for them and a very excited An Lien. "It's going viral," she explained. "The story is going viral even without a video!"

A little later at Jarvis' house, as An Lien was rolling off the hydraulic lift on the side of the van, a pickup truck came around the corner, and then slowed down. The driver stared at them, looking at each one of them in turn, his eyebrows narrowing as he looked at Sidney.

"It's Mr. Dickerson," muttered Giselle, as he gunned the engine and sped down the street away from them.

"Not good," Yameno added, "but I don't know how we could've prevented that."

"Let's do the video," An Lien urged. "Then I can put it online right away."

They chose a spot under a tree in the back yard and soon Giselle and Yameno were busy telling their story to Muriel, who was asked to be the interviewer.

The rest gathered in the living room and talked about the upcoming OET demonstrations. Sidney pointed out that all the kids in his group were going, but the kids in the other groups had been opposed to the demonstration.

"Dirk said that marches and demonstrations were for 'mongrels'." He looked up at the rest of them. "That probably means their 'recruiters' were against the demonstrations."

"And since the demonstrations are against large corporate interests..." added Micah.

Several of the others nodded their heads.

"Could be a connection," agreed Shen Ch'i, "but there's also the sense of all kinds of people working together for a common cause."

"Yes, that's certainly contrary to the idea of 'birds of a feather hanging together' that the recruiters seem to be promoting," added Clare.

"Birds don't really do that," added Micah, who had excused himself from the Synagogue activities for the day.

The video was finished quite quickly. They had all told their stories often enough to be dramatic and precise.

"It's good, I think," An Lien grinned. "Everyone was very earnest, very intense."

Sidney helped her set up the laptop on a desk in the living room. It only took a moment to download the video from the camera and pull it into the editing program. They all gathered around An Lien, and the cat jumped up on An Lien's lap starring at the screen. "He's watching, too," giggled An Lien.

"It's terrific," exclaimed Penny. "Muriel, you're really good at getting straight to the point." The others all nodded.

"Yes, I think it's…"

Suddenly the house resonated like a drum as rocks hit the walls and one came flying through the front window.

"Duck," yelled Jarvis, as the dogs barked wildly and the cat flew down the hall to the back of the house.

"An Lien, get to the back," Shen Ch'i called out as Sidney grabbed her wheelchair and pushed her quickly down the hall toward the bedrooms.

"The video," exclaimed Giselle, grabbing the computer and paraphernalia, and dashing after them. Sidney found a bedroom that faced on the backyard, away from the rock throwers, and An Lien grabbed her computer out of Giselle's hands. "I'll upload the video right now!"

"I'll stay here and protect An Lien." Sidney grabbed a straight backed chair, standing back of An Lien, ready to heft the chair against anyone who broke in and Giselle ran back to the living room where everyone was crouched behind furniture.

Clare was on the phone to the sheriff's office. "They say it will take thirty minutes for the deputy to get here."

Outside rocks were still flying, and the attackers were yelling. "Go home. We don't need no devil worshipers here…" "Yeah, and take your nigger with you…" "And the chinks and ginks and Jews, too."

Another projectile came flying through the window, streaming fire.

Yameno grabbed a sofa cushion, pushing it on top of the flaming bottle as it hit the rug. The others grabbed more sofa and chair cushions, piling them on the first one, and holding them down so the flames would be completely smothered.

There was stunned silence both inside and out before a young voice yelled, "Holy crap, Dickerson. You'll kill someone."

Someone else said, "Shut up, Tom," and again there was silence.

"Did we put it out?" asked Micah.

"I hope so." Yameno looked up from where he was pinning the sofa cushions down over the object. "Do you think we should look and see if it's out?"

Everyone in the room looked bewildered. "I'm afraid none of us has experience with Molotov cocktails," Keegan added dryly, "but since nothing has exploded…"

Coffman's voice broke the silence yelling, "Go home, you fucking mongrels. Take that teacher with you, and your nigger, and go home. And the rest of you, go with them. We don't want you devil worshippers here in Arundel."

There was a lot of car door slamming and engine revving, as the attackers tore off down the street.

Jarvis laughed a little. "Scared themselves, I think."

Afterwards Sidney mentioned the use of the word 'mongrels'. "Same word as the recruiters use with the kids."

"Those news people on TV," explained Dorotea. "They use this word a lot."

"Yes, I've heard it, too," added Micah.

When the deputy sheriff showed up thirty minutes later, he looked over the damage and wrote up a report. He listened to their description of what had happened and who had done it, but never met their eyes. When they showed him the partially melted plastic bottle, still containing some gasoline, he did mutter, "Shit, plastic. What an idiot," and carefully put it in an evidence bag, but otherwise he hardly said a word.

They followed him as he walked back toward his car, the cat padding quietly behind them. "We haven't enough deputies to cover everything that happens in the county and," he looked around at them significantly, "you bring this on yourselves."

Keegan raised his eyebrows at him. "We've told you who the perpetrators are. That should be sufficient to make an arrest."

The deputy shrugged. "It's just their word against yours. I'll file a report, but that's all I can do."

The cat moved between the deputy and his car.

Keegan nodded his head. "I see. And if there are fingerprints on the bottle?"

The deputy shrugged turning back toward his car in time to see the cat standing in front of him staring at him with unblinking eyes, then slowly sitting, curling his tail around himself, the tip flicking back and forth.

"Shit!" The deputy stumbled backwards closing his notebook with a snap. Giving the cat a wide berth, he headed for his car saying – without turning around – "I'll turn in a report."

The rest stood around in the front yard looking at the damage.

Billy turned to Jarvis. "We need to repair the windows. We'll have to get the glass in Robertsville." He grinned. "I don't think we should go to Coffman's Hardware for it!"

Micah went with him and as they passed the hardware store, Micah pointed to the sheriff's car parked on the side street next to the store.

Inside the store, the deputy was reaming out Coffman, who had just finished yelling at Dickerson. "A Molotov cocktail? You know I can't just let that pass. Rein in your people, Coffman, or I'll have to make an arrest. I can't ignore Molotov cocktails, even if the bottle was plastic." He rolled his eyes. "Who do you think you are? Terrorists?"

Tom stood in the doorway to the back room, glaring at them all.

By the time Billy and Micah got back to Jarvis' house, the others had reluctantly decided nothing could be done for Enid and Jesús except to keep trying to get to Ninas Twei every day. They would try again that night.

Dorotea had a gaunt, lost look on her face, but agreed.

"We'll all keeping trying to find another solution," Keegan added. "We must, but let's hope you can find your way back to Ninas Twei soon."

They were more optimistic about the possibilities of the demonstrations. The Arundel and Robertsville group would be marching on the county courthouse where there would be a sit-in demanding that the county park not be sold for logging and fracking. A poster making party was planned for Sunday with Nanda at the Buddhist center, and Muriel had been preparing information on the impact of logging and fracking on the native wildlife and the sacred lands of the Tuwillian people. An Lien showed Muriel how to trace the companies involved back to their parent corporations and how to trace their relationship to problems in other places in the world.

Giselle and Yameno agreed that whether or not there was any connection between the demonstrations and Ninas Twei, the goals of the demonstrations fit the needs of the Weaving Tree. "The connections we form with each other and others in the world will be recorded in the weaving. If we stop some of the destruction of the earth and its peoples, the weaving will get stronger. We'll be closer to becoming a grandsoul and a part of the Tsin Twei."

In a whisper she added, "If it's not too late."

Yameno squeezed her hand.

When they finished talking, Yameno turned to Giselle and Shen Ch'i. "I think you need to go back to Bayomar now, rather than tomorrow. I don't think you'll be safe out at your house. You should leave, and we should make sure that Coffman knows you've left."

Shen Ch'i nodded. "Yes. There's no need to take that risk."

Giselle sighed, and nodded.

Yameno pulled her to him. "Remember," he whispered, "we're together wherever we are."

They left soon after, stopping back at the house so Giselle could pick up some of her things to take back to Bayomar, including, of course, the little wooden Kuan Yin. She hugged Yameno, and with the gray kitty curled in her arms, climbed into the van, closely followed by the dogs.

They arrived back in the city late Saturday night. Shen Ch'i dropped Giselle and Sidney off, and took An Lien home with him, promising – when she wanted to return to her own apartment – he would take her to the Sunday meditation at the Buddhist Center around the corner from her building. She and Giselle would go together to the OET meeting later that evening.

The next morning Giselle brought the dogs and the gray cat, sitting regally on her shoulder, to Shanti Place. The Shanti Place dogs gathered around, wagging their tails and touching noses with the two newcomers.

"Meow," commanded the cat.

The dogs all looked up at the cat and immediately sat, their tails gently sweeping behind them. None of them barked. None of them jumped up on Giselle.

"Weird," muttered Sidney.

"Is that going to work?" Deborah asked.

"My dogs reacted the same way when the cat first came," Giselle laughed. The cat jumped off her shoulder into the midst of the dogs, and walked off down the room, exploring. The dogs watched and wagged, much to the delight of the young people.

Deborah shook her head.

Soon An Lien came rolling in followed by Shen Ch'i. "The video's gone viral. The OET people are excited about it, and telling all their marchers to find pictures and stuff of animals and mythical creatures they identify with, and meditate on them before the march!"

"Speaking of which," Sidney reached down into a bag at his feet. "Miesha, what do you think of this?"

He held out the wood carving of Yemonja.

Miesha's mouth dropped open. She was speechless as she took the sculpture into her hands.

"It's you, Miesha." Sidney smiled. "Isn't it? Giselle's friend Yameno made it for you."

Miesha nodded shyly. "It's Yemonja. Ayoabia said..." her voice faded off. "Anyway, she a totem for the march like An Lien's video talk about, isn't she?"

"Do you have one, Sidney?" asked Rashaun.

"Yup," he replied, pulling out his parrot. "An African Gray Parrot."

Rashaun's eyes narrowed as looked at it.

"You could find yourself a totem, too, Rashaun. You don't have to go with those men. You could join us. We can be African and part of everyone else, too."

Rashaun didn't respond, but as he turned to get his breakfast his brow was furrowed and he was nodding his head.

The three Ikemen Ninjas were also watching. "What about you, Shen Ch'i," one asked. "You have a totem?"

"Yes, I do," he nodded at the boy. "I'm Ti-Tien-Lung, a dragon that's also an oak tree circling the earth. There's a gallery on Hopely

Street that has lots of paintings and sculptures by the same man that made Miesha's Yemonja and Sidney's parrot. Or you can make your own."

He nodded at one of the young men. "Min, you're very good at drawing. You could make totems for yourself and for others. They should be something with qualities you admire. Something that makes you feel strong, and grounded, and capable."

The boy's eyebrows narrowed thoughtfully, but he, too, said nothing more as he joined the food line.

Maria turned, laughing, to Shen Ch'i. "I'm going to be a butterfly. I'm going to be the most beautiful butterfly you've never seen! Full of all kinds of bright colors!"

Shen Ch'i grinned back at her. "You make those wings and fly, dear Maria."

The cat came and wound himself through Maria's legs, giving little mews. Maria leaned down and picked him up. "The cat likes the idea, too," she grinned. "What are you going to be, kitty? A lion?"

In the Cavern: The Listener in the Hall

Luha heard the carillons calling the men.

Shortly after, she heard the triumphal march in the chapel, the singing, and then voices. She couldn't understand them, but they sounded more excited than before, and some had a tone of uncertainty.

Warren went out in the hallway, leaning over the banister to watch the meeting, and when Don returned, he left quickly.

Don barely glanced at Luha as he sat down at his desk and turned on his computer. "We know who you are now, Ha-zel Fra-ya." He spit out her name. "I have a lot to do to counteract the damage you and your friends are doing."

"Oh?" asked Luha.

"You're all over the internet back in the world – you and that Dan Burroughs." He looked up at her. "And where is he? Is he hanging around here some place?"

I wish I knew, she thought, *but I'm not about to tell you that.*

"And where is this Ninas Twei? Is there some way to get there from here? Or did you come here when you died, instead of there?"

When she didn't respond he turned back to his computer and refused to talk at all.

She was aroused just before noon by a distant roaring sound. *The wind,* she thought.

Don looked up and grinned. "More pedalers for our electrical system."

"How many?" she asked.

"I don't know. Who cares?"

"Don't you keep track of them somewhere? On your computers maybe?"

He laughed. "Nah, they come, they work, they die. No need to keep track."

"Why are they kept in the eggs?"

"They're kept separate. No communication. Little communities come here. Little communities can also return."

Oh, yes. That's the way the Giants of God return. A little communal ritual. Well, she thought, *if the wind is still pulling in workers, the Giants of God probably aren't searching over there for a way to Ninas Twei.*

Don glanced at his watch, shut down his computer and stood up, just as the carillon began ringing noon. "See you later!" and he was out the door, and down the hall.

A few minutes later, Marius showed up.

The other Copper who was guarding Sarah with Warren, Luha remembered. He sat on the bench in the hall, staring in the door at her, not saying a word.

Don returned at one o'clock when the carillon rang the end of the lunch hour.

Luha watched as he worked at his desk. "What are you working on?"

"The OET demonstrations this week. It's fun. I get to create lies about the demonstrators, and put them out in a way that stupid people believe them. Gives the police justification for tromping on them. There'll be lots of mayhem."

She shivered. "Ah, yes. I believe I've seen some of your work in the past."

He looked up at her and grinned. "I have a well-known preacher lined up to talk about how all of you're the devil's spawn." He giggled. "Are you the devil's spawn, Hazel Fraya?"

Luha sat back on her haunches and looked at him. "Do you think so, Don?"

He shrugged and turned back to his computer.

"So your computer connects to the internet in the outside world?"

"Nope. We have no access. We can't get out, but more important, they can't get in. We just carry whatever is necessary on external drives when we return."

"That seems inconvenient."

"We can talk freely here – about the Giants of God, for instance, or our real goals. We can write about the Giants, but if we do it's archived here. Whatever we're taking back is checked carefully, so nothing slips out."

He turned back to the computer and refused to talk any more.

Luha sat up a couple of hours later. The clandestine listener was in the hall, but this time he wasn't hiding. He knocked on the open door.

Don turned. "Hey, Ranulf, what's up?"

"I thought maybe you'd like a break from this. I'd be glad to watch her tonight if you'd like." It was the man with the German accent.

"Sure. That'd be great. Warren did it last night, but I don't think he liked it."

"Lots of people are spooked by her, I think," nodded Ranulf.

Don turned and grinned at Luha. "I'll enjoy the evening," he said with great emphasis on the 'enjoy'.

Something churned in the bottom of her stomach.

Ranulf's face was impassive.

Don held up a small portable drive. "I'm finished here. I'll send this back with the group tonight. You need to get anything before I leave?"

"No, I've already eaten, and I have everything I need to get some work done." He held up a small document case.

"Thanks again," Don called out as he walked swiftly down the hall.

They heard chanting in the chapel shortly after he left, and then the carillon rang five o'clock. Luhanada could hear voices up and down the tiers calling out to each other as they headed down the stairs and elevators and out the big front doors.

Ranulf stood watching and listening in the doorway for a long time, and then walked down the hall, first in one direction and then the other.

The building was quiet.

He came back and began silently searching the room, opening drawers, checking the underside of the desk and chairs, even under the sofa and back of the pictures on the wall. When he finished, he went back to the hall and listened again, before returning and sitting in the chair next to her cage, leaning over close to her and speaking in a very soft voice. "Everyone is gone now."

Luha sat on her haunches, her tail wrapped around her feet, and bent her head to the side to lick her shoulder. "This morning you were listening in the hall." She, too, kept her voice low.

He nodded. "Very perceptive."

She flicked her tail. "Are you giving up an evening playing with some little girl to watch me?"

"No." He shuddered. "Not everyone here has such tastes."

Luha nodded. "I see."

"And..." He hesitated for a moment. "I'm not what I appear to be."

"Me, either," she laughed.

He chuckled, too. "No, although I would be hard put to say what it is you appear to be! You don't look like someone named Hazel Fraya."

"I am Luhanada," she replied.

"I don't know who that is, but I've heard enough to know we're on the same side."

"And what side is that?"

He smiled. "It's good to be cautious. What I am is not nearly as clear as that you're not on the side of the Giants of God."

He got up again and checked the hall, and then returned to his seat.

"Have you heard of the organization *Incogni*?" he whispered.

"They're the ones who hack into big corporations and governments, and sometimes release incriminating evidence to *TruthFarm*."

"Yes. We were told about the Giants of God, but we couldn't find a way into this computer system where their most sensitive information is kept. It can only be accessed here, in this strange place. I've spent several years working my way here."

"How did you do that?"

"Well, it helps that my grandfather was a Nazi banker during the Second World War."

"The Giants of God do seem a lot like the Nazis."

"Yes, but they've modified it some. They no longer are as adamant against the Jews, and perhaps admire much of the stereotype they had of them before – and some of them are of Jewish heritage. They're nominally accepting of those of darker ethnicities if they're able to demonstrate power, but the requirements are much higher for these people."

He shook his head. "But mostly they're white and of Christian heritage."

He laughed. "I fit."

"And were you able to access their information?"

"Yes," he nodded. "I have everything from their computers here." He opened the document case and pulled out a small cloth sack. "Flash drives."

He sat back and sighed. "But before we return to the world we're searched – x-rayed to see if we are 'inadvertently' – that's their word – carrying something back that should stay here. External drives like the one Don had can go back, but they check them first. There's no way to get these past their search, so I can't get the information back."

He got up and looked out the door again. He didn't speak until he had returned to his place next to the cage.

"Every time I return to the world, I write down everything I've learned, and that has all been turned over to *TruthFarm*, but they're holding that information until I can bring back the actual files – proof – and until I am safe." He leaned forward. "Perhaps you have some way to take these, if I released you?"

Luha stood up, pacing in the cage. "I don't think I can get back to that world myself. I don't understand it at all. How this place could exist – even how Ninas Twei exists."

"Ah, yes. At the meeting they spoke of this Ninas Twei. But the Giants of God don't know where it is, or how you got here from there, if that is where you come from. They think you came here instead of there."

Luha flicked her tail. "There's no way to know I can trust you."

Ranulf nodded. "You shouldn't tell me anything while I'm here at the City Cave. Too much can go wrong. Too many ways they might get the information from me. I don't think there's a listening device in here, but it could be well hidden."

"If that's the case, you're in trouble."

"I'm taking that chance."

He got up and looked out the door again. When he came back, he sat with his elbows on his knees and his head in his hands. "So, I shouldn't ask you any questions. If you can figure out a way to take the information back, I'll give it to you, and find a way to let you go."

"If you let me go, they'll go after you."

He nodded. "Yes, but the future of the earth depends on this. I must get this information out."

Luhanada paced. *If I leave and take these things to Ninas Twei, maybe Kujakali or Sarah will be able to return to the world with them, but where will they return if they've been here so many years? And I still won't have found the children... or Tata.*

Where is Tata?

A Monkey?

Nima crouched at the bottom of the crevice, looking out into the large cavern. She'd waited until the sun set in Ninas Twei before descending the crevice, but it was always daytime in the large cavern. Across the plateau, and what she knew must be the canyon, she could just barely see the dark City Cave with pinpoints of light in the windows of the houses and apartment buildings and ringing what must be the Nickel circle where the shops and recreation were.

Two flashlights moved up the path toward the tall shadowy building that must be the temple. *The patrol,* she thought.

She looked out at the orange dirt of the plateau. If she stepped out there would she trigger the wind? Would she be swept down into the canyon, into the eggs – trapped?

Or did being dead count? Like Luha, would the wind not sense her step?

She touched the dirt with one finger.

Nothing.

She pressed her whole hand down.

No wind. No sound.

With a sigh she pushed off on her hind legs leaping out onto the plateau and flew in long thrusts to the bridge, her tail a question mark over her back. She looked down into the canyon at the net, and below that the eggs, shuddering, then rushed over the bridge, scrambling over the gate at its end and ducking into the plastic brush of the park.

Staying as close to the back wall as the brush would let her, she felt behind each bush until her hand hit an empty place – the cave entrance.

Carefully she crawled into the cave exploring in the dark with her hands and her nose. Luha's scent was there, but not within the last day.

Nima gave a little moan. Where would Luhanada be?

In the city. She would be in the city, someplace....

Nima would have to go into the city, "and I'm frightened," she whispered to herself. "I'm frightened."

Outside the cave she found an old scent trail – more than a day old – moving under the brush toward the edge of the city. It led to the edge of the radial path called Three. Beneath Luha's scent she could smell men crisscrossing through the bushes. Perhaps this was when they were hunting for Luha and Kuji. There was no man scent more recent than Luha's.

But Luha's scent was more than a day old.

"Where is she?" she whispered, peering down the path to the center of the city, her nostrils flaring. Hugging the brush at the edge of the radial path she loped past the first circle of houses to the first circular path– Sarah had called it the 'Gold Circle.' Dashing across she continued on to the second circle – Silver.

Footsteps close by! She scrambled under the greenery pulling herself into a tight ball with her tail wound around her. She felt her heart thundering in her chest, as two men strode around the circle in front of her, waving their flashlights back and forth across the path, and then disappeared around the back of the city.

She waited, looking and listening down the circle in both directions, before darting over to the greenery on the other side.

Luha's scent continued toward the temple.

Two more blocks, she thought, her heart still beating wildly. *Well, I guess that means I have a heart*, she laughed to herself. *I don't know why I'm so scared. It can't be worse than what I've already endured.*

The Nickel Circle was busy. A few men came out of the restaurant across the path on her left, but they all headed farther down the circle away from her. When the path was empty she took her chances and dashed across.

The carillons rang midnight just as she got to the inner circle. Crouching under the greenery, she listened to a few hurrying footsteps, and the opening and closing of doors that seemed close by. She peered through the branches at the looming dark temple. The sculptures on the facets of the building across from her were dimly lit and deeply shadowed by the light coming from the outer cavern, making the figures into eerie demons.

Nina shivered.

It was getting darker as lights in the apartments around her were turned off and at last the City Cave was dark and very quiet except for the footsteps of the patrol echoing somewhere on the outer circle.

Luha's scent led to a tree next to one of the eight corners of the strange tall temple, but Luha hadn't climbed the tree.

Nima crouched on her haunches and sniffed the ground around the tree following the scent to a door in the wall to the left of the tree where a profusion of chaotic smells met her nose. Luha, men, sweat, a wide swathe of Luha scent flowing in under the door.

Luha was dragged through this door! Dragged!

Quaking with fear, she turned her black velvet face back and forth, listening for the footsteps of the patrol, still on the outer circle, and now on the far side of the city.

She's inside. How will I find her? They… they…

She tried the door. Locked.

She swung her head back and forth and up, looking, her breath coming in short gasps.

The tree.

She leaped back to the tree and scrambled up, resting for a moment in the crotch of the first branch, slowing her breath, focusing on her breath. "*Om tare tuttare ture soha.* Green Tara be with me," she whispered. "*Om tare tuttare ture soha.*"

Swinging out on a branch hanging over the parapet that surrounded the patio atop the bottom tier of the temple, she dropped down, huddling against the wall.

No light. No sound.

She loped on all fours around the octagon, first looking in and then trying each of the glass doors leading into the offices of the second tier. None of them budged.

"Back to the tree," she whispered, climbing the parapet and leaping out to hug the trunk with arms and legs.

She pulled herself up to the branch and then on up to the next branch hanging out farther but not quite over the parapet atop the second tier. The branch bent as she went hand over hand toward its thin end. Reaching up to grab the branch with her prehensile feet she thrust herself out swinging up and down until she could grab the second tier parapet with one hand. Letting go she pulled herself up and over, crouching on the patio floor for a moment to catch her breath.

Here, too, the doors were locked and the interiors dark, but she continued around trying each door hoping one would be open.

She came around a corner and pulled herself abruptly back. A light gleamed on the side of the parapet from around the next corner.

Hugging the wall of the building she moved silently to that corner.

She was shaking again. "*Om tare tuttare ture soha. Om tare tuttare ture soha,*" she whispered.

Slowly, she thought. *Move slowly just enough to see…*

The next door was closed, but there was a light on and someone was talking – almost whispering.

She sniffed the air. Luha's scent. Luhanada was in there!

Smashed up against the wall she moved as close to the door as she could, trying to overhear what was being said.

"Is there some way you could help me escape without them knowing it was you?"

"It would be better if I could do that, then they wouldn't suspect you had the flash drives."

Flash drives? thought Nima. *Computer flash drives?*

She listened a little longer. *It sounds like he's on Luha's side, like they're plotting together.*

What if I'm wrong? But it sounds like…Green Tara give me strength.

She gathered her courage and tapped very gently on the door.

Luha and Ranulf froze.

"Someone's on the patio," whispered Ranulf.

Luha's ears spread open. She opened her nostrils. A faint smell of something animal.

Ranulf moved over to the door and peered out. At first Nima moved back, instinctively hiding against the wall, but then moved slowly out so he could see her.

"A monkey!" exclaimed Ranulf.

"One of us. Let it in," Luha urged him.

He pulled out the piece of plastic holding the door closed and slid it open enough for Nima to slip in. He started to close the door again, but she put a hand on it.

"Don't close it," she whispered. Ranulf nodded, and left the door open.

Luha peered at the monkey from the edge of the cage. "You're from Ninas Twei."

"Yes," whispered Nima, crouching next to the wire. "Kuji and Peeka found me. They've found a lot of us, and we all went to Singing Swan, and then back to Tuwillia. It was decided I was the best equipped to come look for you."

"Are you like Luhanada? Someone who died?" asked Ranulf.

She turned to look at him. "Yes. But who are you?"

"He's from *Incogni*. Do you know what that is? When did you live?"

"Oh, yes, I know of *Incogni*. I've only been dead a few months." She looked at Ranulf speculatively. "You are checking up on these people, these Giants of God."

He nodded. "I've become one of them – for now."

"This is why I heard something about flash drives from outside the door."

He leaned forward eagerly. "Do you think you could get them back to the real world for me?"

Nima looked at Luha, who nodded at her. "I don't know. I can't get back there myself because I'm dead. But Kuji and Sarah…"

"But can they get back to the real world?" asked Luha. "They come from here."

"I don't know."

"I think we must try," Ranulf responded. "There's no other answer. And the internet said there're people who are alive who visit this Ninas Twei. They showed us a video in the meeting, and they spoke of Singing Swan and this turtle..."

"Tuwillia," Nima and Luha responded together.

"Yes, Tuwillia. Tomorrow there're big demonstrations."

"Demonstrations?" Nima asked, and Ranulf explained what he had learned in the Giants of God meeting where they'd looked at An Lien's video and talked about the OET demonstrations.

"People will bring totems and hope to have the chance to travel to this Ninas Twei. Perhaps some will get there. Maybe you'll be able to give them the drives to take back. I put the contact email address with the flash drives. The contact lives in Bayomar."

Nima nodded. "But how about Luha? How will we get her out of here?"

"I can't return to Ninas Twei yet." Luha began to pace. "I need to find the children. They're in the eggs, I'm sure. I need to get them out."

Ranulf nodded his head. "On the video they spoke of the children who fell. You think they're here? In the eggs? If Nima will take the flash drives, you and I can find our way to the cellars under the city and find some way to release the people from the eggs. That would be a very great thing to do."

"Do you have the key to this padlock?" Luha nodded to the lock on her cage.

"No, but..." He pulled something out of his pocket. It was one of those combination tools that fold up to the size of a pocket knife. "This has wire cutters. I don't know if they'll work, but let's try."

"They let you bring things like that through the scanner?" Luha laughed.

"Oh, yes," he grinned. "They're very manly. Many of them carry these. I made sure I had tools of very high quality, and sharp."

He knelt down in front of the cage and tried cutting one of the wires. It snapped with a click. He grinned at Luha.

"Good," she exclaimed, "but give the flash drives to Nima first. She needs to leave before something happens, and she gets caught."

Ranulf stood up and pulled out the little bag. The string that held it closed was long. "I made it so you could put it around your neck," he nodded at Luha. He handed it to Nima. She pulled it over her head and tightened it so it wouldn't fall off.

"Thank you," Ranulf whispered. "You're saving the world."

"We're all saving the world, I hope."

He nodded.

"Luha, we'll all be waiting for you. Hurry."

"I'll bring the children with me, I hope."

Nima made a thumbs-up gesture with her furry hand, and then turned and slipped out the window, loping to the nearest tree and disappearing. Ranulf turned back to the cage, and the wire clippers.

After listening for the patrol and determining it was on one of the outer circles on the other side of the city, Nima climbed down the tree across from radial Two, dashed across the inner path and headed for the park. Except for the distant sound of footsteps everything was quiet, so when she reached Nickel Circle she hesitated only for a second, looking both ways, before she dashed across the path.

As she crossed the middle of the intersection she heard a low voice from above. "Hey, Kurt, look down there."

A man leaning over a balcony high on the building across the path was looking directly at her.

She froze, then ducked into the greenery across from his building, holding very still under the bushes, peering up at the man. A second man came up next to the first one. "What?"

"I saw something cross the circle. It's in the bushes down there."

"One of the women, or one of the children?"

"It looked like a monkey. A black face, silver hair, and a very long tail." He pointed at the greenery. "It's still there. I can see it."

"You watch. I'm going down there," Kurt called as he dashed into the apartment.

Oh, no, thought Nima and took off leaping down the pathway.

When Kurt reached the street, the man on the balcony called out. "It ran toward the park. I'll get help."

Kurt sprinted toward the park.

Nima ducked under the bushes, heading for the pathway next to the canyon and the bridge. *I can't get caught. Not with these flash drives.*

When Kurt got to the end of the path he peered into the dark park, but couldn't see anything. He turned full circle wondering if the creature had turned off at the Silver or Gold Circles.

As he turned back again, he saw a flash of movement to the left, toward the gate to the bridge, but when he turned to look, there was nothing.

He had started for the path to the bridge to check it out, when Todd came running up. "Do you see it?"

Kurt pointed up toward the gate. "I thought I saw something by the gate to the bridge, but..."

"Run up there. See if there's something there." Kurt nodded and continued up the path to the gate.

The bridge was empty.

He turned in a circle calling back to Todd. "I don't see anything. It must be hiding in the park."

More men were running down the paths and Todd threw his arms out yelling to them, "Surround the park."

They ran both ways along the perimeter of the park, surrounding it on three sides, leaving only the back wall unguarded. As more and more men arrived they filled in between the others until there was a man every five feet.

Don arrived, and joined the group on the path by the canyon.

"Don," yelled Todd. "What are you doing here? Who's with the cat?"

"Ranulf's with the cat tonight," Don yelled back.

"Come here." Todd gestured with his whole arm. "Come here."

Don came trotting. Todd lowered his voice. "What if that monkey thing was up there and let the cat out, or hurt Ranulf? Get up there and find out."

Don spun around and headed for the temple.

"Okay," Todd called out. "Some of you go across the back wall there. Start closing the circle pushing it in this direction. Watch your feet. I don't think this thing is very big."

Nima tore across the bridge and the plateau, and didn't pause until she was inside the crevice, where she crouched trying to catch her breath. Looking back at the city she saw someone standing by the bridge, but he had his back to her, and was calling to someone down at the edge of the park.

She took a deep breath and scrambled up to the first ledge.

Ranulf Clips the Wires

Ranulf hadn't been clipping the wires of Luha's cage very long when they heard sounds out in the city. They looked at each other in alarm.

"Nima," whispered Luhanada.

Ranulf went out to the patio and looked over the parapet in the direction of the sounds.

There were men running down the streets toward the park. None seemed to be coming toward the temple.

He hurried back into the room, and picked up the clippers. "They're all headed to the park. Someone must have seen her. Even if they catch her, we need to be out of here to help her."

Clipping the wires of Luhanada's cage seemed a long tedious job, but the clippers were sharp and it was less than five minutes before Ranulf clipped the last wire and lifted out a panel large enough for Luhanada to slip through. She stepped out and he put the panel back, bending a few wires so that it would rest in place.

"It won't be obvious how you got out of the cage," he smiled. "They'll probably blame it on Nima, if they catch her."

He checked the patio – "They all seem to be up at the park. I don't hear anything that sounds like victory." – then the hall again, listening over the balcony hearing only the muffled voices from the park. "We'll go down the stairs, and take the elevator from the bottom floor. They heard the elevator when you came on Saturday."

They had just gotten past the Nickel floor landing when they heard one of the side doors open and slam shut, followed by running feet. Luhanada flew up to the Nickel floor and slid under one of the benches. Ranulf hesitated, then turned to run silently as he could, back up the stairs to the Silver floor. He had just reached the corridor when he heard feet in the chapel, then a voice calling, "Ranulf, are you okay?"

He moved close to the wall, and low, until he was outside of Don's office, then straightened and went over to the balcony. "Yes. Everything's fine here. What's happening? I heard a lot of running and shouting."

"Oh, someone saw something that looked like a monkey wandering in the city. They think they have it cornered in the park." Don laughed. "Weird, huh? Anyway Todd wanted me to check on you to make sure the monkey hadn't let the cat out and done something to you."

Ranulf laughed. "No. No one has let 'the cat out of the bag'." They both laughed.

"Okay, you stay here with the cat, and I'll go back to help catch the monkey." He shook his head. "Although we never had any luck with the cat in that park. They have some kind of escape route."

"Yes," nodded Ranulf. "Very weird."

He waited until he heard Don leave the building before heading back down the stairs. Luha was waiting for him on the Nickel landing.

"I'd better check to make sure he's really gone," he whispered, moving quietly down the stairs to check the Copper office where Don had come in the door. After making a thorough check of the first floor, he came back up the stairs. "You heard?"

Luhanada nodded. "I think she got away. They're searching the park, but she would have run straight for the bridge."

"Should we head for the elevator, or wait and see if she's all right."

Luha licked a paw and ran it over her face. "I think we have to count on her getting away."

Ranulf nodded. "If we can release the people in the eggs... that will create quite a diversion." He grinned, and then took a deep breath. "Let's go."

Luha followed as he moved silently down the stairs to the first floor and the elevator, whose doors stood open, waiting. He pushed the button for Cellar 1, the lowest level. The cab descended and the door slid open into a very long windowless room with thick metal pillars. Dim lights set at intervals in the low ceiling revealed huge batteries in rows coming out from the opposite wall.

"The eggs should be on the other side of this wall," Luhanada pointed out as she padded between two rows of batteries to the wall. At floor level a square metal pipe came out of the wall to the first battery, but there was no way to get through the wall to the eggs.

Ranulf was looking at the elevator set in a wide column at an angle toward the back of the room. "Angled to fit the octagon of the temple," he pointed out. "This room might go the length of the canyon under the whole city."

Luhanada's tail flicked back and forth. "I need to find the children," she growled and trotted down the room looking for an opening to the eggs. They passed the second elevator and continued to the far end of the room, still finding no opening. "And no computers," remarked Ranulf, "but I know this is all run by computers and computerized robots. They've bragged about it. A way to release the prisoners in the eggs might be found on the computers."

"They could be on one of the other floors," Luhanada pointed out, "and there might be a way to get to the eggs." Ranulf nodded, and they ran back to the second elevator.

A Murmuring Sound

Todd watched as the men gradually closed the circle around the park. "The damned monkey has to be in there," he muttered to Don, who had returned from the Temple reassuring him that Ranulf was okay and the cougar was still in her cage.

"Yeah, maybe, but I think they have some kind of escape route in the park somewhere. That's where the cougar headed and the monkey, too, and then they just disappeared."

Todd just shook his head and continued watching the circle close.

Then he added, "Kurt saw something move up by the bridge." His eyes narrowed. "But they couldn't go over the bridge."

"The gate's locked. It hasn't been tampered with."

"No." Todd stood silent for a moment looking up at the bridge. "Maybe a cougar and a monkey could get over the gate."

"But if they reached the plateau they'd be caught by the wind – and we haven't heard the wind."

"No."

"And we know the cougar didn't get caught by the wind, 'cause she's still here."

Todd pushed his hands through his hair, massaging his head for a moment. "Yeah. Wherever they go, it has to be in the park or someone's house."

The circle got smaller and smaller, the men shoulder to shoulder, some dropping back to form a second circle behind them. Finally there were six men and just a little greenery in the middle. One stepped into the middle and pushed his way through the tiny circle of greenery. Nothing was there. Todd let out a wordless growl, stamping his feet and thrusting fisted hands in the air. "Where could it go? Go search all the houses," he yelled at the men, waving his hands toward the city.

"Wait," he called out before they could turn away. "Eric, Kevin, grab a couple of Nickels and go back to the world and report this to Kas."

Eric and Kevin nodded, and grabbing two others, trotted away toward the temple.

"The rest of you go – search the houses. Go!"

He turned to Don. "Not you. You stay with me."

He stared at the park, rocking on his heels, and shaking his head. Except for occasional voices in the city, there was silence – then a different sound – a low intermittent murmuring sound, like whispers.

"Where's that sound coming from?" He turned toward the canyon.

"What sound? I don't hear it."

"No, listen." The two men stood very quietly for a moment.

"It's some of the men talking."

"No, it's not from the city." Todd walked over to the edge of the canyon peering across at the plateau on the other side. "Could they avoid the wind?"

Don peered across the canyon. "I don't see anyone on the plateau."

The murmur came again, very soft, almost not audible.

Todd's eyes got wide. "The canyon. It's down in the canyon." He stared down, looking left and then right.

"Look!" He pointed to the left. "Something moved down that way." Both men ran down the path at the edge of the canyon to the other side of the city. Todd peered through the chain link fence. "There are people down there, and they're doing something to the eggs."

Don joined him. "Are the people in the eggs getting out?"

426

Todd turned toward the temple at a run. Don followed, quickly outpacing him.

"We have to go down to the cellars. Get help," Todd yelled. "Turn out the Coppers – with guns… and if Eric and Kevin are still here, tell them what's happened. Tell them to tell Kas."

Eric and Kevin and the others were standing in the circle, just about to drink from the cups, when Don burst into the temple.

"Stop," he yelled. "People are breaking out of the eggs. Tell Kas," he yelled from the back of the chapel before turning to go get the others.

"Let's go." Eric raised his cup, and they chanted and drank, and disappeared.

2

Last Quarter, Hunter's Moon

After lunch, Shen Ch'i took An Lien to the Buddhist Center. "You don't have to come in with me, dad. Just pick me up at five. I'll stay inside the center with my friends until you come back for me. No one's going to come in the center with everyone else around." Shen Ch'i watched her roll into the center with a couple of her friends before driving back to Shanti Place.

In Arundel on Sunday morning the ministers preached about the upcoming march. Jarvis felt uncommonly enthusiastic, despite the attack on his house the day before. This was the second Sunday since his confessional sermon, and he was pleased to see he still had a reasonably sized congregation, some of them new. He preached on the unity of all life, and the problems of climate change for both humans and the other creatures who share the earth, of the millions of people dying of drought in sub-Saharan Africa, of the islands disappearing in the Indian Ocean, the huge typhoons in the Philippines. He mentioned the OET demonstrations to be held in Robertsville, and all over the world.

Afterwards some of his congregants asked him if he thought it was all right for people to participate in demonstrations. "Yes, certainly," he urged them. "A demonstration is really a form of prayer. We unite for change. If our elected officials won't listen to us, we need to make them listen by being more visible."

Some had seen the video. "I wish," one older woman confessed wistfully, "I could see the Tsin Twei."

Jarvis nodded. "Perhaps you will. Perhaps we all will someday."

She smiled. "I'm going to the demonstrations, and I know my Tla Twei – a hummingbird."

Jarvis laughed. "Yes, that suits you."

Keegan's homily was about creation and stewardship. "The OET demonstrations are really about this. I think most people, regardless of their religious beliefs, understand the need to protect our earth and its life."

Dorotea and Billy sat in the third pew. Their sad, drawn faces told him that the attempt to go to Ninas Twei the night before had not succeeded.

Coffman and his friends were also talking about the demonstration. They were sitting at a big round corner table in the restaurant out on the highway. "Bunch of hippy mongrels," Coffman ranted. "I can't believe there're people in Robertsville actually planning to demonstrate."

"We should do a counter demonstration," urged Harding.

"What's that?" Coffman leaned forward in his chair.

"It's when you demonstrate against the demonstrators."

"Hey, we could do that," exclaimed Dickerson.

Tom wiggled uncomfortably in his chair. "I'll be in school."

His grandfather looked sternly at him. "You could ditch. Some kids are going to ditch to go to the demonstration. You could ditch to go to the counter demonstration."

"I – I don't really want to."

"Well, you're going to." His grandfather nodded, and then turned toward Harding. "So, what do we do at a counter-demonstration?"

In Bayomar, the twenty-two kids who'd been at Shanti Place for breakfast were all choosing totems for their Tla Twein. Giselle didn't know if they'd finally gotten it about the dangers of the recruiters or if they were just excited about the idea of creating totems.

Deborah pulled out all the boxes of recycled and donated art materials from the supply closet, Min had started drawing totem animals for himself and his two Ikemen Ninja friends, and soon all the tables were full of young people creating collages, sculptures made of found objects, drawings, and paintings. Maria was making herself a pair of beautiful wings using scrap cloth donated by some of the women in the church. The gray cat worked his way up and down the middle of the tables, stopping to look at each totem, as if giving his approval. The kids were delighted, and argued about whose art work he liked best.

At six o'clock, just as the sun was setting, Shen Ch'i went to the Buddhist Center to pick up An Lien. He parked in the handicap spot and headed in the door to the main hall. Lots of people were milling around talking, but he couldn't see An Lien anywhere. He grabbed one of her friends. "Where's An Lien?"

The friend looked around. "She was here. Maybe she went to the Ladies."

Another woman looked around, alarmed, and said, "But that was a while ago."

Shen Ch'i moved rapidly to the little hallway back of the main room where the bathrooms were followed by several of the others.

An Lien's wheelchair was sitting empty just outside the door of the bathroom. Down the hall, a door leading to an alley behind the building was propped open. Shen Ch'i yelled, "Call the police!" as he bolted out the open door.

The alley was empty.

The others caught up to him, one still on the phone to the police dispatcher.

"Someone must have carried her," exclaimed one of the men. "Maybe someone saw them." The group scattered up and down the street asking people if they had seen anything.

Shen Ch'i pulled out his phone, punching in Giselle's number.

"They've kidnapped her," he cried out as she answered the phone. "They took her from the Buddhist Center."

"Where are you – where is the Center?" Giselle asked.

"Just a few blocks from you, on Tenth and Washington."

"I'm coming." She turned to Sidney. "They've got An Lien!"

"Who's got An Lien?" Rashaun exclaimed.

"Bad guys. People who are against the march, we think. They tried to take her Tuesday, but I was there and we scared them away. Now somehow they got her from the Buddhist Center."

She grabbed her backpack. "I'm headed there now." The cat barred her way until she picked him up in her arms. He crawled up to her shoulder.

The dogs stayed at her heels.

"I'm with you," Sidney headed to the door.

"Me, too," Miesha jumped from her seat, followed by most of the rest of the kids and their dogs. Giselle held one hand on the cat as she tried to keep up with Sidney, the dogs, and the others who were running down Tenth Street toward the Buddhist Center.

When they turned the corner of Tenth and Washington, a police car was already there.

"Whoa." Sidney held up his hands, pushing the group back around the corner. "They see us, they going to think we trouble, not help."

Giselle nodded. "You stay here.

She dashed around the corner, her dogs at her heels, and down the block to where Shen Ch'i stood talking to the officer, surrounded by An Lien's friends from the Center.

"But this isn't the first attempt," Shen Ch'i was explaining. "They tried to get her on Tuesday, but Giselle stopped them." He gestured toward Giselle as she approached. "She saw the men. They called the police. You have a record of it."

"One of them was a man we caught taking pictures at the OET meeting the night before," added Giselle.

"Why would anyone kidnap An Lien?" one woman asked.

"Because she did the research," explained a woman who had been at the OET meeting. "She traced subsidiary companies doing damage to the earth and humans back to just a few corporations."

"And they're afraid," added Giselle. "They're afraid of what she might find."

The officer glared at her, and then turned back to Shen Ch'i. "As I said, sir," he explained impatiently, "we can't take a missing person report until the person has been gone for twenty-four hours."

He glanced at Giselle and threw out, "Those dogs need to be on a leash."

Giselle signaled the dogs and they sat by her feet.

"This is not a 'missing person' report," Shen Ch'i growled. "She was kidnapped. Her wheelchair is still there. She can't walk away. She had to have been carried."

One of An Lien's friends came running from a store across the street, yelling, "They saw a car in the alley. A black car with tinted windows. It turned right on Washington."

The officer glared at him. "You just jaywalked."

"What?" exclaimed another man. "He's bringing you important information about a kidnapping and you're accusing him of jaywalking? What's your badge number?"

"It's 742," a man facing the officer called out.

"You have no proof of a kidnapping," the officer declared, officiously.

"You should at least come in and look at the empty wheelchair," added one woman.

"There might be fingerprints," another one agreed. "There isn't time to wait until tomorrow."

The officer held his hands up, palms out. "Calm down, all of you. An empty chair doesn't mean she didn't go willingly. We have to wait twenty-four hours."

Giselle stood there listening. *That's bullshit,* she thought. *This guy is stalling.* Some of the others said it out loud, and one added, "Who's paying you?"

She reached a hand out to Shen Ch'i. "We're wasting time. He's not going to help. We need to find her ourselves."

The officer glared at her. "You planning to take the law into your own hands, young lady?"

"I plan to find my friend," she answered, and the music came faintly from the earth beneath the sidewalk in a long crescendo.

> *Breath, flowing through the depths of the earth,*
> *Grow, grow in me.*
> *Grow in me!*

Her eyes bored into the officer and she grew taller, her roots thrusting down through the pavement as the shadow tree formed around her, its leafy crest reaching up and up to tower over the gasping crowd.

The cat perched in the crotch of the lowest branch, very real against the translucent tree.

The officer's eyes got wide and he backed toward his car. Jumping into the driver's seat, he gunned the engine, nearly sideswiping another car as he swerved around the corner.

As soon as the police car was out of sight, Sidney and the Shanti kids ran to join Shen Ch'i. They stared up at the tree, clapping their hands and yelling, "All right, Giselle!"

The rest of the group just stood open-mouthed. One of An Lien's friends, who had seen Giselle in the shadow tree at the OET meeting, turned to the man next to her, whispering, "I told you so."

As the shadow melted away and Giselle became Giselle again, the group broke out into excited talk, quickly silenced when a woman raised a hand and called out, "That's not important right now. We need to find An Lien."

"What should we do?" Miesha asked.

Shen Ch'i just looked at Giselle, tears rolling down his cheeks. He shook his head, "I don't know what to do."

Giselle looked around her at the silent crowd. She closed her eyes and whispered, "Yameno, I need you."

A shadow began to form beside her and the crowd gasped.

She felt a wet nose touch her hand. "An Lien," she whispered to the shadowy wolf. "They've kidnapped An Lien."

> *I'm coming,* he sang, *I am the hunter.*
> *I am the seeker and I'm coming.*

As he sang, the huge umbrous wolf darkened and became real, his head pointing high toward the darkening sky, his voice an eerie howl.

> *I am the lone, the many, the mirror.*
> *My call is like lightning, jagged and bright.*

The crowd backed up in awed silence.

"Show us where she was taken," the wolf demanded, and Shen Ch'i led them down the alley to the back door and into the building where the wheelchair stood forlorn in the hallway.

The dogs formed a pack behind the wolf, pulling their leashed kids behind them. They sniffed the air and the ground in and around the wheelchair and followed the scent into the alley.

"There were two people – one carrying her – and yes, they got into a car. We have their scent and the car's, but it's hard to follow the car – the exhaust fumes destroy the scent."

He looked around at the dogs who wagged their tails and yipped anxiously. "Maybe all of us together…"

The Shanti kids and dogs gathered around Yameno Wolfwind as he outlined a plan. "We'll have to go down the street itself," he pointed out to the young people, Giselle and Shen Ch'i. "You'll have to have lookouts on the sidewalks for cars, and especially the police. Release the dogs."

The kids all unleashed their dogs, and Giselle signaled her two to join them.

More than an hour had passed since An Lien had disappeared.

She thought she was in a dark room, but the blindfold made it hard to know. A musty room. They'd dropped her on the floor, her hands taped in front of her and left. She'd squirmed and her head hit something like a cardboard box. How long would it be before her dad and Giselle would know she'd been taken?

The meditation had ended at five, but her dad wasn't supposed to come 'til six – after the chat and refreshments. She'd gone to the bathroom almost immediately after the meditation and she was just rolling out of the ladies when the men came up behind her, one slapping a large adhesive bandage across her mouth before she even knew he was there. She'd struggled and tried to scream as another grabbed her arms and taped them together, then scooped her out of her chair, running down the hall and down the stairs to the alley. He'd thrust her into the backseat of a car and they got in on either side of her, barely closing the doors before the car moved out of the alley and down Washington Street. One was the man with the camera. While she was staring at him, the other one had tied a scarf over her eyes.

She went back over what she knew about the route they'd taken. Some blocks down Washington, left turn, several blocks, and then right. It wasn't long before they turned left and then parked.

Then they'd lifted her again, and carried her right and then left, then through a door and up an elevator. No way to know how many floors. Then they dumped her in this room. She closed her eyes and waited.

She heard a door open. Someone picked her up again. A big man who smelled of sweat. Out the door and then on carpet a few steps, back in the elevator. Up again.

434

Someone knocked on a door. The door opened with a soft swish – moving over thicker carpet, she thought – and she was carried through and lowered into an armchair. "Take off the mask and the gag," a deep older voice commanded. "And unbind her arms, too."

"She'll see you," one of the men exclaimed.

"She's not going anywhere to tell anyone," responded the deep voice.

Oh, god, thought An Lien, as the scarf was pulled off and then the adhesive ripped painfully off her face and arms. She was sitting in a high backed armchair in front of a huge mahogany desk in a very big, very plush office. Wide windows on three sides looked out at the sea and the city. The two men who'd kidnapped her and the driver remained standing behind her. Two men in suits stood on either side of a white haired man who sat behind the desk. She recognized him from pictures she's seen on the internet – Kasimir Goddard, CEO of Goldstream Oil.

They looked each other over. He spoke first. "I'm sure you know who I am." An Lien just shrugged.

"I know who you are. I know everything about you and your research for OET," he continued.

"She's also the one who put up that video about the Ninas Twei place and the totems and that tree woman," interrupted one man.

Goddard glared at him. "We're not interested in nonsense, Howie."

An Lien turned to look at Howie. He was the man who took the video at the OET meeting. She grinned. "You got to feel the wrath of the Tree Woman, didn't you?"

"Enough!" Kas demanded. "I want to know what information you've already given the OET and what you were going to take to the meeting tonight. It would be wise if you would just tell me." He glanced at her legs. "You've already experienced a lot of violence in your young life. I don't think you're interested in experiencing more."

An Lien laughed. "You've already told these men that I'm not – and I quote – 'going anywhere to tell anyone.'"

"Well, yes," he smiled. "But the difference is how much pain you experience along the way."

An Lien rolled her eyes. "Are you trying to sound like a mob boss?"

Kas slammed a hand on his desk. "That's enough. Doug, do your thing."

The man who'd carried her moved around the chair, pulled her up by the front of her shirt and slapped her hard across the face. She felt tears come into her eyes and blinked rapidly.

"Are you ready to talk?"

She shrugged. "The most exciting stuff I've found has been about Ninas Twei."

Goddard slammed the desk again. "Bullshit! That stuff is a bunch of bullshit. Hit her again."

This time the man back handed her, sending her head into the padded chair with a thump. She couldn't stop the tears.

"What do you want?" she screamed. "I didn't find anything you don't already know. I told most of what I know that night at the meeting and you video'd it. You know what I found."

Goddard just nodded at Doug. This time he hit her in her right breast with his fist, and then the left one. *Oh, my god, that hurts,* she thought, her upper body stiff with pain, tears streaming down her face. *What can I do? What can I do?* Suddenly his fist slammed into her face and she felt herself floating on the edge of consciousness. *Unconscious,* she thought. *If they think I'm unconscious...*

He punched her again smashing her head back. Her head bounced forward, but she forced herself to slump against the back of the chair, willing all her muscles to relax, and letting her mind slip into a meditative state. Her breathing became shallow. Her arms limp. She could feel the blood dripping out of her nose.

Dog Dance

The wolf, the dogs, and the humans formed a strange shadowy choreography as they moved down Washington Street in the deepening night, followed in the van by Shen Ch'i and the gray cat. The wolf and dogs moved back and forth across the right hand lane of the street, some with noses to the ground and others sniffing the air. Occasionally one gave a small howl and the others converged on the spot where a small hint of scent had been found. At the intersections, two dogs branched off to the left and two to the right to make sure the kidnap vehicle had not turned.

The soft patter of running feet and the even softer slow steady padding of the paws formed a rhythmic background to the whispered panting of the dogs:

We are the hunters, the seekers, the finders,
We slip through the night like a shadow.
You leave your essence to spin through the air
And we point our muzzles to follow.

An occasional yip, accented the rhythm as the dogs sighed:

to follow, to follow, to follow.

The humans spread out along the sidewalks, two staying at each corner watching for police until the others reached the intersection and then running quickly to guard the next corners.

When Rashaun sang out, "Police," all of them – dogs, wolf, and humans – melted into alleys and doorways until the patrol car, driving slowly, the officers looking from side to side, disappeared down Washington, finally turning off four or five blocks ahead of them.

"They getting reports of us from some of the drivers passing us," Sidney muttered. The big wolf nodded, as they all moved out into position, and the dance continued:

We are the hunters, the seekers, the finders,
We slip through the night like a shadow.
We follow, we follow, we follow.

Several blocks later, the dogs moving down an intersection to the left, sounded, and they all turned and flowed south on Fifth Street for three blocks before finding the car had turned again, this time west on Cutter Street.

"Cutter Street be less traveled," Sidney informed Shen Ch'i, as the dance continued.

Giselle looked around. "The OET meeting isn't far from here. Maybe someone there will know something helpful," she said, jumping in the van beside Shen Ch'i. He swerved off on Third Street to head to the church where the meeting was held, while the rest continued their search down Cutter St.

"Shit, you knocked her unconscious," Howie exclaimed.

"I guess she's weaker than we thought – because she's a gimp," the driver suggested.

"How long'll she be out?" Kas asked.

"Don't know," Doug muttered.

She heard Kas' desk chair move.

"The hell with this. She's probably telling the truth. She didn't find out anything else."

Soft footsteps on the rug.

"Let's get dinner. Just leave her there. She can't go anywhere without her wheelchair. We'll lock the office. Doug, you go to that OET meeting and find out what's going on there. You two take turns guarding outside the tower door and getting some dinner yourselves. The biggest danger is other people figuring out where she is. Call us if there's a problem. We'll be back in a couple of hours."

There was some shuffling and the door opened and closed.

An Lien stayed still listening for a long time. She couldn't hear any breathing. Slowly she lifted her eyelids a tiny slit to peer out through her eyelashes. No one in front of her. Slowly and stiffly she turned her head and her upper body looking around the room. No one. Sliding off the chair to the floor, she dragged herself to the door, crying as her bruised breasts rubbed against the rug, her bleeding nose dripping on the rug.

She lay still to breathe before straining to reach the knob. It was locked.

Turning toward the nearest windows, she pulled herself slowly, weeping, bleeding, across the long expanse of rug, stopping often to rest and breathe. It was getting harder and harder.

"Come on, An Lien," she whispered to herself. "You're strong. You can do this."

She reached a straight chair close to a window, pulling and pushing it until it sat sideways to the window, and then pulled herself up on it, twisting around so she could look out.

It was a long way down! The windows didn't open and everything was empty – the parking lot, the streets beyond it. If she could find some way to signal, there wasn't anyone out there to see her.

"No, no…" she whimpered.

Looking back at the desk, she could just see a laptop and a cordless phone.

Sobbing, she dropped to the floor and forced herself to drag her body back across the room to Kas' chair, trying hard not to scream out loud as her battered breasts twisted as she pulled.

The chair was on wheels and could be tipped back, making it hard to secure so she could climb up, but finally she managed by propping it against the desk. She sat back with a moan of exhaustion and pain, tears still pouring down her face.

Can't stop, she thought, sitting up, turning the chair to face the desk, and reaching for the phone.

No dial tone.

She pushed different buttons, but nothing happened.

Opening the laptop she pushed the start button. A green light glowed.

While the computer loaded she thought about the password. He thought of himself as the oil king. His company produced 6.2 million barrels a day. There were eight direct subsidiaries, and twenty-two indirect ones. The screen lit up. She tried various combinations, adding some symbols as she went. "Oilking1", "Oilking1!6.2", "6.2oilking1+8", "kingoil1!6.2", and more. Nothing. She sat back. *I give up,* she thought. *I'm just going to die.*

Then she remembered. He had a new grandson named Peter. She tried "peter6.2oilking!".

"Welcome," the computer read.

"Welcome yourself," she whispered, as she searched the desktop for the browser and clicked. The screen flashed, "Server not found."

Oh, god, she muttered, glancing at the bottom of the screen. A big red X over the internet icon. No internet connection. She clicked on the icon, going to the Network and Sharing Center. Nothing listed. *With all these businesses around here, how can there be no wifi?*

Blocked! It's all blocked. They turned off the phone. They turned off the wifi. She sat back in her chair, tears slipping down her face again. There was no way out of here, and no way to communicate with her dad.

Kasimir Goddard. What was he doing here? The main offices of Goldstream Oil were in the Midsouth. She'd never seen an address listed in Bayomar.

There's something important I've never found, she thought. *That's why he kidnapped me. He thinks I know it. On this computer maybe?*

She scrolled through his files. Lots of stuff under Documents, but she couldn't tell what it was.

She searched the desk drawers, holding on with one hand while leaning down to reach into the bottom drawers. At the back of the left bottom drawer she felt something small and oblong, like a pocket knife.

It slipped out of her fingers twice as she tried to pull in out where she could see it. Hanging limp over the arm of the chair she rested just a moment, closing her eyes, breathing. Breathing.

Once again she grabbed the edge of the desk with one hand and reached deep into the drawer, found the object and this time managed to pull it out.

Not a knife. A flash drive.

"Yes," she whispered as she plugged it in.

Empty. But I can use it...

She copied all the documents on to the little drive, then stuffed it into her bra. *Maybe if they kill me they won't find it, and they'll dump my body someplace and someone else will find it. Maybe my dad.*

She pushed the computer back and laid her head on folded arms on the desk and sobbed.

The OET meeting had just started, when Giselle and Shen Ch'i hurried into the room. A young man holding a bicycle helmet was speaking.

"I found out something important. I saw that man who was filming at the last meeting the very next day after the meeting and I think he's connected to some of those corporations An Lien was talking about."

He looked around. "Where is she?"

Giselle interrupted him, running down the aisle and up the ramp to the stage. "An Lien has been kidnapped and that man – the one you're talking about – is connected to it."

She turned to the audience telling them about the attack Tuesday night and about An Lien's disappearance from the Buddhist Center.

"I saw him," repeated the young man, excitedly. "I'm a bike messenger and I saw him at the Seaview Business Park. I was delivering a package to one of the businesses and he got into the elevator in the main tower. And there's more," he called out as the room erupted with noise.

"Go on," Giselle commanded, holding up a hand for silence.

"I looked at the directory and all the offices on the upper floors were just numbers, no names. I asked the receptionist where I was making the delivery about them, and she said she had thought it was weird, too, and had done some investigating. The top floor, she found out is Goldstream Oil. That's one of the corporations An Lien mentioned, but it's located in the Midsouth, and...", he looked around the room, "...on the floors below are offices for Wiebe Armaments and Tutiso Security. The receptionist couldn't find out about any of the others, but she thinks that the LCU – you know, the Legislative Committee for Uhs – holds its executive meetings there. Once a man asked her where the LCU executive meeting was, and someone nearby turned around and pulled the man away from her."

He took a breath. "Not their general meetings. They hold those at big resorts and all the legislators and media executives who come to it are wined and dined."

"But Wiebe Armaments is located in the Southeast," a man called out.

"Yes, I know," the bike messenger answered. "So why do they have an office here, with no name on the directory?"

"Where is this business park?" Shen Ch'i interrupted.

"Right on the water at the end of Cutter Street."

Giselle looked at Shen Ch'i. "Yameno and the kids are on Cutter Street."

"Let's go," Shen Ch'i grabbed Giselle's hand and ran for the van.

The bike messenger yelled, "Come on!" and everyone streamed out the door after him.

They were followed by two silent men, each pulling out a cell phone as he went to his car. One was Doug. "Some bicycle messenger saw Howie there," he was muttering into the phone.

The other one went to an unmarked police car. "They're headed for Seaview Business Park. Standby in case I need backup."

It was dark and silent, as only a deserted Sunday night in a business district can be, when Yameno and the dogs reached the end of Cutter Street and discovered scent at the entrance of the parking lot of the business park. They began a silent search of the dimly lit lot and found the lingering scent of the car in one of the spaces in front of the central tower, but the car was no longer there.

The Wolfwind loped to the locked door of the main entrance. There was no scent of An Lien or either of the two men. He turned as several vehicles pulled into the parking area – Shen Ch'i's van, followed by the bike messenger, a group of runners and other bicyclists, and cars full of OET members.

He loped over to them as they parked, and told Shen Ch'i and Giselle what they had found. The crowd gathered silently around them.

"There must be other doors," Shen Ch'i muttered, moving toward the tower.

Wolfwind nodded and signaled to the dogs.

The Shanti kids and the dogs split and headed around the building.

Several dogs yipped, accompanied by, "Sh-h-h," from their owners.

"Over here," Sidney signaled and they all converged by the side door, where the dogs had a wide-eyed Howie cornered, his cell phone plastered to his ear.

Wolfwind greeted the dogs, licking their muzzles as they wagged anxiously, eyes only for the wolf.

"Good job," he whispered to them, before turning to the humans. "This is one of the men who took An Lien, and the scent of the other man and someone else is strong on the ground here. There's some fainter air scent of An Lien, too."

Howie was whimpering into the phone, "The wolf. It's the wolf." He dropped the hand clutching the phone. "He doesn't believe it, but you're real. You're real."

The wolf grinned at him, tongue hanging out between his large teeth and Howie cowered even closer to the door, his eyes scanning the angry crowd. His hand groped back of him for the handle, jiggling it, and pulling. It was locked.

At the back of the parking lot the plain clothes officer whispered into his phone. "They're trying to break in. Send backup."

"How do we get in?" Miesha asked. She looked around, distracted by the sound of sirens in the distance.

"Search him," demanded Shen Ch'i. "He must have a key."

"No, no, I don't," the man muttered. "He's the only one who has the key, now."

"Who is 'he'?" Wolfwind asked.

"A wolf that talks," the man whined. "He won't believe me."

Giselle moved up to him, the gray cat glaring imperiously from her shoulder. "Just answer."

"Tree woman," the man whispered.

"Who has the key?" she demanded again, grabbing his arm.

"Kasimir. Kasimir Goddard."

"Where is he?"

"Eating dinner. I don't know where. He just said they were going to dinner."

"Is An Lien inside here?"

The man nodded. "Up the elevator. Eighth floor."

Giselle backed up looking at the side of the building. The only light was in the lobby by the front door.

One of the OET members out in the parking lot, called out, "Up there," pointing at the top of the tower.

Giselle backed more until she reached a small dense grove of ornamental firs at the edge of the lot. She saw another very small light, blue-white like the light of a computer screen, on the top floor.

A voice came whispering out of the dark grove behind her.

> *I am the singer, I am the weeper.*
> *You are the leader, the edge of the knife.*

Deep in the shadows, her cloak wrapped tight around her swirling skirts, her big eyes gleaming out at Giselle, was Ayoabia.

Giselle looked up the side of the eight-story building and back at Ayoabia. She reached up to touch the cat and nodded at the woman.

> *I am the leader, the edge of the knife.*

Holding the cat tight to her neck, she ran back to the building. Stretching her arms up the side of the tower, pushing her toes into the sidewalk, she sang out:

> *Breath,*
> *Live in the wind-whipped grasses,*
> *Merge with my feet and let me grow...*

Her roots broke through the cement sinking down, down into the earth. Her branches spread up and up, past the second and third floors. The muffled cheers from the parking lot were just a background hum as she focused on the wall. Her left arm became a thick branch reaching out and up. She found herself peering into the dark fourth floor, and then the fifth, the sixth and seventh, until she reached the window where a small light glowed from a computer on a giant desk across the room.

At the back of the parking lot the policeman was on the phone again. "This is... You won't believe it. Just hurry," he whispered.

On the other side of the lot Doug was also on the phone. "Cops are coming. I'm leaving," and he drove silently away.

The cat let out a large, "Merowl," and An Lien jumped where she sat slumped and dozing in the big desk chair. She turned the chair toward the window and laughed and cried. "Giselle! Giselle!"

Giselle called back. "Stay there. Wait!" as she bent the largest limb – once her right arm – back, twisting the branches at the end into a thick point. The cat scampered up the limb that had been her left arm, climbing high up into the next fork, digging his claws in, and wrapping his tail around the biggest branch. Giselle pulled the right limb back farther and smashed it like a battering ram into the window, pulling it back to smash it again and again. Finally a crack appeared and then a spider's web of cracks with a small hole in the middle. Again and again she hammered at it, until the window shivered into small pieces and fell to the floor. She straightened the limb, stretching it across the room, forking into two sturdy branches as it went. "Come carefully," she called.

As An Lien slipped off the chair, the branches folded around her just under her arms, lifted her above the floor and the shattered glass, and back to the window, bending so that she was pulled into the trunk of the tree just below Giselle's head. The cat scrambled down next to the battered young woman and patted her gently.

"Oh my god, your face," whispered Giselle.

"Oh, my dear An Lien," and she cuddled her close as she shrank back down and down, until she was able to pass An Lien into her father's arms.

"Daddy," whispered An Lien, "don't cry. I'm okay. Don't cry."

"Where's Goddard?" yelled an OET member.

He was echoed by others as the crowd moved forward, angry. "Look what he did to her..." "Is that man one of the kidnappers?"

Howie flattened himself against the door. The distant sirens got louder as they turned onto Cutter Street.

Giselle held up a hand. The Wolf stood next to her as she stood between the crowd and the frightened man. "Remember, we can't let their violence drive us to violence. If we want a world without violence, we must model it!"

444

"I have a flash drive!" An Lien called out triumphantly. "I copied all the files on his computer!"

The crowd laughed and clapped.

Miesha called out, "An Lien, you the best!"

Two police cars, lights flashing, sirens screaming, came roaring into the parking lot honking as they cut a path through the crowd.

The officers jumped out, yelling, "What's going on here?"

Shen Ch'i noticed, wearily, that one of the officers was badge 742.

"An Lien was kidnapped," called out an OET member. "The tree woman rescued her." "They beat her up," yelled another man, and the crowd erupted. "You need to arrest them..." "It was that Kasimir Goddard..." "They have one of them and he can tell you..."

"Shut up! Shut up!" yelled 742 and pulled his gun.

The crowd froze, but the other officer, badge 631, put a hand his shoulder. "Put it away," he muttered in a low voice. "Back up's coming."

He waited until the gun was holstered before turning towards Shen Ch'i and seeing An Lien, still cuddled in her father's arms, for the first time. His eyes narrowed. "Oh my god," he muttered. "What happened to her? What did they do to her?"

The crowd started yelling again. "She was kidnapped..." "Look at her. Look what they did to her..." "Kasimir Goddard..." More sirens were roaring into the parking lot, police emerging from the cars, running to the sides of the crowd, rifles in hand.

Giselle planted her roots, whispering, *Breath, Breath...*

As she grew, she called out, "Stop, please!"

Badge 631's eyes opened wide while 742 yelled at him, "I told you. I told you there was a tree woman."

Two of the police on the perimeter dropped their rifles, while others went into a crouch, aiming at Giselle.

Badge 631 stepped between Giselle and the other police, his arms open. "Put your guns down. These people are peaceful. This woman," he gestured at An Lien, "has been hurt."

"Who hurt her?" a police captain called out as he moved forward, glancing once at the tree woman, and then looking away.

The crowd began shouting, "Kasimir Goddard..." "Some thug of Goddard's..."

The captain turned to the crowd and shouted back, "That's ridiculous. Goddard is a respected business man. You people need to get yourselves under control!"

The woman who had moderated the last OET meeting stepped forward and turned to the crowd, raising her hands for silence. "We have work to do. We have a march to plan. We'll reveal the truth there."

An Lien spoke up. "Please return to the meeting. Please. I need to go home."

The woman turned back to the captain. "We're leaving. Please let us go peacefully."

The captain waved his hands at her and the crowd dismissively. "Go. GO!"

The police lowered their guns and the crowd turned, returning to their cars, offering those who had run a ride back, with the bicyclists leading the way to the church.

The captain turned to Shen Ch'i, grimacing for a moment as he looked at An Lien and then averting his eyes. He seemed to be pretending the huge tree woman and the wolf at her side didn't exist. "You're trespassing here. You'd better get these kids out of here before we arrest them."

Shen Ch'i nodded stiffly and walked to the van. Officer 631 moved ahead of him, opening the door so that Shen Ch'i could place An Lien tenderly on the seat. "I'm so sorry," he whispered. "She needs to go to the hospital. The Captain should have..."

"It's okay," An Lien assured him. "I want to go home."

Sidney and the others slipped back into the shadows to make the trek back to Shanti Place and the police roared out of the parking lot leaving Howie – ignored where he stood flattened against the door – the strange tree woman, and the wolf behind.

"Can you stay? Will you melt away again?" Tree Woman whispered to Yameno her twigs tangled in the fur of his ruff.

"I'll try," he reached up to lick her face.

They loped across the highway to the beach, running through the cleansing sea breezes, weeping, talking, becoming One – earth and tree, wind and wolf and water – before the wolf faded to shadow and disappeared, and Giselle made her way back home, the gray cat cuddled in her arms and the dogs striding on either side of her.

"He'll never believe me," Howie muttered as he waited for Kasimir Goddard to return. "I'll kill them. Someday I'll kill them. When he sees them dead..."

"A wolf with a pack of dogs and kids," Kasimir Goddard yelled. "And the tree again, only this time it's not a shadow. It's real and it grows up tall enough to break my window with a branch and snatch the woman out the window."

He paced back and forth across the office, shivering at the sea breeze coming from the broken window, finally turning back to Howie. "And you expect me to believe this? Are you a spy? Are you in cahoots with these people?"

"No, no," the man pleaded. "I'm not. It's all true. Doug saw it."

"Doug's not here."

"The police saw the tree. And... And..." Howie pointed at the computer, still open on the desk. "She said she'd copied all the files on your computer."

"Who said it?" roared Kasimer, plopping himself in his chair and pulling the computer toward him. He turned to one of the men in suits and pointed to the door. "Go turn the phone connection and the wifi back on."

"The gimp. She told the whole crowd of them after the tree handed her over to her dad."

Goddard ran his finger over the touch pad.

"It's open," he yelled. "She got past my password. How could she get past my password?"

"It's magic," Howie mumbled.

Ridiculous!

Kas called an emergency meeting of all the Golds. Since they needed to meet in person rather than trusting the phones to be secure, they couldn't all get to Bayomar from their offices all over Uhs before Monday night.

"I was stupid," he berated himself. "I underestimated her. And I overestimated Howie. The idiot. We can't report the theft to the police without taking the chance of them believing we kidnapped the girl."

Stuart shook his head. "I know Howie's story sounds… unbelievable, but there is that stuff about the cougar happening at the cavern."

"Also ridiculous, Stuart." Kas glared at Stuart.

"How do you think they got into your office – broke that window?"

"A ladder. I don't know," Kas yelled. He was interrupted as someone hammered on the door. It burst open and Eric and Kevin ran into the room.

"We've come from Todd," exclaimed Kevin.

"Yes?" Kas looked at them expectantly.

"People are breaking out of the eggs!" Eric's eyes were wide.

"And there was a monkey we couldn't catch," added Kevin.

"What?" Stuart shook his head incredulously. "A monkey?"

"Wait, wait." Kas held his hands up for silence. "First, the eggs. Then the monkey."

Kevin looked at Eric who shrugged. "We don't know much. Don just ran into the chapel as we were about to leave to come tell you about the monkey. He yelled we should tell you people were breaking out of the eggs, and then ran out again."

Stuart leaned forward. "They can just turn off the elevators. There's no way anyone can get out of the canyon except by using the elevators."

He turned to Kas. "They should return – or someone should return and tell them to turn off the elevators and guard them right away. Use the elevator key in the slot that says 'On/Off' at the bottom of the panel."

"Yeah," Seb added. "The best defense is at the top of the elevators. I hope they don't try to go down there."

He drummed his fingers on the table top. "I can take some small drones in, send them down the canyon, and wipe them out."

"One of you get some people and get back there to tell them to lock the elevators. Eric, you go. Kevin, you stay to tell us about the monkey. Go…" Kas waved a hand dismissively and Eric took off.

"And now," Kas rolled his eyes and waved Kevin to a chair. "Now, the monkey."

3

Reunion

Enid was shaking as she crouched behind the post listening to the elevator come to a stop. The floor indicator blinked "C2". *This floor,* she thought.

The door opened. Toward the bottom of the elevator, something like a head moved slowly to the edge of the door, turning first one way and then the other.

But what kind of head is that, she thought. *Not human.* It moved a little farther out. *A cougar! It was Aunt Hazel – Luhanada!*

Enid started to jump up. Jesús grabbed her, putting a hand over her mouth, and pulling her back. "A man behind her," he whispered into her ear.

Luha froze and her head started up, facing the direction of the sound. Ranulf stood beside her, holding the elevator door open. *Whispers… and breathing. Lots of breathing all around us.*

She turned her head first one way and then the other, her nostrils flaring. *People. Nervous people. Hiding,* she thought. *Are they lying in wait for us?*

She caught a scent. *Behind that metal column. Enid! And Jesús, too!*

Enid pushed Jesús' hand off her mouth. There were only two of them – Luha and that man. It looked like they were signaling each other with their heads.

Moving her finger in front of her mouth, she pushed down on Jesús' shoulder. *Stay here.*

She stood up and moved out into the room. "Luhanada?"

Luha moved warily out of the elevator. "Enid, are you all right? Is this a trap?"

"Not for you," exclaimed Enid, rushing forward to give her a hug.

Jesús stood up, still wary. "Is that really her? Why is she still a cougar? We changed when we fell here."

Luhanada looked at him, sighing. "It's a long story. Not a happy story."

Dario and the others moved out of their hiding places and stood between the elevator, and Luhanada and Ranulf. "Is this man someone you know?" he asked Enid and Jesús. "Is he on our side? And this animal...?"

Enid stood very straight, a hand on Luhanada's back. "This is my Aunt Hazel. She's a cougar sometimes. She's on our side."

"Your aunt?" Dirk exclaimed incredulously.

Enid folded her arms across her chest, raised her chin and glared at him. "Yes, my aunt."

"It's a cat," he sneered, taking a step toward her just as the small dinging of a watch chiming the hour interrupted.

"Three o'clock," Dario informed them. "Rest period."

Sister Maureen started laughing. "Well, I don't care who she is if she's on our side. We need to find food and a way out of here now. We can find out about the talking aunt cougar later."

"The elevators are the only way down," Luha told them, flicking her tail. "We need to hold the doors open so they can't be called to one of the upper floors."

"The men hardly ever go down here," Ranulf added. "They brag about it being automatic, but that will change as soon as they know Luhanada's escaped and I'm gone."

They propped the doors open on one elevator, and since Luha and Ranulf hadn't seen any food on the first floor, three people took the other one up to C3 propping the door open and pressing the call button for C2 before looking for food.

Soon everyone was talking to Luha as if she were an ordinary human. Enid knelt down to hug her. "Oh, Luhanada, I'm so glad you're here."

"Me, too, Enid," Luha purred. "Me, too."

Todd ran as fast he could up radial One toward the temple, stopping twice to catch his breath and then yell, "To the temple, to the temple." By the time he got to the steps up to the front doors, he had a stitch in his side and was wheezing. He tried to keep moving up the stairs, leaning heavily on the wall.

"Elevators," he managed to say as several men came running up beside him, "meet at the elevators." One of the men stopped to help him, while the others ran on into the building and down the corridors to the elevators. When Todd got to one of the elevators the men were standing outside the door looking at the lit floor indicator above it. "Someone's using it. Look!" The elevator was on C2.

"Call it!" Todd gasped. "Call it up here," and he turned, running down the corridor to the other elevator, careening off the walls as he went around the corners of the octagon. Don came running out of the chapel, and they nearly collided. "They're in that elevator," yelled Todd, pointing back the way he had come. "There's someone down in the cellars using that elevator."

Someone yelled from the other end of the corridor, next to the second elevator. "This one, too. Someone is in this one on C3."

Todd and Don arrived next to them. "Call it!" Todd yelled.

"We have," answered one of the men. "So far it isn't moving."

Todd started slamming a fist against the door, yelling obscenities.

"What's going on?" one man muttered quietly to Don.

"People are breaking out of the eggs. We saw them down in the canyon." All the men's eyes got wide and a few of them added their own expletives to Todd's rant.

Todd got silent and stared up at the ceiling. "That cougar. Is that cougar still in her cage?"

Don headed for the stairs at a run, taking the stairs two at a time, yelling Ranulf's name as he went.

There was no answer.

He reached the Silver tier and stumbled down the corridor to his office, almost falling through the door into the empty room.

No Ranulf, and even more surprising, no cougar.

Tripping over a chair he reached the side of the cage and stared at it. The padlock was still on the door. Locked.

"How did she get out?" he muttered. "How could she get out?" He spun in a circle. "What did she do with Ranulf?"

"Don, what the hell is happening up there?" Todd yelled from the chapel.

He walked numbly out to the corridor and knelt on the bench, looking over the edge and down at Todd.

Leaning heavily on the balustrade, he called out, "They're not here. The padlock is still on the door of the cage, but she's not in it, and Ranulf is not here either. She's done something to Ranulf."

"No!" screamed Todd. "NO!" He ran back into the hallway. "Search the building. All of you. Search the building for the cat and Ranulf." He stopped one man. "Ring the bells. Get everyone here."

He heard chanting in the chapel. *"We are the descendants of those Sons of God, we are the Giants. It is we who shall inherit the earth."*

"Eric's back," Don called from the balcony. Todd leaned against the wall a moment, holding his head, and then turned back to the chapel.

Eric was coming quickly up the aisle to meet him. "They say to lock the elevators," he called out. "If the elevators are locked the people can't get out of the canyon. Sebastian will come later and get them with drones."

Todd turned back to the elevator. He looked along the sides and across the top for a key hole of some kind. "How do I lock the elevator?"

Eric came up next to him. "The lock is inside the cab at the bottom of the panel. You have to call the elevator here.

Todd stared at him incredulously.

"What?" muttered Eric. "What's wrong?"

There was a long silence, and then one of the other men spoke up. "They have the elevators. We've tried calling them, but they won't come. They're in the cellars."

Below them on C2 and C3 the escapees were busy. "Hey, hey," came a muffled shout down the hole above the bay closest to the first elevator. Dario ran over and looked up. One of the men who'd gone up to the third floor was peering down the hole. "The food is up here and we've loaded a lot on the elevator, but they're trying to call the elevator from above. We pushed the C2 button right away when we got up here, and held the door open, so it should go down first, but... We're coming down," the man added. "I hope."

While the small group searched the third floor, Ranulf and Luha had split up and gone to each of the groups still on C2, explaining about the Giants of God. The Avengers – Dirk, Kimberly, and Charlie – listened avidly. When the shouting came from the upper floor Dirk motioned to the other two, and they slipped off into a corner behind the elevator. "I think there was a mistake," Dirk muttered. "We're supposed to be part of these Giants of God, not workers. We're just like them... or most of them."

"We're not powerful." Kimberly looked dubious. "And they're all men. They make women into slaves."

"Well, maybe that's why we got taken to the wrong place," muttered Dirk. "We had women with us."

Kim's eyes narrowed, but she didn't say anything.

Charlie sat very still blinking his eyes. "I don't know, Dirk. I don't think they care about us any more than the others. Those guys were just playing us."

Dirk glared at him. "Well, I don't know about you, but I know I belong with the Giants of God, and I'm going to find a way to join them. You can come with me or not, but you'd better not rat me out."

He looked intensely at Kim. "You either, Kim, or I'll beat the shit out of you."

When, to everyone's relief, the elevator returned safely from C3, Dario made sure Enid and Jesús were given water and food right away. The children sat against the inner wall out of the way of those unloading the elevators, to eat and rest a little. All of a sudden Jesús shouted, "Look! The empty eggs are being brought back just like ours were." They all watched as an egg came slowly in through a bay. There was a noise like some machine had been turned on, and then suddenly a spray hit the egg from a nozzle recessed in the ceiling next to the large hole to the third floor. The egg disintegrated into a fine powder, which was sucked up into another, smaller hole next to the nozzle. A moment later an egg appeared in the next row over and the same thing happened.

The escapees stood staring where the egg had disappeared. Some were trembling. "What if someone was in one of those eggs?" Enid whispered.

Jesús' eyes widened. "That's what they do when there's a break in the work line, when someone stops working." He started shaking. "I'll bet that would have happened to me if I'd kept on refusing to work."

"And that's what happens if someone is too sick to work, or dies," whispered Enid. She looked around at the horrified faces. "We have to get everyone out of the eggs. We have to make the ones who don't want to come out get out."

"Yes," added Jesús. "We have to let them know." He ran toward the ladder.

"Wait," Dario yelled. "Wait." Jesús stopped and looked back at him. Dario gestured at the bay, and Jesús turned to watch wide-eyed as an egg came in and was disintegrated. Taking a deep breath he ran to the next ladder, edged out on to the ledge, and down. Halfway to the bottom, he stopped to look around, amazed at how many people were out of the eggs. There were some people who were lying or sitting next to the eggs they had come out of, too debilitated from their time in the egg to move very much, but there were also teams, scattered among the eggs almost two thirds of the way down the canyon, working to break out more prisoners. At the moment they were all staring at the eggs moving down the tracks to the bays, all of them eggs that were close to the beginning of the lines at the end of the canyon where they had first started releasing prisoners.

He called out to the closest people. "Hey, hey!"

People, Angelino and Pedro among them, came scrambling over the eggs toward him.

"What's happening to those eggs? Did you find a way to release people?" exclaimed one man. Another one called out. "I think they're all empty. I think they're all eggs we've gotten people out of."

"I hope they're empty!" Jesús yelled. He came down another rung. "No, we're not causing this. When the line stops working properly the computers can tell which egg stopped working. They try to get the person in it back to work with the voice and the pain."

They all nodded. They all knew about the voice and the pain.

"When that doesn't work, they take the egg back in and spray it with something that makes it crumble to dust." He paused. "Everything in it crumbles to dust."

"Oh, my god," yelled one woman. "The person in the egg... "

"Yes," nodded Jesús. "You need to make everyone get out of the eggs."

454

"Oh, no!" One man started pushing his way back across the rows of eggs. "There was a man who refused to come out. Help me!" Several others shouted agreement, and headed in his direction.

Jesús turned toward the others who were still looking a little stunned. "Quickly, you've got to get anyone left in the eggs out. Especially in the rows you've already gotten some people out of." He scrambled back up the ladder to report.

Dario looked thoughtfully at the eggs as they came in and disintegrated. "You know," he said. "I'll bet there's no way to release people from the eggs. Or, this is it."

Enid looked at him in horror.

"They don't care about recycling the eggs and the stuff in them. They just use new eggs. Then they don't have to dispose of the bodies."

Ranulf sighed. "Well, that would fit with the rest of their philosophy."

The group moved over to the bays farther down the room from where the eggs were moving in and disintegrating, and looked out into the canyon. Some of the people were working on isolated eggs in the earlier rows, but most were working on the rows in the middle of the canyon.

While they stood there, a man yelled out, "I need Arabic here," and a woman a few rows away yelled, "Coming!"

Ranulf shook his head. "If the Giants manage to get down here, they could use semiautomatic rifles from inside this room and shoot all the people down there. They have no protection."

Luha flicked her tail back and forth, back and forth. "They could do that from the top of the canyon."

"Yes, but it would be harder. The people could shelter against this side of the canyon where the guns couldn't be pointed." Dario and the others nodded their heads soberly.

Kim found tears running down her face, and turned away so no one would see. *I have never been so scared in my life,* she thought.

A cheer came from the computer bank. "They've found something," exclaimed Charlie, and they all started moving down the room.

"What did you find?" asked a tall black woman.

"I've found a file that covers everything about the work in the canyon – the eggs, how the batteries store the electricity generated by the pedaling, all of it – with links to more specific details, operating instructions, and the actual programs that make things work. Everything." Adia grinned.

"All right!" exclaimed Jesús.

"It starts with a game plan for capturing the workers," she added. "Makes me really ashamed."

Ranulf was looking at the files over her shoulder. "These files are not on the upstairs computers. I need to make copies of these and get them out to *Incogni*."

Adia nodded and went on explaining. "The most important thing I've found is about controlling the wind." She clicked a link.

"They must have forgotten they had that," exclaimed Ranulf.

"Well, that's not too surprising," added Luha dryly. "They seemed to be pretty stupid about a lot of the stuff they created themselves!"

"Or had someone create for them." Ranulf laughed. "Then they probably got rid of the creator in one of their power plays."

"That's pretty typical," muttered one of the male techies. "Happens in companies all the time."

Luha sat back on her haunches. "Now we need to find a way to escape up that cliff – a ladder perhaps."

They were all nodding agreement when Kimberly exclaimed, "Where's Dirk?"

"Dirk?" Charlie looked around him wildly. "Did he do it?"

"Do what?" Dario looked sharply at Charlie and Kimberly who looked at each other, their eyes wide.

"What!" Roberto moved over next to Charlie. "What are you talking about?"

Kim looked fearfully at them, but didn't answer.

The tall black woman moved over next to her and gently touched her shoulder. "I'm Andrea. What's your name?"

"Kim," she whispered.

"You seem frightened, Kim."

"He said he'd beat the shit out of me."

Andrea's eyes narrowed. "Who said that?"

Enid thought Andrea looked rather dangerous herself.

"Dirk. He said if I told he'd..." she paused.

"If you told what?"

Kim's looked apprehensively at Charlie.

"I think we should tell," muttered Charlie.

"Tell what," added Dario.

"That Dirk was planning to go over to the Giants of God," Kim whispered.

"What?" several people shouted, and some started moving down toward the elevators.

Luha leapt past them. The first elevator was still there, door propped open. She ran to the next. The door was closed, the elevator still humming. They had just missed catching him.

"Oh, no," yelled Roberto. "They've got an elevator!"

Andrea turned to Kim. "Why did he do this?

"He thinks he belongs with them. He thinks he should be a Giant of God – that we were put in the eggs by accident." She paused. "Well, not 'we', but 'he'. He thinks they put us in the eggs because there were girls with us. Me."

"He's an idiot," muttered Ranulf, "but we need to forget him and deal with the problem. They have guns. We have to be prepared to keep them from getting off this elevator."

Andrea stepped forward. "I think we can stop them." She looked around her. "Pile stuff against this door. Lots of stuff, and piled high. When the elevator comes back down, the doors open, and we push the stuff in. That way we keep the elevator from moving, and block them in it. Then we have to figure out what to do with them." She grinned, and again, Enid thought, *Dangerous. I think I'm glad she's on our side.*

The Gift

Dirk watched the indicator lights on the elevator go slowly up past C3. *He'd made it. I don't think there's any way they can call this elevator back, even if they do figure out I'm gone.*

He shuffled his feet anxiously.

The call light blinked on at C2. *Damn that Kim. I'll bet she told. When I get a hold of her she's dead meat.*

But the elevator kept ascending and he sighed with relief. *Those Giants of God will be grateful to have the elevator. They'll know I'm okay because I'm white. Of course there'd been other white men in the eggs. But I have the elevator. They'll know I'm on their side because I brought them the elevator.*

As the indicator moved to "1" the elevator slowed and stopped. A moment later the doors opened revealing five steel plates circling the elevator door, with five rifle barrels pointing out of slits in them. He raised his hands yelling "friend" just as the deafening "rat-a-tat-tat" of the guns echoed around him. The momentum of the bullets pushed him back against the cabin wall, and he slipped to the floor, his body mangled and bloody.

"Hey," yelled Eric. "Don't let the doors close." He struggled to push the steel barrier away, but the man next to him pushed his barrier forward at the same time, blocking him. He screamed with annoyance as the elevator doors closed. Another man, finally freeing himself from the barrier, ran to push the elevator call button, but it was too late. They could hear the elevator descending.

"What?" screamed Todd when he heard. "Why did you shoot him?"

"But we didn't know there was just one person in there," explained Eric. "You told us to fire when the doors opened to keep them from rushing us."

Todd put his head down in his hands. "Seb will come with drones and get them," he muttered. "Seb will come."

As Andrea made plans for their defense, Enid watched the elevator ascend and stop at "1". The sound of automatic weapons echoed down the shaft.

"No," screamed Kimberly.

The number "1" blinked off and they heard the elevator descending again. "No time for your plan," yelled Dario. "Hide," and they scattered behind nearby columns. The door opened.

At first it seemed empty, then Andrea saw Dirk's body lying on the floor. "Don't let the doors close," she yelled, as she ran over and pushed a hand against the edge of the door. Some moved over to the elevator to look while others hid their eyes.

"They didn't give him a chance," whispered Charlie. "He wanted to help them and they didn't give him a chance."

There was a clunking sound and the machinery behind them started to hum. The food buckets emerged from the metal columns, hooking on to the chain below the belt, and slowly moving out to the eggs. "Five-forty," muttered Dario, looking at his watch.

Too Hot!

"Where is earth?" cried Tata. "Where is my earth?"

"Blue green," whispered the strings, "blue green."

They swooped through the cosmic dust down one arm of the galaxy, past stars, red-yellow and blue-green planets, and roaring comets, flying out until the stars disappeared in a wisp.

"Back, back," called the strings. "Back to the center." Reversing with a swish of energy, they returned to the center, plunging past the massive black hole, to the other spiral arm. Again, they tumbled and soared past stars and planets, peering through the dusty asteroids until at last Tata saw something familiar, a swirl of blue and green, with splashes of white clouds, circled by a small moon that shone silvery white in the sun. "Home," cried Tata to his new friends. "This is my home, my beautiful home." He flew closer, and slid on a sun beam past the moon.

"Warm," came the deep voice of the neutralinos. "Too warm."

"Yes," echoed the Muons and Tauons. "Too warm. Too hot!"

Tata felt it – the waves of heat – too much heat – that wrapped the earth. He watched in horror as the ice caps began to melt, and the water pounded up onto the edges of the land. He turned toward Africa, his ancestral home, and saw the deep burnt yellow of drought creep across the land – and not just there, but in growing patches all across the earth. He watched torrential rains, cyclones, and hurricanes sweeping away homes of people and animals in unprecedented floods. "No, no," he cried. "Not my people. Not my earth."

"Too hot," whispered the Strings. "Too hot," and they turned, dragging Tata with them, to fly back to the edge of the solar system.

Flash Drives?

Nima scrambled as quickly as she could up the cliff. When she got to the last ledge, she saw Kuji, lying on her stomach, reaching two of her arms down to help her over the top edge of the crevice.

"Thanks," she whispered, and then lay quietly, breathing hard and shaking. She pulled herself into a fetal position, her arms and tail wrapped around her legs.

"Are you all right?" asked Sarah, hopping around near her head. Nima nodded, but she felt tears running down her black velvet nose. Finally she sat up, wiping her tears with her front paws

"Is Luha all right?" Kuji asked. "Did you find her?"

"I found Luha. I think she'll be okay, but she's in a precarious situation." She went on to explain about Ranulf, the cage, and their plan to go to the cellars and find the children in the eggs.

"But also, I have the flash drives." She pointed to the bag hanging around her neck. "And I have to tell you about the demonstration because some of them may come here."

"Flash drives?" Singing Swan fluttered his wings. "What are they?"

Tuwillia cleared her throat. "Come, let's move away from this dangerous crevice and let her tell her story. Then we'll all know what these flash drives are and this demonstration."

They followed her over to a place under the tree where there was room for all of them to sit in the shade, and settled down to listen. (All, that is, except the baby ibex who danced around them, running back and forth to the bushes, pulling off leaves, and trying to eat them.)

When she had finished her story, they decided to split up – some would go back to Din Tsin Twei and wait for demonstrators who might come from earth. Some would stay with Tuwillia and plan a rescue of Luhanada and the others in the big cavern. "Go, go," Tuwillia commanded. "It will be morning before you know it."

4

Hunter's Moon, Last Quarter Waning

The Monday morning after the kidnapping, Giselle and the Shanti Place kids huddled together both elated and frightened as they talked about their wild run after the dogs and the rescue of An Lien. The experiences of the night had bonded them.

Giselle thought of the Weaving Tree. *Healing. Healing the weaving.*

That afternoon she was napping in her room, cuddled with the dogs and the little gray cat, when Monica called her. "I saw the video on the internet. Giselle, lots of people believe you. Is it true? Is it really true?"

"Yes. It's true."

"And you're going to this demonstration on Tuesday?"

"Yes."

Monica paused. "Rod and I have decided to come, too. I think the OET people are right. We didn't want to believe our government could be so... Or that corporations would be so... irresponsible, like you've been telling us, but... I mean we always knew some things were wrong, but..."

"You didn't want to believe they were as bad as they are. I understand," Giselle interrupted.

"This business of the..." She paused and took a breath. "The changing – the becoming something else. I don't know, Giselle, but we're trying to understand it. Really, Rod is more ready than I am, but... anyway, we're coming."

In Arundel that last day before the demonstration was a day of preparation for both the demonstrators from the Interfaith Council and the counter demonstrators.

Dorotea joined the others making posters, whispering prayers to Our Lady, and sometimes to the sacred spring that somehow these demonstrations would help bring Jesús and the little girl home.

That night Coffman and his followers met at the Dickersons' house to make their counter demonstration signs. Coffman's grandson, Tom, didn't want to come. "I have homework, Grandpa," he argued. "If you're going to make me miss school tomorrow, I want to make sure I've got everything done."

"You're coming," the older man insisted. "I support you and your mother, and you're going to do what I say. Besides, you kids know more about how to make these signs. You make this stuff for school. Bring your books."

They met in the Dickersons' big family room, spreading the signs out over the floor and dining table. The television was turned to Crevan News. "Hey, there's Reverend Peabody," exclaimed Dickerson. "My wife really likes him."

A silver haired white man stood back of an imposing podium. "God has come to me with dire warnings," preached the minister.

He paused, looking dramatically out at the cameras. "The devil has chosen this time for a mighty battle against Our Lord."

He hit the podium with his fist. "These demonstrations tomorrow are the work of the devil." *Bang!* He hit the podium again. "God has told me so." *Bang!* "The organizers are the Devil's spawn. THE DEVIL'S SPAWN!" This time he hit the podium with both fists. "We cannot allow it."

He leaned forward peering into the camera. "ALL OF US must go out tomorrow to stop this travesty. We must all fight the work of the devil."

"Whoa," Harding exclaimed. "That's pretty heavy."

"Stupid, if you ask me," muttered Tom.

Coffman looked at him. "What did you say, Tom?"

"Nothing."

462

Coffman's eyes narrowed as he looked at the boy for a moment, and then turned back to the rest of the men. "We need to be well prepared tomorrow."

"Well, we're making the signs," grinned Dickerson. "They're pretty good, don't you think?"

"We should make one that calls them 'Devil's spawn'," suggested another man.

"Yeah, yeah," came a chorus of approval.

"Yes," added Coffman, "and we need to go armed."

Tom's book fell to the floor.

The TV kept blaring.

"No, grandpa, that's foolish."

Coffman's hand flew out hitting the boy across the cheek. "Shut up, Tom, and make those signs."

Tom put his hand up to his cheek, tears floating in his eyes, and turned his head away.

Harding was the first to speak. "Okay. I can see it. These people are dangerous. I'll bring a gun."

"Yeah," exclaimed Dickerson. "It's just like the wild west! They're the Indians and we're going to kill them!"

("Too hot, too hot," whispered Tata. "They're destroying the earth," and he turned again, and rushed toward the heat, pulling behind him, like a magnet, hordes of strings – quarks, photons, electrons, leptons, muons, tauons, neutrinos, and trailing at the end, neutralinos. Like new comets, they flew through the air toward the hot planet, whispering as they went, "Too hot, too hot, too hot.")

Flying!

Monday was a day of rest for An Lien, who slept off the distress of her kidnapping. She got up that evening to help make preparations for the demonstration. When bedtime came she slept for a while, but was wide awake at three-fifteen in the morning, full of aches and sharp pains. Pulling herself out of bed and into her chair, she rolled over to the desk, opened her computer, pushed the "on" button, and sat, gingerly touching her swollen face, while she waited for it to load.

Her inbox was packed with email from different organizations urging people to attend the demonstrations. On an alternative news site, she found the demonstrations had already started on the other side of the world.

She stared with delight at the live streams of huge crowds of people packing the streets of cities all over the far side of the world, waving signs full of pictures of animals, gods, goddesses, and mythological characters with the words, "Humans, rejoin the dance of life – the Tsin Twei." Some people wore animal masks and costumes.

One group of ten men and women danced with a beautiful carved and painted Buddha with a magnificent smile, balanced on a platform on their shoulders, singing:

May you be happy.
May you be free.
May you come together as One,
Living together in peace.

In another city, the people sang and danced in unison, fifteen across, down a wide street, many of them beating on drums tucked under their arms, and ululating in high pitched cries. There was a fierce joy in their dance, and An Lien could feel power emanating from the beat of their feet on the street.

"Oh, my," she whispered. "Oh, my," and started moving her wheel chair back and forth in time with the music.

Arise, arise,
Open your heart!
Open your heart to the dance of life.
Arise, arise,
Open your eyes!
See the world in the dance of life.
Beat your feet
To the beat of your heart!
Dance the dance of life!

At Seaview Business Park, Kas was also watching the demonstrations. "This is not good."

Kas ran his fingers through his white hair and looked around at his fellow Gold members of the Giants of God. They were all there, except for Todd.

"This must be disrupted."

Seb leaned forward. "Most of these countries have military ready to surround the demonstrations when they get to their destinations. They're going to fire at will."

"Yes," added Branson. "We've sold drones, and other heavy weapons, to most of them. They'll be eager for a chance to use them."

Reginald grinned, "Did you see Reverend Peabody's sermon on Crevan News last night? I think Don wrote it."

Several of the others nodded their heads.

"It was brilliant. There'll be lots of counter demonstrators out there with weapons." He stretched back in his chair. "Lots."

Kas nodded. "Yes. 'The devil's spawn.' Yes."

He laughed and shook his head. "There's no end to the gullibility of the stupid, but..." he looked at each of them. "But we should not underestimate the power of these demonstrations."

"But they're just as stupid," exclaimed Senator Bailey. "All this ridiculous animal totem stuff! They believe it."

Kas looked at him for a moment. "Well, I thought so, too. But I'm beginning to wonder..."

"Oh, really!" Ottis, Chairman of the Board of the largest bank in the world, laughed and shook his head. "That's just ridiculous."

Kas shrugged. "The way we get to the Cavern is pretty ridiculous, too."

Ottis sat back. "Oh. But that..."

"But 'that' what, Ottis? But that's perfectly rational?" Kas shook his head. "No, it's all weird. All of it."

Seb had been leaning back in his chair just listening. He leaned forward, the front legs of the chair hitting the carpeted floor with a dull thump. "So maybe they are the devil's spawn. I mean if God is on our side – if we're the Giants of God, they must be from the devil."

The rest just turned and looked at him, silently.

An Lien danced her wheelchair back and forth in rhythm with the dancers on the internet and started to sing, first in a small voice, and then louder and louder!

Arise, arise,
Open your heart!
Open your heart to the dance of life.

She watched as a mist swirled around the dancers and flowed out of the computer to surround her as well. She laughed and danced and sang. *The people are transforming,* she thought as she sang. *Look at them! They're growing taller and full of color, like rainbows, like a huge rainbow.* She felt her wings expanding outward, her long tail fanning as she leapt into the air and into the swirling, colorful vortex. The music surrounded her, wrapping her in sound, and then changed, overlapping with another song.

Arise, arise,
Open your heart!
Open your heart to the dance of life.

Come!
Come!
Hammer your feet
to the beat of the drum.

Arise, arise,
Open your eyes!
See the world in the dance of life.

Come!
Come!
Lift up your voice
to answer the One.

Beat your feet
To the beat of your heart!
Dance the dance of life!

Come!
Come!
Answer the call
of the earth and the sun!

The music of the two songs intertwined and blended, twirling and whirling her through the mists, and she flew up and around the other dancers and drummers, adding her own song to the rest:

Peace, peace,
Laughter and dance!
Joy and life for us all.
Sing your tears,
Sing your fears,

Defy oppression through the years,
Peace and justice for us all.

Peace, peace,
Laughter and dance!
Joy and life for us all.
Joy and life for us all.

The mists began to lighten and An Lien found herself flying in a vast round valley, an amphitheater cut in stone out of the towering mountains that enclosed it. She flicked her wings and flew swiftly down to perch on a stone wall next to a path that led into the valley between two smaller hills. Across from her was a ragged crevice where the mountain had cracked in half, creating a jagged rift through the stone steps. She folded her wings and lowered her soft feathery belly to the top of the wall.

Her fellow dancers, each in the form of a different animal or avatar, were dancing and singing on the ground in the center of the amphitheater.

"We are at Ninas Twei," shouted one, and a rousing cheer erupted. The singing and dancing became even more energetic than before.

A Trumpeter Swan came flying up the path with three otters loping along behind him. He perched on the wall next to An Lien. The otters climbed up on the first tier of the amphitheater and stood shakily on their hind legs to peer out at the dancers.

"Welcome!" Singing Swan gave a bow to the little dove and turned to look at the dancers. "I have never seen so many humans here at one time."

"And many more are coming," exclaimed An Lien. "As the sun rises around the world more and more demonstrations will happen, and more and more people will come here!"

She gave a little chuckling laugh. "I shouldn't be here yet, but here I am!"

She cocked her head to one side. "You must be Singing Swan. I'm a friend of Giselle's – of the Tree Woman – from Bayomar. The sun hasn't risen there yet, but I came because I was watching these wonderful people on the internet, and I danced and sang with them, and suddenly I was here!"

"You came by yourself?" asked Singing Swan. "You weren't in a circle sharing water together with others?"

The little dove shook her head. "Nope. I was watching the dancing on the internet at four o'clock in the morning – all by myself." She turned her head toward the dancers. "And those people. They weren't drinking anything. Just dancing and singing."

Singing Swan nodded his head thoughtfully. "I'm learning there are as many different ways to get here as there are different groups of people in the world."

More mist came swirling down into the valley, and another group of demonstrators arrived.

"Oh, it's the ones with the beautiful Buddha," exclaimed An Lien, watching as the ten statue bearers, now ten beautifully decorated white elephants, touched the ground, the platform holding the Buddha balancing on their backs. She listened as their song wove its way through the songs of the earlier dancers and that of Ninas Twei.

> *May you be happy,* they sang.
> *May you be free.*

Singing Swan turned to her. "You're from Bayomar?"

"Yes," she nodded.

"I know why you're here!" he exclaimed, fluttering his wings. "We need something taken to Bayomar. You were sent to us! Come with me."

He took a short run along the top of the wall and launched himself into the air, flying down the path.

An Lien glanced back at the wonderful dance with longing, and then flew after him.

Most of the Gold members of the Giants of God had turned away from the computer to discuss the monkey when Ottis exclaimed, "O my god," pointing at the wide computer screen.

The rest turned in time to see the singing, dancing demonstrators from an island state coalesce into the form of a beautiful, terrible, woman goddess, and begin to flow upward like the eruption of a volcano. The watchers could see both the individual bodies of the people transforming to their Tla Twein and the huge form of the goddess they became.

"They're laughing," muttered Branson. "They're laughing and singing."

"Where's the army?" yelled Kas. "Where're the police?"

"They're there." Seb pointed to the edges of the screen. "See, they're there. They're firing at them. Can't you hear the guns?"

"Sounds like drums to me."

"No. There are drums, but also gunshots. Listen."

"Look," added Dean. "Some of them have fallen."

The huge Goddess figure had swirled away into the atmosphere, and the video cameras turned back toward the ground to show a dozen or more bodies – one human body and many animal bodies, among them a tiger, with a small green bird lying in the crook of its foreleg, some larger birds, a bat, a rat, and a dolphin.

"A dolphin?" exclaimed Reginald. "A dolphin on land?"

Forever Tla Twein

After sending An Lien back to Bayomar with the flash drives, Singing Swan and Sarah Song Thrush perched on the wall by the path to Singing Swan's home watching the demonstrators arrive at Din Tsin Twei. Kujakali sat next to them with Peeka sitting on her shoulder. The otters were crouched on the first tier of the amphitheater where they could rise up on their hind feet to peer at the travelers pouring in.

"Nima, Peeka, and I've made a ladder out of fallen trees," Kuji reported. "It's long enough to reach from each ledge to the next in the crevice. We can move this one from ledge to ledge as we go down or up for now, and keep making more."

"Excellent," nodded Singing Swan.

"I want to go, but I need Luhanada or someone who's dead to carry me. I think I can be Durga down there – Luha and Tata were able to be their Tla Twein in Arundel – but the wind could still get me."

"Perhaps I'm large enough to carry you," suggested Aucapomi, "if it was just across the plateau."

"Perhaps," Kuji said doubtfully, as she looked over the big otter, "but how can an otter get down the crevice, even with a ladder?"

Illari interrupted, "We can't climb down, but we can slide. We can make pads of grass and slide down the ladder."

"Wahoo! That sounds like fun," exclaimed Huayna.

"I think," added Aucapomi, "you need to take a lot of people to do this rescue. We must be a large romp," he laughed. "A multitude."

"But where will we find this multitude?" asked Kujakali.

"There are others here who have died." Singing Swan paced on the top of the wall. "Some are fish in the lake."

"Look! Look!" Huayna pointed up at the sky above the amphitheater. They turned to look as another group swept in, a deep red and black sparkling with bright colors pouring into the amphitheater like lava from a volcano, their island song flowing like an undercurrent through the songs of the others.

We are the land in the sea,
sun cooled by sea breeze.
Bright blossoms,
many-colored joy,
mirrored in darting fish,
corals, and anemone,
in the depths of the clear blue sea.
We come from our creator-destroyer,
fierce goddess, dark beauty,
erupting in fire from the deep,
flowing in red-yellow rivers,
pouring in black writhing smoke,
building our soft gentle island
our land in the sea.
Protect our island.
Protect our sea.
Come, our tempestuous island goddess,
pour your fierce love,
fierce and fiery love, into me.
We come from creation-destruction.
In death, new life will be.
We risk death in defiance.
A sacrifice,
so Gaia can be freed.

A song of joy, and a song of mourning.

As it finished there was a moment of deep silence and into that silence came a tiger and a little green bird; a bat that reminded Sarah of Yoda in Star Wars; a little rat with hard spines down it's back; and a dolphin swimming in the air as if it were water, surrounded by several beautiful fish. Flying around them all was a beautiful, big black butterfly with streaks of white and a suggestion of blue, a multicolored dove, and several sea birds. All the dancers and singers bowed deeply to the newcomers, before returning to the dance.

"Oh, dear," whispered Peeka. "These new ones are dead. They've come like us, because they're dead. Why would some of the demonstrators be dead?"

"Because the police shot them," answered Aucapomi. "They shot them for speaking out for the earth, just as they shot us for protecting the rainforest."

Peeka's little eyes got wide, but he didn't say anything.

As the music resumed, the tiger stood, looking about him, while the little green bird flew circles around him, and then perched on his back. "Dad," chirped the little bird. "Where are we? What happened?"

The tiger spoke. "It's true. The story on the internet is true."

"About becoming animals when we die? Are we dead?" He flew down to sit on the ground looking up at the tiger. The tiger didn't answer.

"We were shot," fluttered the butterfly. "They shot us!"

Singing Swan flew over and landed beside the little bird. "Welcome to Ninas Twei. I, too, am dead. Also shot, but many, many years ago." He sighed. "It's hard to die, but it is good to be able to come here."

No one spoke, and the little bird blinked his eyes several times. Finally he hopped up into the air. "I can fly, dad," he sang. "I'm my favorite bird!"

The tiger chuckled. "Yes, Manua, you can fly, and I can growl."

The little bird laughed. "You can growl at me like a tiger mother. Now you can be both father and mother just like you said!"

The tiger flicked his tail. "I've always loved tigers. It can't be too bad to be a tiger."

He gave a half-hearted growl and the little bird laughed again.

Singing Swan looked appraisingly at him and the others. "I'm Singing Swan."

"I'm Rahiti," answered the tiger. "We heard about you on the internet."

"Yes," the bat chirped. "You've been here a long time."

The butterfly looked wistfully toward the dancers in the amphitheater. "I'll miss my family."

Silence.

Remembering the life left behind.

Finally Singing Swan spoke. "It's hard to leave the world, but for us it's good you're here. You may be the answer to a problem we have – a problem rescuing some people in great need."

The tiger nodded. "That's why we were demonstrating – to rescue an earth in great need. Really, the peoples of the earth in great need, humans and others. Where are these people?"

"Follow me." Singing Swan headed to his home, followed by Rahiti, his son and all the others who had been shot, the otters, and Kujakali.

The Hacker

When she found herself back in her bedroom, sitting in front of the computer, An Lien laughed out loud thrusting her arms above her head. "Unbelievable!" She shook herself a little. It had been a brief but wonderful moment, being a Laughing Dove, flying. *But I'll go again. I know!*

She clicked on her email program, pulled the bag with the flash drives from around her neck, and typed in the email address of the person from *Incogni*. As instructed she put the code word "Giants" in the subject line.

It was five o'clock a.m. When would he look at his email?

She adjusted her screen so that she could see any new email immediately, and watch the alternative news at the same time, turning it on just in time to see a group, marching and singing in the rain somewhere, rise as if they were floating in a mist that swept them laughing away, like a cloud on the wind.

A new email popped up on the screen.

She opened it quickly, but it was just a politician asking for money. Rolling over to the bathroom, she washed and brushed her teeth, checked the computer again, and then rolled to the closet to choose her clothes. She was mostly dressed, wincing with pain as she pulled a shirt over her head, when her computer dinged indicating new email. It was instructions from *Incogniti*.

She met the hacker at six o'clock in a little coffee shop in downtown Bayomar. Her father, who had driven her, sat at the next table pretending to be a stranger. The hacker came rushing into the coffee shop, peering around until he saw An Lien. "I'll be the only one in there using a wheelchair," she had emailed him.

He stood in front of her a moment staring, then said the arranged code. "Are you the bearer of news?"

"Yes. Of giants," she replied, leaning forward to whisper, "Are you from *Incogni*?"

He pulled up a chair, nodding, and she thrust out the bag. "This is from Ranulf."

He opened it and looked in, grinning.

"Thanks. Thanks a lot," he whispered back, shoving his floppy brown hair back from his eyes. He leaned forward talking *soto voce*. "I've already set things in motion. I called my contact at *TruthFarm* and Ranulf's written reports have gone up on the internet by now."

He shook the bag. "These will back up his reports. The *Bayomar Times* has been sitting on a front page story for a month. These files will convince them to print it."

An Lien held out another flash drive. "And this is from me. All the documents from Kasimir Goddard's personal laptop."

The man's eyes got wide. "How did you get them?"

"Not easily," she laughed, taking off sun glasses and pointing to her black eye. "But there's not enough time to tell you now."

He winced, alarmed. "Who did that?" His eyes got wet. "No one should ever hurt you."

"Don't worry," she quickly assured him. "I'll be all right. Just do what's needed with those files."

He nodded, pushing his chair back. "Yes, I have to run and make copies, and get them distributed."

He stood, but he didn't leave.

An Lien felt awkward. "I'll... I'll be watching the paper and the internet."

He bit his lower lip for a moment, then, "You're a beautiful woman, in more ways than one," he declared impulsively, and leaned down and gave her a quick kiss on the cheek before dashing out the door.

Shen Ch'i grinned behind his newspaper.

An Lien sat stunned in her chair, then found herself grinning, too. *Well, he was cute in a sweet nerdy way,* she thought. *And he got teary because I was hurt.*

Suddenly he was back in the door again, leaning close. "Ranulf?" he asked. "Do you know what's happened to Ranulf?"

"The last anyone heard, he was okay, but he's in danger. People – well, sort of people..." She looked a little bewildered as she stumbled around trying to figure out how to tell him. "They're animals," she finally blurted out. "People in their Tla Twei form. They're dead, actually."

"Like that story that's going around the internet?" he asked incredulously.

"Yes. It's true. I posted that story."

"You!" he exclaimed.

She nodded. "And I was a bird when I got those flash drives. A Laughing Dove."

He stared at her, eyes wide.

"But you need to get those files copied. Those people – animals – are helping Ranulf. Go! Go!"

He nodded, turning toward the door. As he left she thought she heard him muttering, "I'll bet you're a beautiful dove."

She grinned all the way through her coffee, and found herself laughing, and rolling at top speed, as she headed for the van and Shanti Place.

"Slow down," her father chuckled striding behind her.

As the sun moved from east to west around the earth, Kas and the other Golds watched with growing trepidation as in demonstration after demonstration in country after country people sang and danced, rose in some misty form into the air, and disappeared, some leaving behind the bodies of animals – the people who had been shot by the police, the army, or counter demonstrators.

"What the hell is going on," Kas shook his head in disbelief. "Where are they going?"

"To Ninas Twei," answered Reginald. "Wherever that is."

Dean's cell phone rang and they all turned to watch him as he answered. "What?" He listened and then, in a loud alarmed voice he exclaimed, "What?" again and turned to Stuart. "Check out *TruthFarm*."

Stuart quickly wrote the *TruthFarm* URL into the computer and they all watched in horror as the headline appeared. "Some Well Known Corporate Moguls Dupe the People, Call Themselves 'Giants of God'."

Kas sat forward in his chair, staring at the screen. "Scroll down. Scroll down. What do they have?"

Incredulous silence choked the room as Stuart slowly scrolled down through a paragraph of general explanation and then a list of links to the files from the Giants of God's computers.

"They have all our names!" Kas exclaimed. "How did they get this? This wasn't on my laptop. It's only on the computers at Cavern City. That An Lien had names of the corporations involved, but not the legislators, judges..."

"Could one of the women have gotten it?" suggested Dean, "Maybe Kujakali?"

Branson looked incredulous. "I don't think she could know anything about computers. She was only a little kid when Eric got her, and she came from off the streets of some slum."

"She's smart though."

Kas took a deep breath. "I think it has to be one of us. One of the men."

"Or that cougar," added Seb. "Maybe that cougar did it."

Kas sat back. "There's no way to know." He swiveled his chair back and forth. "The big question now is what are we going to do to counter this?"

He stood up. "Get Kevin in here."

In the Canyon

Everyone on C2 gathered in silence around Dirk's body, still lying in the elevator cab. Kim sobbed quietly in Charlie's arms. Luhanada leaned against Enid who absently stroked the cougar's neck.

"Well," Dario took a deep breath.

"Yes, we have to..." added Grisha, and then stopped.

Andrea stepped forward. "We need to cover him with something, and put him somewhere out of our way. We can't be stopped by this. We need to feed people. We need to grab the food buckets so we can move faster getting people out of the eggs and we need to find a way out of here."

Sister Maureen stepped forward. "I'll take care of him. Perhaps someone can help me."

"I'll help you," responded Fadil. The rest turned reluctantly away as Sister Maureen and Fadil stepped into the elevator.

It wasn't long before the techies shouted, "The wind is turned off!"

The others took up the cry and called out to the people in the canyon below, "The wind is turned off!" A great cheer erupted from all the captives.

Above the canyon in the City of the Giants, Todd heard the cheer, and shuddered.

5

Ayoabia, Oya of the Winds

T he sun was just rising in Bayomar. Ayoabia Asukiye lay curled up inside a cardboard box in an alley not far from Shanti Place. Something stirred within her, something deep, whirling within her, and her large eyes opened wide.

"The wind," she whispered. "The wind is mine again," and she leapt up, tossing off the cardboard and old blankets that covered her.

Shaking out her skirts, she ran calling, "The wind is mine. I am Ayoabia Asukiye, and I am again Oya of the Winds!" and she began to spin, spinning out to the street, across to the park, faster and faster, until she was just a blur in the eyes of the homeless man who lay awake nearby.

A low hum came from the spinning blur and others awakened, and watched as she stretched herself up and up into the sky, a whirling funnel; a humming, roaring swirling funnel of shades of gray with sudden flashes of greens, blues, reds, and yellows, shining in the newborn sunlight. She pulled up her feet and sailed across the sky, a huge dark cloud with jagged lines of lightning illuminating the bright whirling colors of her skirts.

And the rumbling, roaring wind became a terrible symphony of drums and deep ascending bass, breaking into a high pitched siren of sound. "Let my people go!" she cried:

> *Come winds of judgment,*
> *Winds of change.*
> *Blow fiercely, blow,*
> *Let my people go!*
> *Sink your thunderous lightning teeth*
> *Into the festering bruises of our grief.*

She dived downward, flying with incredible force into the private prison found just north of the city – into all the prisons and immigrant detention centers across Uhs.

With a fierce gentleness she lifted the guards out of her way, setting them down in a nearby field, whispering to them:

> *Grace you are given to cherish and earn.*
> *Remember this gift and offer no harm.*

Even more gently, she lifted the prisoners and set them on the road home, singing again:

> *Grace you are given to live long and free.*
> *Lift up your head, step out and believe,*
> *Care for each other and care you'll receive.*
> *You are love in your soul,*
> *Your life be made whole,*
> *Remember this gift and offer no harm.*
> *Grace you are given to cherish and learn.*

Returning to the empty building she whipped her winds, roaring:

> *Private prisons,*
> *Profiting on sorrow and pain,*
> *Anguish and shame.*
> *Let my winds batter, shatter and cry,*
> *And the place of your evil, crumble and die.*

The shivering treble notes of broken glass sailed across the top of the roaring basses, as if the sound had been released, set free by the shattering of the windows, the crumbling of the walls:

> *Slaves no longer!*
> *Let us go!*
> *Prisoners no longer!*
> *Let us free!*
> *A people born of love and joy!*
> *Love and joy WE WILL BE!!*

Soaring upward again, she tore across the land to all the offices and factories of the largest purveyor of semi-automatic weapons, bombs, and drones – Wiebe Armaments.

> *Security,* the word rumbled in the air.
> *Chaos,* she screamed.
> *Security – Money, money, money for you!*
> *Death and chaos for the rest.*

The night watchmen fled as she let her feet down to drag through the barbed wire fencing, so that the wire flew through the air and spun around, and around the buildings, tightening its grip until they exploded upward, a pounding tympani sounding the bass, the beat of the storm.

She released the wire so that it lay wound through the mass of destruction, a warning to any who would try to salvage the ugly contents.

> *Hear our wailing!*
> *Hear our cries!*
> *Our children march to kill and die.*
> *Enslaved as surely as before*
> *When they march to death and war.*

Her voice slipped to a whisper – almost silence. The center, the eye of the storm.

> *Mothers of murdered children sigh,*
> *Our sweet sons shot, left to die.*
> *Murdered by each other, and...*

Suddenly her voice rose again, thundering, splintered by jags of light piercing the dark roiling clouds.

> *And by YOU!*
> *BY YOU!*

And she whirled, rumbling and tumbling, around the police headquarters of all the cities, sending the burly men and women skidding under desks, huddling under tables.

Moaning and groaning the winds swept over them, this time only a warning:

> *Hear our wailing, hear our cries,*
> *We will not let our children die!*

Then she gathered her skirts around her and strode back across the skies to Seaview Business Park where Kasimir Goddard, and the other Gold members of the Giants of God sat, their eyes glued to the computer screen, watching the live video of her destruction of the prisons and factories, and the menacing of police headquarters.

The early morning sunshine filtering in through the recently repaired windows suddenly disappeared, and darkness, pierced with jagged light, descended on the building. "O my god, it's coming here," yelled Reginald

The men, with Stuart clutching the laptop to his chest, flew from the room, running for the elevators and stairs, tumbling down the eight stories as fast as they could, and down one more to the basement.

Oya laughed and the winds rumbled and screamed.

> *Run, she sang, run,*
> *but you cannot hide.*
> *Beware the winds of judgment,*
> *The winds of change.*
> *Let my people go!*

The glass shattered, and the building shook, the desks flew back and forth in the rooms, the computers crashed to the floor, and the few people who had been in the building at that early hour huddled in the basement wondering if there was a building left above them, if they would get out alive.

Oya smacked her hands against each other, brushing away the debris, the dust and the dirt.

> *Enough, she roared.*
> *Enough, she rumbled and grumbled.*
> *Enough... she whispered,*
> *For now.*

Waning Towards Crescent

Giselle, cat bedecked, with dogs at her heels, arrived at Shanti Place early Tuesday morning, followed almost immediately by An Lien and Shen Ch'i. An Lien had been full of joy as she told (leaving out the part about the kiss) her adventures of the morning. "I'm sure it's on the internet," she added, producing her laptop.

They all crowded around to watch. "Do you think there's a connection between these Giants of God and our disappearing children?" Shen Ch'i wondered.

Giselle nodded her head slowly. "The description of those eggs with workers in them where Luhanada thinks Enid and Jesús might be – I mean inside might look just like that dark place I saw..." Her voice trailed off.

They were just about to turn off the computer when an announcement came about the terrible tornados sweeping the country. They watched the live photography in awe. The storms flew across the mountains and the plains destroying prisons, armament factories and menacing, but not destroying, police stations, but somehow no people were hurt.

"Private prisons and a weapons factories?" Giselle looked at her companions. "Police stations? Doesn't that seem... well, odd?"

Miesha peered closely at the screen, slowly nodding her head, but didn't say anything.

The cat just flicked his tail.

Suddenly the cameras were showing the storm swooping down over the Seaview Business Park. They watched the center tower of the building shake and twist, and the windows break. The building didn't collapse, but by the time the wind had lifted into the sky again the tower looked battered and broken.

Some of the kids cheered.

"The wind sounds like..." An Lien paused. "Well, like…."

"Like it's laughing!" Sidney interrupted. An Lien nodded.

"It's Ayo," muttered Miesha.

"Ayo?" Sidney whispered back to a grinning Miesha.

The storm dissipated, floating in whirls of red, green, blue, and purple across the sky, and was gone.

The children shrugged and turned toward the kitchen for breakfast.

After breakfast they were beginning to gather their signs and banners, bottles of water and snacks to head out for the demonstration when they heard singing in the street.

"Ayoabia," smiled Giselle. The tall woman stood in the middle of the street, dressed in her most colorful skirts, her arms flung wide above her head, and singing. The cars moved carefully around her.

As Miesha came out the door, she beckoned. "Come child," she whispered. "Your time has come."

Miesha nodded, and holding her carving of Yemonja went to stand in the street with Ayo.

Giselle, clutching the little wooden sculpture of Kuan Yin in her jacket pocket, with the gray cat draped over her shoulder, and her dogs trailing behind, joined them.

An Lien, Shen Ch'i, and Sidney, followed by all the rest of the Shanti Place community, including the dogs, came next – a singing, dancing procession to the demonstration parade route.

It was only a few blocks to the business district where the demonstrators were to gather. From there, they would march down Washington Street to where it ended at the edge of the bay in a semi-circular park. City Hall and the other buildings of the civic center all sat on the crescent-shaped city side of the park, facing out toward the ocean.

Car loads of people descending on the city for the march turned off into side streets or pulled over and parked, the drivers hopping out behind the marchers. People streamed out of the subway exits. Bicyclists weaved their way in and out.

Ayo sang, *"Come, come, follow me, follow me,"* gesturing to all the homeless folks along the street, and they each picked up their packs, grabbed their grocery and laundry carts, and pushed their way out to the street to join the march.

Police lined the streets, protecting the skyscrapers that loomed above them, helmets on their heads with smoky plastic covering their eyes, and plastic body shields held in front of them.

As they reached the starting point, Giselle saw Monica and Rod waving their signs, and the gallery owner pushing his way through the crowd to speak to Shen Ch'i and An Lien.

She laughed and waved when she saw her old principal, Samuel, grinning at her from down the street.

Monica and Rod made their way over to Giselle. "I don't like the looks of the police," muttered Rod.

Giselle turned around in a circle. "They look like robots. They're dressed so they don't look human."

She turned to Rod. "But they are human. We need to remember they're human, and we need them, just like we need everyone else, if we're to regain our grandsoul – if we're to become a part of the Tsin Twei."

She walked over in front of a line of officers, staring at the smoky gray of their helmets, and couldn't tell if they were looking at her or not.

She smiled as her feet bored deep below the asphalt, reaching into the water and nutrients hidden below. Her arms stretched up, branching, moving higher and higher above the police, above the crowd. The cat, crouching on a thick branch, stared at them and the dogs sat at the base of her trunk.

With a rustling of leaves and a creaking of limbs, she spoke. "You are one of us."

Her voice cut like a knife through the sounds of the crowd; her branches danced above their heads. The police line faltered a little, and then held still.

She continued, her words resounding off the walls of the skyscrapers that edged the street. . "I know you're afraid for your jobs. I know you believe you're privileged – a part of the corporate strong men, rather than one of us. But they will sacrifice you, and your families, just as quickly as they sacrifice us, the poor, and the quality of the air and the water."

She turned swinging her branches down the line of officers. "Your families will not be spared the cancers that come from pollution, or the illnesses that come from poorly inspected food."

Some of the officers began to shift their feet restlessly.

"When global warming pushes more and more people toward famine and homelessness, your families will also face famine and homelessness."

She looked at the crowd as her words bounced back and forth in the urban canyon, and then back to the police.

"You hide behind these plastic masks trying not to look human, not to look like people who love and hurt, and care about this world. But I know otherwise. I know that you are people of love, just as we are. You're one of us."

The crowd took up the phrase, and repeated it over and over again. "You're people of love. You're one of us. You are one of us!"

The Tree Woman took a deep breath. "If you haven't the courage to take off your masks, lay down your shields, and join us, at least refrain from hurting us," and she grew taller and taller as she spoke.

"When the orders come to shoot us, or beat us, don't. Just don't follow those orders."

"Don't follow those orders," echoed the crowd. "Don't follow those orders."

The Earth Woman Tree Woman began to sing:

> *Remember, we are your family,*
> *Your family!*
> *We are you, and you are us.*

The song echoed off the buildings, climbing higher and higher into the sky, reaching even the helicopters that hovered high above.

> *We are you, and you are us.*
> *We are you, and you are us.*

Amen, sang Ayoabia, her voice deep and resonant. *So be it, amen.*

Back in the basement of the Seaview Business Park tower, Kas and the others listened to the singing on the laptop and Kas whispered, "Holy shit. If they get the police and armies on their side, we're over."

Giselle drew back into her human form, the cat scrambling down the disappearing branches to perch once again on her shoulder. She glanced over at Monica, who stood staring at her, her mouth wide open. She grinned. *Told you so,* she whispered to herself.

Miesha was also staring at her, but her look was more speculative. She'd look at Giselle and then down at the carving of Yemonja in her hand, and then back at Giselle.

Giselle laughed. "Go for it, Miesha!"

Miesha turned to Ayo, questioning.

"Come." Ayo grabbed her hand, and then reached over with her other hand and grabbed Giselle's. "Come. Our time has come. We will lead the march!"

The demonstrators opened a path for them as they moved to the front, and with each step grew taller, taking on more of the attributes of their Tla Twein, until the march was led by the Earth Woman Tree Woman; Oya, Orisha of the winds, whirling in her many skirts like a tornado; and Miesha as Yemonja, Ocean Mother, Mother of Dreams and Secrets, her seven skirts in shades of blue and green, swirling like the waves of the sea, and Yemonja sang:

> *Here am I,*
> *Protector of my people.*
> *Growing from Goddess of the River*
> *to Goddess of the Ocean,*
> *as I travel with my people,*
> *chained beneath the decks of ships,*
> *across the deep and stormy seas.*
> *(Thousands, millions of them, dying at sea.)*
> *I endure with them*
> *as they travel farther and farther*
> *from the homeland,*
> *far from the river of our birth.*
> *Taken in slavery,*
> *whipped,*

separated from their families,
starved into submission,
and even when freed,
subjugated,
beaten down,
ridiculed and battered with lies.
I am with them.
I come to heal.
I come to heal.
I come to love.
Come enter love with me.

The marchers cheered and joined in her chant:

I come to heal.
I come to heal,
I come to love.
Come enter love with me.

A large, brilliantly colored butterfly fluttered around the three women, and behind them, the rest of the Shanti Place community danced into their own Tla Twein.

Sidney became the magnificent African Gray Parrot, swooping above their heads and calling out, "Join the love," in a piercing voice. Ti-Tien-Lung leapt into the air, circling above the crowd, a shimmering protector, the sun gleaming off the greens, browns, and reds of his leaf-like scales. His voice, resonant like Himalayan mountain horns, rumbled a deep "Om-m-m." The fire of his breath warmed the crowd.

Perched on his shoulders was a Laughing Dove, who sometimes flew down to ride on his tail, wings fluttering with the joy of the wild ride, her "chuckling" coos adding a soft treble to the bass of the dragon's deep hum.

A second Laughing Dove flew across the crowd landing next to her.

"The hacker," whispered An Lien.

He smiled. "You said you were a Laughing Dove. I looked it up on the internet, and now I'm one, too!"

They rode the dragon's tail "chuckling" together.

The transformation swirled down through the crowd, sometimes even into the ranks of the police, bringing them striding, hopping, loping, trotting, and flying to the edge of the sea where the three women turned to face them, singing together:

Breath,
live in the wind-whipped grasses,
merge with my feet and keep me dancing.
Breath,
singing through the voice of the wind,
whirl with me, howl with me,
and make me one with you.
Breath,
flowing in the waves of the sea,
creep into my soul and conquer me.

The crowd joined in the song and the city officials, watching from a balcony at city hall, stared wide-eyed as the three women spiraled into a funnel cloud, sweeping up and up into the air in a rainbow of colors, followed by the laughing, singing crowd, whirling and flying, out and out to cover the sky, and then disappear. When the misty cloud had dispersed the officials looked around and found that three of their own were among the missing.

The demonstration in Robertsville drew almost a thousand people, much to the surprise of the local police, who were scattered around the outside edges. They were a wonderful, colorful crowd, some actually dressed as animals found in the local forests, others carrying signs with pictures of animals and plants, children, elders, and families.

They gathered in the park in front of the courthouse steps where, without a microphone, the crowd was repeating the words of the speakers, so they could be heard all the way in the back. Yameno, Dorotea and Billy, Jarvis, and the Chases stood in the front row with Micah, Clare, Keegan, and the other members of the Interfaith Council. The Buddhist nun, Nanda, was speaking.

Coffman and his crew drove to Robertsville in a caravan of pickup trucks, full of men and boys recruited from all over the county. They arrived at the park a half hour or so after the demonstration started, and drove round and round the perimeter of the park, revving their engines and yelling, "Mongrels," and "Devil's spawn," at the crowd.

Each truck had two or three people in the back, holding up their signs. Tom crouched behind the driver's seat in the bed of his grandfather's truck hoping his grandfather wouldn't notice he wasn't participating in the yelling.

The demonstrators ignored the trucks.

Coffman was furious. He double-parked next to the path that crossed the park in front of the courthouse steps. The others pulled up behind him as he climbed out, pulling his twenty-two out of the gun rack in the truck window.

Tom's eyes grew wide. "No!" he yelled, and jumped out of the back of the truck. "Grandpa, stop. Don't take the gun," he pleaded grabbing Coffman's arm.

Coffman shoved him back against the truck. "Coward," he hissed at the boy. "Little mongrel coward." Putting his face right up next to Tom's, he muttered, "Either you come with me, or you don't bother to come home," and turned back toward the crowd, the gun held in both hands in front of him.

The policeman closest to the courthouse saw Coffman emerging with his gun and got on his walkie-talkie to the other officers, who started running toward the courthouse.

The deputy sheriff had been standing leaning against his car on the other side of the park. "Coffman," he yelled when he saw him walking down the path toward him. "Coffman, you idiot!"

He started running toward Coffman.

Nanda turned toward the deputy when he yelled, and then, when she saw the deputy running, looked toward Coffman, now followed by a small crowd of men, all with guns.

She stopped mid- sentence, her eyes going wide, then turned back to the crowd. "Peace!" she called out, raising her arms palm outwards toward them, and they all replied, "Peace! Peace! Peace!" The words traveled to the back of the crowd and finally became an urgent chant. "Peace! Peace! Peace!"

"Stop," yelled Coffman. "Stop that noise." His face got red and he was screaming. "Stop. Stop it. Stop that noise."

The deputy was running as fast as he could, but it felt like he wasn't moving at all.

Nanda, her voice trembling with fear, just kept repeating, "Peace," and the crowd kept echoing her.

Coffman yelled one last "Stop," and raised his gun toward the young woman.

Tom screamed, "No. NO!" and darted in front of his grandfather trying to grab the gun.

The gun went off, and Tom fell to the ground.

He looked at his grandfather, and slowly, laboriously pulled something from where it was tucked in his jacket. It was a small, well loved, stuffed rabbit with a bullet hole going through it. "Nibbles," he whispered.

His grandfather stood frozen over him. "I threw that thing out years ago."

Tom shook his head very slowly, and smiled, as a small red stain appeared on his jacket. "I rescued him."

The deputy, followed closely by Mark Chase, came running up just in time to see Tom transform.

Lying dead on the ground in front of Coffman was a beautiful big jack rabbit, blood still dripping out of the small wound on his chest.

Coffman clutched at Mark. "Please, Dr. Chase," he whispered. "My grandson."

Mark crouched down beside the rabbit. "I'll try," he whispered, shaking his head.

The crowd was silent, stunned, the only sound a breeze moving through the trees that edged the park.

Clare, tears flowing down her cheeks, started to sing, turning slowly in a circle her arms reaching out toward the sheriff, Coffman, and the other men, and finally the crowd.

Dona nobis, pachem, pachem.
Dona nobis, pachem.

Gradually voices in the crowd joined her and they joined hands swaying from side to side, singing the old familiar song. A mist formed around them and the deputy watched in awe as the people stretched into other shapes, birds and flowers, foxes and trees.

Those shapes moved together like puzzle pieces to form a larger shape.

A lily, he thought. The petals trumpeted outward, lacy like flame. *A flaming lily.*

Then the misty lily floated up into the air and vanished, taking with it all the demonstrators, including one small hummingbird.

One of the city police ran up to the deputy. "What happened? Did you see that? What happened?" He looked down at Mark, crouched beside the rabbit, pressing his own t-shirt into the wound, his mouth over the mouth and nose of the rabbit. "A rabbit? What..."

Durga, the Invincible

By the time Kujakali and the others were ready to descend to the cavern, many more people, both living and dead, had arrived at Ninas Twei. Those murdered by police, armies, and vigilantes, including a large jack rabbit, had been recruited for the rescue of the prisoners of the Giants of God, and the workers in the eggs. They were all gathered at the top of the crevice.

Tuwillia sat a little farther away from the edge.

They had decided as many of them as could get down the cliff and be safe, should go. Tina and Singing Swan were back in the amphitheater, riding herd on Djeserit's little kid and watching the amazing forms of the living who were converging on Ninas Twei. The koala, Barega, was intermittently excited and frightened. "But I'll be safe," he kept repeating. "They can't kill me. I'm already dead!" Manua, on the other hand, was delighted to be appointed the message carrier. "I can fly up and down that crevice," he chittered, flapping his wings.

Kuji and Sarah were the only ones not already dead. "If I die," Kuji pointed out, "I'll be in Durga form. I'll come here where I have friends. But," she paused, a wistful look on her face, "It would be nice to live in the real world for a while first."

In the canyon the people were working together and talking together.

Those whose nations had been at war with each other for centuries were hugging and pledging to work for peace between their peoples if they ever returned to their own countries.

Those of different religions or different ethnicities listened to each other and saw how they were more alike than different.

The Rabbi and Imam, sitting next to each other with their backs to the wall as the younger members of their groups worked to release others from the eggs, had slowly begun to talk. "My people were murdered in great numbers – six million! People all over the world were against us. We wanted a place that was our own. We had dreamed of Jerusalem for centuries," explained the Rabbi.

"Yes, I understand," nodded the Imam, "but my people already lived there. Why must my people be pushed out, first from Jerusalem, and then slowly, slowly moved out by your settlements on the land the agreements said was to be ours? If we are to live together, why are we not allowed a part in the governance of the land? Why, if it was done to you, are you willing to turn around and do it to us?"

"Because we're afraid you, too, will kill us – will try to exterminate us."

"But you are exterminating us!"

Both lowered their heads thinking of their own hurts and those of the other. The Rabbi held out his hand and the Imam took it in both of his.

"*Shalom avodah, shalom avodah, shalom, shalom,*" sang the Rabbi.

"*Salaam alaikum,*" chanted the Iman. "*Salaam alaikum.*"

Todd stood behind the chain link fence at the edge of the canyon, alternately peering with his binoculars down at the people and eggs beneath the net, and pulling the binoculars away to look with naked eyes. Either way the net made it hard to see clearly. He swore profusely, started to pick up the semi-automatic rifle leaning against the fence next to him, and then put it back.

Don came running down the path from the temple. "Todd!"

Todd muttered something and turned around to meet him.

"Kevin came back from Kas. *TruthFarm* somehow got the files we keep here – the ultra-secret ones."

"Shit!"

"Yes," Don nodded. "Kas wants me, and all the other media people here, to go back and help with damage control."

"I haven't got enough people to handle this already!"

"He says, hang on. Seb will come with help eventually, but what's going on in the world is big trouble. We need to focus there."

Todd stamped his foot and turned to look back down into the canyon. Don peered through the fence. "What's going on down there?"

Todd shook his head. "I don't know what the hell they're doing."

"There're tons of them. What are they doing over there?" Don pointed to the far wall of the canyon where some people seemed to be building something.

Todd focused his binoculars on them. "Looks like a ladder up to the plateau." He laughed. "They'll get a big surprise when the wind comes and knocks them back into the net, and into eggs."

"Maybe." Don sounded skeptical. "Or maybe they've figured a way around the wind."

"How in the hell would they do that?" yelled Todd. "We can't even figure that out. They'd have to have access to the computers down there that run everything."

He froze and his eyes met Don's. "Oh, my god," he whispered. "They cheered..."

Don turned back toward the canyon his attention caught by movement above it at the back of the plateau. "Shit! What's that?" he yelled, pointing at a tiger emerging from the cavern wall and leaping out onto the plateau.

Todd raised his binoculars. The tiger was huge, and riding on its back was a helmeted woman with eight arms, two holding to the tiger, others waving a lotus flower, a sword, a conch shell, and a thunderbolt triumphantly in the air. "It's one of those Indian monster deities with hundreds of arms."

"Oh, my god," yelled Don. "There're more. How are they coming out of the wall?"

Todd handed the binoculars to Don and stared at the multitude of animals, birds, and fish, who were swimming through the air like water, pouring out of the hidden crevice behind Kuji, now Durga, fierce goddess of justice.

"Otters!" he exclaimed. "Those are huge otters, and look, on the back of one there's a monkey. Is that the monkey we were looking for?"

Don nodded, pointing. "And look at that other otter. Is that a koala on its back?"

"There's a jack rabbit!" Todd grabbed his gun. "Goddamnit, a jack rabbit. I know how to shoot a jack rabbit." The gun chattered, echoing across the canyon, bullets grazing the top of the rabbit's long ears.

The people in the canyon screamed and ducked for cover, but the animals just kept coming, the jack rabbit and the three giant otters thrusting themselves forward in huge leaps, following behind Kujakali and Rahiti to the bridge.

"Go tell Kas," Todd screamed. "We need help!" and Don took off for the temple yelling as he went.

But when Don and his men arrived at the reception area outside Kas's office they found a room full of broken glass and devastation. The windows were gone, but outside the sun shone.

It was a bright beautiful day.

"What the hell happened here?" he shouted, his feet crunching on the glass as he stomped over to Kas's office and looked in. No one was there and the damage was even worse, if that was possible. The others stood where they had landed, looking around them, bewildered.

Don pointed to four of them. "Go back. Tell Todd what happened here. The rest of you, come with me." He headed for the stairs. "We have to find Kas and the others."

When the gun shots stopped, the refugees in the canyon and lining the bays in C2, peered up through the net, trying to see what was happening.

"Birds," exclaimed Ranulf. "They said animals can't live here!"

"That was a dolphin!" exclaimed Jesús. "How can a dolphin fly? And look, there are some fish, too!"

Luha stood, and leaned out of the bay trying to see. "They're from Ninas Twei!"

Enid grabbed the cougar's neck. "Don't fall!"

Luha backed up, turning her head toward Enid, her tail flicking wildly. "We need to tell them about the wind – that the wind won't sweep the living away."

Enid climbed out onto the ladder, scrambling upward. "Someone come here," she yelled through the net. "Help! Come here. We need to tell you something."

A small green bird flew down toward them.

"We've come to rescue you," Manua called out, as he flew back and forth over the top of the net, finally landing on the edge of the bay of C3 just above her head.

"Hooray! And we've shut down the wind," Enid called back. "Tell them we can all go over the plateau now, if we can get out of here past the net – and the women in the city, too."

"Hooray," yelled Manua leaping into the air. "I'll tell them."

He flew around in a wide circle calling, "We've come to rescue you," to the people below, and then off he went, first to his father and Kujakali who were about to cross the bridge to the park, and then back up the crevice to tell the people at Ninas Twei.

The Tree Woman laughed ecstatically as she found herself riding the back of the handsome Wolfwind, his tail flying like a streaming banner, leaping through the swirling mists. The travelers from Robertsville and Arundel joined those from Bayomar and landed at the Din Tsin Twei, adding their voices and their dances to those of the demonstrators from all over the world.

Singing Swan flapped his wings in delight as he saw them, and the travelers gathered around him.

"Have you found a way to rescue the children?" Dorotea cried out.

"Yes," nodded the swan.

"Look!" He pointed at the large crack in the mountainside. "Kujakali and the others have already gone. We have word that the terrible wind that pulls living people into the eggs is no longer working. Go to Tuwillia and she'll give you directions."

The travelers scrambled up the rubble of the broken amphitheater, some flying on the back of the huge dragon, and headed for Tuwillia and the crevice.

Luhanada peered up through the net at the tiger and the goddess on his back.

"It's Kuji in her Durga form!" she called out. And she sang:

> *I am I.*
> *I am now.*
> *I am the protector.*
> *I am the law!*
> *I am I, I am I!*

Kuji heard her and answered:

> *I, daughter of the mountains,*
> *fierce mother of all,*
> *like the lotus I am growing*
> *sounding the great Om with my conch.*
> *Firm as thunder, am I,*
> *striking the demons like lightning*

with my sword of knowledge.
I, daughter of the mountains,
fierce mother of all,
like the tiger I am growing.

She lifted the conch to her mouth, trumpeting her arrival to the residents of the city. The people in the canyon laughed and cheered as she led the animals thundering over the bridge.

Eric and the other men remaining in the city had run out of the temple to the path at the side of the canyon to watch the invasion.

Todd yelled orders, but the men ignored him, some running terrified back to the temple, and others, guns in hand, toward the invaders. He gave up, crouching down next to the fence to watch, his arms pulled tightly around his chest.

Eric stood on the path, frozen, listening to the song.

Kuji lay low across the back of the tiger, birds flying and dolphins swimming as shields on either side of her, two of the tough little Mbuna fish from Lake Malawi swimming high above her. Still, she could feel the wind of the bullets as they whistled past her.

The dolphins leapt past the chattering guns, knocking the men down with their blunt noses. A pod of Orcas followed them, grabbing the guns from the men's hands and mangling them with their teeth. The men, deprived of their weapons and menaced by the teeth of the laughing Orcas, scrambled back to the temple.

The women peeked out the doors and windows, and then, urged to escape by the friendly animals, poured out of the houses, duplexes, and apartments, their small children in their arms, the older girls running beside them.

.Kuji and Rahiti came to a stop next to Eric, who still stood silently on the path to the temple.

"You've come to kill me," he said, his eyes evading hers, his body trembling.

Kujakali, the mighty Durga, waved her sword of knowledge above her head and her voice rang out.

"No, I've come to drive out demons, not to kill."

She brought the sword high in the air, gripped in two of her eight hands. Light poured from its tip, encircling the blade, crackling and

494

spitting sparks out into the air, as she swung it down to touch the top of his head.

He cried out throwing his head back, his eyes meeting hers. His childhood demons, created by the institutionalized bullying and abuse of school mates, the demands and beatings from his father, who was also bullied, and the shaming from his mother, fled from where they crouched in his brain and heart, and he remembered it all – the humiliation, the anger, the hate.

"And I turned it against the women. These blameless women – and the children," he whispered. Anguish, pain, and guilt flowed across his face and he covered it with his hands. His shoulders shook, tears ran down his cheeks, and he fell to the ground sobbing.

"It's a beginning," she told him, "not an end. And Eric," she cautioned, "If you ever touch a child again, I will find you. Lightning will descend upon you!"

Eric nodded, looking up at her. "Kuji, I'm sorry. I... I think I came to love... At least I was proud of you, of your defiance. You taught me many things. I am sorry."

Kuji just shook her head and left him there as she urged Rahiti up the path to the temple, followed by Aucapomi, Djeserit, and her winged and finned protectors.

The little green bird, having delivered his message and returned, was flying laughing circles around them all.

Peeka danced on her shoulder. "Well done, Kuji, well done!"

Todd remained frozen with indecision by the fence, watching the animals pouring across the bridge.

A sound pulled his attention back toward the wall on the other side of the plateau, where the horde had emerged. As he watched, flames came roaring from the cavern wall.

He grabbed the fence with both hands, shaking it. "Fire, fire," he tried to scream, but it came out as a whisper, and faded as he watched the long sinewy body of the dragon emerging from the wall, his back covered with riders.

He circled the cavern, flicking a flaming tongue at Todd as he passed and then swooped down and grabbed the steel net in his claws, ripping it from its anchors. Carrying it to the plateau, he dropped the net in a huge heap to one side of the crevice. The people in the canyon cheered and moved to make room for him, as he spiraled down to the canyon floor.

Todd ran screaming into the temple.

Shen Ch'i landed carefully.

The travelers, perched on his back, called out to the people on the ground, "Don't be afraid. We've come to rescue you," and a majestic gray parrot flew off the dragon's head, circling past the people hanging out of the bays of C2 calling out, "Shanti, shanti."

Enid and Jesús, watching from one of the bays, exclaimed as they saw the Earth Woman Tree Woman and Yameno Wolfwind leap off the dragon's back. Yelling with joy, they scrambled down the ladder to greet them with hugs.

When the big bear with the killdeer on his shoulder called out to Jesús, he turned to peer at them, confused. "Dad?" he asked. "Dad is that you?"

The big bear laughed, and the killdeer flew to the ground and transformed. "*Hijo*," she whispered.

"*Mamá!*" he exclaimed and tears filled his eyes. She took him into her arms and he started to cry. "I can't believe you're here!"

"Shows how much you know," laughed Billy.

The badger was much slower to show himself. Enid was cuddled in Giselle's arms when he lumbered slowly up to her.

Giselle smiled. "Enid," she whispered, "your grandfather is here."

Enid looked at the badger, startled.

Gunther transformed. "Please don't be afraid of me, Enid." He began to cry.

Enid looked at Giselle, eyes wide.

"It's okay," whispered Giselle.

Enid moved over to her grandfather, and they tried a tentative hug, gradually relaxing their fears, both crying.

Sidney laughed as he saw Dario hanging out of one of the bays. "Dario," he called out in his parrot voice. "You're safe!" and he landed on the ledge in front of the boy.

Dario blinked, looking down at the large parrot. "Sidney, is that you?"

The parrot nodded his head. Walking a little farther into the room, he transformed.

"You're alive, aren't you?" asked Dario. "At first I was afraid…"

"Oh, yes. It's okay, Dario. All of us who just came are alive. We've come to rescue you."

"Gracias a dios," whispered Dario, wiping his eyes.

The Wind is Gone

Kuji and the animals spread through the city, calling to the women and children, "The wind is gone. Follow us!"

Most of the women joined them, laughing with joy as they helped their younger children on to the backs of the larger animals, who escorted them back across the bridge to the crevice. There leopards, chimpanzees, and gorillas, directed by Sarah (who remained in human form to be a familiar face for the women), waited to help them up the ledges, some leaping with children on their backs, and others urging them up the ladder, to the first ledge, and then the second, to the top.

But the mothers of the school boys ran to the school where the boys had been locked in to rescue their sons, pounding on the locked doors, and calling out to the animals for help.

Nima, the otters, and some of the Orcas, rushed to their aid.

"Move aside," called out an Orca, and the group scattered away from the doorway as the whale shattered the door with his powerful nose.

The boys and their teachers pressed themselves fearfully against the walls of the classrooms as the Orca swam aside and the smaller animals entered.

Nima urged the teachers toward the temple and an Orca followed them as they ran.

One of the older boys shouted, "Don't do what they say. They're just animals and women. We're to be Giants of God," and some of the others straightened their backs and stood next to him, but the younger boys seemed more than happy to climb on the back of an Orca with their mothers to "swim" across the canyon.

Illari addressed the older boys. "You have a choice – a choice that will define your life. Come with us to Ninas Twei where all the living species dance together – a dance of life – or join your fathers awaiting their fate in the temple. We might say," she added, "that the choice your fathers have made is that of the dance of death."

She looked carefully at each of the boys. "We won't hurt you. It's not your death I'm speaking of, but the death of life itself. Choose."

The boys looked at each other, at their mothers, at the otters, the beautiful langur, and the huge Orcas.

"What a bunch of bullshit," yelled one of the boys, and he and two others ran out the door to the temple, leaving their mothers weeping, but the rest ran to their own mothers, who hugged them, and helped them climb on the backs of the waiting Orcas.

In the temple, with the doors locked and lookouts posted on the parapets of the Silver tier, Todd and some of the men were locked in a hot debate. Todd wanted them all to leave, but Marius was standing up to Todd, insisting they should fight back.

Suddenly they heard chanting, and turned in time to see the four men coming back from the world.

"They've sent you back to help!" exclaimed Todd.

"No, no, it's awful."

They were wild eyed and all yelled at once. "The Seaview tower has been attacked," announced one, while another one yelled, "A bomb!" "Or a tornado," yelled another. "We don't know what happened. The windows were blown in and there's glass everywhere. No one was there."

One of the lookouts came in from the parapet and yelled down from the balcony. "They're coming to the temple – that monster woman – it's Kuji! – and the tiger she's riding, and one of those big otters, and a goat thing."

"Let's get out of here," yelled Todd, and most of the men ran up to the circle in front of the altar.

Marius, Kurt and a few others refused to join them.

Kuji and Rahiti could hear chanting as they came to the front doors of the temple. Kuji tried the doors. "Locked. That chant was the one they use to return to the world."

"I wonder if anyone is left inside?" Rahiti looked up at the tiers of the building.

"We can fly up and look in the window," chirped Manua, launching himself up to the first tier, followed by some of the other birds, a shark, and a dolphin.

They were met by Marius running out one of the sliding doors, his gun at his shoulder. "Rat-a-tat-tat," went the gun, and the birds, the dolphin, and the shark all laughed as the bullets disappeared in their bodies.

The dolphin swam in front of him. "You can't kill those who are already dead," she whistled, and they all surrounded him, the dolphin nosing the gun toward the shark who grabbed the barrel with his powerful teeth and dashed it to the ground.

Marius whirled in a circle, trying to find a way through the crowd of flying and swimming creatures.

Back through the window he saw Kurt, and the few other men who had stayed behind, cowering indecisively in the office. "Fight. Try to find a way to shoot Kujakali," he yelled, turning back and trying to grab the dolphin out of the air.

The shark shot in toward him grabbing his arm in its teeth, holding it, and twisting it, but not biting through. The rest of the men all turned, ran back toward the hall and down the stairs to the sanctuary. A moment later they heard them chanting, "We are the Giants of God..."

The dolphin laughed, and swam back down to the crowd below. "I need a child on my back," she called out. "Someone with fingers who can unlock the doors."

"Take me," cried out a very little girl, who had followed them to the temple.

Djeserit turned her head to look at the child. "Where is your mother?"

Kuji smiled at the little girl.

"She has no mother. She came here like me, from the slums. Let her go. She's smart and brave."

The dolphin swam down close to the ground, Kujakali lifted the child to her back, and they swam back up to the open window.

"Careful," said a raven perched on the parapet. "The child is alive. The guns will kill her."

"We must protect her as we did Kuji," answered a barracuda swimming swiftly to the child's side. Surrounded by fish and birds, the dolphin and the little girl swam carefully into the temple, down through the deserted sanctuary, to the front door.

Loud banging came from one of the smaller back doors.

The two blue Mbuna fish, who'd stayed with Kuji at the front doors, darted around the corner to the back door, hanging menacingly in front of the faces of the two teachers. "Stop where you are," they growled.

"They said we could go to the temple," one of the men whined, raising his arms in front of his face, and cowering back against the door. The other teacher, and the three boys, flattened themselves against the building behind him as the little fish swam back and forth in front of them.

Djeserit came trotting around the corner and her strange yellow eyes narrowed. "You want to join the other men?"

"Yes." The man cringed away from her.

She pawed the ground with her hoof, and she and the Mbuna herded them toward the front doors and Kujakali, who stood next to Rahiti in front of the doors, waiting for them to be opened.

"Kuji?" muttered one of the boys, his eyes widening as he saw her.

"Yes, Harris?" Kuji responded.

He just shook his head.

On the other side of the door, the little girl was busy turning the lock and swinging the heavy door open.

"Peti?" exclaimed another one of the boys.

The child glared at him.

Aucapomi herded the two men and the boys into the sanctuary, where Marius, who had been alternately dragged and poked down the stairs by the shark, sat waiting, rubbing his arm and trying not to look at the shark who swam lazy circles around him.

Kuji and Rahiti talked quietly together. "What should we do with them?"

Rahiti shrugged. "Maybe we should just allow them to go back with the other Giants of God."

"You cast the demons out of Eric. Can you do that with these?" asked Peeka, peeking out from under Kuji's braids.

Kuji shook her head. "He was open. He saw his own guilt. These people are closed. They still think they're right." She sighed. "I need to talk to Luha."

Rahiti called to Manua. "Manua, find a way to bring the cougar to the temple – the one you saw on the ledge in the canyon."

Luha and Ranulf stood at the edge of the bay, gazing out at the reunions happening below. *Everyone is here except Tata,* she whispered to herself.

"Do you know these people?" Ranulf asked.

"Some of them," she replied. "They were part of our original group of travelers. Wolfwind, the Tree Woman, Enid, Jesús, myself, and..." her voice broke, "and Tata. He was a beautiful Red-tailed hawk."

Below them Enid pointed up at Luha, and the Tree Woman and Wolfwind looked up. The Tree Woman began to grow, up and up, until one of her sturdy branches reached into the bay next to Luhanada. Luha laughed and climbed out onto the limb, jumped to the next limb down, and then down to the ground. Ranulf followed down the ladder.

Yameno and Luha touched noses tenderly and then leaned into each other, body to body. Yameno curved his tail over her back, and nuzzled her ears. She licked his muzzle with her rough tongue.

"Tata isn't with you, is he?" asked Yameno.

"No, and he isn't with you either, is he?" whispered Luha.

Yameno shook his head. She looked earnestly at Yameno, tears filling her eyes, and then at the Tree Woman. "I don't know where he is." The Tree Woman wrapped her arms around the cougar and held her for a moment.

(Tata, followed by the streaming cloud of strings of particles, arched around the solar system like a rainbow, spiraling inward toward the sun.

> *Luha, Luhanada,* he whispered to himself. *I'm coming*
> *Look at me!*
> *I am the voice of life,*
> *the song of the One.*
> *High Crier!*

And the rainbow strings joined in:

Look at us!
We are vibrating strings,
vibrating strings of things
Look at us!
Energy, Matter,
We are the universe, the universe!

"And we're coming," whispered Tata. "We're coming.")

When Ranulf got to the bottom of the ladder, and introductions had been made, he said, "I believe you're the answer to our problem. Some are very debilitated – especially those who were in the eggs the longest."

"But they can go out on my back," laughed Ti-Tien-Lung.

The surrounding people, who had been listening, both bewildered and eager, to all the conversations since the dragon landed, started cheering.

Manua joined in as he flew down into the canyon looking for Luhanada.

"There you are!" He landed on her head and peered down at her eyes. "Kuji needs you to help her decide what to do with the last Giants of God. The rest have gone back to the world. They said their chant and poof! Off they went!"

The little bird laughed. "They were scared of Kuji and my dad."

The bird looked around him at all the listening people. "My dad's a tiger!" he exclaimed. "He's a really big tiger, and Kuji's a goddess and she rides on his back."

Eric sat up. He watched for a while as the animals led the women to the bridge, and listened as cheering came from the canyon, then stood up and walked reluctantly to the temple where the birds guarding the doors waved him in. He paused for a moment at the top of the center aisle of the sanctuary and then moved slowly to Kuji, stopping in front of her, his eyes still wet with tears. "I don't know where I belong."

He turned and looked at Marius, the teachers, and the three boys. "We were wrong, you know."

Marius sneered at him. "You were always pretty much a wimp, Eric."

Eric just shook his head and turned back toward Kuji.

Luha came trotting down the aisle, followed by Enid.

Kuji ran to give her a many armed hug and asked her what to do with the men and boys. Luha paced back and forth in front of them stopping in front of the boys. "Are you sure you don't want to go with your mothers?"

The one who had spoken out at the school yelled, "I'm a Giant of God, not a mommy's boy!" but the other two looked at each other a moment, and then looked at Luha with pleading eyes.

"Then go. You go, too," she gestured at Eric.

The dolphin, with Peti still on her back, swam in front of Eric and the two boys. "Follow me," she called, and they ran out of the sanctuary after her.

Luha turned to Kuji. "Send these four back to the world."

Kuji gestured toward the circle in front of the altar and the three men and the boy were soon heard chanting, "We are the Giants of God..."

In the basement of the Seaview Business Park, the men have seen the files An Lien had taken off of Kas' personal computer on TruthFarm. As Stuart scrolls through them the men all turn to look at Kas, horror and anger written across their faces.

"You've betrayed us!" Ottis exclaimed.

"No, no," shouted Kas, his hands palms up in front of him. "No, I was negotiating for us – the Lugas Group. I was trying to get the Lugas Group..."

Luha, Enid, Kuji, and Sarah stood at the edge of the canyon watching Ti-Tien-Lung circling upward with the last of the escapees from the eggs, the weak ones supported by those who were stronger. Luha turned to Sarah and Kuji. "We need to make sure everyone has gone. Every building, all the floors of the cellars and the temple need to be checked." She looked up at the dry roots of the tree hanging down from the roof of the cavern. "Somehow this all will have to be filled in. The roots will have to be covered with soil or the tree won't survive – humanity will not survive."

"How will we do that?" asked Enid.

"I don't know," she whispered.

5

To the Dance!

T he animals had swept through the houses, the temple, the cellars, and the canyon, looking for stragglers, escorting them all to the crevice, and then Ninas Twei. The last group stood looking out the mouth of the crevice up at the dry roots of the tree, shaking their heads. From the top of the crevice a gravelly voice called down, "Come! It's time."

"It's Tuwillia," laughed Kuji. "Let's go!" They leapt, scrambled, and flew up the crevice to Ninas Twei.

"Look," laughed Dario, as he reached the halfway point. "I'm a condor!"

"I'm a wild stallion," exclaimed Angelino, leaping up to the next ledge. "I'll race you to the top!"

The giant wolf, with the Earth Woman Tree Woman riding his back, leapt past him.

> *I am the wild, the freeborn,*
> *earth traveler,* sang the wolf.
> *My soul singing touches the moon and the sun.*
> *Nameless One called for light.*
> *I am the light of wisdom,*

answered the cougar, scrambling up the ledges behind him.

Then there was a burst of childish laughter as Enid and Jesús – Chachuli and Kumni – raised their voices in duet:

> *I am the writer of poetry,*
> *Fluid as the world of dream.*
> *I see the whole in every part.*

I see the things that aren't seen.
I am the echo of creation.
I see the earth in her splendor.
My hands draw the dreams of the universe,
Humanity's heart at its core,
So the joy of humanity can soar.
So the joy of humanity can soar.

The original travelers grew to a wild chorus with the addition of all the others from Arundel, Shanti House, the Cavern City, and the canyon, all tumbling gently through silver swirling mists.

Let the joy of humanity soar, they sang.
Let it soar, let it soar!

Then into a deep silence from very, very far away they heard:

Look at me. I am the key. I am coming!

"Tata!" whispered Luhanada.

Out of the mists the Tree Woman heard a whisper of drums in intricate joyful rhythm:

Arise, arise,
Open your heart!
Open your heart to the dance of life.
Arise, arise,
Open your eyes!
See the world in the dance of life.
Beat your feet
To the beat of your heart!
Dance the dance of life.

"Oh, they're my friends," shouted An Lien.

"And here are our people!" Rahiti and Manua cried, joining in the new song.

We are the land in the sea,
Sun cooled by sea breeze...
We come from creation-destruction.
In death, new life will be.
We risk death in defiance.
A sacrifice, so Gaia can be freed.

One by one, the songs of all the people all over the world who had come to the dance joined together in a wondrous harmony, moving finally to:

Come! Come!
Lift up your voices
to answer the One.
Come! Come!
Answer the call
of the earth and the sun!

"We're so many," whispered the Tree Woman. "Maybe now we can..."

She breathed deeply, and all the others breathed a deep breath, pulling, pulling, pulling them together, until... a sigh, a gasp. A cry.

"No," she whispered. "Again. We must try again."

And they breathed again, a deeper breath, pulling harder, harder, harder... another sigh, a deep whispering gust of a sigh. A moan.

Once more, a grand full breath. A unison breath, pulling, pulling, pulling together, and then! One and many! One awareness! One many bodied being.

Their hearts leapt as a deep voice resonated through them. "We are one. We are many and we are one. We are a grandsoul!"

And then, a sharp pain. A wrenching. A tearing. They separated, flowing out and out – a flinging outward, away from the whole.

Tree Woman felt tears flowing down her cheeks. "Can't we do this?" she whispered. "We must. We must."

She reached for the Weaving Tree – the tree of human lives, tangling her branches in its branches. "The clear ropey strands," she whispered. "Some of them are broken."

Where she saw broken connections she reached out with leafy fingers to weave and weave, tying the insular circles, one to another, and as she wove, more of the clear strands broke loose.

Sticky, she thought. *They're sticky, but not woven in.*

She pulled on them, loosening their bond, and wove some more. Weaving and weaving a deep, complex pattern of light and dark, bright colors and soft subdued colors, weaving and weaving life into the brokenness, weaving joy, hands touching, eyes meeting. Smiles.

Then came a breath as deep as the ocean, as the universe –

a deep, unison breath, filling the lungs of the earth and the sky with precious air –

a full, complete breath thrusting them together in a mighty sigh.

506

They lifted their voices, pulling themselves into one harmony, one voice with many pitches, one dance with many rhythms, flowing together to become a joyous whole, rising to a grand and glorious fullness.

They, the All, felt themselves opening to an amazing awareness, the many as the One. They knew what it was like to live in the slums of Mumbai or the drought laden lands of Northern Africa; what it was like to be persecuted for the color of their skin, their sexual orientation, because they were women, or a myriad of other differences.

They felt the exhilaration of sky diving, the intensity of practice for the basketball player and the rock band, the long distance runner and the concert pianist. They gave joy in the birth of a child, and grieved at the death of another child. They were both themselves and all.

They were a grandsoul.

Softly in the background they began to hear the voices of the Tsin Twei:

We are the One and the many.
We are the life force,
We are the center,
We are the all.
The nameless and the named.
We are the whole, greater than the parts.
We are the kingdom Plantae.
Tracheophyta
Chlorophyta
Phaeophyta
Rhodophyta
Bryophyta
Angiospermae...
We are the kingdom Animalia, they continued beginning a long crescendo:
Metazoa
Cnidari
Platyhelminthes
Orthonectida
Nemertea...

And then, the voices close and resonant:

Chordata
Urochordata
Cephalochordata
Vertebrata
Agnatha

Chondrichthyes.
Amphibia
Reptilia
Aves...

followed by a joyful fortissimo:

Mammalia!

The humans saw them, the *Insectivora*, the *Chiroptera*, the *Edentata*, the *Rodentia*, the *Lagomorpha*, and the giant whales and playful dolphins of the *Cetaceans*. The *Proboscidea* and the *Sirenian*, the *Perissodactyl* and the *Artiodactyls, the Felidae.*

"*Primates,*" sang out the lemurs and monkeys and apes.

And the human grandsoul answered, "*Primates!*"

Papio
Hapalemur
Hylobates
Gorilla
Alouatta
Presbytis
Macaque
Orangatan
Homo sapiens!

"*Homo sapiens, Homo sapiens!*" laughed all the other grandsouls gleefully. "Welcome."

And with a resounding leap of joy the grandsoul of *Homo sapiens* joined the Tsin Twei.

What one grandsoul knew, all the grandsouls knew. *Homo sapiens* felt the despair of the polar bear and the seal seeking an ice floe in a melting ocean. They searched for ever more scarce food with the Artic Fox and the Emperor Penguin. They felt themselves dissolving from acidification of the oceans, like the Staghorn Corals, and cried at the too hot sands of the birthing grounds of the Leatherback Turtles. They tasted the increasing saline, pushing the freshwater dolphins farther and farther up the rivers.

The other grandsouls knew what *Homo sapiens* knew. They saw the overwhelming abundance of poverty, drought, and war. They saw the massive greed of the owners of corporations, the racism, the arrogance, and they learned of the cavern undermining Ninas Twei, and the roots of the Weaving Tree hanging out to dry in that cavern. They all, *Homo sapiens* and all the grandsouls, saw the strings of culpability that spread from the Giants of God, and others like them, to the sufferings of all the species, a sticky web of indifference, and they cried out, a piercing cry for help that reached out beyond the clouds, beyond the moon into the pathways of the solar system.

"Coming," cried Tata, and all the strings of particles. "We are coming," and they spiraled in, circling the earth, a rainbow of energy, spinning around the blue-green sphere sprinkled with the fluffy white of clouds, laughing at the beauty of it, peering closely at all the myriad life forms, rejoicing in the diversity of creation.

They came spiraling through the Tsin Twei, calling out greetings to the grandsouls they had once been a part of, dancing for a time in the midst of the song, their rainbow colors like ribbons weaving in and out of the species.

Then the deep sharp pain came, and they cried out, "Too hot! Too hot," and dove down the crevice to the cavern of the Giants of God.

Circling round and round, swooping over and back, their energy pulled and pulled at the sides of the canyon until the city, undermined, toppled into it.

Pushing in and out of the sides of the cavern, they pulled the dirt up and over the crushed city, up and over the canyon, up and up to the roots of the tree, seeding the soil with nourishment, and packing it close with love. Up and out of the crevice they came, the last of them filling it in behind them.

"Water," cried Tata. "Yameno Wellkeeper – Wolfwind – the tree must have water."

"We are coming," called the Wolfwind, and the Tree Woman gripped his back as he leapt into the air.

> *I am the wild, the freeborn, earth traveler!*
> *My soul singing touches the moon and the sun.*
> *I am the herald, the seeker, the messenger.*
> *I bear the song for those seeking the One.*
> *I am the hunter, the knower, the lover.*
> *My voice like a spear pierces deep in the night.*
> *I am the lone, the many, the mirror.*
> *My call is like lightning, jagged and bright!*

Out of the mists came hundreds of wolves and cougars, swans, coyotes, squirrels, snakes, elk, and eagles, surrounding the Wolf and the Earth Woman Tree Woman.

We are the wild, the wild,
freeborn, earth travelers –
soul singing, earth travelers –
touching the moon and the sun.
We are the commune, the sharers, the lovers,
joining together, ever seeking the One.

It's his nation, Tree Woman realized, *the people of his village who have come here countless times over the years. And more...*

The sound of thousands of drumming circles throbbed through the air as Yameno sang – the indigenous peoples woven into the land of the Americas and all the lands of the earth, drumming and chanting, their feet pounding the ground. Hi, ya! Hi, ya! they called.

Suddenly a jack rabbit leapt into their midst, shoulder to shoulder with the wolf.

"Yes," laughed Yameno. "You, too, are a Wellkeeper, Tom," and he pushed his shoulder gently into that of the rabbit. "Your father was also a guardian of the spring."

He looked again at the rabbit. "You're alive!"

The rabbit nodded. "I was dead. The doctor gave me his breath, and now I live."

He leapt forward. "I know where the water is," he called as he jumped into the lead. "I saw the pipe running through the dry roots of the tree above the bridge as we went to rescue the women."

The quarks and leptons, all the particles of matter and energy that had once been alive, came rushing to the rescue of the water, swarming in to surround the drummers and the chanters with a wild fluting as Tom led them all in a deep dive into Tuwillia's dying pond, spiraling down into the water following an underground stream which had been trapped in a pipe and led away from the tree toward the now destroyed buildings of the city.

Battering it with claws and teeth, matter and light, they broke it apart letting the water flow out and around the roots of the tree, flowing from the pond to the water table under the woods on the far side of the meadow, feeding the tree on its way.

The tree sighed, and drank deeply. The pond filled.

"It is done," cried the particles. "It is done."

The rainbow strings of energy and particles of matter, vibrating strings, quarks, photons, electrons, leptons, muons, tauons, neutrinos, and neutralinos, all swooped their bright colored joy outward, back to the dance of the universe, back to the song of the larger whole.

All but Tata. "Luhanada," he whispered landing between her paws, "come with me."

Weaving the Future

"Is our work done, here?" asked Luha, sitting on her haunches, her tail brushing the floor of the amphitheater where the travelers and the denizens of Ninas Twei had gathered, some sitting on the floor, some perched on the lower steps. "Can those of us who are dead go and join Tata, and the rest of the universe?"

Tata smiled, "To dance for a while as strings of particles and then become again... something. Merging and separating, merging and separating."

"It's not finished for those of us who are living," said Shen Ch'i, his huge dragon body undulating in slow lazy curves above them.

"No," added the fox, swishing his brushy gray tail. "The Giants of God are not defeated. The loss of the cavern, and the disclosure of their actions, will be huge setbacks for them, but not the end."

"And there will be others," added Keegan from his perch on the wall beside the amphitheater.

"So we have our job set out for us," added Sidney, soaring thoughtfully back and forth in front of them.

"Yes, but it's a great job," exclaimed An Lien, pushing her feathered shoulder into that of the hacker, who laughed. "Let me at them!"

Ranulf grinned, "I think we have a convert to *Incogni*!"

"Hazel," asked Jarvis, hesitantly. "Luhanada, before you go, can you forgive me?"

She reached over and licked his scaly horned head. "Yes, Jarvis, let go of the guilt just as you've let go of the hate. It's over now."

"And Dan?" he turned toward the Red-tailed hawk perched on Luha's paw. Tata nodded his head and touched him with the tip of his wing.

Nima stood and turned to Luha, her tail dancing behind her. "I'm not ready to go yet. Perhaps some of us should stay to guard the tree, to guard Ninas Twei, and those who are ready should join that greater dance of the universe."

"Me, too," added Peeka, rubbing up against Kujakali's ear. "I want to stay here. I know I've been here a very long time, but I like it here!"

Djeserit nodded her head and pawed the ground. "I will stay here, too, so I can be close to my kid, who will need to return to the world."

She turned to Kujakali and Sarah. "Can you take him with you? Will you protect him?"

They both nodded. "And Peti, too."

They laughed as they watched the little kid dancing around the amphitheater, first chasing, and then being chased by the little Fishing Cat – Peti, as her Tla Twei.

"We would like to stay here, too," declared Aucapomi, while Illari and Huayna nodded their heads.

"But I will leave." The gravelly voice of Tuwillia broke into the silence from where she sat cuddled next to Sarah in Kujakali's lap. "I've been in this form a very long time. I would like to dance among the stars."

She turned toward Nima, "If you would guard the tree."

"I will," exclaimed Nima. "Gladly."

"And we'll help," added Tinaluirga from where she lay nearby. Barega, curled up next to her with his head on her side, nodded his agreement.

Singing Swan raised his head. "I, too, would like to fly among the stars."

"It would be our great pleasure to guard Din Tsin Twei," Huayna spoke up eagerly.

"And so you shall," agreed Singing Swan.

Gunther lifted his brindled head and looked at Luhanada. "Luhanada, go with Tata. Enid will be safe now."

"And we'll be there to help Gunther," added Billy. "Dorotea and I will be there, and all these others," he swung his head around to include all the other travelers from Robertsville and Arundel.

Yameno Wolfwind moved even closer to Luha, leaning over to lick her ear. "I have missed you both terribly. I will miss you even more." He leaned down, and nosed gently at Tata. "You've been my closest friends." He took a deep breath, letting it out in a slow sigh. "But life is change and we must be willing to change with it."

Chachuli scampered over to Luha and tucked herself under her chin. "Go," she whispered. "I'll think of you every time I see a star."

With an explosion of joy, Tata, Luhanada, Tuwillia, Singing Swan, and many of the others who had died, arched up into the night sky, spinning around in a farewell dance before swooping out past the planets, through the galaxy, a flash of light dancing among the stars.

"And what about us, Ayoabia," asked Miesha. "What shall we do?"

Ayo laughed, and a brisk breeze wafted around them. "We have people to protect, child. This is not the end of the story, you know. There will always be humans who separate themselves from the Tsin Twei, who follow the paths of greed and hate, rather than those of love and caring."

"Why is that, Ayo?"

"Demons," interrupted Kujakali.

"Demons?" questioned Miesha. "But what is the source of the demons?"

"The men I saw at the Giants of God," added Ranulf, "were relentlessly teased and bullied when they were boys to be what their fathers wanted them to be. Bullies produce bullies. Feeling helpless against those who are stronger than they, they're violent and contemptuous against those they perceive as weaker. It's an endless chain unless someone breaks it. My mother stood up to my father. He hit her, and she walked out, taking me with her."

"There're many chains that need to be broken," nodded the Tree Woman. "Mothers, too, have been hurt and turned that hurt on their children. And not just parents... We must make sure every child has their need for love, sustenance and nurture met."

"Want and helplessness," agreed Shen Ch'i. "The source of the demons is unmet needs and feeling helpless against forces perceived as stronger. We must make sure that each person has their need for food, shelter, education, and love met. Most of all love."

"And it has to be done in a way that doesn't destroy the earth," added Kumni. "That's my job. I need to help people find new sustainable ways to do things."

"We have to tell a new story," Chachuli agreed. "I'll help write it."

"The old concept of bread and roses," laughed Shen Ch'i. "Bread and roses sustainably shared equally by all."

"Yes," Ayo replied. "But can we do that?"

The Tree Woman was silent for a long time. "I don't know," she whispered. "I don't know. We can only try."

"Or die," whispered the Tsin Twei. "You must try, or we will all die," and the Tsin Twei swirled around them, sweeping them back to the world.

Hunter's Moon, Waning Crescent

The Bayomar city manager huddled in a corner of the balcony, looking out over the park where the crowd had ascended into the air and disappeared. His cell phone was crammed against his ear and he whispered a frantic report to the CEO of the Lugas Group, turning toward the wall so the others on the balcony couldn't hear.

"Disappeared. They all disappeared."

There was a pause.

"Yes. They turned into animals or goddesses or... something, and then they disappeared."

He moved to the edge of the balcony and looked down. "Oh, my god!" he exclaimed out loud.

The little gray cat sat on a park bench just below their balcony, looking up at them. He was surrounded by dogs in various postures of repose, all with their eyes on the balcony. Was the cat looking at him?

The man shook his head. "That cat... And the dogs... why...?"

"The dogs were on the march," the woman next to him said, pointing down at them. "Look, some have leashes. They're waiting for their owners to come back."

The dogs and the cat waited, and the people on the balcony waited. The dogs laughed and played together. (How could they resist?) And they waited.

And Howie, crouched behind the building with his automatic rifle, waited.

They waited and they watched the sun throw brilliant colors over the sky, and dip into the sea, painting paths of gold from the sun to the city. Stars began to shine faintly on the indigo eastern horizon.

"Listen," exclaimed a man, moving to lean into the railing. A faint music could be heard coming from the sky over the ocean.

The cat stood, and paced back and forth on the bench, head up, tail up, yowling a cat song. The dogs all stood and faced the ocean, adding their howls to the cat's yowls.

The people were returning.

Howie saw them coming, a whirlwind of images across the evening sky, singing as they came, and descending in a sweet blue mist.

The tree woman and the wolf were the first to touch down on the street in front of him. He lifted his rifle, sighted, and pulled the trigger, the drumming sound of the bullets flying through the air and piercing the song.

But the Earth Woman Tree Woman and the Wolfwind did not fall to the ground.

Instead, the tree grew and grew, encompassing the sky and turning to gold in the sunset. The ground shook and the wolf expanded beside her, a silver image next to the golden tree.

Oya of the wind gently blew on the image until it encircled the world and all the marchers, all those who had joined to become the grandsoul of *Homo sapiens*.

They looked up and watched as the wolf danced with the wind and dove down, down into all the fresh water springs of the world, and the Tree Woman melted into the earth and surged upward into the roots and trunks and limbs of all the trees.

The roots mingled with the water, the branches waved through the rain, and the wolf and the tree, now braided into one, rose again into the atmosphere around the earth where Oya blew again until they became a cascade of golden silvery filaments.

The marchers breathed in, and the filaments filled their lungs and wrapped their hearts in a shield of wolf and wind and water, earth and tree, compassion and joy. The last of the filaments sank into the earth, and the earth sighed.

The moon rose, a thin waning crescent rocking gently in the night, and a soft sea breeze whispered past.

"A new moon is coming," it sang. *"A new moon is coming,"* and the moon reached its zenith, a sweet smile in the night.

AFTERWORD

Enid ran laughing down the path to the woods, trying to keep up with Dulcinea, one of Giselle's dogs who had come to live with her. Dulci ran to the not so secret hiding place by the river and dashed full force into Robbie, who was waiting there with Jesús. The two dogs wiggled and rolled around together full of yips and wagging tails, and then dashed off into the woods to explore.

Jesús shook his head, grinning, before calling them back. "Come on, you two. We're meeting the others up at the sacred spring."

He grabbed Enid's hand and they walked on up the hill to the clearing, where they would help Tom rebuild Yameno's little house.

Meanwhile...

Thump! The small blue-gray cat landed on the table under a tree. "What the...?" said the person sitting there enjoying the spring air. The cat sat on its haunches, staring with intense green eyes.

"Well, you're a little spooky. I like your sleek fur." The cat leaned down and licked a shoulder...

Going Forth

Seas crashing,
like thunder rolling,
like drums beating.
A call to the brethren,
a cry to the wary!
The time has come!
Come! Come!
Hammer your feet
to the beat of the drum.
Come! Come!
Lift up your voices
to answer the One.
Come! Come!
Answer the call
of the earth and the sun.

Peace, peace,
Laughter and dance!
Joy and life for us all.
Sing your tears,
Sing your fears,
Defy oppression
through the years,
Dance the dance of life!
Arise, arise,
Open your heart!
Open your heart to the dance of life.
Arise, arise,
Open your eyes!
Dance the dance of life!

APPENDIX I

TERMS RELATING TO THE DANCE OF LIFE:

Tsin Twei – The dance of life, where all of earth's species, except one, dance and sing together to ensure the continuance of life on earth.

Din Tsin Twei – the mountain valley in Ninas Twei where the Tsin Twei takes place.

Ninas Twei – the mystical world of the Tsin Twei.

Tla Twei – the mystical, but corporal form humans must transform to before going to Ninas Twei. Plural is Tla Twein.

Totem – an object that helps a human get in touch with their Tla Twei. A picture, a carving, stuffed animals, etc.

Grandsoul – the souls of the members of a species living today joined together into one grandsoul allowing empathetic understanding between the members of that species.

PLACES AND PEOPLES:

Uhs – (pronounced "ŭs") Nation where story takes place.

Uhsians – (pronounced ŭs -ē-ăn) The people of Uhs.

Bayomar – A large city which sprawls around a crescent shaped bay on the western coast of Uhs.

> ***Kavanaugh House*** – Institution for the mentally unstable and drug addicted.

> ***Shanti Place*** – A homeless shelter for teenagers.

> ***Seaview Business Park*** – A business park next to the bay.

Arundel – Small unincorporated community 200 miles north of Bayomar on the coast road.

Robertsville – Larger community, county seat, inland from Arundel on the Interstate Highway.

Tuwillia River – River near Arundel named after the local Indian word for turtle.

Tuwillian Indians – Native Uhsians who used to have a village on the river near Arundel.

CHARACTERS: *(Tla Twei, if applicable, is in parenthesis)*

Giselle's family and friends, before leaving Bayomar:

Giselle Raphael – Teacher. (Earth Woman Tree Woman).
Monica – Giselle's sister. (Kestrel)
Rod – Monica's husband, a lawyer. (Elk)
Samuel – Giselle's principal in Bayomar.
Ayoabia Asukiye – mysterious homeless woman who sings to Giselle. (Oya of the Wind)

People of Arundel and Robertsville:

Gabriela "Nicki" Nichols – Principal of the small elementary school in Arundel. (Kingfisher)
Penny Waite – Nicki's roommate and lover, an artist. (Tiger Salamander)
Yameno (Wolfwind in Tuwillian) Wellkeeper – keeper of the sacred spring. (Wolf)
Hazel Fraya – Local librarian. (Luhanada Moonmother, Cougar in Tuwillian)
Greta Fraya – Hazel's grandmother. (also Cougar)
Dan Burroughs – Local gardener and scholar. (Tata Sundancer, Red-tailed Hawk in Tuwillian)
Enid Amundsen – A student in Giselle's class and Hazel's niece. (Chachuli Treerunner, squirrel in Tuwillian) (also called Ratatosk, Norse squirrel messenger to the gods)
Jesús McCrae – A student in Giselle's class. (Kumni MakerMan, Coyote in Tuwillian)
Gunther Amundsen – Enid's grandfather. (badger)
Mary Amundsen – Hazel's sister, Gunther's wife, Enid's grandmother. (Tree Swallow)
Emma Amundsen – Enid's mother.
Bidewells – Former owners of Giselle's house.
Humphries – Real estate agent.
Rev. Jarvis Tarrant – Minister at Church of Those Born Again in Jesus. (Horned Lizard)
Muriel Chase – Historian, wife of Mark Chase. (Bumble Bee)
Mark Chase – Retired doctor, Muriel's husband. (Willow Tree)
Rabbi Micah Levinson – Rabbi from Robertsville Interfaith Peace Council. (Gray Fox)
Reverend Clare Yates – Methodist minister from Robertsville Interfaith Peace Council. (Mourning Dove)

Father Keegan Gilchrist – Catholic priest from Robertsville Interfaith Council, specialist in the study of Satanism. (Burrowing Owl)

Coffman – Owner of local hardware store.

Tom – Coffman's grandson. (Jack Rabbit)

Tom's mother – unnamed

Harding – Male teacher at Arundel Elementary School.

Rowena Dickerson – Teacher at Arundel Elementary School.

Dickerson – Rowena Dickerson's husband.

Billy McCrae – Jesús' father. (Black Bear)

Dorotea McCrae – Billy's wife, Jesús' mother. (Killdeer)

Deputy Sheriff – No name.

Nanda – Buddhist nun – (Bird's Eye Gilia - purple flower)

Giaan Singh – Sikh Gayni

Baptist minister – Unnamed

Yono – Tuwillian who may be Tom's father.

Yameno's great aunt – last of the Tuwillians in Arundel until Yameno comes back. Unnamed.

People of Ninas Twei:

Singing Swan – A Tuwillian killed many years ago when white men raided his village. (Trumpeter Swan)

Tuwillia – A Tuwillian who died many, many, many years ago. (Turtle)

Peeka – Former Tuvan shaman. Died at age 12 many, many years ago. Aydemir or moonlight was his human name. (Pika)

Tinaluirga – A Tasmanian aborigine woman killed in an uprising in 1929. (Wombat)

Barega – An Australian aborigine boy, age 9, killed in a massacre in 1926. (Koala)

Nima Rinzen – A Tibetan nun killed while being tortured in Tibet. (Langur)

Djeserit – A shaman killed while demonstrating in Yerainia. (Ibex)

Aucapomi – An indigenous man from the Amazon, shot by lumber company guards during a demonstration. (Giant Otter)

Huayna – Aucapomi's son. (Giant Otter)

Illari – Aucapomi's wife, Huayna's mother. (Giant Otter)

Rahiti – A man from an island, father to Manua. (Tiger)

Manua – Rahiti's son. (Iao or Wattled Honey Eater)

(Swallowtail butterfly)

(Fruit dove)

(Tube nosed bat)
(Spiney rat) And many more.

People of Bayomar:

Shen Ch'i – Physics professor, makes a garden with a sculpture of Kuan Yin at Kavanaugh House. (Dragon of Heaven and Earth, Ti-Tien-Lung)

Shen An Lien – Shen Ch'i's daughter. (Laughing Dove, female)

Sidney – A seventeen year old boy at Shanti Place. (African Gray Parrot)

Miesha – A thirteen year old girl at Shanti Place. (Yemonja)

El Gallitos – The name of a Latino gang at Shanti Place.

Avengers – The name of a White gang at Shanti Place.

Commandos – The name of a Black gang at Shanti Place.

Deborah – A counselor at Shanti Place and rabbi at Temple Shalom Shekinah (Olive Tree w/crescent moon)

Reverend Meg – Garden supervisor at Shanti Place and minister at the UCC church where Shanti Place is located. (Ladybug)

Yasar – A Palestinian man who helps in the garden. (Osprey)

Dirk – The head of the Avengers.

Kimberly – A girl Avenger.

Angelino – The head of Los Gallitos. (Wild Stallion)

Dario – Angelino's cousin. (Condor)

Caldwell – A recruiter of the Avengers.

Blond guy – A recruiter of the Avengers.

Charlie – A member of the Avengers who has a dog.

Bandit – Charlie's dog.

Maria – A Latino transgendered woman, a member of Sid's group. Birth name was Manolo. (Butterfly)

Rashaun – The leader of the Commandos.

Damont – A recruiter of the Commandos.

Pedro and Roberto – Two members of Los Gallitos.

Alberto and Luis – The recruiters of Los Gallitos.

Ikemen Ninjas – The Chinese gang.

Min – An artist member of Ikemen Ninjas.

Bayomar police: First officer, Badge 742, Badge 631

The Hacker – a member of Incogni (Laughing Dove, male)

The Giants of God:

(A secret society created by eight powerful men who have joined forces hoping to rule the world. All listed below are white, but there are some darker skinned members.)

Giants' Sex Slaves:

Deirdre – White, the first woman called to "judgment."

Kujakali – A dark-skinned fourteen year old concubine, sometimes called Kuji. (Durga)

Sarah – Eric's white cook and housekeeper. (Wood Thrush)

Gold: (Eight men, each with a residence.)

Branson Wiebe – A major CEO in the weapons industry. Wiebe Armaments

Todd Uncas – The CEO of Worldwide Media and Communications Corporation. Very black possibly dyed hair.

Reginald – Five-star general in the USEAN armed forces.

Kasimir "Kas" Goddard – CEO of Goldstream Oil, largest oil company in world. Leader of the Gold, white hair.

Sebastian – An owner of Tutiso Security, the biggest company supplying mercenaries,and now involved in electronic surveillance. Shaved head.

Stuart Shaford – Major stockholder in The Shaford Group, the largest conglomerate of all kinds of goods. Gray haired, heavy set.

Ottis – President of the largest bank in the world, The Audamar Corporation.

Dean Bailey – Uhsean politician.

Silver: (Sixteen men, each with a duplex.)

Eric – Kujakali and Sarah's "owner."

Kevin – In charge of privatization of communities.

Donald – In charge of capturing Luhanada.

Nickel: (Forty-eight men, each with a large apartment)

Fenmore

Kurt

Ranulf – member of Incogni

Copper: (Sixty-four men, each with a small apartment, no women.)

Marius and Warren – Sarah's guards.

Others Associated with Giants:

Howie – White spy and infiltrator for TigerSNake Limited

Peters – White liaison between TigerSNake Limited and Kasimir Goddard

Doug – White man, Kas's heavy

Third man – White, driver of kidnap car

Reverend Peabody – White television preacher

People In the Eggs:

> *Imam Labeeb Aalim* – An Imam from Palestine.
> *Rabbi Abraham Cohen* – A rabbi from Israel.
> *Adia* – First techie, female and black.
> *Sister Maureen* – A gray-haired white nun.
> *Fadil* – A short dark man.
> *Grisha* – A tall, thin, white man.
> *Andrea* – A stately black woman.

ORGANIZATIONS:

One Earth Together (OET) – A social and ecological justice group with members all over world.

Giants of God – Secret organization of powerful men.

LifeFriends – A social networking site.

VidYou – An online site where you can post videos.

TruthFarm – An online site that posts information leaked from various sources.

Incogni – A group of hackers who expose important secret information.

Crevan News – A corporate news station.

NIO – National Intelligence Organization

Goldstream Oil – Kasimir Goddard's company.

Lugas Group – a rival conglomerate

LCU – Legislative Committee for Uhs

UhsSA – Uhs Security Administration

TSNL – TigerSNake Limited – a private security company

APPENDIX II

The World of Ninas Twei and the Cavern City:

Ninas Twei and the Cavern City are located in a mystical world connected to our physical earth, but in a different dimension, much like the world of the Interior Castle of St. Teresa of Avila.

<u>RITUALS</u>

In our real world we can find a similarity between the rituals of most religions. All religions create a sense of community for their congregants, but some of these communities are open and accepting, and some are closed. The rituals remain similar – often, but not always, having something to do with the intake of food or drink.

Interestingly, all the major religions encompass both the closed and the open. There are fundamentalists in every group who see their religion as the only right way, and everyone else as "the other" – either evil or unworthy – and there are progressives in each religion who see all the different religions, and seekers who don't identify as religious – even atheists – as on acceptable paths to… whatever.

In *Earth Woman Tree Woman* different groups use different rituals to reach Ninas Twei, or the Cavern of the Giants of God beneath Ninas Twei. By the end we realize that the only thing necessary is community. To get to Ninas Twei you must be part of an open community. Those who are closed to the "other" end up in the Cavern. The Giants of God cleverly use this to bring workers to the eggs.

NINAS TWEI:

Note: *When I use the term "mythical" I do not in any way mean to denigrate the deities of any religion. Mythical does not mean "nonexistent," only that these characters are used to tell the stories of a particular religion or tradition, and usually are more than human.*

<u>TLA TWEI</u> – the mystical, but corporal form humans must transform to before going to Ninas Twei. It can be a mythical character

found in some tradition or one created by the human. In many traditions, such as the Tuwillian tradition, the mythical creatures take the form of animals. They are not real animals, but the tradition's perception of that animal and its powers. Often their names reflect this. In this book the hawk is named Tata Sundancer; the cougar, Luhanada Moonmother. Those humans who choose an animal without associating it with a mythical tradition, give that animal mystical characteristics themselves, making their animal Tla Twei a mythical creature, rather than the "real" animal. Plural is TLA TWEIN.

When a human's Tla Twei is that of a goddess or god, they have not become the actual goddess, but their own perception of that goddess. They become imbued with the perceived powers of the goddess. This is much like the spiritual practice of *Charya Nritya,* "a mental process of seeing oneself as having the appearance, ornaments, inner qualities, and awareness of the deity one is envisioning" practiced by the Newar Buddhist priests of Nepal. http://www.dancemandal.com/dance-mandal-offerings/

TOTEM – an object that helps a human get in touch with their Tla Twei. A picture, a carving, stuffed animals, etc.

GRANDSOUL – the souls of the members of a species living today joined together into one *grandsoul* allowing empathetic understanding between the members of that species. The *grandsoul* is not one member of the species, but most of the members of an entire species in a kind of mind meld. Some may drop out of the *grandsoul,* but if too many leave, their *grandsoul* disintegrates. If most humans open themselves to each other empathetically, they can form a *grandsoul,* even if some do not join.

Members of the nonhuman species don't need a Tla Twei to go to Ninas Twei because they are a part of the *grandsoul* for their species, and therefore part of the Tsin Twei automatically, instantly. They could take a Tla Twei if they wished, but they have no need to. The humans don't need to take their Tla Twei after they've become a grandsoul, but their grandsoul is very tenuous. Using a Tla Twei enhances their ability to be empathetic and will help them stay a grandsoul.

The TSIN TWEI is like a grand-*grandsoul!* In this dance all species have an empathetic understanding of the needs of the other species. It makes possible the grand compromise of life.

BECOMING YOUR TLA TWEI AT DEATH – if a traveler to Ninas Twei dies in her Tla Twei she finds herself at Ninas Twei, a protector of the Tsin Twei.

THE CAVERN:

The Cavern is in the same "dimension" as Ninas Twei. It is located under the roots of the Weaving Tree, the tree of human life, starting as a cavity around the tree's roots caused by human corruption.

<u>THE GIANTS OF GOD</u> is a secret society created by eight powerful men who have joined forces hoping to rule the world. They have based their group on a twisted interpretation of the words in Genesis 6:1-9 of the Judeo/Christian Bible:

There were giants in the earth in those days; and also after that, when the sons of God came in unto the daughters of men, and they bore children to them, the same became mighty men which were of old, men of renown.

Some years before the book begins these eight men performed a secret communal ritual. Because they were a closed community, they ended up in the cavity surrounding the roots of the Weaving Tree rather than Ninas Twei. (As a closed group, they would never understand the need to take a Tla Twei, which is inherently open – accepting of the "other" – so they cannot get to Ninas Twei, and indeed, know nothing about it.)

The eight founders form the Gold Circle of the Giants. They recruit others and form the hierarchical circles of Silver, Nickel, and Copper, subservient to the eight Golds, but seeing themselves as superior to the thousands of lackeys who work for them and know nothing about the Giants. (This idea came to me after reading about a real group of powerful men who formed a prayer circle that grew into a huge secret organization with a very loose and ambiguous religious core.)

<u>THE CITY OF THE GIANTS</u> was built by this group of men. They decided to build a secret retreat center by enlarging the cavity. They are unaware that the cavity surrounds the roots of the tree of human life. Using the rituals that brought them to the cavity, they bring in small bulldozers and other equipment to make the cavern, dig the canyon, and build the city. They harness the energy of thousands of workers in the "eggs" to provide electricity for the little city, and pipe water from an underground stream near the roots of the tree. They can bring in other humans and inanimate objects, but none of the plants or animals who have a *grandsoul* – that is every species except humans.

The city is only about a quarter of a square mile in size and reflects their hierarchy by having four concentric circles of buildings surrounding a central building, the Temple.

The outer circle belongs to the Gold members who each have a one story luxury home of their own. The next circle, the Silver, contains eight two story duplexes with homes for sixteen men. The Nickel circle has eight three story luxury apartment buildings, six apartments per building. The Copper circle, four stories high, also has eight buildings. The first and second floors of these buildings contain communal space – restaurants, game arcades, a brothel and storage. The third and fourth stories have eight smaller apartments. The Gold, Silver, and Nickel members are allowed to have women slaves for sex and household help, and sometimes have children by them. Although we do not hear about the brothel in *Earth Woman, Tree Woman,* it is there for the men of the Copper circle.

The full complement of 136 men are at the City only once a year. Otherwise they rotate in and out when there is a need to meet secretly, and for pleasure, considering the City a "retreat center." All the information about the Giants is kept in computers in the City and not allowed to travel to earth. There is no wi-fi.

<u>THE CANYON</u>, located in the Cavern next to the City, contains 282 rows of individual prisons shaped like eggs, sixteen to a row, containing a little over four thousand people, about the same number as can attend a performance at New York's Metropolitan Opera, half as many as can fit in the University of California Berkeley's Greek Theatre. The eggs, lying on their sides, are eight feet wide and high, and ten feet long – about the same size as an isolation unit at Pelican State Prison in Northern California.

Demons

The demons talked about in EWTW are demons of the mind, "personal demons" not literal "imps". In Sanskrit the name of the goddess *Durga* means "invincible." She is the goddess of victory of good over evil. The first syllable, *du* references the "four devils of poverty, suffering, famine and evil habits." The last syllable *ga* is the destroyer of sins – injustice and cruelty.
(http://www.sanatansociety.org/hindu_gods_and_goddesses/durga.htm - .U5dbJHaQyuI)

Connie Pwll Walck Tyler, activist, teacher, writer, composer, and mystic, received her most important early education working in the civil rights and peace movements in the sixties. This was enhanced by constant "continuing education" in various progressive movements. She taught public school for twenty-one years working with pre-school through high school children from every different background imaginable. She earned an MA/MDiv in Theology and the Arts from the Pacific School of Religion where she did her field education in homeless shelters. She also has a BA and MA in English.

Tyler has set many of the songs in the **Earth Woman Tree Woman Quartet** to music which can be heard at **www.earthwomantreewoman.com.**

She also has a blog at **www.deephum.com.**

You can find her at "Connie Pwll Walck Tyler" and "The Earth Woman Tree Woman Quartet" on Facebook and "Connie Tyler" on Twitter.

Tyler lives in Berkeley, California with her husband, Kenneth; two dogs, Netzakh and Hode; and her cat, Magic; and feeds Little Z, a feral kitty who belongs to herself.